ONE WAY OR ANOTHER

The Snipesville Chronicles, Book 4

Also by Annette Laing

Don't Know Where, Don't Know When
(The Snipesville Chronicles, Book 1)

A Different Day, A Different Destiny
(The Snipesville Chronicles, Book 2)

Look Ahead, Look Back
(The Snipesville Chronicles, Book 3)

ONE WAY OR ANOTHER

By
Annette Laing

CONFUSION
PRESS

Atlanta

In memory of Pam Perrin and Betty Seale
Apology complete, debt everlasting

Copyright © 2017 by Annette Laing.

All rights reserved. Published in the United States by Confusion Press. CONFUSION, CONFUSION PRESS and associated logo are trademarks of Confusion Press.

No part of this publication may be reproduced, or stored in a retrieval system, or transmitted in any form or by any means, electronic, mechanical, photocopying, recording, or otherwise, without express written permission of the publisher. For information regarding permission, write to Confusion Press, P.O. Box 2363, Decatur, GA 30031-2363
Library of Congress Control Number: # 2016906669
ISBN-10: 0-9848101-1-0
ISBN-13: 978-0-9848101-1-6

Printed in the U.S.A.

Graphic design: Deborah Harvey

Author website: AnnetteLaing.com

Contents

ONE
Snipesville, This Year • 1

TWO
The Festival of Britain • 32

THREE
One Way to Snipesville • 45

FOUR
One Way to Balesworth • 77

FIVE
Another Way to Snipesville • 99

SIX
Domestic Matters • 113

SEVEN
Snipesville Matters • 158

EIGHT
Becoming Acquainted • 189

NINE
A Week of Meetings • 214

TEN
So Much Drama • 248

ELEVEN
Testing Circumstances • 277

TWELVE
Balesworth Politics • 305

THIRTEEN
Triumph and Disaster • 326

FOURTEEN
The Truth, Balesworth, 1905 • 346

FIFTEEN
The Truth, Snipesville, 1906 • 384

SIXTEEN
The Truth, Balesworth, 1951 and Snipesville, This Year • 410

Acknowledgments

ONE WAY OR ANOTHER

The Snipesville Chronicles, Book 4

Chapter 1
SNIPESVILLE, THIS YEAR

Saturday Afternoon, Mid-May

"You want this?" Brandon handed his foil-wrapped MegaBurger to his friend Javarius Evans, who looked at him quizzically even as he accepted the warm offering.

Watching Brandon for reassurance that this wasn't a joke, Javarius slowly began to unwrap the sandwich. "You sure you don't want it?" he said. He glanced nervously at the old lady at the counter, seemingly afraid that he was breaking some unwritten rule at Zappy Burger by accepting Brandon's food. "You won't change your mind?"

Brandon shook his head. Javarius quickly finished unwrapping the burger, and sank his teeth into it. With chipmunk cheeks, he said, "Thanks, man."

"You're fine," Brandon said. "Enjoy."

Javarius swallowed noisily, and took a long slurp of soda. Then he burped, lightly spraying Brandon. "Why don't you want it? You feel bad, or something?"

"No," Brandon said, with a shrug. "It's just disgusting, that's all. Like your table manners."

Javarius scowled. "So if you didn't want it, why'd you buy it?"

"I was hungry …." Suddenly, Brandon sat up, his eyes wide. "Wait, I felt it."

"Felt what?" said Javarius, alarmed.

Brandon now had his eyes closed and his nose scrunched up in concentration. He was in pain. He hadn't realized that time travel could be painful.

But he felt as though he had finally found the right place: Peace, balance,

CHAPTER ONE

real, all these words flashed through his head. And then, with a lurch and slight nausea, he fell forward, catching himself just in time before his forehead hit the table.

Javarius looked at Brandon in horror. He grabbed his forearm and shook it. "You okay, cuz? You need help?"

But Brandon had shaken himself out of the ... what was it? ... feeling. "Nah, I'm okay. I'm just ... Nah. I'm okay."

"You sure? I could call your mom to pick you up."

"No, I'm fine. Look, I'll just wait until you're done eating, okay?"

"I'm not hungry anymore," Javarius said, laying down the remains of the burger. "I'm scared you're gonna pass out, or puke on me."

""I'm okay now," said Brandon. He leaned sideways, scaring Javarius again, then reached in his pocket, and pulled out a crumpled sheet of paper. Unfolding it, he handed it to Javarius. "You know about this?"

Javarius squinted at the flyer, his eyes floating back and forth over the text. "No. Why? So what?"

Pageant Of Snipes County Pride

Come Out and Support the Snipesville Players as we Proudly Celebrate Our Local Heritage

Special Living History Performance at SnipePAC
(Snipes County Performing Arts Center)

May 12-17, 7 p.m.

Special Daytime Performances for Schools

See our hometown actors portray prominent leaders of early Snipesville, including **A. P. Hunslow, C. T. Hughes, Benjamin Marshburn, R. H. Gordon**, and many more.

Come out and meet these historic figures!

Presented by Snipes County Historical Society

Sponsored by
The Boiled Peanut Boutique, Zappy Burger, Hotel Duval, and Hunslow's Sippin' Snipe

CHAPTER ONE

Brandon took it back from Javarius, and read it again.

"We're going to this with our class, remember?" Brandon said. "Tell me something, Javarius. How come they never include *us* in their precious heritage?"

"They do sometimes," Javarius said, tapping the flier. "R. H. Gordon, see? I mean, they even named our school after him."

Brandon wasn't impressed. "Yeah, but that was because our school was the all-black school, back when the schools were segregated. That's the only reason it was named for a black guy. Of course, it's still pretty segregated now. Come on, Javarius. Nothing against R. H. Gordon, but he's, like, the only black person in Snipesville history, according to the Snipes County Historical Society." He flicked the flyer away in disgust, and it scudded across the greasy table.

And then Brandon thought about it. Once again, the name *Gordon* had popped up in his life, just as it had again and again on his travels in time. In 1915, he had lived with Mr. Gordon, a dentist in England, in the little town of Balesworth. Hannah had stayed with the Gordon family in Scotland in 1851. All three time travelers, including Alex, had met two Mr. Robert Gordons in Georgia in 1752. Some of these Gordons were related to each other, he knew that much, and it was all very weird.

But Gordon was a common name. It didn't always mean something. R. H. Gordon was black, while all the Gordons they had met time-traveling were white. The only black man named Gordon that Brandon knew was his own father, Gordon Clark. Nobody in Brandon's family had ever told him they were related to R. H. Gordon, but then again, if they were, he thought, it didn't need to be said. He was related to most of the black people in Snipesville.

Meanwhile, Brandon had other things on his mind, like the historical pageant. He looked hard at Javarius. "They never say anything about what happened in 1906, either," he said.

"Ohhh," said Javarius, with a snort. "You mean, *We Don't Talk About That?*

"I do mean *We Don't Talk About That*," said Brandon. "And maybe it's time we *did t*alk about *That*."

Javarius rolled his eyes. "You think it'll make a difference if they do? *We* know about it. My family was here when it happened. That was when my great-great-great-something-grandaddy Evans was the first pastor of Authentic Original First African Baptist, or whatever the church was calling itself back then."

"Oh, seriously, Javarius?" said Brandon in his best sarcastic voice. "I did not know your family started our church. Like, I never heard you mention it, except the 10,000 times you mentioned it before."

"Okay, okay, come on now," said Javarius. "But what difference does it make

CHAPTER ONE

if white people talk about it now or not? The folks in charge will just say that what happened was a long time ago, back in the olden days. They'll say things like that don't happen now. It's all in the past. It doesn't matter. We should stop bringing up stuff like that."

Brandon smiled bitterly. "You mean like they should stop going on about the Civil War?" Anyway, he thought, what were past and present to a time traveler? Not that he could tell Javarius about the time travel. The only person in Snipesville who knew that Brandon, Hannah, and Alex were time travelers was Dr. George Braithwaite, and he had only believed them because he had met them first in England in 1940. But now Brandon remembered that, of course, there was one other person who knew: The Professor.

Monday Morning, Mid-May
There isn't much that's worse, Hannah Dias thought, than being trapped in a class with a teacher who hates you. Except, maybe, being trapped with a teacher who hates you at Snipes Academy, in Snipesville, Georgia. She had asked Mrs. Middleton, the assistant principal, to transfer her, but Mrs. Middleton had said in her slow Southern drawl, "Hannah, why? Mr. Bragg is a fine teacher. All our other students love him."

"Well, I don't," Hannah had said bluntly, and she was rewarded with a detention for something called "insubordination."

She had tried appealing to her dad for help, but he was busier than ever with his job at the bank. "Look, it's not for long," he had said. "The school year ends in—what?—a month? Six weeks?"

He had been right, of course, and now she mentally crossed off each day she spent in Mr. Bragg's class. Now the semester was almost over, but not soon enough for Hannah.

"Okay, everyone," said Mr. Bragg, holding up his hands. "We have a quiz on the War Between the States coming up on Friday, so y'all be sure to review your notes."

Tara Thompson raised her hand. "What about the textbook, sir? Do we study that, too?" Tara was Hannah's only friend at Snipes Academy, and like Hannah, she was a social outcast at school. Although a local, she came from a poor family and had a purple streak in her hair. Hannah was still trying to process the idea that Tara, who looked very white, was Brandon's distant cousin, although they both swore they were related to each other.

Now, Mr. Bragg pushed his greasy glasses back up his nose. "Don't you worry about the textbook, Miss Thompson. I told you all the material you need to know for this class, and you got my study guide with the key terms. Let's finish up the War Between the States, okay?"

Hannah had a headache. Mr. Bragg was boring. He talked all the time about the Civil War, which he always called the War Between the States. She raised her hand. "Excuse me ..." she said.

"Excuse me, *sir*," Mr. Bragg corrected her. "I don't know how you talked to adults in San Francisco, but you address me as *sir*, Miss Dias. I told you before." He was a tall and large man, shaped like a lumpy potato, and yet he walked with steps as delicate as a ballerina. Hannah found everything about him annoying.

"Okay, *sir*," Hannah said slowly, "My question is, why do you call the Civil War the War Between the States?"

"Because that's what *we* call it," said Mr. Bragg.

"Who's *we*?" said Hannah.

Mr. Bragg now looked at her sternly. "It was a war between two sovereign nations, the Confederate States of America, and the Union. It wasn't a war in one country, so it wasn't a Civil War."

"What about the Constitution ... *sir*?"

"What about states' rights, Miss *Dias*?" Mr. Bragg said pointedly. "Now, let's get on." He turned back to the class. "Our guest speaker isn't here yet, so let's review for Friday's test. Ashlee?" He turned to his daughter. "Who was the general, the gentleman from Virginia, who scored a great Confederate victory at Chancellorsville?" He looked hopefully at Ashlee. She rewarded him with a curled lip and a raised eyebrow. "Starts with an R," he hinted under his breath.

"Robert E. Lee," Hannah said loudly, and then she muttered, "like I care."

"I don't believe I was asking you," Mr. Bragg said testily. "Are you looking for attention, Hannah? Because I'm sure Mrs. Middleton will be glad to arrange another detention for you."

Tara whispered, "Let it go, darlin'. Remember what we talked about."

So Hannah bit her tongue, silently counted to ten, and let it go.

"Okay, class," said Mr. Bragg, "I want you to break into pairs, and quiz each other on the material. Keep the noise down."

Tara turned her chair to face Hannah, and said, without enthusiasm, "You want to talk about this stuff?"

"No," said Hannah. "It's a waste of time memorizing battles. There's a lot more to history than trivia ..."

"If you say so," Tara said, shrugging. "I just want to make a B on the test. Hey, you did good keeping your mouth shut with Bragg. Finally."

"Thanks," said Hannah. "I guess. I'm trying. But I'm going to lose my mind if I have to go on like this. I don't want to learn to keep my mouth shut even when I'm right. This isn't normal."

"You mean not like San Francisco?" said Tara, pretending to write something down for Mr. Bragg's benefit.

"I mean like everywhere else," said Hannah, picking up her pencil and following Tara's lead.

"I hate to ask," said Tara, "and you're probably right, but how would you know? You only lived in San Francisco before you came to Georgia."

Oh, Tara, Hannah thought, *if only you knew. I've lived in a city in Scotland in 1851, in a town in England in World War II, and right here, on the land that will one day be Snipesville, in 1752. But Snipesville is the weirdest place I've ever been, and it always, always was.*

Aloud, she said, "You know, if I was superstitious, I would say there's a curse on Snipesville."

Before Tara could reply, the door to the classroom was flung open, and in strolled a small, bespectacled white woman in her fifties, dressed in a smart suit. "Sorry I'm late, Mr. Bragg," she said in an accent with more than a hint of British. "All right if I get started?"

Hannah smiled, and threw down her pencil. She knew this visitor. Dr. Kate Harrower, professor of history at Snipesville State College, was Hannah's mysterious time-traveling mentor. Hannah was genuinely glad to see her. Their relationship had improved from its rocky beginnings last summer, and anyway, whatever the Professor was doing here, Hannah thought, it had to be more interesting than the living death of Mr. Bragg's class.

The Professor beamed at the students, but studiously avoided Hannah's eye.

"Pleased you could make it," said Mr. Bragg. He did not look pleased. Turning to the class, he said, "Okay, now, y'all listen up, and pay attention to what Mrs. Harrower has to say, because there will be questions about it on the test and …"

"Doctor," said the Professor.

"Excuse me?" said Mr. Bragg, astonished at having been interrupted.

"I'm Doctor Harrower. Not Mrs. Harrower."

Mr. Bragg waved away her concern as unimportant. "Excuse me, *Doctor* Harrower." Then he turned back to his students. "This *lady*," he said deliberately, "has come to talk with us about the War Between the States, so this will be …"

"The Civil War," said the Professor, giving him a grim smile.

Now Mr. Bragg looked seriously taken aback. He coughed, cleared his throat, and said, "Maybe I should just have you introduce yourself."

"Thank you," said the Professor.

CHAPTER ONE

Now a hand went up among the students.

"Yes?" The Professor pointed to Natalie Marshburn. She was the daughter of Hannah's dad's boss, and she never let Hannah forget it.

"Are you from England?" Natalie gushed. "I just love your accent."

The Professor gave her a weak smile, but ignored the question. "Let me start by saying that I am not a specialist in the Civil War."

Clifton Hunslow, sitting in the back row, rolled his eyes, then raised his hand. Hannah suddenly felt very protective of the Professor. Clif Hunslow was one of the locals who considered himself a member of Snipesville's elite, and whatever he was going to say, it wasn't going to be welcoming. Without waiting for the Professor to acknowledge him, he said in a lofty tone, "So you're here to tell us the Yankee side of the War?"

"No," the Professor said crisply, "I'm here to give a historian's interpretation. We do argue with each other, but we don't take sides. We deal in facts."

"But you just said you don't know what you're talking about, ma'am," Clif said slyly.

The Professor gave another small smile. Then she said, "Tell me, do you know much about local history, Mr. ...?"

"Hunslow," he said slowly, as if to remind her that a lot of the buildings, businesses, and streets in Snipesville were named for his family, "Clifton Hunslow. And yes, I do, ma'am."

Ashlee Bragg and her friend Natalie Marshburn snickered. Clifton Hunslow smirked.

"That's interesting," said the Professor. "How clever of you to be so well informed about Snipesville's past. You see, even historians have a hard time piecing together the story of Snipes County, because so many documents have either disappeared or," and here she made imaginary quote marks with her fingers, "*disappeared*. But here's a story, Mr. Hunslow, that even someone of your vast knowledge may not know. In 1864, here in Snipes County, a man calling himself James Freeman wrote a letter to President Lincoln, offering his services as a spy in the Civil War."

She paused to let that sink in. The class sat up, some students looking quite alarmed.

Clifton Hunslow raised his hand again, but this time, he was clearly intrigued. "So this guy Freeman, he was a traitor?"

The Professor looked at him keenly. "Mr. Hunslow, what makes you think he was a traitor?"

"Obvious, ain't it?" he said, cracking his knuckles. "He was a traitor to the Confederate Cause, to states' rights."

CHAPTER ONE

The Professor leaned forward, balancing by placing her fingertips on Mr. Bragg's desk. "But what possible loyalty would you expect James Freeman to have to the Confederate cause?"

"He lived in Snipes County, didn't he?" Clif said. "You seen the Confederate statue on the courthouse lawn, right? That's who we fought for."

"James Freeman did indeed live in Snipes County," said the Professor. "What he did was in his own self-interest, in the interests of thousands of people in Snipes County, and nearly half a million people in the state. It was also remarkably courageous."

"Freeman was still a traitor," said Clif, less certainly now. He clearly sensed something was not adding up.

"I don't think he saw it like that," said the Professor with a half-smile. "Oh, and his real name wasn't James Freeman. That was his code name. His real name was Jupiter Gordon, and he was a slave on Kintyre plantation, a place that was right underneath the very room in which you're sitting."

Everyone looked at the floor, as though long-vanished cotton fields had suddenly reappeared at their feet.

The Professor continued. "Unlike most slaves, Jupiter Gordon had taught himself to read and write. He knew that the Confederacy had nothing to offer people like him except an atrocious existence. He had helped his son, Jupiter Junior, to run away, and he feared he would never see him again. And that's why he decided to risk his life, by offering to help the Union cause. Americans like Jupiter faced difficult decisions during the Civil War. And so my questions for today include why did millions of Americans turn guns on each other? Why did they risk their lives? Why did so many white Southerners fight for the Confederacy when three fourths of them did not own slaves? Did states' rights exist as an idea separate from slavery? No, please don't raise your hand, Mr. Hunslow, not yet. Try listening and thinking for a while. You can say all you like at the end."

Mr. Bragg looked positively alarmed. He turned to the Professor, saying in a stage whisper, "Your colleague, Dr. Bryant? He told me you would talk about some of the battles."

"Did he?" said the Professor, looking surprised. "How very awkward. He knows I don't do that. Believe me, this will be much more interesting. Now, where was I?"

As the students left Mr. Bragg's classroom, applause for the Professor was still ringing in Hannah's ears. Even Clifton Hunslow had reluctantly clapped. Pulling her backpack onto her shoulder, Tara said, "Wow, that was way more interesting than listening to Mr. Bragg ramble on about whatever. Did you see his face when Dr. Harrower asked him if she could come back and tell us about suffragettes in England? I hope she does. When I go to Snipesville State, I'm so taking her class. I want to be her."

Even Hannah was impressed. She had never seen the Professor lecture before, and the past hour had given her a lot to think about. But now she wondered: Was the next time-travel adventure going to be in the Civil War? It would be typical of the Professor to have come to her class just to drop a hint.

As she picked up her backpack, Hannah felt a tap on her shoulder, and she turned around.

"I've been meaning to give this to you," said the Professor, holding out a book. Hannah took it, and read the title: *Britain in the Early 20th Century*. By the time she looked up again, the Professor was gone.

Hannah ate her lunch by herself outside, perched on an abandoned cement block around the side of the school. She leafed through the book the Professor had given her, but it was hard to understand, so she decided to read it at home, where she could concentrate. For now, as she picked at the salad she had made for herself, she thought about her dad. Yet again, she wondered what he had done so wrong in his job at the bank in San Francisco. It must have been pretty bad for him to be transferred to Snipesville, Georgia, and so soon after … She didn't want to think about her mother. Her mother, who had died. Her mother, who had left her, who had walked away from her husband and kids. Her mother, who had made it clear that she didn't like Hannah.

Hannah forced herself now to think instead about Snipesville. When she had moved here last summer, she had thought of this as the most boring and unwelcoming town ever. She still did, kind of. But it was also the weirdest, most interesting place on the planet, because her time travel had started here. She didn't know why. She didn't know if it was the Professor's doing, or if it was something to do with Snipesville itself. She didn't know why they kept ending up in Britain, and especially in the little town of Balesworth in Hertfordshire. She didn't know why time travel only happened to her, her brother Alex, Brandon Clark, and, of course, Professor Harrower.

It was always random. But it wasn't all bad: In their first adventure, in Balesworth in World War II, they had lived with Mrs. Devenish, and her granddaughter, Verity Powell, both of whom Hannah had come to adore. But when she and Alex and Brandon were wrenched back to 21st-century Snipesville, it was to a world in which Mrs. Devenish was long dead, and Verity was an old lady. Yet the time travel went on. Soon, Hannah, Brandon, and Alex were in 1851, then in 1752. None of it made sense. At all. Every time, they were separated, yet they always found each other, somehow. Every time Hannah, Alex, and Brandon returned to 21st century Snipesville, they did so at the moment they had left, arriving back with only their memories.

Hannah didn't feel like a kid any more. She didn't even feel like a teen. More and more, she felt like an adult. She had lived so many lives, and experienced things that people like Mr. Bragg couldn't even imagine. She had come face to face with the past as it really was, and it had changed how she thought about everything. Was it time now, Hannah asked herself, to take charge, and decide where and when she went? She thought it was. The only problem was that she still had yet to figure out how to control her travels in time.

Tuesday Morning, Mid-May
Alex was glad his class was going to the downtown theater, no matter how boring the presentation promised to be, because it got him out of school. He took a seat near the back of the bus, and hoped nobody would sit next to him. As the rest of the students boarded, he looked out of the window at the low-slung buildings of Snipes Academy.

"Okay if I sit here?" said someone, and Alex jumped.

A kid named Alex Shaffer was standing by his seat. Alex Dias knew who he was, of course. There weren't many kids at Snipes Academy, and he knew them all at least by sight. People were always mixing him up with Shaffer because of their shared first name. But Alex Dias had never actually talked to Alex Shaffer. He hoped this wasn't going to be one of those conversations about which church he went to. Practically the only reason anyone at the school talked to him, he thought, was to sign him up for their church.

Without asking permission, Shaffer sat down next to him, and then, keeping his voice low, he said, "I was wondering if you were okay."

"What's it to you?" The words slipped out before Alex could stop himself. Now he felt bad. "Hey, I'm sorry, I don't mean to be rude."

"It's okay," Shaffer said. "Look, I do know."

"You do?" Alex was alarmed now. Did Shaffer know he was a time traveler?

"I know Hunslow and Marshburn pick on you," Shaffer said. "So, are you okay?"

"There are worse things in my life than Clif Hunslow and Trey Marshburn," said Alex, and he meant it. "But thanks for asking."

"You're welcome. I don't mean to pry, I just want you to know not everyone around here is like them. Because we're not."

"Just most of you," Alex muttered.

CHAPTER ONE

"That's fair," said Shaffer, shrugging. "But not me. I don't much like Snipes Academy either. Or the Vile."

Alex smiled. "I've heard other people call Snipesville the Vile," he said. "It's pretty funny." As the bus engine roared to life, he and Shaffer shook hands.

But even as they pulled out of the school driveway, Alex still felt uneasy, and not because of the discomfort of sitting bolt upright as the school bus growled and bumped along the uneven road. The reason he could not relax was because he expected at any moment to be snatched away into the distant past, without warning, and without any idea of where he was going.

Much as Alex hated Snipesville, he hated time travel even more. And his adventures kept getting worse. 1752 had been terrifying and dangerous. His sister Hannah was trying to make herself feel better, talking about taking control of the time travel, but this, Alex thought, was delusional. He simply felt helpless, and he dreaded it all happening again.

Alex was too ashamed to tell Brandon of his fears. Brandon was a nice guy, but he was also, Alex thought, the strongest of the three of them. He thought Brandon might make a great leader one day. Alex himself didn't particularly want to lead, or even to follow. He wanted to be left alone.

Soon, with a screech of brakes, the bus pulled to a stop in front of SnipePAC, the new Snipes County Performing Arts Center in downtown Snipesville. It was close to the Confederate soldier statue and the old county courthouse, at the intersection of the two Main Streets, North/South Main, and East/West Main. Before he moved to Snipesville, Alex had never heard of a town with two Main Streets. Now it seemed normal.

Posters out front of the theater advertised upcoming events, including an Elvis impersonator, a beauty pageant (Miss Turpentine), and a touring troupe of acrobats from Bratislava. Today, the marquee announced something called *Pageant of Pride*. Maybe this was what their teacher had called the "special program" they were to see. There was something about the way that adults used the word "special" that made Alex's blood run cold.

The students filed onto the sidewalk and formed a line that snaked from the building, just as another school bus shuddered to a halt behind theirs.

The cavernous auditorium was dark and gloomy. Dusty and threadbare crimson curtains shrouded the stage, and the wooden folding chairs looked hard and uninviting. Alex followed his teacher's pointed finger, and soon he and Shaffer sat alone in their row, empty seats lined up to their left. Alex wondered which strange kids would be their neighbors.

The other school group soon arrived, and, Alex, to his joy, found himself

CHAPTER ONE

seated next to Brandon, who, in turn, was next to Javarius Evans. Alex introduced them both to Alex Shaffer, who gave the two boys an awkward smile.

Javarius pointed at the balcony jutting over their heads. "You know what? They used to call that balcony N-word heaven."

"It's true," said Brandon, leaning forward in his seat. "In segregation days, this was Snipesville's movie theater. Black people were allowed to go to the movies, but they had to go up the staircase in the alley, and sit in the balcony."

"Weird," Alex Shaffer said quietly. "Like a lot of things in those days."

Javarius gave him an intense look. "You think all that sort of thing only happened back then?"

"No, I'm sure he doesn't," Alex Dias said quickly. He felt defensive of Shaffer, the only kid at Snipes Academy who had shown any interest in befriending him.

But Shaffer didn't need defending. "Not exactly," he said calmly to Javarius. "I mean, look at my school." He jerked his head toward the white Snipes Academy students sitting ahead of him. "And then look at yours," he said, nodding at Brandon's and Javarius's classmates from R. H. Gordon Middle and High School, who were a mixture of black, white, Latino, and Asian. "I would be pretty naive to think everything's changed."

Alex said, with a hopefulness he didn't feel, "Even at SA, there are a few students who aren't white."

Javarius smiled like a shark. "You mean like you, Alex Dias? You're a pretty white Mexican."

He didn't say it unkindly, but Alex was still annoyed. "Some Latinos are white," he said haughtily. "But I'm not Mexican. I'm Portuguese."

Brandon intervened to relieve the tension. "Look, guys, one thing has changed. Today, we can all sit together to watch … whatever this is."

"Yes, that's progress," Javarius said dryly. "We can all suffer together."

Brandon smiled and turned back to Alex. "And it's a real pleasure to sit side-by-side with you, dude," he said, elbowing his friend in the ribs. "Hope you took a shower this morning."

Alex threw a mock punch at Brandon, just as a spotlight illuminated the stage, and the house lights went down. An immaculately dressed and made-up middle-aged white woman with hair like a blonde helmet bounced onto the stage. "Good morning, students!" she trilled, clapping her hands together. The audience grunted and stared in response. "Welcome to SnipePAC, the Snipes County Performing Arts Center," she said with a dazzling grin. "As many of you already know, I'm Mrs. Butler, and I'm the director of SnipePAC. We are so happy to have you here, students. We have a *very* special treat for you today."

"Not just special," Brandon muttered. "But *very* special. This is gonna be really bad, huh?"

Alex had to suppress a snort of laughter.

Mrs. Butler continued. "I know you'll want to join me in thanking our friends and special sponsors. Today's performance is made possible by the generous support of Zappy Burger, The Boiled Peanut boutique, The Hotel Duval, and Hunslow's Snipping … Snippy … Snipey … Gosh, I can't even say it, I mean the coffee place over the street."

"Hunslow's Sippin' Snipe," voices yelled helpfully.

"Well, that's right!" Mrs. Butler said. "But first, if anyone representing our wonderful sponsors or any members of the organizing committee are present, please stand and be recognized."

A well-coiffed white woman popped up from the audience to wave with a smug smile, as did an embarrassed-looking black man in a suit, and a young white guy with a ponytail, beard, and many tattoos whom Alex recognized as Ben Hunslow, the owner of the coffeehouse. Only the teachers and a handful of students applauded the sponsors.

"Thank you," Mrs. Butler sang. "Now, I want all of you students to give a respectful welcome to our performers, as they present for you the wonderful history of our very own Snipes County. This is gonna be a wonderful, educational experience for all y'all!"

Alex sighed. Brandon groaned. The show began.

The old white guy in a farmer costume on the stage was rambling on about certain families who he said had settled Snipes County. Alex listened at first, since he had been to Snipes County in 1752, and in 1851, and he hoped to hear the names of people he had actually met. But all the names mentioned were unfamiliar, and so he stopped listening.

He knew the actor. Mr. Marshburn was vice-president of the Bank of Snipesville, the local branch of GrandEstates Bank, and he was his dad's boss. GrandEstates had taken over the Bank of Snipesville a couple of years earlier, but it was the same local people who still ran the bank. Alex wondered about this: Why had GrandEstates sent Bill Dias to Snipesville? And why wasn't his dad the boss of the Bank of Snipesville? Mr. Dias was the only vice-president who wasn't from Georgia, and he always had to suck up to Mr. Marshburn. He always told Alex and Hannah to be nice to Mr. Marshburn's kids, Trey and Natalie, who were awful. Alex also wondered how, while his own dad seemed to work all the time, Mr. Marshburn could make room in his schedule to star in a stage show.

Alex tuned in again to the performance in time to hear Mr. Marshburn say, in an exaggerated Southern accent, "Why, my ancestor, Samuel Marshburn, founded Snipesville when he opened the first hotel here in 1830. Until then, Snipesville was just a clearing in the woods. Samuel Marshburn was a respected and prominent member of the community, and he and his beautiful lady wife, Sarah, were known and loved by all as fine Christian folks. They were kind to their slaves, and treated them like family."

Brandon and Javarius groaned, and Javarius said, "They always say stuff like that. What junk."

Alex raised his hand. He immediately realized that Mr. Marshburn couldn't see him with the house lights dimmed, and so he said loudly, "Excuse me?"

His words caused a slight sensation in the otherwise bored audience: Kids turned to see who was talking, nudged each other, and grinned. Teachers craned their necks anxiously. Mr. Bragg, who was at the end of the row in front, waved downward to tell Alex to lower his hand.

Alex felt like Oliver Twist, but he kept his arm raised. He really wanted to know Mr. Marshburn's answer to his question.

Putting on an obviously phony smile, Mr. Marshburn said, "Yes, young man?"

He doesn't recognize me, Alex thought. "Excuse me, sir," he said. He never called anyone "sir" in San Francisco, but California seemed long ago now. "So how come, if Snipesville was founded in 1830, none of the buildings here are very old?"

Mr. Marshburn peered into the darkness, but he still didn't seem to recognize Alex. "Now that's an excellent question. What's your name, young man?"

Alex could hardly give a fake name with his whole school watching. "Alex Dias," he said.

"You Bill Dias's boy?" said Mr. Marshburn, with the same phony smile. "Yes, I see you now. Well, I sure am glad you're interested in our local heritage, Alex. And that is an excellent question. Yes, it is."

There was a silence.

"Would you mind answering it?" Brandon said loudly. From the other side of the theatre, Ms. Greene, his teacher, hissed, "Brandon Clark, hush."

"I'll be happy to answer," said Mr. Marshburn, although he didn't look happy at all. "The first Snipesville was all log cabins, so the buildings didn't last. And then around about the end of the 1800s, there was a lot of growth, a lot of progress, in Snipesville. The Marshburns, the Hunslows, and other first families, well, we were all involved in that. And," he added awkwardly, looking at Brandon, "so were, um, African-Americans. Yes, people like, um, R. H. Gordon."

Brandon and Javarius groaned again. Alex wasn't quite sure why. Now everyone looked at the troublemakers.

CHAPTER ONE

"What about the violence in nineteen hundred and six?" Brandon called out. Ms. Greene looked ready to have a fit.

Alex couldn't help noticing Mr. Marshburn's features hardening. He stared at Brandon, and then he said, "We're not gonna talk about that today." He cleared his throat, and said hurriedly, "Anyhow, boys and girls, let me introduce all of you to R. H. Gordon himself."

"That's impressive," Javarius said quietly, shifting in his seat. "R. H. must be about 135 years old by now. Guess they'll be wheeling out the casket."

Alex whispered to Brandon, "What's wrong with R. H. Gordon? Why don't you like him?"

"Tell you later," said Brandon. Now, a dark-skinned man in a black frock coat, stand-up collar, and cravat strolled onto the stage.

"Well, that's definitely not R. H. Gordon," Brandon muttered to both Alexes. "That's Cassius Shrupp, the councilman. My dad calls him Suck-Up Shrupp. He doesn't rock the boat with the good old boys who run this town, so they like him."

Mr. Shrupp was speaking now, in the wooden voice of someone who is not comfortable with acting. "You know, back in nineteen hundred and six, I had a dream…"

"I thought Dr. King said that?" Javarius whispered.

"He did," replied Brandon. "I kind of doubt R. H. Gordon beat him to it."

Mr. Shrupp, as R. H. Gordon, continued, " … I had a dream of one day having educational opportunities for African-American individuals …"

"Individuals?" Brandon murmured. "I think he means people."

" … and building a high school for all black youth in Snipes County," Mr. Shrupp droned on. "I would never have imagined that one day, a school would be named for me."

Brandon slumped in his seat. "Nothing to see here," he said. "Everyone move along now."

"You want to hang out at our place after school?" said Alex, who had completely checked out from the performance. "My dad can take you home later."

"Sure," Brandon said. "I'll ask my mom and call you."

Alex suddenly felt bad for neglecting Shaffer, and he turned to him. "So what do you think of the show?"

"Boring," Shaffer whispered. "My family doesn't come from Snipesville. We moved here from Alabama in the Sixties. How long have yours been in Snipes County, Brandon?"

"Since the 18th century," Brandon said.

"Man, you mean the 19th century," said Javarius. "The 1800s."

CHAPTER ONE

"No, I don't," said Brandon. "I mean the 18th. The 1700s." He didn't explain. But Alex knew Brandon was speaking the truth, because he had met some of Brandon's ancestors.

"That show was so stupid," Brandon said later, as they sat in Alex's living room, clutching soda cans. "And can you believe they didn't even mention slavery? It was like they were saying everyone who came to Snipes County was white, free, and thrilled to be here."

"Hey I forgot to ask," said Alex. "Why do you and Javarius have a problem with R. H. Gordon? You said you would tell me."

Brandon cracked open his soda, and took a sip. "I don't have anything against R. H. Gordon. I mean, I don't know much about him, except what old Shrupp said. I don't think anyone does. He's one of those people that you learn exists, but nobody talks much about him, and he died a long time ago. The thing is, whenever white people here want to have a token black in Snipesville history, they talk about R. H. Gordon. Well, him and Old Jimmy McPhee, the guy who shined shoes on the courthouse square."

"Why do they have a historical marker about Jimmy McPhee?" said Alex, crinkling his forehead. "People don't usually put up plaques to guys who shine shoes."

"I think," said Brandon, "it was because he was there a long time, and because not much happens in this town. I heard a man at my church say they put up a plaque because old Jimmy did as he was told, smiled at white people, shined their shoes, and didn't ask awkward questions."

"Not like you and Javarius, then," said Alex with a chuckle. "We might have to wait a while for your plaques. Do you think R. H. Gordon is anything to do with us? The time travel, I mean."

"Man, I hope not," said Brandon.

"Are you related to R. H. Gordon?" Alex said. "Your dad's name is Gordon."

Brandon took a sip of his soda, and burped. "I know, and I'm wondering the same thing. But my Dad said it's just coincidence. Maybe I should ask my grandma. She might know."

"It would be cool if you were related to him," said Alex. "Maybe this is a hint about where we're going next. You could meet R. H. Gordon."

"No, not cool at all," Brandon said emphatically. "The last thing I want is for us to be in Snipesville when R. H. Gordon was around. He was here for the worst time."

Alex was confused. "But they said this morning he was famous in the 20th century, right? That was a long time after slavery ended. How could anything be worse than slavery?"

"I know, right?" said Brandon. "Slavery was terrible, but believe it or not, the early 20th century was even worse."

"How?"

Brandon looked at Alex's face, and realized he couldn't tell him about the lynching. *We Don't Talk About That,* he thought, with an ironic smile. Alex was the youngest, and the most fragile of the three time travelers. He had had the hardest time of them all. It wasn't likely they would end up in 1906 Snipesville on their next adventure, so why scare Alex?

"It just was," he said lamely. "Look, I'm starving. You got anything to eat?"

"Oh, sure," said Alex, hurrying toward the kitchen. "You want chips, or fruit?"

Before Brandon could reply, Alex reappeared in the doorway. "Ever think maybe we're trapped in a bad dream?"

Brandon shrugged. "Hey, speaking of bad dreams, how's your sister?" he said. "I haven't seen her in weeks."

"Okay, I guess," said Alex. "The Professor gave her a history book. She's reading it."

"Wow, that's a shock," said Brandon. "Why?"

"I don't know," said Alex. "I think she just got interested."

"I can't even imagine," said Brandon.

"She's not stupid," Alex said testily. He was loyal to Hannah.

"I never said she was," Brandon said. "She's just not what you think of as a, uh, book person."

"I'm not sure she is," Alex said. "It's just one book."

"Hey, it's a start," said Brandon. "And I can't wait to tell Dr. Braithwaite about it when I see him next."

Tuesday Afternoon, Mid- May

Hannah was practicing her time-travel technique. With her door shut, and wearing her dad's headphones to keep out sound, she closed her eyes and concentrated on feeling something. From what she could figure out, time travel was a trained mental skill, like playing golf, or hitting perfect pitch in song. She felt like she was tuning her brain as though it were a radio, and she was searching out the right frequency.

She experimented with combining mental concentration with physical activity. She made big jumps across the room, then small ones. She tried sitting down, standing up, lying flat, curling in a ball. She tried standing by the wall, then in the middle of the room, then leaning forward. She tried to concentrate after drinking a glass of water.

Now she tried just standing and relaxing. And that was when she felt it.

As soon as Hannah's body and mind went still, something took over. The harmonic sensation lasted only a few seconds, but she felt the ground vanish from beneath her feet, and the air around her become strangely still. Was this it? There was only one way to find out …

Hannah forced herself to calm, closed her eyes, and concentrated once again. Now all around her was light, and darkness, then light again, and a babble of sound, and a whiff of strange smells.

As soon as she opened her eyes, it all stopped, and her legs felt heavy.

Feeling jittery and slightly nauseous, Hannah screwed her eyes tight once again, and shook her head, as if to banish all the strange thoughts and feelings. Once she felt better, she shakily made her way downstairs for a drink. By the time she got there, she was starting to feel energized. She would continue her experiments. She was onto something.

Friday Afternoon, Mid-May

Even as she stood right outside Professor Harrower's office, Hannah fought the urge to flee the campus of Snipesville State College. But if she turned back now, she would regret it, she knew she would. So instead she knocked on the partly-opened door.

"Come in!" The Professor called out cheerfully.

When she entered, the Professor looked up from her laptop screen, her fingers still on the keyboard, and her face lit up. She spun in her chair and clapped her hands together. "Hannah! This is a pleasant surprise. Here, move all the stuff off that chair—onto the floor is fine, anywhere really …"

Hannah picked up a large pile of loose papers and dumped it onto the carpet, to join the other messy heaps of documents and books. Then she sat. "Hi," she said with a nervous smile.

"Hi!" the Professor replied, a little too brightly, drumming her fingers on the armrest of her desk chair. "How are things with you? The semester will be over in a couple of weeks, right?"

"Right. Mostly the usual," Hannah said. "I want to go to England."

"Oh," said the Professor, looking a little disappointed. "That's sudden. What, right now?"

Hannah nodded.

The Professor frowned at her again. "You're in school. And how can you afford the airfare, anyway?"

Hannah gave her an irritated look "You know what I mean!" she said. "Going by time travel. I want to go to 1940, to see Mrs. Devenish, and Verity."

"Oh, of course that's what you meant. No, it can't be done. I can't just make it happen when you feel like it, you know."

But Hannah knew the truth now. She sat up straight, shifted to the edge of her seat, looked the Professor in the eye, and said calmly, "You're lying."

The Professor rubbed her forehead and sighed dramatically. "Hannah, we've been through this before … "

"You're lying," Hannah insisted quietly. "You know how I know you're lying? I started figuring it out when I thought about how you found me in Scotland in 1851. You knew where to look for me, didn't you? Don't say you didn't. In fact, you always find all of us, wherever we are, well, except for that last time, which was scary. But except for that, you always find us, wherever we are, and whenever we are. Do you know how I really know for sure you're lying? Because I can make myself time travel. You've been lying the whole time. Admit it."

There was a long pause, and Hannah again locked eyes with the Professor, who looked pinned to her chair. "Ah," said the Professor.

"Yes, 'ah,'" said Hannah, folding her arms and leaning back. She sensed victory. "Now would you please tell me the truth? I'm not stupid."

The corners of the Professor's mouth twitched. "I know you're not. In fact, you're pretty smart. But it's not as simple as you think."

"I knew that too," said Hannah. "You can't always control the time travel, right?"

"Right," the Professor said. "And I don't always know where you are."

Hannah looked at her. "How do you know at all? Research? Old documents?"

The Professor looked evasive. "Mostly."

"How else?"

Again, the Professor hesitated. "Intuition, I suppose … No, don't look at me like that, intuition absolutely plays a part. Random hunches, experience, that sort of thing."

Hannah still wasn't convinced, but she played along. "Hmm. Can you teach me that?"

"The intuition, no. The research, yes. I can get you started, anyway. In fact, I already did, with the book I loaned you. Look, it will take years for you to learn. The good news is this isn't just about memorizing for tests. But it does mean that you must want to understand the past so much that it hurts, that you're willing to read some of the most badly-written, boring books ever published. You must be willing to ruin your eyesight poring over antique handwriting on microfilm, simply because you want to know. Because you can't sleep without knowing. Because you absolutely, positively, have to know."

CHAPTER ONE

"Okay," Hannah said slowly. "I do want to know. I've been reading that book you gave me, the one about Britain in the 20th century. You're right, it's boring, but I want to be ready for next time. I want to know."

"Here," said the Professor, riffling through a pile of papers on her desk, and pulling out a newspaper. She handed it to Hannah, who looked at the front page. *The Balesworth Examiner*. It looked brand new, as though it had been printed that day, but it was dated October, 1905. Hannah carefully unfolded the tissue-thin newspaper to the second page, and peered at the tiny type. "This is hard to read," she grumbled.

"Not as hard as old handwriting," the Professor shot back. "And you'll have to learn how to read that too, in time. By the way, *The Balesworth Examiner* is available online, so you can read the other issues there and enlarge the type. Look for any mentions of yourself. Remember, you probably won't be called Hannah Dias."

"Of course not," said Hannah. "I'll be Hannah Day, right?" Hannah Day was the name by which she had come to be known on her adventures in the past. She supposed it was because a Portuguese name like "Dias" would stand out in England or early Georgia.

The Professor shrugged. "I can't guarantee what you would be called, or even that you would look like yourself."

"If I didn't have the same name or the same face, how would I know if I found myself?"

"Just look for anything that seems out of the ordinary. Don't forget to look at the pictures. But there will probably be no mention of you at all, even if you are there. Very few people appear in the newspapers. Keep an eye on what else was going on in Balesworth at the time, because that might also be important."

"But it might not?" said Hannah.

"Possibly not. Welcome to history. Frustrating, isn't it? Look, are you sure you want to do research? It really can be very boring. It's needle in a haystack stuff."

Hannah said, "But it's not boring when you're hunting for something you care about, is it?"

"No, then it's addictive. But it can still be frustrating, especially when you realize you're hunting for something that doesn't exist."

Hannah got to her feet, still holding the old newspaper. "Can you give me another book? And don't look too happy that I asked for it?"

The Professor quickly grabbed a thick volume that was sitting on her desk, as though she had been waiting to be asked, and handed it to Hannah. Hannah glanced at the title, *Edwardian England: A Social History*, and put it under her arm. "Have you got anything on, like, 1851?" she said. "I want to know what that was about, too."

The Professor could hardly contain her excitement as she jumped up and ran a finger along a nearby bookshelf. She soon extracted an ancient and crumbling paperback and handed it to Hannah. "It's an oldie but goodie," she said, "It's well-written because it's from the time when historians still worried about writing for normal people, not just other historians."

"And," said Hannah, holding both books and the newspaper in front of her, "can you give me a ride home?"

The Professor pulled a face, but she reached for her purse all the same. "Come on then, pest," she said.

As the Professor locked her office door, Hannah realized that she had not told her the secret. She wondered if she should. Perhaps the Professor would try to stop her if she knew, and Hannah didn't want to be stopped. And anyway, considering how cagey the Professor had always been, Hannah enjoyed having a secret of her own.

TWO WEEKS LATER

Friday Morning, Late May

"Look at this!" Hannah cried. She was standing in the doorway of Alex's room, triumphantly waving a sheet of paper in her right hand, while clutching a book in her left.

"What?" Alex said without interest. He was staring at the computer screen.

Hannah shoved the paper under his nose, so close to his eyes that there was no chance of his being able to read it. He batted it away, then grabbed it from his sister, almost tearing it in the process.

"Hey!" she yelped, "Be careful!"

But Alex was already staring at the printout. "What is this?"

"It's from Balesworth's newspaper, October 20, nineteen hundred and five."

Balesworth. Any mention of this little English town made Alex apprehensive. Their only connection to it was through time travel.

Hannah said, "It's a women's suffrage meeting, you know, people trying to get women the vote. And look who this is." With her finger, she circled a face on a photograph.

Alex looked closely at the photo, his eyes scrunched up. All he saw were lots of serious-looking women wearing humongous hats, and he shook his head. "No idea."

Hannah gave an exasperated sigh, and stabbed her finger at the same face. "This woman here, on the left. It says who she is in the caption." She read it to him. *"Mrs. A. Lewis, president of the Balesworth branch of the Women's Suffrage Association."*

"So, great," said Alex. "Mrs. A. Lewis. ... Fantastic. Who's she?"

"Oh, right," Hannah said. "You never met her, did you? She was a friend of Mrs. Devenish. Well, she was more like Mrs. D.'s mentor, I guess. Even Mrs. D. was scared of her. Me and Verity had tea with her once, remember? I told you about her." Again, Hannah peered at the newspaper photograph. "I don't recognize anyone else in the picture, though. I wonder if one of them is Mrs. D.? Probably not. I don't think she grew up in Balesworth, did she?"

"I don't know," said Alex, returning his attention to the computer.

"Don't you care?" said Hannah, disappointed.

"No, not really," Alex said, tapping repeatedly on the space bar.

"You should care. This newspaper is from 1905. The Professor told me we're going there next."

Alex sighed heavily. "Does Brandon know?"

"I don't think so, or he would have told us. I better call him. Hey, this time should be easy. They have electricity, right? I think they do, anyway. I'm just glad we're going to be closer to today. I don't think I can cope with the eighteenth century again, and I definitely don't think I can handle anything earlier than that. 1905 seems pretty safe. No wars, far as I can figure out, and we're too soon for the Titanic, because that doesn't happen until 1912. Not that I plan going on *that* cruise." She smiled to herself.

And then, she said carefully, "Suppose I told you I can control it?"

"You can't though, can you?"

She looked a little deflated. "No. Not yet."

"Not ever, you mean," Alex said.

"I've been practicing," said Hannah.

"What do you mean, you've been practicing? How?"

"You wouldn't understand. I'll tell you if I get it right, OK?"

"You do that," said Alex, shaking his head. Once again he focused on the screen in front of him.

Friday Afternoon, Late May

"You look disappointed to see me, Dr. Braithwaite," said Brandon.

Old Dr. George Braithwaite's face had indeed fallen when he saw Brandon, but he quickly collected himself, smiled, and opened the door wide to admit his visitor. "Do come in," he said. His accent was still British, even after so many decades in Georgia. Dr. Braithwaite, whom Brandon, Alex, and Hannah had met when he was a small boy in Balesworth during World War II, had grown

CHAPTER ONE

up to become Snipesville's first black doctor, although he was now long retired.

"Wipe your feet," he ordered as Brandon crossed the threshold. "To be honest, dear boy, I was expecting someone else."

Brandon frowned. "So this is a bad time, huh?"

"No, no, come in, come in. Go through to the living room, and I'll bring you tea."

"Sounds good, Dr. B.," Brandon said, "but I'll pass on the tea. I don't want to stay long if you're expecting company."

As they sat down, Dr. Braithwaite saw the worry on Brandon's face. "Brandon, what's wrong?"

"Hannah says the Professor hinted to her that we're going to 1905 next. To England. That's a year before the lynching in Snipesville."

Dr. Braithwaite leaned back and said lightly, "Well, then, nothing to worry about. A year's difference, wrong side of the Atlantic."

Brandon did not find this reassuring. "Okay, but why does nobody talk about what happened in 1906?"

"Oh, we do, once in a while. Black people do, that is. We just don't discuss it much with kids, I suppose because it's very disturbing. So much so, I must confess that I have never enquired too enthusiastically for the details. However, it is just one particularly violent episode in a generally unpleasant history, and it was, after all, a long time ago. We have other things to worry about that are happening right now."

"I guess," Brandon said, thinking to himself that no time was ever long ago for a time traveler. All of it was yesterday, today, or tomorrow. He persisted. "So why don't white people want to talk about it now?"

"Oh, you know the answer to that," said Dr. Braithwaite. "You don't need me to tell you."

At that moment, the doorbell rang. "That must be my guest," said Dr. Braithwaite, as he got to his feet.

Brandon also stood. "I better go then."

"No, no, stay where you are! This is someone who will want to see you."

Brandon hoped he wouldn't have to chat politely with an old person. But then he heard an old woman say in an English accent, "Good Lord, George, that taxi cost me an absolute fortune. You could have warned me. I would have taken the bloody bus."

"There aren't any buses, Verity," Dr. Braithwaite said, chuckling. "I'm in the back of beyond."

"George, I have traveled by bus in India, and in the Sudan, and if that's not the back of beyond, where is? Why would I assume there were no buses in any region of the richest country in the world?"

"Welcome to Snipesville," Dr. Braithwaite said, kissing her cheek. "And wait until you see who I have with me."

But Brandon was already in the hallway, grinning at the very tall, very old white woman before him. He had first met Verity Powell in 1940, when she was even younger than him. Now here she was, shaking out her umbrella on the porch while Dr. Braithwaite picked up her case. She closed the door behind her, and looked delightedly at Brandon, before holding out her arms to him. "Brandon, darling!" she cried.

He gave her a gentle hug, afraid of hurting someone so old and fragile, but Verity surprised him by almost crushing him in her grasp. She wasn't as delicate as she looked.

What Brandon didn't see was that even as they embraced, Verity was looking over his shoulder at Dr. Braithwaite, giving her old friend a very worried and questioning look. In answer to the unspoken question, George Braithwaite nodded, and mouthed "Not yet" to her. Verity frowned.

"Is everything OK?" Brandon said in a muffled voice. "It's just … You're strangling me."

Verity let go, stepped back, and put a hand on his cheek. "I'm sorry, dear, it's just so lovely to see you alive and well."

"You were expecting me to be dead?" Brandon was joking, but he promptly regretted it, because when he looked up into Verity's face, he thought she looked upset, just for a second, and when he turned to look at Dr. Braithwaite, so did he. But perhaps he was imagining things. They were just tired old people.

"Brandon, I think you'll agree that Verity needs to rest after her journey," said Dr. Braithwaite. "And I am ready for my nap. Why don't we meet tomorrow at that new coffee place downtown, the one with the ridiculous name?"

"The Sippin' Snipe? Sounds like a plan," Brandon said. "You want me to ask Hannah and Alex?"

"No," Verity said, a little too quickly. "I'll take the three of you out for lunch while I'm here, but tomorrow, that would simply be too much of a crowd."

Brandon frowned. Why didn't Verity want to see Hannah and Alex? Again, maybe he was just imagining things. He looked at her again. She reminded him so much of Mrs. Devenish. She looked and sounded like an older, modern version of her grandmother, and hardly at all like the young girl he had first met, in 1940 and less than a year ago.

Saturday Morning, Late May

"Boys, I must find a hole in the wall," said Verity. Brandon snorted his cappuccino through his nose. "I'm sorry?" he gasped, grabbing a napkin.

"Oh, don't you call it that? A cashpoint then. Is there a bank nearby?"

"Several banks, in fact," said Dr. Braithwaite, a drained cappuccino on the table before him. "The closest is Bank of Snipesville, or GrandEstates, or whatever it's called now."

"That's where Alex and Hannah's dad works," Brandon told Verity.

"Is it indeed? Then I shall go there when we're ready. But there's no rush. You know, the way you two have spoken about Snipesville, one would think it were a wasteland. But this is pleasant, isn't it?" Verity gave an approving smile to the coffee shop in which they were sitting, with its bright art on the walls, and the sounds of jazz in the air, punctuated by the sharp hiss of the espresso machine. The furniture was strangely unmatched to its surroundings: A battered upright piano which served as a stand for leaflets, and mismatched chairs and tables that seemed to have been rescued from the homes of several old ladies.

The only other customers were two students from Snipesville State College, who pretended to study, but mostly spent their time checking their phones. Behind the bar stood the café's ponytailed barista-owner, Ben Hunslow, who occasionally stole curious glances at Dr. Braithwaite, his white British lady friend, and the black kid who sat with them.

"Perhaps I exaggerated Snipesville's disadvantages just a little," Dr. Braithwaite admitted to Verity, "but not by much. Until this place opened a couple of months ago, I had to go to the college campus for a decent coffee. That said, the eccentric name is a giveaway that this is indeed a Snipes County enterprise."

"What name?" Verity said, and Dr. Braithwaite solemnly raised an index finger to point at the sign over the menu board.

Verity looked over her glasses, and read aloud. "*Hunslow's Sippin' Snipe*? Is that what this place is called? How curious. Whatever does it mean?"

"It's named after Snipes County, and the illustrious local family to whom the owner belongs," said Dr. Braithwaite.

"Good gracious," said Verity. "Well, apart from the preposterous name, I can't honestly say that there's much difference between this place and our coffee shops in Balesworth."

"On the surface, no …" Dr. Braithwaite said slowly. "But, Verity, there's a great deal of difference between here and Balesworth, I assure you, it's just not immediately apparent. It takes time to learn to appreciate the distinctions. Mind you, when I first came to Snipesville, the differences were glaringly obvious. You would have been stunned. People greeted me much as they would have greeted a Martian. Those were the days of segregation, of course. Things have changed a great deal since then, but too many people's attitudes have not. People in Snipesville still don't know what to make of me, of course, because a black Englishman is still quite the novelty here. Mind you, all the Brits in this town say the same thing, that very few of the local whites will admit to being impressed by someone who comes from beyond the boundaries of Snipes County, Georgia."

Brandon sat up at this. "Wait, other British people live here?" This was news to him.

"Oh, certainly," said Dr. Braithwaite. "People from all over the world live in Snipesville these days. How could you not have noticed, Brandon?"

Brandon thought about kids at his school, and realized that Dr. Braithwaite was right. He thought of Erica and Jordan Park, whose parents were from South Korea, and ran the Japanese restaurant … Isabella Sanchez, whose dad owned the town's largest Latino grocery, Supermercado Snipesville … Holly Patel, whose mom was a doctor at Snipesville Family Practice … And, of course, Hannah and Alex Dias from San Francisco, whose dad was a banker at the Bank of Snipesville, and whose ancestry was Portuguese.

In fact, Brandon hadn't thought about Snipesville being diverse, because, even now, most people in Snipesville were white folks and black folks whose families had been there forever. The white families who ran the town were those who had always run the town, and the same black families still tried to seize the few and meagre opportunities that came their way. His own family had built its modest fortunes on the funeral home established by his grandparents. Even before that, starting after slavery had ended, the family had owned a blacksmith's shop until … He didn't want to think about what had happened to it. "Why *would* any Brits come to Snipesville?" he asked.

"Most of us seem to be here by accident," said Dr. Braithwaite. "Let me see. There's Caroline Cross who runs the Duval Hotel—she's from Manchester. And I know a couple of professors at Snipesville State: Mike Hays, Lorna Hebden …. "

"Professor Kate Harrower?" Brandon said.

"No, I don't think so," Dr. Braithwaite said carefully.

"Why?" Brandon said. "She has an accent."

"Don't we all?" said Dr. Braithwaite. "But as to where hers comes from, I couldn't tell you."

Brandon felt a little creeped out by this news. "She's not British?"

Dr. Braithwaite sipped his coffee. "I didn't say that. Look, Brandon, because I worry about you three, I did take the liberty of looking into Professor Harrower's credentials. They do check out. She earned a doctorate in British and American history from Yale, just as she claims. Her undergraduate work was taken at Cambridge University. Verity, she was at Newnham, in fact, just like you."

"Was she?" said Verity, eyebrows raised. She turned to Brandon. "That's my old college at Cambridge. How very interesting. I agree with your instincts, though, George. In my very brief encounter with Kate Harrower, I couldn't tell where she was from."

Brandon felt another chill. He had started to trust Professor Harrower. Now he wasn't so sure he should.

"Then again," said Dr. Braithwaite, with an uncertain chuckle, "I'm sure I sound more American than British, too. I've been over here for more years than I care to count. Of course, Brandon, you have known me for even longer than that."

Ben Hunslow, who had been eavesdropping from behind the counter, stared at the group, but Brandon knew he would never figure out what Dr. Braithwaite had meant. Brandon and seven-year-old George Braithwaite had met first in England in 1940, and how would Ben Hunslow ever know that?

Suddenly, Verity said, "Brandon, this is not purely a social visit. Honestly, I don't travel much these days, and after my nightmare journey to Snipesville, I probably won't be back. But George wanted me here. He was right. It's important."

"What's wrong?" said Brandon.

Dr. Braithwaite gave Verity a meaningful glance, and said, "Nothing is wrong as such, Brandon, it's just that … Remember you told me that time travelers sometimes change what has happened in the past, but they're the only people who know about it when they return to the present? For everyone else, the new circumstances are just the way things have always been?"

Brandon said slowly. "I'm not sure. I think so. The Professor accidentally changed something in 1851, and we changed it back again. Look, why are you asking?"

Dr. Braithwaite glanced at Verity, and she glanced at him. And then he said, "Are you aware that Verity and Eric both time traveled in the 1950s?"

Brandon was shocked. This was absolute news to him. Neither Verity nor her late husband Eric had ever said anything about being time travelers themselves. "I can't believe this … Why didn't you say something before?"

"That's interesting," Dr. Braithwaite said quietly. "So Professor Harrower was right, Verity. Something has changed. You weren't always time travelers, or you would have told the children." To Brandon he said, "This also tells me that you haven't yet had your next adventure. We must not discuss this further until you do."

There was a resounding crash across the room. Ben Hunslow, his mouth hanging open, had dropped a coffee mug.

"Don't worry, son," Dr. Braithwaite called out cheerfully to the shocked young man. "We're all *Doctor Who* fans."

"But what are we going to discuss?" Brandon said.

"What is about to happen," said Dr. Braithwaite, and then he and Verity gave Brandon that worried look again.

"I need to tell Alex and Hannah," said Brandon.

"I don't know if you should," said Dr. Braithwaite. "Why don't you wait?"

Whatever is going on, Brandon thought, *it's freaking me out.*

Monday Morning, Late May

"Hannah," said her grandmother, her picture looking a little fuzzy on the computer screen. "I know you're on break, but is this a bad time to talk?"

"Kind of," said Hannah. "What's up? Everything okay in Sacramento?"

"You know how I've been doing some family history? I found out something that will interest you. Your Grandpa's family, Walker, is old California …"

"I know that," Hannah said impatiently. "Grandpa's always going on about how he could join Native Sons of the Golden West if he wanted."

"Listen, won't you? I started using a family tree website, you know, the one that advertises on TV, and I'm finding out all kinds of things. I discovered my great-grandmother was from New York, and I've been emailing a very interesting lady who has family in common with us, and she and I are going to call each other in a few minutes. Would you believe where …"

But Hannah had stopped listening. "Grandma, that's cool," she said, "but I'm kind of busy. Can I call you back?"

"Not today, sweetheart. Grandpa and I are headed out to the movies with our friends Ed and Loretta, remember them? But maybe tomorrow? Don't forget the time difference."

"OK," said Hannah. "Love you."

"Love you too, sweetheart." The screen popped off.

Hannah smiled. She could only imagine her grandmother's face if she knew what was keeping her so busy.

After she switched off the computer, Hannah gave her full concentration to relaxing. So much so, that she almost fell asleep standing up. But now, something was happening. It felt real, like a dream that doesn't stop after you awaken. She tried to make sense of what she could see, hear, and smell … Straw on dirt, a man's deep voice and a hand grabbing a shovel, a woman laughing raucously, the scent of burning wood … This wasn't a dream, or a hallucina-

CHAPTER ONE

tion. It was really happening, all around her. She just couldn't make sense of it.

She tried again. The same sensations: Random smells, sounds ...

Hannah opened her eyes, and found herself looking right into the face of a strange woman. Frightened, she only had time to register the woman's pale blue eyes, her freckles, the tight bun of her hair, the shock on her face, the smell of the dusty room, and the sound—what was that?—of a horse-drawn cart. The woman opened her mouth (maybe to scream?) and ...

Hannah was back in her room, out of breath, dizzy, scared, and shaking. But she was also exhilarated.

Alex, as usual, was at the computer when Hannah walked into the living room. He hardly noticed her, but she tapped him on the shoulder. He jumped slightly, and then took off his headphones.

"You're looking pleased with yourself," he said grumpily, throwing the headphones down onto the desk.

She smiled, in a smug sort of way. "I can do it. I can time travel."

He looked bored. "That's your news? You can time travel? Well, hey, can't we all ..." But then his eyes widened, and he shot up in his chair. "Wait, you mean ... YOU can time travel? Like *you* can control it?"

Grinning now, Hannah nodded.

When Hannah had finished describing her experiences, Alex no longer looked excited, but worried.

"So what you're saying is you time traveled by yourself but you can't exactly control where you go? Or how long you stay there?"

"Not yet," Hannah said.

"You're scaring me," Alex said. "Suppose you go somewhere and can't get back?"

"I'm scaring myself," Hannah confessed. "I'm worried I'll end up in—I don't know—China in the Stone Age, or something. Somewhere I have no clue how to function."

"You should tell the Professor."

"No," Hannah said quickly. "She'll just try to stop me."

"Yeah, of course she will. It's dangerous."

"You're so negative," Hannah said, her voice rising. "Don't you get what this means? It means that we could live an incredibly long time, because we always come back home at the age we left, no matter how long we're gone. We could do amazing things, and ... and ..."

"And mess up history," Alex said, "And get killed. And get other people killed."

Hannah ignored him. "I can take you with me," she said.

"No, I don't want to go."

"Not even London, 1851? That was okay, wasn't it?"

Hannah held out her hands, and as Alex automatically took them, she closed her eyes, and found the wavelength. As she settled into it, she thought of the Great Exhibition, in 1851, in London. Or tried to.

It all happened in less than three seconds.

Monday, Late May

In Sacramento, California, in a little house that looked like it came from a fairy tale, Ellen Walker, Hannah and Alex Dias's grandmother, had an appointment for 10 a.m. Pacific Time. She typed in a web address from the piece of paper in her hand, and then clicked on the little video camera symbol on the computer.

An English accent said "Hello?" Then a wrinkly neck appeared on the screen, which jiggled about as its owner adjusted the camera. Finally, there appeared the slightly blurry face of a very old white woman.

"Hello, Ellen! How marvelous to see you!"

"And wonderful to see you too," said Ellen. Now, she beamed at the old woman on the screen. "I can't believe all these family relationships between us. Isn't the internet something, Verity?"

"It certainly is extraordinary," said Verity Powell. "I must say that I was delighted to learn that you're interested in tracing all the female lines in your family, just like me. It's trickier than tracing the men, because our names keep changing, but it's much more fun, isn't it?"

Ellen nodded. "Oh, I couldn't agree more. When I realized that all the last names of my women ancestors were really the names of their husbands and fathers, it made me even more determined to learn about the ladies. My maiden name was Hopkins, which is Welsh. But when I started tracing the women in my family, I learned that one of my ancestors, Maggie O'Leary, was born in Ireland, and moved to Scotland during the Irish potato famine. She became a factory worker in a city called Dundee. But by the 1870s, she was in San Francisco, teaching elementary school. What a life that must have been, huh?"

Verity tried to interrupt, but Ellen was on a roll. "Now … I'd like to share with you another Scottish ancestor of mine, my great-great-grandmother. She came from Scotland to New York in 1851, and although she wasn't related to Maggie, she was also from Dundee. Her name was Wilhelmina Gordon, although she also went by Mina, and her married name was Strachan. I think she was distantly related to you, too. You know, until I found Mina and Maggie, I had no idea we had any Scottish ancestry at all …"

CHAPTER ONE

As Grandma looked up at the screen, she looked past Verity, into the bright background, and smiled. "Wow, is that the sun shining in England? It looks like a beautiful day."

"As it happens, Ellen, I'm not in England. I'm in Georgia, visiting a friend."

"Georgia?" exclaimed Grandma, "Oh, for heaven's sake. My grandchildren live there. I wonder if you're anywhere near them?"

"As a matter of fact I am," Verity said, "I'm very near Hannah and Alex. I'm in Snipesville."

Ellen suddenly was on her guard. She realized with a shock that she was talking to a stranger on the internet, to a woman who seemed to know a lot about her. "I'm sorry, but how do you know my grandchildren live in Snipesville?" she said shortly. "And how do you know their names?"

Verity had stopped smiling. Now, behind her, appeared an elderly, light-skinned black man with a mustache, who waved and gave Ellen a tight smile before sitting next to Verity, his face half-appearing on the screen.

"Ellen, this is Dr. George Braithwaite," said Verity. "We have something we wish to discuss with you, and I do hope that you won't think us both demented. But even if you do, please don't hang up. It's very, very important that you hear what we have to say."

Ellen Walker, not knowing how to reply, nodded apprehensively.

Chapter 2
THE FESTIVAL OF BRITAIN

Saturday, May 26, 1851 ... Or 1951 ...Or ?

Hannah opened her eyes to a blur, and heard a babble of voices and footsteps. Then she blinked, and all came into focus. She was standing on a footbridge that ran parallel to a rail bridge, both of them spanning a river. People were walking past her at a brisk pace. As her eyes focused on the spires of the Houses of Parliament, she knew instantly that the river below her feet was the Thames. She was in London. She had done it. She had actually got herself to where she had meant to be. It was fantastic.

But something wasn't right. As Hannah watched the people streaming by, she saw that they were dressed in mid-20th century fashions: men in tailored suits, women in flowery skirts and dresses, everyone in hats. Clapping her hand to her head, Hannah confirmed that she was wearing a hat. Automatically, she looked down, and, to her dismay, saw herself draped in a Victorian dress, complete with hoop skirt. She looked perfect for 1851. Unfortunately, this was definitely *not* 1851. And when she turned to look behind her, she saw a huge white spaceship crouched on the south bank of the Thames.

Hannah gasped. What was a spaceship doing in the middle of twentieth-century London? *And where's Alex?* She looked around frantically. Her brother was nowhere to be seen. She couldn't worry about him now. She forced herself to calm down.

Turning around, she held up her hand, stopping the nearest pedestrian in his tracks, a short young man in his early twenties wearing horn-rim glasses, a button-down shirt, brown tie, corduroy pants, and a pale green sweater.

"Excuse me?" she said, as he tried (and failed) to dodge around her.

"Yes? Can I help you?" He glanced over her shoulder into the distance, to the end of the bridge, then refocused on her.

"What's the date today?" said Hannah.

"Er, Saturday, May 26th," he said, looking over her shoulder again.

"What year?"

"Nineteen fifty one." Hannah smiled at this, but the young man looked annoyed. "I say, is this some kind of joke? Look, I'm on my way to the Festival of Britain." He pointed at the spaceship, which Hannah now guessed probably wasn't a spaceship. "I'm late meeting my fiancée and my mother ... I mean, her grandmother ... Oh, look, I can't stop. Sorry."

With that, he took off at a trot. *No wonder he wanted to get away from me*, Hannah thought, glancing down at her clothes. *I look ridiculous.*

And then she realized. That was Eric. The man she had just talked to was Eric, Mrs. Devenish's adopted son. He was not at all the small kid with the thick London accent Hannah had lived with in England in 1940. He sounded quite posh. But she was almost certain it was him. This couldn't be a coincidence, could it? Out of the millions of people in London in 1951, how could it be a coincidence that she had run into Eric? She knew, just knew, that following him was what she was meant to do now. Hannah picked up her skirts, and began to run along the bridge, apologizing to all the people in suits and hats as she weaved and shoved past them, trying desperately to keep that green sweater in sight.

Eric (if he was Eric) had vanished into the crowd. But this was no longer a crowd walking quickly to their destinations. The pace had slowed, as people began strolling along the riverbank. They were mostly dressed for a day out, in browns, blacks, blues, and grays, the muted drab colors that Hannah remembered from 1940. Some of the women were a little more daring, wearing light blues or floral prints, while a few men sported brightly-colored ties. In the midst of them, Hannah slowed, and then stopped. She had found herself in a place that was so deeply strange, she was starting to think that she really had stumbled into an alternate universe.

Bright colors and alien structures surrounded her. A cement and glass building soared above her head. Giant kabobs strung with globes in bold colors, of blue, red, and yellow, drew Hannah's eye from otherwise gray and somber London. Just a few yards from where she stood, a bizarre aluminum water feature poured and caught water in robotic arms. Ahead of her, spiking toward the sky, a gray torpedo seemed to float in the air, although Hannah quickly spotted the

CHAPTER TWO

wires holding it up.

Dominating the scene was the giant spaceship, astride its spindly metal legs. But now, as the 'spaceship's' walls rippled in the wind, Hannah knew for certain that it wasn't an alien vehicle, or even a building. It was a giant tent.

The people walking around Hannah looked downright cheerful, their slightly embarrassed smiles suggesting that they couldn't believe their luck that they were in London for whatever this event was. Hannah supposed it was the Festival of Britain thing that Eric was headed to. If he was Eric. She now thought of him as Possibly-Eric.

And there he was.

Possibly-Eric was standing in the middle of the crowd, peering at a small map. Looking at him in profile, she felt even more strongly than before that this was, indeed, probably Eric. She called out to him, but he didn't hear her amid the noise. Neatly folding the map and tucking it inside his jacket pocket, he set off toward the 'spaceship.'

Hannah was almost at a run now behind Probably-Eric as he strode into the spaceship that wasn't a spaceship at all. She watched, dismayed, as Almost-Certainly-Eric handed a ticket to a uniformed man in a peaked cap, and pushed through a turnstile. Again, he disappeared from view.

Hannah's way was barred by the same uniformed official and turnstile that had so easily admitted Definitely-Eric. "How do I get in?" she demanded.

"Admission to the Dome of Discovery is five shillings," the man replied patiently, as he dangled a small clipboard by his side. "You buy your ticket outside." He pointed her back the way she had come.

"I don't have time for that," Hannah snapped. She didn't add that she didn't have the money, either.

But the man had noticed her Victorian outfit, and he tapped his clipboard. "Here, half a mo, are you on my list, love? Judging from your get-up, I'd say it was a certainty. You look like you're ready for the Great Exhibition of 1851, not the Festival of Britain, 1951. Impersonating Florence Nightingale, are we?" He laughed, revealing uneven tombstone teeth.

"I might be," Hannah said cautiously. And then she realized he had given her an idea. "I'm supposed to show people what visitors to the Great Exhibition looked like," she said, "and I'm really, really late for work." Genius! She congratulated herself.

The man gave her a conspiratorial wink. "In that case, I shan't make you wait. Here, come through." He tucked his clipboard under his arm, and from his pocket, pulled out a key on a chain, and inserted it into the mechanism of the turnstile. "Now, tell me your name and I'll find you on my list," he said.

"Hannah Dias!" she yelled with a smile as she pushed through the turnstile. "Thanks!"

The official ran his finger down his clipboard, and frowned. "How do you spell that?" he said, looking up. But the girl in mid-Victorian dress was gone, absorbed by the crowds that thronged the Dome of Discovery.

Hannah ran as quickly as she could in her massive gown, to get out of sight before the doorman discovered that her name wasn't on his little clipboard. When she finally stopped to look around her, her heart sank. Possibly-Probably-Definitely-Eric had slipped away.

"Eric, where have you been?" Verity scolded. "Granny and I were almost ready to go on without you. We've been waiting for over half an hour." Mrs. Devenish, tall and fierce-looking, stood by grimly, clutching a large brown purse. Next to them both was a gangly teenager in an ill-fitting suit, whose coffee-colored skin drew curious glances from passers-by. George Braithwaite was used to the stares, because most people in England in 1951 were white, and anybody who was not was bound to attract attention. Sometimes, he pretended to himself that he was a Hollywood film star, and that was why they were looking at him.

"Verity, Granny, George, I am most terribly sorry," Eric said breathlessly to the two glaring women and the shy teen. He wiped over his hair with his hand. "Look, it's not my fault. My train was canceled, and of course it was too late to telephone you at your hotel before you set off."

George came to his rescue. "Mrs. Devenish, the trains were running late when I left Balesworth, and the chap on the platform said something about repairs on the line."

Eric threw George a grateful glance, and said, "Might I buy everyone tea to make amends?"

"We already had tea an hour ago," Mrs. Devenish snapped.

Eric was determined to stick up for himself in the face of the formidable disapproval of his adoptive mother. Mrs. Devenish had taken him in as an evacuee from war-torn London at the beginning of World War II, and raised him alongside Verity, her granddaughter. Unlike most evacuees, he had not returned home at the end of the War. Now that Eric and Verity were engaged to marry, this meant that Mrs. Devenish was both Eric's adoptive mother and his future grandmother-in-law. He found it difficult to know how to introduce her to strangers. To confuse people further, he always addressed Mrs. Devenish as "Granny."

"Come on, Granny," Eric said with an insincere smile, trying to jolly her along, "I did say I was sorry. And it's hardly my fault the nine o'clock from Balesworth was canceled, now, is it?"

Mrs. Devenish was not impressed. "I don't know why you're grinning at me. You should have caught an earlier train as a precaution. Now come along," she said, leading the way. "There is a great deal to see, and precious little time in which to see it. I wish to view the exhibition of nuclear physics, although I daresay I won't understand a word of it. Perhaps you can explain it to me, Eric, so long as you aren't too technical about it. I want to know what you've learned at university, apart from the whereabouts of all the local pubs, that is."

With that, she set off, as George Braithwaite respectfully walked alongside her.

Eric smiled fondly, sighed, and pulled out a cigarette. As he fumbled for his matches, Verity gave his arm a squeeze. "If you can explain nuclear physics to Granny," she said with a mischievous smile, "you might get out of the doghouse by teatime."

He snorted in reply, and exhaled a huge puff of smoke. "If I'm to do that, I shall have to take a crash course in nuclear physics myself. I'm a civil engineering student, not an atomic engineer." He watched as the old woman paused at the next exhibit. "Come on, Verity, we had better catch up with her. She'll be livid if I slow her down again."

But Verity frowned. "Eric, don't be so wet. I was only teasing you. Honestly, the old bat's becoming more difficult by the day. Really, you ought to stand up to her."

"I know," Eric said quietly, "But I'm remarkably tolerant of her jabs because, actually, I'm rather worried about her. Aren't you? She seems, I don't know, a little out of sorts these days. It can't be easy for her, not at her age. I can't believe she's sixty-six years old."

"Hmm," said Verity, as they set off in pursuit of Mrs. Devenish. "I know she's no spring chicken, but I wouldn't fall for her *I'm an old lady* nonsense if I were you. She seems lively enough, rushing about to her WVS and Women's Institute meetings, and still sitting as a magistrate, too, after all these years … I think she's playing on your sympathy."

"Verity," Eric said, perplexed, "I'm not sure whether you're more sensible than me, or just as tough as old boots."

"Both, probably," said Verity. "Now hurry up. I think we've lost her … Not that that's necessarily a bad thing, but we can't leave poor George stuck with her all by himself, can we?"

CHAPTER TWO

❖ ❖ ❖

Hannah still found it hard to believe that she had landed in the past, because this definitely felt like a very weird future. All around her in the Dome of Discovery were more strange shapes, bright colors, and the sheer confusion of an exhibition that seemed to be about everything and nothing. She understood the point of a mannequin helpfully labeled "Charles Darwin." But what was the sculpture of two naked figures pulling a plough supposed to be? Worse, none of the spectators around either exhibit was Eric.

She turned around, and got the shock of her life. In a wall mirror, she saw a strange woman looking at her. It took a second for her brain to register that she was looking at herself. She now appeared to be in her early twenties. She touched her face, and saw the gesture reflected. This had happened before, of course, to Alex and Brandon. But not to her. It would take some getting used to.

Still, Hannah didn't have time to worry about her new appearance. She had to look for Eric. But so many men looked so much like him. Everyone she had seen was white. Everyone was dressed pretty much the same. She positioned herself where she could watch visitors walk along the gangway above her. She scanned the passing faces: A family with small kids, an elderly couple … and then Hannah's heart leaped. She had found Eric, and when she saw who he was with, she could not believe her luck.

Mrs. Devenish looked more wrinkly than Hannah remembered, and her gray hair was now almost white. Otherwise she appeared much the same as she had in 1940. The young woman walking with her had to be Verity: She looked like a twenty-something version of her grandmother. As for the light-skinned black teenager, who else could he be but George Braithwaite? With an excited shout, Hannah charged toward the stairs.

They had reached the Atomic Research exhibit. "This is very colorful, I must say," said Mrs. Devenish. She did not sound approving. She paused to examine a garish mural of two men, one in a gas mask, and the other sporting a giant glass bowl over his head. "Fascinating," she said dryly, "but also rather disturbing, don't you think?"

"Why?" Eric said in a hearty voice, determined to assert himself. "It's the future, Granny. Wonderful stuff. Not disturbing at all. The Festival is the most cheerful thing I've ever seen. I feel as though the War is finally over."

Mrs. Devenish walked on, ignoring him, and Verity elbowed him in the ribs. "You're supposed to be on your best behavior," she giggled. "Remember?"

He winced and rubbed his side. "Steady on, old girl. I was only offering an opinion. And I thought you said I should stand up for myself?"

CHAPTER TWO

"Not now," she muttered. "The old bag is in a bad mood as it is."

"I heard that, my girl," Mrs. Devenish said loudly. "I'll have you know that 'the old bag' isn't deaf."

Blushing, Verity stammered apologies.

Having put Verity in her place, Mrs. Devenish returned her attention to the mural. At that exact moment, a young woman in a vast Victorian dress almost knocked her over, throwing her arms around her, and yelling, "Mrs. D!"

Startled, Mrs. Devenish pushed Hannah away, then hit her hard with her handbag.

"Ow!" said Hannah, clutching her arm. But then she started laughing. It was such a Mrs. Devenish thing to do, she thought, greeting her with mild violence, and it was so wonderful to see her anyway. As far as Hannah was concerned, her beloved foster mother had come back from the dead. "It's me! Hannah! Hey, did you shrink? You look shorter … "

"Who on earth are you?" Mrs. Devenish demanded, stepping away from her.

Hannah frowned. *Of course*, she thought. Mrs. Devenish didn't recognize her because she looked grown up. "I'm Hannah," she said, a little more loudly, in case the old woman was hard of hearing.

But Mrs. Devenish continued to look blank, and now she was shaking her head. "I don't know anyone by that name. And what do you mean by grabbing me like that? I ought to send for the police."

Hannah tried a third time, speaking quickly. "Mrs. D., it's me, Hannah Day," she said, using the name she had used in 1940. "I was your evacuee, remember?"

Suddenly, Verity gasped, and throwing her arms around Hannah, almost lifted her off the ground. "Oh, gosh, Hannah! Is it really you? Oh, imagine finding you here! I say, Eric, George, Granny, isn't this a lovely surprise!"

Mrs. Devenish's eyes had widened in recognition for only a moment before narrowing again in suspicion. She looked Hannah up and down, and muttered, "It's certainly unexpected."

"Don't you look grown up!" said Verity. "Hannah, you remember George Braithwaite?" Shyly, George stepped forward.

"Wow, you got so tall," Hannah said, and George looked more embarrassed than ever.

Mrs. Devenish said sharply, "What accent is that you have?"

Well, Hannah thought, this helped explain why everyone was slow to recognize her. In 1940, she had somehow sounded British. But now, it seemed, she didn't. "My accent's American. That's because I, um, moved to San Francisco … after the War."

Mrs. Devenish nodded curtly, but said nothing. George smiled shyly at Hannah.

Verity, however, had questions, lots of them. "How have you been? And what are you doing back in England? Are you married?"

Hannah laughed. "No, of course I'm not married yet! I'm far too young …"

But Verity interrupted with her own news. "Eric and I are engaged!"

"Oh, yeah, so you are," said Hannah. This wasn't news. She had met Eric and Verity as an elderly couple, not long before Eric's sudden death. She glanced at young Eric now, and thought how weird it was to see him brought back to life.

"How could you possibly know about the engagement?" snapped Mrs. Devenish.

Hannah stayed silent, because "I'm a time traveler" didn't seem like the smartest reply, even if it was true. Anyway, this reunion did not feel right to her. It was not what she had imagined it would be. Suddenly, she felt out of her depth.

It was Eric who broke the silence. "Look, why don't we all have tea at the café outside? My treat." He gave Mrs. Devenish an ingratiating smile.

But she glowered at him. "If we leave this hall, we won't be allowed in again unless we buy more tickets."

"Good point, Granny," Verity said reluctantly. She turned back to her friend. "Hannah, would you mind if we met you later? Would twelve o'clock be all right? We could meet in front of the main doors here."

Hannah now felt crestfallen. "But aren't you worried that I'll be here all on my own?" she said plaintively. Once again, they gave her an odd look.

"Why on earth would we be worried?" Mrs. Devenish said briskly. "I should think that you're old enough to manage. We'll see you at twelve o'clock sharp." With that, she turned on her heel. Eric and George followed her, and only Verity looked back to give Hannah a little wave.

Hannah was weirded out by the entire encounter.

Had Hannah heard what Mrs. Devenish said next, she would have been even more concerned.

"Imagine that girl turning up out of the blue," the old woman grumbled. "Even now she's grown up, she has the cheek of the devil. And did you see how she was dressed? I've never seen anything like it in my life."

Verity sighed. "It was odd. But you shock me, Granny, you really do. Aren't you glad to see Hannah?"

Mrs. Devenish did not reply. She turned to her son. "Eric, explain to me what nuclear fusion means."

CHAPTER TWO

Eric coughed, and rubbed his cheek. "Well, it's like this, Granny. It's a collision of nuclei, in a thermonuclear reaction that, er, releases energy."

"I meant," Mrs. Devenish said sharply, "explain it to me in *English*."

Sitting on a wooden bench in her enormous dress, Hannah stared at the futuristic fountain as it tipped streams of water from one ladle to another. But she didn't really see it. She couldn't stop feeling empty inside. Here she was in 1951, and everything had gone wrong. Bumping into Eric had made her think that meeting him was part of some grand plan. But it probably wasn't. It was just an unfortunate coincidence. And Hannah had been so caught up in the excitement of seeing Verity and Mrs. Devenish again, she had forgotten that she had no idea where her brother was. She had no money, and she had absolutely no idea what to do next. All she had was a noontime appointment that she really wasn't looking forward to. Maybe she should just not show up. Trying not to cry, Hannah stared into her lap, as the water feature clanked and gushed.

At that moment, she realized that she was not alone. To her right, a young man was perched on the edge of a cement planter full of brightly-colored orange flowers. He had his face buried in his hands, he was sobbing, and he had drawn the attention of a helmeted policeman. "I'm sorry, sir," the constable said firmly. "You need to move along. We can't have you making a spectacle of yourself here. Been drinking, have we?"

But Hannah was now standing at the policeman's side. "Excuse me, Officer? Can I handle this?"

"This a friend of yours, miss?" he said, jerking his head toward the distressed man. "Look, he'd best pull himself together, or I'll have to take him down the station."

Hannah leaned toward the young man, trying to see his face clearly. He lifted his head, and said, "H-H-Hannah?"

Hannah turned back to the policeman. "Yes, I know him. This is my brother. He'll be fine. I'll look after him."

Alex gratefully swallowed a gulp of hot, milky tea and cast a dazed eye around the outdoor café. Then he returned his gaze to the strange young woman he was learning to recognize as his sister. "So how did you know I was me?"

"Easy. You look like I imagine you will look when you grow up," said Hannah. "And after what happened last time, I was ready for both of us to look like anyone at all."

Unlike his sister, Alex was dressed for the 1950s. He wore a collared shirt, sweater, jacket, and pressed pants. A trilby hat lay on the table in front of him.

CHAPTER TWO

"Alex, you got any cash? I'm broke, and someone needs to pay for this." Hannah touched the empty teapot.

Alex pulled a brown leather wallet from his pocket, and peered inside. "I've got two ten shilling notes," he said, holding up a bill with a picture of King George VI etched on it in brown ink. Hannah took it from him. She had a pretty good idea that it wasn't enough money to keep them in meals for long, and certainly not in hotels.

"How much do you have altogether?" she said.

He looked in his wallet again. "That's it."

"Two ten bob notes? That's all?"

"At least we can find jobs if we have to," Alex said. "We both look like adults."

"Alex, we don't need to worry about jobs," said Hannah. "I think I can get us home, back to the 21st century. But I don't want to leave right away, not until I sort things out with Mrs. D."

Alex looked at her doubtfully. "I don't know, sis. Maybe we best leave things as they are. I don't think we're supposed to be here. And what about Brandon? Is he here too?"

Hannah was alarmed by the suggestion that she also had dragged their friend into this, but she calmed down as she thought it through. "No, I don't think so. It was me, not the Professor, who brought us here, and I didn't even think about Brandon."

She looked over Alex's shoulder and stiffened. "Oh, no. Here comes Mrs. D. Look, remember our last name is Day."

"Of course I remember," Alex muttered. "I'm not stupid."

They both stood up at the approach of George, Verity, Eric, and Mrs. Devenish.

"Good Lord, is this Alex?" Eric said delightedly. He extended a hand to Alex, who hesitated before accepting the handshake. "How marvelous," Eric said. "You remember George Braithwaite, I hope? And Verity?" Alex offered Verity another awkward handshake.

"And, of course," said Eric, "You can hardly forget Granny … I mean, Mrs. Devenish."

The old woman leaned her head forward in greeting. Without thinking, Alex tried to give her a hug. She promptly stepped away from him.

Eric borrowed two extra chairs, and they all crowded round a small café table.

"So how are you, George?" Hannah said. George smiled and nodded.

"George here goes up to Oxford this autumn," said Eric. "He's been awarded an exhibition at Brasenose to read biology."

CHAPTER TWO

Hannah and Alex looked puzzled, so Eric explained. "I mean, he's going to Oxford University to, er, I believe the American expression is to major in biology. And he has a scholarship."

Alex and Hannah offered their congratulations to George, who nodded awkwardly. Now Eric clapped his hands together. "Alex, did your sister tell you our news? Verity and I are to be married next year!" Alex did his best to act surprised. He already knew Verity and Eric would get married. He also knew they would have two kids, Mark and Lizzie. He knew more about their lives than they did.

Verity glanced at the small menu. Then she said brightly, "So! You two emigrated to America?"

Hannah was very aware that the conversation had now moved into dangerous waters. She hated lying to her friends, but what else could she do? They wouldn't believe her if she told them the truth. She and Alex would have to make up a story on the spot, and they could easily contradict each other. Hannah took charge. "We moved to San Francisco after the War," she said, lightly stepping on Alex's foot under the table to tell him to keep quiet.

"Gosh, how exciting!" Verity said.

Mrs. Devenish sniffed loudly. "Indeed," she said sourly, then turned to gaze at passersby.

Now Hannah was certain that something was very wrong. What was the matter with Mrs. Devenish?

The pained silence was broken by the waitress's arrival. Without asking anyone what they wanted, Mrs. Devenish turned to her, and ordered tea and biscuits for all.

As the waitress walked away, Hannah said carefully, "Look, is everything okay?"

"Of course it is!" Verity said. "It's just that you do sound very American, Hannah. It takes a little getting used to." She turned to her grandmother and said pointedly, "Doesn't it, Granny?"

Mrs. Devenish shrugged and looked away again. And then, she looked right at Hannah. "Actually, the truth is, I don't remember you. It was so long ago. You were only with me such a short time, and you were a little girl. I didn't even recognize you today."

Hannah felt her stomach drop, and her temperature fall to a cold sweat. *Mrs. D. has forgotten me?* Tears sprang to her eyes, and she glanced upward to get rid of them.

Verity threw her grandmother an angry glare, and leaned toward Hannah. With a forced smile, she said, "Tell us about life in America, do."

CHAPTER TWO

"Not much to tell," said Hannah, feeling empty and sick as she grasped at her thoughts. "It's kind of boring. Alex and me, we decided to move to England, and … um … look for work here."

Alex shot her an alarmed look that said, *Where are you going with this?* Eric and Verity exchanged confused glances. Mrs. Devenish narrowed her eyes suspiciously. Hannah knew she had said something that didn't sound true. Now what? She ploughed on, because there was nothing else to do. "Fact is, we need someplace to stay. We're kind of desperate. Otherwise, we have to go back to California."

"What a pity," Mrs. Devenish said shortly, as the waitress brought their tea. "Never mind. From what I read, I should say there are a great many more opportunities waiting for you in America." She turned and called over her shoulder to the departing waitress, "I say, you've forgotten the milk."

Hannah desperately tried to get the conversation back on track. She pointed to her dress. "I liked *this* job, but unfortunately, this is my last day. I'm supposed to remind people about the Great Exhibition in 1851. I'm dressed like a Victorian."

Mrs. Devenish was not moved. "Yes, I can see that. Did you get sacked?"

Once again, Verity gave her grandmother a dirty look.

Hannah shook her head, and started to babble nervously. "No, I quit. It won't be much longer before another job turns up. I heard there's lots of jobs in England, and especially in Balesworth."

"Really?" Verity said. Even she was incredulous now. "That's news to me. Mind you, I found a job for this summer, before I go back to Cambridge. I'm to help in a grocer's shop in Ickswade. Perhaps you ought to look for something of that sort, you know, working in a shop?"

Maybe, Hannah thought frantically, it was time to tell them all the truth. But then, the unexpected happened. Mrs. Devenish, as she started pouring tea into Eric's cup, said casually, "I might have beds for you at Weston Cottage … " She paused significantly. "Provided you don't stay too long."

Hannah could cheerfully have leapt across the table and hugged the old woman. An invitation to stay was Mrs. Devenish's version of a hug, and it felt like one to Hannah.

Pouring tea for Verity, Mrs. Devenish continued, "Eric is mainly staying in London this summer. So I have plenty of room." She carried on laying out her plans as she filled George's teacup. "Alex can take Eric's room. Verity, I don't expect you to share. Hannah could sleep in the spare bedroom."

"I wouldn't mind sharing my room with Hannah," Verity said cheerfully, "but of course she should have her privacy. Still, it will be lovely to catch up, won't it, Hannah? We girls have so much to talk about!"

"Do we?" said Hannah. "I mean, yes, we do! Of course!"

Even to herself, she sounded hysterical. She was relieved by Mrs. Devenish's abrupt shift in attitude, but she was also slightly freaked. She watched as the old woman calmly poured tea for Alex. When Mrs. Devenish returned her gaze, her eyes bored into Hannah's soul. What was she up to?

Chapter 3
ONE WAY TO SNIPESVILLE

Monday Afternoon, Late May, This Year

School was out for summer, but Brandon had a lot on his mind. Time travel, for one thing. And, for another, why were Verity and Dr. Braithwaite acting so weird? But his attention snapped back to home when he was summoned to an emergency family meeting. He knew immediately that it was news about Clark and Sons Home of Eternal Rest, Inc., and that it would not be good news.

Brandon wasn't the first to arrive at the funeral home. His grumpy Aunt Marcia (or as he thought of her, Aunt Morticia) was already in the conference room. Aunt Morticia pretty much ran the funeral home these days. She was his mom's sister, and she had started out as the receptionist, back when Brandon's grandparents, were still in charge. Technically, Brandon's dad, Gordon, and Gordon's brother, Uncle Sam Clark, were the funeral home's owners and managers. But Gordon was busy with his insurance company, and Uncle Sam's health had not been good lately.

That was why Aunt Morticia was more in charge than ever. Nobody could ever tell if she was happy or not, since she always looked sour and angry, like a ferocious prune. Sitting uncomfortably across from her, Brandon wished he had arrived later. Nervously, he cracked his knuckles until she barked at him to stop, and then he stared at the door, willing the others to show up soon.

To his great relief, the door finally swung open. His grandparents arrived first. For Grandma and Grandpa to turn up, Brandon thought, this meeting had to be a very big deal indeed. Right behind them were Brandon's parents, his Uncle Sam, and his cousins, Ivory and Brooklynn Simone. The looks on the

CHAPTER THREE

adults' faces dashed his remaining hopes. Only Brooklynn Simone, who was the same age as Brandon, looked as puzzled as he felt. She raised her eyebrows at him, and he shrugged his shoulders to show her that he didn't know what the meeting was about, either. Aunt Morticia now silently passed out notepads and pens.

"What are these for?" said Brandon's grandma, holding up a notepad. "And what are little Brandon and Brooklynn Simone doing here?"

"Brandon and Brooklynn Simone aren't so little anymore, Mrs. Clark," Aunt Morticia said. "This is their inheritance we're talking about. They need to be in the discussion."

Brandon was surprised: Aunt Morticia had never showed any interest in his opinions before. Brooklynn Simone sat up straight, and leaned forward in her chair, suddenly looking self-important. Brandon caught himself doing the same thing. "And Mrs. Clark," said Aunt Morticia, "The notepads are for in case you want to write anything down."

Old Mrs. Clark harrumphed, and set her chin firmly at Aunt Morticia. Brandon thought she had never disguised her opinion that her daughter-in-law's sister was an interloper, even though it was she who had hired Morticia in the first place, and the two women had a lot in common. "I don't need to write down anything," she said grumpily. "I already came to a decision. We all did."

Aunt Morticia looked at her for a second, then looked away and nodded. There was an awkward silence in the room.

"Okay then," Aunt Morticia said finally, looking around at the serious faces, before holding her gaze on Brandon's dad. "Gordon, what do you want to say?"

"Oh, no," Brandon's dad said anxiously, "I don't want to be the deciding vote." He looked to Brandon's mom, but she said quietly, "Not my decision," and pushed her chair back from the table. He looked at Brandon's grandpa, who stoically looked back at him, and shifted slightly in his chair.

"Excuse me?" Brandon said. "What's going on? I mean, I thought you wanted my opinion, but I don't even know what we're discussing."

His dad looked at him uneasily. "We're deciding whether to shut down the funeral home."

Even though he had half-expected this, Brandon was still shocked. "But we can't do that," he blurted out. *What am I saying?* he thought. *I never wanted to go into the family business. Never.* Yet now he heard himself say, "We just can't. It's too important to the community. I mean, people depend on us, especially those folks who can't afford much for funerals."

"That's part of the problem right there," said Aunt Morticia, stabbing a finger at him. "We have to pay taxes and utilities and such, all the costs of doing business. And I don't take much income, but I have my own bills to pay. More and more people just don't have the money. And every year, a few more black folk leave Snipesville than arrive. I've tried to get white folks to turn to us in their hour of need, but nothing doing. They're not interested."

Brandon had never considered before how hard Aunt Morticia worked.

Now Brandon's dad, Gordon, chimed in. "Not to mention that folks these days can buy their caskets from the discount stores or online, and we have to let them use them even when we arrange the funeral."

"That, too," said Aunt Morticia. She turned to look at everyone around the table in turn. "Now we all love this place. Sam and Gordon grew up in the business, and we all put a lot of sweat into it, starting with you, Mr. and Mrs. Clark. But we have got to face facts. There's a time for everything, and the time for Clark and Sons Home of Eternal Rest, Incorporated … Well, it's ending. Gordon, you could move the insurance company in here. Save money on rent."

"Why close it down? Did people stop dying?" said Brandon. Everyone looked at him in horror: Nobody ever said "dying" in Snipesville. Nobody in Snipesville ever died. They "passed." They "went home." But they did not die. However, Brandon was a time traveler who had recently spent a lot of time around English people who didn't mince words. So "dying" was what he said.

"Brandon, that's rude," said Aunt Morticia, when she recovered from hearing the D word. "Didn't you listen to a thing I said?"

"Yes, ma'am, I heard," Brandon said. "But we're the only black funeral home left in Snipesville."

"Brandon, I get what you're concerned about," said Brooklynn Simone. "But who will take over the business when Aunt Marcia retires?"

Aunt Morticia shifted uncomfortably in her chair. "Hey, I'm not ready to retire," she growled.

"I'm just saying," said Brooklynn Simone. "I know I'm not staying in Snipesville after high school. And I know you won't, Brandon. So it's over."

"It's not like the old days, son," Brandon's grandfather said softly. "Black folks can go to white funeral homes now. Trouble is, it doesn't seem to be working the other way."

"It might," said Brandon stubbornly. "It could."

"Brandon, you're just being difficult," Aunt Morticia said irritably.

But now Brandon's dad was looking at him with new appreciation. "Brandon, I never thought you were interested in the funeral home."

Neither did I, thought Brandon. But losing the family business seemed like losing the family soul, the thing that kept them rooted in the community, and bound them all together.

CHAPTER THREE

Aunt Morticia sighed. "Look, Brandon, we're not just the last black-owned funeral home in Snipesville. We're the last independent mortuary in town. Even the white homes are joining with big corporations. Just last week, Thompson-Hunslow sold out to Eternal Interment, Incorporated. Young Mr. Hunslow will be general manager, and old Mr. Hunslow is retiring."

"I know that, but who wants to be buried by a corporation?" Brandon said. "Have you talked to the churches about this?"

Everyone looked at him, impressed. Nobody had known Brandon was so passionate about the funeral home. His dad cleared his throat. "Well, of course, I told our pastor at Authentic Original First African Baptist Church."

Brandon shook his head impatiently. "Yeah, but I'm talking about all the other pastors, and white churches, too, especially the integrated ones, like the Catholics and the Episcopalians. We could ask to make a presentation, and go talk to them about keeping things, you know, local. The professors at the college like to support local stuff. I could speak at the Hispanic churches, have someone translate for me. And can't we stay open even if people use discount caskets, so long as we get more customers?"

"I guess," Aunt Morticia said uncertainly. "I mean, I've been thinking of working part-time at the college to help support myself. That's something I could combine with working at the home, at least for now."

Brandon seized on this. "So you do want to keep it open, Aunt Marcia?" he said. "Hey, I can help you after school." Everyone looked at him, amazed. It was well known that Brandon and Aunt Morticia had never really gotten along.

"Look, Brandon, we're all pleased by your concern," his dad said, "But we have to face facts. We know you want to leave Snipesville after college."

"Before," said Brandon. "I want to leave before college. I'm not going to Snipesville State."

"Whatever you decide," Aunt Morticia said. "It's your life. But why do you want to save the home all of a sudden, especially if you're planning to leave Snipesville?"

Brandon blanked. "I have no idea," he said. "But give me a chance."

Brandon's mom rolled her eyes, but Brandon couldn't help noticing that, for the first time ever, Aunt Morticia had lost her "prune" face. Now, she was wearing a truly terrifying expression. *Wow,* Brandon thought, *So that's what Aunt Morticia smiling looks like.*

Now Grandma came to Brandon's aid. "Give the boy a chance," she said. "But, Brandon, don't you give me your cheery look. You have got to understand something: We would be saving the home for *you*. Now if you don't want to go to Snipesville State, we understand. After all, your Grandpa went

CHAPTER THREE

to Fisk,"—Old Mr. Clark nodded to confirm this—"and your daddy went to Morehouse. We understand. If you want us to try to keep the home going until you graduate, we might be able to do that, although that's a few years away. But we own the building, so it's possible. And I have to say, I know the family has operated businesses in Snipesville all the way back to the end of slavery times, so you're speaking to my heart. The question is, should we try? Do you really think you would come back to Snipesville?"

She looked at Brandon keenly, but he had no answer. That was a decision he thought he had already made, long ago. Now, he was not so sure.

The light was fading. Clutching huge soda cups, Javarius and Brandon strolled from the convenience store up the dirt trail that served as a sidewalk on Snipesville's West Main Street. A huge truck thundered past, followed by a line of cars. The boys were headed to the coffee shop, not far beyond the courthouse, and just past the crisscrossed tangle of railroad tracks that lay near the heart of town.

Javarius wasn't talking. Neither was Brandon. Finally, it was Javarius who broke the silence. "You OK?" he said. "You look sick again, like you did at Zappy Burger."

"No, I'm fine," said Brandon, kicking at a rock. He considered telling his friend about the funeral home's trouble, and then decided not to. Until he had a chance to develop his strategy for the business, he didn't want rumors that Clark and Sons Home of Eternal Rest, Inc. would soon close its doors forever. He wanted to refine his ideas. He wanted to ask for Dr. Braithwaite's advice. And then he realized he could also ask Verity, who was a sensible, wise person. How strange it was, he thought, that a well-raised Southern kid like him had never called Verity "Mrs. Powell," or "ma'am," or even "Miss Verity." It just didn't seem right to call her any of these things, and he was sure that if he did, she would laugh at him. Of course, in 1940, the very idea of addressing Verity's grandmother, Mrs. Devenish, as "Elizabeth" would have been unthinkable. Even calling her "Mrs. D." had felt daring. Different rules, he thought, for different times and places. Things are always changing. He said to Javarius, "Let's pass on going to the Sippin' Snipe. There's someone I want you to meet. Let's go this way."

Javarius frowned. "Who? Where are we going?"

"Dr. Braithwaite's house," Brandon said.

"I already know Dr. Braithwaite," Javarius said, adding resentfully, "I was kind of looking forward to my latte."And then it happened. It happened so fast, Brandon's first desperate thought was he had been mugged. Someone …

CHAPTER THREE

something … yanked him backward by the arm, and then he was walking with Javarius again—or at least he was for one more step, before he fell to his knees—but Javarius was no longer with him. Did Javarius really do that? Brandon looked down at his own clothes, and they looked as though they had sprung from an old photograph.

No. This was Brandon's thought. Not just, "No, Javarius didn't just yank me backwards," but …

No.

Not this.

It was still early evening. Brandon was still in Snipesville, kneeling in the dirt on the edge of downtown. The courthouse was still ahead of him. But it looked different without white paint, and it was surrounded with dirt roads and trees. Two rows of shops he had known all of his life were there, but the paint colors and shop signs were all wrong, and he saw other buildings that were completely unfamiliar and covered boardwalks on South Main Street. Three horses tethered to buggies drank from a red brick trough, and a horse-drawn wagon rolled by.

This was Snipesville, Brandon's hometown. But this was not his Snipesville. This was Snipesville, he feared, at the worst time in its history.

Wednesday, January 24, 1906

Harnessed to a parked buggy by the covered boardwalk, the horse shook its mane, jangled its reins, and once again lowered its head to lap up water from the trough. A heavy white man in a derby hat stepped off the boardwalk, and ambled along the dirt road toward the horse and carriage, his feet kicking up puffs of sandy dust. Quickly, he unharnessed his horse, then spat into the street. Brandon watched him, standing still for fear of drawing attention, but the man never even glanced his way, as he heaved himself into the driver's seat, and took up the horse's reins.

In the dusk, downtown Snipesville looked like an old sepia postcard come to life. Ahead of him, Brandon spotted the office of *The Snipesville News*, a *Closed* placard hanging inside its glass door. He jumped up onto the boardwalk, and peered through the window. His greatest fear was realized when he saw a wall calendar for 1906: This was indeed the year of *We Don't Talk About That*.

As twilight began to descend, the streets of Snipesville burst into a blaze of electric lights. Electricity in Snipesville in 1906? Brandon never would have guessed that. But nightfall meant he needed a safe place to sleep. Acting as casually as he could, he walked toward the Hotel Duval, hoping it was open for business, and felt around in his pockets for money. He found only two nickels.

CHAPTER THREE

That was when he realized it made no difference. He couldn't stay in the Hotel Duval in 1906, no matter how much money he had. He was black.

As Brandon turned back toward West Main Street, he saw the city lights come to an abrupt end at the edge of downtown. Beyond Snipesville itself there was no artificial light.

Brandon was an experienced time traveler. Without electric light, without even a lantern or flashlight, he knew, walking after sunset would be beyond dangerous. He also knew he had to leave downtown to find sanctuary. It was time to hurry. He immediately set off down the block, reversing the route he had been walking with Javarius minutes earlier, before everything changed. He was headed for West Snipesville, his neighborhood, which began at the foot of the hill on which downtown Snipesville rose. But as he carried on downhill and peered into the gloom, he saw that his neighborhood wasn't there. Only the location at the foot of the hill, and the pecan orchard that would one day become George Braithwaite Park, told him where he was. Where houses and the funeral home should have been were pine trees, and fields beyond. Only one modest house, and a barn-like structure next to it, stood next to the pecan orchard. Excitedly, Brandon realized that the barn was on the exact spot of his grandparents' first funeral home. Above the large doors of the barn was a sign: *E. T. Clark, General Blacksmith, Wagon and Buggy Repair*, and nailed below it, a rough shingle on which was hand-scrawled, *"Bicycle Repair."*

Brandon looked in awe upon the workshop. This was his family's first business, founded by an ancestor newly freed from slavery. He was pretty sure the house next door also belonged to the family. But if he knocked, what would he tell them? He could hardly say, "Hi, I'm your great-great-whatever who just stopped by from the future, can I stay?"

Standing in the gathering gloom, Brandon began to think up a back story for himself. He could tell people he was from England. Hey, he could put on a pretty good English accent, or at least Alex had told him he could. *Anyway,* Brandon thought, *nobody in Georgia in 1906 knows what an English accent sounds like. There's no TV or radio, and even if they have movies in Snipesville, they're silent.*

Butterflies in his stomach, Brandon climbed onto the porch of the little house, and knocked loudly. No lights glimmered inside, nor was there any sound. Walking on, he found three more houses ahead of him, but he could already see from the absence of lights that nobody was home. Continuing on the dirt road in the gathering darkness, he was increasingly afraid. He tried to calm down, reminding himself that this was home, that this land had once belonged to Kintyre Plantation, where generations of his ancestors had lived in slavery, and where his family had lived ever since. Somewhere in the gloom were people who, even though they would be strangers to him, were his people. It was a comforting thought.

It was almost completely dark, and Brandon shivered, from fear as well as cold. If he kept walking, he knew, he might end up in a ditch, or a pond, or worse. Maybe he should turn back, he thought, and wait for people to return to the houses he had passed. Where were they anyway?

Now Brandon heard singing. Quickly, he headed in the direction of the voices. His spirits lifted as he saw a kerosene lamp flicker in the window of a large wooden building. There was no sign, but he knew what this was, and his heart leaped. Voices in harmony leaked from the gaps in the clapboards, as he stumped up the uneven wooden steps. He pushed through the creaky door, and emerged into the light. Brandon had found a church. He had found his people. He was home.

The singing faltered slightly as all eyes turned on Brandon, and although the singers quickly recovered, they stole curious glances at him as he hovered in the doorway. Trying not to stare back, he looked over their heads at the church interior, its backless pews illuminated only by a few oil lamps. He searched for somewhere to sit.

To his huge relief, an old woman gestured to a spot next to her, while the well-dressed dark-skinned young man at her side shifted down to make room for him. Brandon happily inserted himself between them. He took a discreet glance at the woman, who was so light-skinned she could have passed for white. In fact, if they hadn't been sitting in this church, Brandon would have assumed she *was* white.

The pastor, a slim middle-aged man in a slightly frayed suit, cleared his throat as he prepared to address the congregation. "Brethren, sisters, and visitors," he said in a mild voice. Here he paused and looked at Brandon. All eyes turned in Brandon's direction. This was awkward. He slumped slightly in his seat, and tried to look modest. The preacher continued, "I would like to recognize a gentleman in our congregation at Snipesville African Baptist Church. Kindly extend a sincere welcome…."

My church! Brandon thought. *That's my church's original name! I'm going to be welcomed by my own church in 1906!* He jumped to his feet, just as the minister announced, "… to our brother in Christ, Mr. R. H. Gordon, who is newly graduated with a Bachelor of Arts degree from Atlanta Baptist College. Please welcome him home."

Brandon sat down again, while the young man next to him rose, and nodded gravely as the congregation applauded.

CHAPTER THREE

Feeling very silly now, Brandon lowered his head in embarrassment. But then he realized what the preacher had said: *R. H. Gordon*. Was THE R. H. Gordon sitting right next to him? Shyly, Brandon turned his head slightly to study the young man, who at that moment, pulled out a pocket watch from his vest and examined it. In that pose, he looked exactly like the portrait of R. H. Gordon hanging on the wall of Brandon's school. It was all Brandon could do not to stare open-mouthed.

When the service ended, Brandon was watching Mr. Gordon standing at the end of the pew, surrounded by well-wishers, when the old woman at his side asked him in a distinctly Northern accent, "Are you a floater?" She pronounced it *floatah*.

"Ma'am?" Brandon said distractedly. He had no idea what a floater was, and anyway, he did not want to talk to the old lady. He wanted to speak with Mr. Gordon.

But the old woman kept talking. "You don't know what a floater is? Are you traveling in search of work?"

"No, ma'am, I don't live here," he said impatiently. "I'm from England. And yes, I'm looking for work."

The old lady smiled. By now, Mr. Gordon was halfway across the floor, and Brandon rose to follow him. But at the end of the pew, he was stopped by an elderly couple. "You look mighty familiar," said the grizzled dark-skinned old man who looked amazingly like Brandon's grandfather. "Are you a Clark?"

Brandon was startled. He could not admit that he was a member of the Clark family. If he did, he would have to explain that he hadn't yet been born. "No, I'm not," he said. "My name is, uh, George Braithwaite." Dr. Braithwaite's name had sprung automatically to his lips, and Brandon cursed himself for his stupidity in not having planned a better fake name. It wasn't easy to say or spell Braithwaite. He said, "Is *your* name Clark, sir?"

The old man tilted his head. "Yes, why, yes, it is. I am Mr. Elias Thomas Clark, Senior. You sure you not kin to me? We sure look like we're related."

"Yes, sir, we sure do," Brandon said, adding, untruthfully, "but we're not related." He knew who the old man was, of course. Elias Thomas Clark, Senior, was his great-great-great-great-grandfather, and Brandon had heard his name all his life. Elias Senior was the slave who had worked as a blacksmith on Kintyre plantation until he became free. It was he who had started the first family business at the end of the Civil War. Now, Mr. Clark introduced Brandon to his great-great-great-great-grandmother, a shy little old lady, who gave him a warm smile. Brandon was so excited, he almost bowed to her.

"And this is my grandson Thomas, and his wife," the old man said. He grabbed the arm of a stocky, dark-skinned young man. The wife appeared much more assertive than the husband, and she looked Brandon in the eye. "I'm Elias Thomas Clark, the Third," said the young man, who appeared awkward and shy. He nodded to Brandon, who knew now that he had also met his great-great-grandparents.

As Brandon reveled in this amazing realization, he felt a tug on his sleeve. He turned to find the old lady with the New England accent. *Boy, she's persistent,* he thought. "Come with me, if you please," she quietly ordered him. Something in her tone made him comply. As she led him through the church, she extended her other arm to clear a way through the crowd, which parted respectfully. Whoever the old woman was, Brandon realized, she was someone important in the community.

He soon found himself standing before R. H. Gordon, and he shook hands with him. "Pleased to meet you, Mr. Gordon," Brandon said politely, feeling a bit weird to be calling a guy in his early twenties "Mister," even if he was a legend.

Mr. Gordon said to the old lady, "Aunt Julia, to whom do I have the pleasure of being introduced?"

"Well, my goodness," she said helplessly, "I have no idea." She turned to Brandon. "I am Miss Julia Russell. What is your name, young man?"

"George," Brandon said, trying to get used to his time-travel name, "George Braithwaite."

"And you say you're from England?" Miss Russell said.

"That's right," said Brandon. He watched her eyes narrow slightly in the oil lamp-lit gloom of the church.

"Where, exactly?" Miss Russell asked carefully. Now Brandon could tell she was testing him. He had been dumb to assume that nobody in Snipesville would know an English accent.

"North of London," he said. "I lived there for a couple of years, but I'm an American. I've come home."

"You're so very young to have had such an interesting life," Miss Russell said. "But where …"

Desperately seizing the reins of conversation, Brandon said, "Mr. Gordon, where is Atlanta Baptist College? I never heard of it."

"In Atlanta," Mr. Gordon said, deadpan.

Brandon inwardly kicked himself, but he pushed on. "Where in Atlanta, I mean?"

"You know Atlanta?" Mr. Gordon was clearly skeptical.

"I've been there," said Brandon. Which was true, only his visits lay more than a hundred years in the future.

Mr. Gordon now looked at him very suspiciously. "You know Atlanta, but you don't know where Atlanta Baptist College is?"

"I might," said Brandon, obviously bluffing now. "Is it near Georgia Tech?"

Mr. Gordon looked baffled. And then he said, "The Georgia School of Technology, you mean?"

"Yes," said Brandon. "My cousin went there."

Mr. Gordon's eyebrows shot through his hairline.

Another goof, Brandon thought. *Of course, Georgia Tech is still for whites only. I hope he thinks I have a white cousin.* He desperately started reeling off the names of historically black colleges. "Is your school near Morehouse?" His dad had taken him to visit Morehouse once. It was the only college in the world dedicated to educating black men. Dr. Martin Luther King, Jr., graduated from there. So did Brandon's dad and brother. He hoped Mr. Gordon was impressed that he knew it.

Mr. Gordon was not impressed. "I have never heard of the institution you mention. Atlanta Baptist College is across the street from Spelman Seminary."

"But that's where Morehouse is," said Brandon. "Across the street from Spelman College." And then the penny dropped. Atlanta Baptist College was the original name of Morehouse. Mr. Gordon was now looking at Brandon as though he had three heads. Brandon inwardly shriveled.

Miss Russell, noticing the conversation lag, put a hand on Brandon's arm, and said, "Have you a place to sleep, George?"

Mr. Gordon sniffed, clearly questioning the wisdom of Miss Russell offering hospitality to this lying kid. Brandon noticed his sour face, and couldn't blame him. If he were Mr. Gordon, he would think he was a liar or crazy. Who would have thought, after all his travels in time, that the hardest place to fake his identity would have been in his own hometown? "I don't have someplace to stay," he said, glancing at the evidently disapproving Mr. Gordon. "Is there a … um … colored hotel around here?"

Miss Russell shook her head, and said firmly, "You come home with me, George, and I will give you a meal and a place to stay."

"Yes, ma'am," Brandon said gratefully.

"First," she said, "Allow me to introduce you to Reverend and Mrs. Evans."

Javarius's ancestors, Brandon thought with a smile. What a shame it was, he thought, that he'd never be able to brag about this to Javarius.

Lying in the dark guest room of Miss Julia Russell's house in Snipes County in 1906, Brandon was wide awake. He didn't know why he was here, where Hannah and Alex were, or whether any of them were even in the same era, much less the same year. Maybe his friends were in England, maybe in Balesworth. On every adventure, always, and eventually, the three of them were drawn back to Snipesville and Balesworth. For now, Alex and Hannah could be anywhere.

Hannah had told him that she was starting to have some control over time travel. Maybe he did, too? That strange feeling that came over him sometimes was time rushing past, he was certain, time waiting for him to grab it, or to jump in. But he didn't dare try: Who knows where he would end up? Then again, could anywhere be worse than Snipesville in 1906? He could wait for the Professor to show up, if she ever did. He knew now that even she could barely control her own travels in time. What hope for him? Or Hannah and Alex?

In the morning, Brandon still lay in bed, still awake, and still not ready to face his new reality. In the past year, he had survived two world wars, coal mining in Victorian England, and life with slavery in colonial Georgia. He had thought he was ready for anything that time travel threw at him. He was wrong. He wasn't ready for Snipesville in 1906. He just wanted to go home or, barring that, pull the covers over his head and go back to sleep. But now he heard a knock, followed by Miss Russell popping her head round his door with an offer of breakfast. Seeing her made everything real. He could no longer avoid life. Reluctantly, he got out of bed.

Having washed with cold water in the basin and put on his ill-fitting 1906 clothes, Brandon was seated at the breakfast table. Despite the lavish feast set before him, of country ham, fried eggs, and warm biscuits with butter and cane syrup, he was not enjoying himself. He was being interrogated by R.H. Gordon.

"So what brings you to Georgia?" Mr. Gordon said, giving him a baleful stare.

"Passing through, mostly," said Brandon. "Just doing some traveling before I settle down."

Mr. Gordon did not look convinced, and he replied through a mouthful of bacon, which earned him a reproving glance from Miss Russell. "Why did you leave England?"

Brandon knew he was being tested. After his gaffe over Morehouse the night before, Mr. Gordon didn't believe a word he said, and who could blame him? So in his room the previous night, Brandon had devised a more detailed life story for himself. Sounding as confident as he could, he now said, "I was a servant, and I got tired of the work." That much at least was true.

Mr. Gordon lobbed back at him, "You were a servant? Then how did you pay for your Atlantic voyage?"

Brandon hadn't anticipated this question. There was a painful silence. Finally he said, "It's a long story."

"Hmm, I'm sure it is," said Mr. Gordon, cutting a piece of ham and laying it across a biscuit. Then he said sharply, "You're not on the run from the law, are you?"

"No," Brandon said. That was true, but he felt guilty anyway. Making up stories to tell the famous R. H. Gordon felt very wrong, even though he knew he had no choice. "Look, I'm just traveling and exploring after my time in England. I stopped in Snipesville because I was interested in seeing it, and I got caught at nightfall without a place to stay. If you want me to leave … "

Miss Julia Russell came to Brandon's rescue. "You seem like a well-educated young man," she said kindly. "Your time in England no doubt had a salutary effect on your education. And I doubt that your arrival here is a coincidence. I believe it may be a blessing for us all. Unless you're in a hurry to move on, why not stay here with me awhile, and see if it suits you?"

Brandon was astonished by Miss Russell's generosity, and also deeply relieved. He had no idea where else he would go, and he had no money to get there. "That's very kind of you, Miss Julia," he said. Mr. Gordon, hearing Brandon use her first name, gave him a hard stare. Brandon said, "You are a stranger here like me, aren't you, ma'am?"

Miss Julia nodded. "That's right. I was born in Boston, and lived some years in New York."

"But why would you leave New York and come here?" Brandon said. "Snipesville is a backwater."

Rather than allow Miss Julia to speak for herself, Mr. Gordon replied. "That was certainly true when Miss Russell arrived, many years ago," he said. "But in 1906, Snipesville is the talk of Georgia. It's becoming a bustling city."

Brandon almost laughed at this. "Snipesville? A bustling city?"

Mr. Gordon frowned. "Surely you saw the new courthouse?"

Brandon raised his eyebrows. "Yes, I did. Why?"

"You do not appear impressed," said Mr. Gordon, steepling his fingers and leaning back in his chair. "Why don't you come for a walk around town with me?"

"Great, I'd like that a lot," said Brandon, and he meant it. He seized on this offer of hospitality from Mr. Gordon, and anyway, touring 1906 Snipesville in the company of R. H. Gordon was too good an offer to pass up.

Miss Julia said, "Robert, why don't you show George the schools?"

Robert? thought Brandon. *R. H. Gordon's name is Robert?* Time travel and the name Gordon, especially Robert Gordon, always seemed to coincide. In 1915 Brandon had worked for a Scottish dentist named Robert Gordon. In 1752, he had met two Robert Gordons. And Hannah had stayed with a Scottish family called Gordon in 1851, and wasn't one of them Robert? How many Robert Gordons could there be? What, if anything, did it mean?

Brandon wiped his mouth with his cloth napkin, and folded it neatly before placing it on the table. "Thanks for the great breakfast, Miss Julia."

"Oh, George, I don't cook," Miss Julia said. "Alberta is my housekeeper. Why don't you take your plate through to the kitchen and thank her yourself?"

Somehow, Brandon hadn't expected Miss Julia to employ a servant. But when the kitchen door swung open, it revealed a dark-skinned, gray-headed woman in an apron standing at the sink. He coughed, and the old woman turned her head. "Can I help with the dishes, Miss Alberta?" he said.

"You Mr. George, ain't you? No, sir," said Miss Alberta, shaking her head, and holding out her wet hands. "I'll wash 'em. That's my job."

Reluctantly, he handed over his plate and silverware. He had been a servant in his travels in time often enough, but he had never been served by one. It felt awkward. He tried to sound grateful. "Thanks for the food. It was great. How long have you been a cook?" As soon as he'd said it, Brandon felt like he was talking down to her.

"All my life. Soon as I could walk," said Miss Alberta. "My mama died when I was seven years old, and my daddy put an old wood box in front of the stove, so's I could stand on it and cook for him and my brothers and little sister, and them. I never cooked afore that."

"Wow. So how did you learn?"

Miss Alberta looked up, and pointed to the ceiling. Then she said. "*He* taught me everything. The Lord has been good to me."

Brandon nodded. He could imagine Hannah laughing about divine cooking lessons, but he knew what Miss Alberta meant, and he respected and shared her faith. "So when did you start working for Miss Julia?"

"Near on forty years ago, I reckon," said Miss Alberta. "Afore that, when freedom come, I worked a spell for a white lady, but she was mean. When Miss Julia come to Snipesville, and made known she needed a cook, why, I jumped at the chance. We about the same age, and she been good to me, like I been good to her. I taught her a little cooking, and she taught me to read. She's a teacher, you know."

"I didn't know," Brandon said, but then he remembered Miss Julia urging Mr. Gordon to take him to see the "schools."

CHAPTER THREE

Miss Alberta folded her arms. "Why yes indeed, Mr. George. Miss Julia come here after the War, and start a school for our children. My husband and me, we didn't have no money to pay her, but we brought sweet potatoes, collards, and a chicken to eat, and so forth, and she accepted them. But then," and here she laughed, "Miss Julia say to us, she say she don't know how to cook! So she hired me on right then and there. I been working for her ever since. She tell me you lived in England, is that right? And you a servant there?"

Brandon nodded.

"You an educated young man," said Miss Alberta. "I know that just listening to you. Miss Julia, she tell me always to speak the Queen's English, although she said it's now the King's English, because that Queen Victoria is dead. But sometimes," and she looked around her in case Miss Julia was listening, "I can't be troubled with the King's English. It's not how my kin and friends talk, and they think I put on airs and graces when I try to talk like Miss Julia." And she giggled to herself. But then she looked seriously at Brandon. "But you an educated young man, and you can make something of yourself in this world. You know what you ought to do?"

"No, ma'am," Brandon said.

Now Miss Alberta looked at him in deadly earnest, and with a nervous glance toward the parlor, she said, "You ought to do what I always tell Mr. Robert to do, the same thing. You both ought to leave Snipes County, go to the North. This is no place for a smart young colored man."

Brandon felt a chill go down his back. But Mr. Gordon seemed optimistic about Snipesville, didn't he? And a guy with a college degree had to have some idea of what he was talking about. But why did he think so well of it? Brandon hoped to find out on his tour.

Brandon and Mr. Gordon paused in silence at the intersection of Snipesville's two Main Streets, with wagons and buggies clattering around them. "Where's the Confederate soldier statue?" said Brandon.

"There isn't one," said Mr. Gordon. "Not yet."

"The Civil War ended in 1865," said Brandon, "but they haven't built the statue yet?"

Mr. Gordon sniffed. "Why are you so concerned? Anyhow, as we speak, Confederate statues are going up all over Georgia. Now that the veterans are passing on, white Southern ladies are acting to memorialize them. And there are plans to erect a statue here." He cleared his throat, drew himself up, and shifted into tour guide mode. "This courthouse is the most visible sign of Snipesville's progress," he said. "Only two years ago, Snipes County was holding court in a log shack." Brandon understood that Mr. Gordon meant for him to be awed by the courthouse, a building he had known all his life. He tried to look impressed, and failed. "And you see the electrical and telephone lines?" Mr. Gordon drew his finger along the thin black wires hanging droopily over their heads. "They are opening Snipesville to the world, even more than did the telegraph."

Now he swept a hand toward the row of stores along the boardwalk on South Main Street. "The world is also coming to Snipesville. The laundry is owned by a Chinaman," he said, "and Sweitzer's, that general store, belongs to a German Jew." He pointed up East Main Street toward Hotel Duval. "A Frenchman built the new hotel. And you see the Bank of Snipesville, and *The Snipesville News?* Both were founded by an Englishman, who recently was elected our mayor."

This caught Brandon's attention, because, in his experience, whenever England was mentioned, there was a possibility that this could lead to a clue about why he was traveling in time. He tried to ask Mr. Gordon about the English mayor, but Mr. Gordon was not easily interrupted. "You can see that Snipesville is fast becoming a metropolis, and all these people bring new ideas and new life. This is a time of profound change and …" But here Mr. Gordon added in a quieter and less confident voice, "it should be a time of opportunity for colored folk, too."

Brandon tried again. "So you said Snipesville's mayor is English?"

"He is, and … that reminds me, George. There are plans afoot to create Agricultural and Mechanical Schools throughout Georgia, and the Mayor intends to bid for one of them to be built in Snipesville."

Brandon already knew that this fancily-named high school would be the first incarnation of Snipesville State College. But … "Isn't the school going to be for whites only?"

Mr. Gordon shrugged. "Of course, but if Snipesville builds a high school for white youths, we will find it easier to argue that colored youth should also have a high school. It is helpful that the Mayor is already friendly to the colored community. Of course, colored folk cannot rely only on his goodwill. We must do whatever we can to ensure that we have a place in Snipesville's future." He lowered his voice again, "And not just as poor laborers in the cotton fields and turpentine camps of Snipes County." He looked around nervously to see if anyone had heard him.

Inspiring though Mr. Gordon's vision was, Brandon thought that his nervousness was a better indication of Snipesville's future. Still, he was intrigued by this alternative, better Snipesville. "So Mr. Gordon, what do you think Snipesville will look like a hundred years from now?"

CHAPTER THREE

Mr. Gordon replied confidently. "Oh, that is not a matter of opinion. It is plain to see. Snipesville will soon be a huge and prospering city, just like Atlanta, with streetcars, and automobiles, and railroad trains going this way and that, and with our people taking a share in its prosperity. A colored high school will prepare our children for a rewarding life."

"Well, except for the segregated high school, that sounds great," Brandon said. Of course, school segregation would eventually end, sort of, at least officially. Otherwise, it seemed a shame to pop Mr. Gordon's bubble, but somebody had to do it. "Tell me," said Brandon, "What would you say if I told you that a hundred years from now, Snipesville will be a boring little town, that the high school will become a college that nobody ever heard of, that very little business will happen here, and that our people will hardly run anything at all?"

Mr. Gordon was deeply offended. "Don't be absurd. How dare you mock me?"

"I'm not mocking you," Brandon rushed to assure him. "I'm just kind of skeptical." He already knew he had gone too far, but it was so hard holding in the truth.

"George, you are a stranger, newly arrived in Snipesville. How can you presume to predict the future?"

Brandon could hardly admit that he was a time traveler. But suppose he could not only predict Snipesville's future, but change it? Professor Harrower had made it clear that the future could be changed. Even she was not always willing just to let things take their course. Why not try to make Snipesville a better place? He looked steadily at Mr. Gordon. "I don't just want to assume that things will get better. I want to change things here."

"Do you indeed?" said Mr. Gordon. "And how do you propose to do that?"

Brandon did not reply, because he had no idea. But what Mr. Gordon said next took him by surprise. "I don't know who you are, George, or where you came from. The story you tell of yourself is unconvincing. But you are clearly an interesting and educated young man, and I sense genuine good in you. I hope my faith is not misplaced."

"It's not," Brandon said eagerly. "And I do appreciate you giving me a chance."

"Never forget," Mr. Gordon warned him, "that as far as I am concerned, you are staying with Miss Russell on trial. You must prove yourself, as I have done in earning a Bachelor of Arts degree, meeting the highest standards of scholarship and character. This is why I am accorded so much respect here in Snipesville. You, George, have an inflated opinion of yourself, but to us, you are a stranger. I repeat, you must prove yourself, and not only to my cousin

CHAPTER THREE

Miss Julia Russell, but to me." He gave Brandon a hard look.

Brandon suddenly felt deeply inadequate. Then he shook himself. "No, I'm not qualified like you are," he said. "Or old enough to make much of a difference to Snipesville. And I'm pretty much broke, as you probably guessed. I lost all my money on the way here. But you're not wrong about me, Mr. Gordon. I am a good person, and I would like to help. Look, can I buy you a coffee?" He had already seen the *CAFÉ* sign on the building that would one day house Hunslow's Sippin' Snipe. "Is that place any good?" he asked.

Through clenched teeth, Mr. Gordon said, "Are you out of your mind?"

"Why?" Brandon said. "Is it expensive?"

Mr. Gordon's eyebrows practically zoomed through the stratosphere. "George, you have obviously spent too much time in England."

It took a second, and then the truth dawned. Of course they couldn't go into the café. It was for whites only. "But there's no sign," Brandon said helplessly. "It doesn't say it's segregated."

"There doesn't need to be a sign," Mr. Gordon said. "Don't you understand? Everyone in Snipesville knows. Everyone in the South knows, except for you. Truthfully, we could step around to the entrance on the alley, and purchase coffee to drink on the street. But why would I patronize an establishment that won't treat me respectfully? No, George, let us forgo that dubious pleasure."

When Brandon had learned about segregation at school, his teacher mostly talked about separate drinking fountains. He had never understood what segregation actually felt like. He got it now. It felt sad, like not being allowed into a party he could see through a window. It felt humiliating, like being told he just wasn't good enough even to spend his money how he wanted. It felt like being imprisoned, because he was shut out of the good things in life, even the simple pleasure of a cup of coffee. And it was also very inconvenient, because he was thirsty, as he now told Mr. Gordon.

Mr. Gordon sighed. "Very well. Wait here." He hopped onto the boardwalk, and disappeared into Wheeler's Apothecary, soon emerging with two bottles of soda. "Don't tell Miss Russell," he said as he handed one to Brandon. "She considers eating and drinking on the street to be vulgar."

Brandon took a swig of his cola, which tasted weird. "So how come you went in the, what is it, the drugstore? Isn't it segregated?"

"Of course it is," said Mr. Gordon. "But the owner is from the North, and he speaks to me with some respect, at least. But, George, I have to steel myself before I enter any white-owned establishment. At least in Atlanta there are colored cafés where I may be sure of a warm welcome."

"So," said Brandon, "Everything in Snipesville isn't perfect, then?"

CHAPTER THREE

"No," said Mr. Gordon, taking a sip of soda. "I never claimed it was. I have no intention of staying here myself. Like you, I'm just passing through."

They walked and drank their sodas, as Mr. Gordon continued the tour down South Main Street. "That's the new library," he said, pointing to a small brick building with white columns that looked like a miniature plantation house. "The millionaire Andrew Carnegie has built libraries across the United States. Unfortunately, Snipesville's Carnegie library is for whites only. Miss Russell has written to Mr. Carnegie to protest, and she has also started a petition."

But Brandon was no longer listening. He was looking at the five plantation-style mansions on South Main Street. Only two of them would survive until the 21st century: One as a bed and breakfast inn, the other as a lawyers' office. "Why are all those plantation houses built together?" he said. "Where's the land where their slaves worked?"

"Oh, these were never plantation houses," said Mr. Gordon. "They were built only recently, while I was at college. That one over there belongs to the dentist, that one to the doctor, and across the street, that one belongs to Mr. Thompson, who owns the department store. Now you see what I mean about Snipesville's prosperity."

Brandon did indeed.

As they walked back along the dirt road toward Miss Julia Russell's house, Brandon mentally colored in his 21st century neighborhood. One future day, a subdivision of smart houses would appear in the cotton field on the right. The convenience store and café would replace the cotton field on the left, and next to it, Mr. Eddie would plant neat rows of collards, corn, and turnip greens in his field. When they arrived at Miss Julia's house, Brandon finally recognized it by daylight. By the 21st century, it was old and run down, and belonged to an elderly friend of his grandma, but it was still standing.

Mr. Gordon was about to step onto the porch, when he suddenly stopped, and snapped his fingers. "I forgot! I promised Miss Russell I would take you to view the schools." Brandon wasn't really interested, but he had little choice but to follow Mr. Gordon. As they resumed their walk, he continued silently comparing what he saw before him with 21st century West Snipesville. One day, the three old shacks and cotton field would be replaced by the squat brick buildings and football fields of R. H. Gordon Middle and High School. Now he caught sight of a large but tumbledown blue-painted two-story farmhouse he didn't recognize. It looked like it could use some work. "Is that the school?" he said, confused.

"Of course not," said Mr. Gordon. "That's the old big house of Kintyre

Plantation."

Brandon was astonished. "But that's not a plantation house."

Mr. Gordon squinted at him. "And what should a plantation house look like?"

"White paint, columns, you know, said Brandon "like the big mansions we saw downtown."

"Those houses downtown imitate the old plantation houses you'll find in the wealthy areas near Atlanta," said Mr. Gordon. "There was nothing so impressive built here in Snipes County before the War. Georgia's wealthiest plantations were elsewhere, because the soil here is pretty bad for farming. Still, Kintyre was the largest plantation in this area. It belonged for a long time to the Gordon family, as did the members of my family, including my parents. When my father became free, he chose to keep the Gordon name. I don't know why. The Gordons lost the property even before the War. Kintyre passed to a family in England, and they still own it."

Brandon's nose twitched. This news rang bells. He had heard the story of Kintyre, because the Professor had talked about it, but he couldn't remember all the details. "Who are the English family who own it? What's their name?"

"I have no idea," Mr. Gordon said. "They never come here. I know they collect rent from their Negro tenant farmers. Or at least, they used to collect rent. Nobody has asked the farmers for money in years. Nobody has lived in the house, either, not since before the War. For a long time, we thought that perhaps the owner had forgotten it, or that he had died without heirs. But then, my uncle received a letter from England, together with a bank draft, instructing him to maintain the house, to stop it from going utterly to ruin. So he keeps it up, and that provides a little work to our people. Do you see that building over there next to our church?" He pointed across the dirt road to the African Baptist church. Next to the wooden church building was an unpainted barn raised on blocks. "That's Miss Russell's school," said Mr. Gordon. "She has hundreds of students divided between separate morning and afternoon sessions. Miss Russell can only teach them half a day to sixth grade, at most, before they must leave for good, and meanwhile, they are often taken from school to work in the fields. But our children are lucky to have any education at all."

Thinking about it, Brandon realized that Miss Julia Russell was probably the first black teacher in Snipesville ever, and yet he had never heard of her. Now Mr. Gordon was pointing to the foundation of a modest brick building next to the school. "And that is to be the high school," he said, without enthusiasm.

"It's kind of small," said Brandon. "When's it gonna be ready?"

Mr. Gordon shook his head. "No one knows," he said. "A high school is too expensive for the colored people of Snipesville. There's no shortage of volunteers to help build it, but we lack materials, and even if it were built, it is beyond our means to sustain it. Establishing a high school will take so much more than a building. It will require a great deal of money. Truthfully, Miss Russell needs a man to plead her cause with wealthy philanthropists."

Brandon translated the last sentence for himself. "So you're saying rich guys might be willing to help pay for the school, but they don't take Miss Russell seriously because she's a woman? And she needs a man to help her?"

Mr. Gordon nodded, and looked slightly guilty. "She hopes I will agree to be that man, and to be the principal of the high school. That is why she invited me down to Snipesville to visit. I wrote to refuse her, but she was so obviously disappointed in her reply, I agreed to come. However, I will not stay permanently in Snipesville, even though my father has also tried to convince me to remain."

"So why don't you?" said Brandon. "You said yourself how the town is growing, how progressive it is."

"I did," sighed Mr. Gordon. "I admit that I am ambitious, and perhaps a little selfish. I've always intended to live in Boston or New York. When I left Snipes County for Atlanta, I shook its dust from my shoes. In Georgia, even a progressive, growing town is a difficult place for an educated man of color."

"I do understand," Brandon said with feeling. He couldn't tell Mr. Gordon the truth, of course, of how he had always dreamed of leaving, and of how his adventures in time had made him more determined than ever to have a life beyond Snipesville, Georgia.

Mr. Gordon looked across the cotton fields to the little town on the hill. "I will confess to you that I have not ruled out returning one day, once I have made something of myself, and have achieved some form of financial independence, just like Miss Russell," he said. "I am very impressed by Snipesville's growth, and if conditions for colored people do change for the better, I daresay I would consider coming back. This is my home, after all."

"How can I help?" Brandon said suddenly. "With the school, I mean."

Mr. Gordon was looking curiously at him. "That's the second time you have claimed you can help Snipesville. You are very young, George. I really don't see how you *can* help."

Brandon felt insulted. R. H. Gordon suddenly looked like an arrogant, immature young man, not an icon of Brandon's boyhood. He drew himself up. "Let me tell you something, Robert."

Mr. Gordon tried to interrupt. "I don't believe I gave you permission to use my Christian name … "

But Brandon stood his ground. "While you've been sitting in a classroom, I've been working. I know I look young, but I'm at least your age when you

CHAPTER THREE

consider my life experiences, maybe older. So, yes, I think I can help. I can figure out a way to get a high school started for my … For these people."

"Haven't you been listening, George?" Robert Gordon said angrily. "Aunt Julia … Miss Russell needs money to finish the high school, and pay a staff. These are the plain facts. Unless you can write a check for several thousand dollars, or know someone who can, you are no help at all."

Suddenly, Brandon realized he was out of his depth. There was still so much he didn't know. But no matter what, he wasn't going back to calling Robert "Mr. Gordon." It was time to follow Hannah's example of confident attitude. It was well past time to stop being so obedient, and to think of himself not as a boy, but as a man.

After the tour, Miss Alberta served a lunch of pork chops and greens. Miss Julia asked Brandon, "Did you enjoy your tour of Snipesville?"

"It was very interesting," he said, choosing his words carefully.

Miss Julia put down her knife and fork. "Your skepticism is evident, George. You are right to be skeptical. Few businesses here are owned by colored folk. Young Thomas Clark's blacksmith shop is one of the exceptions, but he caters almost exclusively to whites …"

Brandon was shocked. "Wait, what? Are you telling me my … I mean … Mr. Clark discriminates against black people?"

Miss Julia did not seem to share his surprise. "Thomas serves colored people, but whites are always served first and given the best treatment, because they have far more money to spend, and because … Well, that is the way of Georgia. The most important problem is that white people have almost all the money to be had. George, you are too young to remember this, but when our people were freed from slavery, they were never compensated for their lifetimes of unpaid work. Most freedmen took nothing from slavery except the ragged clothes on their backs. Old Elias Clark was fortunate, because he had something he could take with him, and that was knowledge of a skilled trade. He was a blacksmith. His shop on the plantation was destroyed in General Sherman's march through Snipes County at the end of the War, but, fortunately, Elias's services were much valued in the area, and a white man loaned him money to rebuild on that area of Kintyre plantation that's closest to Snipesville."

"Old Elias was one of the lucky few," Robert Gordon added. "As well as a trade, he had a little education. His father had secretly taught him to read, and as you may know, it was against Georgia law for slaves to read or write. But most freedmen were not so lucky. As slaves, people worked in the fields, from sun-up to sun-down, and the only thing they learned in slavery was how to pick cotton, which is neither an education nor a skill."

"But the Civil War ended, like, forty years ago," Brandon said. "Haven't things got better at all?"

Miss Julia shook her head. "White farmers keep our people in their place, picking cotton. Even if a colored sharecropper or tenant farmer is able to save money, it's very hard for him to buy land: Banks won't make us loans, and even when our people offer to pay cash for land, they are refused. They don't like to see land pass from white hands to colored, you see, and since Reconstruction ended, our hands are tied …"

"And that, George," Robert said, "is why our people's future lies with making a break from the past, by leaving the land, and taking up opportunities in cities and towns like Snipesville."

Miss Julia took up the story again. "George, education can prepare our children for the future that Robert describes. Even though many children spend but a small part of the year in my overcrowded classroom, they benefit by it. They would benefit even more by a high school education."

This was a pretty strong hint, and Brandon could see that Robert looked uncomfortable. Once again, Brandon was troubled by his own knowledge of the future. "Miss Julia, don't you think white folks might have a problem with black kids getting an education?"

It was Robert who answered. "The white men now arriving in Snipesville see things a little differently than the few local white families who have been here for a long time. Our Mayor was until recently a stranger, but he has practically created Snipesville from nothing. When he came here, the town was comprised of a few white families living in shacks. It was he who enticed the railroad to build a branch line to Snipesville, and he boosts Snipesville as a center for cotton buying and selling. He is keen to develop this little town into a large and prosperous city."

"Indeed, Robert," said Miss Julia. "The Mayor has told me that Negroes will find much opportunity here. He has even subscribed to the building of our colored high school, and already has made a substantial contribution."

Brandon was really astonished now. "Wow, the Mayor actually gave you money for the high school? Why would he do that?"

Miss Julia did not answer Brandon's question directly. "That's not all. He has a plan to build a prosperous Negro neighborhood in the area between this house and Thomas Clark's blacksmith shop. He says he will sell plots of land to colored families who can afford to purchase them, and build good houses to rent to others."

"And you trust this guy?" said Brandon, who strongly suspected that Snipes-

CHAPTER THREE

ville's mayor was not doing all these things from the goodness of his heart.

"It is hardly a question of trust," Miss Julia said evasively. "It is a matter of our doing whatever can be done to advance our race. If good homes and the high school are built, there will be many more Negro citizens who come to Snipesville, and who will be able to buy their own homes and open businesses here. That will strengthen our community."

This, Brandon decided, all sounded very different from his vague memories of Snipesville's history. But it also kind of made sense: West Snipesville was a real place, and his own house had been built around this time. His grandparents had opened their funeral home there eventually, right? He had so much to think about. What he said was, "Robert, sounds like you should stay in Snipesville."

"We shall see," Robert shot back defensively. "If the high school is built soon, I may stay a short while."

Miss Julia allowed herself a small smile. Clearly, this was the first she had heard of Robert considering a change of plans. Robert saw her smile, and added hurriedly, "But my greater ambition is to apply for further study, for a doctor of philosophy degree, in Boston or New York. That will allow me to make my mark in life on a wider stage than that of Snipesville, Georgia."

Brandon couldn't understand why Robert Gordon was being so selfish. He was a clever man. He obviously wanted to do good things. And the R. H. Gordon that Brandon had always been taught about was a pretty selfless guy who lived his life for the good of others. "Why would you want to do that?" he asked.

"Why would I not? Why should a Negro not earn the highest academic honors? Have you never heard of Dr. Du Bois, George?"

"You mean W. E. B. Du Bois?" Brandon said. "Sure." After all, Du Bois was one of the stars of Black History Month at school. Not that Brandon knew much about him, except that he and Booker T. Washington (about whom he knew even less) had two different ideas of what black people should do, and that they didn't get along with each other. Or something.

"Dr. Du Bois is a great man," said Robert. "He urged me to pursue my studies in the North."

Brandon could barely breathe. "You *know* W. E. B. Du Bois?"

"Of course," Mr. Gordon said proudly. "I had his special permission to enroll in his philosophy course at Atlanta University."

Brandon looked at Robert Gordon with new respect.

As he watched the rain stream down Miss Julia's parlor window, Brandon was thinking. Much as he loved church in the 21st century, it was a lifesaver now. Otherwise, he thought, he might never leave this house. Although services at First African Baptist in 1906 were very boring, at least church was something to do, and he got to spend a few hours in a place where black people were treated with respect. Admittedly, it was hard to keep up his false story while chatting with people after church. He spent much of his time in the evenings developing a complete autobiography that he could present to others. But church was a place he could socialize, and it was a refuge from segregation, which ate at his soul.

Miss Julia joined him at the window. "I suppose you are thinking of moving on," she said.

Brandon tensed. "Yes, ma'am," he said reluctantly. "I guess so."

"You have nowhere to go, do you?" she said quietly. "Nor any money."

"No, ma'am," Brandon said.

"I may soon have occasion to employ you myself. But," she added hurriedly, "not at present." Brandon didn't know what to say, and he gave her a nervous smile. Out of the corner of his eye, he could see her thinking. Finally, she said decisively, "George, you may stay here. If you find work, you can pay me room and board. If you do not, I will keep you, but you must make every effort to find suitable employment. I don't expect you to pick cotton, but perhaps there may be work for you in a business downtown, or in domestic service."

Brandon silently drew the line at ever being a house servant again. If Robert was correct, he could find good work in Snipesville in 1906. He did not have to be somebody's skivvy.

Nodding toward the door, Miss Julia said, "There is no time like the present, is there, George? I see the weather is turning." It was true: The rain had ended as abruptly as it had begun, and the sun was already bursting through the clouds. Brandon understood that his job search began now.

"May I borrow your umbrella, ma'am?" he said.

Miss Julia looked slightly embarrassed. "I'm sorry, but I don't think that would be wise for, um, someone in your position to carry an umbrella, George. Not in Georgia." She didn't explain.

An hour later, Brandon had taken a deliberate detour from the direction of downtown. The clouds had begun to dissipate moments after he had left Miss Julia's, and both his mood and sense of urgency had lightened with the skies. Strangely, he had felt drawn to the future site of Snipesville State College. It was absurd to think the Professor would be there, of course, but somehow, this crazy thought drove him along. Unfortunately, Georgia weather was the same as it ever was, and the clouds had soon returned for an encore. Having been unable to shelter from this second downpour, Brandon now squelched along the dirt road in his wet shoes, wondering how he would land a decent job with sodden footwear, and also concerned because he had somehow gotten lost. He decided to ask directions at the small farmhouse up ahead: In the yard, a barefoot white woman stirred clothes with a wooden paddle in a giant black kettle, while her little girl played nearby. Brandon smiled politely as he approached. "Excuse me, ma'am, but do you know if this is the way to the college? I mean, the place where they plan to build the, um, Agricultural and Mechanical School?"

To his astonishment, the woman suddenly dropped her paddle, and backed away from him. "Who are you?" she yelped. "You one of them floaters?"

He didn't know how to answer, he was so surprised. He was only asking for directions, and hadn't expected to frighten her. Surely there was nothing wrong with that? And he still didn't know what "floater" meant. As he stared at her, trying to figure out what to say, the woman picked up her daughter, and ran for the house.

Afraid she was going to fetch a gun, or alert a gun-toting husband, Brandon started to run. He was no longer worried whether he was headed the right way. He was desperate to put as much distance as possible between himself and the madwoman.

Standing in what he was pretty sure was the middle of the Snipesville State College campus, Brandon looked around him. It was only a clearing in the woods. Hearing footsteps through the forest behind him, he whirled around in fear, expecting to see a white man with a gun.

But to his relief and surprise, it was the Professor. "Too soon, Brandon," she said. "1906 is the year Georgia passes a law to create the Agricultural and Mechanical Schools. They're not built yet. Look, close your eyes, relax, and think of this place in 1910."

He did as she ordered. And when he opened his eyes again, he was alone. Even most of the trees had disappeared.

He found himself looking at the two original brick buildings of Snipesville's Agricultural and Mechanical School. They still stood in the 21st century, but by then they would be joined by dozens more structures on the campus of Snipesville State College, along with paved roads, parking lots, and sidewalks. What would one day be a pleasant park was now a muddy field, a pen full of pigs at its center. A young white man was leaving the pig pen, carrying a tin bucket. He closed the gate behind him, set down his pail, and saw Brandon staring at him. "What you want, boy?" he said.

Brandon knew that "boy" was a deliberate insult directed at him because he was black. He also knew that in 1910 he would need to pick his battles carefully. So he pretended to himself that he was being called "boy" because he was a kid. "Do you know where I could find the history department?" he said.

"The what?" The young man looked mystified.

"Never mind," Brandon said. "Thanks anyway."

The young man shrugged, and walked off, back toward the smaller brick building, leaving the empty bucket on the ground. This gave Brandon an idea. He picked it up, and headed toward the larger of the two buildings.

Nobody greeted Brandon in the lobby. He knocked at a door and opened it, only to find an empty closet. However, before he closed the door again, he spotted a bunched-up rag on a shelf inside, and he grabbed it, completing his disguise just as he heard creaking steps on the floor above, and glimpsed legs walking down the lobby staircase. He decided to gaze out of the window, hoping that these people would just pass him by.

But the footsteps and voices came to a halt. "Who are you?" a woman's voice said sharply. "What are you doing in here?" He turned to look at the young white woman who had spoken, and as he did, she saw the bucket and cloth in his hand.

"Oh, did Isaac send you to wash the windows?"

Brandon nodded. "Yes, ma'am. I'm supposed to start in the history department."

She looked puzzled. "You sure about that? There's no such place. There are history teachers on the third floor. Why don't you try up there?"

His heart in his mouth, Brandon tried to look casual as he climbed the creaky wooden staircase. On the third floor, he found a long corridor that stretched down the length of the building. Anxiously, he walked past the closed office and classroom doors, until he found one door that was wide open. Inside was a woman at a desk, her back to him. He hesitated, and then knocked.

"Come in," she said in a slight British accent, and turning to face him, she gave him a huge smile. He was stunned. The Professor looked many years younger than she had when he met her in the woods a few minutes earlier. This Professor Harrower appeared to be in her early forties. As a younger woman, he thought, she also seemed familiar in another way he couldn't quite figure out. It was puzzling. "I've been expecting you. Sit down," the Professor said briskly. "But stand up if someone knocks. Otherwise, it will be a little awkward to explain why a black kid is sitting in my presence."

CHAPTER THREE

Brandon looked around the tiny office, with its bare desk, and single bookshelf. "So this place is still a high school? Not a college yet?"

"You got it," she said. "Before these Agricultural and Mechanical Schools were built, there were only about a dozen public high schools in Georgia, all for whites, and all in richer cities, mostly Atlanta. But a few years from now, this school will evolve into a teacher-training college, and Snipesville will build a new white high school to replace it."

Listening to the Professor, Brandon had a sudden, strange thought. "You've always been here, haven't you?" he said. "You've been at Snipesville State since the very beginning."

"No, not exactly. I'm not Dracula," she said. "I don't live forever. And I'm not always here: It would be too time-consuming. I teach a class now and then, every few years, then I take a break and return under a different name. People forget me, or they retire, or they die, and between me changing names and the record-keeping being so bad, nobody notices that my teaching career here spans over a century. There are photos of me at various times, but either people don't look at them closely, or, if they do, they don't believe I'm the same person."

"This is creepy," said Brandon. "You're younger than you were when we first met. How do you even know who I am?"

There was a pause, and then she said evasively, "Just a hunch."

"I don't believe you," he said.

"I know you don't," she replied. "But that can't be helped." She turned away, and folded a sheet of paper. "So, what can I do for you, Brandon?"

"The usual questions. Why am I here? Why Snipesville? Why now?"

"You have work to do," she said. "I assumed you would know what you were doing here by now. And did you find a job yet?"

"No. I only just started looking," he said. "Most of the jobs here are working in the fields, growing cotton or whatever, or being a house servant. I won't do it. I refuse. It's demeaning."

"I believe we've also had this conversation before," the Professor said. "What makes you think you're too good to do a horrible job? Remember what I told you: Nobody is too good for a horrible job. Nobody."

"Easy for you to say," Brandon retorted. "You're white, and you have your choice of jobs." He glanced around her office. "This one looks like a cushy gig."

She didn't seem to take offense, but gave him a kindly smile. "Actually, landing any gig isn't a piece of cake," she said, "but for what it's worth, no, love, I don't expect you to feel sorry for me. I want you to know something important: At your age, you can accomplish things without having to prove yourself first. Most kids and teens don't understand that, and I wish you did. Important people are much more likely to listen to you than to me, to pay attention to what you have to say, to try to help you, because they like to nurture young people. All you have to do to open doors is to give them a light push. Now, I had better get on, and so had you." She turned back to her desk.

"So that's it?" said Brandon. "What use is that? There aren't any really important people round here. You won't tell me anything else? You brought me here to tell me to suck up to people, and otherwise suck it up?"

"I didn't bring you here," she said shortly, without turning to face him. "But do think about it, Brandon: Nobody is too good to work the most humble jobs, and nobody should be denied an education. You can help with that, because important people will listen to young people. Just be careful that you speak to the right important people. Do you think it's fair that the only high school in town is for white kids? And that the very same school is intended to train ordinary whites to stay down on the farm? Who wins?"

"Not black people, that's for sure," Brandon said. "Or, from what you're telling me, too many white people, either. Is that what you want me to think about? How does that help me?"

"Good luck," said the Professor.

Suddenly, Brandon lost his temper. "Who do you think you are?" he said, his voice rising.

"I wish I knew," said the Professor quietly. "Now you have to go. This isn't a good time for us to talk."

As if on cue, there was a knock at the door. The Professor urgently gestured to Brandon to stand up. He did, almost knocking over his bucket in the process, just as she called, "Come in."

A white man in a suit and bow tie was standing in the doorway, papers in one hand, and a pencil in the other, his glasses perched the end of his nose. "Miss Calder, I have a question about this English class you intend to teach …" He suddenly stopped and stared at Brandon. "What's this boy doing here?"

"He came to wash the windows," said the Professor.

"Without water?" the man said suspiciously.

Brandon looked at his empty bucket. "I was just going to fetch some," he said.

As he left the room, he heard the man say, "He thought he was going to wash windows without water! Ha! Now, I want to talk with you about your ideas …"

Brandon could hear no more of the conversation, because he was soon halfway down the stairs, headed for the exit. Abandoning the bucket in the hallway, he shoved open the heavy glass and wooden door, and headed outside under darkening skies. He had just walked past the pigs' enclosure when he

CHAPTER THREE

remembered that this was still 1910. Panicking, he wheeled around toward the college.

But the college was gone. The pigs were gone. Only a clearing among the pine trees remained. The Professor, once again in her mid-fifties, was standing near him. "You're back in 1906," she said. "Remember, Miss Julia is trying to build a black high school before plans have even been finalized for a white high school. Think about that."

To his astonishment, she vanished into thin air. He'd never seen her do that before.

Brandon was so freaked out by the encounter with the Professor he forgot all about looking for a job until he reached the outskirts of downtown. Now, he realized, he needed to pull himself together and start asking around for work. But as he approached the large mansions on South Main Street, he made a mental commitment to himself: Under no circumstances would he become anyone's domestic servant.

Walking into downtown Snipesville, Brandon tried to remember all the rules of segregation. *Take off your hat if a white person talks to you*, he reminded himself. *Step off the sidewalk if you see white people coming toward you. Don't stare at white women. Try not to look white people in the eye.*

He had read all the rules in history books. They made fascinating reading, but actually living with them? Terrifying, and also surprisingly hard to remember. Following the rules hadn't seemed quite so difficult when he was with Robert Gordon, because he just followed what Robert did. But now, by himself, Brandon had to think of almost nothing else but the rules in order to stay safe. It reminded him of The Talk, of what his parents had told him to do if he was ever stopped by the police. Exhausted by the effort, he paused outside the courthouse, and took stock of the businesses that lined the courthouse square: The café, an agricultural supply store, the department store, lawyers' offices, the hotel … And so many more. Surely, one of these places would have a job for him? And then Brandon remembered one business in which he had a lot of relevant experience: Dentistry. In 1915, he had been a dentist's apprentice in England.

Less than a minute later, he stood on the boardwalk before a small sign advertising *Dr. Samuel H. Marshburn, DENTIST*. An arrow pointed up the flight of stairs, between the drugstore and the grocery. Anxiously, he climbed the dark wooden stairway, his footsteps echoing loudly.

The dentist's office was a familiar place to Brandon. Just as in Balesworth in

CHAPTER THREE

1915, scary instruments were lined up on a table. In the middle of the small room was an examination chair, its arm rests' leather upholstery worn out where thousands of terrified patients had gripped for comfort. But Brandon also took note of how dirty the walls were, spattered with who-knew-what. Dr. Marshburn stood at the small sink, washing his hands with a white block of soap. He was stocky, with balding red hair, a neat ginger mustache, and eyes that popped alarmingly.

Shaking his hands to dry them, he turned to Brandon. "Yes?" he said sharply.

"I'm looking for a job. I …"

"No jobs," Dr. Marshburn snapped. He reached for a towel on a hook by the sink, and dried his hands. When he turned back again, he seemed shocked that Brandon was still there. "I said, no jobs," he repeated, his eyes popping out even more.

"The thing is," Brandon said, "I was a dentist's apprentice. I already … "

"You were *what?*"

"A dentist's apprentice," said Brandon, less certainly now. Under the dentist's hostile glare, he was starting not to believe it himself.

"You expect me to believe you?" the dentist sneered. "Now where was that?"

"England," said Brandon.

Dr. Marshburn laughed, but then he saw Brandon's face, and his laughter faded away. "So you came all the way from England, huh? Well, that makes you a foreigner, and you can drop any uppity ideas you got there, boy." He slung the towel back onto its hook. "If I hire on an apprentice, he'll be a white boy from Snipesville. This is a white man's job. Although I did hear there's a National Association of Colored Dentists that got formed a few years ago, up in Washington, D.C." He paused. Brandon was hoping Dr. Marshburn was about to direct him to a black dentist in town. But then the dentist added, with a malicious smile, "I hear they couldn't find enough members to keep their little club going. What does that tell you? So let me do you a favor, and give you some advice. There's plenty of jobs in Snipes County for a young buck like you, chopping cotton or tapping turpentine. That's the jobs for your kind. Who do you think you are? Get out."

Brandon fled. By the time he was downstairs, he was out of breath, feeling as though he had been punched in the gut, and his hands were shaking. He had to talk himself out of running all the way back to Miss Julia's house. Instead, he forced himself to calm down, took a deep breath, and walked into the grocery store below the dentist's office. One look at the old white couple in there, though, and he already knew the answer. He asked for a job anyway, because he thought with a sudden surge of anger, *I am not going to let these*

CHAPTER THREE

people scare me.

By noontime, Brandon had walked the length and breadth of downtown Snipesville, and visited almost every business in search of a job. Everyone he spoke with had answered him dismissively, and many were sour about it. The only people who had refused him politely were Mr. Wong at the laundry, Mr. Wheeler at the drugstore, and Mr. Duval at the hotel, who suggested he stop by again the following month if he still needed work. The only business Brandon hadn't yet checked was the town newspaper.

The doorbell jangled as he entered. A thin white man in shirtsleeves with a pencil tucked behind his ear looked around the doorpost from the adjoining room. "Yeah, what do you want?" he said.

"I'm looking for work," Brandon said. "Any jobs going here, sir?"

The man shook his head. "Not for you. Just jobs for white men."

As Brandon turned away, the man said, not unkindly, "You could wait and ask the boss when he gets back. I been hoping to hire a boy to sweep the floors."

Brandon wasn't interested in sweeping floors, but, encouraged by the man's friendly tone, he said, "Those jobs for white men you mentioned? What are they? I read and write really well."

The man's features hardened. "I done told you, no work. Who do you think you are?"

Brandon had had enough. "I could say the same to you," he said.

The man suddenly darted toward him, but Brandon was already halfway out the door. This time, he ran down the street, as fast as he could. But he was glad he had said what he had said, scary though it was. Hopefully, the man wouldn't recognize him again. However, Brandon also realized that there was a price to be paid for sticking up for himself: he had lost the chance of a job at the newspaper. And then he wondered. He was right to ask about better jobs, not just to allow himself to be pushed into something beneath him. But the Professor was right, too. He was young, and not qualified to be a newspaper reporter. Maybe sweeping floors wasn't so demeaning after all. It was so hard to know what was normal, what was right, in Snipesville in 1906. He wondered where Alex and Hannah were, and what they were doing. If he knew Hannah, they were in Balesworth in 1940, having a great time with Eric, Verity, and Mrs. Devenish. Brandon felt a powerful pang of jealousy.

Chapter 4:
ONE WAY TO BALESWORTH

Saturday, May 26, 1951

Hannah stood next to a grubby pillar in London's busy King's Cross railway station, watching her brother at the ticket window. Alex was trying too hard to act like a grown-up, she thought pityingly. He looked utterly ill at ease, shifty even, in his adult body and clothes. He hopped from one foot to the other, gesturing wildly with his arms. Really, he looked like a kid playing dress-up. It was lucky, she thought, that nobody would ever suspect the truth about him: He *was* a kid playing dress-up.

They were on their own. After tea, Eric, Verity, George, and Mrs. Devenish had left to continue their tour of the Festival of Britain, but not before Mrs. Devenish had instructed Hannah and Alex to present themselves at Weston Cottage in Balesworth after six that evening. By then, she said, she expected to be home to receive them.

It was probably just as well, Hannah thought. She had needed to get out of her ridiculous Victorian hoopskirt. So they had taken Verity's advice, and headed to the Portobello Road street market in the East End of London, in search of cheap used clothes.

Hannah found clothes to buy, but she could find nowhere in the poor and bomb-damaged East End to change into them. So the two of them had taken the Tube back into central London. Carrying her clothes in a thin brown paper bag, Hannah had slipped into the restroom of a huge Lyon's Corner House restaurant, and changed into her brown wool skirt and white blouse. Meeting Alex at the entrance to the building, she suggested they eat their overdue lunch

CHAPTER FOUR

in Lyons Corner House, because it was basically a giant food court, with several restaurants on multiple floors. But a quick look at a menu confirmed that even though each of them could have had a meal for only three shillings, that was still too pricey: They only had ten shillings left after buying Hannah's clothes. So instead, they eased their hunger pains with bars of chocolate they bought from a little newsstand.

With time to kill on a beautiful day, and wanting to save money on Tube fares, Hannah and Alex walked to Kings Cross on a route that took them past Buckingham Palace. "Come on, Hannah, wave to the Queen!" Alex joked.

"Sure," said Hannah, "but don't forget to wave to the King, too."

"Huh?" said Alex.

"The King," said Hannah. "King George. This is 1951, remember? Isn't King George still alive?"

"I think so," Alex said. "I think he dies next year, though. I guess I better wave now." He began waving with both arms in the direction of the Palace, like a human windmill, earning odd looks and smiles from passersby. Hannah laughed.

They strolled through Green Park, and on to Hyde Park, admiring the colorful spring gardens, before stopping to watch soldiers in bright red uniforms and gleaming gold helmets practice elaborate drills on horseback. As a horse and rider cantered past, Alex turned to his sister, and said, "If time travel was always this much fun, I would never want it to stop."

Now, Hannah was leaning against the dirty pillar in the dingy ticket hall at Kings Cross, remembering the soldiers in their scarlet costumes, and thinking how great it had been to see color in drab and depressing post-war London. Weed-strewn empty lots throughout the city marked the many places where bombs had fallen during World War II. People everywhere wore dull and threadbare clothes. Brandon had talked about how he had read that Britain took a long time to get over the war, and now Hannah could see for herself. She wished Brandon were here now. He could be seriously annoying, but although she hated to admit it, he was interesting. He knew way more about history than she did, although, she thought happily, she was at least starting to catch up.

At the window, Alex gathered up his tickets and change, and returned to his sister. "Here's your ticket," he said self-importantly, as he handed Hannah a tiny rectangle of blue cardboard. He was clearly enjoying his new role as an adult, however incompetent he looked in the part. "Good job I had those ten bob notes," he said. "It would have been awkward to ask Mrs. D. for money for the train."

CHAPTER FOUR

Hannah turned over the ticket in her fingers. "No joke," she said. "It was bad enough when the waitress brought the check for tea. You know what it's like in England. We're adults, so we're supposed to argue and pretend we want to pay. But when Mrs. D. went to pay, we just let her. It was embarrassing."

"Never mind," said Alex, "Let's go get the train."

Hannah pointed over Alex's head to the huge black signboard listing the scheduled trains and their stops. "Looks like the five o'clock to Cambridge stops at Balesworth, and it's already at Platform 10. You want to see if we can catch it?"

As the steam engine hissed loudly, Hannah closed the window so the sooty smoke wouldn't enter their carriage. She flopped down next to the window and across the small compartment from her brother. Running her fingers along the familiar coarse fabric of the seat, she glanced up at the suitcases and bowler hats perched on the netting of the luggage rack over Alex's head. They were not alone. Three men in suits hid behind their newspapers, and an old lady sitting by the door was peering through her thick-lensed glasses at a paperback book with an orange cover.

Alex said, "So what do you want to do when we get to Weston Cottage?"

"Just hang out with Verity and Mrs. D. How about you?"

Alex grimaced. "I don't know. Eric won't be there, and even if he was, he's way older than me now. Even George Braithwaite is way older than me."

Hannah noticed one of the businessmen lower his newspaper for a moment to look at Alex in puzzlement. Suddenly, Alex leaned across the aisle, and whispered to his sister. "Look, Hannah, this feels all wrong. The Professor didn't send us. Both of us look grown up. And I think we're changing things in time that we shouldn't be changing. When we met old Verity, she never said anything about meeting us again in 1951. And you saw how Mrs. D. acted."

"No," Hannah said shortly. She didn't want to continue this conversation. Alex was right, but it was just too awful to admit it, even to herself. Trouble was, she wasn't sure she could get them home. She couldn't tell her brother that, of course. He would be crushed. Thinking about this made her feel sick. She had to think positively. "You'll be fine," she said. "Don't worry about Mrs. D. She'll change her mind. Eventually."

While Alex and Hannah's train steamed toward Balesworth, Elizabeth Devenish was trying to unlock the front door of Weston Cottage. She wiggled the key in the lock, and then twisted it this way and that, but it would not budge. "I really must have that little man come back and repair the bolt," she said to Verity, as she shook out the cramp in her hand. "He made an absolute mess of it."

"Would you like me to have a go?" Verity said, watching her grandmother struggle again with the key.

"No, no, I can manage," said Mrs. Devenish, and with that, the lock clicked open. She pushed open the door.

As she followed her grandmother inside, Verity said, "I don't know why you've taken to keeping the front door locked. Do you really expect an enormous increase in crime, Granny? In Balesworth?"

"You obviously haven't been reading the newspaper," Mrs. Devenish said. "And do wipe your feet, Verity."

Verity glowered at the old woman. She had always been close to her grandmother, despite Mrs. Devenish's prickly personality. But, lately, their relationship had grown strained. *The old girl*, she thought, *is becoming impossibly cantankerous*. Mrs. Devenish's constant carping was very annoying, and especially when it was directed at her. She, Verity, would soon be a Cambridge University graduate, and a married woman. She did not care to be treated as a child.

Ignoring her granddaughter's pouting, Mrs. Devenish set down her small suitcase in the hallway, and flipped a tiny brass light switch on the wall. "Balesworth has a severe problem with what is termed juvenile delinquency," she said. "It all began with fathers being absent from home during the War, while mothers spent all those long hours doing war work."

Verity looked at her skeptically. "But, Granny, even if that were true, the War has been over for almost six years."

"Yes, yes," Mrs. Devenish said impatiently. "But that was when the trouble started, you see. A boy now turning 21 was a child of ten in 1940, and he started life as a child with absent parents."

"Just like Eric," said Verity, smirking. "He's almost 21, and he got in trouble when he was 10. And I was in trouble with him. Don't you remember Mrs. Lewis telling you that you should have hauled us up before your magistrates' court? Just think, Granny, I'm a reformed juvenile delinquent. If I remember correctly, so are you."

Mrs. Devenish glared at her. "Don't be facetious, Verity."

"Actually, I'm not joking," Verity said, suddenly serious. "If that policeman hadn't come round and had a quiet word with you, and if you hadn't been a magistrate with a great deal of power and influence in Balesworth, things would have been very different for Eric and me, wouldn't they? Instead of you giving us a good hiding, we would have had criminal records, and our lives might have been ruined. It's only because we're middle class that it didn't happen. It's very unfair, really."

CHAPTER FOUR

Mrs. Devenish sniffed. "Fair or unfair, I do see more and more cases of juvenile crime in court. We have had a number of cases of thieving recently, and a burglary, all by young people. And, of course, most of the young people come from New Balesworth. It really is an absolutely dreadful place."

This was Mrs. Devenish's favorite new complaint, Verity thought with an inward sigh. She was obsessed with the awfulness of New Balesworth. New Balesworth was one of the so-called 'New Towns' that the government was building near London, to house people whose homes in the city had been destroyed by bombing in World War II. Mrs. Devenish had been very much in favor of 'New Towns,' until one of them was built on the edge of Balesworth.

Glancing back at their cases, still sitting in the hall, Mrs. Devenish said, "Verity, take our bags upstairs, won't you? I'll put the kettle on."

Verity, irked at being ordered around, almost asked Mrs. Devenish if she missed having a maid. But she held her sarcastic tongue just in time. She knew that her grandmother had, in fact, grown up in a house with several servants. But that, Verity reflected, had been a very long time ago. Britain in Mrs. Devenish's youth had been a hugely different place. Why, even in Verity's own short lifetime, she had seen enormous change. She remembered when her parents' maid had left to work in a factory during the War, and her mother had been unable to replace her. Nobody they knew in 1951 kept servants. But even before the War, so far as Verity knew, her grandmother had never employed a maid, which was very unusual for a woman of her age and class. Thinking about it now, Verity wondered why not. It was rather odd.

As Verity placed her case next to her bed, she thought about the unexpected return of Alex and Hannah Day. Truthfully, it had been a shock. She had never expected to see them again. Now she wondered why Hannah and Alex had never contacted them.

But, she reminded herself, people don't always stay in touch. And Alex and Hannah surely had family members in England they needed to visit, like grandparents, aunts, uncles … But if they had a family here, why had they been sent to live with strangers during the War? Now Verity realized that there were so many unanswered questions about Hannah and Alex Day.

As she pondered these troubling thoughts, Verity wandered through to the kitchen, where she found that Mrs. Devenish had set out cups, saucers, and spoons, and was glaring fiercely at the steaming teakettle.

"Granny, what's wrong? You're going to terrify the poor old kettle, glowering at it like that."

Mrs. Devenish said, "I suppose you want biscuits with your tea? I only have shop-bought."

CHAPTER FOUR

Verity frowned, and picked up a pack of cigarettes and a small box of matches from the corner of the counter. "Granny, why are you in such a bad mood?"

"Don't talk rubbish. Biscuits or not?"

"Biscuits, please," Verity said, lighting a cigarette.

"I don't know how you can afford to smoke," said Mrs. Devenish, looking disapprovingly at her.

"Actually," said Verity, waving the cigarette in the air, "it's one of yours. I'll give it back tomorrow."

"Next time, ask me. That's dreadfully rude of you just to help yourself."

"Oh, for heaven's sake," Verity said angrily, "Nobody can do anything right today. First it was poor Eric daring to have an opinion of his own, then it was Hannah and Alex having the gall to speak to you, then it was all about the New Town. What's wrong with the New Town, anyway? I thought you liked the idea of working-class people having somewhere nice to live after the War? I think it's quite exciting, myself."

There was a brief silence.

"I just didn't want one built here, that's all," Mrs. Devenish muttered.

Verity sensed that she had the upper hand. She said in a condescending voice, "Well, where do you think New Towns should be built, then?"

"I don't know," said Mrs. Devenish, pouting childishly.

Verity tasted victory in their argument. "Granny, you are a terrible old hypocrite."

Her grandmother aimed a slap at the back of Verity's head, but Verity ducked sideways and laughed when she missed. That broke the ice, and Mrs. Devenish smiled ruefully.

"I'm sorry, Verity," she said, as she sat down at the kitchen table, then briefly rested her head on her hand. The kettle boiled, and as Verity poured water into the pot, Mrs. Devenish said, "I know I am in the most dreadful funk, and our visit to London didn't cheer me up as much as I had hoped. I really do want to believe in the Festival of Britain's rosy vision of the future. But the New Town isn't what I thought it would be. Or where I thought it would be, which was nowhere near us. Poor old Balesworth."

"So that *is* what is upsetting you," Verity said sympathetically. For Mrs. Devenish to reveal her feelings like this was alarming. She sat down next to her grandmother, and put her hand over hers. Mrs. Devenish did not pull away.

"I suppose," Mrs. Devenish said slowly, "I suppose I was unduly optimistic … Naive, even. I do speak with people in the course of my duties as a magistrate, and I cannot help noticing that so many of the young families in New Balesworth have left behind their elderly relatives and friends in London. Their

CHAPTER FOUR

children are growing up without aunts, uncles, or grandparents. This muddled society is even worse than it was during the War. That's why crime is going up. Young people need adults in their lives, and not just their parents."

"I know," Verity said quietly. "I cannot imagine what Mummy and Daddy and I would have done during the War without you to help bring me up."

Mrs. Devenish ignored the compliment. "For working-class people to have lovely new houses and parks, and so forth, is all well and good," she said. "But I am afraid that not only has New Balesworth no soul, but that it is stealing the soul from Old Balesworth, too. Do you know, the plans call for the New Town eventually to surround the old town entirely? What will happen to Balesworth then?"

Without thinking, Verity said, "Hopefully, by the time that comes to pass, you will be ..." Then she realized what she was saying, and blushed.

"Dead?" Mrs. Devenish finished for her. "Well, thank you very much, Verity. Let's have some tea. Your cup is the one on the left, the one with the rat poison in it."

Verity laughed and gave her grandmother an awkward pat on the shoulder. "Granny, think of all these people coming to New Balesworth, and what it means to them. Whole families who have been existing in a single squalid room or two in London now live in proper houses with bathrooms and lavatories—two lavatories even!—and lovely gardens. And they are so happy. I do wish you would take the time to get to know them, not just those of them who end up in court. These are people just like Eric, and they come from such wretched conditions in the East End. Do you remember what Eric was like when he got here?"

"Don't remind me," said Mrs. Devenish with a shudder. "That poor little boy. I had to burn all his clothes, because of the fleas and heaven knows what else. The day he came to me, I sent him back to the bathroom three times to wash himself. He had only ever washed in a tin bath before, when he had bathed at all, and he was terrified of the bath taps."

Verity smiled sadly. "Mummy recalls you ringing her in an absolute panic, wondering what on earth you were going to do with Eric. And look at him now, Granny. He's super."

"I still think you're both too young to marry," Mrs. Devenish said sharply.

Now it was Verity's turn to ignore her, and change the subject. "Anyway, wasn't the New Town what you wanted? To make sure that things were better for everybody after the War?"

Mrs. Devenish sighed, and Verity knew she had won. "Now, Miss Clever Clogs," said her grandmother ruefully, "what on earth am I going to do with our American visitors?"

"What you always do," Verity said gently. "You'll make Hannah and Alex feel right at home."

Mrs. Devenish's expression grew dark again. "But it was so long ago. All I remember about Hannah is that she was a bloody nuisance."

Clearly, Mrs. Devenish's mood had not improved as much as Verity had hoped. "Granny, Hannah adored you, and I thought you were fond of her?"

"It really was all a very long time ago," Mrs. Devenish said distantly, "I don't remember."

Verity was puzzled. She remembered Hannah and Alex very well indeed. And, in her experience, her grandmother never forgot *anything*. How on earth could she have forgotten Hannah? Was her mind beginning to go?

"Weston Cottage is the only thing in Balesworth that stays exactly the same," Alex said to his sister as they stood across the road from Mrs. Devenish's house.

"Exactly the same?" Hannah said.

"Well, okay, the tree in the back is taller," said Alex, "and the bushes are a bit bushier, but otherwise ..."

"Shut up, Alex," Hannah said, not unkindly, as she gazed across the street. "Just let me enjoy this moment, okay? I've been looking forward to this for months."

Alex turned to her and said, all in a rush, "We don't have to do this if you don't want to."

Hannah stared at him. "What are you talking about?"

"We can walk away right now," he said. "Look, it won't be the same. Maybe we should just ..." Suddenly, in mid-speech, he grabbed Hannah's arm and turned her to face him. "Hannah, I love Mrs. D. too, but she's not our mother."

Hannah angrily pulled away from this giant, grown-up version of her brother. "Why would you even say that? You ... you jerk." With that, she crossed the road.

As he reluctantly followed, Alex thought silently to himself, *Poor Hannah. It just won't be the same.*

When Mrs. Devenish opened the door to Hannah and Alex, she said politely, "Do come in."

She's talking to us like we're strangers, Hannah thought. It was very disconcerting.

Three dogs suddenly appeared at Hannah's feet. *At least we're getting a warm welcome from someone,* she thought. She crouched down to pet a little dog she

CHAPTER FOUR

recognized right away, a gray-muzzled Cavalier King Charles spaniel. "Emmeline!" she cried, "you're still here!"

"Yes, she's still here," Mrs. Devenish said gruffly. "Now, come upstairs, and I will show you to your rooms."

But I don't need a tour. I know this house, Hannah thought, *every room in it. I have been here so many times in my head these past months. I don't need you to show me. Just tell me where to go.*

"You will remember where to find the bathroom and the lavatory, I presume?" Mrs. Devenish said, handing Hannah towels. "Supper will be ready soon. Are you still fussy about food?"

So she remembers something about me, Hannah thought, her heart leaping, *even if it's just that I'm picky.* "No," she said, "I pretty much eat anything now." And it was true. After some of the terrible foods she had eaten on her adventures, she was pretty easy to please. "But I still hate Brussels sprouts," she added.

"Fortunately, Brussels sprouts aren't on tonight's bill of fare," Mrs. Devenish said acidly. "I'm making sausages and mash."

With that, she turned back toward the stairs, just as Hannah said, "Mrs. D? I want to tell you something."

The old woman looked at her sourly. "Yes?"

Hannah wanted to say that she was so happy to see her former foster mother, and that she had missed her terribly. But faced with Mrs. Devenish's impatient stare, she lost courage, and said only, "Thanks."

Mrs. Devenish gave her a frosty half-smile. "I have the Women's Institute meeting tonight, and I have already eaten my supper. Verity will serve yours. I trust that will do."

"Oh, sure," said Hannah. She was trying not to show her disappointment. It was her first visit with Mrs. Devenish in eleven years, or at least it was eleven years for Mrs. Devenish, and yet she wouldn't even skip a meeting to visit with her?

Hannah tried to tell herself that being back in Balesworth was at least a start. But nothing about this reunion was going as she had hoped and planned.

The following morning, Mrs. Devenish placed a hot plate of British bacon, fried eggs, and half a fresh tomato in front of Hannah, who was very hungry. She hadn't eaten much at supper the night before: The sausages Verity had served were dry and gristly, and the mashed potatoes were lumpy and unseasoned.

"Where's your brother?" Mrs. Devenish demanded sharply. Verity, sitting across from Hannah, looked up, startled by her grandmother's tone of voice.

"Alex is still in bed," Hannah said nervously. "He's exhausted."

"Well, he'll miss his breakfast," Mrs. Devenish snapped. "I am not running a restaurant." Returning to the stove, she served herself, clattering the spatula on the frying pan, then sat down alongside Verity.

"So, Verity," Hannah said, turning to the only friendly face at the table. "Do you want to hang out this morning?"

"Hang out?" Verity said with a giggle, "What on earth do you mean by that?"

Oh, right. Hannah remembered once again that her American words, like her accent, were no longer being magically translated into 20th century British English, as they had been in 1940. "I mean, like, just … We could have tea and, um, biscuits, and talk about stuff."

"Sorry, Hannah," Verity said with evident regret, "I really can't. I have an appointment." Hannah's face fell, and Verity added hurriedly, "But we can go out together this evening, if you like. We could pop down to the pub after it opens at 7 o'clock."

"Yes, great idea," Hannah said, feeling better already.

As she ate her last mouthful of breakfast, Verity placed her knife and fork neatly on her plate, and, picking up her purse from the floor, began to rummage through it. Pulling out a small bright red rectangular can, she flipped it open, and offered the cigarettes inside to her grandmother, who took one. "Take two, Granny," Verity said. "I found these in my room, and I owe you one, remember?"

With a questioning look, Verity now offered the cigarettes to Hannah.

Hannah shook her head in disgust. "When did you start smoking?" she exclaimed.

"At university," Verity replied, taking out a cigarette and closing the can. "Why? Does it matter?"

"Yes, it does," said Hannah, as Verity lit her cigarette, and then passed it quickly to Mrs. Devenish, who used it to light her own. "It matters a lot. Didn't I tell you? Cigarettes are really, really bad for you."

"Oh, Hannah, I forgot," said Verity, as Mrs. Devenish puffed out a cloud of smoke. "I should have remembered that you disapprove of tobacco."

"No," said Hannah, exasperated, "it's not just because I don't like the smell. Look, smoking's really bad because …"

"Will you and your brother start looking for jobs today?" Mrs. Devenish interrupted, giving Hannah a stern look. "I can't afford to have you live here rent-free for more than a few days."

Crushed, Hannah bowed her head. She didn't see Verity pull an angry face at her grandmother.

Hannah's offer to help wash the breakfast dishes having been brusquely refused, she wandered off alone to the drawing room.

At least the drawing room hasn't changed, she thought. The wooden radio still sat on the little table in the corner, next to the gramophone player and the pile of records. The bookcase was still neatly stuffed with books. Mrs. Devenish's letters were still arranged tidily on the desk as they had been in 1940. There was still no television. Hannah tested the old sofa to see if it felt the same as she remembered. It did, right down to the uncomfortable broken spring.

What am I doing here? Hannah thought desperately. Her happy memories of life at Weston Cottage had dwindled away. Now all she could think about were her clashes with Mrs. Devenish. She recalled their first raging argument, and of how Mrs. Devenish had later shocked her with the first whipping of her entire life. It was at the precise moment at which Hannah reminded herself of how humiliated she had been, that the drawing room door flew open, and Mrs. Devenish walked in. She ignored Hannah and sat at her desk, where she began shuffling through her correspondence. Picking up a dagger-like letter opener, she sliced open an envelope.

Suddenly, Hannah Dias hated Elizabeth Devenish. *Hated* her. It was as though a switch had been thrown. She struggled to remain calm and polite. "May I borrow one of your books?"

"Only if you don't take it with you when you leave." Mrs. Devenish picked up another envelope from the pile on the desk.

"Of course I wouldn't steal it," Hannah said, bewildered.

Still speaking over her shoulder, Mrs. Devenish said, "Well, you were the ringleader of most of the wicked behavior in this house during your stay. You really were the most dreadful girl."

Now, without warning, Hannah lost her temper. "Why are you acting like this?" she snapped. "Why are you being so mean to me?"

Mrs. Devenish turned to look her in the eye. "I hardly think I am being mean, as you put it. I have invited you and your brother to stay, even though I hardly remember you. It's like having strangers in the house."

"But it's been eleven years!" Hannah said furiously. "Of course it's a long time. So what? Why be rude? We were glad to see you. Why are you pretending you don't even remember us?"

"Because," Mrs. Devenish said gravely, "I really don't."

Hannah gasped. And then she broke down, crying as hard as she had done in 1940, on the night that she and Alex had turned up on the doorstep of

CHAPTER FOUR

Weston Cottage. Then, a kindly Mrs. Devenish had taken an exhausted Hannah onto her lap and comforted her. Now, she turned her back on her.

"Well, that's one way in which you haven't changed a bit," she grumbled. "Still looking for attention, I see."

Hannah jumped to her feet. "I hate you!" she screamed. "I hate you so much. You're an old *witch*." With that, she stormed from the room.

If Hannah had looked back before she slammed the door behind her, she would have seen Mrs. Devenish bite her lip, and look thoroughly ashamed of herself.

Now Verity put her head round the door of the drawing-room. "Granny, I overheard what you said. That was simply dreadful of you. You really must go after her. And if you won't, I will."

Hannah lay on her bed, sobbing uncontrollably. Since her dramatic exit from the drawing room a few minutes earlier, she had tried to think of how to fix things with Mrs. Devenish, and she had failed. There was really only one thing left to do.

Alex was still asleep, and Hannah didn't want to wake him to explain. He had been right, after all. It had been a mistake to come here. Kneeling next to his bed, beneath the painting of yellow tulips in a blue vase, Hannah gently took both of his hands, closed her eyes, and forced herself to relax until she found the correct wavelength. She started thinking of Snipesville. But then thoughts of Balesworth intruded, and thoughts of how difficult Mrs. Devenish had become, and so did thoughts of wanting to be a kid again, and wanting to go home, but not really knowing where home was. *But the Professor once told me that Mrs. Devenish cares about me,* Hannah thought with a sob. *How could she have stopped?* And when Hannah finally felt herself rushed away, her concentration was so fractured, she had no idea where or when she was going, or with whom.

Mrs. Devenish knocked softly on the bedroom door. "Hannah?" she said gently. "May I come in? I am sorry for what I said. It was wicked of me." When there was no reply, she slowly pushed the door open, only to see that the room was deserted. Puzzled, and sensing that all was not well, she almost ran the few steps to Alex's room. Finding that he, too, had gone, Mrs. Devenish sat down on his bed, and sighed heavily. "Elizabeth Hughes," she said angrily to herself, "You are a bloody fool." And then she realized that it had been a very long time since she had addressed herself by her maiden name. How odd that she should do so now.

CHAPTER FOUR

❖ ❖ ❖

Hannah's eyes fluttered open. She was lying flat on her back on a hard floor, looking at the ceiling. *It didn't work*, she thought desperately. *I'm still in Weston Cottage*. But then she began to take in the silence around her, and an unfamiliar smell of damp. This was strange. She opened her eyes, and lifted her head.

With a shock, she realized that the room had changed. Yes, the bed was still in the same place, more or less, but it was not the same bed. The walls were now whitewashed, not wallpapered, and the tulip painting had vanished. Hannah felt heavy fabric brush against her knee, and, lifting up her leg, saw she was wearing a long dress. She groaned. This was definitely Weston Cottage. But this was not 1951.

Dazed, she sat up, and looked at the bed. On it was only a dirty old mattress, stripped of sheets and pillows. Her brother was gone. Now, she started to panic. She had lost Alex. He could be anywhere. She tried to calm down, reminding herself that they had found each other in 1951, and she pushed aside the uncomfortable thought that the Professor had not arranged this particular adventure, either, and that she might not be so lucky this time.

She drifted out into the hallway. The house smelled dusty and earthy, not like a living home at all. She wandered into what had been her bedroom. It was empty, except for an old brown shoe and a crumpled sheet of paper that rested on the wooden floorboards.

The light from the window was fading. Hannah peeked through the window for clues to the time she was in, but the view, of fields of grain in the dusk, left her none the wiser. She set off downstairs.

Gone were Mrs. Devenish's hall stand and its attendant hats, coats, and umbrellas. Gone was the little table on which the clunky black rotary phone had rested. Reaching the end of the hall, Hannah pushed open the kitchen door … And got the shock of her life. A pair of eyes stared back at her, dimly lit by gas lamps affixed to the wall. She opened her mouth to scream, but nothing came out.

"It's all right, Hannah," said the Professor.

Hannah had never been so happy to see her, and she ran over, flung her arms around her neck, and burst into tears. Stroking the girl's hair, the Professor said soothingly, "You've done very well. It's all right. I'm here now."

Hannah's tea was hot, sweet, milky, and very strong, and she sipped it gratefully. She was safe, and the Professor had told her that Alex was safe, too, although she wouldn't say where he was.

But everything was not okay. Hannah still occupied an unfamiliar adult body. She still wasn't at home. And worst of all, her reunion with Mrs. Devenish in Balesworth had ended in disaster. She felt as bad as she had when her mother died, only different. She was grieving for her friendships with Verity and Mrs. Devenish. She knew she would never see them again.

Now, she didn't even know what year she was in. She didn't really want to know. She didn't much care. She was just going to live in the moment.

And the moment, as it happened, featured food. The Professor was bustling around Hannah, setting out a feast on the huge kitchen table: massive sandwiches of fresh crusty bread filled with ham, a vanilla sandwich sponge cake dusted with sugar, and a steaming pot of tea.

"I really can't eat all this," Hannah said. "I just had a big breakfast. But Victoria sponge is my favorite cake ever. You made it?"

"I did! I know it's your favorite," said the Professor. "Mine, too. Anyway, lots of sugar is good for shock, if nothing else."

Hannah picked up a knife from the table, and hacked off a ragged slice of cake. As she sank her teeth into the soft, buttery sponge, it oozed raspberry jam down her chin.

The Professor poured herself a cup of tea, and took a seat at the table. "I would suggest we go sit in the drawing room, but there's no point. There's no furniture. These kitchen chairs and the beds are the only furniture in the house, at least for now. Nobody has lived here in years. The roof in one of the bedrooms is leaking, and the owner hasn't got the money to fix it. "

Hannah tried to snap out of her depression, and listen to the Professor. *Live in the moment,* she thought. *That has definitely got to be my new motto.* "The last people left this?" she said, patting the vast kitchen table.

"Tell me, Hannah," said the Professor, setting down her teacup, "how would you propose getting it out of the room?"

"Huh. No clue. What year is this, anyway?"

"Nineteen hundred and five," said the Professor. "September 11th, to be precise."

Hannah wiped another stray spot of jam from her lip. "Good thing I read that book you gave me about Edwardian England. It was interesting, what I read of it. Which was," she added hurriedly, "quite a lot."

The Professor gave her a knowing smile. "I'm sure you did your best. You know, in the future, a lot of people imagine that 1905 was a quiet time in Britain. It wasn't. It only seemed calm viewed from what happened next, the storm of the First World War. At the time, this period was full of upheaval."

Hannah nodded, and there was a brief silence. Then the Professor said, "I'm renting this house. The owners are a family called Hughes."

Suddenly, Hannah felt anxious again. She knew the name Hughes. She knew what this probably meant. The Professor continued. "Mrs. Hughes lives in a large home in the next county, with her three daughters. Her eldest is named Victoria Halley, and she is 28. She recently returned home after her husband died just two years after they married. Her second oldest, Margaret, is 26, single, and likely to remain so. A single lady in 1905 does not live in her own apartment, but stays with her parents. Neither Margaret nor Victoria has much chance of finding a husband. Victoria is already on the old side, even at 28. Margaret has no personality that I can see. Talking to Margaret is about as much fun as watching paint dry."

Hannah said slowly, "You said Mrs. Hughes has three daughters."

"I did," said the Professor, "And I was just getting to the youngest. She's 19, just a little younger than you appear to be right now, Hannah."

Hannah said in a very small voice, "Let me guess. Her name's Elizabeth, right?"

"That's right," said the Professor, looking at her kindly. "Elizabeth Hughes is the girl who will one day be Mrs. Devenish … Are you all right?"

"I'm fine," said Hannah, suddenly feeling very tired. And then she blurted out, "Please don't make me do this."

A troubled look passed across the Professor's face, but then she continued briskly, "I've arranged you a job as a house-parlormaid with the Hughes family. I recommended you very highly."

Hannah briefly rested her head on her hand, and tried to collect herself. "Housemaid? Again? Why do I have to be the housemaid?"

"Because it's the only way to get you into the house, and among the family," said the Professor. "Look, if I just send you into town with orders to befriend Elizabeth Hughes, it won't happen. Middle-class Edwardian English people don't invite casual acquaintances into their lives, much less strangers. People must be introduced, and it can take a long time for them to really get to know each other. But a servant moves into the home, and quickly becomes intimately familiar with the family. Who knows more about the private life of a middle-class Edwardian family than their servant? And as it happens, I also have a feeling that you will like Elizabeth."

"I don't know," Hannah said. "I don't think we'll have anything in common." Truthfully, she couldn't even imagine a young Mrs. Devenish. It was mindboggling.

"Nonsense," said the Professor. "In her eyes, you're close to the same age, and you already sort of know her. But never forget that you are the maid, and that you are not the social equal of the Hughes family. Your role as a servant will

CHAPTER FOUR

require you to think carefully about how to gain Elizabeth's trust."

"Why would I need to get her trust?" Hannah said, and she thought, *Why would I want to?*

The Professor leaned forward, and said urgently, "Hannah, this is an important job."

"Being a housemaid?" Now Hannah wasn't just doubtful, but incredulous.

"Look, you remember you met Mrs. Devenish's mother in 1851 …"

Hannah looked blank.

"Sarah," the Professor reminded her. "Sarah Chatsfield."

"Oh, *her*," said Hannah, curling her lip at the memory. She had indeed met Mrs. Devenish's mother, Sarah Chatsfield, as Mrs. Hughes was then, a wealthy girl living in Balesworth Hall, the manor house nearby. "She's the most stuck-up little monster ever."

"She hasn't become more likable with age, I'm afraid," said the Professor. "But do try to have a little sympathy, Hannah. She has had a hard life, has Sarah Chatsfield Hughes. And as for her youngest daughter, Elizabeth Hughes, the future Mrs. Devenish, well … Look, the fact is, Hannah, that Elizabeth's family love her, but she is very much a square peg in a round hole. She's a bit lost. Just as …" and here the Professor paused, appearing to struggle with her thoughts.

"Yes?" said Hannah curiously. "What were you about to say?"

"Nothing," said the Professor. "Like I said, you'll see."

Hannah folded her arms. "Look, just tell me what you were going to say. Why do you have to be so mysterious? Is this just you going off on a power trip again?"

"I do understand why you think that, but no," said the Professor. "You see, if I try to get you to do something specific, there's a huge chance I will get it wrong, and that I will be more likely to steer you away from what you really should be doing. It's a bit like trying to … I don't know … perform a golf swing for you by holding onto your arms. It just doesn't work. That's why I give you as much freedom as I can."

Hannah was desperately trying to understand. "Freedom to do what?"

The Professor looked at her steadily. "I don't know. The time travel is a point in itself, remember? And bear in mind, Hannah, the old saying, *the child is father to the man.*"

Hannah was totally lost now. "Meaning?"

"I promise you this," said the Professor. "Once you have helped Elizabeth, you can ask all the questions you like, and I will try very hard to answer them."

Hannah was beyond exasperated. "But why not now?"

CHAPTER FOUR

"Because it's not the time," said the Professor. "Now, one more thing, and this is a tiny bit awkward, but you might want to look in the other bedroom upstairs, Mrs. D.'s room. There's someone in there you've brought with you."

Hannah jumped to her feet, ran upstairs to the largest bedroom, called her brother's name, and threw open the door. It was dark, and she reached automatically for the light switch. But as she fumbled, she remembered that Weston Cottage in 1905 was lit by gaslight. She had no idea how to switch on gaslight.

"Who's that?" called out a sleepy voice. "Is that you, Granny?"

It couldn't be. But it was. Somehow, Hannah had brought Verity from 1951. How was this possible? She had held hands with Alex, and Verity wasn't even in the room. But somehow, Verity was here in 1905.

Hannah swallowed her rising alarm. She was going to have to break the news to her friend. "No," she said softly, "It's not. It's me, Hannah."

Verity said sleepily, "Oh. Hallo, Hannah. I say, would you mind switching the light on? I have no idea how I ended up in bed. How odd. I must have been most dreadfully tired."

Hannah was panicking now. Maybe she could get the Professor to break the bad news to Verity? "Look, why don't you get more sleep?"

"No," said Verity, struggling to her feet. "I'm up now, and I'm supposed to be going out. Gosh, I hope I'm not late. Where's my alarm clock? But ... What on earth am I doing in here? This isn't my room. Where am I?" She sat up. "Switch on the light, won't you?"

"I can't," Hannah said. "I think the bulb has died. In fact, all the lights are out."

"Good grief," Verity said quietly, and before Hannah could stop her, she had pushed past her, and into the hallway.

Verity stared at the gas lamp. "What is that? What's going on? This isn't Granny's house."

"Yes, it is," Hannah said quickly. "Only it's in 1905. We're in 1905, Verity."

"Don't be ridiculous ..." But then Verity looked around again. And then she fell to her knees, openmouthed.

"Well played, Hannah," said the Professor, who had her arm around a blanket-draped Verity, trying to coax her to sip from a cup of hot tea laced with whisky.

Calming down Verity had taken some time. Once she could stand up, she had run from the house, then dashed back inside screaming, before collapsing in a curled-up heap.

"It was a shock, of course," said the Professor. "But I suppose her zooming around in hysterics outside did cut down a bit on the need for explanations. Drink up, Verity, there's a good girl. Nothing like tea for shock, especially when it's topped up with something a little bit stronger."

Verity nodded silently, her eyes dull.

"I think it might be best if Verity were to get a good night's sleep," the Professor said decisively. "Then we can work on getting her home. What do you think, Verity?"

Once again, Verity nodded.

But Hannah was busily thinking about her new mission. "So I sound American, like I did in 1951?" she said. "It might be kind of hard to explain an American maid."

"No, I fixed that for you," said the Professor. "The only people who hear you speaking in an American accent are Verity and me. Here's a bit of advice, though. Next time you time travel by yourself, bear your accent in mind. When you concentrate, try to think of flipping through a binder full of items you need, like your accent change, and do it quickly but in a focused way, over and over. That works best for me, but then I've been doing this for a long time. It's hard to explain, but don't worry, you'll get the hang of it."

The Professor rose to her feet, and patted a still-silent Verity on the shoulder. "Would you like something to eat?" she said.

Verity quickly shook her head.

The Professor looked dubious. "What, not even a nice bar of chocolate?"

This got Verity's attention, and she turned to look at the Professor with new interest.

The Professor reached into her bag, and pulled out a candy bar wrapped in purple paper illustrated with a wooden milk pail. "Classic British milk chocolate, brand new this summer, 1905," she said, tantalizingly waving it in the air before placing it in Verity's outstretched hand.

Verity quickly tore it open, broke off a square, and popped it in her mouth.

"Wartime candy rationing in Britain doesn't end until 1953," the Professor explained to Hannah.

Hannah was astonished. "But World War Two ended in 1945!"

"It's a long story," said the Professor. "Look it up."

Verity, who had eaten several pieces of chocolate meanwhile, swallowed, and sputtered, "Don't tell me when chocolate is going to come off the ration. I don't want to know the future, thank you."

"Fair enough," said the Professor, "Hannah, don't talk to Verity about the future. And, Verity, it's good to see you with color as well as chocolate back in your cheeks. I'll make you another cup of tea, and then you should get some rest. Even time travelers can get jet lag."

"What on earth is jet lag?" said Verity.

It was strange to be in 1905, Hannah thought. But it was even stranger to be in 1905 with someone from 1951.

Early the next morning, Hannah sat on the bed, leaning on her knees, and watching the sunlight filter through the threadbare curtains of her room. Thinking about what was to come made her anxious, and so she jumped at the knock on her bedroom door. The Professor walked in, wished her a good morning, and held up a small case in one hand, and a maid's uniform in the other. The uniform was a long black dress, with white frilly pinafore apron, collar, and fancy lace cap. Hannah grabbed the cap, jammed it low on her head, and pulled a silly face.

"I don't blame you for hating the cap on sight," the Professor said. "Edwardian maids all hate their caps. They find them humiliating. Look, just put the uniform in your bag, and wear the street clothes in the wardrobe for the train."

"Should I have a bath first?"

The Professor looked at her curiously. "When did you last take a bath?"

Hannah had to think about it. "I guess it was a couple of days ago."

"In that case, a cold sponge bath will do," said the Professor. "It will have to. I don't have running hot water. Anyway, you know as well as I do that you'll be most authentic if you take a proper bath no more than once a week. Go use the washstand in my room. I'll get you one of your own this week."

Hannah, who had been so fastidious in her life before time travel, found this perfectly acceptable. In 1752, she had hardly washed at all, and nobody had said anything, because everyone smelled. *After a while,* she thought, *you stop noticing.*

And in any case, bathing was the least of her worries. How, she thought, could teenage Hannah Dias, pretending to be a maid, help formidable Elizabeth Hughes Devenish navigate life? The idea would have been laughable, if she had found it funny.

The Professor waved a hand toward the hot breakfast on the table. "Lovely back bacon, fried eggs, mushrooms, tomatoes, fresh bread, and a pot of tea to wash it all down," she said proudly.

Hannah needed no introduction to her breakfast, and she tucked in, pausing only to slather butter on bread, and slurp her tea.

"Now, you've got the address?" the Professor said eagerly.

Hannah nodded, then used her knife to push eggs onto the back of her fork, British-style. She didn't want to stand out like a sore thumb in England. In 1940, Mrs. Devenish had corrected her table manners, not realizing that Hannah ate normally for an American. After Hannah wrangled the precariously balanced eggs into her mouth and swallowed, she said, "By the way, this is delicious."

"Oh, it's only a fry-up," the Professor said modestly. "Now listen. The Hugheses live in Ickswade."

The corners of Hannah's mouth twitched. "Ickswade?"

"I agree, it's a silly name. Ickswade is in Bedfordshire. That's the county next to Hertfordshire."

"Yes, I know about Beds and Herts," said Hannah, pronouncing the abbreviation for Hertfordshire as "hearts," to show off her local knowledge.

The Professor continued. "Mrs. Hughes owns Willowbank, a late-Victorian home in Ickswade. Mr. Hughes was a lawyer, so he built a house suitable to his station in life. You'll be living in the servants' quarters in the attic, but you'll get every Wednesday afternoon off…"

Hannah scowled. "So servants still get just one afternoon off a week? It's such a rip-off…"

"Agreed," said the Professor, "It's exploitation. That's why I took advantage of the current servant shortage in Ickswade to negotiate a special deal for you. I got Mrs. Hughes to agree that you can stay here at Weston Cottage overnight on Wednesdays. She thinks you have to visit your aged mother. Go ahead and stay in Ickswade this first Wednesday, so you have a chance to settle in, but we'll start your Wednesday visits here next week."

Hannah grimaced. "It must be pretty bad there if you think I need a break every week."

"All of us need a break, Hannah, and we're all entitled to a life, something that privileged people did not acknowledge in 1905. But actually, I think you'll like working for the Hugheses. And if you don't, you will at least get downtime here every week. If I'm around, I'll cook for you. If not, help yourself to what's in the larder. You should consider Weston Cottage your home, Hannah. But I think you already do, don't you?"

"Got it," Hannah said abruptly, picking up her fork. She didn't want to think of Weston Cottage, Mrs. Devenish's home, as her own. Not anymore. "Now, tell me again what exactly you want me to do."

The Professor held up an index finger. "First and foremost, get to know Elizabeth," she said. "But remember that she's not yet Mrs. D., and you're not you. You're a servant, so you must always address her as Miss Elizabeth, and don't overstep your bounds. It won't be easy."

"Nothing involving her is ever easy," Hannah said. "And you still haven't told me the whole point of being nice to her."

"Hannah," the Professor said quietly, putting her hand to her head, "please just go along with it." But then she seemed to collect herself, and she looked at Hannah kindly. "Listen, darling, here's the key. Just be yourself."

In her normal 21st century life, nobody ever told Hannah Dias to be herself. The only people who had ever seemed to appreciate her for who she was were her friends in the past. Now, the Professor was urging Hannah to just be herself. In a small voice, Hannah said, "You don't really mean that, do you?"

"Actually," the Professor said gently, "for once, I really, really do."

"Be myself? Really? That's all?" Hannah couldn't quite grasp it.

"Really," said the Professor. "Don't you understand? Look, at some point in life, we all have to stop making frantic plans, and looking for the approval of others, and start having confidence in ourselves. When we have confidence, real confidence, it makes us the people we really ought to be …"

Hannah wanted to cry. "Maybe, but now? I'm still a kid."

"Yes, now," said the Professor. "You're ready for this, Hannah. I promise."

Hannah looked at her anxiously. "So what do you want me to do, exactly?"

"I told you. I want you to help Elizabeth Hughes become Mrs. Devenish."

"But what if I make poor choices?"

The Professor sighed heavily. "One of the things I hate most about modern life," she said, "is all this twaddle about poor choices. Some of the most brilliant things people have ever done were regarded at the time as poor choices. Some of the most interesting people would never have got their lives off the ground if they had only made so-called good choices. Hannah, let me try to explain. After you and Verity went along with Eric chucking a stone through that window in 1940, Mrs. Devenish spanked you, so that must have been a bad choice, right? But if you and Verity had stopped Eric from throwing that stone, you would never have rescued George Braithwaite, and his life would have been a misery. So tell me, was the stone-throwing a good choice, or a bad one? Hmm? All I can tell you is that I have complete faith in you, mistakes and all."

Hannah put her knife and fork together on the plate. She would have to think about what the Professor had said. Then she jerked her head toward the ceiling. "What are we gonna do about Verity?"

"Leave Verity to me," said the Professor. "I'll look after her. You get going to Ickswade. Oh, and here's some money." She pushed a small coin purse across the table at Hannah, who took it and tipped out clunky coins in bronze and silver. Examining the change, she realized it wasn't much. "How generous," she said sarcastically.

"If I were to give you a lot of money," the Professor said patiently, "and the Hugheses were to see it, they would assume you had stolen it. Remember, you're a maid. You don't have lots of money. And you won't need it anyway."

"Why not?"

"You'll see," the Professor said. "And by the way, you can't go by Hannah Dias, obviously, because there aren't many Spanish names in England …"

"Portuguese," Hannah corrected her.

The Professor ignored her. "And you can't go by Hannah Day, because … Well, time-travel reasons. So I had to think of another name in a hurry. I told Mrs. Hughes your name is May."

Hannah stared at her. And then she half-gasped, half-laughed, "Are you telling me my name's *May Day*?"

"No. Your name is May Harrower," said the Professor, looking embarrassed. "It was the best I could do. Sorry. Now, off you go. Here's the address and a map. It's not hard to find. As I said, it's near the railway station. Keep in touch, dear."

"I will if you will," Hannah said, and her eyes pleaded, *Please don't leave me alone here. I have no idea what I'm doing.* She was too proud to say it aloud.

Chapter 5:
ANOTHER WAY TO SNIPESVILLE

Tuesday, January 30, 1906

Alex sat perfectly still, his eyes closed tight. He was trying to understand what had happened to him. He clearly remembered lying in bed in Weston Cottage in 1951. Now he was outdoors, in a sitting position, propped against a wall on hard ground. He had not yet opened his eyes, because he was pretty sure that what he was about to see would disturb him.

Even with his eyes shut, Alex knew he was not in Balesworth, or in England, or in 1951: He heard horses' hooves trotting back and forth, and people talking in American accents. Suddenly, he was startled by the crash and jangle of coins hitting the ground, and he looked.

An overturned hat lay crumpled and slack on the sidewalk in front of him, and loose coins were scattered in and around it. As he looked at the coins, Alex looked down at himself: His snazzy 1950s summer outfit was gone, replaced with a mud-colored suit of thick wool. He looked up. A dark-skinned man in a hat strolled by, smoking a pipe, and dressed in an outfit that appeared to be two sizes too small. Two young light-skinned black girls in long skirts and puffy white blouses paused to admire the window display of a nearby store. Craning his neck to look down the street, he saw signs: *MOORES PHOTOGRAPHS, KROUSKOFF BROS & CO. HATS & CLOTHING,* and, most interesting of all, *NEW YORK DENTAL PARLORS.*

But if Alex was in New York, why was every accent he heard Southern? He looked for more clues. A streetcar jolted by, and a spark sprang from the wires overhead. More people passed him: A stocky white man sporting a bushy

CHAPTER FIVE

mustache and wire-rimmed glasses, carrying a paper-wrapped bottle … A thin white guy driving past in a horse-drawn carriage … A young black kid struggling to push a heavy handcart in a straight line … An old white woman wearing a long dress and enormous fancy hat. She dropped coins in Alex's cap on the sidewalk, without breaking her stride.

Tilting back his head until his neck ached, Alex read the massive sign over his head: *SAVANNAH ELECTRIC CO, EDISON LIGHT*. Savannah, then. Not New York. And electricity. That meant he had to be in the 20th century, yes? It had been less than a minute since he had opened his eyes, and he already felt overwhelmed. But now he recognized where he was. "Is this Broughton Street?" he called out to a small white boy running along the pavement. The kid turned, nodded, and ran on.

So that was it, then. He really was in Savannah, Georgia, the closest "big city" to Snipesville. Judging from everything around him, he was somewhere between 1851 and 1951. Maybe halfway? 1901? He scrambled to his feet, and brushed himself off. Picking up the cap and loose coins from the sidewalk, he tipped the change into his palm, then put on the hat, and turned around to check out his reflection in the shop window. He still looked like he was in his early 20s, which he decided, was probably a good thing. Alex felt the last thing he would have expected in these circumstances: a burst of confidence. Sure, he had time traveled. But dreading the time travel had been much worse than just getting on with it. Okay, so 1951 hadn't gone so well, with Mrs. Devenish being such a grump, and his awkward interactions with a grown-up Eric, but at least it hadn't been scary. Now he was in Savannah, and probably in the late Victorian era. He could deal with this, too.

Feeling something press against his chest, Alex reached inside his jacket pocket, and pulled out a wallet that was full of crisp dollar bills. He looked around to be sure nobody on the street had seen his stash of money, but no one was paying the slightest attention to him. Alex smiled. He was tired of being afraid, of dreading his life. This time, he had money, he had skills, and he looked like an adult. He was going to take charge, and trust that the Professor would find him when necessary. She always did. Why worry?

Standing on the platform of the Savannah Railroad Depot, Alex waited for the next train to Snipesville. He had bought a newspaper on Broughton Street, so he now knew this was January, 1906. The year rang a bell, but it was only when he repeated it aloud to himself that he realized why: the San Francisco Earthquake was in 1906. For the first time since leaving California, he felt glad to be a long way away.

CHAPTER FIVE

Alex wasn't sure why he felt drawn to Snipesville now. He knew nobody in 1906 Snipesville. He had no clear idea of what he would do when he got there. He just knew, somehow, that going there was what he must do. Not that he was too worried. He could find somewhere in town for a meal, and a place to stay for the night, right? He was pretty sure the Hotel Duval was in business by 1906. And he was pretty sure he could find a job. After all, he had experience working as a lawyer's clerk, even if that experience had been in 1851. Alex felt in control. He was living in the moment.

And at this moment, he heard rapid echoing footsteps approach behind him. He turned to look. A young white man was bent double in the station entryway, puffing and trying to regain his breath after running, his head down and his hands flat on his knees.

If that guy was here to catch the Snipesville train, Alex thought, he had made it just in time. The huge engine was chuffing toward the platform, steam pouring from its massive funnel. Alex checked his ticket once more as the locomotive slowly rolled to a halt, and exhaled a burst of steam and smoke. As passengers disembarked, Alex stepped forward, and politely held open a carriage door for a well-dressed young dark-skinned man behind him. The man gave him a startled look, and then hurried down the platform to board another carriage. Puzzled, Alex took a seat.

He wondered again why he was headed to Snipesville. Why go there when he had a much larger city under his nose? His dad had done the same thing in the 21st century, of course. Bill Dias had transferred from San Francisco to Snipesville. Alex wondered now if his dad had had no choice. Maybe he had messed up in San Francisco. That was a worrying thought.

He was just opening his newspaper when he felt a tap on his shoulder.

"Excuse me, sorry to bother you, but I'm terribly lost," said a hesitant English voice.

Astonished, he turned to look at the speaker. It was Eric from 1951.

They stared at each other, then Eric held out a trembling hand for him to shake, and said quietly, and desperately, "Help me. Please. Help me."

It took about half of the rattling, bumping train journey for Eric to calm down. He was clearly in shock, and he kept asking for tea and cigarettes. Finally, he found cigarettes in his pocket, and to Alex's dismay, he lit one. When the conductor came through the open carriage, staggering like a drunk as the train jolted forward, Alex bought Eric a ticket, and learned from the conductor that they should change trains at Clacton. Alex watched as Eric looked desperately at the conductor when Clacton was mentioned, as if he were hoping that

CHAPTER FIVE

this had all been a terrible mistake, and that he was really on a train headed toward Clacton, England.

But there was no mistake, as Alex knew all too well, and while Eric slumped glassy-eyed on the hard seat of the carriage, Alex quietly told him the story of his time-traveling life or, rather, selected highlights. In telling Eric his story, Alex also told it to himself. His confidence grew as he realized how much he had survived, and the good he had done, and the experiences he had enjoyed as well as those which had frightened him out of his wits. And now, here he was, helping Eric.

Eric had no idea how young Alex really was, until Alex told him that, too. "But … You're the same age you were in 1940? You're eleven? You look like you're my age," he stammered.

"I know," said Alex. "Now people treat me differently. Better, mostly."

"I'll be one of them," Eric said. "I'm going to have to depend on you, Alex, believe me. I've never been to America before, much less … this."

By the time the train chugged into Clacton, Alex was feeling great. He even had a fleeting fantasy of becoming a successful businessman in 1906, until he realized that this would mean never going home again. As they waited for the second train to Snipesville, he said to Eric, "I almost forgot. I gotta tell you all about the Professor."

"Professor?" said Eric. "What Professor?"

"So this is where you live, then, is it?" said Eric, his eyes shining as they got off the train in Snipesville. He had cheered up enormously since learning about the Professor, and how Alex, Hannah, and Brandon had returned safely from their previous time-travel journeys. "Does Snipesville look at all like this in the 21st century?"

"Kind of," said Alex. "Well, the railroad depot … I mean, the railway station, that's gonna be a hair salon."

Eric looked confused. "You mean the train station closed and became a hairdresser's? How do you manage without trains?"

"We all have cars," Alex said.

"Goodness," Eric said. "Granny was quite the pioneer with her old Austin Seven, but I've never dreamed that *everyone* would have a car. What, even the working classes? Goodness. So what else has changed?"

As they strolled into downtown, Alex peered along East Main Street.

"Huh, it's not so different," he said. "Well, okay, they have dirt roads. And they have a lot more trees than we've got. And I don't recognize some of the buildings … But you know what? Snipesville doesn't look so sad in 1906. They

CHAPTER FIVE

actually have real businesses downtown, like over there, see the signs? Look, there's a café, and a department store, and a hardware store …"

But Eric was confused again. "What do you mean, real businesses?"

"In my Snipesville, most of the downtown shops sell useless stuff. They don't sell stuff you really need. They're all, like, antique stores, and gift shops."

"Gift shops?" said Eric. "What does a gift shop sell?"

"Gifts," Alex said. "Pointless junk. I guess people buy most stuff online now."

"Online?" Eric said. "What's that?"

But Alex was finding the endless explanations exhausting. And he had enough to do, wrapping his head around Snipesville in 1906. "Hey, see the hotel? It's still around in the future."

"*The Hotel Duval* …" said Eric, wrinkling his nose. "It sounds French."

"I guess," said Alex. He really hadn't thought about it.

Alex looked across the street to a grand building on which was engraved in stone, *BANK OF SNIPESVILLE*. "That's my dad's bank!" he cried. "And there's the courthouse!" Something was missing, but he couldn't think what it was. He looked down in dismay at the dust covering his shoes and the cuffs of his pants. "If they would just pave the roads, this Snipesville would be amazing. Of course, Snipes County still has a lot of dirt roads in the 21st century."

"That's not terribly reassuring," said Eric, running his hand over his hair. "Anyhow, I don't really want to know about the future. Well, except perhaps the good news. Tell me about science. Has anyone flown a spaceship yet?"

"Oh, sure, moon landings, space shuttles, the works," Alex said matter-of-factly. "Robots on Mars. Robots on a comet."

Beaming, Eric hurried after Alex, who was striding up the steps of the Hotel Duval.

When Alex pushed open the swinging doors, he stopped in amazement. The hotel lobby was elegant, with white columns, plush red carpets, and a vase of colorful fresh flowers on the reception desk. Beyond, he glimpsed the dining room's white tablecloths, sparkling silverware, and yet more vases of flowers on every table. Electric lights hung everywhere. He didn't know what he was expecting, but this probably wasn't it.

Behind the reception desk, a young white man stood to attention, and said, "How may I help you, gentlemen?" His accent was not Southern. That was unexpected, too.

"How much for a room?" said Alex.

"Seventy-five cents a night, sir."

Alex reached for his wallet. "In that case, I'll take two of them," he said cheerfully, handing over two crisp dollar bills.

CHAPTER FIVE

"Are you sure?" said Eric, adding under his breath, "Do we have enough money?"

"Of course," Alex said. The clerk shoved a heavy book across the desk to him, just as the hotel phone started ringing. "What's this book for?"

"Registration," Eric explained in a whisper. "We write in our details."

As the clerk took the phone call, Alex grabbed the pen lying in the spine of the registration book, and scrawled both their names.

"Alex," whispered Eric, "My name's Scrivener. Not Powell. Powell is Verity's name."

"Oh. I forgot about that," said Alex. "Look, I always think of you as Eric Powell now, because you took Verity's name when you got married."

"I did?" squeaked Eric. "I mean, I will? Why?"

"I dunno," said Alex. "Anyway, let's go with Eric Powell. It'll just be easier."

"Not for me, it won't," Eric muttered.

The clerk hung up the phone, and glanced at the hotel register. He looked shocked by Alex's awful handwriting, which contrasted painfully with the beautiful signatures of previous guests, but he said nothing. Taking two keys from the hook board behind him, he picked up a small brass bell, then paused, and looked over the desk at Alex's and Eric's feet. "You have no baggage, sirs?"

"No, we don't," said Alex. "Our bags were stolen in, um, Savannah. Is there somewhere around here we can buy clothes?"

The clerk said crisply, "Yes, sir. I recommend Thompson's department store on South Main Street, just across from the courthouse, or Greenberg's Men's Store."

"Splendid," said Eric. "Thank you very much."

Hearing Eric's accent, the clerk smiled. "Excuse me, I hope you don't mind my asking, sir, but where are you from?"

"I'm from London," said Eric.

"And you, too, sir?" the clerk said to Alex. Alex opened his mouth to say "No," and then changed his mind halfway through. What came out was "Nye-ess."

"Isn't that interesting," said the clerk. "I'm from Massachusetts myself. My name's Charles, Charles Zilinski, and if I may be of service to you gentlemen, please don't hesitate to ask for me. Welcome to Georgia, gentlemen. Allow me to show you to your rooms."

Alex had assumed that everybody living in Snipesville in 1906 was from the South. Meeting a guy from Boston with an Eastern European name was quite a surprise.

Their hotel rooms were not nearly as luxurious as the lobby. A single bed, a

CHAPTER FIVE

washstand, a simple chair, and small wardrobe were all the furnishings. But neither Alex, seasoned time traveler, nor Eric, citizen of impoverished post-World War Two Britain, was too disappointed. Their standards weren't very high.

Alex sat on the bed for a minute, and tried to think. Now that he was in Snipesville, the plans that had so inspired him on the train platform in Savannah suddenly seemed really, really hard. Truth was, he had never had to look for a job anywhere before, much less in 1906. Maybe Eric could help. He wandered into the hallway, and knocked on Eric's door. "So, I guess after we get some new clothes, we should find jobs," he said as Eric opened the door. "Just in case, you know."

"No, I don't know," Eric said. "What do you mean, exactly?"

Alex bit his lip. "In case it takes a long time before we can go home."

Eric looked worried now. "And how long do you think it might take?"

"I don't know," said Alex.

"I see," said Eric, although it was clear to Alex that he didn't. "What sorts of jobs do you think we might we find here? Is there a labor exchange in Snipesville?"

Alex didn't know what a labor exchange was, but he didn't want to say "I don't know" again, and he tried to look self-assured by cracking his knuckles. Eric cringed at the sound. Then Alex remembered the newspaper he had bought in Savannah. "We can look at the job listings in the newspaper. If they have a newspaper here."

Eric looked at him uncertainly. "Of course, we could always return to Savannah," he said. "That was obviously a much larger town. It ought to have more jobs."

Alex knew Eric was right, but he was determined to make the decisions. He was an experienced time traveler, after all, and he was from a time with more technology than Eric was, which had to count for something. Plus he was American, and he had actually lived in Snipesville and Savannah, so he definitely knew more. He also didn't want to admit to Eric that coming to Snipesville had probably been a huge mistake. "Let's find something in Snipesville," he said. "First, though, let's go buy some clothes."

"So long as we don't spend too much money," Eric muttered. "Alex, might I be treasurer of this expedition?"

"What do you mean?" said Alex.

"I mean," said Eric, holding out a hand, "why don't you let me look after the money?"

"Oh, that's not necessary," Alex said, patting his wallet.

CHAPTER FIVE

Eric did not look convinced.

Alex knew this building. In the 21st century, it would be home to The Boiled Peanut boutique. Now, in 1906, it housed Thompson's Department Store. He and Eric stepped from the dusty street onto the covered boardwalk to admire the stylish Edwardian clothes through the plate glass window. As they did so, two white men left the store. One was young, and dressed in a derby hat, smart suit, and tie, while the older man wore shabby farmers' overalls and a broad-brimmed black hat that had seen better days. "I wish I didn't shop in Thompson's," said the older man, removing his crumpled hat and inspecting it sadly.

"Well, why do you?" said the younger man. The pair was apparently unaware that they had a fascinated audience in Alex and Eric, who lurked a few feet away.

"Same as everyone," said the older man. "Thompson and me reckon up how much I owe him for goods I bought from him on credit this past year, and I come up short again. So I got to keep buying from him, cause I ain't got the cash to buy from nobody else. How come I always end up owing him?"

The young man shook his head ruefully. "Might have something to do with you always spending your money by the time you get out of his store," he said. "You ought to live within your means, Father."

"Easy for you to say, son," his father said. "In your fancy clothes with your fancy ways, and your fancy job working in the bank."

"Well, maybe you should quit the farm, come to work in town, too," said the son, in a slightly malicious tone.

Looking ashamed, the old farmer glanced at his feet, then looked away. "Now, you know I can't do that. I owe Thompson, and I don't know how to read and write, hardly."

"That's never stopped old Thompson," said the son. "He can't read nor write at all, and he makes a fortune, doesn't he?"

"Look how he makes his money," the older man said sharply. "Stealing from the likes of me. Don't think I don't know what he's doing. And you and your pals at the Bank of Snipesville help him do it, giving him credit so he can keep up this racket."

But now the younger man had noticed Eric and Alex staring at them. "Say, can I help you gentlemen?"

Eric was embarrassed. "No, no, not at all," he said, and as a good Englishman, took refuge in talking about the weather. "Lovely weather we're having, isn't it? Barely a cloud in the sky. I can hardly believe it's winter."

"Well, listen to that fancy accent!" said the farmer father. He peered at Eric.

CHAPTER FIVE

"You a Yankee?"

"No, I'm English," Eric said, baffled. "I'm not American."

Alex tapped Eric's arm, and translated, "He means, are you from the Northern states?"

Eric said, slightly more loudly, as if the farmer were deaf, "No, I'm from England."

"England, huh?" the son said. "You oughta know our newspaper editor, then."

"Should I?" Eric said. He and Alex exchanged confused looks.

"You might find him over yonder," said the older man, pointing across to the boardwalk opposite, and an office bearing the sign *THE SNIPESVILLE NEWS*.

"Thank you very much," said Eric.

The men nodded, and solemnly tipped their hats to him. Eric, looking awkward, returned the gesture. "Just observing local customs," he said to Alex, who suspected the two men were making fun of his friend.

Alex said, "Why do they think we should meet the editor of *The Snipesville News?*"

"I haven't the foggiest," said Eric. "Still, it's not the daftest idea. We need to get acquainted with people if we're to find work. At the very least, we can pick up the newspaper and have a look at the situations vacant."

"You mean job listings?" said Alex.

"Do I? Oh. First, though, we must get ourselves properly dressed." He held open the door of Thompson's department store for Alex, before following him inside.

Carrying a stack of white paper-and-string-wrapped department store boxes of new clothes, Alex was about to step from the covered boardwalk onto the dirt road, when Eric threw out an arm to stop him. "Look where you're going," he yelped, and pointed to a slow-moving horse and wagon.

"Please," Alex snorted. "I would have to be crawling across the road to get run down by that. I'm a man, not a sloth."

They were halfway across the street when the wagon passed them, casting up a mud puddle that sprayed all over Eric's pants.

Standing on the boardwalk, Eric was looking forlornly at the speckled mess on his trousers. He brushed at the dirt, which only rubbed it deeper into the fabric. "Good job we bought new clothes," he said. "But I shall need to get these cleaned. I suppose the hotel can do that for me, for a price."

Alex, balancing his purchases on one arm, pointed to the shop next to the newspaper office. Painted on the window was *H. WONG. LAUNDRY. WASHING AND IRONING.*

"How very convenient," Eric said with a grin.

"Good afternoon, gentlemen, how may I help you?" Mr. Wong, the laundryman, was in his twenties, wore a pair of pince-nez glasses dangling from a ribbon on his front, and spoke in a strong Georgia accent. The front area of his shop was tiny. One pile of bags made of knotted white sheets sat on the counter, and another lay on the floor, along with buckets and large tubs, some filled with soaking laundry. Behind Mr. Wong, belts and pulleys hung from the ceiling. Bedsheets spilled from a large wicker hamper, next to an iron wringer for wet clothes. Standing at one of the high counters that lined the side of the room, an Asian woman in a long apron was silently folding linens. A baby careened around the room in a wheeled wooden walker.

Alex had known Asian people in San Francisco, of course, and had run into a few Southerners of Asian ancestry in 21st-century Snipesville. But he was astonished to meet Asians in Snipesville in 1906. "Where are you from?" he squeaked.

Mr. Wong gave a tolerant sort of smile, as though he had fielded this question thousands of times before. "Augusta," he said, and then added quickly as if to head off an inevitable question, "My father came to Georgia from China to work on the canals." He noticed Eric's pants. "Do you need those cleaned, sir?"

Eric nodded, and Mr. Wong pointed him to a side room where he could change. Then he carefully slotted his glasses on the bridge of his nose, and began writing out a ticket on a small notepad.

"So how long have you been in Snipesville?" Alex said brightly.

"Only a few months," Mr. Wong said, giving Alex a polite smile.

This was followed by an awkward silence.

"So," said Alex, "Why did you come here?"

Mr. Wong moved a bag full of clothes from the counter to a small pile nearby, and then said reluctantly, "My uncle showed me a pamphlet from the Snipesville Chamber of Commerce, asking for businesses to set up here. My father helped me establish this laundry."

"Do you like it here?" Alex really wanted to know.

Mr. Wong hesitated for just a second, and then he said, "Snipesville is prospering. I'm pleased to be here."

Alex had a pretty good idea of what Mr. Wong really thought. Living in Snipesville wasn't easy for someone who didn't belong. He knew all about that. He extended a hand, and Mr. Wong, a little surprised, shook it. "My name's

Alex …um …Day," he said. "I just got here, and I'm looking for a job."

Mr. Wong hurriedly withdrew his hand from Alex's grip. "I'm sorry, I need no help," he said.

"Oh, wow, I didn't mean I was asking you for work," Alex said truthfully. "I just thought, well, if you want to go for coffee with us and hang out sometime …"

"Coffee?" Mr. Wong blinked. "That's very kind of you, Mr. Day."

"Alex, call me Alex. What's your name?"

"Mr. Wong," said a puzzled Mr. Wong, who apparently didn't hand out his first name to strangers. Alex wasn't sure if this was because he was Asian-American, or because this was 1906. Meanwhile, Eric had emerged from the back room, wearing his new pants, and holding up the muddy pair. Mr. Wong took them from him and threw them in a wicker basket. "They will be ready on Friday," he said, sliding the paper ticket across the counter to Eric. Even before Eric and Alex had left the counter, Mr. Wong had returned to sorting out clothes. Somehow, Alex doubted that he had time to hang out with them, or trusted them enough to turn up for coffee.

Peering through the window of the offices of *The Snipesville News,* Alex could see a gray-haired white man with a large, neat mustache, in shirt sleeves and cravat, sitting at a wooden desk, surrounded by bundles of newspapers stacked on the floor, and a massive wooden cabinet displaying row after row of metal printing type. He was smoking a cigar, and leaning forward in his seat to examine the enormous leather-bound accounts book lying open in front of him.

As Alex and Eric entered, the doorbell jangled, and the man looked up. "How may I help you?" he said.

Both Eric and Alex looked at him, looked at each other, and then back at him. He didn't sound Southern. In fact, if Alex wasn't mistaken, he was English. "We just arrived in Snipesville," Alex said. "We're staying at the hotel. We're looking for work."

The man steepled his fingers below his chin, and leaned backward in his wooden chair, which creaked. "And who is "we"? Are you gentlemen drummers?" he said.

There was no doubt about it now. He was English. But what was a drummer? "No," said Alex. "I don't play drums. Do you play drums, Eric?"

"No," Eric said quietly, "I don't think that's quite what this gentleman means. Do you, sir?"

As soon as Eric spoke, the man sat up straight, and grinned. "Well, I'll be … You're an Englishman!"

CHAPTER FIVE

"I am sir, a Londoner," said Eric. "Well, I was born in London, but I was …"

"Where in London?" the man said eagerly.

"Bethnal Green," said Eric.

The newspaperman looked baffled. "Good Lord. You don't sound as though you're from the East End. You're very well-spoken. Was your father the local vicar?"

"Not exactly," Eric said. "I was adopted, and went to live in the country. It was my adoptive mother who taught me to speak like this, sir."

"Goodness gracious!" said the newspaperman. "And your friend here? Are you an Englishman?"

Alex said, "I'm from California. San Francisco."

"From California? Good Lord. How far afield. What brings you both to Snipesville, pray?"

Alex and Eric had no idea. They looked awkwardly at each other.

"No matter," said the man as they stood in embarrassed silence, "Like you, I came to Snipesville without any idea of the place, but it most certainly has proven as marvelous a town for business as one could desire."

Eric stepped forward, his hand outstretched. "Pleased to make your acquaintance, sir. This is Alexander Day, and I'm Eric … um … Powell."

"How do you do," said the newspaperman. "My name's Hughes. Charles Hughes."

"Hughes? That's my mother's maiden name," Eric said. "My adoptive mother, that is. Perhaps you're related?"

Charles Hughes smiled. "I very much doubt it. Hughes is an extremely common name."

Alex looked around at the small office and then out through the window at downtown Snipesville. "And you seriously like it here?" he said, incredulous.

"Oh, absolutely," said Mr. Hughes. "My wife and I have recently moved into our new house. We have modern plumbing, electricity, telephones, trains …" He ticked off these items on his fingers. "We are more progressive here in Snipesville than is practically any town in England. America is a country with great room for ambition, and it rewards every man who works hard. You saw our new hotel? The county courthouse is new, the Bank of Snipesville is new, and we have hopes of persuading the State of Georgia to establish an Agricultural and Mechanical School here. Oh, and *The Snipesville News*, of which I am publisher and editor, prints not only the news in town and throughout Snipes County, but in the state and nation. Our readership reaches almost to Savannah."

"Impressive," said Eric, and he seemed to mean it. "Mr. Hughes, do you

CHAPTER FIVE

happen to know of any jobs in town?"

"What sort of employment do you seek?" said Mr. Hughes. "Our most promising opportunities are for businessmen. Are you sure you don't intend to open your own business? It will thrive, I promise you."

Alex frowned. "I don't think we have enough money to start a business."

Mr. Hughes looked appraisingly at Alex and Eric. "As it happens, gentlemen, I require two reporters and a clerk. So many gentlemen come to Snipesville to begin their own ventures that we have a shortage of literate men needing waged work. Our local men seldom possess business skills, you see. Most are farmers, and while their sons are interested in jobs in Snipesville, they seldom start as suitable employees, and require a great deal of training."

"I can be a clerk," said Alex eagerly. "I've done that before. In Savannah."

Mr. Hughes looked at him sharply. "Who was your employer?"

"A lawyer, Mr. Jeremy Thornhill," Alex said promptly. Then he remembered that Mr. Thornhill had been dead for more than a half-century. Quickly, he added, "But he went to live somewhere else."

Eric cleared his throat. "I have never been a newspaper reporter," he said. "But I would be willing to have a go."

"That settles it," said Mr. Hughes, slapping his hand on the desk. "You are both employed, but on trial, mind. Day, take a look at my accounts," he shoved the large book toward Alex. "And Powell, you can begin by interviewing the Mayor of Snipesville about the planned building of houses to the west of the city."

Eric looked a little daunted. "First, I need to know where to find the Mayor."

"That should not present difficulties," said Mr. Hughes. "You're looking at him." Eric gulped slightly as Mr. Hughes indicated that he should pull up a chair. "Do a good job, Powell, and perhaps, in a year or two, the Bank of Snipesville can loan you the capital to start your own enterprise. Did I mention that I'm the bank's president?"

As Alex and Eric strolled back along the covered boardwalk on their way to the hotel, two elderly black men stepped onto the dirt road to allow them to pass, averting their eyes as they did so. Eric tipped his hat to them and said "Thank you, but really, you shouldn't have done that. Too kind."

They glanced fearfully at him.

"What's wrong with those two old chaps?" Eric said. "There was no need for them to get off the pavement and walk in the street. Plenty of room on the pavement for all of us. I say, Americans call pavements sidewalks, don't they?"

"Eric," Alex said quietly. "People are staring at us."

It was true. As soon as Eric had tipped his hat at the old men, several people

❖ 111 ❖

CHAPTER FIVE

on the street, black and white, had stopped to gaze at him in astonishment. One white man was now talking animatedly to another, and gesturing toward Eric and Alex. "Okay," Alex said to Eric, "I don't know what this is about, but let's get to the hotel. I don't like how they're looking at us. This is like the start of a horror movie, or something."

Chapter 6:
DOMESTIC MATTERS

Balesworth, Tuesday, September 12, 1905

Rain began to fall just as Hannah took her seat in the ladies-only carriage, ready to depart Balesworth for Ickswade, and her new job. Slowly, the steam train started moving. Hannah looked out the window, and as she watched, a smartly-uniformed porter loaded a travel trunk onto his barrow, and started pushing it down the platform. Having waved off the driver, the station guard dropped his little red flag to his side, and twiddled it between his fingers as he stepped back to watch the train depart. Glancing at his chained pocket watch before tucking it back into his vest pocket, he opened a door in the station wall. As the train moved away, Hannah briefly caught a glimpse of a roaring fire in his office when he slipped inside, pulling off his cap.

Probably going for his morning cup of tea, she thought, as the train left Balesworth behind. Nervous though she was about her new job, she already felt jazzed about being in 1905. She really did love just being in England in the 20th century. It was a world away from modern Snipesville. It was just a shame, she thought, that time travel always came with so much drama that she didn't plan, and couldn't control.

Hannah sheltered beneath her umbrella as she splashed along the soaked and rutted dirt road, following the Professor's scrawled map and directions to the house named Willowbank. The town of Ickswade looked very much like Balesworth, composed as it was mostly of houses, shops, and the occasional church.

The closer Hannah got to Willowbank, the more apprehensive she became. She had been imagining a young Elizabeth Hughes Devenish: a very proper Victorian girl with strict rules, and very likely no sense of humor. Hannah

CHAPTER SIX

knew Elizabeth would find fault with everything she did, and boss her about mercilessly. How could Hannah, a mere servant, have any influence on this terrifying teenage Elizabeth? What would either of them get out of an attempted friendship? Hannah had a sense of impending doom about the whole venture. And what made it even worse was that she had to start thinking of herself as the humble maid called May Harrower. Her heart sank.

The rain fell more heavily as Hannah continued her walk, and she picked up her pace as she splashed along Station Road, with her case and soggy map clutched in one hand, and her umbrella in the other. She passed a large brick house on which roofers were working in cloth caps, not helmets, climbing rickety ladders while toting roofing slates on long poles. Their job was clearly dangerous, and she hoped hers would not be, but in 1905, anything was possible.

As Hannah reached the intersection, she saw that the last brick house on her left had a shop front, with two large plate glass windows in which were stacked elaborate pyramids of canned and packaged foods. Above the door, a sign: GORDON N. BAKER FAMILY GROCER & PROVISION MERCHANTS. The idea of a grocer named Baker made Hannah smile. Looking up at the building's second story, she saw, with a jolt, the sign for *Church End Road*. She took another look at the Professor's crudely-drawn map, and swallowed hard. This was the street. Willowbank was the third house on the right.

At the top of the drive, she again made sure she was in the right place, by checking the name of the house on the gate. But the Professor's directions had not let her down. This was indeed Willowbank. The strange thing was that it also looked very familiar. But Hannah had never visited Ickswade before, so how could that be?

And then she saw the monkey puzzle tree in the garden. She *had* been here before, in 1940. Mrs. Devenish had driven Hannah, Alex, and Eric through the countryside to this house for Verity's birthday party. After a long drive, it was almost dark when they arrived. Hannah had never thought to ask where they were, but she definitely remembered Mrs. Devenish pointing out the funny old monkey puzzle tree. Now she knew that Verity had grown up in her grandmother's childhood home.

Wet gravel crunched under Hannah's feet as she trudged up the short drive. Standing under the covered porch, she shook out her umbrella, closed it, and, her hand shaking, pressed the doorbell, which was helpfully labeled *PRESS*. She silently wished herself luck.

The grim-faced old woman who answered the door wore a maid's uniform that was almost identical to the one in Hannah's bag.

CHAPTER SIX

"I'm Han ... I mean, I'm May. I'm the new maid."

"Are you now?" said the old woman, grinning maliciously at her. "Then you'll be cleaning the kitchen, the bedrooms, the bathroom, and," she said with glee, "the water closet."

"You mean I get to clean the toilet?" Hannah said, wrinkling her nose.

"That's right," said the old maid.

"Okay," said Hannah, still hovering on the doorstep. "Can I come in first?"

"No," she said. "This ain't the servants' entrance. Come round the back to the kitchen door. That's where you come in." She crooked a finger to indicate the gravel path that ran up the side of the house, and then closed the door in Hannah's face.

Hannah opened her umbrella again, before squatting to pick up her bag. "This should be a ton of fun," she muttered to herself, stomping off with gravel crunching and puddles splashing underfoot.

Not that she had expected anything better from this job than drudgery and humiliation. She had too much experience in domestic service over the centuries to harbor any illusions. That was the thing about time travel: Hannah was proud of being a time traveler, and it was an amazing life, but calling it fun would have been a flat-out lie.

When she reached the back door, the old woman was there to greet her. "Here, haven't we met before?" she said, still keeping Hannah on the doorstep.

"Yes," Hannah said, "At the front door. Thirty seconds ago."

"No, no, no," she said, waving her hand in Hannah's face. "I mean a long time ago. I'm Flora."

Hannah looked at her closely. There was no denying it. This was the same Flora with whom she had worked in 1851. She now looked about 70 years old. How could Hannah explain her own resemblance to her 1851 self? "My grandmother was in service at Balesworth Hall," she said. "Maybe you met her?"

There was a pause while Flora thought about this. Hannah could see the effort written on her face. "Might've done. What was her name?"

"Um, Hannah," said Hannah.

"I might remember someone of that name," said Flora. "But that were a long time ago. Come in, then."

She held the door open just wide enough to admit Hannah and her case. Hannah gave her umbrella one last shake, and squeezed inside. Irked by Flora's rudeness, she said angrily, "Honestly, I'm surprised you haven't retired."

"Retired?" Flora said. "I should be so lucky. I haven't got tuppence to rub together. Anyway, I would never leave Mrs. Hughes. No, that I would not." She nodded to a thin and angular woman who was standing at the kitchen table, peeling apples. "This here is Mrs. Morris, our cook-housekeeper. Mrs. Morris? This here is May, the new tweeny ... I mean, junior house-parlormaid."

Tweeny? Hannah thought.

"May is junior house-parlormaid *and* kitchenmaid," Mrs. Morris said firmly. "Good morning, May. Put your bag down over there in the corner for now."

Mrs. Morris didn't look much like Hannah's idea of a cook. She had sharp features and graying black hair, and resembled an aging crow. Grabbing a wooden spoon and a white dishcloth from the kitchen table, Mrs. Morris stepped smartly to the huge black cooking range. There, she picked up the lid from a large copper pot with the wadded dishcloth in one hand, while stirring the steaming contents with a wooden spoon in the other. "Have you been in service before?" she said abruptly, replacing the pot lid with a clang.

"Yes," said Hannah. "I used to work at Balesworth Hall…" Flora shot her a quizzical look, and she added hurriedly, "I mean, I used to work at a house in Balesworth. Not Balesworth Hall." Actually, she was already regretting even having admitted to any experience as a servant. When she had worked with Flora at Balesworth Hall in 1851, she had been one of a large staff, all of whom performed specialized tasks. At Willowbank, with only three servants, she already knew she would have to do a lot of jobs.

She must have looked worried, because Mrs. Morris said, "Well, I'm sure there will be much for you to learn, May. Flora will take you round the house and explain your duties, but Mrs. Hughes will want to see you first. Flora, tell Mrs. Hughes that May is here."

"Madam already knows," Flora said, tutting. "This silly girl came round the front door."

"Did she now?" said Mrs. Morris. "Well, you didn't get off on the right foot then, did you, May?"

Hannah inwardly rolled her eyes. She thought how stupid it was for two grown women to make such a fuss about which door she used. After all, both doors led into the same house. But then she reminded herself that she was in early 20th century England, where people seemed to care very much about doing things properly, and that these women decided what "properly" meant. She told herself not to take any of it personally.

PING! A high-pitched bell sounded over Hannah's head, startling her. She looked up. Over the kitchen door hung a small framed glassed-in board with tiny square windows, each labeled after a room in the house: *Dining Room, Bedroom 3, Front Door,* and more. In the square labeled *Drawing Room,* a little flag the size of a large postage stamp was rocking back and forth.

"See?" Flora said, nodding toward it, "Mrs. Hughes knows you're here."

CHAPTER SIX

❖ ❖ ❖

Mrs. Hughes was a small, brittle-looking woman wearing a black dress and a sour expression, and she matched her surroundings perfectly. She sat bolt upright on a stiff dark brown armchair. The rest of the drawing-room furniture was also dark brown, the large rug was a dark burgundy, the walls were covered in flocked dark green wallpaper, and the upright piano was topped with a limp and leafy dark potted plant that seemed to be losing the will to live. Hissing gas lamps extended from the walls, spreading an unpleasant smell through the room (and indeed through the whole house), while generating barely any light.

If Hannah was unenthusiastic about meeting Mrs. Hughes, Mrs. Hughes was evidently unenthusiastic about meeting Hannah. "You have experience as a housemaid and as a kitchenmaid, I understand," she said, sounding as though she didn't believe any of it. "I am not accustomed to employing my servants sight unseen. But our last maid selfishly left us at short notice, and you come highly recommended by the agency that wrote to me. Heaven knows how they knew I needed a maid, but I received their letter the very day the last girl departed."

Hannah was standing on the rug with her hands demurely tucked behind her, as the Professor had instructed her to do. She knew who the "agency" was, but she wondered nervously why her predecessor had fled.

"As you may have been informed, you are a between maid. You are to divide your time and duties between assisting Flora as junior house-parlormaid until 11 o'clock in the morning, and as kitchenmaid and scullerymaid to Mrs. Morris in the afternoon. Flora is our senior house-parlormaid, but she is not as young as she was, and you will also perform many of her duties."

Hannah silently cursed the Professor, who had failed to mention that this was a "between maid" or "tweeny" job. Whatever she was to be called, Hannah knew this meant that she would do almost all the housework.

Mrs. Hughes continued. "Flora has served me well and faithfully for many years, and I will not have her distressed. You are to follow orders from her to the best of your ability, but Mrs. Morris's orders take precedence over Flora's. Let me be quite clear: This position requires some tact in dealing with Flora, which I hope a young girl like you can somehow muster. Do you understand?"

Hannah nodded and tried to look super-mature. She understood, all right. She just didn't like it. No matter who was giving the orders, she would be doing Flora's work for her.

"I told your agency that your half-day off is Wednesday, but apparently you require time off from Wednesday afternoon until early Thursday morning, to visit your aged mother in Balesworth. Since you come highly recommended,

CHAPTER SIX

I am willing to accommodate this inconvenient arrangement, provided your work is otherwise satisfactory. I need not tell you that you may bring no followers to this house."

Hannah knew what "no followers" meant: No boyfriends, or, indeed, friends of any kind could visit her. She considered saying something snarky, but decided against it. "Very good, Mrs. Hughes," she said.

"Then I shall expect good conduct from you," Mrs. Hughes said, in a snobbish tone. Hannah gritted her teeth and reminded herself that she was here to help the young Mrs. Devenish. This thought, however, did not make her feel better. Young Elizabeth was sure to be as bossy as her mother. She wasn't looking forward to both of them ordering her about.

At that moment, the door flew open with a bang. A gangly girl in her late teens careened into the room, all arms and legs, carrying an untidy stack of papers and envelopes. Large cloth bags were slung over each of her shoulders, and a pencil was clamped between her teeth. Her narrow green skirt accentuated her height, while her long brown hair was haphazardly arranged in a puffy Edwardian pompadour, stray strands bursting out all over. Without ceremony or introduction, she dropped everything she was carrying in the middle of the drawing room, and sheets of paper wafted in every direction. For the finale, she spat out the pencil onto the carpet.

Mrs. Hughes stared at her. "Elizabeth," she said faintly. "What on earth …?"

"Yes, Mother," Elizabeth said distractedly. She had dropped onto her hands and knees, and was scrambling to corral all the stray papers.

Hannah looked upon the scene open-mouthed. Here, not five feet from her, was the future Mrs. Devenish. Elizabeth Hughes was nothing like she had imagined. She had thought Elizabeth would be disciplined, polite, and grave … Right now, she looked anything but. She was a mess. Not that Hannah was disappointed: Young Elizabeth looked fun, and not at all scary. In fact, Hannah suddenly felt a tiny bit superior to her.

"Elizabeth," Mrs. Hughes said in a strained voice. "This is the new maid. Her name is May." On her knees with her legs tucked underneath her, Elizabeth focused on shuffling her papers. But after a second's awkward silence, she glanced up and gave Hannah a quick smile. "Hello, May! I say, Mother, whatever happened to the last maid? You never said."

"Pas devant la domestique," her mother said quietly.

"What?" Elizabeth said. "Pah de vont? Oh, you mean I shouldn't talk in front of the servant! Oops, gosh, I say, sorry, too late. My French is pretty awful, Mother, you know that. Mademoiselle Lafarge told both of us that on all my school reports, ridiculous old woman."

CHAPTER SIX

Mrs. Hughes gave a sharp intake of breath, and stared thin-lipped at her youngest daughter. Hannah, meanwhile, was beaming at Elizabeth. This was definitely someone she wanted to know.

"May," Mrs. Hughes said sharply, noticing with disapproval her new maid's amused grin. "I hope you will be happy in your position here. Flora will show you your room and explain your duties. You may go."

To get out of the drawing room, Hannah practically had to step over Elizabeth. She thought to herself that one thing was for sure: Living in this house was going to be interesting.

As Hannah arrived in the kitchen, Mrs. Morris dropped a glistening shelled hardboiled egg into a basin of water with a small splash. "Flora has gone upstairs for a nap," she said, wiping her hands together. "Did Mrs. Hughes tell you about Flora? She oughtn't to be working at all, not at her age. But Mrs. Hughes isn't prepared to pay Flora a proper pension, and her sister died last year, so there's nobody she can go and live with. That's why Mrs. Hughes keeps her on here." Suddenly, she seemed to realize that she was gossiping, and as she started peeling another egg, she said, "Now, my girl, I don't want you repeating nothing I just said to no one, you hear?" Hannah nodded. "Good," said Mrs. Morris. "I hope Mrs. Hughes told you that you must treat Flora with respect. She is your elder and better." Hannah again nodded politely, and Mrs. Morris continued, lowering her voice slightly, "Still, if you have any troubles with her, you just come to me. This job isn't to everyone's liking, I warn you. You'll be a housemaid sometimes, and a kitchenmaid others. You do as I tell you, and we'll get along all right, but any sign of idleness, and you'll find me a tartar to be reckoned with, understand?"

Hannah nodded. Historical British battleaxes of the cooking variety weren't a new experience for her, and Mrs. Morris didn't scare her. The cook-housekeeper looked fierce, but the more she spoke, the more Hannah liked her.

"Now, get your bag out of that corner," Mrs. Morris said, "and give me a moment to put this pie in the oven. Flora will show you your room."

"Do I have to share a room with Flora?" Hannah said, alarmed.

"No, you have your own, lucky girl. My first place, when I started in service, there was only one big room for six servants, and we slept two to a bed, three beds in all. But the attic rooms in Willowbank are small, and there's just the two of them. I live out with my husband in our cottage, and Flora gets her own room on account of her age. So you will have a room all to yourself."

Hannah thought, *I bet it's some poky little nook in the attic, but so long as it's a Flora-free zone, that works.*

CHAPTER SIX

Hannah's room was indeed a poky little nook in the attic. She had to walk through it with her head cocked to one side, to avoid bashing her skull against the rafters. The space was hardly big enough for the saggy and narrow iron-framed bed, and the decrepit chest of drawers. Crammed alongside them was a washstand with chipped basin, cracked water jug, and thin worn-out towel on a rail. A small, flattened and faded rag rug lay on the bare floorboards. The only decoration on the wall was a framed needlepoint with a message: *Whatsoever Thy Hand Findeth To Do, Do It With Thy Might.* Creeping damp in the walls bubbled the paint in the top corner of the room, completing the dismal picture.

Hannah looked around her with resignation. One thing was for sure: No matter what year it was, people who hired her as a servant did so to make themselves comfortable, and put as little money as possible into making her life pleasant. She took her uniform from her bag and set it aside, and then folded the other clothes neatly, and laid them in a drawer in the chest, before starting to change.

Grimacing, she pulled on her huge frilly underwear. She had argued with the Professor about whether she should have to wear this awful garment instead of modern underpants: Who would know what she was wearing under her uniform? But the Professor had said that modern underpants would lead to awkward questions when they appeared in the laundry. So here she was, wrestling with long cloth strings attached to enormous drawers. Carefully, she tied the strings firmly at the knees and waist with double knots, thinking that she didn't need her underwear falling down in the middle of serving dinner. She giggled to herself at the thought of Mrs. Hughes's reaction to that.

Hannah still wasn't keen on the dorky cap with its silly streamers and the multiple black hair grips attached to it. Before she could put it on, she had to do something with her hair. Girls in 1905 wore their hair loose or in braids, but all the grown women she had seen wore theirs in buns, and since she looked to the world like a woman, not a girl, she had to wear a bun, too. Trouble was, Hannah had never made a bun before, not properly. She really wished at that moment for a video on emergency bun construction. Since that wasn't happening, she was just going to have to do her best.

Ten minutes later, she inspected her hairdressing effort in the cracked and fading mirror propped on the chest of drawers. Observing her many stray hairs and prickly black grips, she thought, *I look like a demented porcupine.* It would just have to do. But that thought stopped her in her tracks. Since when did Hannah Dias not care about her appearance? And why did that seem like a good thing? She laughed, feeling strangely happy and relieved.

Mrs. Morris gasped. "What have you done to your hair? Oh, what a sight. Come over here, and I'll put it right for you. Oh, I never did see the like …"

She hurriedly wiped her floury hands on her apron, and advanced on Hannah, twirling a bony finger to order her to turn around. Hannah obeyed, wincing as Mrs. Morris roughly tore off her cap and hair grips, taking several strands of hair with them, and then grabbed her hair with both hands, pulling it into a tight ponytail. "Don't tell me you don't know how to put up your own hair," she grumbled. "Anyone would think you was a fine lady."

"My mother always did my hair for me," Hannah said, pleased with herself for instantly coming up with a plausible, if untrue, explanation for her incompetence. She flinched as Mrs. Morris started vigorously twisting her hair into shape.

"And she never taught you how to do your hair for yourself?" Mrs. Morris exclaimed. "Good heavens, girl. I hope this don't mean that all your work is lacking. I can't spend all my time putting up your hair. Look, once I have the dinner made, I'll teach you. Nothing fancy, a simple bun. *There*," she said, yanking hard one last time, then bringing tears to Hannah's eyes as she rasped hairpins across her scalp. "You look almost respectable. Now, go and peel those potatoes, and look sharp." Hannah's hair and face were now drawn so tight, she felt like she had a facelift.

Monday, September 18, 1905
Within a week, Hannah had settled into the routine of the Hughes household. This morning, bleary-eyed, she rose at 6 a.m., as she did each and every morning, awoken by the light of dawn through the thin curtains, even before she heard the morning bell rung by Mrs. Hughes, who always went back to sleep once this duty was performed.

Hannah did not have the luxury of going back to sleep. She rose with the bell, because Mrs. Hughes did not have a snooze button. Before Mrs. Morris arrived, around 7 o'clock, Hannah had started the fire in the kitchen range, swept out the fireplaces in the drawing and dining rooms, laid fires with coal and newspaper, and cleaned both rooms with dustpan, brush, and cloths. Next, she cleaned the carpets on the stairs and the long narrow hallway rugs by spreading on them a layer of damp used tea leaves, and then brushing these off, hoping to pick up dust in the process. Her last job before breakfast was to take cans of hot water from the bathroom to each bedroom, knocking on the doors to wake the Hugheses. The water was for the ladies' sponge baths, because nobody took a real bath more than once a week. Hannah checked the chamberpot under each bed, and if one had been used, took it quickly to the toilet, while trying not to look at or breathe in the contents. There was a modern toilet on the second floor, but Mrs. Hughes had forbidden everyone to use what was called the "lavatory" at night, in case a flush awoke her.

By the time the grandfather clock on the landing struck the first chime of 8, Hannah was starving. She raced to the kitchen, tore off her dirty apron and threw it into the kitchen hamper, and then took her place at the table. She ate breakfast with Flora and Mrs. Morris, and they all tucked into large plates of back bacon, eggs, and toast, and bowls of thick oatmeal. They ate in silence, except for the scrape of knives, forks, and spoons, the loud ticking of the kitchen clock, and the distant thumps overhead as the Hughes family got washed and dressed.

When the servants' breakfast was done, Hannah collected and washed the dishes in the scullery-room sink, adding washing soda crystals to hot water, before taking up a little white mop on a wooden stick. The washing soda made her hands bright red, and she worried that it was toxic, so she rinsed every dish carefully, for fear of otherwise poisoning everyone, even though Mrs. Morris poked fun at her for constantly running the tap.

At 9 a.m. precisely, Flora served the family their breakfast. By this time, Hannah felt that half the day had gone by. But since none of the family had jobs, she thought irritably, they probably thought nine o'clock was early. Mrs. Morris next began preparations for lunch, and Hannah did her second round of dishwashing, before heading upstairs to make the beds (with Flora's occasional help) and clean the bedrooms. As Hannah scrubbed Margaret Hughes's floor on her hands and knees, she halfheartedly reminded herself that she was getting a good workout. She also thought wistfully of how much easier her life would be with a vacuum cleaner (preferably the robot kind that operated itself) and a dishwasher.

All of this housework occupied Hannah until 11 a.m., when she returned to the kitchen, donned her apron, and became Mrs. Morris's kitchen maid. The servants ate lunch, which Mrs. Morris called dinner, at 12 noon. The Hughes family ate their lunch, which Mrs. Morris called luncheon, at 1 p.m. By then, Hannah's working day was less than half over.

Once the heaviest cleaning was done, one of Hannah's duties was to help Flora answer the call bells whenever the family rang to order them to do something. It was usually Flora who answered the front door to important visitors; all three servants shared the job of opening the back door to visiting tradesmen, who

CHAPTER SIX

arrived frequently, usually delivering food. The butcher's boy brought meat, the baker's boy brought bread, the greengrocer's man brought vegetables, and the milkman, who was never seen, left milk and eggs on the doorstep early each morning. The fish man visited twice a week.

At four o'clock most days, Flora and Hannah changed into fresh caps and aprons to serve afternoon tea. Usually, Flora served the Hugheses, while Hannah served Flora and Mrs. Morris. Every evening, after supper, Hannah cleaned the dining room (again) and checked the drawing room (again). There were other tasks, duties, and demands.

And then, after a too-brief sleep on her uncomfortable bed, Hannah would start all over again.

In her first week, she was already tired of the drudgery and routine. And how would she ever accomplish her mission, whatever it was? The Professor had made it sound so easy for her to get to know Elizabeth, as if they would instantly become firm friends because they lived under the same roof. But Hannah had discovered that an Edwardian household didn't work like that.

Yes, she lived in the same house as Elizabeth Hughes, but she also lived quite separately from her. Hannah's world was composed of the large kitchen, which also doubled as the servants' social hall, her poky little attic room, only used for sleeping, and the two staircases, the larger of which was also used by the family. The steep and claustrophobic upper staircase that led to the attic was used only by Hannah and Flora.

Hannah's world did cross with that of Elizabeth, of course: Every day, she visited almost every room in the house. But it wasn't like she could spend her spare time lounging around in the drawing room with a cup of tea like the Hughes women did. She was only allowed into the drawing room to clean it. She often glanced jealously at the upholstered furniture on which the Hughes family spent many hours sitting.

Elizabeth was often around, and yet Hannah had barely spoken at all with her. She was not supposed to speak to any of the family unless they spoke to her, but they did not start conversations with her. They didn't seem mean. They just didn't seem interested in their servants, and especially not in "May," the newest and youngest of the domestic staff.

Even if Hannah could pluck up the courage to speak to Elizabeth, she thought, it never seemed like the right time. Elizabeth always seemed to be busy, and she never walked anywhere: Whenever Hannah saw her, she was practically running, usually out of the house to go to some appointment or errand … or something. The Mrs. Devenish Hannah knew was brisk, but as a young woman, she was a total whirlwind of activity. Not that it was necessarily organized activity. Hannah had no idea what Elizabeth actually did with her time. She wondered if she had ADHD, but when she asked Mrs. Morris about Elizabeth's ADHD, she got a blank look.

This morning, Hannah was slowly walking downstairs, when Elizabeth passed her on the landing, said "Good morning, May," and hurried on. This was the first time Elizabeth had greeted her by name. *It's a start,* she thought. But it was only a start. Mrs. Devenish was a private person who had seldom revealed her emotions, and surely Elizabeth was the same way, so it wasn't going to be easy to get to know her. Who could tell Hannah more about her, if not Elizabeth herself? The answer came to her, quick as a flash: Mrs. Morris.

In the late afternoon, as Hannah scraped a small dull knife across yet another potato, she said casually, "I met Elizabeth this morning."

"That's Miss Elizabeth to you, May," Mrs. Morris said, not looking up as she rubbed lard into flour in a bowl. Hannah knew she was playing a dangerous game, trying to get Mrs. Morris to gossip. But she had to try something. "Miss Elizabeth seems like a lot of fun," she said.

"Fun? I've never heard that word used in this house," said Mrs. Morris, dusting off her hands, and wiping them on a dishtowel. "I never have, not about her or nothing else."

"So she's *not* fun?" Hannah said in an innocent voice.

"Now then, I never said that," said Mrs. Morris, pouring a splash of milk into her mixing bowl, and picking up a wooden spoon. "She's a good girl, Miss Elizabeth. She's just a little … Well, high-spirited, I suppose is the word. Ooh, you should have met her when I first did, nine years ago! She was a naughty little imp then, always getting into mischief. But she's a fine-looking young lady now, no matter her temperament."

"Does she have a boyfriend?" Hannah asked calmly, trying not to sound like she was dying to know.

"No gentlemen callers, not yet," said Mrs. Morris, grabbing a handful of flour from a crock, and sprinkling it across a small area of the kitchen table. "I daresay we shall have gentlemen calling for her soon, now that she has left school." She picked up the bowl and lowered her voice. "Mind you, I expect Mrs. Hughes hopes that Miss Elizabeth will find a husband sooner rather than later. Mrs. Hughes has enough worries, what with Miss Victoria and Miss Margaret both stuck at home without marriage prospects. Now, that said, I don't know what sort of a man would want to marry a girl like Miss Elizabeth. She's such a beanpole, and she talks of nothing but votes for women, and all that

CHAPTER SIX

sort of foolishness." With that, Mrs. Morris tipped out a large glop of dough onto the floured table.

"Foolishness?" Hannah said encouragingly, hoping to keep Mrs. Morris talking.

Mrs. Morris paused from kneading the dough to wipe her forehead with the back of a floury hand. She picked up a round cutter with which she began to stamp out the dough as she talked. "A few years ago, Miss Elizabeth got herself involved with that Mrs. Lewis in Balesworth, and her women's suffrage palaver. Mrs. Hughes did her best to forbid Miss Elizabeth from joining that nonsense, but she should have known that it's nigh impossible to put a stop to anything that Miss Elizabeth puts her mind to."

As Mrs. Morris laid her pastries on a baking tray, and then slipped it into the oven, Hannah was on full alert. She was thinking about the very familiar name the cook had mentioned: Mrs. Devenish's old friend and mentor, Mrs. Lewis. Hannah had met her in 1940, by which time she was in her eighties. Her forbidding manner had even intimidated Mrs. Devenish, to Hannah's and Verity's great amusement.

What on earth would Mrs. Lewis be like in her early fifties? Hannah was curious to find out, so long as she didn't have to get too close. After her awful encounter with Mrs. Devenish in 1951, she had had her fill of bossy old English ladies.

Tuesday, September 19, 1905
Laden down with cleaning tools, Hannah staggered to the top of the stairs, threw open the door of Elizabeth's bedroom, and accidentally dropped her broom, metal dustpan, wooden brush, and feather duster with a loud clatter. "Oh, crud," she grumbled loudly to herself.

She had just leaned down to pick up her equipment when a familiar voice said, "I say … "

Startled, Hannah straightened up suddenly, and promptly hit the back of her head on the doorknob. "Owwww…" she cried, and doubled over again, one hand on her head, the other steadying herself on the door. When she took her hand off her head and looked at her fingers, she saw blood, and Elizabeth saw it, too.

Setting down her pen, Elizabeth got to her feet, took Hannah by the elbow, and guided her to sit on the armchair next to the desk. Then she yanked open a drawer in the chest, pulled out a small folded handkerchief, and flapped it open. "Move your hand out of the way," she ordered, "And tilt your head … No, no, the other way, toward me." Hannah did as she was told, and Elizabeth,

CHAPTER SIX

leaning over her, dabbed at her scalp with the handkerchief. Examining the result, she said, "It's nothing, really. Only a light gash. It should heal of its own accord in no time at all. Just don't pick at it."

"But it hurts," Hannah insisted. She meant it, too.

Elizabeth looked at her gravely. "You don't feel faint, do you?" she said.

"No, but …"

"In that case," Elizabeth said, raising her voice to drown out Hannah's complaints, "you'll be right as rain. But leave your broom and whatnot here, and I will take care of this room."

"I can't just leave my cleaning stuff," said Hannah. "I've gotta clean all the other rooms."

Elizabeth sighed. "Very well, carry on, but if you do begin to feel ill, tell Mrs. Morris at once."

In fact, Hannah's head was feeling better already. Now she was thinking about how to prolong this conversation, if receiving first aid from Elizabeth actually qualified as a conversation. This wasn't how she had planned to get acquainted, but it would have to do. She remained sitting on the chair next to the desk, watching as Elizabeth picked up her pen, and started scribbling away. She seemed to be doing accounts, working with numbers in columns on a sheet of paper. Hannah also noticed an envelope on the desk, but when she tried to read the address, Elizabeth saw her doing it, and flipped the envelope upside down.

"Miss Elizabeth?" It felt so weird to call her that.

"Hmm?" Elizabeth didn't look up.

"Could I, like, borrow a pen and some paper off of you? Maybe an envelope?"

"Whatever for?" Elizabeth said absently.

"To write a letter. To my mother," said Hannah. Which was sort of true, except that by "Mother" she meant "The Professor."

"Yes, very well," Elizabeth said impatiently. "Look, there's a spare bit of ink in the desk downstairs. Ask my mother or sisters for it. Here's some paper, will two sheets do? And an envelope, and you may borrow my old pen, but bring it back, won't you? Oh, and here's a bit of blotting paper."

"How about a stamp?" said Hannah.

Elizabeth stared at her. Hannah added hurriedly, "Please?"

Without another word, Elizabeth gave a small nod, reached into a nook in the desk, and pulled out a red stamp, which she handed to Hannah.

"Thanks," Hannah said, glancing at the stamp with its etching of King Edward. "Okay if I take all this to my room before I start work again? I'll come back for my stuff." Again, Elizabeth nodded impatiently.

CHAPTER SIX

How serious Elizabeth looked when she sat at her desk, Hannah thought. Perhaps she had misread the crazy, hyper girl she had met on her first day.

Late in the evening, when all her domestic chores were done, Hannah brought her writing paraphernalia downstairs to the kitchen, which she now had all to herself. It was good to finally have "alone time."

Settling at the kitchen table, she poured herself still-warm tea from a fat brown china pot, and unscrewed the ink bottle that she had earlier begged from Margaret Hughes. Carefully dipping the ink pen into the black liquid, she began to write. Immediately, a large blot of ink fell from her pen onto the paper. Sighing, she grabbed the blotting paper, and patted the ink puddle with it, to soak up the mess. She would have started again with a fresh sheet of paper, but she only had two sheets.

It was not a long letter: Hannah briefly reminded the Professor that she would be arriving at Weston Cottage on Wednesday afternoon. It probably wasn't necessary, she thought, but it was fun to write. When she was done, she slipped out of the house with the sealed envelope, and looked at it one more time under the streetlights before she dropped it through the slot in the red pillar mailbox on the street corner. Streetlights, she thought with a smile, were a great improvement from 1851, and even from 1940, when the wartime blackout kept the streets pitch dark.

As she closed and locked the front door behind her, Hannah was startled to realize that this little excursion had been her first journey off the Hughes' property since her arrival at Willowbank. She was looking forward to visiting Balesworth, and, she was surprised to realize, to seeing the Professor.

Wednesday, September 20 – Thursday, September 21, 1905

On her walk to Weston Cottage, Hannah swung the basket in which Mrs. Morris had packed her lunch: meat paste sandwiches wrapped in crackly white paper, an apple, a hardboiled egg, a small wedge of cheese, and a bottle of milk, all crammed together under a linen cloth. But the basket was empty now. Hannah had eaten all the food on the train.

Walking in England always helped Hannah relax, and the break from the hard work at Willowbank was a definite plus. As she plodded through Balesworth in the drizzling rain, she glanced at the shops she passed. Some, like the baker's and the greengrocer's, would still be around in 1940, and owned by the same families. She also noticed the old pubs on the High Street, and one pub in particular, the Balesworth Arms. Hannah felt a slight pang of sadness as she passed it. She had lived and worked there in the eighteenth century. Now

CHAPTER SIX

it seemed like an alien place.

Reaching the northern edge of town, Hannah picked up her pace, passing the boys' grammar school that George Braithwaite and Eric had attended, and, beyond it, on the other side of the road, she saw Weston Cottage. She really couldn't wait to get there. She had so much to tell the Professor.

Hannah found her in the kitchen, rolling out pie pastry in a halo of flour on the vast kitchen table. Dropping the empty picnic basket, she greeted her with an awkward hug. "What are you making for supper?"

"Hungry already?" the Professor said with a mischievous glint in her eye, "Is that basket on the floor empty, or do we need to have a little chat about wasting food?"

Despite herself, Hannah smiled at the Professor's sly reference to a fight she had had with Mrs. Devenish in 1940. "I ate the lot, so I hope you didn't make me lunch. But I'll be hungry by suppertime, so go on, tell me. What are you making?"

"Would you believe steak and kidney pie?"

Hannah's face fell.

"Just teasing," the Professor laughed, draping the sheet of dough over her rolling pin, then deftly transferring it to a pie pan, "I hate steak and kidney. I'm making chicken and mushroom."

"My favorite!" Hannah cried.

"I know," the Professor said, as she pressed the pastry into the pan, "and it's one of mine, too. Here, fetch me that chopped chicken there … Thanks. There's nothing very exotic or exciting about good old British cooking, but it does hit the spot, doesn't it?"

"Hmm," Hannah agreed. As the Professor spooned the chicken into the pie pan, Hannah picked up a tiny piece of leftover dough, and stretched it between her fingers. She almost jumped out of her skin when she saw someone standing in the kitchen doorway. "Verity!" she gasped, "What are you still doing here?"

The Professor picked up her rolling pin. "I gave Verity a choice either to return to 1951, or to stay with us awhile in 1905. You won't be surprised that she chose to stay."

"Oh, I'm having a simply marvelous time!" Verity said cheerfully, as she poured Hannah a cup of tea. "Kate here has explained everything to me."

"Everything?" Hannah said. *Kate?* She thought.

"Everything, you know, the time travel, and all that. It's fascinating. Hannah, I simply can't believe that you're from America in the 21st century, and

CHAPTER SIX

your surname isn't really Day, but something in Spanish, is that right?"

"More or less," Hannah said. "My last name is Dias, but it's Portuguese, not Spanish. So what have you been up to while I was in Ickswade?" Feeling a little superior to her friend, Hannah sipped her tea.

"Oh, gosh, it's been wonderful," Verity said. "Well, except for almost being run over by a horse. My word, London traffic is a nightmare! Motor cars and horse-drawn vehicles are not a good combination."

"You visited London?" Hannah felt a pang of envy.

"Kate suggested it," said Verity. "It's such a treat to see the city as it was before the World Wars. I've visited several of the churches that will be destroyed in the Blitz, and I went shopping at Harrods. Such fun!"

"Hey, how come I don't get to do that?" Hannah asked the Professor, trying (and failing) not to sound whiny.

The Professor gave her a sidelong look. "Verity deserves a holiday after all those years of war and food rationing. Hannah, you will have plenty of time for fun and games later. Right now, you have a job to do, and, as it happens, so does Verity. She will be working part-time in a grocer's shop, just as she plans to do in the summer of 1951. However, unlike you, she doesn't have living accommodation provided by her employer, so she'll be taking the train each day to Ickswade."

"Ickswade? Is the shop anywhere near the Hughes's house?" Hannah said.

"Of course it is," said the Professor. "It's Baker's the grocers, at the top of your street. That's why I got her that job, so you two might have a chance to visit."

Hannah frowned. "But I haven't been to Baker's even once. Mrs. Morris gets food delivered."

"Don't worry," said the Professor. She carefully rolled the top crust onto the pie, and started to seal it. "Mrs. Morris will eventually forget to order something, or run out of something, or … Well, something. And then you can pop down to the shop and see Verity. Now, Hannah, how is life as a house-parlor-maid slash kitchenmaid, or whatever you are? How do you get along with Mrs. Hughes?"

"As little as possible," Hannah said. "She's even more boring and stuck up than she was in 1851. And before you ask, I haven't seen much of Elizabeth, either. She always says 'hi,' well, sort of 'hi,' and asks how I'm doing, but our first actual conversation was yesterday, when I hit my head on a doorknob and she looked after me."

"Oh, how sweet of her," said Verity. "Do you like young Granny?"

"She was nice, but it wasn't a deep discussion or anything. I'm not allowed to start a conversation with the Hugheses. I even got in trouble for saying good morning to Elizabeth's sister. She told me off for calling her Miss Victoria like Flora does, instead of calling her Mrs. Halley."

"I know it's frustrating. Have patience," said the Professor. With a folded kitchen towel, she slid the finished pie into the range oven, and closed the door with a clang. "Now, how about another nice cup of tea?"

"That would be great," Hannah said, yawning. "But I need a nap. My job is exhausting." She flashed a sleepy smile, and scraped back the chair. "Give me twenty minutes, and then I would love some tea."

But Hannah got no farther than the doorway when she heard Verity say to the Professor, "Kate, could you teach me to time travel?" Hannah stopped where she was, and turned back to listen.

"No," said the Professor. "Sorry to be so blunt, Verity, but it's a bit of a gift, like rolling your tongue. I can help Hannah learn how to manage it, but that's all. Hannah can take you with her, as can I, but you can't do it by yourself."

"Oh, how disappointing," Verity said, frowning. Hannah felt strangely relieved.

"That reminds me," said Hannah. "I'm confused about something. When I met you as an old lady, Verity …"

"Wait," said Verity, clapping her hands to her ears. "No, I mean it. Stop. I don't want to know anything of the future."

"Too late," said Hannah. "I met you in the 21st century, and you … Old Verity, that is, you hadn't met me in 1951. You said we hadn't met since 1940."

The Professor tutted. "Hannah, how could you have forgotten? Things change, remember? When you return to your time, Verity will have every recollection of what has happened here, and of the time travel."

Verity blinked slowly. "Oh, how strange," she said. "Do you mean to tell me you have changed my future?"

"Sure," said the Professor. "Happens all the time. Of course, I don't really get it at all. I'm no scientist."

"But I thought we weren't supposed to change things?" Hannah said.

"What makes you think they were right to begin with?" said the Professor.

"You make my brain hurt," said Hannah. "I'm going to bed."

When Hannah awoke, it was already dark. She stumbled out of bed, pulled the curtains closed, and headed downstairs. On the kitchen table, she found a large, warm slice of chicken pie under a cloth, along with a note: "Hope you slept well. Verity went to bed early. I've gone out for a bit. Eat this and anything else you want from the larder. Love, Kate xx"

Kate? She wants me to call her Kate? That was going to take getting used to,

Hannah thought, but she could hardly stand by and let Verity act all buddy-buddy with the Professor while she herself still addressed her as … Nothing. Now Hannah thought about it, she never addressed the Professor by any name. So she would have to start calling her Kate. Huh.

She ate her supper in silence, and with a vague sense of unease. She still didn't know how, exactly, she was supposed to help Elizabeth, who seemed pretty competent. What was the Professor not telling her?

Thursday, September 21, 1905

By mid-morning, rain was pouring down. Hannah's gloomy mood was not helped by having risen extra-early to take the train from Balesworth to Ickswade. Now, here she was in the kitchen once again, emptying out her pail of water, after scrubbing Margaret's bedroom floor on her hands and knees. She felt doomed to spend all her time in 1905 cooking, cleaning, and running around after the Hughes family.

The call bell rang. Hannah glanced up. It was ringing for *Bedroom No. 3*, Margaret's room. She looked hopefully at Flora, who was sitting by the fireplace.

"It's not my place to answer that, May," Flora said. "You know I only take upstairs calls when you're busy."

Hannah sighed, and pointed to her bucket. "You don't think I'm busy, Flora?" All the same, she went, climbing the stairs just as the grandfather clock on the landing struck ten.

Margaret was at her dressing table, brushing her hair, when Hannah arrived.

"May, you did not close the window," she said, waving vaguely behind her. "Attend to it."

I hate her, and her silly little girl voice, Hannah thought. Silently cursing Margaret, Hannah pulled the window shut with a bang, and left without saying a word. As she trotted downstairs, she suddenly found her way blocked by Elizabeth. Hannah really wasn't in the mood for more orders. "Yes, Miss Elizabeth?" she said, with barely-concealed irritation.

"I say, May, are you about to clean my bedroom? I have not yet made my bed, and I should very much like to do so beforehand."

In her jaundiced mood, Hannah had not listened carefully, and thought Elizabeth was criticizing her for not having made the bed. Muttering insincere apologies, she turned and headed back upstairs.

But Elizabeth followed her. "No, no, no," she said. "You didn't hear me, May. I told you. I shall make my own bed."

This was odd. After all, Hannah thought, middle-class Edwardians employed servants to do every tedious chore. Why would Elizabeth want to make

CHAPTER SIX

her own bed? "Sure, um ... Thank you," she stammered. But immediately she had second thoughts. "Look,' she said, "It's a nice offer, but maybe I better make it for you. It's my job."

Elizabeth gave Hannah a small smile, and brushed past her.

Hannah didn't know what to do. She followed, and tried to insist on helping. Her own skills as a bed-maker were pretty good: Mrs. Devenish herself had taught her in 1940, after witnessing Hannah's sloppy and inept efforts to wrangle sheets, blankets, and pillowcases into some kind of orderly arrangement. But now Elizabeth simply ignored her, and began making the bed in a take-charge manner. Hovering anxiously behind her, Hannah briefly saw another spark of a future Mrs. Devenish. She wondered how Elizabeth had ever learned to make beds, having been brought up with servants. She decided to ask.

Elizabeth laughed at the question. "Really, May, I'm hardly a delicate Victorian creature! I went to boarding school, and our matron's rule was that we made our own beds perfectly, which was a jolly good thing. I can't say I relish bed-making, but there is something childish about always expecting others to wait on one, hand and foot. Don't you agree?"

"Oh, sure!" Hannah agreed enthusiastically.

"I applaud your spirit, May," Elizabeth said. "It's especially remarkable in a girl of our age."

Elizabeth pulled the bedspread up over the pillow and patted it, then, rubbing her hands together, she asked Hannah to bring her a broom, a request which Hannah gladly obliged.

But just as Elizabeth began sweeping the floor, Flora, passing in the hallway, stopped to stare at the peculiar sight of her young mistress cleaning her own room while the junior housemaid watched. "Miss Elizabeth, what *are* you doing?"

"Don't fuss, Flora," Elizabeth said firmly, continuing to sweep with gusto. "What does it look like I'm doing?"

Flora persisted. "You ought to leave that sort of thing alone. That's not work for a lady." She moved to take the broom from Elizabeth, but Elizabeth pulled it away, and gave Flora a hard stare, before resuming her sweeping.

"To be sure," Flora said, anxiously wringing her hands, "I don't know what Mrs. Hughes will say."

"Don't tell her, Flora," Elizabeth said, without looking up. "Then she won't say anything, will she?"

Flora jerked her head in Hannah's direction. "I hope this lazy girl didn't put the idea in your head, Miss Elizabeth."

"No, I did not!" Hannah exclaimed. "Anyway, it's no big deal. Miss Elizabeth just offered to give me a hand. And why not? I think it's cool."

CHAPTER SIX

"Good for you, May," said Elizabeth. She turned to Flora and said curtly, "Flora, go and chase after my mother and sisters. I'm sure none will object to you slaving for them."

Hannah was starting to really like Elizabeth, and had to remind herself that she still hated Mrs. Devenish. It was all so complicated.

It was also too good to be true, of course. Ten minutes later, Mrs. Morris was scolding Hannah in the kitchen. "May, you should never have stood by and let her do housework," she said sharply.

"But I keep telling you, Mrs. Morris," Hannah protested, "Elizabeth insisted on making her bed."

Flora, who was clearly enjoying the sight of "May" in trouble, chimed in. "That's not an excuse for getting above your station. You encouraged her! And that's *Miss* Elizabeth to you."

"I did *not* encourage her," Hannah grumbled, trying to keep her temper. She didn't want to get fired for being rude to Flora. Not yet, anyway. She was also now annoyed with Elizabeth for causing this trouble. It wasn't as if "May," a lowly servant, could have done anything but play along. Elizabeth should have known better.

Apparently, Mrs. Morris thought so, too, because suddenly her attitude softened. "Are you sure Miss Elizabeth insisted, May? Are you telling the truth?"

"Yes, Mrs. Morris," Hannah said. "She did."

"All right," Mrs. Morris said in a decisive tone. She removed her apron, and checked her hair in the mirror on the wall, before turning to Flora. "Is Mrs. Hughes in the drawing room?"

Flora said eagerly, "Are you going to tell her what May did?"

"In a manner of speaking," said the cook, looking sideways at the old woman. "I'll return shortly."

Hannah sighed, and sat down heavily in Flora's chair by the fire, ignoring Flora's irritated tutting as she did so. If she was about to be fired, she was at least going to have a few moments of comfortable rest before she had to pack up her stuff, and head to Weston Cottage. Perhaps after that she could go home, back to the 21st century, back to Snipesville, and forget all about Mrs. Devenish?

Somehow, though, that thought was frightening, too, as if something would be lost, forever. How strange. It wasn't like Elizabeth really needed her. She even wanted to make her own bed. Once again, Hannah asked herself what possible good she could do for a smart, independent, and organized 19-year-old woman?

CHAPTER SIX

As the Hugheses were finishing dinner that evening, Mrs. Morris said, "You go and clear the dinner table, May." She pointed Hannah toward the dining room. "And whatever you do, don't stack the plates on the table. Take them and the cutlery to the sideboard, scrape any leftovers onto one plate, stack them, not too high mind, and then bring them to the scullery."

"Here, now," Flora protested from her seat by the fireplace, "That's my job, that is, serving the family meals."

"You've done enough for one day, Flora," Mrs. Morris said. It wasn't entirely clear what she meant, but Hannah suspected that Mrs. Morris wasn't just talking about housework.

While Hannah collected the family's plates, Mrs. Hughes cleared her throat, and announced that she had a serious matter to discuss with her daughters.

"Will it take long?" Elizabeth said. "I have a great deal of work to do."

Mrs. Hughes sniffed. "Elizabeth, your work, as you call your women's suffrage nonsense, can wait. What I have in mind is far more important. I wish to address our domestic harmony."

"Gosh, Mother," Elizabeth said in a mocking tone, "that *does* sound important."

Hannah almost dropped the plates she was carrying. Her ears felt like they were on stalks. *Wait, was Elizabeth just rude to her mom? Whoa.* Elizabeth's sisters, meanwhile, had sat up expectantly. Margaret looked mystified, while Victoria gave Elizabeth a pitying look.

Mrs. Hughes cleared her throat, and said, "It has come to my attention, Elizabeth, that you have interfered in the servants' work."

All eyes, including Hannah's, swiveled to Elizabeth. "What on *earth* can you mean?" Elizabeth said, sounding more annoyed than apologetic.

Mrs. Hughes's face hardened. "I mean, Elizabeth, that you placed a servant in an extremely awkward position when you insisted, for reasons I cannot imagine, on making your own bed, and cleaning your bedroom."

Elizabeth raised her eyes heavenward, then said "Mother, what became of *pas devant les domestiques?*" She nodded in Hannah's direction.

Mrs. Hughes stiffened even more. "This happens to be May's business. You have caused her no end of trouble today."

Hannah continued to collect the plates. It was so weird, she thought, how English people of the 20th century could make her feel so tense and embarrassed over the stupidest little things. Apparently, Elizabeth felt much the same way, because she said, "Oh, Mother, this is ridiculous."

"No, it is not," said Mrs. Hughes, holding up her chin, "I only wish your father were still with us. He would know what to do with you, I'm sure. What will happen if it becomes generally known that my own daughter does the work of servants? I shall never be able to show my face."

Glancing in the mirror above the sideboard, Hannah saw Elizabeth's expression turn troubled, and then angry. "Mother, you're being absurd," Elizabeth said, her voice rising. "And it is most unfair of you to reprimand me for everything I do of which you do not approve. There is *nothing* morally wrong with my making my own bed. Quite the reverse in fact. And if you were entirely honest, you would admit that I am right." She threw down her napkin on the table, aiming it toward her mother, then noisily scraped back her chair. "I shall be upstairs," she announced, and marched from the room, slamming the door behind her.

Hannah had found herself pointlessly rearranging dirty silverware as an excuse to stay and hear what was said next. She could hardly contain her joy. Young Elizabeth was as outspoken and difficult as … Oh, this was hard … *As I am,* she thought. It was like Elizabeth was two different people at once.

Victoria turned to her mother. "Mama, you simply cannot allow Elizabeth to behave like this. She will never find a husband so long as she acts like a petulant child."

"You're quite right, Victoria," Mrs. Hughes said, "but I have so little influence over your sister. She is no longer a little girl, and even when she was … Perhaps she would listen to you?"

"Don't look at me, Mama," said Victoria. "The last time I tried to take Elizabeth to task for her conduct, she threw a rolled-up newspaper at me. But if I might make a suggestion … I have the impression that she behaves much better in Mrs. Lewis's presence. Perhaps Mrs. Lewis might help my sister to see sense?"

Mrs. Hughes didn't like this idea at all. "If you think for one moment that I would invite that frightful woman to intervene in our family's private affairs … Victoria, the Lewis woman is a social climber and incomer, from Manchester I believe, or somewhere of that sort. I don't doubt Mrs. Lewis's only interest in your sister is to fill her head with nonsensical ideas about women's suffrage, and to worm her way into an acquaintance with this family. I tried forbidding Elizabeth to associate with her last year."

"I remember," Victoria said, raising an eyebrow.

"We should never have sent you girls to that school," said Mrs. Hughes, in a sudden change of subject.

Victoria was baffled by this. "What has our school to do with Elizabeth's conduct? Margaret and I were both pupils, and didn't we turn out all right?"

"Yes, of course you did," Mrs. Hughes said, tapping the table. "But the tone of the school lowered after you left. I blame the new headmistress. That woman arrived at the same time as your little sister, and she is a notorious suffragist, one of those dreadful persons who is led by Emmeline Pankhurst to demand the vote for women in a most unladylike fashion. I am sure she filled all the girls' heads with nonsense. Mark my words, Victoria, all Elizabeth needs is a firm hand. What she needs is a husband. And I intend to see that she finds one, by every means at my disposal."

Hannah was furious. Mrs. Hughes wanted to marry Elizabeth to someone who would crush her spirit? Awful. But she also knew that it would be a disaster to express her own opinion to Mrs. Hughes. So she kept her mouth shut, and took up the large pile of dirty dishes and silverware, startling Mrs. Hughes, who had apparently forgotten that she was still in the room. As she opened the dining room door, she heard Mrs. Hughes say that she had invited a gentleman to Sunday lunch. She didn't give his name.

In that instant, Hannah knew that her job wasn't just to be nice to Elizabeth. It was to prevent Elizabeth Hughes from being married off to the wrong man.

Friday, September 22, 1905

At mid-morning, as Hannah flicked her feather duster over Elizabeth's bookcase, she kept glancing at the letters and diary lying on her desk. It would be so interesting and helpful to see what Elizabeth wrote … But no, Hannah corrected herself, it was evil to look at people's private stuff, and anyway, she wasn't sure that she wanted to know Elizabeth's personal thoughts. Instead, she started reading the titles of the leather-bound books on the bookshelves. She thought most of them looked boring: Works of history, a complete set of Shakespeare's plays, and several of Charles Dickens's novels, which she had tried to read several times in the past, and found too difficult. But the name H. G. Wells was familiar, and she liked the title of his book, *Love and Mr. Lewisham*. Laying down her feather duster, she plucked it from the shelf, and started to read.

Hannah was already on the third page when Elizabeth walked in, startling her. "Sorry," Hannah said, dropping the book down to waist level. "The book just looked interesting. I hope you don't mind."

"Do you like to read, May?"

Hannah had to think about this. "Sometimes," she said cautiously. "It depends on the book, I guess."

Nodding at the volume in Hannah's hands, Elizabeth said, "That you care to read at all is remarkable when you no doubt attended a mediocre elementary school whose purpose was to keep you ignorant and in your place. And it is even more admirable that you are interested in something other than penny novels of the worst sort. I have learned a great deal, you see, from talking with other working-class women, as well as to those ladies who strive to better your condition."

Hannah had no idea what Elizabeth was talking about. But she nodded and tried to look interested.

"May, what are you doing this afternoon?" said Elizabeth. "Around two o'clock, I mean?"

Well, that's a stupid question, Hannah thought. What was she ever doing? "Working, Miss Elizabeth," she said. "At that time of day, I'll be in the kitchen, doing whatever Mrs. Morris tells me to do."

Elizabeth briefly pursed her lips. "I'm well aware of how hard you work. Good Lord, does Flora do nothing at all?"

Not much, Hannah thought, but she said carefully, "I'm sure she does what she can."

"I shall tell Mrs. Morris that I require your services," Elizabeth said decisively.

"Doing what, Miss Elizabeth?"

"Oh, I'm sure I can think of something to tell Mrs. Morris and my mother. But what we shall actually be doing is visiting Balesworth. I have some business there. Meanwhile, I shall leave you to get on with your work. You may borrow *Love and Mr. Lewisham,* but return it when you're finished with it, won't you?"

"Yes, Miss Elizabeth," said Hannah. "Thank you." And she meant it.

All the same, Hannah wondered. Why was Elizabeth being so kind to "May", the new maid? Then again, why had Mrs. Devenish been kind to Hannah, the wartime evacuee? Now Hannah's heart sank. Mrs. Devenish's interest in her had ended badly, she told herself, and so would Miss Elizabeth's concern for her now. She couldn't trust or depend on her.

"It's not as though I have any choice but to let you go, May," Mrs. Morris grumbled, "not when Mrs. Hughes says you have to chaperone."

"Chaperone?" Hannah was astounded. "Who am I chaperoning?"

"Miss Elizabeth, of course," said Mrs. Morris. "You can hardly expect a young lady to wander the streets of Balesworth by herself."

"*I'm* young, and *I* walk in Balesworth by myself."

"Yes, but you're not a lady, are you, May? Although it must be said, and not that I approve, but since young ladies took up bicycles, a lot of them do without chaperones. Even Miss Elizabeth does without when she goes to Mrs. Lewis's meetings. Never mind. You go and enjoy your day out."

CHAPTER SIX

The train ride between Ickswade and Balesworth was not the most exciting journey ever, but Hannah loved every minute of it, because she had finally escaped the four walls of Willowbank. She had been going stir crazy. And this outing was her best opportunity yet to get to know Elizabeth Hughes.

Tall and poised, in a smart long coat and enormous and elegant silk hat, Elizabeth looked every inch the Edwardian lady, while Hannah, so much shorter than Elizabeth, and dressed in threadbare street clothes and crushed little hat, looked every inch the Edwardian maid. Hannah worried at first that they wouldn't have anything to say to each other. But she soon realized that she should have known better: Elizabeth was already a great talker, and on the train to Balesworth, she immediately put Hannah at ease, without asking "May" too many personal questions. She chattered about the sights they passed and, now, as the train slowed on its approach to Balesworth, she rapped the window with her knuckles, and said, "May, you must know the story of the Six Hills, surely?"

Hannah looked for hills in the distance, and saw none. But then she saw what Elizabeth was talking about: Six grassy mounds by the side of the train track.

"Six Hills?" Hannah said. "Six pimples is more like it. What's the big deal?"

"They're not natural hills, of course," said Elizabeth. "I expect they are ancient burial sites, or something of that sort, or at least that's what my father used to say. But you're local, aren't you? You must know the story that the country people tell?"

Hannah shook her head, leaving it an open question whether she was saying that she wasn't local, or that she didn't know the story.

"The tale is that the Devil was angry at the people traveling on the Great North Road," said Elizabeth. Hannah knew the Great North Road, the highway from London to Scotland, which was known as the High Street as it passed through Balesworth. Elizabeth continued. "The Devil grew so incensed, he grabbed great chunks of soil, and flung them at passers-by. Six times he missed, but as his missiles landed, they became the Six Hills. He threw a seventh which hit St. Swithins Church and bent the steeple. I don't know if you know this, but the steeple really was bent for a very long time. It was only repaired about twenty years ago."

"Great story," Hannah said, getting to her feet. Now, the train shuddered to a halt at Balesworth Station, and the steam engine let off a mighty hiss.

"So now we're here, what are we doing?"

"You'll see," Elizabeth said breezily. "Come along, May, we haven't all day."

CHAPTER SIX

As they walked up the High Street, Elizabeth drew Hannah's attention up an alley, and to an ancient white-washed building that bore a shiny new sign reading *Tudor Tea Rooms*. "How very exciting that Balesworth now has a tea room, May," she said. Hannah smiled. In 1940, the Tudor Tea Rooms was the very first place she had eaten as a time traveler, although by then the establishment was not nice at all. She hoped the food would be better and the waitresses less rude in 1905.

Farther up the High Street, Elizabeth stopped in front of a shop. "I assume you have been here before, May?" she said. Hannah wasn't sure, and she read the small sign by the door:

> **INGLE-GILLIS BROS.**
> (*formerly* JAMES COTTER & SONS)
> **BOOKSELLERS OF BALESWORTH, HERTS.**
> **BOOKS AND PRINTS BOUGHT AND SOLD**

"No, never," she said. "Never been here."

"Not even when it was owned by Mr. Cotter?" said Elizabeth.

Hannah thought quickly. She remembered she was supposed to be a Balesworth local. "Well, I passed it by," she said. "But I can't afford to spend money on books." That, at least, was true.

As the doorbell jangled, Elizabeth held open the door for Hannah. The shop was a small dark room crammed with books from floor to ceiling. Books in every subdued color possible, from black to navy blue to burgundy, were slotted and stacked in bookcases and shelves, piled this way and that: Vertically, horizontally, diagonally, right-side up, upside-down, spine out, cover out …

A strong smell of dust hung in the air. Hannah's inner housemaid wanted to grab a feather duster and get to work, but at this point, she figured, all that would do was to rearrange the dirt. The only reason any light filtered into the room at all was because the tottering piles of books could not quite blot out the sun from the bay windows. And yet there was something quite cheerful about the bookstore, too, as though it were well-loved despite all the mess and neglect.

"Be with you in a minute!" called a young man's slightly muffled baritone voice. He sounded as though he had his mouth full. Elizabeth unpinned her

CHAPTER SIX

hat, strode past Hannah toward the adjoining room, and knocked on the doorpost to announce her imminent arrival.

"Mr. Ingle-Gillis?" she called to someone Hannah could not see. "Tell me you're not eating pudding and custard. Every time I pay a call on you, you ..."

The owner of the deep voice cleared his throat. "Of course I'm eating pudding and custard," he said. "Good afternoon, Miss Hughes. How delightful of you to visit." Then he called to someone else, "Pierce? Make tea, would you?"

"Certainly," said another young male voice.

Elizabeth stepped backward, pursued by the baritone, a tall and strikingly handsome dark-haired young man in a blue vest and bright red bow tie, who was carrying a small steaming bowl. As Hannah gazed in rapture at the gorgeous newcomer, a heavenly scent of sharp fruit and sugar and milk wafted under her nose.

"This is our new maid," Elizabeth said, "May ..."

"Day," Hannah blurted out.

The corners of the young man's mouth twitched. "Your name is May Day?"

"No," Hannah said, thinking fast. "I meant Good Day. Good Day to you. My name is May Harrower." She inwardly cursed the Professor for giving her such a stupid fake name.

"Ah, I see," said the young man, obviously trying not to mock her. "Do you care for reading, May?"

Hannah nodded.

"Jolly good. My name's Mr. Ingle-Gillis," he said, and then returned his attention to Elizabeth. "I don't know whether you've heard, Miss Hughes, but my brother has decided, for some unaccountable reason, that he prefers to spend his days in London, and so he has abandoned ship, or rather, shop. This leaves me as sole proprietor, but it's far too much work for one." As he gestured at the doorway, a short dark-haired young man with crumbs on his chin appeared, smiling sheepishly. "I have employed Reid Pierce here as manager," said Mr. Ingle-Gillis. "You may recall that Pierce and I were at Haileybury together." Hannah guessed that "Haileybury" was a boarding school: Mr. Ingle-Gillis certainly sounded just as posh as Elizabeth, so it made sense that, like her, he had attended a posh school.

Elizabeth said politely, "Mr. Pierce, how good to see you again. Are you also living in Balesworth now?"

"No, Miss Hughes," said Mr. Pierce, "I take the train each day from Ickswade."

"Do give my regards to your mother, won't you?" Elizabeth said, and Mr. Pierce thanked her for her concern.

CHAPTER SIX

Mr. Ingle-Gillis suddenly had a moment of inspiration. "I say, Miss Hughes, would you and your maid care for rhubarb crumble and custard? It's another of our cook's splendid recipes."

Hannah had thought he would never ask, and nodded frantically, but Mr. Ingle-Gillis did not swing into action until Elizabeth said, "That would be most kind of you."

"Two chairs and two puddings for our customer, Mr. Pierce! And don't forget the tea!"

"Yes, Mr. Ingle-Gillis," Mr. Pierce replied cheerfully, before ducking into the back room. He reappeared almost immediately, carrying two chairs, which he placed by the window.

Hannah marveled at how these young people appeared to be in their late teens or early twenties, and yet called each other by titles and last names. She was the exception: As a servant, she was addressed only as "May," if anything at all.

Mr. Ingle-Gillis made a show of brushing off the chairs, sending clouds of dust into the air. He gestured to Hannah and Elizabeth to sit down, and Hannah made sure to sit where she had the best possible view of the adorable Mr. Ingle-Gillis. Then Mr. Pierce brought the promised desserts.

"Oh, Good Lord, have you no table?" Elizabeth yelped as Mr. Pierce tried to hand her a bowl. "Really, it is most unseemly to eat from one's lap in the middle of a shop and I ..."

At that moment, Hannah thought, Elizabeth sounded quite like Mrs. Hughes. Or Mrs. Devenish.

"Now, Elizabeth, you never said whether you would care for tea?" Mr. Ingle-Gillis said smoothly, cutting off Elizabeth's complaint. "Would you?"

For a second, she looked charmed by him. But then she glanced about her and said dryly, "Of course I would. But where do you propose I put my teacup?"

"No idea," he said, looking quite unconcerned and flashing her a grin. "But you are welcome to try balancing it on a pile of books."

"Please don't spill it, though," said Mr. Pierce, who appeared more anxious than his boss for the fate of their merchandise.

With a skeptical glance at the two men, Elizabeth accepted a bowl of dessert and spoon. As promised, Mr. Pierce soon served two cups of tea, after Mr. Ingle-Gillis placed a small table at Elizabeth's elbow to receive her teacup.

Left to her own devices, Hannah carefully put her teacup in the only space left in the bay window, where it fit perfectly among the books, then took a bite of warm rhubarb crumble and custard. "Not bad," she said. "It could use a bit

CHAPTER SIX

more sugar."

Everyone frowned at her. "May," Elizabeth said lightly, "Manners, please."

Hannah was taken aback, not because Elizabeth had told her off, but because she had done so gently. In 1940, Mrs. Devenish would have barked at her for being rude, there would have been no "please," and possibly a light slap would have been aimed at Hannah's head. It was almost as though Elizabeth expected little better of a maid, while Mrs. Devenish had treated Hannah just as strictly as she had Verity, her granddaughter.

"Sorry," Hannah said sheepishly. "It's good." And then she added, holding out her bowl, "May I have some more custard, please?"

"Aha!" cried Mr. Ingle-Gillis, "We have Olivia Twist in our midst!" He muttered to himself, "My word, what a splendid rhyme … " Then he said, "Pierce, fetch the custard jug, if you would."

Hannah watched Mr. Ingle-Gillis as he perched precariously on the edge of a table, leaning against several stacks of books. He somehow looked even more handsome in this pose. "Now, Miss Hughes, to what do we owe the pleasure of your company? Is there a book you wish me to obtain for you, or would you like me to suggest a title or two?"

As Mr. Pierce poured her more custard sauce, Hannah couldn't help the discouraging thought that Mr. Ingle-Gillis didn't really speak to her, but only to Elizabeth. "Good Lord, no," Elizabeth said. "I don't travel all the way to Balesworth merely in pursuit of books, Arthur. I come here for scrumptious puddings. Really, you ought to rename your establishment *The Brothers Ingle-Gillis Book and Custard Shop.*"

"I shall take your suggestion to heart, Elizabeth," Mr. Ingle-Gillis said, with a twinkle in his eye.

"Good," Elizabeth said firmly. "Now, to business. My maid here is a reader. I wish to purchase a second-hand book for her."

Hannah suddenly felt emotional. Mrs. Devenish … Elizabeth … was going to buy her a book?

"Nothing too expensive, mind," Elizabeth said hurriedly. Hannah smiled at that. *It's so like Mrs. D. to be both generous and thrifty all at once,* she thought.

Now Hannah had a helpful idea to keep down costs.

"Do you have any paperbacks?" she asked Mr. Ingle-Gillis. "They're cheaper."

Elizabeth, Mr. Ingle-Gillis, and Mr. Pierce all stared at Hannah. Looking around, Hannah realized that there were no paperbacks in the store. Paperbacks, it seemed, had not been invented yet.

"I'm sure we can come up with something suitable," said Mr. Ingle-Gillis. "Pierce, what would you suggest for a maid with an enthusiasm for reading?"

CHAPTER SIX

Mr. Pierce said kindly, "What do you like to read, May?"

"Nothing too boring," Hannah replied.

Mr. Pierce suppressed a laugh. "Well, let's see what we can do, shall we?" He began to inspect the crammed bookcases.

"No penny novels, Mr. Pierce," Elizabeth said sharply. "May here has begun to discover modern literature, and I wish to cultivate her interest."

Mr. Ingle-Gillis said, "I have been meaning to write you, Miss Hughes. If you wouldn't mind, I have two new poems I would so much like you to read."

"Mind? Not at all, Arthur," said Elizabeth, setting aside her tea cup.

"I was hoping you would say that," said Mr. Ingle-Gillis. "I have already taken the liberty of copying them out in anticipation of your visit." He quickly reached into his inside jacket pocket, and extracted an envelope, which he handed to Elizabeth. "Oh, and Elizabeth, you really ought to attend one of the meetings of our newly-formed little band of radical young folk in Balesworth. This month's meeting has already passed, but our next will take place on a Tuesday, October the twenty-fourth if memory serves. Would you care for me to arrange an invitation? We have hopes of a talk from Annie Kenney. You must know of Miss Kenney? She's the Lancashire mill-girl who is now an associate of the Pankhursts."

Elizabeth looked regretful. "I'm sorry, Arthur, but I am already committed to Mrs. Lewis's Women's Suffrage Association. I cannot possibly spare the time to involve myself with another organization."

"I did not mean to suggest you make any sort of commitment, Elizabeth," Mr. Ingle-Gillis said with a frown. "I simply suggested you come to hear a lecture among friends. I'm sure it will be terribly interesting. Miss Kenney is a remarkable speaker."

"Thank you," Elizabeth said in a firm tone. "But to repeat, my loyalties are to the moderate suffrage movement, and to Mrs. Lewis."

Mr. Ingle-Gillis sighed heavily, and muttered, "That woman …"

Elizabeth looked angry now. "I will have you know that Mrs. Lewis has done more to advance the cause of women's suffrage than all your Pankhursts put together. While Mrs. Pankhurst was still dabbling in socialism, Mrs. Lewis had already been advocating for the women's vote for decades."

"I don't deny Mrs. Lewis works hard," Mr. Ingle-Gillis said, sounding exasperated, "But you really ought to spend more time in the company of people of your own age, Miss Hughes."

Hannah, who was still waiting for Mr. Pierce to finish pulling books for her attention, watched Elizabeth from the corner of her eye. Her eyes were blazing the infamous Death Rays of Mrs. Devenish. It was pretty obvious that

CHAPTER SIX

Mr. Ingle-Gillis found the death rays scary, because Hannah saw his effortless confidence waver. Then he said quietly, and in his most charming voice, " I am so sorry. That was rude of me. Please say you will forgive me."

Elizabeth gave a small smile, and inclined her head toward him. *No question,* Hannah thought, *Elizabeth really likes Mr. Ingle-Gillis, the bookseller and poet. She likes him a lot.*

Uh-oh.

For one crazy moment, Hannah hoped that "Ingle-Gillis" was a weird way of pronouncing "Devenish." But no, she decided, probably not. Not only did she have to stop Elizabeth from marrying some guy her mother had picked out for her, but she also had to stop her from marrying the man she loved.

Oblivious to the turmoil going through her maid's mind, Elizabeth turned the tables on her gentleman friend. "Will you attend Mrs. Lewis's meeting on October 4th, Mr. Ingle-Gillis?"

"I cannot say I have been invited," he said.

"I am inviting you. It begins at four o'clock. Do say you will come. I think a closer acquaintance with Mrs. Lewis will persuade you of her tremendous wisdom."

Mr. Ingle-Gillis was clearly reluctant. But finally he said, "Of course. The meeting will take place at her house, I presume?"

Elizabeth nodded happily.

Then Mr. Ingle-Gillis gave a wicked smile. "If I attend your meeting, perhaps you will attend mine?"

"Perhaps," Elizabeth said, and sniffed.

On the train home, Elizabeth and Hannah sat across from each other in the otherwise empty carriage. Hannah eagerly turned over the parcel containing her book, which Mr. Pierce had carefully wrapped in brown paper and tied neatly with string. Finally, she couldn't wait any longer, and she tore it open.

She held up the book to show Elizabeth, and Elizabeth fumbled in her elegant little purse, before pulling out a small glasses case, from which she extracted a pair of pince-nez spectacles. Unreeling a ribbon hidden in her brooch, she attached her glasses to it before slipping them on. Hannah watched this performance with fascination. "It is an interesting choice, May," Elizabeth said with a small smile, as she carefully turned the pages of Hannah's book. "I trust you will be happy with it."

She handed the book back to Hannah, who again held it up to admire the bright red cover, with its ornate gold-embossed swirled patterns, and dark silhouette of a giant dog set against a full moon. *THE HOUND OF THE*

CHAPTER SIX

BASKERVILLES announced the title, and below the illustration, *CONAN DOYLE*.

Hannah glanced through her book. She had considered Mr. Pierce's suggestion of *Five Children and It*, but it was too childish. She had thought of reading more H. G. Wells, because she had enjoyed *Love and Mr. Lewisham*. And Mr. Pierce had spoken highly of *Where Angels Fear to Tread*, by a new author named E. M. Forster. However, Sherlock Holmes looked like the most fun. Plus, Hannah had watched Sherlock Holmes dramas on TV, so she had a head start in understanding the story. But the real reason the book felt special, she thought, was because Mrs. Devenish, Elizabeth, had cared enough to buy it for her. She had to remind herself that she hated Mrs. Devenish now.

When Hannah looked up from her book, she saw that Elizabeth appeared lost in thought as she gazed out of the train window.

"He's nice," said Hannah.

"Who?"

"Mr. Ingle-Gillis. He's really cute. Are you guys, you know, a couple?"

But Hannah had gone too far. Elizabeth gave her a massive burst of death rays. "My personal life," she said sternly, "is none of your business."

Chastened, Hannah sank in her seat, and returned to her book. Now she understood why the Professor had warned her that she should never forget that she was not Elizabeth's social equal.

Saturday, September 23, 1905

"Morning, Mrs. Morris!" Hannah barely glanced at the figure standing by the kitchen table as she swung through the kitchen door, and put down her bucket. "What's for breakfast? Can I help ... Oh!"

The woman standing in the kitchen wasn't Mrs. Morris. She was Elizabeth, and she was clasping the handle of a black iron frying pan that was lying on the kitchen table. She looked uncomfortable. "Mrs. Morris will return shortly, May," she said.

Hannah didn't reply. She just stared at the pan in Elizabeth's hand.

"I was, um, looking at this," Elizabeth said awkwardly. Using both hands, she held up the heavy pan with difficulty, and examined it as though it were a fine antique.

"Yes, I can see that, Miss Elizabeth," said Hannah, trying not to smile at Elizabeth's obvious discomfort.

Elizabeth again rested the pan on the kitchen table, and gave it a little shove as she did so, as though, Hannah thought with an inner giggle, she was trying to pretend that they weren't actually together. Just then, Mrs. Morris reappeared. "Miss Elizabeth, I'm sorry to keep you waiting ... May, fetch the bacon and eggs from the larder, quickly now ... Now then, Miss Elizabeth, are you sure about this?"

"Indeed, Mrs. Morris," Elizabeth said eagerly. "Very sure."

"And you're not planning to dismiss me from my position in this house?" Mrs. Morris said with a nervous laugh.

"No," said Elizabeth, sounding a little less certain. "My mother is your employer, not I."

Mrs. Morris gave her a long look, and then said in a subdued voice, "In that case, we had best begin with breakfast." She turned to Hannah, who had put on her apron, and was watching the curious scene. "May! Don't just stand there gawking. Go and fetch the bacon and eggs, like I told you."

Hannah hustled into the larder, which was where food was kept cold since home refrigerators had yet to be invented. It was a damp and chilly little room with shelf-lined walls, and a mesh-covered window that allowed in the cold autumn air. She grabbed the eggs in their straw-filled basket, and the paper-wrapped bacon from its place on a shelf.

By the time Hannah returned, Mrs. Morris was using a long iron tool to drop a doughnut-shaped metal ring onto one of the burners on the hot stove. She stooped to flip open the drawer beneath the stovetop, and, with a small shovel, dropped coal inside. Taking the frying pan from Elizabeth, she slid it onto the burner.

"You'll want the pan moderate for bacon," Mrs. Morris told Elizabeth, who looked puzzled. "You'll learn what that means by practice. Here, we put the bacon in first, while the pan's cold. When the bacon is cooked, we cool it down a bit, the pan I mean, and add plenty of fat for the eggs, else they'll get crispy, and I don't care for a crispy egg."

Elizabeth nodded, but Hannah recognized the look on her face. It was the facial expression that Mrs. Devenish made when she was completely confused.

Mrs. Morris continued. "Now, Miss Elizabeth, please fetch yourself a pinafore, so you won't get your clothes dirty. You'll find my spare pinnies over there, that's right, in that cupboard, as long as May has done the ironing like I told her. May," Mrs. Morris called over her shoulder. "Fetch me the lard, and be quick about it, then you can cut a few rounds of the loaf for toast."

As Hannah returned to the larder, she realized with a start why so many of Mrs. Morris's recipes tasted familiar, as if she had eaten her cooking before. Now she knew that she had. Mrs. Morris had taught Elizabeth Hughes Devenish how to cook, and much of the food that Mrs. Devenish fed Hannah in 1940 must have been from the same recipes that Mrs. Morris taught her. But

CHAPTER SIX

why would Elizabeth want to cook and clean, Hannah thought, when she had servants to do everything? *Weird,* she thought. *I wouldn't bother if I was her.*

Elizabeth helped Mrs. Morris prepare breakfast, or rather, got in the way while Mrs. Morris worked. She asked lots of questions. Afterward, she thanked the cook, hung up her borrowed pinafore apron, and quietly left the kitchen.

Returning from serving breakfast to the family, Hannah said to Mrs. Morris, "What was that about?"

"What do you mean?" said Mrs. Morris, who was stamping out scones with a round cutter.

Hannah rephrased her question. "Why is Miss Elizabeth learning to cook?"

Mrs. Morris did not reply. She patted the dough flat again, and expertly cut out more circles of dough, then lifted them onto a greased baking sheet.

"I mean," Hannah said slyly, "she'll put us all out of work if she looks after the family herself."

But Mrs. Morris didn't take the bait. "That I doubt," she said firmly. "She's keen, but she's hopeless."

"Yes, I could see that," said Hannah, smiling at the very idea of a Mrs. Devenish who couldn't cook. "But why is she interested?"

"May, I have no idea," Mrs. Morris said with a sigh, "and it's none of your business or mine if Miss Elizabeth decides to do servants' work."

But Hannah persisted. "Do you think she'll come back to learn more?"

"She says she wants to," said Mrs. Morris, gathering up the leftover dough and patting it flat again in a puff of flour. "Now stop pestering me, and go and start the ironing. The washerwoman sent round the laundry on the wagon."

"I wanted to ask you about that," Hannah said. "Why is it my job to iron clothes? I'm supposed to be a housemaid and a kitchenmaid, not a laundrymaid, too."

"Between maid, that's what you was told, and that's what you are," Mrs. Morris said firmly. "This isn't a big house with an army of staff. Now less of your cheek, and do as you're told."

But these were all good questions, Hannah thought. She had so many questions about how hard she had to work for how little she was paid, and about the people and life of Willowbank. Individually, her concerns seemed petty, but together, they suggested that things were not as they should be. Not at all.

By noon, it was raining heavily, and it had been an unusually slow morning at Gordon N. Baker, Family Grocer and Provision Merchants of Station Road, Ickswade, Bedfordshire. Assistant Shopkeeper Verity Powell had spent

CHAPTER SIX

the morning busying herself as best she could, dusting shelves and rearranging displays of canned goods into intricate stacks. So she was delighted to see a customer for the first time in twenty minutes, a young man carrying a straw hat, who asked for half a pound of butter.

Verity loved to sell butter. Happily, she plucked two little ribbed wooden butter paddles from the water-filled crock in which they were stored. A paddle in each hand, she pried off a lump of deep golden butter from the mountain that sat uncovered on a large marble slab on the counter. The slab was helpfully gold-embossed on one side with the word BUTTER, just in case it was ever suspected of being for some other use.

Dropping the dollop of butter on the scale, Verity saw with satisfaction she had hacked off exactly half a pound. Picking up the butter with the pats, she carried it to the open part of the marble slab, and set to work, slapping the golden lump into shape, just as Mr. Baker had taught her. Soon, the butter was a crooked rectangle, stamped on all sides with lines formed from the ribs of the pats.

Verity deftly wrapped the block of butter in white paper, sealed it with paper tape, and said to her customer, "Anything else? Cigarettes? Bacon?" This was something else she had learned from Mr. Baker. He had impressed upon her the importance of encouraging customers to buy more than they had planned to do.

"Yes, please," the young man said cheerfully. "A packet of Woodbines, and, um, a tin of golden syrup."

Verity fetched the pack of cigarettes first, placing them on the counter before she climbed the high wooden stepladder. Just as she reached to the very top shelf for a green and gold syrup can, the doorbell rang, and Verity turned to greet the arriving customer. She smiled when she saw Hannah, but when a teenage Elizabeth Hughes, her own grandmother, walked in, she was literally almost floored: With a shriek, Verity lost her footing on the ladder. She now hung in the air by one arm, her feet frantically pedaling in an effort to find a step.

"I say," Elizabeth cried, rushing to her aid, just as the young man dropped his straw hat on the counter, and vaulted over it. Each of them grabbed Verity by an ankle, and helped her to clamber back onto a rung.

Panting slightly, Verity looked down and grinned at Elizabeth. There was no mistaking her grandmother: She looked just like Verity. "Thank you," Verity said warmly to Elizabeth. Then she remembered her other savior, the young man, who was fidgeting with his hat, and stammering, "I say, I'm awfully sorry, I hope you don't think me forward, I just …"

CHAPTER SIX

Verity burst out laughing. "No, no, of course not! Both of you were just trying to help. Thank you." She returned to smiling at her future grandmother.

Elizabeth looked slightly alarmed by the wildly grinning shopgirl, and turned away from her. Now Mr. Baker came rushing into the shop, blinking worriedly over his walrus mustache. "Everything is well, I hope? I was upstairs, and heard a cry."

Verity carefully climbed down the ladder, a can of syrup in one hand, and her long skirt gathered in the other. She placed the syrup can on the counter. "Don't concern yourself, Mr. Baker. I almost took a tumble, but this, er, lady and this gentleman came to my rescue."

Mr. Baker nodded, and returned to the back room. The young man waiting for his syrup coughed, looked embarrassed, and tugged with one finger at the stiff upright collar around his neck. Then he looked at Elizabeth. Then Verity. And then Elizabeth again.

"I do hope you don't mind my asking," he said hesitantly, "but are you ladies by any chance related to one another?"

"Excuse me, I don't think we have been introduced," Elizabeth replied, looking at him steely-eyed. But then she turned to Verity and gave her a searching look.

Hannah was afraid that Verity would suddenly lose her mind and announce, "Guess what? I'm your granddaughter," but fortunately she did no such thing. Instead she said nervously, "I very much doubt we're related."

But Elizabeth wasn't so sure. She peered at Verity. "We do look rather alike, it must be said. What is your name?"

Verity told her.

"Verity?" said Elizabeth, as though she had heard something very weird.

"Yes," Verity said uncertainly. "It's unusual. I know. The name was your … I mean, my grandmother's idea."

"I don't know anyone by the name of Powell," said Elizabeth, "so the resemblance between us is doubtless coincidental."

"Yes, doubtless," said Verity, no longer eager to prolong the conversation.

The young man and his can of syrup had been forgotten. Now, he cleared his throat and placed a shilling on the counter. Verity quickly retrieved the coin, and made change from the massive brass cash register. "Do you want anything else?"

"No, no," he said. "This will be all." He added unnecessarily, "I am rather partial to syrup on buttered toast," and then, when nobody responded, he gave a quick grin, and ducked out of the shop.

Standing behind Elizabeth, Hannah glanced pointedly at her back, then

CHAPTER SIX

mouthed "Talk to her" to Verity. But Verity was completely daunted in her youthful grandmother's presence, and continued to smile insanely at Elizabeth. Finally, having failed to think of anything else to say, she said, "Do you care for syrup on your toast, Miss … er … Hughes?"

Hannah put her face in her hands.

"How do you know my name?" Elizabeth snapped.

Somehow, this pulled Verity from her trance. "It's a pleasure to meet you, Miss Hughes," she said hastily, "I'm sorry, I should have explained. I have heard so much about you from Hannah."

"And who is Hannah?"

Hannah thought fast. "It's her nickname for me," she said.

Elizabeth was not giving up her interrogation. "How curious that I should be the subject of gossip between a maid and a shopgirl. And what sorts of things have you heard about me, Miss Powell? Do tell. I should very much like to know."

Verity and Hannah exchanged glances, not sure for a second whether to laugh or cringe. They both realized that Elizabeth was demonstrating how she was well on her way to becoming Mrs. Devenish. There was an awkward silence as both girls fought the giggles.

"Cat got your tongue?" said Elizabeth, annoyed now.

In a strangled voice that came from trying not to burst into laughter, Verity said, "I understand, er, Miss Hughes, that you are involved in the women's suffrage movement? I should like to learn more about that."

"Would you?" Elizabeth said guardedly. She clearly knew she was the butt of some secret joke.

"Indeed, I would," said Verity. "I am a great admirer of, er, Millicent Garrett Fawcett."

Finally, Verity had said the right thing, Hannah thought, because Elizabeth was looking at her future granddaughter through softer eyes. "You seem remarkably well informed for a shop assistant," she said. "Now, I should like to purchase some writing paper. Have you any? Nothing too fussy."

From behind the counter, Verity quickly produced a paper-wrapped pack tied with string, and handed it to Elizabeth, who pulled a few coins from her purse. As she gave Verity the money, she said, "There is a meeting of the Women's Suffrage Association on Tuesday, October 4th. It will begin at four o'clock sharp at Oaks Lodge, Mrs. Alice Lewis's house in Balesworth. If you wish to attend, perhaps you could take the train with me. May will also accompany me."

"Will I?" Hannah said. It was the first she had heard of it. Elizabeth ignored her.

CHAPTER SIX

"I would love to go," Verity said, with genuine enthusiasm. "I live in Balesworth, so perhaps I could just meet you there?"

"Good," Elizabeth said. "Do you know Mrs. Lewis?"

"Oh, of course ..." Verity started to say, but Hannah frantically shook her head, so Verity finished lamely, "Not. No, I mean, I've heard of her. But I'm just a shopgirl, as you say. So I'm not her friend. Not at all."

"In that case," Elizabeth said, "I will meet you at Balesworth Station at half past three o'clock sharp."

Verity flashed her a smile. She was enjoying her adventure, Hannah could see that, and taking it in her stride. But then she didn't have to work as a maid, did she? Hannah felt another pang of resentment toward her friend, and tried to suppress the thought.

Sunday, September 24, 1905
"Bet you're excited to get this afternoon off," Hannah said to Mrs. Morris as she tied on her kitchen apron.

"I'll be staying late today," Mrs. Morris said shortly. "There's a guest for luncheon. May, fetch me the joint of beef from the larder. We'll serve it with roasted potatoes and carrots. Which reminds me, why didn't you set out my vegetables?"

"The carrots and potatoes are on the table, Mrs. Morris," Hannah said. "So who's the special guest?"

"I don't know his name," said Mrs. Morris, "but I understand that we are to seat him next to Miss Elizabeth. Did you hear that, Flora?" Flora grunted from her seat next to the fireplace.

Hannah realized now that this must be the guest that Mrs. Hughes had mentioned a few days earlier, the man she intended Elizabeth to marry. Maybe, Hannah thought excitedly, the guest was Mr. Devenish. It would certainly make things easier if he were just to turn up for lunch.

Mrs. Morris and Hannah were making final preparations for the meal, and Flora was dozing in her chair, when the servant bell rang. All three of them automatically looked up at the indicator board. The *Front Door* flag was waggling madly.

"I'll go," Flora murmured.

"I can go," said Hannah. Putting down her potato-peeling knife, she began to untie her apron. She was dying to see the guest.

"No, you don't," barked Flora, fully awake now, and struggling to heave herself out of her chair. "I'm the parlormaid. I open the door to visitors."

CHAPTER SIX

Mrs. Morris nudged Hannah, and said quietly, "You stay here, May, and help me get the plates ready." As soon as Flora closed the kitchen door, Mrs. Morris said gently, "Flora needs to feel useful, poor old soul. But don't worry, you'll get a good look at him soon enough. I need you to wait at table. I'll tell Flora to have a rest once she has helped serve the meal, and you can stay in the dining room to wait on the family."

But Hannah had more important matters to consider. "What do you think this guy looks like?"

"I have no idea, I'm sure," said Mrs. Morris. "But I hope he's suitable to Miss Elizabeth. From what I can gather, Mrs. Hughes sees him as the answer to her prayers."

Hannah headed slowly toward the dining room, carefully carrying a platter on which rested a large well-cooked roast beef garnished with sprigs of parsley, and surrounded with golden brown roasted potatoes. It smelled delicious. Ahead of her, Flora was transporting a dish of boiled carrots, topped with a pat of melting butter.

Having placed the vegetable plate on the table, Flora left the room, her duty done. As Hannah gently set down the roast, she scanned the faces at table. Margaret, Victoria, and Mrs. Hughes were all present and correct, along with an old man who sported a little red hair on a mostly bald head. Hannah had no idea that there was to be another guest. Maybe this was the father of Elizabeth's potential boyfriend? Come to think of it, where was Elizabeth?

At that exact moment, Elizabeth exploded into the room, all arms and legs.

"Sorry I'm late, Mother," she said cheerily, not sounding sorry at all. She pulled out a chair next to Mrs. Hughes. "I quite forgot the time."

Mrs. Hughes smiled thinly at her daughter, but her eyes blazed fury.

Hannah, as she had been instructed, remained to wait on the family during the meal. Her position at the sideboard gave her a great view of what happened next.

"Elizabeth," Mrs. Hughes said with more than a touch of frost in her voice, "This is Mr. Collins." She indicated the old man at the other end of the table. "Why don't you take the chair to his left?"

Elizabeth looked astonished. She clearly had not been told that there was to be a guest at lunch.

Hannah, meanwhile, had finally figured out that the old man was the only guest. *This* was the boyfriend to be? He was at least fifty. He was more than old enough to be Miss Elizabeth's father. Hannah was shocked.

"Delighted to meet you, Miss Hughes," said Mr. Collins, nodding to Elizabeth. Elizabeth smiled politely, then turned away so that he couldn't see her expression, and pulled an *Are you serious?* face at her mother.

"Mr. Collins is a gentleman learned in the law," said Mrs. Hughes, glaring at Elizabeth. "Am I right, Mr. Collins?"

"In a manner of speaking, Mrs. Hughes," he said modestly, twiddling his ginger mustache and looking very satisfied with himself. "I am a solicitor."

A lawyer, Hannah thought.

"That must be terribly exciting," Elizabeth said, and Hannah heard the sarcasm in her tone. Then, after a small pause, she ambushed Mr. Collins with a dangerous question. "Tell me, are you in favor of votes for women?"

Mr. Collins's mustache twitched. Hannah thought how clever Elizabeth was. If Mr. Collins said he supported women having the right to vote, he would offend Mrs. Hughes. If he said he opposed it, then Elizabeth would have a great excuse to strike him off her potential husband list.

Mr. Collins, however, was no fool. He smiled politely, and said, "I do prefer not to spoil everyone's digestion with talk of politics. I say, Mrs. Hughes, should I carve?" He nodded toward the roast, and Mrs. Hughes simpered that she would be much obliged if he would do so.

"I wonder, Mr. Collins," Elizabeth said as he carved a thin slice of meat, "are you a friend of my mother's? I ask, because you appear to be around the same age as she."

After that, Mr. Collins mostly talked to Elizabeth's sister Victoria.

It was four o'clock that afternoon when Hannah closed the front door behind the departing Mr. Collins. As she did so, she heard a loud discussion begin in the drawing room.

Victoria spoke first. "Elizabeth, you were terribly rude to poor Mr. Collins."

"He's far too old for me," Elizabeth protested. "I'm only nineteen. I don't even need or want a husband now. And I would have to be desperate to marry a man in his dotage."

"Elizabeth!" her mother exclaimed. "That is unfair and unkind. Mr. Collins is a good and well-connected man … "

"Well-connected, you say?" Elizabeth said it in a mocking tone. "I thought he was falling apart. Oh, honestly, Mother, there is more to marriage than attaching oneself to the first available man with a substantial income. Perhaps Mr. Collins is a good, kind man, but I cannot say I find him in the least attractive …"

Hannah heard Flora's unmistakable slow gait begin to descend the stairs from the top landing, and, regretfully, decided that any further eavesdropping might get her in trouble. She quickly retreated toward the kitchen. When would Mr. Devenish make an appearance? Soon, she hoped. Very soon.

Wednesday, September 27, 1905

"Pass me a leg, please, Verity," said Hannah, nodding at the plate of golden roasted chicken pieces as she handed her friend a bowl of roasted potatoes. "What a treat to have a roast on a weeknight. This is great food," she said to the Professor. "Do you have someone secretly cooking for you, Kate?"

"Oh, hush," said the Professor, spooning potatoes onto her own plate. "You have the cheek of the devil, Hannah. Of course I can cook."

"Well, it's great," Hannah said. Verity, her cheeks stuffed, could only nod in agreement. "In fact," Hannah added, "It's even better than Mrs. Morris's."

"I have learned lots of tips from the internet," the Professor said.

"I don't know what internet means," Verity said, "But this conversation reminds me of something. There's a cook who comes into the shop almost every morning, and she's the oddest creature. She always brings her mistress's little dog for what she calls an airing, and …"

Hannah stopped listening. She felt creeping jealousy whenever Verity talked about her job. *She* wasn't stuck in a house all day, doing exhausting housework. *She* had very little physical work to do at all, and she met lots of different people. Most annoying of all, Verity got evenings and weekends off, and the Professor looked after her.

Hannah's mood improved slightly when the Professor produced a dessert she called profiteroles, a mountain of little golden pastry puffs, each of them stuffed with thick whipped cream, and the whole pile drizzled with warm chocolate sauce. As Hannah generously helped herself, she complimented the Professor on managing such an elaborate dish without electricity. "Oh, I cheated," said the Professor. "I popped home to the 21st century and made them there."

"You can bring back food?" Hannah blinked rapidly. "Can *I* do that?"

"Not yet," said the Professor. "But perhaps in a year or two."

Hannah bit into a soft chocolate-drizzled cream puff and considered this prospect. What other time-travel tips and tricks could she learn from the Professor?

After dinner, Hannah showed Verity and the Professor her copy of *The Hound of the Baskervilles*. "Elizabeth gave me this," she said proudly, handing the red book to the Professor. "She bought it for me at the bookstore in Balesworth."

"Very nice, dear," the Professor said. Thoughtfully, she ran her fingertips over the cover, opened it up and looked through it, a small smile playing around her lips. Then she carefully handed the book to Verity.

CHAPTER SIX

"Young Granny bought you a book, Hannah?" said Verity. "How very kind of her. And how super that there's a bookshop in Balesworth, because there isn't in 1951. I always have to buy my books in Cambridge, or London … You know, now I think of it, I do remember Granny saying once that there was a bookshop on Balesworth High Street when she was young. What's the name of it? She never said."

"Ingle-Gillis," Hannah said promptly.

"Ingle-Gillis, did you say?" said Verity. "That name does sound familiar."

But Hannah suddenly remembered she had something much more important to tell Verity. "Oh, my gosh!" she exclaimed. "Big news! Elizabeth's mom is trying to get her hitched to random guys. I'm keeping an eye out for your grandpa, Verity, but I don't know what he looks like. Can you describe him?"

Verity frowned. "Grandfather Devenish? No, I have no idea. He died in the Great War, the First World War, and that was long before I was born. Granny never talked about him. She didn't even have a photograph on the wall, or anything like that. You know how unsentimental she is."

"Do you know when they got married?"

"No, sorry," Verity said. "I suppose sometime before 1908, because that's when my mother was born."

"She can't be getting married yet, can she?" Hannah said. "She's only nineteen."

"I don't see why she can't marry at nineteen," Verity said shortly. "That's not much younger than I am, and I'm supposed to be married next year, as soon as Eric and I find somewhere to live. There's such a shortage of flats and houses since the War."

Hannah said, "I think it's so funny you're gonna marry Eric."

"Funny ha-ha or funny peculiar?" Verity said sharply.

"Sorry, I don't mean to offend you," Hannah said. "It's just that you guys grew up together like brother and sister, and you're older than him …"

"Not by much," Verity snapped. "So what? And it's not your business, is it? Let's talk about Granny, shall we?"

Hannah wondered briefly why Verity was so touchy on the subject of her own marriage, but she let the moment pass.

"The thing is," Hannah said carefully, "Elizabeth has some … um … issues that maybe she needs to address before she gets married."

"Issues?" said Verity. "What do you mean, issues?"

"You know … She has problems … Personal problems," Hannah said, suspecting that this wasn't the right thing to say to Verity, especially at this moment. It wasn't.

CHAPTER SIX

"What are you implying? I know Granny can be difficult, but she's not barking mad."

Now the Professor stepped in. "Of course she's not mad, Verity," she said calmly. "Hannah is just being an early 21st century person with all our ideas about psychology. I'm sorry. It's hard to explain to you."

Hannah, feeling a little safer with the Professor's support, said, "Elizabeth is really nice, but kind of immature around her family. She's always losing her temper and being rude to her mother."

"That's hardly a surprise," Verity muttered, opening a pack of cigarettes.

"Verity, I've told you before," the Professor said sternly, looking pointedly at the cigarette she had already put between her lips. "Not in the house, please, and preferably, not at all."

"Oh, all right," Verity grumbled, stuffing the cigarette back into its pack. "But I'm terribly on edge, I'll have you know. I can't smoke in public because women smoking is just not the done thing in 1905, and now you say I can't even smoke in here. Anyway, I don't know what all the fuss is about, and I don't just mean my cigarettes. Look, Hannah, why are you so worried that my great-grandmother is trying to arrange my grandmother's marriage? Why would that concern you so much? We all know who she married. She married Tom Devenish."

There was an awkward silence. Hannah didn't know how to tell her the problem, and bit her lip. Finally, Verity said, "What's wrong?"

Hannah took a deep breath. "Don't you remember that conversation we had, last time I was here? About things changing?" She looked for support to the Professor, who nodded gravely in agreement.

Verity sat motionless, the color draining from her face. Weakly, she said, "Are you trying to tell me that Granny might marry someone else? Or nobody at all?"

The Professor and Hannah nodded again.

"But surely not?" Verity said faintly. "I mean, I'm here, aren't I, and I wouldn't be if my grandparents had never met … Would I?"

"Look, Verity, it's probably OK," the Professor said, in an unconvincingly upbeat voice.

"That's all very well for you to say," Verity said angrily, "But I don't want to return to 1951 and discover I don't exist."

Hannah, also trying to sound cheerful, said, "She's bound to come across Mr. Devenish, and then marry him, although hopefully not too soon, and things will carry on as they …" Suppose they didn't? Hannah got a cold chill. Suppose Elizabeth married someone else?

CHAPTER SIX

So, Hannah realized, her mission in 1905 wasn't just to prevent Elizabeth from marrying the wrong man, and it wasn't just to prevent her from marrying Arthur Ingle-Gillis, whom she obviously adored. It was also to make sure that Elizabeth Hughes became Mrs. Devenish. But first she had to find Mr. Devenish. And she would. She *would* find him. Then she would persuade Elizabeth to get to know him, and help her somehow to grow up enough to get married.

But what then? Mr. Devenish would die in the First World War. Elizabeth would become a young widow with two small daughters. And saddest of all, she would never remarry. She would be alone for the rest of her life. Maybe, Hannah wondered, Elizabeth could have a better, happier life, with someone who would stick around? Who wouldn't get himself killed? Maybe Arthur Ingle-Gillis? But if Elizabeth married him, what would happen to her daughters, to Verity, and Eric, and Hannah and Alex and Brandon and George Braithwaite, to every kid whom the widowed Mrs. Devenish would one day care for?

Hannah now had a truly awful thought … What if Verity and her mother and aunt really weren't supposed to have been born? Suppose there were other people who should have been Elizabeth's children and grandchildren, but who had not been born … That couldn't be right, she thought. It just couldn't. What on earth was she going to do?

She looked at the Professor, who gave her a supportive smile, but Hannah could see that she was anxious, too *She knows*, Hannah thought. *She knows, and she doesn't know what to tell me. Not that she would tell me if she could.*

The Professor got to her feet. "How about some tea?" she said.

"Yes, I would like tea, thanks, Kate."

As the Professor walked past Hannah's chair, she leaned down and said quietly, "You don't need to tell me. That thing you were just thinking about, I know. And you're right. I haven't a clue. It's your call."

Hannah felt a chill. So Kate Harrower was a witch, after all. And the time travel? It was magic.

Chapter 7:
SNIPESVILLE MATTERS

Monday, February 5, 1906

As soon as Eric and Alex walked into the newspaper office, Mr. Hughes sat up in his chair. "Powell, I want you to interview the owner of the new drug store and soda fountain."

Eric looked mystified. "I'm sorry, Mr. Hughes, but I haven't a clue what a drug fountain is."

Mr. Hughes chuckled. "My word, Powell, you are green!"

"I feel fine," said Eric, looking even more confused. "I'm not ill at all."

Mr. Hughes shook his head. "No, no. Not green as in *ill*. Green is what we call a recent immigrant who is as yet unused to American ways."

Sitting down at his desk, Alex quietly explained to Eric. "A drug store is what you call a chemist's shop in England, and a soda fountain is an ice cream café that also sells fizzy drinks."

"But what do medicines and fizzy drinks have in common?" Eric said, mostly to himself.

Ignoring the conversation, Mr. Hughes continued, "The drugstore's owner is Mr. Wheeler. He's from Pennsylvania."

"Pennsylvania?" Eric said blankly. Mr. Hughes sighed, and muttering the word "green," pulled a bulky book from the shelf behind his desk. Opening it up, he jabbed his index finger onto a page. Eric leaned in close for a look, his nose only inches from the paper. Then he straightened up again. "So that's where Pennsylvania is," he said. "It's, um, quite near to Snipesville, is it?"

Mr. Hughes closed the book and replaced it on the shelf. "No, it's not," he said. "America is vast, Powell, apparently so vast that it is beyond your ability to imagine."

"I can't help noticing," said Eric, looking pained by Mr. Hughes's putdown, "that none of the business owners I have met thus far are from Snipesville, and that several of them, like you sir, are not American."

"Snipesville draws men from far and wide," said Mr. Hughes. "As I said, the local men are farmers, not businessmen. That's why it's important for our economic progress that Snipes County is chosen as the site of an Agricultural and Mechanical School, and that is why I spend much time up in Atlanta, pleading our case. The school will also train local farmers in modern scientific agriculture. It's a practical modern high school for a practical modern nation …"

"Yes, super," Eric said hurriedly. Alex already knew that Eric thought Mr. Hughes was a blowhard. "But, Mr. Hughes, are none of Snipesville's business owners actually from Snipesville?"

"Some are," said Mr. Hughes. "Dr. Hunslow is from Snipes County. Mr. Thompson is also from Snipes County …"

"Thompson? The department store chap? The fellow who can't read or write?"

"That's the man. He's from here, a farmer's son. In any event, Powell, let us return to the subject at hand. I want you to write about Wheeler's Apothecary, and specifically about the soda fountain, because that's a modern sort of place, a real feather in the cap for Snipesville. Get something on my desk by four o'clock sharp."

"Right then," said Eric, grabbing his notebook and hat. "No time to lose."

"Sir, can I go with him?" Alex asked. "I need a break, and there might be free samples of ice cream."

His boss sighed and nodded. "Cut along, then. Powell might need you to translate into English for him."

Mr. Wheeler, the drugstore owner, was large and tough-looking, but also polite and shy. While Eric interviewed him at one of the spindly café tables, Alex had a look around. He eagerly studied the metal soda fountain with its many silver taps, and the ice cream freezer. He marveled at the three huge unlabeled bottles of colored liquid on the counter. On the shelves behind them sat rows of small medicine bottles with ornate labels. Coca-Cola posters hung on the walls. At the back of the shop, a tight wooden grille that ran from floor to ceiling closed off an area from the café. It was broken only by two service windows, one labeled PRESCRIPTIONS, and the other marked OFFICE. Most importantly, a sign behind the counter advertised ice creams for a nickel. Alex knew that this wasn't the bargain it sounded, considering how little he and Eric were being paid. But it was good to finally arrive in a time when ice cream was available.

"So," Eric said to Mr. Wheeler, "What brings you all the way to Snipesville from, um, Gettysburg, was it?"

"A cousin of mine showed me that little booklet Mr. Hughes published," Mr. Wheeler said, "all about the business opportunities in Snipesville. Mind, my family and friends think I'm a little crazy to move to the South, on account of my father having served in the Union army in the War, but I sure like it here."

"And what sorts of … um … food will you serve?" said Eric.

Mr. Wheeler began listing off menu items on his fingers. "Sodas … ice cream … ice cream sodas … sandwiches … hot dogs … candy."

Eric blinked. "Candy? You mean sweets?"

"Well, now, Mr. Powell, I don't know of candy that ain't sweet, do you?"

Eric smiled uneasily. Alex, watching, could tell he felt stupid, when all he had been doing was translating for himself into British English. But he quickly recovered. "So what sorts of, um, candy do you sell, Mr. Wheeler?"

"I got home-made caramels," he said. "Only a nickel a bag."

"I'll take two," Eric quickly replied.

"On the house," said Mr. Wheeler with a grin. "And more where that came from if you give me a good write-up!" He laughed, but Alex had the impression he wasn't joking.

"What else do you sell?" Eric asked eagerly.

Alex smiled to himself at Eric's happiness at finding candy on sale. He remembered Eric's sweet tooth from 1940, and Eric had told him that candy was still rationed in England in 1951, even though World War II was long over. Now, Alex thought, Eric really did look like a kid in a candy store.

They were no sooner out the front door of the drugstore, when Eric opened his white paper cone of candy, eagerly unwrapped a caramel, and popped it in his mouth. He stopped right in the middle of the street, and a look of bliss came over his face. "Oh, lovely," he said through a mouthful of sticky sugar, then offered the bag to Alex. "Would you like… Ah!"

Suddenly, Eric clamped his hand to his cheek and rolled around the contents of his mouth as he pulled his cloth handkerchief from his pocket. Spitting the caramel into it, he examined the sticky mess. A look of horror came over his face. "Oh, no … I've lost part of a tooth. Is there a dentist in town?"

"Honestly, Eric," said Alex, "every time we go outside, some disaster happens to you." But as he looked over Eric's shoulder, he saw the small sign: *Dr. Samuel H. Marshburn, DENTIST.*

CHAPTER SEVEN

Eric glanced over the dentist's chair that looked like it belonged in a medieval dungeon, the scary dental tools, and the white beadboard wall spattered with nameless substances. He gulped. In a tone of forced calm that Alex knew meant Eric was panicking, he said, "I say, Alex, would you mind keeping me company? I never have much cared for dentists."

Alex sat on a stool in the corner of the office as Dr. Marshburn washed his hands with soap and water, and instructed Eric to open wide, before tapping the tooth with a metal tool. "That hurt?"

"Gah," said Eric. This apparently meant "No."

The dentist prodded at the tooth with his pick. "How about this?"

"Gah," Eric said again.

The dentist kept tapping the tooth. Finally, he said, "It doesn't hurt at all?"

Eric shook his head. The dentist sniffed, and said, "Then you can either have it out or leave it. It's up to you, sir."

Eric lifted his head, and in a tremulous voice said, "I will just leave it for now. If you think that's advisable."

Dr. Marshburn nodded. "I do think so," he said. "No hurry, Mr. Powell. Oh, and some very impressive fillings you got there. You have those done in England? How about that. Look, you'll find me here from nine in the morning until half past eight at night, and if you have an emergency outside those hours, I have a home telephone installed now, and I'll give you my card, just in case. You're new to Snipesville, aren't you? Well, welcome to town. I'm a Snipes County native, and I can't believe how much this place has grown these last few years. I'm pretty pleased, though. My daddy worked hard to set me up in business, and it's good to set up practice in my own hometown. You know, my grandparents were the first settlers in Snipesville, way back before the War Between the States. They kept a hotel."

Alex frowned. So this talkative dentist was the grandson of the Marshburns who ran the awful inn where he stayed in 1851. That meant that Dr. Marshburn was also likely an ancestor of his dad's boss at the bank. Looking at Dr. Marshburn's beefy face, he could see the family resemblance.

"We sure are glad to have you here," Dr. Marshburn said. "All the way from England, huh? You know, this will make you laugh, but there was a colored boy here just last week, claimed he once apprenticed to a dentist in England. Of course, that was nonsense, but I think maybe he must have overheard you speaking …"

Alex looked at Eric. Eric looked at Alex. At exactly the same time, they said "Brandon!"

❖ 161 ❖

CHAPTER SEVEN

Dr. Marshburn gave them a very odd look.

"I still have a space in tomorrow's paper," Mr. Hughes said. "Powell, have you finished that piece on the drugstore?"

"Just about, Mr. Hughes," Eric said, painstakingly pecking with two fingers at the typewriter, a lit cigarette hanging from the corner of his lower lip. Alex had been amazed that Eric couldn't type, but when he had said so, Eric had blustered something about typing being work for secretaries, not engineers. Alex didn't have the heart to tell him about computers.

"Let me see what you've written," Mr. Hughes said, standing next to Eric's desk and snapping his fingers then extending them toward the typewriter. Reluctantly, Eric unrolled the paper, and handed it to him.

Reading over the draft, Mr. Hughes grunted a couple of times, and winced once. "Your writing's competent, but this story is dull. Liven it up. Do it again." He threw the paper onto Eric's typewriter, and Eric stared at it miserably.

Mr. Hughes now turned his attention to his accountant. "Day, I found five errors in your arithmetic this morning. I've made a note of them. If this continues, gentlemen, we will need to reconsider your employment. I have a meeting at the bank shortly, and I expect to see progress by the time I return."

When Mr. Hughes left the office, Eric stubbed out his cigarette, picked up his manuscript, crushed it into a ball, and launched it at the wastepaper basket. He missed.

"Hey, don't do that," Alex said kindly. "At least let me try to fix it."

"Oh, I doubt you can," Eric said, exasperated. "I mean, English wasn't my strong subject at school, but I am a bit older and certainly better educated than you are."

Alex gave him a lofty stare. "I got an A on my last English paper, and I edited a lawyer's letters in 1851. Look, how about I read over your article, and you check my accounting?"

Eric hesitated. But then he said, "We can certainly do that. I was treasurer of the university chess club, I'll have you know."

"So you keep saying," Alex said. "Let's trade, okay? This gives me a chance to get out of the office and look for Brandon. You probably don't remember him well, but I know what he looks like. At least I think I do."

Later that afternoon, Mr. Hughes finished reading the draft that Alex had handed him. "This is much improved over Powell's," he said.

"Great," said Alex. "Sir, Eric and I would like to trade jobs. He's way better at accounting than I am."

"Why not?" said Mr. Hughes. "We can but try."

Tuesday, February 6, 1906

As Brandon and Robert Gordon sat reading on the uncomfortable, upright sofa, Miss Julia laid down her ink pen and groaned. They both looked at her. "This is the third time I have written to Mr. Booker T. Washington for assistance with building our high school," she said. "But all I have received in reply has been a series of polite refusals. I suppose so many people ask Mr. Washington for funds to build schools, and he can only oblige so many of us. It may help our cause if Mr. Hughes is successful in persuading the legislature to establish an Agricultural and Mechanical School for white children in Snipesville. But how can I argue for a proper classical education for colored children when even whites are taught to know their place as farmers and mechanics?" She sighed again.

Maybe another problem, Brandon thought, was what Robert had hinted at. Perhaps the famous educator Booker T. Washington didn't take Miss Julia seriously because she was a woman. Brandon recalled reading about the Progressive era in America, and how much was written about "manliness" in the early 1900s. At the time, he had joked about it, saying "manly" in his deepest voice every chance he got, but he knew it was no joke. As he had explained to an uninterested Javarius, women were ready to lead in the Progressive era, but men didn't take them seriously. As if to contradict his silent thoughts, Miss Julia said, "George, I am to be a delegate to the Equal Rights convention in Macon, and Robert will accompany me. All sorts of important men will be present. Bishop Turner … Professor Hope …" Brandon had no idea who these people were, and he was just returning his attention to his book when Miss Julia said, "Professor Du Bois …"

Brandon's head jerked up. "Wait, did you say Professor *Du Bois?* W. E. B. Du Bois will be there?"

"Indeed," said Miss Julia.

Robert picked up an apple from the fruit bowl on the coffee table, and said, "I look forward to representing Snipesville in Macon, Aunt Julia." He bit into his apple, and then, spitting fruit fragments into the air, added, "Am I required to make a speech?"

"Of course not," Miss Julia said sharply. "You are to be an observer, not a delegate."

Brandon said slyly, "And your prize will be two days listening to speeches in Macon."

Robert chuckled despite himself. Miss Julia looked frostily at both of them.

CHAPTER SEVEN

"I would appreciate less flippancy from both of you. This is an extremely important meeting," she said. "Even as colored people are coming into our own, setting up businesses, churches, and schools, we are increasingly denied our rights as citizens. Does neither of you think it important that we have the right to vote? That colored men sit on juries? That colored people not be arrested on the smallest pretext and enslaved as convict laborers? These and more are matters we will address at this convention."

Robert said, "Aunt Julia, you should make a report of the proceedings to *The Snipesville News*." Brandon at first thought this was a joke, but when he turned to look at him, he saw Robert was serious.

"Perhaps Mr. Hughes will be interested," said Miss Julia, "and if he is not, well, his lack of interest is also useful to know."

"Who's Mr. Hughes?" Brandon said.

"George, surely I have told you of Mr. Hughes?" said Robert. "He is Snipesville's mayor, banker, newspaper publisher, and greatest booster. It is thanks to him that Snipesville is the thriving town you see now. Oh, and since you have lived in England, you really ought to meet him. He is English, you know."

Brandon's head was spinning. How could he have forgotten what Robert had told him the first time, that the Mayor was a Brit? And now he had learned that the Mayor's name was Hughes. He had a sudden sense of foreboding. He had heard that name before. Hughes was a very common name in England, he knew that much. But still … "I guess I should introduce myself to Mr. Hughes, then," he said.

"George, it would be best if I were to introduce you," said Robert, throwing his apple core into the nearest wastepaper basket (which earned him a disapproving tut from Miss Julia). He grabbed his jacket from the coat rack. "I have a reputation in this town as one of the better sorts of Negro."

Brandon stared at Robert in shock. Did he really just say that? *One of the better sorts of Negro?* Apparently he did. And he wasn't joking. Brandon was embarrassed for him.

Brandon followed Robert into the office of *The Snipesville News,* hoping nervously that he would not run into the man who had chased him into the street when he asked about jobs.

"Good afternoon, sir," Robert said to Mr. Hughes. They nodded to each other. Brandon noticed that neither of them tried to shake hands, but Mr. Hughes seemed genuinely pleased to see Robert. "Now, sir, as to my business," said Robert. "Miss Julia Russell and I are delegates to a meeting in Macon of the best colored men in Georgia. I wondered if you would wish us to submit a report for the newspaper?"

"By all means," said Mr. Hughes. "Will Booker T. Washington be present?"

"That, I don't know, sir," Robert admitted.

"Well, I will be interested to read the proceedings all the same."

"Thank you, sir. Oh, and kindly allow me to introduce George Braithwaite. He's recently arrived in town, and he comes to us all the way from England, where he has lived for some years, he says."

Mr. Hughes looked astonished, and then suspicious. He toyed with the pen on his desk, rolling it around. "And where, precisely, are you from, George?"

Brandon knew Mr. Hughes was testing him, but he could also test Mr. Hughes. Without hesitation, he said "Balesworth." Did he see Mr. Hughes's eyes widen, just for an instant? Or was that his imagination?

But immediately Mr. Hughes's face turned blank. "The name sounds familiar," he said. "In which county?"

"Hertfordshire," Brandon said. "About thirty-five miles north of London …"

"Ah yes, of course," said Mr. Hughes. "I have passed through Balesworth on the train."

"Where are you from, sir?" said Brandon.

Mr. Hughes nudged at his nose with a crooked finger. "I lived in London for some years. But tell me, what brings you here to Snipesville?"

"Probably the same reason you're here, sir," said Brandon, and he noticed Mr. Hughes flinch. Or was he just seeing things?

As they were leaving the newspaper office, Robert grabbed Brandon by the upper arm, and hustled him off the boardwalk. Brandon almost fell as he stepped down awkwardly onto the muddy road. "Hey, what did you do that for …" he protested. But as he turned to face Robert, he immediately saw why. Two young white women swept by them on the boardwalk, as Robert removed his hat, and Brandon stood in the mud. Brandon stared after them, until Robert grabbed him by the shoulder, and turned him away.

He leaned toward Brandon's ear. "That's the reason," he said quietly. "Never be seen not to make way for white women. And don't stare at them, either."

Brandon was furious with himself. Of course, he knew this from his reading. He hated it, but he knew it. He stepped back up onto the boardwalk, and began scraping mud off his shoes, scowling furiously. Robert stepped up to join him. "You ask why I hesitate to stay here?" he said. "That is why. Even in Atlanta, I am at least not expected to step off the sidewalk, at least not yet. Snipesville will show progress, but I don't know if I have the patience for it. Now, have you any other business downtown, George?"

CHAPTER SEVEN

"Not really," Brandon said forlornly. "I'll just head back to Miss Julia's, I guess."

"Very well, I shall see you there," said Robert, putting his hat back on his head. "I promised to call in on my uncle."

As he walked away, Brandon wondered how he could ever have complained that 21st century Snipesville was boring. Sure, the bowling alley was kind of a dump, and, true, the owner did let his pit bull run around while he was fixing the machinery, but still, the town had a bowling alley … And there was Snipe-PAC, the performing arts center downtown … There was the multiplex movie theatre over by the Mall, even if your feet did stick to the floor. There was the Snipesville Mall itself, which was so tiny, people called it the Small. There was Zappy Burger, of course. And now there was a coffeeshop, even if Hunslow's Sippin' Snipe was the dumbest coffeeshop name on the planet. But in 1906, Snipesville had none of these things, only a solitary café, and it would not serve Brandon, not unless he was willing to wait in a dirty alley for his order from the 'colored' window.

Longingly, he looked over at the café, wishing for an entertainment as simple as sitting with a cup of coffee at a table in a public place. At that moment, a short young white man bumped into him. Losing his footing, Brandon fell forward, catching himself on his hands on the boardwalk. As he picked himself up and dusted himself off, he suddenly felt angry. How could this guy have just walked into him like that, and not even bothered to apologize?

"I am terribly sorry," the man said in an English accent, as Brandon brushed off his knees. "I wasn't looking where I was going. Are you all right?"

"Sure, I'm fine," said Brandon, startled. "No problem. It was just an accident. But who …"

"That's very good of you," said the man. "I say, are you sure you're all right?"

Now another white man was at his side, and he hissed at the Englishman in an American accent, "Eric, I told you, don't apologize to black people. Even when you should." He turned to Brandon, and said, "He's from England. He doesn't … Brandon!"

The American man gave Brandon a huge smile, even as Brandon stared at him, agog. "It's me, Alex. And this is Eric. You know? Eric from 1940?"

Brandon continued to stare.

"Come with us," Alex said quietly. "I know where we can go talk."

It was Mr. Duval himself who led Alex, Brandon, and Eric to a small room off the kitchen of the Hotel Duval. "You cannot sit together in the public dining room," he said apologetically in French-accented English. "You eating and drinking together, even here, the people do not like it, and it cause me difficulty."

"It's okay, Mr. Duval," Alex said soothingly. "I do understand, and I'm grateful for your consideration. As I explained to your assistant Charles, I'm interviewing this boy for a story I'm writing."

Brandon knew Alex meant nothing by calling him a boy, but he still cringed inwardly.

As they sat down at the table, Eric said, "Mr. Duval, I wonder if we could have a nice cup of tea. Or rather," he added hurriedly, "coffee." Alex smiled. He knew what Eric thought of American tea.

Mr. Duval inclined his head. "I will tell Charles to see to it." As soon as he closed the door behind him, the three time travelers relaxed, and Eric lit a cigarette, to sour looks from Brandon and Alex.

"So, Brandon," said Alex, tapping his fingers on the tablecloth. "What do you think?"

"About the hotel? Nice," Brandon said. "I'm jealous."

"No," said Alex, "Not the hotel. About everything. About being here." He swept his arms. "What are we doing here? Is Hannah with you?"

Brandon frowned. "You're asking me if your sister, a white girl, is hanging out with me in 1906 Snipesville? No, of course she's not. Don't be stupid."

"I had to ask. We all thought we were alone at first," Alex said. And then he explained what had happened, beginning his story in 1951.

Brandon sipped his coffee, then asked Alex, "So you think Hannah is still with Mrs. D. in 1951?"

"I guess so," Alex said anxiously. "I hope so."

Eric said, "I hope Verity and Granny aren't worried about us."

"They won't be," Alex said, "because we'll arrive back right after we left. Nobody will know we went anywhere, unless we tell them."

"Oh, I won't tell them," said Eric. "I cannot imagine Verity or Granny believing a word about time travel."

Something was bothering Alex. "The thing is, even the Professor doesn't know we're here."

"Yes, she does," Brandon said. And then he told them about his meeting in the forest clearing in 1906 that magically became a high school campus in 1910.

The coffee cups lay drained, except for Alex's. Brandon, with a quizzical look, pointed to the half-cup of cold beige liquid with a skin sitting by his friend's elbow. "I don't much like coffee," Alex said, "even this milky sweet stuff."

"It's like a latte," said Brandon.

"Milky coffee," said Eric. "We call it milky coffee in England."

"Why are you both looking at me like that?" said Alex.

"It's quite a treat, you know, Alex," said Eric. "You shouldn't waste it."

"What Eric said," said Brandon. And then he changed the subject. "Eric, do you think Mr. Hughes is related to Mrs. D?"

Eric shook his head. "I cannot think of how he could possibly be related to Granny."

"Maybe he could be an uncle, or a cousin?" Alex said.

"Granny never mentioned any relatives moving to America. Her father died when she was a teenager, and she had an unmarried aunt on her father's side, but she really didn't know her. I'm sorry, Brandon, but if you think Mr. Hughes is a clue to what we're doing here, think again. Hughes is a very common name, you know."

Frustrated, Brandon ground his foot against the floor. "I know it is, but we have to think of something. This place is creeping me out. I just want to figure out the mystery, then go."

Eric said, "You know, it's not that bad. I rather like Snipesville."

"That's because you're white," said Brandon sourly. "It's not the same place for me as it is for you."

"White privilege," Alex said suddenly, and Brandon nodded.

"What's that?" Eric said, puzzled.

"Something we've got, and Brandon doesn't," said Alex.

Eric looked embarrassed. "I'm terribly sorry," he said to Brandon. "It was a stupid thing to say. That was very inconsiderate of me."

Brandon gave him a wan smile. "You know what? The hardest thing about segregation for me is just trying not to deal with it. I hardly ever leave Miss Julia's house except to go to church. Reading is about the only thing stopping me from going stir-crazy. It's just good luck for me that Miss Julia has one of the best book collections in town. Apart from that, the only interesting thing to do is to think about how I can help Miss Julia's plans for the high school. Still, I need to get a job so I can make enough money to pay her some rent. But I'm pretty scared of spending more time out of the house, honestly, because then I'll be dealing with segregation all the time, all day and every day."

"Perhaps we can help you," Eric said. "I could have a word with Mr. Hughes. Perhaps he can engage you as a reporter of news among the colored people, or some such? Then you could at least work alongside us."

"Not happening," said Brandon. "Don't you get it, Eric? Good jobs go to whites. I bet even the folks who deliver *The Snipesville News* are white. Am I right?"

CHAPTER SEVEN

Eric had to admit that he was. Then he said, "Perhaps you could, perhaps, sweep the floors or something of that sort. At least we would all be together."

Brandon's face hardened. "So while you learn to be an accountant, and Alex is learning to be a reporter, I learn how to use a floor mop? No thanks." He got to his feet. "I'll keep looking for work. Thanks for the coffee, you guys. Go ahead and throw my cup in the trash, because if you don't, Mr. Duval will. They won't re-use a cup a black person drank out of. I guess I should go out by the back door, huh? Out into the alley like a good Negro."

As he turned to leave, Alex said, "Brandon, it's not our fault, what's happening. Don't blame us."

Brandon did not look back. He carried on walking. But as he reached the hotel lobby, he suddenly found himself flanked by Eric and Alex. Alex grabbed one arm, Eric grabbed the other, and they both walked with him toward the front door.

"We're coming with you," Alex said. "We're not gonna let you be alone in this. Introduce us to Miss Julia, oh, and I wanna meet R. H. Gordon. At least I'll find out if Shrupp did a good job of pretending to be him."

As they pushed through the doors to the Hotel Duval's front porch, Brandon, softening, protested mildly, "I can't take you guys to Miss Julia's. It's too dangerous for all of us."

"Nonsense," Eric said. "We're only paying a brief call."

Brandon looked doubtful. "You don't understand."

"No, probably not," Eric said firmly, tightening his grip on Brandon's arm. "But I would very much like to."

"Me, too," said Alex, and he let go of Brandon's arm, and slapped him on the back.

"Okay, I'll introduce you guys to Miss Julia and Robert," Brandon said, "But you have to call me George."

"George?" said Eric and Alex, and Alex added, "Again?"

"Yep," said Brandon. "I borrowed Dr. Braithwaite's name again. George Braithwaite, that's me."

Alex and Eric laughed, but their smiles faded when they noticed two white men staring at them. It was time to go.

They made an odd sight in Snipesville, Georgia, in 1906: A tall white guy, a short white guy, and a black kid, who walked and talked together as though they were equals. As they passed Elias Thomas Clark's blacksmith's shop, an old man sitting outside on a bench made from a log waved to them. The tall white man called out "Hello!" and the other two waved back politely. None of them

❖ 169 ❖

greeted him as "Uncle" or "Boy," which added to the strange impression they made. The old man smiled and nodded at this peculiar trio, and he continued to watch them as they walked by, especially the tall blond fellow.

Thomas Clark, the young blacksmith, came out into the sunlight, wiping off his hands on a towel, and stood next to the old man, watching the strangers walk away. "You recognize any of them, Thomas?"

Thomas squinted into the sunshine. The old man said, "I'm not sure. I didn't get a good look at them. Why?"

"No reason," said the old man.

"You all right, Uncle?"

The old man didn't mind the young man calling him Uncle because, after all, Thomas was his grand-nephew. "I'm fine, Thomas," he said. "But I just saw the strangest thing. I do believe I just saw a ghost."

Thomas burst into laughter. "It's 1906, Uncle. I don't believe there's ghosts."

"You would be surprised," the old man murmured. "I think so… Yes, you would, Thomas. You would be surprised."

Brandon knew that Miss Julia had to be amazed to find two white men on her front porch, but she didn't show it. Instead, she invited them politely into her parlor.

As Alex and Eric sat down on the sofa, Brandon watched Miss Julia struggle with what to say and do. Finally, she said, "Can I offer you gentlemen coffee?" They agreed to coffee, and Miss Julia called for Alberta. Even the normally taciturn Miss Alberta allowed her jaw to drop slightly at the sight of Eric and Alex.

While Miss Julia instructed Miss Alberta on the refreshments, Brandon saw Eric look around him at Miss Julia's heavy Victorian furniture, her dark wooden wall clock, her bookcase, her framed prints of flowers and maps, and under a glass dome, her creepy dried flower arrangement with a stuffed bird perched on a small branch. Brandon guessed that this was Eric's first visit to any American home, much less one in 1906.

Now there was an uncomfortable silence. Eric rubbed his hands together nervously. "I understand that, um, George is your lodger, Miss Russell?" he said to Miss Julia.

"In a manner of speaking, Mr. Powell," Miss Julia said politely. "George is presently my guest."

Brandon felt embarrassed. He was indeed a guest, and not a boarder, because he was staying for free. He had not yet found a job, and he couldn't pay Miss Julia any rent until he had money.

Eric cleared his throat. "Miss Russell, Mr. Day and I are staying at the Duval

Hotel, and it is rather expensive. We are now employed by *The Snipesville News*, and so we've been thinking that we ought to seek more suitable accommodation. I don't suppose you have other rooms for rent?"

Miss Julia looked at him with curiosity. "Mr. Powell, I do not have other rooms to rent, but even if I had … Forgive me for asking … Are you and Mr. Day aware that I am a Negro? My light complexion and Northern accent cause me to be taken for white, you see …"

Eric blushed furiously, and he looked confused as well as embarrassed. He clearly didn't know what to say, so Alex spoke for him. "Yes, we know you're black," he said. "Why? Aren't we allowed to live in a house with you?"

Brandon cringed at Alex's indelicacy, but he respected his honesty.

"I do not wish to put you to any inconvenience, gentlemen," Miss Julia said, "nor cause any harm to your reputation. I wanted to be sure that you're aware that you are being entertained in a colored home. I know that circumstances to do with race in England are not as they are here. Ah, Alberta, please put the coffee on the table. Do you gentlemen still wish to take coffee with me?"

Eric mumbled, "Of course, of course," but he was staring at Miss Julia, clearly trying to figure out how she was black.

Miss Julia poured coffee from a large silver pot. "Now, as I said, I cannot board you two gentlemen. However, a boardinghouse has opened near here, and I daresay the proprietress would welcome your enquiry. I will direct you."

"Thank you, Miss Russell," said Eric, quickly recovering the manners he had learned under Mrs. Devenish's stern tutelage. "That would be very good of you."

Just then, Robert appeared in the doorway, and Miss Julia introduced him to her guests. Alex beamed at this Snipesville celebrity returned from the dead, who did indeed look nothing like Cassius Shrupp. Seeing R. H. Gordon gave Alex an idea. "Miss Russell, Mr. Gordon, I have a question. Bran … I mean … George, he said you're trying to raise funds to build a high school. May I interview you for the newspaper?"

"Of course, sir," Robert said eagerly. He sat down, tugging at his pants legs, and then folded his hands in front of him, making ready for an interview. Miss Julia frowned at him.

Alex said hurriedly, "Of course, I shall have to write some questions first and then make an appointment to meet with you. Um, George? Can you take us to the boardinghouse?"

As Brandon, Eric, and Alex stood before the boarding house, Alex recognized it at once.

CHAPTER SEVEN

"It's Kintyre plantation house," he said. "I came here in 1851."

Brandon screwed up his eyes against the sun. "I bet if we dug around here, we would find evidence that this house is on the exact spot of the original Kintyre house where Hannah lived in 1752. I'm not making this up. Judging from how far this is from the top of the hill in downtown Snipesville, I think it's the exact same place."

Eric turned to Brandon. "I assume Georgia had slavery in 1752. That must have been a terrible time to be a colored person here, even worse than now."

Brandon hesitated. "Of course it was awful. But it still wasn't as bad as … Never mind."

Now Alex was startled. "Not as bad as *what?*" he said.

"Forget it," said Brandon, keen to get off the subject. "So, Alex," he said, "does the house look the same as fifty years ago?"

"More or less," said Alex. "It could use some new paint, but otherwise, this is pretty much what I remember."

"Do you know who owns it?" asked Brandon, as he led the way across the yard.

"Who owns it now, you mean? In 1906?" Alex said. "No. Why would I know that?"

Brandon knocked on the front door. It was answered by his great-great-grandmother, the wife of Elias Thomas Clark III. The young woman looked slightly alarmed to see two white men with Brandon on the doorstep. "Can I help you gentlemen?" she said to Alex and Eric.

"We're here about renting rooms," said Eric. "Have you any available?"

"Are you from England?" she replied. It was odd, Brandon thought, how she asked that question. She didn't seem to be asking out of curiosity, or because of Eric's accent. It was as though she had asked them for a secret password. And when Eric replied that he was from England, she invited them in.

As the little group followed Mrs. Clark into the parlor, Eric took off his hat, and nudged Alex to do the same. Brandon, hatless, closed the door behind them. He wrinkled his nose: The smell of kerosene lamps was obnoxious. "You gentlemen just go upstairs," said Mrs. Clark, pointing to a narrow stairwell. "The two rooms on the left of the hallway are available. And call if you need me. My name's Caroline."

As Brandon moved to follow his friends, Caroline stopped him with a hand to his chest, cornering him at the door. "I know you. You come to our church," she said. "First African Baptist Church."

"Yes, I do. And you're Caroline," Brandon said.

"To you, I'm Mrs. Clark," she said firmly. She ran her hand over her belly,

CHAPTER SEVEN

and Brandon, reminded that she was pregnant, remembered what was to become of mother and baby. He suddenly felt his eyes fill with tears.

"Are you unwell?" said Caroline.

"I'm sorry," he said, wiping his eyes with his sleeve. "I've got allergies ... Hay fever." He could hardly tell her the truth. He wondered again if he was here to prevent what would happen in 1906 from happening to Caroline. But he didn't want to think about that right now.

He and Caroline both looked up as they heard footsteps, and Alex and Eric emerged from the short staircase. Alex gazed forlornly at the spartan, low-ceilinged, and dimly-lit parlor, and sighed. Reluctantly, he said to Caroline, "We'll take the rooms, I guess."

"I'm going to miss the hotel," Alex complained, as he, Brandon, and Eric walked back toward Miss Julia's house and Snipesville.

"I bet," said Brandon, without sympathy. "You got used to all that luxury, huh? Hey, that reminds me ... I need you to check out some books for me at the new Carnegie library downtown."

"Why can't you borrow your own library books?" Alex said.

Brandon looked pityingly at him. "Because, genius, they don't allow black people in there. Miss Julia is really mad about it, and she's started a petition to open it up to us, but for now, we're shut out. Miss Julia needs all the books she can get. You don't stop learning new things if you're a good teacher."

"Wow, that's hard," said Alex. "Maybe I could borrow books for Miss Julia and R. H. Gordon?"

"Awesome," said Brandon. "Robert's a huge reader, too. How about we stop by the house on our way downtown, and ask them what they want?"

"Mr. Gordon ain't ... isn't here," Miss Alberta said when she answered the door.

Now Miss Julia was behind Miss Alberta at the door. "He's gone to the repair shop to ask if my buggy's ready. Would you like me to give him a message?"

"Where is the repair shop, ma'am?" Brandon asked.

"You know it, George. It's young Thomas Clark's blacksmith's shop. You really ought to meet Thomas properly. He's a very impressive young man." She turned to Alex and Eric. "Did you gentlemen meet Thomas's wife Caroline at the boardinghouse?"

"Yes, ma'am, we met her," Brandon said.

"And did you meet the proprietress?"

"Isn't Mrs. Clark the owner?" Alex said.

CHAPTER SEVEN

"Of course not," tutted Miss Julia. "I would hardly have recommended the place to two white gentlemen had that been the case. No, Mrs. Clark is the housekeeper. The owner is a white woman."

Alex asked if he could borrow books for Miss Julia from the library, but she looked worried. "I would prefer you wait until we see the success of our petition," she said, "and then we may borrow books for ourselves."

Although he didn't say so, Brandon had no faith in the success of Miss Julia's petition. He realized that he knew too much about the future, that things would get worse long before they got better.

Elias Thomas Clark III was in front of his workshop making repairs, but not to Miss Julia's buggy. He was instead busy under the hood of an open-top automobile. A ruddy-faced white man in his fifties, the car's owner, leaned on the side of the vehicle, clutching a brown glass bottle, and watching the mechanic at work.

Eric pointed to the white man's bottle. "Excuse me, I'm sorry to bother you, but is that beer? Where might I buy a beer in Snipesville?"

The man stood up straight. "Nowhere around here, sir," he said with a smile. "You must be a stranger. Snipesville is a dry town, and this is a soda."

Thomas popped his head round the side of the car hood. "Be with you gentlemen shortly," he said to Alex and Eric. He didn't look at Brandon. Brandon couldn't help noticing how even black people ignored him when he was with Alex and Eric.

"Would you gentlemen care for a soda?" the white man said. "I have some more in the trunk, still cold."

"Don't drink it," Alex whispered to Eric and Brandon out of the corner of his mouth.

"Why not?" said Brandon.

"It's got drugs in it," Alex muttered.

"Coca, you mean?" said Brandon quietly. "No, I went to a museum in Atlanta, and they said all the drugs were taken out of it by now. I think."

"Good thing," Alex said. "Look at Eric."

Eric, who could not resist sugar in any form, was already chugging down a soda. The white man handed another bottle to Alex.

"Do you have any more?" said Alex, indicating Brandon.

"For your servant?" said the white man. "Sure." He handed a bottle to Brandon, who glowered at him.

Just then a tremulous voice called out, "You got one more bottle for me, sir?"

Everyone turned to look at the old dark-skinned man sitting on the bench in front of the workshop, leaning on his walking stick.

"Sure, uncle," the white man said, and he opened a bottle for him.

The old man took a swig, and smacked his lips. "Sure is refreshing," he said. "Thank you, sir."

Brandon cringed throughout this little scene. It took all his self-control not to say something. When white people called old black men "uncle," it was a put-down, a condescending leftover from slavery. The white man was old enough to have been a slave owner, and the old man was old enough to have been his slave, which might explain, Brandon thought, why he was acting so humbly. Either way, it was embarrassing and degrading.

Eric apparently hadn't noticed any of this. He raised his bottle, and said, "Thank you again for the drink, Mr. … um …"

"Doctor Asa Hunslow, sir. And you are?"

"Powell," Eric said, and Alex noticed how he no longer hesitated when giving his new name. "Mr. Eric Powell, and this is Mr. Alexander Day. We're visiting … Well, not exactly visiting, since we both live in Snipesville now." He did not introduce Brandon, and Brandon could have kicked him.

"New to town, eh?" Dr. Hunslow said cheerfully. "Like a lot of folks these days. Not that I mind, of course, because more citizens means more patients for my hospital."

"I hear you're building a bigger hospital, Doctor," said Thomas. "You going to treat Negroes, sir?"

"Well, sure," the doctor said uneasily, and then, with exaggerated enthusiasm, "One of these days, I'm gonna have a ward for you people, with colored nurses."

"But no Negro doctors, huh?" Thomas said carefully. He moved out from behind the car, and wiped his oily hands on a tattered rag, before tossing it back on its hook on the workshop's outer wall.

Brandon was amazed by his ancestor's outspokenness. He didn't think black people in 1906 dared to challenge white people. Maybe they normally didn't, he thought. Maybe Thomas was taking a huge risk.

But Dr. Hunslow gave a short laugh, and he clapped Thomas on the back. "Might be one day, we'll see," he said. "I hear you people have hopes for a Negro high school. Whatever next?"

Thomas said nothing, but turned to Alex and Eric. "Now, how can I help you gentlemen?"

"Actually, we're looking for Robert Gordon," said Alex.

"Oh, he came by here already," said Thomas. "But that buggy ain't ready, so he went into town on another errand. If you wait here a spell, you might catch him on his way back." Now he looked at Brandon. "Hey, you're the young man called George who used to live in England, ain't you? You come to our church. You're staying with Miss Russell, ain't that right?" Now he turned and looked at Eric and Alex, "Oh, hey, are you gentlemen from England, too?"

"That's right," said Eric. "Well, I am, anyway."

"How about that! What do you make of this, Doctor?" Thomas turned to Dr. Hunslow.

"I say it's not the Yankees who're invading Snipesville," the doctor said with a smile. "The British are coming!"

"I used to live in England," said the old man on the bench. Everyone turned to stare at him.

"What's that you say, uncle?" said Dr. Hunslow. "You sure you don't have that confused?"

"No, sir," the old man said calmly. "I was in England."

"Were you now," said Dr. Hunslow, clearly skeptical. He turned back to Thomas. "Send for me when the car is ready. I'm proud of my little jalopy, but I think a trip to Savannah was a little too much for her."

"Would you like me to run you into town on my buggy, sir?" said Thomas.

"No, Thomas, that won't be necessary. It's only up the hill." Turning back to Eric and Alex, the doctor said, "Good day to you, gentlemen." He still ignored Brandon.

After the doctor was gone, Brandon said to Thomas, "So you fix cars? I thought you were a blacksmith."

"I *am* a blacksmith," said Thomas, "But I reckon the horses will all be retired someday soon." He pointed over his head, and Brandon saw the new wooden slate on which was scrawled *"Auto-Repair."*

Thomas continued, "Only two automobiles in Snipesville yet. Mr. Hughes owns the other, and he pays a Savannah mechanic to take the train here. But Dr. Hunslow said it's cheaper and easier for him if I learn automobile repair, so he bought me some books, and I've been studying them."

"Dr. Hunslow seems to like you," Brandon said disapprovingly.

"Yes, he has kind of what you might call a sentimental attachment to my mother's family," Thomas said with a shrug. "My grandparents were his house slaves. But I don't depend on him for all my business. I already heard that more gentlemen in Snipesville are planning to buy cars. So I am hoping one day to move my shop into downtown Snipesville. That way, they won't have to drive back up the hill and test my repair job too soon." He chuckled to himself.

"Will you sell cars, too?" Brandon said.

Thomas considered this. "Maybe," he said. "But that's expensive to set up in business, and I don't have the money, nor credit. Anyhow, I reckon it's a matter of time before the Snipesville Buggy Company starts selling automobiles, and I'm not sure white folks would buy a car from a Negro when they can buy from a white man. No, I just want to fix cars, like I fix buggies and bicycles. That should be a very good business indeed."

Brandon felt proud to be descended from this savvy and ambitious man. But a thought kept niggling at him, the thought that Thomas was not being allowed to be *too* ambitious. He said, casually, "Don't you think you should leave Snipesville? You know, seek your fortunes somewhere better?"

"Why would I do that?" said Thomas, but he didn't seem sure. He sounded, Brandon thought, almost like he had to persuade himself. "I got my family here, and my wife's, too. This is our home. People say things have got worse again for colored folk these last few years, but I don't remember what it was like in Reconstruction times, when they say things were better, so I don't know about that."

Behind him, the old man snorted. "You oughta listen, Thomas. I'll tell you."

"So you say, Uncle," said Thomas, giving him a smile before returning his attention to Brandon. "I reckon there's enough opportunity in Snipesville, if you know where to look."

While Brandon was chatting with Thomas, Eric approached the old man on the bench, and said in the friendly but patronizing voice that young people often use with old people, "So where did you live in England, sir?"

"Oh, here and there, sir," the old man said vaguely. "Just here and there, yes, sir."

"That's nice," Eric said awkwardly.

But the old man really wasn't paying attention to Eric. He called out to Alex. "You believe in ghosts, sir?"

"Maybe," said Alex. "Why?"

"You look like one to me, sir. You know why?"

"No," said Alex, embarrassed by this odd conversation. "I don't."

"Me, neither," said the old man, and he gave a toothless laugh. "Me, neither."

Hearing the word "ghost," Brandon glanced curiously at the old man. Thomas saw the question on Brandon's face. "That's my great-uncle," Thomas sighed. "He's my grandfather's older brother, and he's kind of a character. He was a slave, but he ran away from Kintyre plantation. He tells people he ran all the way to England, but I don't believe it. He married a white woman in New York, and they came back here after the War, right when Reconstruction started and things looked like they might get better. I think he was crazy to come back, but he said he always promised to come home to Snipes County.

CHAPTER SEVEN

But when he got here, even my grandfather hardly knew his brother, because he was born after Uncle Jupiter left Georgia …"

"Wait," said Brandon, feeling a rush of adrenaline. "What did you say his name was?"

"My grandfather? Elias Thomas Clark …"

"No," Brandon said urgently, "your great-uncle. His name is Jupiter?"

"That's right," said Thomas. "Jupiter Gordon. He stuck with the name of the white folks who once owned our family, while my grandfather chose a new name, Clark, like a lot of folks did after slavery."

"Excuse me," said Brandon. He ran over to Alex, and grabbed him by the shoulder. "You are so not going to believe this," he said quietly. "The old guy? It's Jupiter. It's Jupe."

Alex whirled around to look at Jupiter, who smiled back at him. Could this old man really be Jupe, the teenage runaway slave who had been his companion in 1851? He called over, "Sir, your name is Jupiter?" he said. "Jupe?"

"That's right," Jupe said agreeably.

"And you lived in England? You remember where?"

"Here and there," said Jupe with a smile. "Here and there, yes, sir."

Brandon was at Alex's side now. "He won't tell you because you're white, remember?" he murmured. "Let me talk to him."

Alex nodded, and turned to watch Thomas working on Miss Julia's buggy.

"So your name is Jupiter, sir?" Brandon said.

"That's right," he replied. "But I'm Mr. Gordon to you, son." In an instant, the old man had changed from a cagey and smiling old fool to a real person. Brandon already knew why. Jupiter could not trust white people. He had to act like a demented old man around them. His pretending was really self-preservation.

"Yes, sir," Brandon said. "May I ask, Mr. Gordon, where did you live in England?"

"Several places," said the old man, "But the first place was a big old plantation house."

Brandon knew that there were no plantation houses in England, not exactly, but he knew what Jupe meant. "And where was that? Do you remember, sir?"

"Oh, sure, of course I do," said Jupe. "I just reckoned you wouldn't know it, but I hear you're from England, is that right? It was called Balesworth Hall, near London. I was a servant there for a very short time, but the English lady who hired me paid my passage back to America. So I went to live with my Aunt Betsy and Uncle Joseph Russell in Massachusetts."

Now Brandon was even more excited. He had figured out a long time ago that he was related to Jupe, but surely this meant … "You're related to Miss Julia Russell?"

"Of course I am," said the old man. "She's my cousin. I lived with her and my aunt and uncle until I was 21, first in Massachusetts, and then in upstate New York, when Uncle Joseph took a job preaching there. Then, after the War, everything seemed to be looking up in the South, so I decided to make good on my promise to my Daddy that I would come home. By then, I was married, so my wife and I sold up our little grocery store and came down here. My wife Wilhelmina, she was a white woman. She was a lot younger than me, and we used to joke about how we were already related, because her mother was a Gordon, too."

Brandon found this jarring. *Another* Gordon who was related to him? This one white?

Jupe continued. "Now Wilhelmina, she wasn't happy in Georgia, especially after the Reconstruction ended. We led a quiet life, because we was afraid we would be prosecuted for being married. But it was hard for us to leave, what with our family here and all, and we couldn't afford to move back to New York. Anyhow, Wilhelmina died in childbed. It's been more than twenty years."

"I'm so sorry," Brandon said, and he meant it.

Jupe nodded and gave a small smile. "I'm all right. I got my brother Elias Clark and my cousin Julia Russell here. When Miss Russell told me at the end of the War that she wanted to start a school in the South, I asked her to come to Snipesville. My daddy, Jupiter Senior, lived long enough to see her start her school. He said it was the best day of his life."

Out of the corner of his eye, Brandon could see Alex listening to the conversation. He was glad. Alex needed to hear this.

Jupe continued his story. "I joined my brother Elias Clark, Thomas's grandfather, in this blacksmith shop. I took care of the business side. We had a lot of customers after slavery ended. White men remembered our father, Jupiter, because he was respected. He was the only black overseer in charge of a plantation in these parts, you know. Blacksmithing was a good trade, and for my nephew, too, but he's right to be learning about motor cars. Times are changing, sure enough. I sure hope Miss Julia's high school gets built, because we need somewhere to educate our children, although I expect my own son thinks he's too good to teach in it …"

Brandon's ears perked up again. But before he could ask Jupe about his son, Jupe said, "Say, who's that tall white man you're with?"

"That's Alex," said Brandon. "Alex Day."

"That can't be," Jupiter exclaimed. "Either he's a ghost, or I knew his grand-

CHAPTER SEVEN

daddy." Brandon said nothing. It was probably simpler to let Jupe think that Alex was his own grandson. It was easier than convincing the old man of the existence of time travel.

Now Robert Gordon walked toward them, and Jupe called out amiably, "Afternoon, son."

Brandon and Alex were astonished. "Robert Gordon is Jupe's *son*?" Alex squeaked.

Robert nodded curtly in greeting to his elderly father, looking embarrassed by him. Then he said to his cousin, "Have you had time to finish work on Aunt Julia's buggy?" Thomas glanced at Robert with disdain, and Brandon saw immediately that the two cousins did not get along.

"No, it's not ready," Thomas said abruptly. "Anyway, like I told you, it just needs a little tightening here and there, that's all. You could have done the job yourself."

Did Brandon hear a slight sneer in Thomas's voice as he spoke to Robert? If so, Robert Gordon ignored Thomas's jibe.

Now Brandon remembered why they were there. "Robert? Alex … Mr. Day has offered to check out some books from the Carnegie library for us. Did you want to make a list?"

Robert's face lit up, and he thanked Alex profusely. Thomas, meanwhile, watched the scene impassively from the shadow of the automobile.

Standing in the stacks of the Snipesville Carnegie Library, Alex peered at two lists. One was for Robert Gordon. It was long and detailed, carefully written out in Robert's elegant handwriting. The other, Brandon's list, was scrawled and brief. It read, *Anything that doesn't look boring.*

No question, Robert's list had been easier to handle, even though it was long. The card catalog made it simple for Alex to discover that only one of the books Robert had requested was in the library, and it was a novel. He drew a blank on the scholarly works on Robert's lengthy list.

But Brandon's apparently simple request was anything but. Alex spent a long time browsing, agonizing over the small library collection, before he finally found something he hoped Brandon might enjoy.

When he returned outside, he found Brandon alone. "Eric went back to the office," he said.

"Okay," Alex said. "Here." He tried to give Brandon's book to him, but Brandon quickly pushed it away, looking around to be sure that nobody had seen Alex offering him a book. Then, quick as a flash, he said loudly, "May I carry those for you, sir?"

CHAPTER SEVEN

"What?" Alex said. And then he figured it out, and said loudly, "Oh, um, sure. You may carry my books. If you insist."

"I do," Brandon said emphatically.

As soon as they were on the road to the west of town, walking toward Miss Julia's and the boardinghouse, Brandon took a good look at the red-covered volume Alex had chosen for him. *"The Hound of the Baskervilles?"* he said dubiously. "A Sherlock Holmes novel?"

"Best I could do," said Alex. "It was either Conan Doyle or Charles Dickens. I never heard of most of the other authors, and they looked pretty awful."

Brandon flipped through the book. "Thanks, anyway," he said. "I never read Sherlock Holmes before. I might as well start now. It's not like I have anything better to do."

"Miss Julia has a lot of books," Alex said. "I saw them in the parlor. You read all of those?"

"They're mostly theology, you know, books on religion," Brandon said, "and they are really hard to understand."

Alex smiled. "Miss Julia is bound to show off the serious books in the parlor, so people admire her learning and good taste. But I bet she has trashy novels somewhere. Why don't you ask her?"

"That thumping sound you hear?" Brandon said with a chuckle, "That's me kicking myself. You're a genius."

Eric found Mr. Hughes alone at the office, reading a British newspaper. "Is that *The Times?*" he said, puffing out a cloud of cigarette smoke. "However did you arrange for it to be delivered to America?"

"It's from a fortnight ago," said Mr. Hughes. "A friend in London sends it me occasionally. Would you like me to pass it along to you?"

"Thank you, sir," Eric said. "I do need to catch up with the news from England." That's when he remembered that the news would, for him, be almost a half-century out of date.

"It is odd not to know what is happening at home, isn't it?" Mr. Hughes said.

"Indeed, sir," Eric sympathized, and then he took another puff of his cigarette. "I hope you don't mind my asking, Mr. Hughes, but how do you fit in here? I feel like a fish out of water. It's jolly difficult to persuade local people to talk to me at all."

Mr. Hughes looked very pleased to be asked. "Powell, I will confess that I enjoy certain advantages. For one thing, I am a Master Mason. I joined Snipes Lodge 202 of the Free and Accepted Masons. I am aware you are not a freemason, but you should apply. You will find that freemasonry confers many benefits upon men of business. I also don't mind confessing to you that I brought capital from London …"

"Capital?" said Eric. "Oh! You mean money."

"Yes," said Mr. Hughes, who evidently did not like being interrupted. "I also brought knowledge and business relationships that allowed me to attract more investment in Snipesville from as far away as London. By persuading the railroad company to run trains through Snipesville, I guaranteed the city's prosperity. But my masterstroke was becoming a member of Snipesville's First Baptist Church."

"Gosh, are you a Baptist, sir?" Eric was genuinely surprised.

"Of course I wasn't when I arrived," said Mr. Hughes. "I was a member of the Church of England. But had I remained so, I should not have forged such strong relationships with men of influence in Snipesville. Powell, you're a clever young man, and I would like to help you rise. But it has not escaped notice that you never attend church."

Eric, who was not a keen churchgoer, grew flustered. "Ah, well, yes, sir, well, you see, my mother is always nagging me to go to church, but …"

"You have no need to make excuses," said Mr. Hughes. "But I strongly suggest that you join First Baptist Church. Perhaps there you will find yourself a suitable wife, as I have done."

"Mrs. Hughes is from Snipesville, is she?" said Eric, flicking ash into the trash can.

"What do you mean by that?" Mr. Hughes said sharply.

Eric couldn't imagine how he had offended his boss. Perhaps Mr. Hughes had misheard? "Your wife. You said she is a local lady."

"Oh! Yes, I see. She is indeed. She was the widow of an eminent farmer in Snipes County, and she is in her own right a prominent member of local society. As chairman of the United Daughters of the Confederacy in Snipesville, she has promoted the planting of a Confederate memorial statue on the courthouse square."

Eric tried to make a mental note of everything Mr. Hughes had told him, not because he wanted to take his advice and settle in Snipesville, but because he wanted to repeat all of it to Alex. What Mr. Hughes had said probably wasn't important, Eric thought. But then again, from what Alex had told him, returning home would require both of them to play the detective. It was very important that no possible clue be left unexamined.

On his way into the boardinghouse, Alex met Mrs. Clark on her way out, wearing an enormous hat. She must have caught his questioning look, because she said, "I'm late to church. But the proprietress, she's here, if you need anything."

With that she quickly crossed the front yard, clutching her hat to her head, and leaving Alex to wonder who the "proprietress" was. He didn't have to wonder long. As he closed the front door behind him, he heard a slow, steady creaking from the room next to the parlor.

"Hello?" he called out nervously.

"Come in," said a woman's voice. When he opened the door, he wasn't entirely surprised by what, or rather who, he saw.

"Hi, Alex," the Professor said. She was spinning cotton, standing at an enormous wheel. "You look very grown-up, I must say."

"Thank you," said Alex.

"You're welcome. I'm your landlady. Did you remember I own Kintyre?"

"Actually, I did forget that," Alex said.

"This house is a bit of a wreck," said the Professor, "but I'm hiring some local people to help me get it back into shape. I have to keep that quiet, though. I don't think the local white tradesmen would be too happy to know that I hired black tradesmen to fix the place up. They don't want competition. They want all the money to come to them. That's really what racism is about, you see. It's not about skin color, and it's not about innate differences among human beings, which is nonsense. It's not even about different cultures. It's about money. People don't understand that, or they refuse to believe it, but there you have it. So I have hired Mr. Early from Savannah to fix the leaky roof, and I am paying him quite a lot of money to take on a Snipesville lad as his apprentice, a kid named James Shrupp."

"James Shrupp?" Alex said. "Any relation to the city councilman, Mr. Shrupp?"

"Of course they're related," said the Professor, "But James is a great kid. Why should I hold the poor boy responsible for his descendant, the obnoxious Cassius?"

But Alex had a worrying thought. "Hey, if James Shrupp likes Savannah, maybe he'll stay there, and Cassius Shrupp won't even come to Snipesville. Won't that mess things up?"

"No," said the Professor, "Won't happen. It's in the documents, you see, all of it. I'm just playing my part. And the Roofing Shrupps, as people call them, will be well known in Snipes County, right into the 21st century. They do great work, and it all starts with James. By the way, Cassius embarrasses the family. They can't stand him. They were all relieved when he bought a carwash instead of joining them in the roofing trade. Anyhow … I have chicken pot pie with biscuits in the oven for you and Eric."

Alex hoped the Professor knew how to cook. "I thought your maid would do all the cooking," he said.

"Caroline isn't my maid," said the Professor. "She's my assistant. We do the cooking and cleaning together, and she also helps with some of my historical research. Right now, she's transcribing some documents that I know will otherwise, um, *go missing* in the 20th century. They will disappear because what they say becomes inconvenient to powerful people in Snipesville. Oh, and do know that although Caroline knows I'm not really a boardinghouse keeper, she doesn't know about the time travel. She thinks I'm a professor who works with Dr. Du Bois at Atlanta University. She thinks you two are my associates, working undercover. She's sworn to secrecy."

Alex looked at her doubtfully. "Professor, why are we in Snipesville in 1906?"

"I can't tell you, Alex. That's not the way it works. You must try your very best to understand what's going on around you, and then you will know what to do when you see it. Or perhaps not. But if I tell you too much, it will mess things up, I promise."

"That's all you can tell me?"

The only sound in reply was the whirr and creak of the spinning wheel.

"Okay," Alex said finally. "But at least tell me about Hannah. Is she okay?"

"Oh, Hannah," said the Professor with a smile, "She's a completely different story."

Returning to Kintyre, Eric found Alex using a pair of tongs and a folded dishtowel to take a chicken pot pie out of the range oven. As they prepared to eat, Alex told him about the Professor, and what she had said about Hannah.

Eric sat down at the dining room table, exhaled a stream of cigarette smoke, and grinned. "How splendid that Hannah is with Granny! And what I would give to meet Granny when she was a girl. I bet she was a force to be reckoned with, even then. You know, I'm sorry I didn't get to meet your professor, but I'm delighted to hear she's turned up again."

"Why are you so happy?" Alex said, confused.

"It's obvious, young Alex," said Eric. "It confirms that we're not here by accident, or by ourselves. Things will be fine."

But Alex was determined to set his friend straight. "You don't get it," he said bluntly. "Just because she shows up doesn't mean everything is fine. We don't even know who she is, not really, and she never, ever gives us a straight answer. So if you think our problems are over, you're wrong. We don't even know why we're here, and I bet our problems are just starting." By the time he ended this speech, Alex realized he was shouting. He had shocked himself: He hadn't realized how stressed out he was.

Eric opened and closed his mouth wordlessly, like a goldfish, and then swallowed. "I see," he said, although it was clear to Alex that he didn't see, not really. "Well," he said, nodding at the pie, "At least she made us supper."

Despite himself, Alex had to laugh at this.

Alex laid down his knife and fork on his empty plate. Eating a good meal had made him feel better about everything, and he had had time to think. "I'm not sure what we're supposed to do," he said, "but maybe we are supposed to help Brandon, Mr. Gordon and Miss Russell set up the school."

"I see no harm in that," said Eric. "What do you have in mind?"

"Well, I can interview Mr. Gordon like I promised."

"Yes, good," said Eric. "And?"

"And apart from that," Alex said. "I have no clue. That's what worries me. It's almost like I'm not supposed to be here."

Wednesday, February 7, 1906

Carefully, Brandon placed a bookmark in *The Hound of the Baskervilles,* and laid it down on Miss Julia's sofa.

"This is the hardest thing I've ever done, being here," he said. "I'm proud to be black, but it's never easy, and here, it's just a nightmare. Going through tough times in our last journeys was nothing compared to this. Here, it feels like so many people are trying to make me feel like I'm worthless."

"It's not worse than 1851," Alex said, jealously eying Brandon's book.

"How would you know, Alex?" Brandon said bitterly. He resented that Alex had ignored his complaint, and that he was looking enviously at his book.

"Because I was in Georgia with Jupe in 1851, remember?"

"I know," Brandon said. "And we were both here in 1752, and that was awful, too. But . . . Look, would you stop looking at my book like all I do is read, okay?"

Brandon was exhausted, and feeling on edge all the time had left him with a short fuse. He was running out of patience with his friend, who seemed to understand little and care less about what he was going through. "Alex, please try to understand. You can go for a sandwich when you want to, and do a job that's interesting. I can't. I can't go anywhere without being careful not to look at white people the wrong way. I can't find a job. The only job I've heard about so far was a gig processing sugar cane, but Miss Julia wouldn't let me apply, because she said I could get my arm ripped off. She also won't hear of me picking cotton, or making turpentine. So I don't have any money to pay her rent, or do anything, and even if I did, nothing much in town is open to black folks. That's why I stay here and read. It keeps me busy, and gets me out of my head."

"Can I help?" Alex said, and pulled out his wallet.

But Brandon held up his hand. "No, I appreciate it, but I don't want your money. Don't you get it? I feel ashamed to have to depend on you for something as basic as going to the library, or buying a soda. My problem isn't the money itself. It's about Snipesville constantly eating away at me, at my self-respect. If I didn't have the black community, I would fall apart. I mean, you know, that we come back to the 21st century looking physically like nothing happened, but inside . . . "

"Please," Alex said desperately, wanting Brandon to stop talking, and to let him help, somehow. He held out five crisp one-dollar bills. "Take it. I didn't earn this money through work. It's money I found in my clothes when I got here. It's yours." Brandon took the cash. "Thanks," he said. "I'll set it by for later."

"I thought you needed it for rent or a soda?" Alex said.

"Now you're telling me what to do with the money?" Brandon snapped. Then he forced himself to calm down. "Look, I'll buy a treat with it, and give most of the rest to Miss Julia. But there's another problem. It's killing me, but I'm going to have to leave Miss Julia's, anyway. She and Robert Gordon are going to Macon next week, and Robert hinted they don't want to leave me alone in the house. I'm still a stranger to them, and I don't blame them if they're worried I might rob them while they're gone, or whatever's worrying them."

"I get it, but, hey, just wondering, why are they going to Macon? What's in Macon?"

"I don't know about the 21st century. But this is the early 20th century, and Robert says Macon has a big and important black community. The Georgia Equal Rights Convention is happening there. Lots of important people are going, even W. E. B. Du Bois."

Alex looked blank, and then he said. "Du Bois? The Black History Month guy, right?"

Brandon mentally face-palmed himself, then said sarcastically, "Yes, Alex. The Black History Month guy."

"That's cool," said Alex, trying to sound excited.

"Yes, it is," said Brandon. "But I'm not invited. So I might have to go find a job and someplace to live in Savannah."

"Does that mean it's going to take longer for us to get home?" Alex said, looking downcast.

CHAPTER SEVEN

"Not everything is about us getting home."

"It is for me. Nobody asked if I wanted to do any of this."

"Excuse me while I interrupt your self-pity," Brandon said angrily. "But I want to make a difference here, because this is my town, and my family, and my life. And how do you think it makes me feel when I have to pretend to be your servant to do anything? When I have to go to the back doors of white businesses to get served, and still get treated like garbage, even while they take my money? When the only way to get money is do a dangerous job, or beg from you? I'm seriously thinking I might not leave here alive. I mean, how do you think that feels?"

"Pretty bad," said Alex. "I know how it felt last time."

"I know," Brandon said with a sigh. "Look, Alex, I know we're in way over our heads with the time travel. But I want to try to do something, to fix something in Snipesville now, in 1906, so people don't have to wait a hundred years or more for things to change. If there's any chance I can help, I'm taking it." Suddenly, he sat up, a light in his eyes. "Wait ... I can't believe I didn't think of this. I don't have to go to Savannah. I'm going to use your money, and tag along with Miss Julia and Robert to the Equal Rights Convention in Macon. I'm going to ask Dr. Du Bois to help get money to build the high school. I bet he would love the idea of a real high school. He's all about black kids getting a real education, and learning science, and English, and math, and history, not just training for some lowly job."

"But if you start meeting famous people, won't you change history?" Alex said.

"I don't know, and I don't care," said Brandon. "I'm doing what I know I'm supposed to be doing. Isn't that what the Professor always tells us we should do?"

"Yes, but did you tell her what you plan to do? How do you know this is your mission?"

Brandon couldn't lie. "No, I didn't tell her," he said. "I prayed about it. That's how I know."

Alex was embarrassed. He wasn't very religious, and never knew what to say when Brandon mentioned prayer. "So what are *we* supposed to be doing? Me and Eric, I mean? Can't we help? We want to."

"Maybe," Brandon said. "I don't know. Maybe you should pray about it, too. Do what you think is best. But I don't think I can work together with you guys. I'm sorry. Not here, not now."

"But why?" Alex said plaintively.

Finally, Brandon exploded. "Because being with white people is a pain!"

The shocked silence hung heavily in the room.

CHAPTER SEVEN

Brandon felt sick. He had not meant to say that. He had meant to say that for the three of them to work together would be hard in the middle of a segregated Snipesville. What he had said was honest, but it was not what he had meant to say. "It's not you, Alex. It's not personal. It's history. It's this place. It's 1906. It's really getting to me."

Alex put a hand on Brandon's shoulder. He was almost in tears. "Please let me try to help, Brandon."

"I don't know what you can do, Alex," Brandon said, shaking his head. "You and Eric need to figure it out. It's not for me to decide. I'm not you. I've never felt so strongly that this time, each of us, you, me, and Hannah, we're on our own in figuring things out for ourselves."

Chapter 8:
BECOMING ACQUAINTED

Monday, October 2, 1905

Hannah woke up knowing that she could not, would not, abandon Verity Powell. She would not stand by and allow her friend to return to a 1951 in which she did not exist. Verity might not be an important person in history, Hannah thought, *but she's my friend, and she doesn't deserve that.* Hannah would find Tom Devenish. She would persuade Elizabeth to marry Tom. She would do these things, and she would do them soon. Somehow.

As soon as Mrs. Morris arrived in the morning, her junior maid began to pepper her with questions. She was not pleased.

"I told you, May. I ain't never heard of no Tom Devenish," Mrs. Morris muttered. "Why do you keep asking?"

Hannah hadn't counted on that question. "No reason," she said.

"He's not a lad, is he, May?"

"He's a boy, yeah," said Hannah.

"Now you know the rules," Mrs. Morris warned her. "No followers, and that's that. If you want to court a young man, you best meet him at home in Balesworth. There's not a respectable house in all of England where the mistress will tolerate servants' followers. And don't think I don't know you have a friend who works at Mr. Baker's shop, but he's a soft man, is Mr. Baker, allowing you two to stand there yapping. Don't you get your friend in trouble with your gossiping, my girl. I'm not sure I should put up with your dilly-dallying there, neither."

"How did you know I talk with Verity?" Hannah said with a frown.

"There's not much happens on this street that I don't know about," Mrs. Morris said.

"Well, in that case," said Hannah, "if you hear anything about Thomas Devenish, will you let me know?"

"You're a cheeky one!" said Mrs. Morris. "Now, aren't you supposed to be doing your work?"

Hannah pouted. "Oh, right. Flora asked me to trade places with her today, so I guess I better go dust the drawing room."

Mrs. Morris gave her a stern but fond look. "Yes, May, I suppose you better ought."

As Hannah dusted, she saw that a fat book had fallen onto the floor behind a small tea table that stood against the wall. Fishing it out, she saw the title: *KELLY'S DIRECTORY OF HERTFORDSHIRE 1904*. Intrigued, she leafed through the pages. It was like an old-fashioned telephone book, except without telephone numbers. She looked up Balesworth: *Miss Smith, Lime Street*, she read. *Rev. M. Jones, Rectory, St. Swithins*. She was excited to see the name of Brandon's old boss from 1915, *Mr. R. Gordon, Dental Surgeon, 57, High Street, Balesworth*. She even spotted Elizabeth's mentor, *Mrs. Lewis, Oaks Lodge, Balesworth*. But nobody by the name of Devenish was listed as living in Balesworth. Hannah, desperately wishing she had internet access, went page by page through the directory, checking town after town, but no Devenish was listed as living anywhere in the entire county of Hertfordshire. Hearing Flora's footsteps coming downstairs, Hannah quickly shoved the directory back behind the table, feeling very discouraged.

Tuesday, October 4, 1905

If there had been such a thing as an online meeting in 1905, Hannah thought, she would probably never have escaped from Willowbank. So there were some good things about not having computers, because she was on her way to an actual, real-life meeting. She was walking with Verity under overcast skies, following Elizabeth Hughes through Balesworth to Mrs. Lewis's house. Elizabeth was several yards ahead, a bag of paperwork slung over her shoulder.

"My goodness, look at Granny go," Verity said quietly. "She's charging ahead of us as usual, just like when we were children."

"Yeah, I don't get why she does that," Hannah said sharply. "We're not kids anymore. Isn't she being kind of rude, not walking with us?"

"Perhaps, but, you see, we're still not her equals. We're a maid and a shop-

CHAPTER EIGHT

girl," said Verity. "I hate to say it, but despite her best efforts, Elizabeth's a snob. It's just how people are in 1905, I suppose. Granny is still the tiniest bit snobby in 1951, although she would be very cross to hear me say it. She won't admit that the reason she doesn't like so many people coming to live in New Balesworth is because they're working class. Don't think too ill of her, though, for we have to take her age into account, and now you see the times in which she grew up. Many of us younger folk think differently in 1951. Heavens, even Granny has changed. The War had an enormous effect on how we all think. Eric, especially, has helped my family see the world through the eyes of working-class people. And who would have dreamt before the War that we would have elected a Labour government? I certainly would never have imagined that Granny would have voted for it. Although she does miss Mr. Churchill, and I expect she'll vote Conservative at the next election."

Hannah didn't have a clue about politics, so she kept quiet. Verity continued. "I must say, I am looking forward to Mrs. Lewis's meeting. How exciting to witness history! We shall see women gathered together to demand the vote for themselves. I wonder whether Mrs. Lewis ever invites famous speakers? Oh, how I should love to hear Emmeline Pankhurst. She was apparently an extraordinary lecturer. So was her daughter, Christabel, although I read recently, in 1951 that is, that Christabel has now joined a peculiar American religion and lives in California."

Hannah was hardly listening, because she something Verity had said had given her an idea. "So, your granny's little dog Emmeline is named for ..."

"Emmeline Pankhurst, yes," said Verity. "It was Granny's joke, you see, naming a silly miniature spaniel after Mrs. Pankhurst. If Mrs. Pankhurst were to be reborn as a dog, the *last* sort of dog she would be is a miniature spaniel."

Hannah laughed. "So you think Mrs. Pankhurst should have been a pit bull?"

"I have no idea what sort of dog that is," she said. "It must be American. Is it very fierce?"

"Very," said Hannah.

The moment Hannah saw Oaks Lodge, she recognized it as Mrs. Lewis's house. She had visited it a few months earlier, during World War II, and it looked little different in 1905. She also knew the cottage next door, and she nudged Verity, saying, "Hey, there's Mrs. Smith's place."

"What a hoot!" Verity said. "I wonder if she already lives there? We ought to chuck another stone through her window, dreadful woman." She giggled.

"Not funny, Verity," Hannah said sourly. For Verity, the stone-throwing incident was an amusing memory. For Hannah, it was painfully recent history.

CHAPTER EIGHT

"Don't be a bore, Hannah," Verity said. "How can I be sensible? Everything feels like a very peculiar dream. You look like you're my age, when really, you're the same age you were in 1940. Granny is younger than I am now. And all three of us are on our way to see Mrs. Lewis in 1905. It's absolutely batty." She laughed again.

Hannah gave Verity's arm a hard pinch.

"Ow, what was that for?" Verity said.

"See? That hurt. It's real," said Hannah. "Now promise me you won't say anything stupid at the meeting."

"I can't promise that," Verity said, trying not to laugh.

"No, I mean it. This is important, Verity. We don't want to mess up and do the wrong thing."

"But how will we know what the wrong thing is?" Verity said, suddenly serious.

"That's the problem," Hannah said. "I'm not sure. But don't do anything obviously stupid. This time travel? It's real. It matters. It can change things. We've got a part to play."

"Indeed," said Verity. "Although it would be helpful if we knew what our lines were."

Around three dozen people were crammed into Mrs. Lewis's drawing room, many on folding wooden chairs. Most were women, but a few men were dotted about the room, and one of them, a young blond, looked familiar to Hannah. She just couldn't think why. Before she had a chance to ask Verity about him, Elizabeth was hustling both of them over to meet Mrs. Lewis.

Except for her short height, the lively fifty-something Mrs. Lewis whom Hannah saw before her now was hardly recognizable as the fierce old lady she had met during World War II. Hannah wondered, *How many different people can one person be in a lifetime?*

Elizabeth tactlessly introduced Hannah and Verity to Mrs. Lewis as "my maid and the girl from our local grocer's shop." Mrs. Lewis greeted them both distantly, and said in a briskly polite voice, "Go to the kitchen, and Cook will give you your tea."

But Elizabeth intervened. "Oh, no, Mrs. Lewis" she said, frowning. "These girls aren't here as my servants. They've come to attend your meeting, at my invitation."

"Have they indeed?" Mrs. Lewis said, with a cold smile and just the slightest snap of frost in her tone. "In that case, you two young people must help yourselves to tea in the dining room. Elizabeth, I need a word, if you please …" She took Elizabeth by the arm and escorted her away, saying, "I have just received a letter from an old friend in America …"

Hannah did not have time to take offense at Mrs. Lewis's dismissive treatment of her and Verity, because she was now all ears. Any mention of America had to be a clue about Snipesville, right? This had to be connected with the time travel. Before she could follow Elizabeth and Mrs. Lewis, however, Verity tapped her shoulder. "Let's get some tea. I wonder if there will be sandwiches and cream cakes later? Mrs. Lewis has a reputation for putting on quite a spread, or at least she will have a reputation for it someday."

But Hannah pushed her away. "Just get me tea, okay?" she muttered. "I've got work to do." She hurried to get within earshot of Elizabeth's and Mrs. Lewis's conversation.

By now, Mrs. Lewis was in mid-sentence. "… and I urged her to move to England permanently, but she said that America, for all its faults, is her home. A remarkable woman. Do you think we might find a way to assist her?"

"Perhaps," said Elizabeth, "But I have other pressing questions on my mind for the present."

Mrs. Lewis frowned. "I must say I am disappointed with your lack of enthusiasm. I do hope you will reconsider. Now, I must have you meet another old friend of mine." She led Elizabeth toward a gray-haired lady. "This is Mrs. Fitch, who has recently moved to Balesworth from Manchester, where we were childhood friends. Mrs. Fitch, this is Miss Hughes."

Mrs. Fitch gave Elizabeth a warm smile. "I have heard a great deal about you, Miss Hughes," she said as she grabbed the forearm of a blonde teenager skulking behind her, and pulled her into the conversation. "Miss Hughes, may I introduce my niece, Miss Millicent Cooke?"

Elizabeth and Millicent Cooke nodded shyly to each other, although only Miss Cooke was smiling. "Delighted to meet you Miss Hughes," said Miss Cooke. "I say, I do hope we can be friends!"

Elizabeth looked a little taken aback, and gave a polite nod. Hannah smiled. Mrs. Devenish had never seemed comfortable around gushy people, although Hannah suspected she liked them anyway.

Mrs. Lewis said proudly, "I am sure Elizabeth can explain our work to you, Miss Cooke."

Now it was Miss Cooke's turn to smile politely. Hannah wondered, where had she heard the name "Millicent Cooke" before? She couldn't think.

As Hannah watched, Verity came to join her, silently handing her a china cup and saucer. Trying not to appear as though they were taking an interest in the conversation, they both nonetheless made an attentive audience.

CHAPTER EIGHT

"Elizabeth has been such a help to me these last few years," Mrs. Lewis said to Mrs. Fitch and Miss Cooke. "She has faithfully traveled to my meetings all the way by train from Bedfordshire, and she ably assists with a great deal of the Women's Suffrage Association's correspondence."

"Remind me, Mrs. Lewis," said Mrs. Fitch, "how did you and Miss Hughes become acquainted?"

"I gave a lecture on women's suffrage at Miss Hughes's school some years ago," said Mrs. Lewis. "She wrote me a very kind letter afterward, and I invited her to luncheon. I found her such a breath of fresh air. How old were you then, Elizabeth?"

"Thirteen," Elizabeth said shyly. "Mrs. Lewis has greatly encouraged my interest in the cause."

"Elizabeth has more than repaid my time and attention," said Mrs. Lewis. "She works very hard for the Association, and to a very high standard."

"Wow," Hannah whispered to Verity. "This is quite a lovefest."

Verity considered this. "Hmm, I think I understand what you mean by that," she said. "Granny ... Oh, I can't call her that, she's only nineteen ... *Elizabeth* is basking in the attention, isn't she?. I honestly never knew that Mrs. Lewis ever praised her for anything. The old bat died last year, and she was telling off Granny right to the very end ... Hannah, I need a cigarette. Let's go into the garden."

"Is that a good idea? You know they'll all be shocked if they see a woman smoke. And please don't call me Hannah. People know me as May. Honestly, Verity, you don't have the hang of this time travel thing yet, do you?"

"No, I don't suppose I do," Verity said irritably. "In any event, they look ready to start the meeting. My fag will have to wait. Blast."

Hannah was both pleased and dismayed to see the handsome Mr. Ingle-Gillis in the audience, sitting alongside his friend Mr. Pierce, and apparently unaware of the admiring looks from the young women around him. Hannah wondered if she and Verity should distract Mr. Ingle-Gillis from chatting with Elizabeth during the meeting. And who *was* that young blond man in the back of the room? Now, with a pang of disappointment, she remembered. He was Syrup Guy, the customer in Baker's grocery the day that Verity met Elizabeth. Sure enough, he and Verity now caught each other's eyes, and exchanged smiles and nods.

Time crawled by as the ladies proposed and voted on motion after motion, mostly agreeing that they should write letters to politicians, and to other women's suffrage groups throughout Britain. Elizabeth did not seem to be bored

CHAPTER EIGHT

at all. She was seated at a small table next to Mrs. Lewis, who conducted the meeting, and she furiously scribbled notes, occasionally interrupting to ask a speaker to explain a point.

Here, Hannah thought, it was much easier to see Elizabeth as the future Mrs. Devenish. She came across as a mature young woman who was highly disciplined in her habits, and confident in dealing with adults. But Hannah knew all too well that Elizabeth was also the rebellious, mouthy, and weird teenager who lived at Willowbank. She seemed to be both of these very different people at once. Why?

During a break in the meeting, two maids wheeled in a tea urn and trays of snacks. The audience eagerly got to their feet, and started helping themselves to steaming cups of tea, and plates of little sandwiches and cookies. Only Elizabeth remained where she was, at the front of the room, still writing.

Hannah and Verity slipped out through the French doors into the garden, each holding a cup of tea and plate of goodies. Others did not follow them, and Hannah immediately found out why. "It's freezing out here," she gasped, as they walked around the side of the house.

"Hmm," said Verity, lighting up a cigarette, then shaking out her match as she exhaled a swirling cloud of smoke. "It is a bit chilly. All the same, what a relief to escape from that room. This meeting is not at all what I had hoped." She took another deep drag on her cigarette, and exhaled through her nose.

"Do you *have* to?" Hannah said, coughing and waving away the smoke cloud.

Verity ignored her. Looking thoughtful, she said, "Elizabeth is so self-important and dutiful. That's just like Granny. It's such fun to watch her as a young woman."

"It's also bizarre," said Hannah.

"What do you mean by that?" Verity said sharply.

Hannah explained Elizabeth's conduct at home.

"Perhaps Elizabeth behaves better in the presence of Mrs. Lewis?" Verity said. "The old bag obviously thinks the world of her. Didn't you see how she showed her off? And evidently Elizabeth wants to please her, although it does make her look rather a toady, don't you think?"

"Toady?" Hannah had never heard this word before.

"Someone who sucks up," Verity explained.

"Huh. Maybe. When Brandon met your granny and Mrs. Lewis in 1915," she said, "they weren't getting along at all."

"Brandon met Granny and Mrs. Lewis during the First World War?" Verity

CHAPTER EIGHT

was impressed.

"Yes, he did," said Hannah, "and they were having a huge fight. He said your granny was rude to Mrs. Lewis, and then Mrs. Lewis went all ballistic, and they decided not to see each other again. But I guess they made up again by the time I met Mrs. Lewis in 1940. Sort of. Your granny still seemed kind of afraid of her then, didn't she?"

Verity exhaled smoke as she laughed. "Oh, I know. Granny was dutiful toward the old dragon, but she was always a bit scared of her. They stayed in touch, you know, but they never seemed all that close. Granny rarely mentioned her. Mummy said she always wondered when they were going to drop each other for good. Apparently, that was a constant possibility. Once, they quarrelled so badly, they didn't speak for years."

"Not much danger of that right now, though," Hannah said. "I wonder if that's a good thing or a bad thing?"

Just then, Millicent Cooke sidled around the corner of the house. Because she was looking behind her to make sure she wasn't seen, she did not at first notice Verity and Hannah. Having assured herself that the coast was clear, she pulled a cigarette and matches from her bag, and lit up. She was just shaking out the match when she turned her head and almost jumped out of her skin at the sight of the two young women.

"Hi, there," Hannah said cheerfully. "How are you?"

"Very well, th-thank you," Miss Cooke stammered, then she looked with relief at Verity's cigarette.

Verity extended her free hand to shake Miss Cooke's. "I don't believe we have been introduced. I'm Verity Powell," she said, "and this is my friend Hannah … I mean, May Harrower."

"Pleased to meet you both. My name's Millicent Cooke, Cooke with an *E*. I'm here with my aunt, Mrs. Fitch. She and Mrs. Lewis were girlhood chums in Lancashire. Look, you won't mention this to either of them, will you?" She held up her cigarette. "There will be a fearful row if Auntie hears about it."

"Why do you think we're standing out here in the freezing cold, Miss Cooke?" said Verity, holding up her own cigarette.

"Speak for yourself," Hannah muttered.

Verity rolled her eyes. "Miss, um, Harrower here doesn't approve of tobacco. But you are a co-conspirator with us, aren't you, Miss Harrower? Standing out here, keeping us company."

"Just try not to blow smoke at me," Hannah grumbled.

Miss Cooke tilted her head in apology, then said, "What do both of you think of the meeting?"

"Boring," said Hannah.

"Deadly," said Verity.

"Oh, I am so pleased you agree," Miss Cooke sighed with evident relief, and then she began talking rapidly. "You see, when we moved here from Manchester, I foolishly mentioned to Auntie that I was interested in the Women's Suffrage Association in Balesworth, and she told Mrs. Lewis. I'm trying to decide whether to remain involved. I shall probably have to grin and bear it, so as not to offend Auntie and Mrs. Lewis. But honestly, I do wonder whether I ought to join Mrs. Pankhurst's Women's Social and Political Union. Do you know any of the other young people in Balesworth? A pleasant young man here told me that there's a group of our age who are sympathetic to the Pankhursts, and who meet regularly. They sound so much more exciting than this rather stuffy bunch. Then again, the WSPU may be a little too exciting for me. I don't know that I am terribly keen on being arrested, *Deeds Not Words,* and all that. Do you know, I actually met Christabel Pankhurst in Manchester? I didn't like her. Far too conceited. A frightfully good speaker, though." Hannah wondered if Miss Cooke had drawn breath even once during this entire speech.

Just then, an older woman's voice called, "Millie? Are you in the garden? Millie?"

"Oh, gosh, trouble," Miss Cooke said, stubbing out her cigarette. "Coming, Auntie!" she cried, then turned back to Verity and Hannah. "Auntie and I live in Waldley Cottage, on Sish Row, off the High Street," she said. "Please come for tea, both of you. *Do* say you will visit, and *do* call me Millie! There are so few girls of our age in the Women's Suffrage Association. You two seem far more amusing than Miss Elizabeth Hughes. She looks so terribly serious, and she's quite the apple of Mrs. Lewis's eye. Oh, gosh, I hope she isn't a friend of yours! You will think me awful. But I must go, or my aunt will be beside herself. I shall see you inside, more's the pity for all of us."

After she was gone, Verity said, "My word, what a chatterbox! But it is a shame she seems to have taken against Elizabeth. I think Millie might have been good for Granny. Still, I'm sure Granny has lots of friends in Ickswade."

"No, I don't think she does," said Hannah. "I mail letters for her to her old boarding school friends, but she doesn't seem to know local girls of her own age. She's like someone in my time who only has friends online … I mean, on the computer …"

Verity looked baffled.

"Oh, never mind," said Hannah. "Maybe I'm not being fair. It's just that nobody comes to the house, and Elizabeth doesn't talk about hanging out … you know, visiting … with anyone. Well, except for Mr. Ingle-Gillis, and I don't want to encourage *that* friendship."

Verity picked up her teacup and plate from the lawn, and, grinding out her cigarette in the grass with her foot, said with a twitch of her nose, "Now you mention it, Granny hasn't got any true friends in Balesworth in 1951, not since Mrs. Lewis died, if we count her. And Mummy says that Granny always puts family first, and she is rather shy with new people who want to befriend her. Millie's obviously not interested in getting to know Elizabeth, either. Perhaps it's just as well if Elizabeth's not the social sort, and doesn't really need friends."

If that was true, Hannah wondered, maybe this explained Mrs. Devenish's attitude in 1951. If she was an introvert around adults, maybe she just didn't want to be friends with an adult Hannah. That thought did not make her any more happy.

As the meeting reconvened, Millie said, "See over there? That's the man who organizes the gatherings of young people to discuss politics." Hannah and Verity followed her gaze, and found themselves looking at Syrup Guy.

Suddenly, Hannah felt a burst of adrenaline. "What's his name?"

"Tom," said Millie. "Tom Devenish. Do you know him?"

Simultaneously, Hannah and Verity took a sharp intake of breath, and Hannah felt Verity jump in her seat as she craned her neck to get a good look at Mr. Devenish. "But that's the chap who helped Elizabeth rescue me from …"

"I know," Hannah said.

As they both stared at him, Tom Devenish turned slightly in his seat, and, finding himself the center of feminine attention, gave them a twitchy smile. When Hannah looked at Verity, she saw she had tears in her eyes. "My grandfather," she murmured. Millie gave her an odd look, Mrs. Fitch whispered at them all to shush, and the meeting resumed.

It was music to Hannah's ears when she heard Mrs. Lewis finally say the magic words, "Is there any other business before we adjourn?"

Elizabeth's hand shot up.

"Yes, Miss Hughes?" Mrs. Lewis said, frowning. *For some reason,* Hannah thought, *she doesn't want to call on Elizabeth. Why?*

Elizabeth took a deep breath. "I wish to know what the Balesworth Women's Suffrage Association intends to do to involve working-class women in our cause."

When Mrs. Lewis replied, her voice took on a slight edge. "You and I have talked of this before, Miss Hughes. Much as we should like to include working-class women in our proceedings, my drawing-room is hardly a suitable place for a large attendance of that sort."

Elizabeth gave her a piercing look. "Mrs. Lewis, do you mean that you don't want working-class women in your house?"

There was a slight sensation in the room. Some of the young people laughed nervously, including, Hannah noticed, Millie Cooke. The older ladies, among them Mrs. Fitch, tutted at Elizabeth's boldness. "No," Mrs. Lewis said, in a chilly voice, "That is not what I said, Miss Hughes. It is a question of my not having sufficient room, as you and I have already discussed. Now if we might move on …"

"If inadequate space is the difficulty," said Elizabeth, determined to press her point, "Why do we not hold our meetings elsewhere?"

There were some murmurs of agreement among the company, and Mrs. Lewis quickly moved to close the floor to further discussion, a motion that Mrs. Fitch seconded. As the meeting broke up, Elizabeth remained seated at the front of the room, looking quite put out. Mrs. Lewis, stern-faced, leaned forward, tapped her hand, and said something to her. Elizabeth started to protest, but then Mrs. Lewis very quietly said something else. Whatever it was she said, it silenced Elizabeth, and left her looking red-faced and resentful.

"Oh, dear, trouble in paradise," Verity said cheerfully, nodding toward the scene. "If we stick around, Hannah, we might see fireworks. This isn't in the same time-travel league as witnessing the Fall of Rome, I suppose, but it ought to be entertaining."

But Hannah ignored Verity and approached Elizabeth, who sat alone now, gathering together her pencils and notes. "Is everything all right, Miss Elizabeth?" she said.

"Yes, of course," Elizabeth said briskly. "Why would it not be? Did you find the meeting interesting?"

"Very," lied Hannah. "You guys seem to get a lot done."

"Perhaps," said Elizabeth, shuffling her papers. And then she looked up at Hannah. "I think we would accomplish a great deal more if we were less exclusive. May, this is why I brought you with me tonight. Working-class girls like you have the most to gain from the vote. Useless ladies like me who sit around drawing rooms, sipping tea, at least have the opportunity to lead more interesting lives. But girls like you have so little chance to escape drudgery and poverty, and that is why we should welcome you. With the vote, we women can change this country for the better, and for everyone."

Hannah wondered if this was why Elizabeth was trying her hand at cooking and cleaning, to get a better idea of how life was for working-class women. But then she remembered her mission. "Miss Elizabeth, I have a couple of people

CHAPTER EIGHT

I want you to meet ..."

When Hannah turned around, almost the entire crowd was migrating toward the hall and out the door. However, Millie Cooke was talking animatedly with Verity and Tom Devenish. Just as Hannah was about to hurry Elizabeth over to join them, Mrs. Lewis, catching Elizabeth's eye, beckoned to her, and not in a good way.

"Perhaps later," said Elizabeth. "But first I suppose I must face the music." She gathered up her belongings, and reluctantly approached Mrs. Lewis.

If Hannah could get Tom's immediate attention, she thought, she still might have a chance to introduce him to Elizabeth, and at the same time save Elizabeth from a scolding. She rushed over to the young people.

Millie was saying, "You know, Mr. Devenish is a newcomer to Balesworth, just like me."

Mr. Devenish smiled. "Not quite a newcomer, Miss Cooke, because I was already at boarding school in Hertfordshire before Mother moved us up from Devon."

"Where did you say you are from, Millie?" said Verity.

Hannah tried to interrupt. "Mr. Devenish? I have someone I want you to ..."

But Millie replied to Verity, drowning out Hannah's words. "Auntie and I are from Manchester," she said.

"I would be most interested in learning more of Manchester politics," Mr. Devenish said eagerly. He turned back to Verity. "Are you familiar with Manchester's radical history, Miss Powell?"

"Oh, yes, I have read the history ... I mean the newspapers. Most interesting. Not long ago, I read about the Peterloo Massacre."

"That was hardly today or yesterday," said Millie, as if Verity had said something slightly stupid. "Wasn't that nearly a century ago?"

"No, it wasn't," Hannah said hurriedly, "But I need to introduce Mr... "

"In 1819 as I recall," said Verity, tapping Hannah on the arm to shut her up. "I believe I have an ancestor who was involved in it."

"As do I!" said Mr. Devenish. "On my mother's side of the family."

"Perhaps the same person," Verity said with a sly smile. "We might be related, Mr. Devenish."

Hannah, frustrated with being ignored, looked back across the room for Elizabeth. Apparently, her conversation with Mrs. Lewis had already ended, because she was now chatting happily with Mr. Ingle-Gillis. This was not good, either. Hannah finally lost patience. "Mr. Devenish, I really, really need to introduce ..."

But Mrs. Lewis chose this moment to appear at Hannah's side, and everyone

CHAPTER EIGHT

turned respectfully to her. "I don't wish to hurry all of you young people, but I have an invitation to dinner and must prepare."

Immediately, everyone stammered apologies, and the group broke up. Finally, Hannah thought, she had her chance: Elizabeth and Mr. Ingle-Gillis were saying goodbye to each other. Desperately, she turned back to grab Mr. Devenish. But Tom Devenish was walking out through the front door, with Millie right behind him. Only Verity stayed behind. Hannah had missed her chance.

"Well, thanks a lot for that," she grumbled to Verity.

"What did I do?" Verity protested. "I was having a wonderful time talking with my grandfather."

"You idiot, I was trying to get him to meet your grandmother," Hannah hissed. "You could have helped me introduce him to Elizabeth, because at least you fit in with these people. They all ignore me. I'm just some maid. You might be a shopgirl, but you act like a duchess. I can't speak fluent posh. You can. And I need your help to get those two together."

"Perhaps it just wasn't the right time?" Verity said tentatively. "It might not be wise to rush things."

"Or maybe you just messed up," Hannah snapped. Without waiting for a reply, she went to get her coat.

On the walk through Balesworth from Mrs. Lewis's house, Verity once again trailed behind Elizabeth, but Hannah, still mad about what had happened at the end of the meeting, trailed behind Verity. Now she noticed that they were almost at the other end of the High Street. "Hey," she called out, running to catch up to Verity, "I thought we were going to the railway station?"

Verity shook her head. "Elizabeth is walking me to Weston Cottage first, because it's getting dark."

"But that means …"

"Yes," Verity said. "It means we're taking Elizabeth to visit her future home."

As they approached Weston Cottage, the Professor opened the door, as though she had been expecting them. She beamed at Elizabeth. "Miss Hughes, I presume?"

"Yes, that's right," said Elizabeth, startled. "I'm sorry to have to ask, but have we met before?"

"Oh, eventually," the Professor replied breezily. "Thank you for walking Verity home. I am Miss Powell, her, um …"

"Aunt," Verity said helpfully.

"Yes," said the Professor, shooting Verity a grateful look, "Verity's aunt.

CHAPTER EIGHT

Would you care for tea?"

"Thank you, but it is rather late," Elizabeth said, "so I really ought to be going." But then she looked up at the house. "I say, I know this place," she exclaimed. "It's Weston Cottage, isn't it? I haven't been here in years! Good heavens. I sometimes came here as a child. My mother owns it, you know."

Everyone tried to act surprised.

"I pay the rent to a leasing agent, so I had *no* idea who owns it," lied the Professor, all wide-eyed innocence. "I say, Miss Hughes, would you care to take a peek inside for old times' sake?"

Elizabeth stepped backward. "Oh, no, it would be far too much of an imposition."

"Not at all, Miss Hughes," said the Professor, opening the door wide.

Verity and Hannah exchanged looks. What was she up to?

Like a slick real estate agent, the Professor shepherded Elizabeth around Weston Cottage, pointing out all the house's features.

"And a large bedroom, here, you see!" She flung open a door. "There's not a bathroom in the house yet, but it can easily be added on. Do come downstairs and let me show you the best feature of the entire house."

Elizabeth was clearly hooked. "And what is that, Miss Powell?"

The Professor gave her a big smile. "The kitchen, of course."

As they trooped down the stairs, Verity muttered to Hannah, "She's playing Elizabeth like a violin. She obviously knows her very well."

Arriving in the kitchen, the Professor flung open her arms to indicate the huge kitchen table, and said, "Isn't this magnificent? As you can see, it's terribly practical, a veritable island for food preparation."

Hannah thought, *Did she seriously just call that antique a kitchen island?*

The Professor continued in sales mode. "The kitchen is also equipped with a large and airy larder, and the range is so easy to cook upon."

"Do you cook, Miss Powell?" Elizabeth said keenly.

"I dabble," the Professor said modestly. "Don't I, Verity and, er, May?" The girls smiled on cue.

Elizabeth said to the Professor, "Tell me, Miss Powell, have you lived in this house long?"

"No," said the Professor, "Nor do I intend to remain here a great deal longer. But this is a perfect house, and I shall miss it very much. However, I intend to move away soon to live with my sister."

"So the house will be vacant," Elizabeth said thoughtfully.

"It will not remain so for long, I'm sure," said the Professor, slipping back into her real estate agent persona. "It is a most desirable and charming property."

Verity whispered to Hannah, "Why *is* she trying to sell Granny her own house?"

Hannah shrugged. "Beats me. For her own amusement, I guess."

Elizabeth was still gazing around the kitchen, but suddenly she snapped out of her daydream. "Well, I must be leaving if we are to be home before dark," she said hurriedly. "But thank you for showing me the house, Miss Powell. I do hope we meet again."

"Oh, you may be sure of it," the Professor said.

Elizabeth now turned to Verity. "And I hope I shall see you at our next meeting, Miss Powell."

"That would be, um, lovely!" Verity said. "I shall make my best effort to attend." As Elizabeth stepped outside, Verity added under her breath, "If I'm not washing my hair that night."

Grinning, Hannah rushed to follow Elizabeth, who was striding down the garden path as though she owned it. Which, Hannah thought, she sort of did.

Wednesday, October 4, 1905

Hannah poked at the blazing fire in Weston Cottage's drawing room, then settled into the comfortable new armchair with a cup of sweet milky coffee, and the new book the Professor had given her. It was about the militant women's suffrage movement, and its leader, Emmeline Pankhurst.

At first, Hannah found the book too hard to understand, and so she looked at the pictures. Soon, she was so enthralled by the story told by the images that she was reading more and more of the words. She learned that Mrs. Pankhurst, her daughters, and their Women's Social and Political Union wanted women to have the vote, but that they were nothing like Mrs. Lewis and her polite Women's Suffrage Association. The Pankhursts' followers called themselves suffragettes. They attacked politicians with whips, fought the police, smashed shop windows with rocks … One suffragette died when, to draw attention to her cause, she threw herself in front of a horse at a famous race.

Hannah read breathlessly of Edwardian ladies arrested and thrown in prison, where they continued to protest by refusing to eat. As a time traveler, Hannah had been exposed to and endured many terrible things. But when she read that prison doctors forcibly fed suffragettes by pouring liquids through long rubber tubes up their noses, down their throats, and directly into their stomachs, she had to put down her book.

She closed her eyes and listened to the ticking of the drawing room clock, stunned and horrified by what she had read.

CHAPTER EIGHT

"Enjoying your book?" said a voice.

Hannah jumped slightly. She hadn't heard the Professor come in. But there she was, sitting on the new sofa, opening up a laptop. Her computer looked completely out of place in 1905.

Hannah grimaced. "I can't exactly say I'm enjoying the book, no."

"Oh, you must be reading about forcible feeding," the Professor said sympathetically. "Yes, it's horrible, and that's not a word I use lightly. Some of the suffragettes were very proper posh ladies, which I always think makes it seem worse somehow. I feel odd saying that, but they were so innocent, you see."

Hannah thought about this. These terrible things had not yet happened, but they would happen soon. Suddenly, the suffragettes she was reading about seemed real and alive. Bad enough that tough working-class girls suffered, but the dignified and proper ladies she saw around her in 1905 subjected to such horrors? Hannah didn't want to dwell on it. She needed to think about something less disturbing. "I like the new furniture," she said.

The Professor stopped typing. "Good. I bought all of it in London last week. I popped into Heal's on the Tottenham Court Road. I love Edwardian department stores. I get to throw around a bit of attitude. Not to say I'm rude, just that I act posher than I really am, and the salesmen fall over themselves to wait on me. They arranged for everything to arrive yesterday. I thought about saving money by bringing cheap furniture from the 21st century, but it's tricky to bring furniture through time. Plus I would have had to explain the weird modern style to any visitors we might have, like Elizabeth. I guess I could have told people that my flat-pack furniture was Charles Rennie Mackintosh's latest design, or something. Not that many people in 1905 have heard of Charles Rennie Mackintosh, even in Glasgow."

"Well, I like the stuff you bought," said Hannah, who had never heard of Charles Rennie Mackintosh, either. "I feel really at home in this chair."

"That's because you've sat in it before," said the Professor. "It's going to be Mrs. Devenish's favorite armchair in 1940. I'll leave it in the attic for her when I move out, and that's how she'll acquire it. If you don't recognize it, that's because Mrs. D. had it re-covered."

Hannah felt a sudden wicked joy at knowing that she was sitting in Mrs. Devenish's armchair. In 1940, any kid who dared settle in it was kicked out the moment Mrs. Devenish entered the room: It was hers, and hers alone. Now it was Hannah's.

But Hannah's smile quickly faded. It was so hard to have any good thoughts about Mrs. Devenish. Bad memories kept bubbling up to take their place. She had coped with knowing Elizabeth by thinking of her as someone else. And pretty much, most of the time, she was.

At that very moment, out of the corner of her eye, she saw someone enter the room, and Hannah thought, with a start, that it was Mrs. Devenish herself. But it was only Verity, holding a cup and saucer. "I say, this coffee you made is rather good, Kate," she said. "Is it the real thing? I've only ever had chicory coffee before."

"What's chicory coffee?" said Hannah.

The Professor answered. "A sort of coffee-like substance, made from the root of the chicory plant. It's vile stuff that people in England started drinking during World War One, when there were coffee shortages."

"And of course we still don't have real coffee in Britain in 1951," said Verity, "because we have had rationing since the War."

"Don't make excuses, Verity," said the Professor. "Brits don't understand coffee. You ought to stick to making tea."

That use of "you" caught Hannah's attention. "Kate, are *you* British?" she said. "I've always wondered."

"So have I," said the Professor with a chuckle. But she did not explain. She stood up, and tugged at the waistband of her Edwardian dress. "Now, if you girls will excuse me, I must finish making supper."

"May I help with the cooking, Kate?" Verity asked, starting to get to her feet.

"That's very polite of you, Verity, but I think I can manage."

Hannah watched the Professor go, and as soon as she was safely out of hearing range, she sputtered to Verity, "Why didn't she ask me to help? I bet I'm way better at cooking than you are."

"Doubtless," Verity said, "but I offered to help, and you didn't. Anyway, I think you'll find she has absolute bags of faith in you."

"Yeah, right," said Hannah, and she sipped her coffee, only to find it was now cold.

Verity glanced at the cover of Hannah's book, lying on the arm of her chair. "I see you're reading about the suffragettes. You know, the women's suffrage movement is one of the most exciting episodes in British history, but you wouldn't have known it from Mrs. Lewis's meeting last night. I just wanted to wave my arms, and shout, *Go home, ladies of Balesworth! This is a waste of time! You'll get the vote anyway!*"

"It's good you didn't," Hannah said, pulling a face. "People get weirded out when time travelers tell them about the future. Don't you remember the awful thing your granny said to me in 1940 when I told her Britain was going to win the war, no matter how I behaved?"

"No," she said shortly, "I don't remember what Granny said to you. But I can make a good guess based on all the tellings-off she gave me over the years: A few choice words, including an empty threat to smack your bottom. Am I right?"

There was a silence.

"Wait," Hannah said slowly, "You mean she never planned to hit me?"

"Hannah, I hate to intrude on your persistent self-pity, but Granny is not the horrific dragon of your imagination. You realize it was just your hard luck that you got mixed up with Eric and me on our window-breaking escapade, because that was the one and only time Granny ever seriously walloped either of us."

Suddenly, Hannah's memories were being changed, not by anything in the past having changed, but because of how Verity was interpreting that past.

"Now don't look so pitiful," Verity said firmly. "I'm not forever harmed by that day, and neither were you."

Without warning, Hannah felt a surge of raw anger. "How do you know?" she snapped. "I mean, how do you know what I went through? I'm not you. I was humiliated. In my time, most adults I know think it's wrong to hit kids, and for her to do what she did … She would get arrested for that in the 21st century, and …"

Verity cut her off. "Who cares? I certainly don't. I don't live in your time, Hannah. I don't think like you think. I don't care what you think. Of course you were humiliated. That was Granny's point, wasn't it? To take you down a peg or two, and show you that you weren't boss. It was bad enough listening to you complain then, but I won't hear you insulting Granny now. She is an absolute heroine as far as I'm concerned. She raised Mummy and my aunt all by herself, while she worked at a hospital *and* looked after her mother."

Hannah opened her mouth to argue, but Verity held up a hand. "No, Hannah Day, don't you *dare* interrupt me. Listen. Granny has been a wonderful mother to Eric. She looked after me during the War. And to cap it all off, she rescued you and your brother and your friend, complete strangers, and she treated you as members of our family. She is very fond of you, Hannah. So I don't want to hear from you ever again that a hiding from Elizabeth Devenish was the worst event of your entire life, even if you truly think that it was, because *I don't care.*"

Hannah's temper was cooling, and she felt drained. Her anger had surprised her almost as much as it had annoyed Verity, and she already knew that her fury had nothing to do with what had happened in 1940. She just couldn't bring herself to tell Verity the truth: That she was devastated by Mrs. Devenish's rejection of her in 1951, and by her realization that neither Verity, nor Eric, nor Mrs. Devenish herself really considered Hannah part of their family.

CHAPTER EIGHT

It was just too much.

She tried to explain. "People in my time …"

"… sound very foolish to me," Verity finished for her. "Assuming that you are qualified to speak for them all, of course. How would I know?"

Hannah was still struggling with what she wanted to say. She tried again. "Look, I'm just so angry, and …"

"Fine," Verity snapped. "I'm going to help Kate in the kitchen, whether she wants my help or not. But Hannah, I don't want to hear you speak again about your childish bitterness towards my grandmother. I have better things to do than dwell selfishly on past wrongs. I only wish you thought the same way."

With that, she left Hannah staring into the fire, feeling sad and alone. It seemed to Hannah that her friendship with Verity was ending, because nothing she said seemed to please her at all. Hannah started to think that she needed somehow to get closure. That was it. She needed to make peace with Mrs. Devenish, even though she would never see her again, and with Verity, too.

Yet Hannah knew she still cared very much about Verity, even if they were no longer to be friends. How awful it would be if she just ceased to exist. But maybe Verity wouldn't vanish if Hannah Dias couldn't persuade Elizabeth Hughes and Tom Devenish to marry each other. Maybe everything would go wrong in some other universe, while Verity would be fine. But Hannah couldn't risk it. She had to find a way to bring Tom and Elizabeth together. That meant she had to make an extra effort to get to know Elizabeth, to find out what she and her future husband might have in common. This gave her an idea.

Thursday October 5, 1905

"Would you care for tea, Miss Elizabeth?" Hannah was holding a tray as she stood in the doorway. It was late in the afternoon, and Elizabeth had spent the entire day shut away in her room.

"Yes, May, provided I need not come downstairs for it," said Elizabeth, without looking up. "I am rather busy." She didn't look busy. She was sitting on the bed, reading a book.

Hannah suspected, not for the first time, that Elizabeth used her suffrage work as an excuse to avoid spending time with her mother and sisters. She also suspected that much of the time when Elizabeth was hiding out in her room, she was reading books, not writing letters.

It was time to try to get to know Elizabeth better. That was why Hannah's tray was loaded not only with a silver teapot, sugar bowl, milk jug, and plate of cookies, but also two teacups and saucers.

Sliding the tray onto the tea table, she said, "What are you reading?"

"Oh, just a book," Elizabeth said, turning a page.

"Yes, I can see that, Miss Elizabeth," Hannah said, a slight note of irritation creeping into her voice. "What's it about?"

Elizabeth still didn't look up, but said slowly, "It's about women agitating for the right to vote in America. Mrs. Lewis loaned it to me. A friend of hers sent it from the United States."

Hannah brightened. "Oh, I thought it was a novel. You mean it's about women's suffrage in the States? Susan B. Anthony, Elizabeth Cady Stanton, all those people?"

Elizabeth looked up in astonishment, and put her book down in her lap. "You know about the American suffragists, May?"

Not really, thought Hannah. She had only a vague idea from Women's History Month at school. But she wasn't about to admit that to Elizabeth.

"A little," said Hannah in what she hoped was a modest voice. "But I always thought they were kind of boring. You know," she added with enthusiasm, "I'm way more interested in what I'm reading about Mrs. Pankhurst and her daughters."

Elizabeth sat up and leaned forward, resting her arms on her bent knees. "I only wish a book had yet been written about the Pankhursts. Perhaps it has. I should ask Mr. Ingle-Gillis. May, do sit down." She pointed to the desk chair. "Have you a moment to join me for tea? Oh. I see you brought two cups."

"Yes, I did," said Hannah, "Just in case you wanted to chat. But don't let Flora see me, okay? She thinks we shouldn't talk to each other."

"Oh, Flora," Elizabeth said, tutting. "Don't mind Flora. She's old."

Hannah sat down, and poured cups of tea for them both. Elizabeth said, "I am pleased to see you take such an interest in suffrage, May. But don't you think the WSPU are too radical? Mrs. Pankhurst is a socialist, I hear, and even Mrs. Lewis, who is very progressive in her ideas, finds her worrisome. On this matter, I am inclined to agree with Mrs. Lewis."

Hannah felt a little out of her depth in this conversation, but her reading had made her keen to talk about the suffragettes. "I don't know about that. I just think they're cool," she said. "It's awesome that they started throwing rocks through windows."

"They certainly are brave …" said Elizabeth. Then she frowned. "I'm sorry, what did you say?"

"Throwing rocks," said Hannah. "You heard about that, right?"

"Oh, but of course!" Elizabeth said after a split-second pause. "I'm sorry, May, I didn't hear you. Yes, of course I have heard about that. But I am not sure that I approve."

CHAPTER EIGHT

"Why not?" said Hannah, and she sipped her tea.

Elizabeth struggled with what to say. "Mr. Ingle-Gillis is a great admirer of the Pankhursts, but Mrs. Lewis certainly won't … Doesn't approve of such extreme measures …"

"I'm not asking for Mrs. Lewis's opinion, or Mr. Ingle-Gillis's," said Hannah. "I'm asking for yours."

Elizabeth considered this, as she nibbled on a cookie. "If I'm to be honest, like you, I don't know," she said slowly, wiping stray crumbs from her lip. "I think Mrs. Lewis is right to be cautious, but …"

"Women don't have the vote yet, do we?" said Hannah. "I mean, how many hours have you spent at that desk, writing letter after letter to who knows who? And where has it got you?"

Elizabeth's eyes shone. "Oh, no, May, you're wrong about that. We have made progress. Truly, we have. A few months ago, Mrs. Lewis's Member of Parliament received a deputation of ladies from the Balesworth branch of the Women's Suffrage Association, including me. He listened respectfully to us, and he received our petition."

"Yes, I bet he did," said Hannah, "but did he actually do anything about it? You know, try to change the law, or anything?"

There was a pained silence. "No," Elizabeth finally admitted. "You're right. It was all rather frustrating. At times like that, I find that I do admire Mrs. Pankhurst's courage and outspokenness. I just don't know whose side I should be on. Mrs. Lewis is an admirable woman, but sometimes she doesn't want me to hold views contrary to hers. Perhaps that's because she is certain of her opinions, and she does have knowledge and wisdom that I lack."

Hannah had no such doubts. She was fired up by the book she had been reading, and the stories of suffragettes being arrested, attacked, imprisoned, and tortured. "But don't you see, Miss Elizabeth? The Pankhursts are right. Sometimes, a rock through a window really get the message across better and faster than words."

"Perhaps," Elizabeth said uncertainly. "I admire Mrs. Pankhurst and her daughters for their forthright attitudes, but I do think everyone should obey the law."

At that moment, Hannah suspected that she shouldn't push her point any further. Dropping her eyes, she said, "As you say, Miss Elizabeth, Mrs. Lewis would not approve."

"No," said Elizabeth, picking up her book. "You're quite right about that. Mrs. Lewis is a deeply sensible lady. She very definitely does not approve of vandalism and violence, and I have no interest in quarreling with her on that

CHAPTER EIGHT

score. I say, won't Mrs. Morris be wondering where you are?"

Hannah reluctantly agreed that she probably was.

Mrs. Morris was not at all happy with "May."

"You only had to deliver Miss Elizabeth her tea, May. Why did it take you so long?"

"She wanted to talk," Hannah said wearily, washing her hands at the sink.

She jumped when she heard Flora's voice behind her. "You meant to do that, May. I saw you take up two teacups, one for yourself. I saw you. And it's not the first time. You got no business acting like Miss Elizabeth's your friend."

Hannah turned on the old woman. "Yes, I *did* talk to her," she snapped, and just stopped herself in time from saying "So sue me."

She returned to pleading her case with Mrs. Morris. "Miss Elizabeth is lonely," she said. "She doesn't have any friends as far as I can see, and …"

But Mrs. Morris leaned one hand on the kitchen table, and waved a finger at Hannah. "Now you just listen to me, my girl. You're not Miss Elizabeth's friend. You are a servant. Any more of this, and I will tell Mrs. Hughes of your conduct."

Hannah knew that if she really had been "May Harrower," her situation was now very dangerous: In 1905, a servant girl who was fired without a "character," a good reference from her employer, faced a very bleak future. She had to remind herself that she was not "May." Still, even as Hannah Dias the time-traveler, she knew it was important not to get fired.

Mrs. Morris said sharply, "Go through to the scullery and iron the linens while they're still damp."

Hannah hated the scullery. It was a cramped, cold, miserable little room off the kitchen, where she washed the dishes. "Can't I iron someplace else?" she said. "It's freezing in there."

She fully expected another rebuke, but Mrs. Morris surprised her. "As you please," she said with a sigh. "But I don't want you setting up in here … Why don't you iron in the pantry?"

Hannah was confused. She was pretty sure that "pantry" was the American word for "larder." That seemed like a weird place to iron. But it wasn't what Mrs. Morris meant. Seeing Hannah's confusion, she said, "You've probably never been in there, May. It's a little room between here and the drawing room, the one that looks like a cupboard from the outside. It's never used, because the family never holds large dinner parties, and they swapped the dining room for the drawing room years ago. But there's a fireplace in there to heat your irons and keep you warm, and plenty of room for your ironing board. You'll have to lay a fire, mind."

"No problem," Hannah said gratefully. "Thanks, Mrs. Morris."

Mrs. Morris, glancing at a now-snoozing Flora, said gently, "May, I didn't mean to scold you quite so hard about Miss Elizabeth, and that. But I'm warning you that the Hugheses, they're not your friends. There's a lot of bad blood among these ladies, and it's best the likes of us don't get involved. I know you're a kind girl, but you keep your distance from Miss Elizabeth Hughes."

Great, Hannah thought grumpily, as she went to fetch the ironing board from the scullery. She was under orders from the Professor to get involved in Elizabeth's life. And now Mrs. Morris was ordering her to stay away. This was going to be complicated.

The windowless little pantry was cold and damp, but at least, Hannah thought, it would give her some peace and quiet to think about her ever more complicated mission. She built a fire with the coal, newspaper, and kindling stored next to the hearth. She had only just placed her irons at the fire to heat, when she heard people entering the drawing room next door. As she got to her feet, dusting off her knees, she realized that she could hear Mrs. Hughes and Margaret talking about the weather. How was it possible to hear so much of their conversation?

Hannah lifted up the decorative fabric banner hanging on the pantry wall, and found a serving hatch. She had no idea it was there, because it was covered by a mirror on the drawing room side. Carefully, she pulled open the hatch door, praying it wouldn't creak. It didn't. It silently swung inward a few inches, and Hannah found herself looking at the back of the mirror. She allowed the banner to drop back into place. Now, she no longer had to strain to listen to the conversation next door. Footsteps echoed as someone came into the drawing room.

"Elizabeth," said Mrs. Hughes's voice. "I have not seen you all day."

"I'm busy, Mother," Elizabeth said in a dull tone.

"Be that as it may, you must not expect Mrs. Morris to send up your meals on a tray unless you are unwell. I expect to see you at luncheon tomorrow."

"Why?" Elizabeth said.

"Never mind why," said Mrs. Hughes, but then she added, "I have invited a guest."

"We have another guest? Very well, Mother," Elizabeth said, "It's not as though I have a surplus of social engagements. And how exciting to have a surprise visitor! I wonder who *he* might be."

Hannah heard Elizabeth chuckling wickedly to herself.

CHAPTER EIGHT

Friday, October 6, 1905

In the afternoon, the arrival of a short, skinny middle-aged man with darting eyes brought Hannah more disappointment. Mrs. Hughes had drafted another potential husband for her youngest daughter, and, as Hannah could see for herself while serving lunch, he certainly wasn't Tom Devenish.

"How do you do, Mr. Cooper?" Elizabeth said confidently, extending her hand for him to shake. "How kind of you to visit. Tell me, what is your business?"

He looked terrified by her. "I am a solicitor," he stammered.

"*Another* member of the legal profession?" Elizabeth said. "Law is a terribly interesting subject, is it not? Do you think women ought to have the vote? Do tell me your views, Mr. Cooper. "

Mr. Cooper gave her a noncommittal smile, and quickly turned to Margaret, who appeared rabbit-like with fear as he spoke to her. "Tell me, Miss Hughes. What do *you* think of this business of votes for women?"

Margaret actually did have an opinion on the subject, even if it was her mother's. "Oh, I am quite opposed to women's suffrage," she squeaked. "I believe a lady should always be guided by her father, her mother, and, um, her husband."

Mr. Cooper looked intrigued. "I take it that you do not approve of Mrs. Pankhurst and her followers?"

Margaret looked shocked by the very idea. "Certainly not," she said. "No, Mr. Cooper, they are quite beyond the pale. Dreadful."

Mrs. Hughes, meanwhile, was giving Elizabeth a long stare that reminded Hannah of Mrs. Devenish at her most terrifying. Elizabeth, still undaunted by her mother's anger, took another big mouthful of dinner.

After this initial interrogation, Mr. Cooper seemed to relax, but, through the rest of the meal, he spoke mostly to Margaret. Margaret, who was clearly flattered by his attention, responded happily. Elizabeth continued to eat her dinner with relish, and contributed as little as possible to the conversation at table.

As Hannah cleared away the dishes, she speculated on whether Mrs. Hughes would invite Arthur Ingle-Gillis as a possible suitor for Elizabeth. Did Mrs. Hughes even know that he existed, and that Elizabeth visited him at his bookstore? Surely not. Otherwise, why would Mrs. Hughes not try to arrange for him to marry her youngest daughter? He was good-looking, and he had his own business. Hannah idly wondered if she should find a way to hint to Mrs. Hughes ... But then she came to her senses. *I'm supposed to get Elizabeth to marry Tom Devenish, not Arthur, even if Arthur is way cooler ...* And, she thought in dismay, this also assumed that shy Tom would have interest at all in the complicated Miss Elizabeth Hughes. *What a pain.*

Chapter 9:
A WEEK OF MEETINGS

Monday, February 12, 1906 – Tuesday, Feb 13, 1906

Brandon was carrying Miss Julia's bag in one hand, and his own in the other, as he awkwardly descended from the steam train onto the platform in Macon. Dropping both cases, he offered up his arm to Miss Julia, and helped her down the carriage steps.

"Such a pity that Robert has caught a cold," Miss Julia said, "but I'm very glad you are able to escort me, George, especially since Reverend and Mrs. Evans traveled here early. I should not have liked to travel alone."

"Ma'am, I'm just happy to be off that train," Brandon muttered, brushing off his coat. "We paid just as much money for our tickets as the white people did, but we had to sit in a crummy overcrowded carriage right behind the engine. I can't believe the other half of our car was for white guys who wanted to smoke. And what was up with those white men wandering through to our part of the car and staring at us? They made some of the young ladies really uncomfortable. And I don't think the railroad company ever cleans the colored car, do they, ma'am?"

"I don't doubt you're right," Miss Julia said briskly. "Keeping the car in that disgraceful state allows the train company to claim that our people are dirty. Now stop grumbling, George, and do come along."

Brandon picked up the bags. "So you know where we're going, ma'am?"

"No, not exactly, but I have this map that Reverend Evans drew for me. He is quite the cartographer." She paused to examine the paper in her hand, then carefully refolded it, nodding to herself. "We're staying with a Mrs. Fellows on

CHAPTER NINE

Chestnut Street. Her home is only a short walk from the Georgia Equal Rights Convention at Steward Chapel."

Brandon followed behind Miss Julia, wrangling her bag and his own. He was becoming very fond of the old woman and ever more respectful of her. Beneath her sometimes dithery exterior, he knew now, she was as sharp and steely as a knife.

Mrs. Fellows, their hostess, was a widow who, unfortunately, only had one guest bed in her home. Miss Julia got it, while Brandon was assigned to sleep on the parlor rug. What the kindly Mrs. Fellows lacked in accommodation, however, she made up for in hospitality. She clearly felt honored to host Miss Julia Russell and her companion, and she fussed over them both in a motherly way. Mrs. Fellows' meals were feasts of Southern cooking. Supper in the evening was pork chops, sweet potatoes, cabbage, and cornbread, and breakfast featured bacon, sausage, eggs, biscuits, and grits. Brandon, a true Southerner, loved grits, and these were the best he had ever tasted. He slurped down several portions, to Mrs. Fellows' evident pleasure. "I never saw such an appetite," she marveled, removing his dishes after he scraped them clean. When he thanked her, he heard his voice suddenly go squeaky. Miss Julia gave him a knowing look, but Brandon was embarrassed: Was puberty a thing you could talk about in 1906? Probably not, he decided.

The journey on foot from Mrs. Fellows' home to Steward Chapel African Methodist Episcopal Church was about ten blocks, not quite the short walk that Miss Julia had forecast. Still Brandon was enjoying getting out and about, well away from Snipesville. There was a spirit of optimism in the larger town of Macon that was missing among black people in Snipesville, and he and Miss Julia were among friends: Miss Julia recognized and warmly greeted several visiting delegates as they walked to Steward Chapel. When they were almost at the church, she apologized to Brandon for not introducing him to everyone they had met on the way. "I cannot always recall people's names," she said, "and so introductions can be awkward. I see these ladies and gentlemen so seldom, you see. It is very isolating to live in a town as remote as Snipesville."

You can say that again, Brandon thought.

Steward Chapel AME Church was an imposing late Victorian red brick edifice with a tall tower and intricate stained glass windows. While some horses and buggies were parked outside in the dirt lot, most delegates were arriving on foot. A few people went straight into the church, but because it was pleasant weather, especially for February, and the meeting didn't begin for another half hour, many others gathered to chat in the parking lot.

Miss Julia pointed out famous people to Brandon. "I don't yet see Dr. Du Bois," she said. "But there is Bishop Turner, over there … Have you heard of him, George? Bishop Henry McNeal Turner? He is a very important gentleman."

Without thinking, Brandon muttered, "I think so, yeah, Black History Month."

Miss Julia shot him an odd look, and he hastily changed the subject. "Ma'am, are all of these people delegates?"

"No, not everyone, no more than you are," Miss Julia said. "There will be a roll call, I am sure. Several representatives have come from each of the eleven congressional districts in Georgia. Now, I must find Reverend and Mrs. Evans …"

Smiling vaguely, she wandered off into the crowd. Brandon thought to follow, but he immediately lost sight of her, even though, as one of the few women, she stood out. Now, alone among hundreds of people, he reckoned it was a good time for him to mingle, to introduce himself to men—and he knew they likely would be men-- who could help him fundraise for the school. But deciding to network, and actually doing it, were two different things. Brandon felt awkward. He was young, short, and not very well dressed. All the people around him were adults, they radiated a lot more confidence than he felt, and they were all in their sharpest clothes, conducting themselves with great dignity. Everyone seemed to know everyone else, except him. He felt invisible.

Just then, as he hovered on the edge of the crowd, he caught the eye of a short dark-skinned man sporting a mustache and clergyman's dog collar. The man gave him a kindly smile, and called out, "Are you looking for someone, young man?"

"Kind of, sir," said Brandon. "I'm hoping to talk to people who can help me start a high school."

The man looked pleasantly surprised. "Do tell me more," he said.

When Brandon had finished his pitch, the clergyman asked, "What's your name, young man?"

"George, sir," he said. "George Braithwaite." Every time he said Dr. Braithwaite's name, he felt like an imposter.

"George, I am Reverend Walker, Charles T. Walker, and I am pastor of Mount Olivet Baptist Church in New York. But I began life as a slave near Augusta, Georgia. I was born in a cabin in a place called Hephzibah."

Brandon nodded at the name, remembering the day he and his dad had gone to a church meeting in Hephzibah.

Rev. Walker continued his story. "My father was a coach driver, and he was much trusted by his master and his fellow slaves. But he died before I was born, and my mother died when I was a boy. I could have spent my life chopping cotton in the fields. But a school for freedmen begun after the War gave me an education. What you are trying to accomplish is admirable, George, and it deserves the greatest encouragement."

Brandon waited for Rev. Walker to offer to write him a check. But he didn't. Instead, he offered advice. "I know exactly who can help you," he said. "I suggest you lay your proposal before Mr. Booker T. Washington."

Brandon's hopes for this conversation were dashed. He thought of Miss Julia's fruitless efforts to persuade the famous Booker T. Washington to give her a grant for the school. But Rev. Walker continued, "Be warned that Mr. Washington is a practical man. I do advise you to set aside your impractical idea of a largely academic course of study for students. Propose instead an industrial high school."

Brandon didn't like the sound of an "industrial high school," and what did it matter when writing to Booker T. Washington was clearly a dead end anyway? With more politeness than enthusiasm, he thanked Rev. Walker.

Brandon spotted Miss Julia sitting with Reverend and Mrs. Evans near the back of the crowded church, and she beckoned to him to join them. "I'm glad you finally decided to come inside, George," she said disapprovingly. "I was afraid I could not save you a seat for very much longer." By now, every pew on the floor and in the gallery was overflowing with delegates, and some were standing in the back. The loud buzz of conversation filled the church. But suddenly, a hush fell as a minister on the platform rose to his feet and approached the pulpit.

The minister asked the assembled delegates to bow their heads in prayer. Brandon prayed fervently for success, not only for the convention, but also for himself in helping to bring a high school to Snipesville. If he failed, would that mean the school was never built? That was scary. He prayed harder.

As soon as the assembly had chorused a resounding "Amen," another delegate introduced the Reverend William White of Augusta as the convention president. Rev. White shuffled his notes at the podium, and began to read his speech in a strong voice. "Forty years have lapsed since President Lincoln's emancipation proclamation was made effective in Georgia by the surrender of the Confederate Army …"

At that moment, Brandon stopped listening, because he had spotted a very famous face on the stage. His heart was pounding. There was no mistaking that trim goatee and mustache: W. E. B. Du Bois was in the house. Since Du Bois was always mentioned at school in the same breath as Booker T. Washington, Brandon half-expected Washington to be sitting right next to him, but he didn't seem to be on the stage at all. Surely Booker T. Washington would have wanted to be here, talking about civil rights? Maybe, Brandon thought, he wasn't present because this was a meeting about Georgia, and Washington lived in Tuskegee, Alabama. That had to be the reason.

Looking again at Dr. Du Bois, Brandon realized that the great man was giving his full attention to the speaker, and so he figured maybe he should do the same. Unfortunately, he had already lost track of what Rev. White was talking about.

But then Rev. White said, "Legal and illegal discriminations against the colored man are being multiplied by the ruling element of the white people of the South, until the condition, already alarming, is becoming more so every day. It is no idle question that we are asking ourselves, what shall I do?"

That got Brandon's attention. Every word Rev. White had just said resonated with his life in 1906 Snipesville. He started to listen more carefully. But then he lost track again. *It's so hard to listen to Victorians and Edwardians give speeches,* he thought. *It takes more concentration than us modern people have.*

Now, Rev. White was saying something about men being manly, and Brandon felt Miss Julia stiffen disapprovingly next to him in the pew. But Brandon really picked up the thread of the speech again when he heard, "The white people are not educating the colored children, but the colored people are helping to educate the white children of the state."

Brandon's first impulse was to holler "YES!" But he stayed quiet. And then he started to worry. He had watched documentaries from the civil rights era of the 1950s and 60s, of raging mobs of white people screaming outside churches full of peacefully-protesting black people. So far as Brandon had seen, white people in 1906 Macon neither knew nor cared that this meeting was taking place in their city. But were they actually here, spying?

Just as he had this disturbing thought, a white man walked into the church, and Brandon flinched. Then he recognized the newcomer. What was Alex doing here, of all places?

An usher stopped Alex, apparently asking him if he needed help. But Alex simply smiled, and waved a notepad and pencil at the man. Looking a little flustered, the usher turned to the congregation to appeal silently for help with this awkward situation. A young man reluctantly gave up his place to Alex, who looked a little confused by the gesture, but accepted the seat.

Brandon figured out that Alex got this special treatment because he was the only white person in the room. Or was he? Brandon saw a man sitting on the stage who appeared to be white. During a break in the speech, when everyone was applauding and stamping their feet, he quickly asked Miss Julia, "Who's that light-skinned guy up there? Is he white?"

She peered at the stage. "Oh, you mean Professor John Hope. He's president of Atlanta Baptist College. No, he's colored. His father was a white man from Scotland, and he lived in Augusta with Professor Hope's mother, a free colored woman, although they could not marry under Georgia law, of course. Professor Hope is often mistaken for a white person, as am I. We both choose to acknowledge that we are colored."

Meanwhile, Rev. White had started talking about segregation on public transport. Thanks to Brandon's awful experience on the train to Macon, this was another subject close to his heart, and he turned his full attention back to the speech.

Mid-morning, the meeting took a break, and everyone spilled out of the building into the parking lot, where ladies waited with steaming urns of coffee. Brandon, impatient to push his way through the crowd and meet with W. E. B. Du Bois, nonetheless first made a beeline for Alex, who had just ended a brief chat with Professor Hope when Brandon caught up with him.

"What are you doing here?" Brandon hissed at his friend.

"Writing a story for Mr. Hughes," said Alex. "He said he might be interested in what I write, so long as I do research on my own time, so I took the day off."

Brandon wasn't sure whether to facepalm himself or punch Alex. "You idiot! You're acting like a spy. Don't you see you're the only white person here?"

"What about Professor Hope?" Alex said. "He's a nice guy. When I told him I had lived in England, he said his dad was from Scotland."

"He was," said Brandon, "but Professor Hope is still black. Look, I'll explain later. Just try not to do anything dumb, ok? I have to go try to meet W. E. B. Du Bois."

Alex's ears perked up at this. "The Black History Month guy? Can I come with you?"

"No," Brandon said flatly. "You can't." Turning his back on Alex, he pushed his way through the crowd.

"Obviously, I am delighted that the Niagara Movement is having such an effect here in Georgia," W. E. B. Du Bois said to John Hope. Brandon, standing behind them, didn't quite understand the conversation, and he was astonished by Du Bois's voice, which was so posh, it was almost English. Oblivious to the starstruck eavesdropping kid behind him, Dr. Du Bois continued. "However, I am concerned that unless we have influential white supporters for this and the Niagara Movement in general, we will make little progress, and our voices will be suppressed by the Tuskegee machine. But let us see how this meeting proceeds."

As Professor Hope walked away, Brandon said nervously, "Excuse me, Mr. Du Bois?"

"That is DOCTOR Du Bois," the professor corrected him, as he wheeled around.

Brandon was petrified, and mortified at having said the wrong thing. He blurted out, "Sir, what you were saying, what about the NAACP? They have white members."

He felt nauseous when he realized what he had just done. He had told the founder of the NAACP about the NAACP, which probably didn't exist yet. There was nothing for it but to soldier on. "I mean, sir, how about a National Association for the, um, Advancement of, um, Colored People? With whites allowed to be members?"

Dr. Du Bois gave him a piercing look. "And what is your name, young man?"

"Brandon Clark. I mean, George Braithwaite, sir."

"You're not even sure of your own name," Dr. Du Bois said acidly, "and yet you devise a clever idea for an organization? That's impressive."

Brandon seized the moment. "Sir, may I ask you a question?"

Dr. Du Bois glanced at the crowd filing back into the church. "Be quick. Professor Hope may not save me a seat," he said with a sardonic smile.

"Yes, sir," said Brandon. "Look, a lady called Julia Russell is running an elementary school in Snipesville, and …"

Dr. Du Bois was again glancing impatiently at the church door. Brandon cut to the chase. "Well, sir, the thing is, she's trying to finish building a high school, and there isn't enough money, and I was kind of hoping …"

Brandon looked into the face of W. E. B. Du Bois, and realized he was talking to W. E. B. Du Bois. His nerve left him. "So I was … That is … I want to help Miss Russell build a real high school, with academic subjects."

Dr. Du Bois regarded him keenly. "Another impressive idea. However, George is it? George, while I sympathize with your cause, you have come to the wrong person in one crucial respect, for I have little enough funding for my own scholarly work. Why don't you state your case to Alonzo Herndon, the barber in Atlanta? He's the wealthiest colored man I know." Under his breath, he added, "And he owes me $50."

Brandon was desperate now. "But, sir, suppose Mr. Herndon says no?"

"Then, I suppose, George," said Dr. Du Bois, starting to walk away, "You will have to go and see the Wizard."

CHAPTER NINE

Well, that's cruel, Brandon thought. *Telling me to go see the Wizard of Oz.*

But Alex was standing behind Brandon now, and he quickly muttered in his ear, "He means Booker T. Washington. That's Washington's nickname, the 'Wizard of Tuskegee'. I remember that from Black History Month."

Brandon's eyes widened, and he called after Dr. Du Bois, "Sir? Is Mr. Washington here?"

Dr. Du Bois turned around and stared at him again. "Here?" he said in an incredulous voice. "At this meeting? Of course he's not here. This is hardly Mr. Washington's cup of tea." With that, he trotted up the steps.

As Dr. Du Bois disappeared into the church, Brandon turned to Alex. "W. E. B. Du Bois and Booker T. Washington hate each other, right?"

"That's what I heard," said Alex.

"So why does Dr. Du Bois want me to go ask Booker T. Washington for money?"

Alex shrugged. "I guess maybe because Washington has got money. Wasn't he all buddy-buddy with Andrew Carnegie, the rich Scottish guy who owned all the steel mills and paid for all the libraries? Carnegie gives him money to give away, right? That's why you should go see Washington."

"You know what?" Brandon said with a grin, "You're not as dumb as you look, Dias. The important word is *go*. Not just *write*. So if I actually go to Tuskegee, in person … Wait. Why does Dr. Du Bois want me to go see Alonzo Herndon first?"

"No idea," said Alex, who now felt completely out of his depth, historically speaking. "Who's Alonzo Herndon again?"

"Another Black History Month dude. Rich black guy in Atlanta," said Brandon. "He had, like, a barber's shop."

"He got rich from cutting hair?" said Alex. "That makes no sense."

"No, I never understood that either," said Brandon. "But I think he sold insurance, too, kind of like my dad. He had two jobs. I guess I'll head to Atlanta and start with Alonzo Herndon. Anyway, let's get inside. They're restarting the meeting."

"Before you take off for Atlanta," said Alex. "Shouldn't you ask Miss Russell first? It's her high school."

"I can't ask Miss Julia," Brandon said firmly. "She might say no. I'm just hoping to surprise her with a big huge donation. Hey, do you mind escorting her back to Snipesville tomorrow while I go to Atlanta?"

"I would if I could," said Alex reluctantly.

"Why can't you? Are you going home today?"

"No, that's not the problem. I booked a room for tonight at the Hotel Lanier downtown. But the thing is, I sit in the white train car, remember? If I'm going to travel with Miss Russell, I would have to tell the conductor I'm a very, very light-skinned black person."

"You can travel in the colored car," Brandon said. "White men come in there to gamble and make fun of us, so I guess you can sit with Miss Julia. And if the conductor kicks you out, at least you guys will be on the same train. Meanwhile, I have to hope I get some money from Herndon. After I pay for my ticket, I won't have much left."

"Okay, so consider this a donation from a supporter," Alex said, handing him $10.

Brandon grunted a half-hearted "thanks," taking the two five dollar bills, and shoving them in his pocket. Ten bucks was a lot of money in 1906. But he needed it, especially because he strongly expected that Atlanta was not his final destination. He was pretty sure he was going to go all the way to Tuskegee, Alabama, to see the Wizard.

Wednesday, February 14, 1906

Looking again at the crumpled, hand-scrawled map in his hands, Brandon wished he had not come to Atlanta by himself. He should have asked Miss Julia's permission. He should have … But he hadn't. Now here he was, feeling very alone on Valentine's Day. The only familiar city landmark was a tall, white L-shaped building that his dad had once pointed out as Atlanta's oldest skyscraper, built by the guy who made his money from Coca-Cola.

Brandon was standing between Atlanta Union railroad station, and a massive red brick building that looked like a castle. Turning his map around, he tried to figure out if the building was on it. He looked back and forth between map and building, still confused about where he was.

A young white boy in a cap approached him, chewing an unlit cigar and carrying a shoulder bag filled with newspapers. "You lost, nigger?" he said. Before Brandon could tell the kid to get lost, the boy pointed to the red brick building and said, "That's the Kimball House, right there." With that, he skipped away across the street, dodging carriages, a car, and horses parked at the curb with their tilted barrows loaded with sacks. Brandon lost sight of the boy while a streetcar rattled past, and when he saw him again, he was standing on the busy corner next to the Kimball House, shouting the name of his newspaper to passersby.

Brandon looked again at his map, and sure enough, next to the station, Rev. Evans had drawn a large rectangle and labeled it *Kimball House Hotel*. Now that he had his bearings, it was only a matter of walking half a block up

CHAPTER NINE

Peachtree Street to reach his destination. He was glad it was a short journey, because it looked like it would rain, and he had no umbrella. Miss Julia had advised him against carrying an umbrella in Snipesville because it would make him seem like he didn't know his "place" as a black kid, but here in Atlanta, he saw lots of well-dressed black folk carrying them, without being harassed.

Reaching in his pocket, Brandon felt his letter of recommendation, which Reverend Evans had handwritten on a sheet of Steward Chapel AME Church notepaper. He had read the letter on the train so many times, he had memorized it. The minister had been careful to point out that he had only recently made "George Braithwaite's" acquaintance, and that any money intended for the school should be mailed directly to Miss Julia Russell in Snipesville. Brandon couldn't blame Rev. Evans for not trusting him. Much as he hated to admit it, he was a stranger in his own hometown.

Two streetcars passed Brandon in opposite directions, one of them followed by an automobile. He walked by a cluster of white people dressed in fine clothes. Nobody paid any attention to him, but he was relieved all the same to reach his destination, which was marked on his map as *Herndon's Crystal Palace*. A red, white, and blue pole was affixed by the door, and a sign hanging from the second floor proclaimed *HERNDON*.

Nervous now, Brandon peered through the window at the huge barber shop. It didn't resemble the real Crystal Palace in London in 1851, but it was still very flashy. Dotted around the large room were barbers dressed smartly in white linens, and all the barbers were black men. Two were chatting, and one was operating the cash register, but most were busily attending to customers, cutting hair, buffing fingernails, and wielding scary enormous cut-throat razors as they shaved chins slathered in white foam. A black barber shop! Here, Brandon thought, was a safe place in 1906.

Confidently, he pushed through the dark wood and plate-glass door, and found himself in the gleaming interior. The barbershop looked even more impressive now he was inside. He took in the white ceramic tiles on the floor, mirror-lined walls, white-painted tin ceiling, luxurious padded benches, and wood and metal chairs upholstered in gleaming green leather. Immediately, one of the white-jacketed barbers rushed to greet him.

"Good afternoon," Brandon said. "I'm here to see Mr. Alonzo Herndon?"

The barber looked Brandon up and down, and then spoke sharply. "Mr. Herndon is not here," he said. "Likely, he's over at one of his other businesses, either Atlanta Mutual Insurance Association, or another of his barbershops. Is he expecting you?"

"No, sir," Brandon said, suddenly feeling very let down.

CHAPTER NINE

"Are you looking for employment? If you are, there's no available positions ..."

Brandon shook his head. "No, sir, I just want a word with Mr. Herndon on, um, educational matters."

"You'll have to return later," the barber said curtly, extending a hand toward the door.

Brandon was disappointed, but now he had another idea. How cool would it be to be to get a haircut in the most famous barbershop in Georgia history? It would be worth a splurge, just to be able to tell Dr. Braithwaite about it later. "Hey, how much is a haircut?" he said.

"Who is the customer?" said the barber.

"Me," Brandon said brightly. "Who else would it be?"

The barber looked sour. "We don't serve colored in here. Not even Mr. Herndon himself can have a shave or a haircut in his establishment. There's a place down on Decatur Street. It's the closest for colored. You can go there."

Brandon was absolutely stunned. Now he took a really good look around the barbershop. Sure enough, all the customers being shaved and shorn were white men. He tried to understand. "You're owned by a black man, all your staff are black, and you don't cut black people's hair? Not even your own boss's?"

"That's right," said the barber. "You obviously aren't from here."

"No, sir," Brandon said, "I've been living in England."

The barber flicked his fingertips at Brandon. "Look, I told you where you might find Mr. Herndon. You go along now, and don't make a fuss. We have important gentlemen getting served here, and we don't want our customers disturbed."

As Brandon, in a shocked daze, prepared to leave, he held the door open for a light-skinned mustached man to enter, and then watched as he removed his derby hat, revealing neatly-parted hair. Brandon saw how several barbers had perked up at this man's arrival, and the barber who had just dismissed him was already fawning over the newcomer. "How are you today, Mr. Herndon? How is business?"

"I came to ask you that," Alonzo Herndon said sharply, handing his umbrella to his manager. "You're late with this week's reports, and you know how that irritates me."

The manager nodded frantically. "Yes, sir, I will have the reports to you by the day's end," he said, and then, eager to change the subject, he nodded toward Brandon, still standing in the doorway. "This young man wants to see you."

Alonzo Herndon gave Brandon the same sort of look Dr. Du Bois had given him, the look of a busy and important man who didn't like having his time wasted. Quickly, Brandon stepped forward, pulling from his pocket his letter of introduction from Rev. Evans, and handed it to Mr. Herndon. Mr. Herndon slipped on his wire-rimmed glasses, read over the letter, frowning, and then handed it back.

"I take it," he said, "that you are George Braithwaite?"

"Yes, sir."

Mr. Herndon sniffed. "I cannot give money to someone who solicits me at my place of business. And I am not familiar with either your Mr. Evans, or Snipesville. Is that near Macon?"

"No, sir," Brandon said. "Closer to Savannah."

"Then," said Mr. Herndon, "I am baffled as to why this letter would be written on stationery from a church in Macon."

"We were at the Georgia Equal Rights Convention," Brandon said, and immediately, he knew he had said the right thing. Alonzo Herndon's eyes lit up.

"Were you indeed? I was sorry to miss it, but I have three barber shops and a new insurance company to attend."

"You sound like my dad, sir," Brandon said. "He's always busy. He runs a funeral home and an insurance company."

"Really?" Mr. Herndon looked interested now. "In, um, Snipesville, is that? Perhaps you could have your father send me his business card. But you say you were at the Convention in Macon. You are too young to have been a delegate, surely?"

"I wasn't a delegate. I was just along for the ride with Reverend and Mrs. Evans, and Miss Julia Russell."

"Miss Russell? The lady mentioned in Mr. Evans' note, I take it?" said Mr. Herndon, eyeing him keenly.

"Yes, sir," Brandon said.

"I see," said Mr. Herndon. "George, as I said, I don't encourage soliciting at any of my places of business, and while I am a philanthropist, I mainly support causes and enterprises here in Atlanta. However, you have shown initiative coming all the way here to see me, and I believe in the saying that he who ventures, gains. If you would send me a letter care of Bumstead Cottage at Atlanta University, I will consider your request. "

Brandon wondered if he was getting the runaround. He was used to vague addresses in his travels in time, but Bumstead Cottage was such an obviously ridiculous name, and why would Mr. Herndon be living on a college campus? "Bumstead Cottage, Atlanta University?" he repeated.

"Yes, that's my home address." Mr. Herndon said, and he did not appear to be joking. "No promises, mind. Have you approached Booker Washington? He might be able to offer some assistance."

CHAPTER NINE

"No," said Brandon. "But I met W. E. B. Du Bois in Macon, and he suggested I talk to Mr. Washington and to you." Then he smiled. "Oh, and Dr. Du Bois said you owe him fifty bucks."

Alonzo Herndon's expression grew hard, and Brandon realized he had gone too far. "I'm sorry, sir," he stammered, "I- I thought he was joking."

"No, he was not," said Mr. Herndon shortly. "As it happens, that's quite true. Good day to you, young man."

Brandon memorized Alonzo Herndon's unlikely address, but without much optimism. He was mad at himself for making that stupid joke about the debt Mr. Herndon owed Dr. Du Bois. Now he was all alone and discouraged in Atlanta, and he had only one more chance to succeed. He either had to go to Alabama to try to meet with Booker T. Washington, or else he would have to give up, and go back to Snipesville. Since coming back empty-handed did not appeal to him, Alabama it was.

But first, he needed to eat. It was the middle of the afternoon, he hadn't had lunch, and he was hungry. As a friendly-looking white woman walked by him on the street, Brandon asked her, without thinking, "Excuse me, ma'am, but I need a meal, and I wondered …" The rest went unsaid. The woman's expression instantly became both offended and frightened, and she picked up her pace down the sidewalk.

Brandon had realized that he had blown it, the moment the words had left his lips. Now two young white men had stopped to stare at him, just as a middle-aged black man in a suit grabbed him by the arm, shook him, and growled, "What are you doing panhandling her? You never talk to a white woman you don't know. Never."

Brandon was embarrassed and afraid, and his fear grew rapidly as he saw the two young white men walking slowly in his direction. "Get out of here," the man in the suit said, and gave him a shove. Brandon didn't need telling twice. He quickly stepped into the thick of a passing crowd, then broke into a run, taking the first left turn from Peachtree Street onto an alley, and then a right onto Decatur Street. He tried to remember the street names so he could make his way back to the train depot. Only after ensuring he had not been followed did he start to take stock of where he was. He walked down the street, pedestrians streaming by him, most of them black men in dusty work clothes, and past storefront windows, each of which featured hand-printed signs that read *Colored Only*. Stopping in front of one establishment, he pressed his face to the glass to see if it was a café. He saw men drinking beer, smoking cigarettes, and playing pool. One of the pool players laughed when he saw Brandon staring, took the cigarette out of his mouth, and gave him a friendly wave with his pool cue. Flustered, Brandon stepped back and looked up to see a sign over the door: *SALOON*.

It didn't take him long to realize that he was in a sketchy part of town, and he quickly retreated toward Peachtree Street and the business district. But he still needed directions to a restaurant, and this time, he stopped a middle-aged black man for advice. The man pointed south, and said, "You need Miss Mattie Adams' place, up on Peters Street. Most of those houses and businesses up there, they're white. Mrs. Adams's is the only place you can safely have a meal."

And that little episode, Brandon thought as he headed toward Peters Street, pretty much summed up Georgia in 1906: A forbidding and frightening place, where he felt constantly in danger, and was always looking for the next warm and safe refuge for people who looked like him.

As he walked, Brandon remembered his grandfather reminiscing about the *Green Book* that black people carried wherever they traveled in the 1950s and 60s. The *Green Book* held state-by-state listings of places where black travelers could eat, sleep, visit, or simply find safety if they were in danger. "Sometimes, the listing was out of date," his grandfather had recalled. "And we would show up to find the Negro motel or restaurant had gone out of business. But there was always a local family, usually an old widow, who would accommodate us. She would throw open her door and turn her home into a temporary home for us tourists, for total strangers. We made some lifelong friends that way."

Brandon now realized that Miss Julia Russell had done exactly this for him. She had invited him, a stranger, into her home, and looked after him. And then he remembered that the same was true of Sukey, his ancestor, who had cared for Alex in 1752, and even of Mrs. Devenish in 1940, who had looked after all those strange kids, including three time-traveling Americans, as well as Eric, and the real George Braithwaite. There was love and kindness and self-sacrifice in the world, Brandon decided, and he wanted to be part of it.

Fifteen minutes later, Brandon was seated at one of the rickety little tables in Miss Mattie Adams's parlor, which served as her restaurant. He caught a glimpse of an older woman whom he assumed was Miss Mattie herself, bustling about in an apron and carrying a bowl of greens from the kitchen. His server was a woman called Alice, whom he heard address Miss Mattie as "Mama."

Soon, Brandon was digging into a meal of pork chop, collard greens, and golden-crusted biscuits. Everything was tasty, and the whole meal cost only a nickel. "Haven't seen you before," Alice said. "You stay in Atlanta?"

He shook his head, his cheeks stuffed with greens, then took a sip of water from his glass before he replied. "No, ma'am, I live in Snipesville. It's down near Savannah."

"Oh, you come a long way," she said. "You go to one of the colleges here?"

"No, ma'am. I'm on my way to Tuskegee."

"To see Mr. Booker T. Washington, huh?" she said. Brandon feared she was mocking him, and shook his head. But Alice smiled kindly, and said only, "How's that pork chop?"

"Delicious," Brandon said, and he meant it. "So ... Has the restaurant been here awhile?"

She nodded. "Mama's been serving meals for, oh, twenty years now, but there are some who would like to see her out of business. She competes with white folks, like that William Jaillette, the man that keeps the restaurant across the road."

"But he can't stop her, can he?" Brandon said. Alice shrugged in reply.

He glanced at the wall clock. "Ma'am, I need to send a letter today. Can I buy paper, envelopes, and a stamp anywhere around here?"

Alice called out "George!" Brandon jumped, thinking she meant him.

A young man appeared. "This here's my son," she said, and then turned back to young George. "Go get me a bit paper, stamp, and envelope."

Brandon added hopefully, "And a pen?"

"And a pencil," Alice said. "George don't loan out his pen to nobody, it's too expensive."

When George returned with the supplies, Brandon pulled out a $5 bill to pay for his meal, but Alice wouldn't take it. "I can't change that," she said. "And you ought not to be waving round that kind of money. Put it away. No, you just be sure and stop back by and see us next time you're in the city. You can pay me then."

Brandon sputtered his thanks, but Alice said only, "Oh, it's nothing. That was a bit of food left that needed eating."

Brandon thanked Alice, then quickly addressed the envelope to *Mr. Alonzo Herndon, Bumstead Cottage, Atlanta University.*

Thursday, February 15, 1906

Following an uncomfortable night on the floor of an overcrowded "colored" boardinghouse, Brandon was on the move, aboard the colored car of a Western Railway of Alabama train headed southwest. To get to Tuskegee, he would have to leave the train well before Montgomery, and change at someplace called Chehaw.

The colored car was right behind the engine. Nobody dared open the win-

CHAPTER NINE

dows for fear of letting in soot and smoke. While the few white passengers on board could spread out in their mostly empty cars, the colored car was tightly packed with people. Brandon was crushed up against an old woman with two small wriggling children.

Dreading the onboard restroom, he delayed going as long as he could, but the journey was several hours, and finally, he had no choice. When he found the single bathroom, it was filthy beyond belief, and he could barely bring himself to step inside.

As Brandon returned to his seat, the old lady next to him noticed the disgusted look on his face. She said quietly, "'Scuse me for mentioning this, but you know, they don't never clean it. That way, they can say that the colored are dirty."

This was exactly what Miss Julia had told him. But he did wonder about something. Train restrooms were always kind of disgusting in England, where most people were white. "Ma'am, do you think the white people's restrooms on this train are clean?" he asked.

"Yes, indeed," she replied. "They ain't perfect, but they's much cleaner. I know, because I used to be nurse to a little white child, and I would take him to relieve himself. Used it myself until he was old enough to tell tales. Compared to ours, those are palaces. They clean them all the time."

"So are you headed to Montgomery, ma'am?"

"I am," she said. "Montgomery is where I stay, and I'm taking my grandchildren home with me. Their mama is a widow woman, and she's sick, so she asked me and my husband to care for them."

Brandon wondered why the old woman didn't stay with her daughter, rather than separating the kids from their mother. Then he realized that she probably needed to get back to her job. The only retired black person he had met in 1906 was Jupe.

The old woman was on her feet now, taking down a shoebox from the overhead rack. When she sat down and opened it, Brandon could see golden pieces of cold fried chicken, and fluffy biscuits. By now, his breakfast in Atlanta was a distant memory. His mouth started watering. "Excuse me, ma'am," he said, "But do you know if there's, like, a snack bar on the train? Somewhere I can get something to eat?"

She looked surprised. "Why, of course, there's a restaurant car, but it's white only. You from the North?"

He gave a tight smile. "No, ma'am. I just lived in England a while."

She held out the shoebox to him, and said in a motherly tone, "Here, you take a biscuit, and a piece of chicken. These two children don't eat much. We can spare it."

CHAPTER NINE

Two hours later, Brandon felt guilty for having accepted the food from the old lady, because her grandchildren were complaining of hunger. The train journey from Atlanta to Chehaw was supposed to have taken four and a half hours, but it had taken six: The train hit a mule on the line, and the journey was suspended while farmer and engine driver argued over who should pay for the damage to train and mule.

As the train slowed on its approach to Chehaw, Brandon said goodbye to the old woman, and took down his bag from the overhead rack. He and a few other people, all of them black, disembarked in what looked like a remote forest. There was not even the smallest of railroad stations, or a platform. All Brandon could see in the misty and rapidly darkening evening, apart from trees, were two small houses on a dirt road next to the railroad tracks. But he wasn't worried. The little one-car Tuskegee shuttle train was waiting for them.

Brandon and his fellow travelers were approaching the shuttle, when the conductor jumped down. "You're welcome to board," he said, "but we got to wait for the delayed train from the south to connect. This is the last train to Tuskegee tonight, and we can't leave those folks stranded in Chehaw."

"How long before it's due?" asked one middle-aged man. He was dressed like a professional, in a raincoat, suit, and tie, and his accent sounded Northern.

"About two or three hours," said the conductor. The would-be passengers groaned at the news.

"Look, is there some place we can get food or drink?" asked another well-dressed man with a Northern accent.

The conductor shook his head. "No, there's not, nor is there any other form of conveyance, unless you want to walk. Now, if you had took the through train from the north, it goes direct to Tuskegee without you changing here. But because you came from the east, well, you have to wait."

One man hopped aboard the Tuskegee train, but then immediately returned outside. "Say, conductor, it's freezing in there. Can you switch on a heater?"

The conductor had yet more bad news. "We got no heating on the Tuskegee train."

Brandon said, "So how far is it from here to Tuskegee?"

"Five miles to the Institute," said the conductor. "Takes a half hour each way by train."

The first man had had enough. "Say, Conductor, can't you just take us there, and then come back for the passengers from the later train?" He pulled out his wallet, and held up two dollars. "How about a little compensation for your trouble?"

CHAPTER NINE

But the conductor refused the bribe. Now Brandon made a suggestion. "Why don't we walk?" he said to the grumbling passengers.

"I can loan you a lantern," the conductor said. "Just bring it to the station in the morning."

As they walked away from Chehaw, Brandon glanced back and saw signs for "White" and "Colored" in the windows of the tiny shuttle train. Even for a few miles on the way to a famous black college, it seemed, black people were not allowed to forget that they were not the equals of whites.

It was a wearying walk along the railroad tracks, especially in stiff leather shoes, and by the time Brandon limped onto the campus of the Tuskegee Institute, he had a blister on his heel. Still, he felt honored to be there. Tuskegee Institute, the college founded by Booker T. Washington, was a legend, as was the man he intended to meet.

Brandon's companions from the train saw him as far as The Oaks, Washington's house on campus, and then bid him farewell as they headed off to their boardinghouses, taking the lantern with them. Only after he had waved them goodbye did Brandon, left standing in the dark, realize that he did not have a clue where he would stay that night. He looked up at the imposing two-story house. It did not look welcoming.

Now he was really anxious. He hated to knock on the famous man's door at nine o'clock at night, but he had no choice. Taking a deep breath, he rapped loudly. Soon, he heard the door being unlocked, and he steeled himself for an encounter with the Wizard himself.

But the person who now looked enquiringly at Brandon was a middle-aged maid.

"I've come to see Mr. Washington," Brandon said, trying to sound confident.

She looked him up and down, and noticed his bag. "Is he expecting you?" she said, frowning.

"No," said Brandon. He knew that explanations were seldom helpful.

Now a large and imposing light-skinned middle-aged woman, wearing pince-nez spectacles and hair arranged in a large bun, was standing behind the maid. "Who is calling at this late hour?" she said sharply.

The maid turned to her, "I don't know, Mrs. Washington."

Brandon leaned sideways so Mrs. Washington could see his face, and said in his best sort-of posh, sort-of English accent, "Mrs. Washington, ma'am, my name's George Braithwaite. I have come on behalf of the community of Snipesville, Georgia." With that, he held out Rev. Evans's now-tattered letter.

Dismissing her maid, Mrs. Washington invited Brandon inside, took his letter, and glanced over it. Then she said to him, "Wait here," pointing to a bench in the hall. Gratefully, Brandon took a seat, and promptly wished he hadn't, because now he really noticed how much his feet were hurting.

Mrs. Washington had gone upstairs, and, a few seconds later, Brandon heard knocking on a door, followed by a brief conversation he could not quite hear. She soon returned, handed back his letter, and said quietly, "George, Mr. Washington will see you, but he is very busy, so state your business quickly. You will find him in the den, the far corner room. Oh, but do wait a few minutes, while he finishes his correspondence."

As she passed in front of him without another word, and closed a door behind her, Brandon was left confused. Was he supposed to wait five minutes? Ten? Or was he supposed to go upstairs immediately, and wait there? He was too embarrassed to knock on the door through which Mrs. Washington had passed, and beyond which he supposed were the private family quarters. He hovered uncertainly. Just then the door opened, and Mrs. Washington reappeared. "I take it from your bag that you are staying the night in Tuskegee?"

"I guess so, ma'am," Brandon said, "I mean, yes, ma'am, I just don't …"

"You arrived in the night without any idea of where you would stay, George?" She looked at him sternly. There was something about her that made him think of Mrs. Devenish, a combination of kindness, strictness, and not suffering fools gladly.

"No, ma'am," he admitted. "Do you know where I can get a room?"

"You may stay here tonight," she said briskly. "Leave your bag here, and knock on this door when you have met with Mr. Washington."

Brandon thanked her profusely.

Five minutes later, his knees knocking, he stood outside Mr. Washington's den, still wondering whether now was the right time. Through the crack in the door, he heard a deep voice saying, "One last letter, Mr. Scott. To Mr. Andrew Carnegie. Dear Mr. Carnegie …"

Brandon was thrilled. He really was in the presence of greatness: Booker T. Washington was dictating a letter to Andrew Carnegie, the steel guy from Scotland, the factory owner who gave money to build all those libraries. Wow. He didn't want to interrupt this.

Mr. Washington continued. "Thank you for your letter. I am delighted that you and Mrs. Carnegie have accepted my invitation to visit Tuskegee on April 1 for the celebration of the 25th anniversary of the founding of the Institute. It is very kind of you to take time to visit us, and I look forward to seeing you both. I hope and trust you will very much enjoy seeing the fine results of your kind assistance. Very truly yours, et cetera."

Just as Brandon had not expected W. E. B. Du Bois to sound almost like an upper-class Englishman, neither had he expected Booker T. Washington to sound like one. Washington was born into slavery in Virginia, yet there was hardly a trace of the South in his voice.

Now Mr. Washington said, "Read that back to me, Mr. Scott."

"Excuse me, Mr. Washington, but what of the young man Mrs. Washington said is waiting for you?"

"Oh, heavens, Scott, I forgot all about him. What a nuisance. Where is he?"

"Right outside the door, I expect," said Mr. Scott.

Booker T. Washington sounded even more annoyed by this news. "Scott, why didn't you tell me?" he said, and then, more loudly, "Enter."

Awkwardly, Brandon sidled into the room. "Good evening, Mr. Washington, sir," he said to the man at the desk in the middle of the office, realizing a split-second later that this young man, with his neatly parted hair and bowtie, looked nothing like any photo of Booker T. Washington he had ever seen.

Brandon's eyes flicked across the room. And there was the Wizard himself, straight out of Black History Month, reclining in his chair, with his back to a grand wooden Victorian rolltop desk that was covered in papers and topped with a brass candlestick phone. Mr. Washington glanced at Brandon, then grunted, "Take a seat," gesturing to a leather and wood sofa on the other side of the room, as Mr. Scott, at a nod from his boss, picked up his notebook, and slipped out.

As Brandon stared at him open-mouthed, Mr. Washington removed his glasses, and stared back at him with piercing gray eyes.

He said, "Now, Master um ..."

"Clark," said Brandon. "I mean, Braithwaite, sir."

"Quite," said Mr. Washington, lifting an eyebrow. "Whatever your name is, would you please tell me concisely, that is, in as few words as possible, what brings you to my door at this late hour?"

Brandon gulped. "My train got delayed, so I walked from Chehaw ..." He immediately felt stupid, because Mr. Washington sighed heavily, and shook his head.

"No, I meant what cause brings you here? I gather from your letter of introduction, if indeed it was your letter of introduction, that you are advocating for a school in, where was it? Ah, yes, Snipesville, Georgia."

"I am, sir," Brandon said, and then, taking a deep breath, he explained what he was trying to do. Mr. Washington listened carefully.

"You have good timing, Master Braithwaite. I have the promise of funds from a benefactor who intends them to be used for the establishment of rural schools." Seeing Brandon perk up, he added hurriedly, "*But* she means to fund elementary schools. What is more, your Snipesville, as I understand it, is a rapidly-growing small city. Whether it may be described as rural is an open question."

Brandon thought fast. "Yes, sir, but the school is being built just outside the city limits, in Snipes County," he said.

"And what sort of school is it?" said Mr. Washington.

"A high school," Brandon said uncertainly.

"An industrial high school?" Mr. Washington asked hopefully.

Brandon still wasn't sure what an "industrial" high school was. He said, "It's going to be a high school with subjects like history and science. It will prepare kids for college, but I guess we could have courses in, um, becoming a plumber, or an electrician. Or a chef. Something like that."

Mr. Washington looked at him keenly. "Perhaps you ought to find out what an industrial high school is, Master Braithwaite, and why such a school is better suited to the circumstances of colored people in the South than is a school with a largely academic course of study."

Brandon was desperately trying to remember what he knew from his school textbook about the differences between Booker T. Washington and W. E. B. Du Bois. Not much, was the answer, and it was all kind of mixed up. All he could remember was something to do with black folks being self-sufficient, getting the vote, and Washington's famous speech to white people in Atlanta, which, for some reason, was about fingers in a glove. Or something.

"George … That is your first name, George? Why don't we discuss in the morning what is meant by industrial education." said Mr. Washington. "You may accompany me on my morning walk. Where are you staying tonight?"

"Your wife, sir, I mean, Mrs. Washington, she said I can stay here."

"Did she indeed? My wife is principal of the Institute, and generally a good judge of character. Don't disappoint us. I will see you in the morning, at eight sharp." With that, he pressed a bell on the wall to summon the maid.

Friday, February 16, 1906

By daylight, Brandon had a much better view of The Oaks, and of the trees surrounding the house that gave it its name. The Oaks, he thought, would not have looked out of place in 20th-century Balesworth. The maid served him a generous breakfast of ham, eggs, and grits in the dining room. He ate alone, but he couldn't complain: He knew he was lucky to be a houseguest at all.

As they set off across campus at a brisk pace, Mr. Washington gestured to the gaggle of smartly-dressed students entering one of the several red brick buildings. "Most of our students take academic classes in the morning, and industrial classes in the afternoon."

"So in the afternoon, they learn to be, like, carpenters and blacksmiths?" said Brandon. He was still vague about what Mr. Washington meant by the word "industrial," but it had to mean classes that trained people for jobs, right?

"Sometimes," said Mr. Washington, without elaborating. "But all students perform physical labor. You see these classroom buildings? They were built by Tuskegee Institute students, yes, as was my house. Students even made the bricks. We grow our own food, and grow more for sale."

Brandon was really wondering about all this. It was impressive, and yet something about it didn't make sense. And then he saw two young ladies leading a neat line of tiny kids carrying hoes.

"Are those kids learning to garden?" he said.

"In a manner of speaking. They are our kindergarten class, and they are going to learn orderly fieldwork."

Brandon's eyes narrowed. "So what do the children actually learn from that, sir?"

"Steady work habits and discipline," Mr. Washington said.

"Just like slaves on the plantation," blurted out Brandon. It had been the first thing that popped into his head, but he hadn't meant to say it aloud.

Mr. Washington looked steadily at Brandon. "Let me tell you something, George. Wealthy men support Tuskegee because they are confident that we prepare young colored people to be good workers. And they are right. We do. We dovetail our academic subjects with our industry: Whenever we can, we teach mathematics through carpentry. Our students write essays about plowing fields and preparing the soil for turnips. Our female students compose essays about baking bread and cooking greens. And in so doing, our students gain practical skills for their lives."

So this was what "industrial" meant. As far as Brandon could see, the Institute used its students as cheap labor, and prevented them from getting a real education, or even real job training. "So, Mr. Washington, your students do all this work around campus for free?"

"Oh, no, of course not," said Mr. Washington. "We pay them."

This was a relief. But Brandon was afraid to ask his next question. "How much?"

"A dollar," said Mr. Washington.

"A dollar an hour ..." Brandon repeated, and he thought to himself with relief that this was pretty good for 1906.

"No, not a dollar an hour," said Mr. Washington. "A dollar for every forty hours."

Brandon's face registered his shock. Mr. Washington, however, was undaunted. "Our students benefit from the discipline of manual labor, and they also receive a fine academic education. Our teachers come from the best colleges. Do you see young Mr. Houston over there?" He pointed to a serious-looking man in a suit. "He teaches English, and is a graduate of Harvard College. But George, our people need poetry less than they need practical means to advance in society. So tell me, this high school you hope to build in Snipesville, is it to be an industrial school?"

"I don't know yet, sir," Brandon said, watching the students walking by. They all looked very serious, and Brandon wondered if they had any joy in their lives at all. "Miss Julia Russell is in charge," he said. "She'll decide, I guess."

Mr. Washington gave Brandon another hard look. "I suggest your Miss Russell considers that an industrial school would be in the best interests of her students. If she decides to follow Tuskegee's industrial model, have her write to me, and I shall do my best to find funds for her."

But Brandon had misgivings. "Sir, if you're going to teach people job skills, why don't you teach them really useful skills? Like, I don't know, how to be carpenters and bricklayers?"

"We do," said Mr. Washington. "I told you. Students built these buildings."

"Yes, sir, but you didn't really make a big deal about that, or about their academic work, about, you know, becoming educated for education's sake. I mean, I know how much better my life is because I like to read. I would go crazy if I didn't have books. But mostly you're telling me about the students doing grunt work, you know, mindless unskilled labor."

Mr. Washington gave Brandon a cautious but knowing smile. "George, I shall tell you something else, but you must not repeat it, and if you do, I will deny having said it. A great many white men in the South do not wish the education of colored people to go any further than it has. And as our economy becomes more technical, I believe they will soon feel more alarmed by the prospect of the rise of large numbers of colored carpenters than by colored poets. A colored carpenter, contractor, or architect competes with whites in a way that colored teachers and ministers do not. This will be the challenge for Tuskegee. We already train teachers and ministers, as well as carpenters and brickmasons. It will be a battle not to draw too much attention to our successes. It is vital that whatever we do, we remain cautious and circumspect, so that we do not cause a backlash. Do I make myself clear?"

Brandon nodded to show that he had understood, at least sort of. What

CHAPTER NINE

Brandon heard was that black people should not be too successful, too fast, or bad things might happen. That wasn't a cheerful thought.

They walked in silence as they headed back toward The Oaks. Then Mr. Washington said casually, "I believe you attended the Georgia Equal Rights Convention?"

Brandon was surprised. He was sure he hadn't mentioned the Convention to anyone in Tuskegee. He remembered what Dr. Du Bois had said, that a meeting about civil rights wasn't really Mr. Washington's "cup of tea."

"Yes, sir. How did you know about that?" he asked.

"A friend of mine was there, and happened to mention your name. What did you hear discussed? I am very interested to learn of the proceedings."

"I wasn't a delegate, sir," said Brandon. "And I wasn't always listening. But they talked about voting, and how black people are treated like second-class citizens."

"Interesting," said Mr. Washington. "Go on."

Brandon realized that Booker T. Washington was plugging him for information. The Macon conference was about the kind of ideas W. E. B. Du Bois liked and Booker T. Washington opposed, like black people getting involved in politics, and pushing hard for civil rights, rather than just waiting for them to happen. But what did Mr. Washington have against black people demanding the vote? This was Brandon's chance to find out. "Sir, I hope you don't mind my asking, but why don't you want black people to have the same rights that white people have?"

Mr. Washington considered this, and answered carefully. "You're asking a very complicated question, George. I have dedicated my life to helping our people rise, and I have no doubt that what we teach and practice at Tuskegee is necessary for raising the race to claim our rightful place as Americans. It will take time."

"But W. E. B. Du Bois says …"

"Dr. Du Bois," Mr. Washington said abruptly, "is from Massachusetts. He is neither comfortable in the South, nor familiar with its ways."

Brandon knew that this was the sort of put-down that Southern white people often said to outsiders, to Hannah and Alex. It bothered him. "But Dr. Du Bois does live in Georgia, right?" Brandon persisted. "So I guess he knows it pretty well. And what's wrong with black people getting involved in politics, anyway? Why should we wait? I mean, right now in Georgia, white politicians are trying to stop our people being able to vote at all."

"Du Bois has become an agitator," said Mr. Washington, "and he is fast making a fool of himself. When he stuck to the business of scientific investigation, he was a success. You should take this to heart, George."

So Mr. Washington didn't like Dr. Du Bois. That wasn't a surprise. Still, Brandon couldn't help thinking that there was something not quite right about Mr. Washington's idea that things would gradually get better for black people if they just kept their heads down and worked hard. "Sir, what about all the violence against black folks? The lynchings?"

They paused in front of The Oaks. "I understand your concern, young man," Mr. Washington said shortly. "The Negro cannot rise when limits are placed upon him, or when the mob rules. That is indeed a very serious problem. Now, I must get on with my work, and you must collect your belongings. Have your Miss Russell write to me when you return to Snipesville. And do stay in touch, George. I would like to hear of your progress."

Brandon considered that perhaps Booker T. Washington and W. E. B. Du Bois weren't as far apart as they seemed. It also seemed to him that the Professor had been right after all: That powerful people listened to young people, and tried to help them. That was good to know. He doubted Miss Julia, an old lady who was little known outside Snipesville, Georgia, would have gotten the same attention from Booker T. Washington.

Friday, February 16, 1906

It had been a busy day. Alex had helped Eric send out all the bills to subscribers of *The Snipesville News,* and his lunch had been a ham sandwich eaten hastily at the drugstore. By the time they returned to Kintyre, he was starving. The tempting aroma of fried chicken greeted him at the door. He inhaled deeply, and practically ran to the kitchen, with Eric right behind him.

But the Professor was not the cook. A wiry middle-aged white woman was stirring buttermilk into flour in a long, narrow wooden trencher, while Caroline Clark pushed pieces of chicken around a large black skillet on the stove. The cook dusted the flour off her hands, then wiped them on her apron. "You Mr. Day and Mr. Powell? I'm Mrs. Hudgins. I been hired to run this place."

Alex glanced at Eric, who seemed as perplexed as he was, then said to Mrs. Hudgins, "Where's, um, Miss Harrower?"

"Why? You need to speak with her?"

Alex nodded.

"I don't know," Mrs. Hudgins said. "But she done paid me a month's wages in advance, so I ain't too worried. Anyhow, she said you gentlemen work at the newspaper, and I thought maybe you could help me put a new advertisement there."

"She asked you to do that?" Alex said, alarmed at the idea of sharing the boardinghouse with a succession of traveling salesmen. He liked that he and Eric had the place to themselves.

"Sure she did," said Mrs. Hudgins. "I don't know why. This place is too far from town, and the rent's too high, if you don't mind my saying."

"We don't mind," said Alex. Mrs. Hudgins pushed her glasses back onto the bridge of her nose, leaving a slight smudge of flour on one of the lenses. "Anyhow, I told her myself, but she just said something like she needs to have a record that this place is here. I don't know what she means. Do you?"

Alex and Eric exchanged looks again. "No clue," Alex said. Honestly, though, he did have a hunch. He had heard the Professor say things like this before. It was as though she was leaving a paper trail so she could find her way back again through the past.

As Mrs. Hudgins served supper, she chatted with Eric and Alex. "I been a widow for many a year," she said. "Ever since my husband died, a long time ago, I been struggling. My son went off to Savannah to look for work. So I had to give up the farm, and I didn't have quite enough money to get by. I been keeping house for an elderly gentleman, but then he died. I was like to move to Savannah to look for work when I got a knock on the door, and there was Miss Harrower, asking me if I wanted this position as a cook-housekeeper. So I took it."

She turned back to Caroline, who was standing at the sink. "You not done with them dishes yet, Caroline?" she said sharply. Alex instantly felt annoyed. He had noticed that Caroline Clark never spoke while Mrs. Hudgins was in the room. Mrs. Hudgins was obviously a racist, and what was Caroline doing the housework for? That wasn't her job. The Professor had said so.

"I'm almost done," said Caroline. "This reminds me, we got a letter from my brother. You want me to read it to you, Mama?"

Mama? Alex's mouth fell open. Maybe he had misheard. "Wait, you two? Mrs. Hudgins and Caroline? You're mother and daughter?"

They didn't have to answer. It was obvious now that he looked at them.

Saturday, February 17, 1906

Now that he was back in Atlanta, Brandon realized what had been bugging him about the city. He had never felt very comfortable there, even as a 21st century tourist, because of the crazy traffic, and because the place was just so big. But in 1906, segregation made Atlanta feel downright sinister. Standing at the corner of Mitchell and Peachtree Streets, he watched streetcars rattle past him, attached to overhead electrical wires. Every streetcar was set up like the

CHAPTER NINE

little Tuskegee shuttle train, with black people seated and standing in the back, and whites seated in the front. He did not see any whites standing on board.

Brandon had no intention of breaking the rules of segregation, or "Jim Crow," to use the nickname by which people called it. He was afraid that standing up to "Jim Crow" might prove fatal. The street car conductors were all white men, and they mostly looked mean. For the very first time, he really understood how brave Claudette Colvin and Rosa Parks must have been.

Now he caught sight of the streetcar that would take him to Atlanta University as it rolled down the block, past the ornate Victorian buildings of Peachtree Street. As Brandon boarded, he paid his nickel to the conductor in exchange for a grunt and a sour look. Nervously, he made his way down the aisle, past the empty seats reserved for white people. Every seat in the "colored" section was full, so he joined the other black passengers standing in the back. Traveling alongside Brandon was a workman in dusty clothes, as well as several men in suits, ties, and derby hats, and two elegantly-dressed young girls, one carrying a beribboned box that showed she had been shopping.

At the next stop, a huge crowd was waiting to board. The conductor yelled, "Move down there, niggers!" Brandon closed his eyes. He felt anger and shame as a physical pain. And he couldn't show it. He knew that. He bottled it all up, and it hurt even more, like a giant rock in his belly, pushing against his chest and throat.

The young workman standing next to Brandon called up the aisle to the conductor, "Sir, could you please bring the color line forward? There's no white people on here." That much was obvious, but Brandon thought the man was brave to point it out. Since there were no signs showing where the "white" and "colored" sections began and ended, it seemed that it was up to the conductor where the invisible line dividing white and black people started.

The conductor was not impressed with the young man's courage. He yelled back, "Don't you sass me, nigger!" And now the car jolted forward, as the passengers clung on as best they could, crammed together like sardines. Brandon, trying not to fall, resisted accidentally grabbing the arm of one of the two pretty young women standing next to him. The taller girl now muttered angrily to her friend that they ought to get off and take the next car. But her friend said quietly, "Ada, you know it won't be any better."

Ada sniffed in reply. "Bazoline, I wouldn't have come downtown at all if you hadn't needed a chaperone while you went shopping."

"I know," Bazoline said frostily, "But if you get off this streetcar, I will have to join you, and then I will be late for class." She contented herself with glaring at the conductor's back. Brandon found himself gawping at the striking-looking Bazoline. She was very thin, with large eyes, and she was beautiful, in a very exotic way. Most of all, she gave off an aura of being quietly in charge.

Arriving at Atlanta University, Brandon must have looked lost, because the girl called Bazoline turned to him at the trolley stop, and asked if he needed help. When he told her he was looking for W. E. B. Du Bois, her face lit up. "I can take you straight to his apartment," she said. "It's in South Hall, the boys' dorm."

Brandon was taken aback. "What? No, I don't want to bother Dr. Du Bois at home," he said. "Where's his office?"

"In his apartment," Bazoline replied. "That's where he works."

"Okay, then," Brandon said reluctantly, and he followed her. "So are you a student here?"

"Yes, for now," said Bazoline. "But I'm graduating at the end of this term with a degree in mathematics."

Brandon said bashfully, "My name is George Braithwaite, by the way. Your name is Bazoline, right?"

"Miss Bazoline Usher to you," she said.

"That's a nice name," Brandon said, feeling like a doofus as soon as he said it.

But Bazoline didn't seem to notice that her new acquaintance was lovestruck. "My mother called me Basil," she said, tossing back her hair, "because she loved the smell of the herb when she was cooking. But Basil is really a man's name, so I changed it to Bazoline when I enrolled here."

"Do you know Dr. Du Bois?" Brandon asked. "Did you ever take a class from him?"

"Oh, several classes," she said, and Brandon was thrilled. "Mathematics is my favorite subject, but I took history and economics from Dr. Du Bois. He's my favorite teacher. When I was a freshman, I earned a little money by looking after Dr. and Mrs. Du Bois's daughter on Saturdays. Are you planning to enroll at Atlanta University?"

Brandon told her why he had come, and she listened carefully. "I am glad you're helping your Miss Russell," she said. "I don't think there's any higher calling than education. More than anything, education is what will lift up the race, you mark my words."

There was a dignity as well as cleverness about Bazoline Usher that impressed Brandon. Meanwhile, her confidence made him feel inadequate next to her. But then feeling inadequate had always been his demon, hadn't it? Not feeling quite good enough, as if he were an imposter whenever he tried to do something out of the ordinary. Considering the extraordinary life he was leading

CHAPTER NINE

now, he thought, he really needed to get over his self-doubts. And when he thought about what the Professor had told him, about seizing the opportunity to meet important people and do important things while he was still young, the more he knew that she was right. He started to overcome his fear of meeting with Dr. Du Bois. He wondered if Miss Usher could introduce him to more people.

"I hope you don't mind my asking, Miss Usher," he said, "but are you from a prominent family in Atlanta?"

"Oh, no," she said with a smile. "I'm just a country girl from Walton County, Georgia. But my father was determined that I would have the best education we could find. I started at the preparatory school here on campus when I was 14, and I've been here ever since."

With Brandon standing beside her, Miss Usher knocked at the door of the Du Bois's quarters in South Hall. It opened a split-second later, to reveal two women, one white and one black, both in high-necked blouses and with upswept hair. They were startled by the visitors on the doorstep.

"Bazoline, what a surprise!" Mrs. Du Bois exclaimed. "You know my friend Miss Lizzie Pingree? She's the dorm matron, lives across the hall."

In a thick New England accent that made Brandon think of Miss Julia, Miss Pingree said, "Why, of course I know Bazoline! How are you, dear? I can hardly believe I talk with you so rarely, for this is such a small campus, but we all lead such busy lives, I'm sure …"

As Miss Pingree prattled on, Bazoline's face grew set. Brandon realized that she thought Lizzie Pingree was a bit of an idiot, and she wasn't doing a very good job of hiding her feelings.

Finally, when Miss Pingree stopped to draw breath, Bazoline introduced Brandon. "Mrs. Du Bois, I'm sorry to disturb you, but this boy's name is George Braithwaite, and he's come all the way from south Georgia to meet Dr. Du Bois."

Mrs. Du Bois frowned. "Is my husband expecting you, George?"

"No, he's not," said Brandon, "I have a letter of introduction."

He handed her Rev. Evans's letter, which was by now in tatters. Holding it carefully in both hands, she looked it over. Then, to Brandon's dismay, she said, "Dr. Du Bois is very busy." She folded the letter and handed it back. "Perhaps you could write to him."

Brandon was not going to give up that easily. He decided to play his trump card. "I just came from meeting Mr. Washington in Tuskegee," he said importantly, "and before that, I met Dr. Du Bois at the Georgia Equal Rights Convention in Macon."

CHAPTER NINE

Mrs. Du Bois hesitated, then said, "I will ask my husband if he will receive you. Oh, and thank you, Bazoline."

"Yes, ma'am," Bazoline said before turning to Brandon with a smile, "Please excuse me, but I have to go to class." And then, under her breath, she said, "Well done, George." With that, she headed toward the stairs, pausing only to turn and call back, "I enjoyed meeting you, Mr. Braithwaite. Good luck with your school. If I can help you at all, write to me, Bazoline Usher, Atlanta University. It should find me. I'm planning to be a teacher, here in Atlanta, but we never know what will happen, do we?"

"Yes, of course I remember you," said W. E. B. Du Bois. He gestured to Brandon to shut the office door behind him and sit down. Then he stood, and pulled a window closed.

Sitting on the other side of the great man's desk, Brandon grew excited as he looked around. He was in W. E. B. Du Bois's study at Atlanta University, and it was a total mess: papers were strewn across the desk, books were piled in open filing cabinet drawers, and there was general disarray. It was at least as messy as Brandon's room in the 21st century, possibly even *more* messy. Brandon was overjoyed. Somehow, it made the great Dr. Du Bois seem more human.

Dr. Du Bois leaned back in his chair. "Did you have any luck with Herndon? How about the Wizard?"

While Brandon told a polite and heavily edited version of his trip to Tuskegee, Dr. Du Bois stroked his goatee, and said, "Hmm," "I see," and "Go on." If he had an opinion, he didn't betray it. Finally, when Brandon finished speaking, Dr. Du Bois asked him casually, "What did you think of Tuskegee?"

Brandon hesitated. Just as he had known that Mr. Washington was pressing him for information about the Georgia Equal Rights Convention, he was equally sure that he had to be careful what he said to Dr. Du Bois. It was, after all, Booker T. Washington, and not W. E. B. Du Bois, who would provide the money for Miss Julia's school, if anyone did.

"It's interesting," Brandon said slowly, "what Mr. Washington is trying to do there."

"George, a word to the wise," said Dr. Du Bois, "Did you notice that I had you shut the door, and that I closed that window the moment you arrived? Do you know why that is? Allow me to explain. It is for your protection. Almost every Negro in America is afraid to criticize Mr. Washington—except me, of course. He already knows my opinion of him and his work. But most of those who fear him are right to be afraid: Whites consider him the leader of our people. He uses the money they give him to wield great power, and his word carries tremendous weight. He even has spies. He can and does destroy anyone who threatens him."

"Except you?" said Brandon.

"Except me," said Dr. Du Bois. "Although I will not pretend that my criticism has not cost me and this university. Now, you seem like a very mature young man. I can tell that you have decided to be discreet in what you say. So I shall say it for you. Let me suggest that Washington told you that industrial schools are in the best interests of Southern Negroes. I say that's claptrap. Our people need political power even to earn a living wage. We cannot have one without the other. And we have rights as United States citizens, including the right to vote, and the right to a true education, not merely a training in subservience."

Finally, a detail Brandon had learned in Black History Month popped into his head. "But if everyone has the right to good education," he said, "Why do you always say that only ten out of a hundred black people are smart enough to go to college? Why do you talk all the time about the Talented Tenth?"

Dr. Du Bois looked startled. "I don't say that we're not intelligent, or have the potential to be so. I think only ten percent of us are presently prepared for higher education. If we educate the best of our people, however, they can go out into the world, and educate others."

Brandon thought of Bazoline Usher. But something was still bugging him. "Isn't that what Mr. Washington wants, too?"

"Not at all, no," said Dr. Du Bois. "He's more concerned with the things of the world, with practical matters of making a living and getting ahead, not with, as I might put it, the souls of black folk. Tell me, George, do you read only to get ahead of the other fellow?"

"No," Brandon said truthfully. "No, I don't."

"Which book are you reading presently?"

"Sherlock Holmes," said Brandon, a little embarrassed. *"The Hound of the Baskervilles."* He added hurriedly, "A white friend borrowed it for me from the Snipesville Carnegie library. It was all they had."

"Don't be ashamed of reading a novel. That's my point. It is your right to read as you please," Dr. Du Bois said emphatically. "You have the right to read for leisure and pleasure, as well as for edification and enlightenment, just as our white brethren do. That is my point, George. Nothing should be denied us. And neither you nor anyone else should be required to use a white person as an intermediary to borrow books from one of Carnegie's libraries. Did you know that I led a delegation to the Atlanta Carnegie Library to demand that they admit Negroes? The best they would do was to promise a separate library for us. That was four years ago, and there is no sign of it yet."

Brandon finally plucked up the courage to be blunt. "I kind of think Mr. Washington agrees with you more than you know," he said.

"Do you now?" said Dr. Du Bois, a smile twitching at the corners of his mouth.

"Well, his students take academic classes in the mornings. And some of his professors studied at Harvard."

Dr. Du Bois exhaled sharply. "George, Washington's academic teachers are all terrified of him. He pays them badly and treats them like dogs. Even his wife Maggie has begged him to raise their salaries, or so I hear. Washington hems in his students and teachers with ridiculous and humiliating rules, so as to impress upon his wealthy white friends that he is running a tight ship."

"Well, he kinda has to do that, I guess," Brandon said slowly. "Because if rich white people like Andrew Carnegie get scared off, and don't give Mr. Washington money, who will? I mean, if Alonzo Herndon is the richest black man in America, and he isn't all that rich, we kind of need white people's money, right?"

Dr. Du Bois didn't reply, but again gave the tiniest of smiles. Brandon wondered again if there was more to his relationship with Booker T. Washington than met the eye. Meanwhile, Dr. Du Bois reached into his desk, and pulled out a small booklet. After writing in it, he tore out a slip of paper, and handed it to Brandon. It was a signed blank check for fifty dollars. "Fill in the name of the lady who is leading the building of your high school," Dr. Du Bois directed him.

"That's Miss Julia Russell," said Brandon, and Dr. Du Bois handed him a pen to write the name himself.

"Alonzo Herndon finally repaid me my fifty dollars," said Dr. Du Bois, "I gather that you had something to do with jogging his memory. And so I am passing the debt on to you. I want to see you build that school. Call it an industrial school if you must, but," and here he looked Brandon in the eye and tapped his desk hard for emphasis, "do your best to persuade your Miss Russell that our young people must be given the chance to cultivate a life of the mind. Persuade her to hire her teachers from Atlanta University and from Atlanta Baptist College, not just from Tuskegee. Tell her to write to my friend Professor John Hope at Atlanta Baptist College. He can advise her on whom she might employ, and how to tread carefully with Booker T. Washington. Now off you go, George. I have a great many pressing matters to which I must attend."

Brandon stood up. As he shook hands with W. E. B. Du Bois, he suddenly remembered something very important. "Dr. Du Bois?" he said sheepishly, "Could you loan me the train fare back to Snipesville?"

Rolling his eyes, Dr. Du Bois reached for his wallet. As he handed Brandon a dollar, he said, "Remember what I told you. And keep in touch. You know, you ought to consider applying to study here at Atlanta University, or the Baptist College. Professor Hope and I would welcome a clever and enterprising young man like you."

Brandon was reluctant to leave. He had a question. "Dr. Du Bois, you're from the North, right?"

Dr. Du Bois nodded. "Born and raised in Great Barrington, Massachusetts."

"There's racism up in the North, right?"

"Indeed, there is," said Dr. Du Bois.

"Is it just as bad as here?"

Dr. Du Bois exhaled sharply, then glanced out the window, and back at Brandon. "I suggest you travel, and then you can decide for yourself. But … look, do you see the green lawns of Atlanta University, George? Someone said that this campus is like a green oasis in a sea of dull red. It is an oasis in more ways than one. On this campus, a black man is treated with respect, as a human being, as he ought. But not so beyond the edge of campus. That is why I seldom leave Atlanta University, except to leave the South. I have my work, of course, and it keeps me very busy. But you will appreciate that my work is not the only reason I prefer to spend much of my time in South Hall."

He opened the door for Brandon, and said, "Oh, and your idea for a national association to promote the rights of colored men? It was already beginning to form when we spoke in Macon. I don't recall if I mentioned it to you, but I was one of several prominent men of color who met at Niagara Falls last year, to discuss how we might organize to end segregation, and achieve voting rights. William Trotter, Professor Hope, and Alonzo Herndon were among those present. Booker T. Washington is working hard to suppress us, even censoring any mention of us in the black newspapers. But we are pushing forward, as you saw in Macon."

"But you keep talking about colored men," said Brandon. "Women, too, right?"

"Yes, of course," said Dr. Du Bois, with a smile. "That is implicit. We have been hammering out that very issue lately, the admission of women to our movement. Trotter opposes it, but I support it, and I am adamant. Good luck, George."

As the sad-eyed Mrs. Du Bois showed him out, Brandon thought about what life must be like for her. She was cooped up in an apartment, and he wondered what she did while her husband worked at his desk. Like all the men he had met in 1906, Dr. Du Bois hadn't talked about women until he was asked. Brandon almost asked Mrs. Du Bois himself about her life, but the look

CHAPTER NINE

in her eyes told him what, really, he already knew. Brandon sympathized with both Dr. and Mrs. Du Bois. He wasn't looking forward to being cooped up in Miss Julia's house once again. He now knew what it was to be hemmed in, to be limited, to be confined, now and, perhaps, forever.

Chapter 10:
SO MUCH DRAMA

Thursday, October 12, 1905

Hannah imagined changing out of her uniform, walking out of the front door of Willowbank, and escaping from Ickswade forever. Maybe she could take a train to London, or Edinburgh, or anywhere else. But every time she had a daydream like this, she would savor it for a moment, then pull herself together. Too much was riding on her remaining in the Hugheses' stuffy and oppressive home, she knew that. She couldn't prevent either World War, or get women the vote, but if she did her best to ensure that things in this house happened as they were meant to, she could save several lives, maybe even her own. Still, that didn't mean she wasn't frustrated. And now she had just learned she would be the only servant on duty this coming Sunday.

Both Flora and Mrs. Morris had asked for Sunday off. Mrs. Hughes had easily given Flora permission to visit her sister in Balesworth. But when Mrs. Morris asked to spend Sunday with her grandchildren, her mistress was not so agreeable, and the cook returned from the drawing room in a foul mood. She slammed a saucepan onto the kitchen table with a loud clang, then turned to a startled Hannah and described what had happened.

"And," she added with a self-satisfied expression, "I told Mrs. Hughes plainly that I have prospects for another position. That put the wind up her. She knows I'm a good cook, and good cooks are hard to find. But then Miss Elizabeth told her mother that she should let me visit my family, because she—Miss Elizabeth, that is—could cook the lunch herself. Imagine!"

Hannah's eyes widened. "Wow. So what did Mrs. Hughes say to that?"

"She said I could have the day off after all. But then Mrs. Hughes had words with Miss Elizabeth in some foreign language so I couldn't understand her, and Miss Elizabeth went off in a huff again. I expect Mrs. Hughes reminded her again that she's a lady, not a servant. Now, May, with me gone, that means you'll have to make Sunday lunch and supper."

"Me?" Hannah was alarmed. "I can't make Sunday lunch. That's like roasted meat, and stuff." Cooking on a range was an art. It didn't have a thermostat to regulate the temperature, and Hannah knew she still needed help.

"Calm down, girl," said Mrs. Morris. "Nobody expects a proper roast from you. I will make a chicken on Saturday, for a cold Sunday supper. I told Mrs. Hughes you could serve a nice bit of soup and a home-made loaf for a light lunch. I told you, May, these ladies eat like birds."

Sunday, October 15, 1905
Making soup wasn't the worst way to spend part of the morning, Hannah thought. She had stripped the meat off the chicken carcass and set it aside for the evening meal. Now she chopped several carrots, two onions, and a turnip to add to the chicken bones for the soup broth. A loaf of bread she had made from scratch was making its final rise in a cloth-covered bowl near the fire. Hannah marveled at her own confidence with cooking, and how much she had learned in her travels in time. She could be out having fun, just like Verity, but this was better, somehow. Her work was the most important thing, she told herself, whatever that work happened to be. It was what gave her life purpose.

Now the servant bell rang. Hannah looked up at the indicator board, saw that she was required in the drawing room, and, with a sigh, removed her apron.

By the time Hannah left the kitchen, Mrs. Hughes and her two elder daughters were standing in the hallway. They were dressed for church in elegant coats and huge hats, with prayer books, purses, and umbrellas in hand.

"May, we shall return no later than twelve o'clock," said Mrs. Hughes. "Miss Margaret and Miss Victoria, that is, Mrs. Halley, have an afternoon engagement, and so we shall take luncheon early. Are you certain you will not attend church with us?"

"No, I'm sorry, madam," Hannah said, trying to look disappointed. The sermons at the Hugheses' church were beyond boring. "I have to get lunch ready." And, after all, that was true.

Mrs. Hughes nodded, and called upstairs for Elizabeth. From overhead came a muffled response, and the sound of hurried preparations. Victoria, Margaret, and their mother exchanged exasperated looks.

CHAPTER TEN

Forty minutes later, while everyone else was at church, Hannah saw that her soup was bubbling away nicely. She gingerly pulled the heavy loaf pan from the oven, and tipped her hot, golden-brown bread onto the cooling rack, inhaling the warm, yeasty fragrance with great satisfaction. Her loaf was perfect. Maybe the Hugheses would invite her to eat it with them?

No, she thought sadly, *get real, Hannah. This is Edwardian England. Servants never eat with their employers.* This rule she knew, was one that even the radical Miss Elizabeth was unlikely to test, beyond taking the occasional (and daring) cup of tea with her young maid, "May". Hannah consoled herself with the thought that eating lunch alone would allow her a bit of much-needed peace and quiet. And anyway, making polite conversation with the posh people would not be fun. Or so she told herself. Hannah felt excluded from this strange and difficult family, and now she thought about it, she couldn't figure out why it bothered her.

The Hughes's return was so quiet, they did not disturb Hannah from her nap in the chair by the kitchen fire. But the servant bell awoke her. Rubbing her eyes, she hurried into the drawing room, where all the Hugheses were sitting in tense silence. Something had happened while they were out, that was clear.

"You may serve luncheon in a quarter of an hour, May," said Mrs. Hughes in a strained voice.

Hannah couldn't wait to find out what was going on, and since the soup was already warm on the stove, and the only preparation she needed to do was to slice up the bread, she didn't return to the kitchen. Instead, she slipped into the pantry, to listen to the conversation in the drawing room. At first, her spying felt like a waste of time, because the family continued to sit without speaking. Hannah stood very still, trying not to breathe too loudly.

Finally, Victoria broke the silence. "Margaret and I are taking the train to see Emily Plaskitt in Balesworth this afternoon, but Mr. Plaskitt has kindly promised to run us home in his motor car after supper."

"How kind of him," Elizabeth said, "and how kind of the Plaskitts not to invite me."

Victoria ignored her sister. "Mama, perhaps we could all take a brief walk after luncheon? I think a little more fresh air would do all of us good."

"No, thank you," Elizabeth said.

"Honestly, Elizabeth," said Victoria, "There is no need to sulk."

"I am not sulking," Elizabeth said sulkily.

"Yes, you are," Victoria insisted. "Whether or not you approve, Mama is entitled to her views on women's suffrage."

"No, she is not," Elizabeth retorted. "Voting is and ought to be the right of all adults in a free society, whatever Mother's views on the subject."

Mrs. Hughes said, in a tremulous voice, "I do not care for being spoken of as though I were not in the room. Elizabeth, will you or will you not take a brief walk with us after lunch, before your sisters go to Balesworth?"

"No, I will not," snapped Elizabeth.

"Then, in that case," said Mrs. Hughes, "go to your room and remain there until you find a civil tongue in your head."

Hannah grimaced. She could feel Elizabeth's humiliation radiating through the serving hatch.

"Mother, I am not a child." said Elizabeth, clearly struggling to keep her temper. "I will go to my room after lunch, but only because I choose to do so."

"Good," said Mrs. Hughes. "We shall walk without you. I am going upstairs before luncheon."

The moment the door closed behind Mrs. Hughes, Hannah heard Victoria take her younger sister to task. "Elizabeth, Mama is being ridiculous, but so are you. Why on earth does it matter so greatly to you whether Mama favors women's suffrage? Really, this dispute is out of all proportion."

Elizabeth glowered at her. "Because I must live with her."

"Elizabeth, I love you dearly, but you really must act your age," Victoria said gently. "Mama is elderly, and she cannot be expected to conform to your new ideas."

"Mother ought to move with the times in which she lives," Elizabeth grumbled.

"Why should she do any such thing?" Victoria said. "No, I am in earnest, Elizabeth, why should she? She is a lady of the nineteenth century. And who is to say that she is wrong?"

"I am," Elizabeth said angrily. "You *know* what happened with Papa. Mother lives in a dream world that has nothing to do with life, her *real* life. Meanwhile, the world has changed, Victoria, and nothing will change it back. All of us, you, me, and you too, Margaret, we must be prepared to support ourselves in work, and not just depend on men. Yet we have nothing to offer the world. We have no skills or means of support beyond Mother's paltry income, and your meager inheritance from your late husband, Victoria."

Victoria said, "That is a cruel and wicked thing to say, as I am sure Margaret will agree."

Margaret said nothing, as usual, but Hannah imagined her nodding.

"You know, Elizabeth, Mama is right," Victoria said. "You ought to be banished to your room like a naughty child."

CHAPTER TEN

In the pantry, Hannah heard Elizabeth slam out of the dining room and stomp upstairs. After waiting a few seconds until the coast was clear, she silently slipped out of the pantry, and returned to the kitchen.

Once the family was served in the dining room, and a tray taken upstairs to Elizabeth on Mrs. Hughes's instructions, Hannah prepared herself a bowl of soup and a chunk of bread. As she ate her solitary lunch, she wondered yet again how the impulsive, hot-tempered and disrespectful Elizabeth had ever morphed into the disciplined and calm Mrs. Devenish. The calmest that Hannah had seen Elizabeth was at Mrs. Lewis's meeting, and even then, she had managed to infuriate Mrs. Lewis. Hannah was sure Elizabeth had deliberately angered her mentor, but why?

People change as they mature, Hannah thought, and Elizabeth must have changed a lot between the ages of 19 and 55. No wonder that Mrs. Devenish at the age of 66 was different again. *That has to be why she doesn't like me anymore,* Hannah thought sadly, as she lifted a chunk of bread to her lips. *People change as they get older.* But if that were true, how could she ever depend on anyone? She put the bread down. She suddenly wasn't hungry anymore.

When the grandfather clock on the landing chimed one, Mrs. Hughes and her two elder daughters had left on their walk, Elizabeth was quietly in her room, and all was again peaceful at Willowbank. Hannah had decided to enjoy having the almost-deserted house to herself for the next half-hour. Since Elizabeth was unlikely to come downstairs, Hannah felt free to make herself at home.

Hannah inhaled the drawing room's distinctive smell, a heady mixture of air-freshening rose potpourri from the bowl on the sideboard, wax floor polish, and ever-present dust. Closing the door behind her with a well-aimed foot, she set down her teacup and copy of *Hound of the Baskervilles* on the small table that sat by the largest of the overstuffed armchairs. Then she added a couple of lumps of coal to the fireplace, and poked at the guttering fire. Cluttered and gloomy though the drawing room was, Hannah thought, this was easily the nicest room in the house. It was so much more pleasant than the spartan kitchen where she spent most of her limited free time, or the cramped attic room where she slept. She flopped down into the big armchair, lifted her feet onto a footstool, and, awkwardly reaching back, rearranged the pillows behind her.

What would happen if she were discovered, she wondered? Elizabeth probably wouldn't care. *If Mrs. Hughes returns early, she might scold me,* Hannah thought, *but that's no big deal.* She knew from Mrs. Morris that Mrs. Hughes was pleased with her work as a maid, and unlikely to fire her. *Of course she's*

CHAPTER TEN

satisfied, Hannah thought. *She's getting all this work out of me for really low pay.* Hannah had decided some time ago to take pleasure in doing a good job for her own sake, not for Mrs. Hughes's.

She listened to the coal blazing and crackling in the hearth, and the gentle tick-tock of the mantle clock, and she felt herself relax. Her life in Willowbank was mostly dull, but the lack of drama had helped her appreciate little things and moments in life: A crispy and smoky chicken wing from the coal-fired oven. The pure joy of inhaling fresh air and the scents of trees, grass, raw dirt, and coal smoke mixed with mist on her rare moments in the winter garden. Her pride when Mrs. Morris complimented her pastry-making. A hot, sweet cup of tea with home-baked bread and farm-made butter. A good book, like *Hound of the Baskervilles*. Victoria Halley's awesome piano-playing, and what had Mrs. Halley called that tune? *Salut d'Amour*, that was it. She had told Hannah that the composer, a man called Edward Elgar, had written it for his girlfriend, which made it even more lovely. How simple and precious life had become.

As Hannah admired the view through the drawing room window, a tiny little red-breasted English robin, half the size of its American cousin, landed on a branch of the monkey puzzle tree. Tilting its head this way and that, it appeared to be watching Hannah. Hannah, blissfully calm, smiled back at it.

A split-second later, a tall figure leaped between Hannah and the robin, and before she could understand who or what she was seeing, the window exploded with an almighty crash, shattering into a thousand pieces. Hannah screamed and flinched as an object landed with a thud on the carpet, right in front of her. Terrified, her first horrific thought was that this was a terrorist attack. She thought to run in case the object was a bomb, but she could not will her legs to move. She sat motionless, in shock.

In a daze, Hannah remembered that this was 1905. How could this be terrorism? Did they have terrorists in 1905? Maybe, but in *Ickswade*? She looked down, and although she neither saw blood nor felt pain, she saw shards of broken glass at her feet, and on her apron. She looked at the bomb, or whatever it was. It was square, wrapped in paper, and tied with string.

And that was when Hannah Dias realized that this was no bomb.

In 1940, Mrs. Devenish had confessed to Hannah and Verity that, as a teenager, she had once flung a half-brick through her family's front window. Now, in 1905, Hannah had witnessed the deed itself. But laughing about it as a funny story told by an adult to children, many years after the fact, and actually experiencing the event, were two very different things.

Furious, Hannah jumped out of her seat, spraying broken glass onto the

CHAPTER TEN

carpet, and dashed into the hallway. Wrenching open the heavy front door, she sprinted down the gravel drive, and emerged onto the sidewalk just in time to see the inimitable figure of Elizabeth Hughes loping down the street, one hand clasping her enormous Edwardian hat to her head.

"You could have killed me, you moron!" Hannah yelled after her, but Elizabeth had already vanished round the corner by Baker's grocery.

Seconds later, Mr. Hastings, the neighbor from across the street, came hurrying over. "Is anyone hurt?" he said breathlessly. "What happened? I heard breaking glass."

"Nobody's hurt, but ..." Hannah almost said "Elizabeth" and realized this was maybe not such a good idea. "Someone threw a brick through our window."

"Who on earth would do such a wicked thing?" he said, looking outraged.

Now old Mrs. Owen arrived from next door, pulling her shawl around her shoulders. "Mr. Hastings, did you see that girl?" she said, pointing in the direction Elizabeth had fled.

"What girl?" he said.

"The girl who ran down the street," said Mrs. Owen. "I am sure I saw a girl. If I didn't know better, I would say it was Elizabeth Hughes."

Hannah decided that now would be a very good time for her to withdraw to the house. She would sweep up the mess, remove the evidence that she had been lounging around the drawing room, and await further developments. But it was too late: Mrs. Hughes, trailed by Victoria and Margaret, was walking rapidly toward her, and she called out, "Is something the matter?"

"Now, May," said Mrs. Hughes. "I see from the presence of your novel and tea cup that you were sitting in the drawing room during our absence. I will overlook your insolence, but it is very important that you tell me the truth about what happened. Who threw this?" She held up the half-brick in one hand, and in the other, the crumpled and grubby piece of paper in which it had been wrapped. Even as the paper trembled in Mrs. Hughes's grasp, Hannah could see scrawled upon in it, in terrible handwriting that looked like a child's, *VOTES FOR WOMEN, a message from The Women's Suffrage Association.*

Something told Hannah that siding with Mrs. Hughes against Elizabeth was a bad idea. But right now, she wasn't in the mood to defend Elizabeth, either. She decided to remain neutral. "Like I said before, whoever it was, I didn't really see who did it, Mrs. Hughes," she said with as much conviction as she could. "It all happened so fast."

"I see," said Mrs. Hughes. Her lips had gone very thin.

CHAPTER TEN

"Could I see that note, please, Mama?" said Victoria. She read it, and then read it again. As she did, her expression grew more and more grave. "It was Elizabeth," she said briskly, handing the paper back to her mother. "That silly little fool. She has tried to disguise her handwriting, I see, probably by writing with her left hand."

"I was afraid of this," said Mrs. Hughes. "That is why I have not sent May for the police. Why on earth would Elizabeth do such a thing?"

"I have no idea," said Victoria. "But it's very worrying. Mama, please ask Mrs. Lewis to intervene. Elizabeth would, I am sure, listen to a dose of common sense from Mrs. Lewis."

"Oh, I couldn't possibly," Mrs. Hughes protested. "I hardly know the woman."

Victoria gave her mother a shrewd look. "Given what an influence Mrs. Lewis is upon your daughter, perhaps it's time you made her acquaintance."

Mrs. Hughes did not reply, but said, "May, that will be all. Bring us tea."

As Hannah left the room, she glanced at the front door, and was startled to see Elizabeth's silhouette through the frosted glass. Quickly and quietly, she opened the door, and Elizabeth slipped back into the house with an apologetic grimace to Hannah. She put a finger to her lips, and her eyes begged "May" to remain silent. As Elizabeth unpinned her hat, Hannah stared angrily at her. But they had not been quiet enough. Mrs. Hughes now startled them both.

"Elizabeth," she said in a voice that was at once angry and anxious, "I know that you are responsible."

"I'm going to my room, Mother," Elizabeth said, rapidly walking to the foot of the staircase. "I am rather tired."

"And I am absolutely beside myself," Mrs. Hughes protested weakly, even as Elizabeth began climbing the stairs. Hannah saw that Mrs. Hughes was almost in tears. "I have no idea what to do," she said to herself, "or where to turn."

Elizabeth had paused on the landing next to the grandfather clock. She looked back at her mother. "I lost my temper, Mother, because of your antique attitudes and ... well, everything. You know what I mean. You are beside yourself, you say? Well, I am simply overwhelmed. But do not concern yourself with the damage. I will pay for a new window."

"Pay with what, pray?" Mrs. Hughes said. "And what am I to tell the neighbors? Did you not consider your family's reputation?"

"I have far weightier matters to consider than what the neighbors think," Elizabeth said, "And don't you know, Mother? Mrs. Pankhurst and her ladies are now committing acts of protest exactly like mine. Throwing stones through windows is hardly a novelty."

"What the dreadful Mrs. Pankhurst might or might not do is none of my concern," said Mrs. Hughes. "What you have done this afternoon is very much my concern. I shall have to think of what to do about it."

"Why don't you, Mother," Elizabeth said scornfully, resuming her journey upstairs. "I am going to lie down."

Neither of them had paid any attention to Hannah, who was now lurking just inside the kitchen, listening. Quietly closing the door, Hannah tried to process what had happened. What Elizabeth had done, throwing a brick through her family's drawing-room window, simply didn't make sense. And why did she feel "overwhelmed"? Sure, her sisters were annoying, and Mrs. Hughes was about as warm as a refrigerator, but Elizabeth's home life wasn't that bad. She was rich, she had servants at her beck and call, and when she cooked or cleaned, she was just playing at it. She could choose to read books and write letters while others cooked her meals and did housework. What was more, she was deftly resisting her mother's efforts to marry her off … What *did* Elizabeth have to feel overwhelmed about, Hannah asked herself resentfully?

She thought about Victoria's suggestion, that Mrs. Hughes summon Mrs. Lewis to speak with Elizabeth. She remembered from Mrs. Devenish's recollection of this day, in 1940, that Mrs. Lewis *did* become involved, and that she had said something that Elizabeth Devenish would still remember with a cringe, thirty-five years later. Suddenly, Hannah realized that perhaps it was her job to get Mrs. Lewis to Willowbank … And, she thought with a grim smile, it would be her pleasure. It would give her a chance to get a harmless revenge on Mrs. Devenish for hurting her. This, Hannah decided, was the closure she had been looking for. The time was now.

Hannah poked her head around the drawing room door, to find Mrs. Hughes alone. "Excuse me, madam? I just wondered if you want me to do any more baking, or anything?"

Mrs. Hughes said stiffly, "Had I needed anything further from you, May, I should have said so. Mrs. Halley and Miss Margaret have gone to Balesworth, and so I only require supper for two this evening. Take Miss Elizabeth's meal up to her on a tray."

Hannah said, "Sure. I'll do all that, Mrs. Hughes. But is it okay if I go on a walk?"

"A walk?" Mrs. Hughes was astonished. "Whatever for?"

Hannah guessed that Mrs. Hughes thought pleasant walks weren't necessary for working-class people like "May." After all, she got plenty of exercise from her job. However, Hannah's plans required her to leave the house. She made up an excuse. "I have a headache," she said.

CHAPTER TEN

"Then perhaps you ought to lie down," said Mrs. Hughes. "That seems to be the fashion this afternoon."

"Nope," said Hannah. "Walking is better for me. I want some fresh air, madam."

The fresh air argument worked. Hannah knew that Edwardians fervently believed in the health benefits of fresh air, and with Hannah the only servant available today, Mrs. Hughes wouldn't want to risk "May" becoming ill. "Oh, very well," Mrs. Hughes said irritably. "But don't take too long about it."

"Very good, Mrs. Hughes," said Hannah, and she trotted back to the kitchen to take off her apron, jangling the coins in her skirt pocket as she did so.

Shortly before five o'clock, Hannah was dusting in the dining room when she happened to look out of the window. With a flutter of nervous excitement, she saw Mrs. Lewis exit from a horse-drawn taxi into the rain, open her umbrella, pay the driver, and hurry to the front door. Drama! It was really happening. There was going to be drama. Hannah smiled smugly to herself.

Before the small woman in the enormous hat had a chance to knock, Hannah yanked open the door. "Welcome, Mrs. Lewis," she said joyfully. "I saw you coming!"

"Did you now?" Mrs. Lewis said as she stepped inside. She shook off and folded her wet umbrella, before handing it to Hannah. Hannah popped it into the wooden hall stand, and took Mrs. Lewis's coat before showing her into the drawing room.

"It's Mrs. Lewis, Madam," Hannah said triumphantly, as if she were announcing the arrival of Queen Alexandra herself.

"Please do sit down, Mrs. Lewis," Mrs. Hughes said politely. "This is a surprise. Would you care for tea?"

"No, thank you, Mrs. Hughes," Mrs. Lewis said, looking puzzled.

"May, that will be all," Mrs. Hughes said to Hannah. "You may go."

Hannah was careful to leave the drawing room door cracked open. She ducked back into the dining room and grabbed her dusting rag, then returned to the hallway, where she began polishing the stair banister, to give herself an excuse to lurk outside the drawing room. In the otherwise still silence of the house, it wasn't hard to overhear the ladies' conversation, and through the cracked-open door, she could see a little, too.

"I received your telegram, Mrs. Hughes," Mrs. Lewis said anxiously, "and I immediately sent my servant to fetch a taxicab to the station. What can be the matter? Is Elizabeth all right? Is she ill?"

Mrs. Hughes's reply was a stunned silence. And then, her voice faltering, she said, "I sent no telegram, Mrs. Lewis. What did it say?"

"The message was quite specific. It asked me to come at once."

"Mrs. Lewis, Elizabeth is perfectly well. I have no idea who summoned you, but I promise you I will find out. Regardless, I confess that I am glad of your presence. I would very much appreciate your advice, and your discretion."

"Of course," said Mrs. Lewis, as she unpinned her hat, placing it in her lap.

Mrs. Hughes continued, "This afternoon, Elizabeth did something rather curious. While her sisters and I were taking a stroll, she threw a … a brick through our window, breaking it, as you can see."

There was a brief pause while Mrs. Lewis inspected the broken window. "A brick?" She sounded deeply shocked.

Mrs. Hughes said weakly, "I am quite at a loss to explain her conduct."

Mrs. Lewis regarded her with a disapproving look. "But what makes you think that I might be of assistance? Surely, Mrs. Hughes, this is a matter for you and your daughter? I cannot say that I am pleased to have been summoned all this way for such a peculiar reason, and by some unknown person. That telegram gave me quite a fright. I really do think …"

Mrs. Hughes interrupted her. "I assure you, I sent no telegram, and I do not know who did. But there is an important detail I have failed to mention, and it will explain why this unfortunate incident involves you. You see, the brick was enclosed within a piece of paper on which was written the words *Votes for Women* and *The Women's Suffrage Association*. I am none the wiser as to who sent for you, but now that you are here … I wonder if you might cast light upon this affair?"

In a voice like thunder, Mrs. Lewis said, "Mrs. Hughes, I hope you are not implying that Elizabeth performed this ridiculous and wicked act at my suggestion?"

Mrs. Hughes was clearly alarmed by Mrs. Lewis's reaction. "No, not at all," she said anxiously. "I merely …"

But now Mrs. Lewis was in a state of high dudgeon. "I would *never* suggest such a thing. I am offended, indeed outraged, that you would even think it of me."

Mrs. Hughes put up her hands to calm her, "Again, I do apologize," she said hastily, "I am in a terrible muddle. I hoped you might help me, Mrs. Lewis. You see, Elizabeth is a rather difficult young woman …"

"Oh, believe me," Mrs. Lewis said with feeling, "you have no need to explain that."

"And," continued Mrs. Hughes, "you and I are insufficiently acquainted with each other for me to feel entitled to make accusations of any sort. I know you principally by your fine reputation."

For a second, Mrs. Lewis preened at this flattery, but then Hannah glimpsed her eying Mrs. Hughes with renewed suspicion.

"I am well aware that my daughter holds you in high regard, Mrs. Lewis," Mrs. Hughes persisted. "And now that you are here, I rather hope," she was almost pleading now, "that you might have a word with Elizabeth? That you might help her to see sense?"

Mrs. Lewis did not reply.

With an air of defeat, Mrs. Hughes said, "Mrs. Lewis, I am sorry to say that if you cannot persuade Elizabeth to behave herself, I am rather at a loss to say who can."

"You are her mother," Mrs. Lewis said sharply. But now she seemed to come to a decision. "However, since Elizabeth has implicated the Association in this nonsense, I will speak with her. Where is she?"

"Upstairs," said Mrs. Hughes. "I'll send for her." She rang the servant bell.

"May I please speak with her alone, Mrs. Hughes?" Mrs. Lewis said.

"Yes, of course," said Mrs. Hughes, sounding very grateful to be allowed to vanish. "Do call when you require my presence."

Hearing the bell ring from the kitchen, Hannah was careful not to reveal that she had been right outside, listening. She counted a few seconds, pushed open the door, and looked to Mrs. Hughes for instructions. "May," said Mrs. Hughes, "kindly inform Miss Elizabeth that she is to come at once to the drawing room to meet with Mrs. Lewis."

Hannah said, with a little too much enthusiasm, "Yes, Mrs. Hughes, at *once*."

She waited until she was halfway up the stairs before she broke into a gleeful grin, and danced a little jig on the steps. So it was going to happen, the scene that Mrs. Devenish had briefly described in 1940. *And*, she thought, *I arranged it!* She hadn't expected to be quite this happy, but she was. She was about to get payback, and not only for almost being seriously injured by Elizabeth Hughes' brick. This would also be sweet revenge for the damage that Elizabeth Hughes Devenish had inflicted on her pride (and her backside) during World War II. Hannah Dias intended to have a ringside seat for the Great Scolding of 1905.

"Excuse me, Miss Elizabeth," Hannah said cheerfully. Elizabeth was sitting on her bed, propped up on the pillows, reading a book.

"Yes, May, what is it?" she said, without looking up.

Hannah beamed at her. "Your mother, Miss Elizabeth. She wants you to come down to the drawing room." It was only kind to warn her, Hannah

CHAPTER TEN

thought devilishly, so after a pause, she added, "Mrs. Lewis is here."

"Mrs. Lewis?" said Elizabeth, looking alarmed, and putting down her book. "Is she? May, do you know why? Is it about the, um, events of this afternoon?"

"You think?" Hannah said before she could stop herself, but she managed to turn her exclamation into a cough.

Elizabeth didn't seem to hear what Hannah had said, and she reluctantly got to her feet. "How ghastly. I am quite unprepared for another scene. But I suppose I had better go downstairs, and pour oil on troubled waters. Oh, dear."

"Yes, Miss Elizabeth," Hannah said, as she eagerly opened the door to speed the young woman's appointment with doom, in the shape of a bad-tempered little lady named Mrs. Alice Lewis. On their way downstairs, Mrs. Hughes passed them, averting her eyes from her daughter.

When Elizabeth entered the drawing room, shadowed by Hannah, she found Mrs. Lewis standing. "Elizabeth," she said somberly. "I wish to speak with you about this afternoon. Sit down." Now she noticed Hannah lurking in the doorway, and barked, "You, girl! Go about your business."

Hannah hastily retreated, remembering just in time to leave the door very slightly open. Looking about her nervously, she grabbed her polishing cloth from the hall table, and dropped to her knees, keeping one eye out for Mrs. Hughes's return. Despite the risk of being caught eavesdropping, Hannah couldn't miss out on the scene she had made possible, of the future Mrs. Devenish getting her comeuppance, not for all the world. *If only we had popcorn in England in 1905,* she thought, *I would be all set for the show.*

But Elizabeth did something unexpected. She ignored Mrs. Lewis's instruction to sit down. Instead, she immediately took charge of the situation, speaking in a very calm, grown-up voice. "Before you say anything, Mrs. Lewis, I do apologize for your having been drawn into this odd little affair," she said smoothly, clapping her hands together, and standing up straight, her nose raised to accentuate how much taller she was than Mrs. Lewis. "I assure you that this matter has nothing to do with you. I am quite mystified as to why my mother would summon you all the way from Balesworth. What a pity that you have wasted your journey. Would you care for tea? I shall ring for tea, shall I?" She moved toward the servant bell handle on the wall.

Brilliant, thought Hannah, admiring Elizabeth's style even as she felt cheated of the hoped-for scene.

But to Hannah's surprise and joy, Mrs. Lewis did not play along. "Let's stop pretending, shall we?" she said abruptly.

"I'm sorry?" said Elizabeth. Through the crack in the door, Hannah thought she saw the young woman gulp.

Mrs. Lewis, whose slight Manchester accent now grew far more pronounced, advanced on the much taller figure of Elizabeth. "How dare you try to mollify me? And how dare you associate me and my cause with your childish behavior?"

Elizabeth was backing away from her in alarm, but she managed to maintain the same haughty voice. "Kindly remain calm, Mrs. Lewis," she said, "I have no intention of doing any such thing. Really, you do have a most exasperating tendency to misunderstand … Oh!"

Elizabeth had been silenced by a sharp slap on the bottom.

Crouching at the keyhole, Hannah gave a delighted wince under her breath. So, she realized, Mrs. Devenish had not told her and Verity the whole truth in 1940. Even after thirty-five years, she must still have been too embarrassed to admit that Mrs. Lewis had swatted her.

While Elizabeth bit her lip and discreetly rubbed her backside, Mrs. Lewis raged at her, and her words seemed strangely familiar to Hannah. "How dare you condescend to me? You spoiled, silly, and deceptive girl … Oh, I see from your expression that you think yourself insulted. Well, I don't care a fig for your absurd self-regard. So, I say again, how dare you associate your stupidity with me? This dreadful exhibition of yours is an embarrassment to the very idea of women's equality. For heaven's sake, what man would have done such a thing?"

Elizabeth stuck out her chin and said in a less confident but still defiant voice, "As I recall, workingmen rioted for their vote, and broke windows. Is this so very different?"

"I doubt they rioted in their own homes," Mrs. Lewis said, her voice rising, "and smashed their mothers' front windows."

"Yes, but …"

"Hold your tongue! I will not debate you, Elizabeth Hughes. I have been summoned all the way from Balesworth on a Sunday because of your peculiar and disgraceful behavior. I am not interested in your preposterous explanations. If word spreads about what you have done, you will ruin the reputation of the Balesworth Women's Suffrage Association. And what on earth has come over you lately? I deeply resent your rudeness at my meetings, showing me up in front of all my ladies and gentlemen. No, don't deny it. Well, this is the last straw. If you intend to return to my good graces, you had better act your age. And the very first thing that you will do is to apologize to your mother for your outrageous act this afternoon."

"No!" Elizabeth exclaimed. "No, that I cannot do! I won't! It's too awful." She sounded much younger than her years, and Hannah almost felt sorry for her.

CHAPTER TEN

"Oh, yes, you will," Mrs. Lewis said firmly. "For once, Elizabeth Hughes, you will do as you are told, because, you see, here is what *I* am prepared to do on your behalf in return. I am prepared to defend your behavior to everyone, to compromise my integrity, and to tell falsehoods to protect you, your family, and the Women's Suffrage Association. The very least you can do to thank me is to apologize to your mother." She walked to the wall, and rang the servant bell.

When Hannah opened the door, pretending to have come from the kitchen, Mrs. Lewis ordered her to notify Elizabeth's mother that her presence was required.

As Mrs. Hughes arrived in the drawing room, she closed the door firmly behind her. Hannah, desperate to see what happened next, fell to her knees at the door, and peered through the keyhole.

"Mrs. Hughes, I will shortly take my leave," Mrs. Lewis said calmly, while Elizabeth stood gazing into space, clutching her hands in front of her. "Elizabeth tells me that she momentarily lost her senses this afternoon. I suggest that, if anyone asks, we represent what has happened as nothing more than a misunderstanding. Perhaps we could imply that Elizabeth was locked out of the house, that the servants did not hear her, and that she broke a window to get in? That might be for the best, I think. After all, I have the Association's reputation to consider. Now, Elizabeth has something to say to you, Mrs. Hughes."

Elizabeth, now staring fixedly at the rug, remained silent.

"Elizabeth!" snapped Mrs. Lewis.

Elizabeth jumped slightly. Then, almost without drawing breath, she said mechanically, "My action was nothing to do with the women's suffrage movement or with you, Mother. I apologize."

"And what of Mrs. Lewis?" Mrs. Hughes said anxiously. "Does not she deserve an apology, for having come all the way from Balesworth on your account?"

Elizabeth's only response was to twitch her nose, and grunt something that might or might not have been "Yes."

Mrs. Lewis threw Elizabeth a furious look. "If I were you, Mrs. Hughes," she said angrily, "I would give her a good hiding."

From the keyhole, Hannah took in everything that happened next. Mrs. Hughes turned her attention to the window. Elizabeth seemed ready to sink through an imaginary hole in the floor. Mrs. Lewis looked more offended than ever by the awkward silence of mother and daughter that followed her suggestion. In fact, the only person enjoying the scene was Hannah, who almost fell over backwards in the hallway in silent mirth, her hand clamped to her mouth to stifle the giggles.

Mrs. Lewis flung one last withering stare at a mortified Elizabeth, and then said to nobody in particular, "I wish you a good evening. Now, if you will excuse me, I must catch the Balesworth train."

Without a word, Mrs. Hughes rang the servant bell. Hannah jumped up from her crouch, and opened the drawing room door just in time for Mrs. Lewis to stalk out. Rushing to the hall stand, Hannah grabbed Mrs. Lewis's coat and umbrella. As she thrust them at the irate little woman, she had a huge smile on her face.

Mrs. Lewis glared at her. "What are you grinning at, you insolent girl?" she said. "Do you find this amusing?" She threw Hannah a withering look of contempt, and said, "You ought to be ashamed of yourself." With that, she launched herself down the gravel driveway.

Hannah felt as though Mrs. Lewis had punched her in the gut. In an instant, she knew she had been wrong. The scene had not been meant for her entertainment: Elizabeth was humiliated, and Hannah suddenly felt her shame. How was it possible, she wondered, to feel so deeply sorry for Elizabeth and yet bitterly angry toward Mrs. Devenish at the exact same time? But that was precisely what was going through her mind.

As Hannah walked slowly toward the kitchen, she heard Mrs. Hughes exclaim loudly to Elizabeth, "Well! What a dreadfully common thing of her to say! Is your Mrs. Lewis always so blunt?"

"Oh, Mother," cried Elizabeth, her voice cracking, "You are such a frightful snob!" With that, she burst into tears, and flew out of the room, past Hannah. Hannah could see the utter misery on Elizabeth's face, and her mood turned completely to ashes.

When Victoria and Margaret returned that evening, Hannah, working in the kitchen with the door open, heard Mrs. Hughes stop Victoria in the hallway. "I shall say little of what you did today," she said. "But I will say this. I know what you did, and I resent it."

"I have no idea what you are talking about, Mama," Victoria said, in genuine confusion.

Hannah's stomach lurched. Unlike Victoria, she knew exactly what Mrs. Hughes was talking about. It was the telegram to Mrs. Lewis. Hopefully, she would take a while to figure out that it was not her eldest daughter who had sent for Mrs. Lewis, but her new maid, a nobody.

Afraid though Hannah was of discovery, she was far more ashamed of herself, just as Mrs. Lewis had told her she should be.

CHAPTER TEN

Later, still feeling sick as she arranged cold cuts of chicken on a serving plate, Hannah thought yet again how stupid she had been to meddle in Elizabeth's life purely for her own reasons, and without considering the effect her actions would have on Elizabeth. Revenge wasn't sweet at all: It was ugly and miserable, and made her feel like a terrible person. After all, if Elizabeth had felt driven to something as drastic as chucking a brick through her family's front window, there was obviously something really wrong with her life.

As she washed her hands at the kitchen sink, Hannah had another, very different thought. When, in 1940, Mrs. Devenish had recounted the story of this day's events, she had said that both of her parents were present. Hannah was sure of it. But how could that possibly be, when Mr. Hughes was already dead?

Monday, October 16, 1905

Hannah couldn't wait until her Wednesday off to tell Verity what had happened, although she was worried that her friend was still mad at her. She had to find an excuse to go on an errand to Mr. Baker's shop. But what?

"Put the kettle on, May," said Mrs. Morris, who was sifting flour into a bowl. "I need hot water."

Hannah turned on the tap, and went to fetch the huge black iron tea kettle from the range. Mrs. Morris nodded toward the little can of Borwick's Baking Powder sitting on the table. "Here, May, before you put that kettle on the stove, measure out a teaspoon of baking powder for me."

Resting the kettle on the wooden draining board by the side of the sink, Hannah grabbed the baking powder and a teaspoon, and started to measure it out over Mrs. Morris's dough bowl. But Mrs. Morris would have none of that.

"Not over the bowl," she scolded, lightly slapping Hannah's hand away. "If you drop in too much, you'll ruin my mixture. No, go and measure it over the sink."

Rolling her eyes, Hannah took the can of baking powder and teaspoon back to the sink. At that moment, she had an idea. She scooped out a teaspoon of fine white powder, leveling it off with her finger, and set it aside for the cook. Glancing over her shoulder to make sure Mrs. Morris wasn't watching, she knocked the open can into the sink. "Oh, no!" she announced dramatically. "I am so sorry, Mrs. Morris! I dropped the baking powder."

"Well, fish it out then," Mrs. Morris said vaguely, as she tried to soften butter by stabbing at a slab of it with a wooden spoon.

Behind her, Hannah was busily scattering the last of the baking soda from the can into the sink, while running water to swill it away. "No, I'm sorry, but it all fell out," she said. "I'm rinsing the sink. I did manage to save you a teaspoonful for your recipe."

"Oh, my giddy aunt," tutted Mrs. Morris. "You clumsy girl. Go down the corner shop and fetch some more, then."

Hannah ran all the way down the street to Baker's grocery store, and pushed open the door to the accompanying jangle of the bell. Mr. Baker was up on the ladder, arranging cans of tomatoes in a pyramid on a high shelf, and Verity was standing at the huge brass cash register.

With a smile, she said, "Hello, um, May. How can I help you?"

"Borwick's Baking Powder, please," said Hannah.

"That's pronounced Borricks," Verity said. "Not Bore-wicks." But then, she leaned forward, and whispered, "Because English makes no sense, that's why."

Hannah felt a great surge of relief. Her friend had forgiven her for their argument. "Verity, can I talk to you? In private?"

"Not now," Verity said quickly, glancing at Mr. Baker. "Perhaps after work?"

Hannah couldn't wait to tell Verity, and knew she couldn't come back later, but she was afraid to say too much in front of Verity's boss. She certainly couldn't use Elizabeth's name. So she said, as casually as she could, "It's about our friend."

"Our friend?" said Verity, brow furrowed.

"Yes," Hannah said significantly, "Our friend. Betty."

"Betty?" said Verity, still confused.

"Yes, Betty," Hannah repeated.

Suddenly, Verity got the joke. Betty. Elizabeth. Hannah saw the corners of Verity's mouth twitch, as she tried desperately not to laugh at the idea of her very proper grandmother being addressed as Betty. "I assume," she said, "you mean …"

"Betty," said Hannah, now trying to make Verity laugh. "You know, the girl from the Dragon Factory."

Verity exploded into laughter, and Hannah started giggling. Mr. Baker tried to look like he wasn't really paying attention as he descended the ladder, and he began stacking small yellow boxes of matches on the counter. Verity, meanwhile, was making choking sounds, trying to regain her composure. "Are you all right, Miss Powell?" said Mr. Baker. "Would you care for a cup of tea?"

Verity managed a frantic nod, her lips firmly pressed together, and Mr. Baker disappeared into the back of the shop, toward the kitchen. But at that moment, the shop doorbell jangled, and Verity, looking over Hannah's shoulder at the door, whispered, "Oh, gosh, look who the cat dragged in."

CHAPTER TEN

"Good afternoon, Miss Powell," said Tom Devenish. "I am glad to see you're not risking your life on the ladder today."

"Oh, I'm fine," Verity said with a smile. "But it was kind of you to save me from what I am quite sure was certain death ... No, I'm just joking, Mr. Devenish. No need to look so concerned. Now, how may I help you?"

"A packet of Nut Brown tobacco, please, a small box of matches, and ... What was it again?" He seemed lost for a moment. "I have quite forgotten," he said, and looked hopefully at Verity.

"Well, if you don't know," she said, "I certainly don't."

He looked downward, thinking, and then suddenly, his head shot up. "A quarter pound of boiled ham!" he said triumphantly. "If you please."

"Hey, how are you today?" Hannah said to Tom. He looked surprised that she had spoken to him, and she mentally kicked herself. Of course he didn't remember her. She was Elizabeth's maid, not anyone important.

Verity, having cut ham with a very dangerous-looking meat-slicer, deftly wrapped the thick, dark pink slabs of meat in white paper, sealed the package with paper tape, and placed it on the counter with Mr. Devenish's other purchases.

"Anything else?" she said.

He shuffled awkwardly. "I, um ... I ...um ...so ..."

"I'm sorry?" Verity said, looking puzzled.

"I'm sorry," he said, "What I mean to say, um, that is ... You do know Miss Cooke, of course?"

"Of course! Millie!" said Verity. "Yes, we met at Mrs. Lewis's meeting."

"The thing is," Mr. Devenish rushed on, "We, that is, a group of young gentlemen and ladies, are holding a meeting to discuss politics at Waldley Cottage, that is, Millie Cooke's home in Balesworth, a week from tomorrow, and I wondered whether you would care to attend? Miss Cooke speaks highly of you, Miss Powell, and I am sure she would be gratified by your attendance. Miss Cooke's aunt will chaperone, of course."

"Oh, of course she will," said Verity. "We wouldn't want innocent young ladies being unsupervised for a moment, would we? They might have independent thoughts, and then where would we be?"

Hannah caught Verity's sarcasm, which seemed to go over Tom Devenish's head, and then coughed pointedly. Verity took the hint. "Can I bring Miss Harrower here?" she said. Mr. Devenish glanced at Hannah in her servant uniform and hesitated. Then he said, without enthusiasm, "Certainly, of course," before quickly returning his attention to Verity. "I must say, I am delighted that you will join us, Miss Powell."

CHAPTER TEN

"Can I bring another friend?" Verity said.

"That should be all right," Tom said reluctantly. "May I ask her name so I can mention her to Miss Cooke?"

"Elizabeth," said Hannah. "Elizabeth Dev … I mean, Elizabeth Hughes."

Mr. Devenish scratched his head. "Hmm, yes. I'm afraid that might present difficulties at present."

Verity stared at him. "Why?" she said sharply.

He looked embarrassed. "I am not well-acquainted with Miss Hughes myself, but just this morning, Miss Cooke warned me … You see … The thing is, Miss Hughes does seem rather … Well, I shall say no more."

The two girls glared at him in silence.

"Oh, dear," he said in dismay. "I do seem to have dropped a brick, rather. Ah. So …"

"Dropped a brick?" Hannah said, confused.

"Mr. Devenish means he has put his foot in it," Verity said shortly.

"I'm sorry," Tom said. "It's just that, well, Miss Cooke, for some reason, has suddenly taken against Miss Hughes. Whether that is fair or not …"

As Verity rang up his purchases, she said stonily, "Now, if you will excuse me, Mr. Devenish, I have to give Mr. Baker a hand sorting out some stock that's just been delivered. Please give the details of the meeting to Miss Harrower, Mr. Devenish." With that, she hurried into the back of the shop. Hannah figured out that Verity was pretty freaked by this conversation. She had always been her grandmother's fiercest defender, as Hannah knew all too well. Now she was having to defend her against her grandfather, which had to feel very strange.

Tom Devenish picked up a pencil and paper bag from the counter and wrote down the address, date, and time of the meeting. Hannah had a question. "Do you live in Ickswade?"

"No, actually," he said, "I live in Balesworth. My mother and I moved there quite recently."

He was a new arrival in the area. This explained why he wasn't listed in the Hertfordshire directory, Hannah thought, but there was something else it did not explain. "So why do you come all the way to Bedfordshire to buy tobacco and matches?"

"I was just passing …" he said unconvincingly.

Hannah suddenly knew exactly why he had come all the way to Baker's shop, and it had nothing to do with needing smoking supplies.

As soon as Mr. Devenish left, Verity slipped back behind the counter. "I say, Hannah, it wasn't my imagination …"

CHAPTER TEN

"No, it wasn't," said Hannah, "You heard right. Your grandpa is asking you out. You look a lot like your granny. But don't worry. Now we have a chance to fix up your grandparents."

"We had better," said Verity, picking up the address and looking at it. "It's a great pity that Tom Devenish and Millie Cooke think Elizabeth is barmy. I have no idea why. She seems perfectly normal to me, and you would think they would approve of her standing up to bossy old Mrs. Lewis at the last meeting."

"Barmy?" said Hannah. Here was a British word she hadn't heard before. She had a bad feeling about this.

Verity explained. "Potty. Batty. Mad."

"Oh," said Hannah. "Nuts. Um, yeah. Look, that's what I came to talk with you about …"

But Mr. Baker picked this moment to return with tea. Hannah's news would have to wait until Wednesday, after all.

Tuesday, October 17, 1905

Early morning found Hannah, as usual, filling cans with warm water in the massive claw-footed bathtub, before delivering them to the bedrooms. As usual, each of the Hugheses greeted her when she knocked on their bedroom doors to wake them and deliver the water. But for the second day in a row, Elizabeth, who usually said a groggy "Good morning, May," only grunted, as if reluctant to do any more than demonstrate that she had not died in the night.

Until this moment, Hannah had assumed that Elizabeth was just sulking since Sunday's events, too ashamed after the brick-throwing and Mrs. Lewis's fierce scolding to show her face to anyone. Now, she wondered whether Elizabeth was angry with her. After all, Hannah was the only witness to the deed, and while Elizabeth probably wouldn't figure out that she had sent the telegram, maybe she thought Hannah had ratted her out to Mrs. Hughes. Later, when Elizabeth passed her in the hallway, Hannah said "Good morning, Miss Elizabeth." But Elizabeth did not reply, and closed the drawing room door firmly behind her. *So it's not my imagination,* Hannah thought grimly. *She's not talking to me.*

But Hannah's attitude toward Elizabeth had hardened since the fateful day. Elizabeth *had* thrown the brick. It was obvious to everyone that she had done it. She had even admitted to it. How was this Hannah's fault? *How childish and spiteful,* Hannah thought. *She needs to grow up and get a life.* And then she felt guilty. It was so much easier to blame Elizabeth than it was to admit her own role in adding to the young woman's misery.

CHAPTER TEN

Wednesday, October 18, 1905

On this rainy evening, as they sat before a brightly-burning coal fire in the drawing room of Weston Cottage, Hannah finally had a chance to tell Verity the full details of the brick-throwing crisis at Willowbank. Hannah was somber and sympathetic to Elizabeth in the telling, but Verity nonetheless found her tale very entertaining. When Hannah repeated Mrs. Lewis's parting advice to Elizabeth's mother, Verity laughed loudly. "So it really happened!" she said. "Just like Granny told us. But she never told us that the old bat walloped her, did she? Ha! Oh, how marvelous. I do wish I could have been a fly on the wall! What fun!"

But Hannah didn't share the joke. "Look, Verity, I know it sounds funny, but it's not. Elizabeth won't talk to me, and when I'm honest with myself, I realize this is my fault. I mean, okay, she threw the brick, but I shouldn't have sent the telegram. Whatever is going on with Elizabeth right now, she needs Mrs. Lewis's support. If Mrs. Lewis stops talking to her, that's not good."

Verity brushed off Hannah's worries. "Don't worry so. I told you before, something like this was bound to happen. Granny and Mrs. Lewis were always falling out and making up again. Honestly, I think Mrs. Lewis never really accepted Granny being a grown-up and having her own opinions. She always thought of her as the little girl she first took under her wing, you see. But that's not real life, is it? Young people grow up. They don't just do what adults tell them, and the world would be very dull and very strange if they did. Mrs. Lewis should have had the good sense to know that."

"I guess," Hannah said. She couldn't help thinking of Mrs. Devenish at that moment, but before she could wonder why, she finally voiced what had been weighing heavily on her mind. "Suppose Elizabeth doesn't want Mrs. Lewis to think of her as an adult? Suppose throwing the brick was a cry for help?"

"No, that's not something Granny would do," Verity said firmly. "She's always been the most grown-up person in our family."

But Hannah was not so sure. "Well, she isn't acting grown-up right now. Grown-up people don't deliberately break the windows of their own houses. She's acting so immature. She behaves like a spoiled brat."

"What's the matter, Hannah?" Verity said briskly. "Don't you like the competition?"

Hannah was stung by Verity's remark, but she didn't argue. She was afraid that Verity might be right. Instead, she said, "I'm worried that Tom and Millie think Elizabeth's crazy, and she's not, although she is kind of strung out. But here's what confuses me: I don't know how Tom and Millie would know about the brick, or about how Elizabeth behaves at home. Neither of them lives in

CHAPTER TEN

Ickswade, and without phones, I don't see how the news would have traveled that fast. And if it's not the brick that's worrying them, I don't know what else it would be. Usually, Elizabeth's on her best behavior in public."

"You don't think Mrs. Lewis spilled the beans?" said Verity. "You know, about the brick and all that?"

"No, I don't think that at all," said Hannah. "Mrs. Lewis will keep her mouth shut, and she would even if she wasn't worried about the reputation of the Women's Suffrage Association Your granny always respected Mrs. Lewis because she's got, I dunno the word...."

"Integrity?" suggested Verity.

"Yes, that's it," Hannah said. "Integrity. Just like your granny ... Wow, her throwing a brick really is weird, isn't it?"

Verity frowned. "You're quite right, Hannah. It's really not funny at all. Poor Elizabeth. Oh, gosh."

"What is it?" Hannah said.

"Nothing. Just something I overheard Mummy say to Daddy, ages ago." She fell silent.

"So what is it?" Hannah repeated.

"I can't tell you," Verity said. "My lips are sealed."

"Oh, come on, Verity ..."

Verity hesitated, and then she said, "What Mummy said to Daddy about Granny wasn't meant for my ears, and Mummy swore me to secrecy when she realized I had overheard. She would be furious if she knew I told anyone, even now. It's private."

Hannah gave Verity a stern look. "Your mom hasn't been born yet, and she won't be if we don't sort out Elizabeth. Tell me."

Verity took a deep breath. "Mummy said that Granny is very fragile."

Hannah couldn't help grinning at the very idea. "We are talking about your granny, right? Mrs. Devenish? She's about as fragile as a tractor-trailer."

"No, Hannah, don't make me cross. That's what Mummy said, and I believe it. Look, I know it makes no sense. Granny can be terribly fierce, but that's because she's like a hedgehog. She's a sweet little thing inside, but if someone gets too close, or makes her feel threatened, she gets all prickly. Oh, I shouldn't be telling you this ..."

Hannah wasn't sure she wanted to hear it either. Mrs. Devenish had been her hero, and she already felt deeply let down by her. Now, she was starting to think she had never known her at all. She decided to change the subject. "Verity, I need your help," she said. "I think Elizabeth has to be at the meeting, but Tom never actually invited her, so somebody else has to do that."

CHAPTER TEN

"Don't look at me," Verity said adamantly. "I'm just a shop girl, remember? I can't invite Elizabeth to the house of someone I hardly know, someone who doesn't even like her."

"What if Elizabeth got an invitation in the mail?"

"I suppose we could try to persuade Tom or Millie to send one," Verity said uncertainly.

"No, I don't mean that," Hannah said, "I'll send it and sign it from Millie."

"You mean you would forge a letter?" Verity looked shocked, and started fumbling in her purse for her cigarettes.

"Actually, my handwriting isn't good enough for 1905," said Hannah. "I need you to forge it."

"I know we're desperate, and it's a clever idea," Verity said, popping a cigarette between her lips, and reaching in her bag for her matches. "But is it the right thing to do?" She lit her cigarette, and blew out a puff of smoke while waving out her match. "Hannah, Granny is a person of great moral convictions. Imagine what she would say if she knew we were forging letters on her behalf. She would be livid, and I daresay, very disappointed in me."

Hannah said nothing, but gave Verity a long, questioning look. Then Verity said quietly, "But she's not Granny yet, is she? And she won't be, not if we don't somehow arrange for her to marry Tom. Hmm. Needs must when the Devil drives, I suppose."

"That's a bizarre expression," Hannah said. "But I think I know what you mean, and yes, we do need to send that faked invitation. Oh, and Verity?"

"Yes?"

"No smoking in the house."

Verity frowned. "Speaking of moral convictions ..." she said. She took one last puff, then tossed the cigarette in the fireplace, before reluctantly following it with her entire cigarette pack. "Oh, well. I was thinking of giving it up, anyway. Come on, let's see what Kate has to say about all this. About Granny, I mean. Sending anonymous telegrams? Forging letters? I'm worried that we're both getting out of our depth."

Hannah and Verity were sitting with steaming cups of tea set before them. They had explained everything to the Professor, who stood at the other end of the kitchen table, using her bare hands to stuff a raw chicken with a breadcrumb and onion mixture. They now awaited her advice.

The Professor disappointed them. "I cannot advise you about Elizabeth, or Mrs. Lewis, or Mr. Devenish," she said, as she dumped the chicken into a roasting pan. "Just remember, there's always more than one way to skin a cat.

CHAPTER TEN

Or stuff a chicken."

"*Why* can't you give us advice?" said Verity. "Or was that it?"

"I can't give you more advice than I have," said the Professor, wiping her hands on a cloth, "because I'm not even supposed to be here. I would tell you the wrong thing to do, I'm sure of it."

This strange speech was too much for Hannah, who felt her recent goodwill toward the Professor evaporating. "What are you talking about now, Kate? I thought you promised not to be so mysterious?"

The Professor sighed, and pointed to herself. "Do I look the same to you two as I did last time you saw me?"

Hannah looked the Professor up and down. In fact, there *was* something odd about her, but she couldn't figure out what.

Verity said, "Now you mention it, you do look different, Kate. And I only saw you this morning."

"That's because I was two years younger this morning," the Professor said. "Two years ago, my time, I forgot to come back here to look after you two. I finally realized my mistake a few hours ago, so I've popped back to make dinner."

"How confusing this time travel lark is," Verity said. "By the way, it's very kind of you to go to the trouble, but I'm sure Hannah and I would have managed to cobble together a bit of supper."

"Possibly," said the Professor, "So long as you left the cooking to Hannah."

"Cheek!" Verity exclaimed. But then her shoulders slumped. "Oh, all right. It's probably just as well you're cooking, Kate. I admit, I'm hopeless at it."

"I know," said the Professor. "Your cooking lessons with your grandmother in 1945 ended rather badly, as I recall."

"Burnt sausages," Verity said wistfully, gazing at the empty space in the kitchen where Mrs. Devenish's modern stove would be installed one day in the future. "After hours of careful instruction, Granny left me by myself to cook dinner for her and Mummy. It was supposed to be a simple meal of sausages and mash. I absolutely carbonized them ... The sausages, that is, not Mummy and Granny. And I ruined her best saucepan burning the potatoes, too, all because I was reading a terrifically good book and completely forgot about the food. When they came home expecting a meal, they found a mess. I was sent off in disgrace to buy fish and chips out of my own money. Granny was especially miffed because she had been showing off to Mummy about how well she had taught me. Mummy thought it was a hoot, of course, but Granny would barely speak to me for days. Of course, Mummy is a terrible cook, too. That's why she sent me to Granny for lessons. Granny thinks we're both pitiful. But at

CHAPTER TEN

least I can make scones. Sometimes. Poor Eric. When we are married, we shall live on fish and chips."

Hannah had laughed through the whole story. "Don't worry, Verity, someone will invent microwaves, Chinese take-out, and frozen dinners, and you'll be all set."

"Now don't tell me about the future!" Verity cried, but then she added quickly, "Mind you, I like the sound of all that, whatever it means."

Hannah looked at Verity seriously now. "Verity, are you and Eric sure you're ready to get married? I mean, I know people used to get married younger than they do in the 21st century, but you just don't look sure. You're not really all that interested in cooking and cleaning, and stuff that women in the Fifties are supposed to like. Maybe you're meant to wait. I don't know when you will get married, I just know that you do. Maybe you should have a career first."

"I'm not sure about getting married quite so soon," Verity said quietly. "I don't suppose it does any harm to tell you both that. I have been thinking about it."

To Hannah's great surprise, the Professor said, "I shouldn't interfere, I know I shouldn't, but I do know why you and Eric are marrying young. Lots of young people got married in the 1950s. There were lots of jobs, and so they could afford to set up homes. And it wasn't like your time, Hannah. Unmarried couples didn't live together, not if they were respectable. Plus, in 1951 you weren't legally an adult in Britain until you were 21, and young people, especially girls, didn't go get apartments of their own like they do now. So many young people pretty much lived under the thumb of their parents until they got married, which was a powerful incentive for them to get hitched and start a home of their own. But then when they did marry, as you guessed, middle-class wives were expected to stay at home."

"That's all quite right, Kate," said Verity, looking very serious. "I'll be all right. I suppose I can do lots of voluntary work, just like Granny always has, until we have children. But I do want to help Eric, you see. I don't mind living with Mummy and Daddy, but Granny's rule is rather oppressive. She nags, and unlike me, poor Eric feels more obliged to stay with her. Although he only has to live with her during the university vacations, he really can't become his own man until he leaves home."

Hannah couldn't help smiling at this. "But Verity, when he does leave home, won't you run his life instead?"

Verity looked at her primly. "I don't know that I like your tone, Hannah Day, or whatever your name is. I love Eric, and I do respect him. I know how our relationship must look to you, because I know that I am a bit bossy, but

CHAPTER TEN

I assure you, nothing would make me happier than to see Eric stand up for himself. And when he does stand up to Granny, it will do her a world of good as well. She's become so rude to everyone lately. Mummy says it's just a matter of time before someone tells her off."

"So you're going to marry Eric soon, then?" Hannah said.

"Of course," said Verity, sounding to Hannah more resigned than happy. "And I have to, don't I? You should know that. I have to carry out my part in the play. Or else I might change things, for us, and our children, and for you, and Alex, and Brandon. I can't have that on my conscience. Don't worry, Hannah. Eric and I will be fine, won't we?"

Hannah didn't answer. She couldn't be sure that Eric was the best husband for Verity, but she didn't want to be responsible for such an important decision. She turned to the Professor with another question that had been bothering her. "How did you know about Verity's cooking lessons with Mrs. D.?"

But Verity intervened. "Never you mind how she knows that. Kate Harrower knows a great deal more about all of us than you could possibly imagine."

Hannah wanted to know more, but she had other, more pressing questions, and little time in which to ask them. She knew from experience that the Professor would leave if necessary to avoid answering her. "Look, Kate, you said I have to do something for Elizabeth, and for myself, whatever that means. Am I supposed to make sure she marries Mr. Devenish? Is that part of my job?"

"Don't ask me for advice, remember," the Professor said firmly, as she snapped green beans in half. "Remember, there are many ways to help Elizabeth."

"Hannah, don't forget," Verity said. "You have already done something for Granny that I expect was meant to happen."

Hannah sighed heavily. "What?"

"Let me ask you this. Who gave her the idea to chuck a brick though the front room window?"

"Not me," Hannah said. "I mean, we talked about Mrs. Pankhurst, and the suffragettes smashing windows, but I didn't tell her to go break a window herself. She already knew about the suffragettes, anyway."

Verity leaned forward in her chair. "Hannah, you do realize that this is the year 1905?"

"Yes, of course I know," Hannah said impatiently. "I'm sure that your granny throws the brick this year. Don't you remember? When she told us about it in 1940, she said she threw it in 1905."

Verity looked like she was dying to tell Hannah the punchline. "You're missing the point."

Hannah was really frustrated now. "What point?"

CHAPTER TEN

Verity gave her a self-satisfied smile. "I have read a great deal about the history of the women's suffrage movement," she said. "In 1905, Mrs. Pankhurst's Women's Social and Political Union began to use militant tactics to get the vote. What that means is that they decided to stop acting like Victorian ladies, always doing as they were told. Instead, they started to speak out. They interrupted politicians' meetings, and some of the women, including Christabel Pankhurst, were arrested and imprisoned. But ..." and then she paused significantly.

"But?" said Hannah.

"*But*," said Verity, "I am absolutely, positively certain that they didn't break any windows until 1908. I'm right, aren't I, Kate?"

The Professor's mouth twitched slightly.

Hannah stared dumbfounded at Verity. And then the other shoe dropped. She said slowly, "Verity, are you trying to tell me that I gave your granny the idea to throw the brick?"

"That," said Verity, with a broad grin, "is exactly what I am trying to tell you."

Hannah was having a hard time taking this in. "It wasn't the suffragettes? It was me?"

Verity nodded again.

"Oh, no ..." Hannah groaned. She laid her arms on the table, and her forehead on her arms. In a muffled voice, she moaned, "What have I done? I turned Mrs. D. into the first suffragette ..."

"And in other news, girls," the Professor said, "I have an apple pie in the larder for supper. Your granny's recipe, Verity, as a matter of fact."

"Super!" said Verity. "Thank you!"

Hannah raised her head from her folded arms. "Do total idiots get some, too?"

Verity and the Professor laughed. "Of course they do, Hannah," said the Professor. "And even an extra helping, if they wish."

"Thank you," said Hannah with as much dignity as she could muster.

"And, no, Hannah, you're not an idiot," said the Professor, "much less a total idiot. I'm delighted you know as much as you do about women's suffrage and the suffragettes. Anyway, I'm hopeless with dates myself, so I shan't point a finger at you."

"You're bad at dates?" said Hannah, not believing her ears. "Wait ... What? You're a history professor."

"Exactly," said the Professor, as she placed an apple pie on the table, its bumpy, glossy golden crust topped with three little pastry leaves. It was enough of a distraction for Hannah, who needed something to take her mind off the complicated tasks she had been set.

Hannah wiped her mouth, and gave a little burp. "That was delicious. Thank you, Kate. Now, Verity, how are we going to get Elizabeth married to the right man?

Verity looked troubled. "Yes, I've been thinking about this. The thing is … What do you think of Mr. Ingle-Gillis?"

"Oh, he's awesome," Hannah said. "He's funny, and he's cute. What about him?"

"Cute?" Verity said curiously.

"Um, good-looking," Hannah explained.

"Oh, I see," said Verity. "Because, well, Tom Devenish is quite handsome, too, isn't he?"

"Yes," said Hannah with less enthusiasm, "I guess so."

"But he's not *cute*, is he?" Verity said. "Not in the same way that I suspect you mean. If you ask me, Tom's a bit wet. Boring, I mean. Why on earth would Granny choose him over Mr. Ingle-Gillis?"

"Honestly, Verity?" said Hannah. "I have no idea."

Just in time, she stopped herself from saying the next thing that popped into her head, which was *Verity, why on earth are you marrying Eric?*

Chapter 11:
TESTING CIRCUMSTANCES

Monday, February 19, 1906

Alex enjoyed hanging up his hat when he walked into the office, because it made him feel like an adult, as did his job. It was fun to get out and write stories about people he had met. The only sour note was that Mr. Hughes tended to rewrite everything he wrote until he no longer recognized it himself. Still, that was better than Mr. Hughes telling him exactly what to write in the first place. It was more interesting, Alex thought, to follow his instincts and learn from his mistakes than to follow some kind of script.

"You look pleased with yourself," said Eric, who sat at his desk with his usual cigarette clamped between his fingers.

"I just did a great interview with the owner of the Snipesville Buggy Company," Alex said. "Mr. Bragg, the owner? He's kind of an idiot. He thinks automobiles are just a passing fad for rich people, and he says most people will never give up horses."

"Does he now?" Eric laughed.

"Yeah. But I gave him some advice, you know, man to man."

"Man to man, eh?" Eric said, taking another puff.

"Yes. I told him cars are really taking off everywhere, and there's a guy called Henry Ford up north who's talking about making cars so cheap, farmers will be able to afford them. I remember that from fifth grade social studies. I don't actually know if Henry Ford invented the Model T yet, but I think he's already around. Anyhow, Mr. Bragg looked kind of worried."

"Good show," Eric mumbled distractedly as he added a note to the account book, his cigarette dangling between his lips.

"I gotta write up my story before I forget," Alex said. "Nobody's using the typewriter, right?"

But before Eric could reply, Mr. Hughes walked in. "Day!" he barked, "Just the man I need to see. I've decided to take the train to a national convention on building good roads. I'm going to argue that any national road planned for the South should be routed through Snipesville. Now, I should be gone for some time, more than a fortnight, since I have other business in the North, so I am leaving you two in charge, starting with the Friday edition. If there's an emergency, you may telegraph me at the Palmer House, Chicago."

"Wait, you're leaving us in charge of the paper?" Eric said in alarm. "Is that wise?"

"You boys seem perfectly capable to me," said Mr. Hughes. "You have Jimmy to do the layout and run the presses, and of course, to handle the advertising. All you need to do is fill the blank spaces with copy, and you know most of our copy comes on the wire from Atlanta newspapers. I'm sure you can come up with a few local stories, eh?"

"Oh, I'll be fine," Alex said. He was in a very confident mood. "There's, like, lots going on here. It's a really interesting place, Snipesville. I just interviewed Mr. Bragg at …"

"It is indeed," Mr. Hughes interrupted. "Now, if you'll excuse me, boys, I must go home and pack for my trip, because the weather looks distinctly unpromising. Day, follow me with a box of Snipesville's promotional pamphlets. You'll find them in the cabinet at the back of the printing room. Quick as you can."

Spurred on by Mr. Hughes's energy, Alex dashed to the print room, and soon returned, struggling under a large and heavy box of advertising literature. He followed his boss out the door. As soon as they left, Eric stepped onto the boardwalk to take a look at the weather. The clouds were indeed dark and gray, and Snipesville looked dark and gray beneath them. He sighed. He had always imagined that time travel would be full of danger and excitement, but Snipesville, which had at first seemed strangely charming, was mostly boring, except, of course, for the unpleasant sense of unease it induced.

Mr. Hughes's house was not the largest in town, he told Alex: That honor, he said, belonged to Dr. Hunslow's white-painted mansion. "That's the sort of house that may be yours someday, if you're ambitious and work hard," he said. "Dr. Hunslow keeps a small hospital inside, but he plans to build new quarters for his patients in his back garden."

Mr. Hughes's house was not as large as Dr. Hunslow's, but it was still big.

CHAPTER ELEVEN

A sprawling two-story mansion, with gingerbread trimmings and decorative swirls, it was painted in bold shades of blue and purple. Small panes of colorful stained glass bordered the windows. Alex had expected something more restrained, especially in the home of a 20th century Englishman, and Mr. Hughes caught the surprised look on his face. "The colors are my wife's choosing," he said with an awkward chuckle.

As he stepped into the house, Alex caught a scent of flowers and dust that smelled like the lobby of the Hotel Duval. He set down the box of brochures. When he straightened up again, he could see, through the flowers on the circular hall table, a white woman he assumed to be Mrs. Hughes, sitting in the parlor. Catching his eye, she rose to her feet. She looked to be in her early forties, much younger than Mr. Hughes, and she wore a lacy, high-necked white blouse. "Good afternoon," she said in a South Georgia accent. This was another surprise. Alex had assumed Mrs. Hughes would be English, just like her husband.

"This is Alexander Day, my new reporter," said Mr. Hughes.

Mrs. Hughes said politely, "I have heard so much about you, Mr. Day. I hear you're from California?"

Alex nodded, but before he could answer her properly, Mr. Hughes interrupted. "Day, do set the boxes on that bench.".

"I like your house," Alex said to Mrs. Hughes as he obeyed Mr. Hughes's order.

Mr. Hughes answered on his wife's behalf. "That houses such as this even exist in Snipesville would come as quite a surprise to people in Atlanta."

"And even more so to people in London, I imagine," said his wife.

Mr. Hughes gave her a half smile. "Thank you, my dear," he said without enthusiasm, as if annoyed that she had spoken at all. "Don't let us detain you." Alex cringed a little at seeing Mrs. Hughes dismissed like that, but she didn't seem surprised. Meekly, she retreated to the parlor.

"Now, Day," said Mr. Hughes, "I want you to interview my wife about the Confederate memorial statue downtown, because it will be in place by the end of the week, thanks to Mrs. Hughes and the other ladies. And I trust that you and Powell will keep the wheels humming at my newspaper in my absence. As I said, you may telegraph me at my hotel, the Palmer House."

It was at moments like these that Alex really missed the web. "How do I get the address for the hotel?"

Mr. Hughes exhaled sharply. "You will hardly need it. I'm staying at the grandest hotel in the city. Simply message *Charles Hughes, Palmer House, Chicago*, and your telegram will find me. But don't telegraph me except in the direst of emergencies. I expect you and Powell to hold the fort, and Jimmy can show you any ropes you don't already know. Now, off you go." He dismissed Alex with a nod.

Not for the first time, Alex thought that Mr. Hughes reminded of someone, although he couldn't think who. Either way, he was excited by his boss's confidence in him. And did Mr. Hughes really think that he, Alex, could one day afford a mansion of his own? That was quite a compliment. He looked forward to writing stories that would not only impress Mr. Hughes, but send *The Snipesville News's* circulation skyrocketing.

And then a voice in his head said, *What about Brandon?* That was when Alex realized that he was falling into the same trap he had in 1851, blindly following a charismatic leader. And he was being drawn in by greed, instead of focusing on doing the right thing. On the spot, Alex decided he would be his own man, and write exciting stories that would truly make a difference, and would help the black community. Of course, he thought guiltily, writing good stories would still increase newspaper subscription sales, and please Mr. Hughes.

For most of the long train journey back from Atlanta, Brandon had looked forward to telling Miss Julia of his success. But now, as he disembarked from the "colored" car in Snipesville in the overcast early evening, his anxiety returned. What he felt was a more intense version of what he had felt his whole life, the fear of being trapped in this suffocating town. Brandon's gloom only deepened as drizzling rain began to fall while he walked up East Main Street.

Two men were digging a hole in the courthouse lawn. For a moment, Brandon wondered what they were doing. And then he realized he had a pretty good idea. They were working on the exact spot where the Confederate soldier memorial would stand in the 21st century, and he remembered that Robert had mentioned the plans for it during their tour of the town. But why build a memorial now? The Civil War had been over for forty years. Most of the veterans were dead. He had thought about this, and it made no sense.

The rain suddenly turned heavy, and so Brandon took temporary shelter on the boardwalk on South Main Street.

It was a quiet time of day. Most businesses were closed, and so he was alone on the street, listening to the patter of rain on the cover overhead, and the distant, plaintive howl of a train horn. He shivered. On impulse, he looked behind him, through the window of *The Snipesville News*, and saw Eric.

As the doorbell rang, Eric looked up from his massive accounts book, and leaned back in his heavy wooden chair, smiling. "Well, hallo there! The happy wanderer returns! How was your holiday, Brandon?"

Eric's warm welcome instantly made Brandon feel human again. "It was awesome," he said excitedly. "I met Booker T. Washington and W. E. B. Du Bois."

"Did you? Tremendous!" said Eric. After a moment's pause, he added, "And who might they be?"

Brandon laughed. He should have guessed that Eric from 1951 England wouldn't have a clue who Washington and Du Bois were. "I'll tell you, but it will take a long … Whoa, what's that?"

Looking beyond Eric into the print room, Brandon had glimpsed a massive black iron printing press with wheels, rollers, and pulleys. Eric turned to see what he was gawping at. "Oh, you see our new press? It's very impressive, if you'll forgive the pun. It can print up to 2,000 copies of the newspaper in only one hour. That's much faster than we need at present, but our Mr. Hughes thinks we'll need it soon, what with the town expanding at such a terrific rate. Lots of new readers, you see. Our Mr. Hughes is quite the go-getter."

Brandon had heard this slightly sarcastic tone before from Brits, including from Eric himself. He knew what it meant. It meant that Eric did not approve of Mr. Hughes. "Eric, is everything okay?" he said.

"To be honest, no," said Eric, his shoulders sagging. "Look, I can't say I'm happy with some of the stories we're publishing in the newspaper. I'm not talking about the articles Alex is writing, which are pretty harmless nonsense about local people. I'm talking about the articles telegraphed on the wire to us from the newspapers in Atlanta, the ones that we reprint. Mr. Hughes insists that those wire stories appear on the front page."

Brandon was frowning. "What stories from Atlanta?"

"Stories about the election," said Eric. "Oh, don't you know about that? There's to be an election this year for governor of Georgia, and both of the men standing for office are newspapermen, like Mr. Hughes. Tell me, are American politicians always journalists, too?"

"I don't think so," Brandon said. "But, look, tell me what the problem is, before someone else comes in." Brandon was keenly aware that they could not have this conversation in front of white people, who would wonder why Eric was discussing politics with a black teen. "Tell me about the stories."

"I'm getting to that," Eric said. "This chap Clark Howell is one of the two candidates. He's the editor of the *Atlanta Constitution* newspaper. The other candidate is a chap by the peculiar name of Hoke Smith. He owns the *Atlanta Journal*. They're arguing about which of them is most willing and able to stop colored men from voting. And, well, there are a lot of very nasty things being said."

"I'm not surprised," Brandon said, shaking his head.

But Eric looked dismayed. "It's dreadful. One proposal I read said that colored people must be educated before they are to be allowed to vote, but you and I know there's very little education available for colored people."

"Okay, so this is one more reason why we need the high school," said Brandon.

Eric looked doubtful. "Yes, well, these two men don't seem terribly keen on educating colored men to be voters."

"I'll bet," said Brandon, making a mental note to ask Miss Julia and Robert about the election. "Where's Alex?"

"Out," said Eric. "He was carrying something to Mr. Hughes's house, so he should be back soon. Honestly, I'm not sure it was such a good idea for him and me to exchange jobs. Alex's story ideas have been pretty feeble. He's always interviewing some local farmer about cotton prices, or something of that sort, nothing especially exciting. I keep telling him that everyone has an interesting story if you ask the right questions, but I'm not sure he grasps what I mean."

Brandon didn't really want to listen to Eric complain about Alex, and now that the rain was letting up, he was eager to take his own news to Miss Julia. "I'll catch you later," he said.

Miss Julia opened the front door to Brandon, and while she was clearly delighted to see him, he suspected she was relieved that he had returned at all. His hunch was confirmed when Miss Alberta bustled down the hallway, wiped her wet hands on her apron, and said, "You come back! We didn't think you would." Brandon smiled. He often thought that Miss Alberta's blunt honesty was far preferable to the elaborate game of Victorian manners that haunted his conversations with Miss Julia. Miss Julia, meanwhile, looked embarrassed.

"Miss Julia, Miss Alberta, I don't blame you for thinking I wouldn't come back," Brandon said. "But here I am, and I've got good news."

"Have you, indeed?" The voice was Robert's, and he did not sound pleased. He appeared in the parlor doorway. "Come in here. I want a word with you, George Braithwaite." For the first time, Brandon thought, Robert sounded very much like a high school principal.

Robert did not invite Brandon to sit, but Miss Julia did. "Now, tell me about your adventure," she said, leaning forward, as Brandon settled onto the uncomfortable sofa.

"Not just yet," said Robert, who was still standing. Brandon immediately got back on his feet. He felt guilty, even though he had done nothing wrong.

"Braithwaite, if that is indeed your name," Robert said, in a very self-important voice, "Miss Russell trusted you to escort her to the Equal Rights Convention. You repaid her trust by absconding on some wild goose chase, supposedly to seek funds for the high school. Not only were you given no authority to do such a thing, but you never even informed Miss Russell of your departure, much less its purpose. What's more, you convinced Reverend Evans to set aside his own scruples, and write a letter on your behalf. Now, no doubt, you have returned with some poppycock about having raised money, although I am sure this is simply a ruse to defraud Miss Russell, just as you have defrauded her since your arrival in this house."

Brandon thought about all the things he could say to defend himself, but he knew that his actions would speak louder than words. In reply, he simply reached inside his jacket, pulled out Dr. Du Bois's now-crumpled check, and handed it to Robert.

Robert looked it over, wide-eyed, and passed it to Miss Julia. She glanced over it with evident pleasure, and then looked up and beamed at Brandon, before turning to her young cousin. "Robert, I am sorry I did not tell you this, but I received another check for this exact sum from Mr. Alonzo Herndon not an hour ago. George, you have rewarded my faith in you."

Brandon and Miss Julia both looked at Robert, who blustered, "Well, how was I to know?"

Brandon was quick to reassure him. "No, it's okay, Robert," he said. "I apologize for not telling you my plans. Everything you said was true, except that I'm not trying to rip off Miss Julia, and I really am helping raise funds for the school. I hope I can win your trust."

"We shall see," Robert said sourly. "Even if I accept that you meant well, George, it wasn't your place to approach anyone for money. Now, if you will excuse me, I have an appointment in town."

When Robert left, Brandon sank down onto the sofa again. But Miss Julia was excited to share some news of her own. "George, I received another letter today, and it is from my friend in England." She held a small envelope under Brandon's nose, and Brandon, curious now, recognized King Edward's face on the red and green stamps. As usual with British mail, there was no return address on the envelope. "How did you get a friend in England, ma'am?" he said. Now he remembered Miss Julia mentioning her before.

"I have known this lady for many years," said Miss Julia. "When I was a member of the National Women's Suffrage Association, I was among those who opened a correspondence with the Women's Suffrage Association in England. But then, around fifteen years ago, I'm sorry to say that the American suffrage movement turned in a deplorable direction. You see, our former

CHAPTER ELEVEN

leaders were Northern women like Mrs. Stanton and Miss Anthony, who had helped to fight slavery as well as for women's rights. When they retired, more white women from the South then began to join our cause, and they took a very dim view of colored women's participation in the movement. Our new leaders saw that they would draw more Southern support for women's suffrage if they abandoned colored women, and indeed, that is what they did, to their great shame. So we colored women left them to it, and formed the National Association of Colored Women. But, be that as it may, through all these tumultuous years, I have maintained my correspondence with my fellow suffragist in England, Mrs. Lewis."

Brandon gasped. Surely not …

"Mrs. Lewis? *That* Mrs. Lewis?"

"I'm sorry, George," said Miss Julia, "But I don't know who you mean."

Brandon couldn't for the life of him think of Mrs. Lewis's first name. He wondered if she even had a first name, apart from "Mrs." He tried again. "I met this lady called Mrs. Lewis in England, in Balesworth … Little lady, right? Talkative?"

Miss Julia's eyes lit up. "Mrs. Alice Lewis, George! And she does indeed live in Balesworth. What an extraordinary coincidence that you two should have met."

"Have you ever met her in person?" Brandon said, "Did Mrs. Lewis come to Georgia?"

"No, George, I traveled to England seven years ago. I was there for two months, and I stayed with Mrs. Lewis in her home for three weeks. It was a thoroughly enjoyable visit. We shared much in common. I have invited her to Snipesville, although I am sorry to say it is very unlikely that she will accept my invitation to come all the way to America. And as I explained to her, I cannot receive her at my home. As a respectable white woman, she would have to stay in a hotel, not in the home of a colored lady."

Brandon could only imagine Mrs. Lewis's reaction to someone telling her who she could and could not stay with. However, it made sense that she and Miss Julia were friends. And it also reminded him of something. "Has Mrs. Lewis ever mentioned someone called Mrs. Devenish in her letters?"

"No, I don't believe so," Miss Julia said. "Why, is that lady a mutual friend of yours?"

Brandon realized that, as ever, he had to tread carefully. He didn't answer the question directly. "Maybe … ," he said slowly. Perhaps, he thought, Mrs. Lewis had fallen out with Mrs. Devenish? It wouldn't be the last time, and probably was not the first. Then he remembered that in 1906, Mrs. Devenish was probably not yet Mrs. Devenish. He said, "Has Mrs. Lewis ever mentioned a young woman called Hughes, you know, the same as the Mayor of Snipesville?"

Miss Julia looked thoughtful. "Mrs. Lewis often mentions a young woman in her letters, but only by her first name, Elizabeth."

"That's her!" Brandon exclaimed happily. "Elizabeth Hughes!"

"If Elizabeth's a friend of yours, George, do know that Mrs. Lewis is fond of the girl, and thinks very highly of her. I think she worries about her much as a mother would, and with some justification."

Brandon waited for Miss Julia to offer more information. But Miss Julia was no gossip, and so he was disappointed. Now that he knew of her Balesworth connection, however, he had another question. "Miss Julia, you know Jupe, right?"

"Jupe?" She blinked a couple of times. "You mean Jupiter Gordon? Robert's father? Of course I know him. We're cousins. Why do you ask?"

"You know he used to live near Balesworth?"

"I did not," Miss Julia gasped. "He lived with my family for several years, but it has been a long time since I paid any attention to his stories."

"Well, don't you think it's strange that you and Jupe would have this one town in common?"

"I suppose so," she said. "Jupiter and I have little else in common, you see, beyond blood and Balesworth." She smiled grimly at her own joke.

Blood and Balesworth. Brandon was struck by the expression, and filed it away in his head. *Blood and Balesworth,* he thought. *Blood and Balesworth.*

Tuesday, February 20, 1906

"Thomas, I am so sorry Caroline is feeling unwell and was unable to join us, but how good of you to come for tea and share in our celebration," Miss Julia said, as she showed off Dr. Du Bois's check yet again. Sitting with her were Brandon, a prim and silent Robert Gordon, and his cousin Elias Thomas Clark, III, who looked deeply uncomfortable in a suit.

After carefully laying the check flat on the coffee table so everyone could continue to admire it, Miss Julia poured Brandon another cup of coffee. "When George went traveling in search of funds, she, said I confess I was much concerned. But then I received a check from Mr. Alonzo Herndon for $50, which he attributed to George's visit to him in Atlanta, and then George brought me Dr. Du Bois's check. He also tells me that Booker T. Washington himself is interested in taking up our case."

Brandon nodded happily to confirm Miss Julia's words, but on seeing Thomas's polite smile and Robert's irritated expression, he slumped down a little, trying to look modest.

CHAPTER ELEVEN

"And what conditions does Mr. Washington attach to his support?" said Robert.

Brandon shifted uneasily in his seat. "He wants it to be an industrial high school."

"Of course he does," Robert said smugly. "He and his wealthy friends think that cotton-picking is the only work of which we are worthy."

"Come now, Robert," Miss Julia said quietly, "That's not only disrespectful, but untrue."

"It's as good as true," Robert shot back. "The man's a philistine. He has no interest in Negroes becoming educated, only that we are trained in manual labor and continue to know our place for the foreseeable future."

Thomas was looking crossly at Robert now. "What's wrong with working with your hands?" he said, gingerly holding onto his coffee cup with oil-stained fingers. "Poetry ain't ... begging your pardon, Aunt Julia ... Poetry *isn't* gonna feed my wife and child. I mean, I understand what you say, Robert, and maybe one day, my children or grandchildren can go to one of your fancy colleges and study Shakespeare, but we need money and property first."

Robert glared at him. "You seem very sure that your money and property are secure. Don't you ever read a newspaper, cousin? Don't you know what happened eight years ago in Wilmington, North Carolina?"

Brandon had no idea what Robert was talking about, and judging from his face, neither did Thomas. Robert sighed, and proceeded to explain. "This is why we need education, Thomas, because you are utterly unaware of something very important that took place only a few years ago, as though it had never taken place at all. So allow me to instruct you. In 1898, in the town of Wilmington, North Carolina, Negroes and some white citizens together voted for a local government that included colored representatives. Other whites, including prominent men, rioted in protest, attacking colored people. We believe that at least sixty colored people died, maybe hundreds. And the fact that many of the colored men who were attacked owned businesses and were respectable?" He rapped out his words on the table with his knuckles, "That did not help them one bit."

Thomas looked at him warily. "That was in North Carolina?"

Robert exhaled sharply. "And because it was not in Georgia, that makes it irrelevant to you, is that what you think, Thomas? Very well. There are examples of violence against colored folk elsewhere, including in Georgia. You cannot possibly be unaware of the terrible lynchings all over the South. Even you, Thomas, cannot claim such willful ignorance."

"And what do you propose I do about it?" Thomas shot back, his voice rising. "Close up my business and go read books?"

"Gentlemen!" Miss Julia said sharply, and they both sank back in their chairs, rebuked. "Stop all this arguing at once. The important thing is that Mr. Washington may be willing to find us support for our high school, and I say that any kind of high school is better than none at all. Really, Robert, look at the plans being discussed for an Agricultural and Mechanical School for white students in Snipesville. It is hardly a college of the New England sort, but it will do much to train young white people for employment, and I daresay to educate them, too. Our young colored people deserve at least the same, do they not?"

Robert sniffed, in what Brandon assumed was grudging agreement.

Thomas looked smug, but now Miss Julia dealt with him. "And may I remind you, Thomas, that whatever Mr. Washington's private or public views on academic work, his students take academic classes for several hours a day. He sees the value of a liberal arts education, whether he confesses it or not. Now I daresay, and none of you must repeat this, that Robert is correct that Tuskegee students' work is not always as worthwhile as we might hope. But all of us can do only what we can to raise the race in these very trying times. That includes Mr. Booker T. Washington. George, tell us what you saw at Tuskegee."

Brandon thought, not for the first time, that Miss Julia was a very smart woman. She already knew what he would say, because he had earlier described to her his impressions of Tuskegee. She wanted him to repeat it to make her point for her, so that she didn't appear to be taking sides between the cousins.

"Some of the work Mr. Washington's students do is kind of useless, honestly," Brandon said. "It shocked me at times. Do you know that Tuskegee Institute holds a kindergarten class, and they take those little kids out to a cotton field, and make them weed with hoes? It was like they're training them to be slaves."

"Quite," said Robert, and even Thomas, who was looking down into his coffee cup, did not disagree with him. But Miss Julia said carefully, "I believe Mr. Washington's purpose in requiring such tasks is to acquaint young people with the routine of work, so that they might lead disciplined and purposeful lives. However, I daresay that there is a limit to the usefulness of such a scheme. George, how do you think we should proceed with our plans?"

"Mr. Washington is our best hope," said Brandon. "I think you should ask him for money again, and tell him it's for an industrial school. Call it something like the Snipesville Industrial High School." He heard Robert sniff in contempt. Thomas, meanwhile, was looking up.

"Then I propose," said Miss Julia, "that we call our school the Snipesville Industrial High School for Colored Youth."

But Brandon hadn't made his most important point, and he continued, looking at Robert from the corner of his eye, "Then let's do what we have to, to keep Mr. Washington and his donors happy. But then we should also make sure that the academic classes are really good. That means we need really, really good teachers. We need top graduates, like from the colleges in Atlanta."

Brandon saw Robert lick his lip with the tip of his tongue. He was hooked, and Brandon knew it. Miss Julia said, "I think that's a splendid idea, George. I shall write to President Bumstead, and …"

"I'm sorry," Brandon said, "Did you say Bumstead?"

"Yes," Miss Julia said, slightly puzzled by his smirk, "Reverend Dr. Horace Bumstead. He's the president of Atlanta University. He's a white gentleman from Boston, and an old friend of mine." Brandon could hardly tell her that, to anyone who had lived in England, Dr. Bumstead had a pretty funny name. He tried to look mature.

Robert now was sitting forward in his chair, one finger raised politely in the air to catch Miss Julia's attention. "If I might, Aunt Julia? I daresay I would be willing to consider taking on the job of principal. If you were to consider me."

Miss Julia tried to look surprised. "Why, Robert, are you applying for the post? I would be most pleased if you were. Perhaps you could help me draft the letter to Mr. Washington, requesting his support."

Robert's face fell. He now seemed to realize that he had just been manipulated into committing himself to staying in Snipesville. "I would be willing to entertain becoming the founding principal," he said hastily, "for a year or two."

Thomas smiled, and again looked down into his coffee, this time to disguise a grin. Brandon tried not to break into a smile himself. Robert's ego had triumphed over his own objections. He would remain in Snipesville after all, and it was Brandon's doing. But Brandon now wondered uneasily if that had been a kind thought. He himself desperately wanted not to be trapped in his hometown. It seemed very cruel to trap someone else in Snipesville, especially in 1906.

Wednesday, February 21, 1906

Sitting with Miss Julia in the parlor in the evening, Brandon was finding it hard to concentrate on his reading. He felt embarrassed to still be unemployed, and he was just deciding that he would make a renewed effort to find a job, when he heard a knock at the front door.

Alex and Eric were on the doorstep. The second he saw Brandon, Alex said, "I thought you said black people and white people can't marry each other here?"

CHAPTER ELEVEN

"Would you like to come in?" Brandon said. "Will I ask Miss Alberta to fix us some coffee? How about, hello, Brandon, did you have a good trip? So, what's this about?"

"We were on our way home," Alex said, wiping his feet. "And I have some questions."

"Great," Brandon said, with a glance behind him. "But maybe we need to talk outdoors." He lowered his voice. "This isn't a conversation I think we can have in front of these folks."

As Brandon walked Alex and Eric back to Kintyre, they talked. Alex told Brandon about the arrival of Mrs. Hudgins, and the shocking news that she was Caroline Clark's mother.

But Brandon didn't look shocked, just amused. "So you met one of my white ancestors. I didn't know this one's name, or where she fit on the family tree. I just knew that she existed."

"You know, now you mention it," Alex said, "Hannah said something about you being related to her friend Tara."

"Oh yeah, Tara Thompson is my cousin, because we're related through this … Mrs. Hudgins, is that her name? She was my great-great-something-grand …"

Alex interrupted. "But how come they could get married? A white woman and a black man? I thought that was illegal."

"It is," Brandon said, "They just kind of married themselves and lived together. It probably happened before Reconstruction ended, and Southern whites took control back from the Federal Government. It's seriously risky for them to be married now. Is Mr. Hudgins still alive?"

"No, she said he died not long after Caroline was born," said Alex.

"That explains a lot. Otherwise, they might have ended up in jail for being married."

"It's all crazy," Alex said.

"I know," said Brandon. "Racism is always crazy, and it makes people do crazy things. But it's real, and it exists in England, too. I mean, don't you ever wonder why George Braithwaite left England and came over here?"

Eric was startled. "George left England? I mean, he does? When?"

"Yeah, he does," Brandon said. "I don't know when. Sometime in the Fifties."

"Will he leave before Verity and I get married?" Eric said anxiously. "I want him to be my best man."

"No, he's definitely at your wedding," said Brandon.

But Eric was very concerned now. "Why would George Braithwaite emigrate to America? No, don't tell me. I'm not sure I want to know all about the future. It goes to show, though, you never know someone as well as you think you do. He's my best friend, you know." Eric looked deeply saddened.

By now, they had reached the boardinghouse. Eric wished Brandon goodnight, and stepped inside, but Alex held back. "Hey, do you want to meet Mrs. Hudgins?" he said to Brandon.

"Later," he said. "Look, I want to know what you think. I still don't have a job. Got any ideas?"

"Why don't you just come stay with us here? The Professor won't charge you rent."

"No, I think I'm supposed to stay with Miss Julia," Brandon said. The truth was, he wasn't sure he wanted to spend all his time talking about race and racism with Alex and Eric. There was very little else to discuss, except, maybe, all the interesting things Alex and Eric could do because they were white. "And anyway," he said firmly. "I'm black, and you're white, remember? We can't live in the same boardinghouse."

"You could pretend to be a servant," Alex said brightly. Brandon's eyes narrowed. "I mean," Alex said all in a rush, "Just when people ask. So you can live with us."

Brandon pulled a face. He knew Alex meant well, but it was just all so obnoxious. "I think," he said coldly, "I am going to ask my great-great-granddaddy for a job."

Thursday February 22, 1906

Brandon heard the raised voice well before he could tell who it belonged to. As he drew nearer to Thomas Clark's workshop, he saw Dr. Marshburn, the dentist, and Thomas facing each other across an automobile. Jupe was sitting in his usual spot in front of the workshop, leaning on his walking stick. Dr. Marshburn was doing all the yelling.

"This is just not good enough, boy!" he yelled at Thomas. "I only brought you my brand new automobile to fix because Dr. Hunslow recommended you. You better believe I regret that."

Brandon hesitated. Angry white men in 1906 Snipesville were intimidating: They had so much power. He hoped Dr. Marshburn wouldn't remember him from that day he visited the office in search of a job. Deciding that he was mostly invisible to white men, and would not be recognized, Brandon took a seat on the bench next to old Jupe. They exchanged deliberately blank looks. Both knew that it was dangerous to be seen expressing an opinion about the argument taking place a few feet away. Brandon focused on making patterns in the dirt with his feet, while listening to the quarrel.

"Dr. Marshburn, sir?" Thomas said. "Beg pardon, sir, but I gotta tell you something. Now I don't know what the seller told you, but this here is not a new car. This here is last year's model, a 1905 Wayne, two-seater, 16 horsepower …"

"You think I'm a fool, boy?" exclaimed the angry dentist. "You answering me back now? This car here done cost me a thousand dollars. You think I would spend a thousand dollars on some old piece of junk?"

Feeling tense, Brandon could see Thomas struggling between telling the dentist what he wanted to hear, and telling him the truth. Thomas said, "No, sir, I don't think you would make a bad bargain. I'm just saying I'm not sure I can fix it without ordering you a new engine."

"Looks to me like you don't know what you're talking about," growled Dr. Marshburn, dropping his cigar at Thomas's feet, and grinding it out with his shoe. "I shoulda known better than to bring my car to a nigger mechanic. Now, you have your horse tow this automobile back to my house by nightfall, and I'll have one of my *white* auto repair fellows from Savannah come out and fetch it. You can forget any more of my business."

As Dr. Marshburn stomped off toward downtown, Thomas said quietly to himself, "You done paid a thousand dollars for this car? But it only cost $800 new."

"It's not your fault," Brandon said, getting to his feet behind Thomas. "Sound like the car's a lemon."

"Waynes are pretty good, I read," said Thomas. "But you're right, not this one. Whoever sold it to Dr. Marshburn cheated him."

"That's not really your problem, is it?" said Brandon.

"No, I guess not," Thomas said, fiddling with the engine as he spoke, as if somehow hoping for a miraculous recovery. "But Dr. Marshburn telling people I don't know what I'm doing? Now *that* is a problem."

Brandon was worried now. "You don't get a lot of people coming to you for car repair, do you? There are only, like, three cars in town, including this one. It's not a big part of your business."

"That's true for now," Thomas said. "But there's gonna be a heap more, you watch, and I don't want people to give up on me as an auto mechanic when I just got started. I'm thankful that at least Dr. Hunslow is well pleased with my work on his car. Anyhow, George, what do you need?"

"Thomas, I hate to ask," Brandon said hesitantly, "And this is probably a bad time, but have you got any jobs going?"

Thomas gave him a sideways look. "You got any skill as a blacksmith,

CHAPTER ELEVEN

George?"

Brandon shook his head.

"Or know anything about carriage repair?"

Brandon shook his head again. But this time he said, "I could learn."

"You could learn, I'm sure, from all I hear of you," said Thomas. "Miss Russell thinks highly of you, that I know, and Robert says you're a bright young man. Trouble is, I got to take time to teach you, and I can't afford to pay you."

Right then and there, Brandon almost offered to work for free. But then he remembered that this would not pay his rent.

"I don't know how desperate you are," Thomas said, "but the turpentine farm might could be hiring. That's pretty nasty work, mind. A lot of them working out there are convicts, and floaters like yourself."

"What is a floater, anyway?" said Brandon.

"You don't know? Floater's someone who goes from place to place, looking for work. That's dangerous for colored folk. You was lucky Miss Russell took you in, and nobody picked you up for vagrancy and put you in jail."

"Vagrancy? But I'm not a beggar," said Brandon.

Suddenly, Jupe chimed in. "You don't got to be a beggar to be a vagrant, boy! You just got to be walking in a place where they don't know you. That's the Jim Crow law, that's how it works."

"He's right," said Thomas. "If a lawman sees you walking in the road, and he don't recognize you, and you can't account for where you belong, he can arrest you. Before you know it, he lease you out as a convict to some man, and he work you to death. And when I say, *work you to death*, I'm not lying."

Brandon had thought that life in 1906 Snipesville couldn't get worse, but it just had. Involuntarily, he glanced over his shoulder, looking for some invisible sheriff coming to arrest him. He wondered how close he had already come to this terrible fate while on his travels through Georgia and Alabama.

"Don't worry, George," Thomas said casually. "People in Snipesville know you stay with Aunt Julia, and that will protect you." Brandon gave him a wan smile.

But now Thomas, looking conflicted, said, "Look, George, don't go work in turpentine like I said. If I hear of any good jobs for an educated young fellow like you," he said, "I'll send word. See, none of us really knows who you are, or why you're here, but we like you. Even my cousin Robert likes you. There's something about you, George, that everyone likes, and lots of colored folk in Snipesville are glad that George Braithwaite is our neighbor. Maybe you was sent." He pointed at the sky, and Brandon broke into a smile.

"Maybe," he said. "But I'm no miracle-worker."

And then he remembered who Thomas was, and tears sprang to his eyes. He was, indeed, no miracle-worker. There were some things in Snipesville that he might not be able to fix, and he wasn't thinking of Dr. Marshburn's car. *Then again,* he thought, *through God, all things are possible.* What he needed, he decided, was stronger faith.

Monday, February 26, 1906
Brandon hated going into downtown Snipesville. But he needed a job, and he told himself firmly that he had dragged his feet for far too long. Now, as he arrived at the courthouse square on this unusually warm morning in winter, he found people gathered around the new Confederate soldier statue. Still wanting to put off job hunting, he watched from the edge of the crowd. About a dozen young white girls in white dresses, wearing blood-red sashes, stood behind Mr. Hughes while he addressed the people, but Brandon couldn't quite hear him. He moved closer just as Mr. Hughes introduced his wife as the representative of the United Daughters of the Confederacy of Snipesville, but he couldn't hear her either, because she spoke very quietly. By the time Mr. Hughes started introducing an old Civil War veteran to the crowd, Brandon had decided he had to get on with his day.

After several refusals from business-owners, most of them rude, Brandon reckoned he deserved the treat for which he had been saving some of his dwindling stock of money. But even a brief stop for ice cream at Wheeler's Apothecary was stressful. It required that he act with great awareness and care. A few days earlier, he had prepared for this moment by asking Robert's advice, and Robert had explained how he should behave.

So Brandon already knew that he could not thoughtlessly wander into Wheeler's Apothecary for an ice cream, like he could in the 21st century. He knew he would need to step inside the drugstore, because it didn't have a take-out window. He knew he couldn't sit down in the café and enjoy an ice cream or soda from real glass dishes, but would have to order a cone to go instead. He knew he had to get everything right, or else risk humiliation, injury, or even death. He remembered the photo in his history textbook, of a 1960s sit-in where young black and white students defied segregation. They sat together at a lunch counter, while a scary crowd of angry whites poured ketchup, sugar, and mustard on their heads, for the terrible crime of sitting down in a public restaurant to eat. Faced with the reality of segregation now, in 1906, he could not imagine their courage.

Gingerly, he passed two white women who sat primly at a table by the window, but they paid no attention to him. He stepped up to the end of the long white marble counter that was closest to the door. Above the end of the counter a small sign reading COLORED hung from the ceiling. If he hadn't been looking for that sign, he might have missed it.

Mr. Wheeler, having brought the girls their ice cream sundaes, now returned to the counter and smiled. "How can I help you, young man?"

Brandon was surprised by the druggist's enthusiastic greeting, but then he remembered that Mr. Wheeler was from the North. Maybe a white Northerner wasn't quite so racist? But then, Brandon thought cynically, he was here to spend money. Of course Mr. Wheeler was pleased to see him.

Brandon said none of these things aloud. What he said was, "Scoop of vanilla on a cone, please, sir."

"You bet," said the pharmacist, taking Brandon's nickel from him. While Brandon waited for his cone, Dr. Hunslow walked up to the front of the counter, and started tapping a folded copy of *The Snipesville News* against the marble to catch Mr. Wheeler's attention. Mr. Wheeler, who had just started scooping Brandon's ice cream, stopped at the sight of Dr. Hunslow. Dropping his scoop into a crock of water, he wiped his hands on a towel. "Yes, sir, can I help you?" he said brightly.

The doctor nodded. "I'll take a vanilla ice cream cone," he said.

The pharmacist resumed his scooping, and quickly produced a cone. Brandon leaned forward, ready to receive it. But the pharmacist handed it to Dr. Hunslow instead.

Brandon knew his part in this play. He knew that he should say nothing. He knew that he should meekly wait his turn. And he knew he would be disgusted with himself if he did. "Excuse me, sir," he said firmly to Mr. Wheeler. "I believe I was being served?"

Startled, the pharmacist turned to look at him, and said, "Yes, sonny, indeed you are." And quickly, he began making another cone.

Dr. Hunslow frowned, and sidled over to Brandon. With the rolled-up newspaper, he again tapped the counter near Brandon's hand. "I remember you," he said. "Our young colored man from England. You were at Thomas's blacksmith shop the other day."

Brandon nodded. Dr. Hunslow, looking steadily at him, took a lick of ice cream. There was an awkward silence. Finally, Brandon said, "How's your car, sir?"

This was a subject that was obviously close to the doctor's heart. "It's running fine, since you ask. Thomas did a good job with it."

"I know Thomas would be very grateful if you would spread the word about his work, sir."

Dr. Hunslow said, "Aha. Thomas put you up to this, did he?"

"No, sir," said Brandon.

"I happen to know," said the doctor, pausing mid-sentence to slurp down more of his ice cream, "that our dentist Dr. Marshburn is none too happy with the work Thomas did for him."

Brandon hesitated to say anything else. He did not trust Dr. Hunslow at all.

"You tell Thomas not to worry," said Dr. Hunslow. "I'll take care of things. I'll see him right. He's a good boy."

Brandon felt his inner lip curl, not only at the word "boy" and Dr. Hunslow's condescending attitude, but at the idea that a black man should have to rely on a white man to protect him. Suddenly, he deeply regretted asking for the doctor's support for Thomas.

Meanwhile, Dr. Hunslow lifted his rolled newspaper from the counter, and then pointed it at Brandon. "You see, boy, Thomas's family and mine have a history. His great-granny was my slave mammy, who looked after me from the day I was born. So I look out for him. Thomas is ambitious for a Negro, but he doesn't step out of his place. He belongs in this country. He's not the sort of uppity young buck who thinks he should be served ice cream before a white man."

Brandon's blood ran ice cold. He had not missed the thinly-veiled warning. As he watched Dr. Hunslow stroll away, Mr. Wheeler handed him his ice cream, and said very quietly, "Listen, you shouldn't ought to do that, you know, complaining about not being served. That's not a good idea. Now, before you say anything, I know you're not from Georgia, but they got their customs, and it's best to follow their ways if you know what's good for you."

Brandon sighed. "Mr. Wheeler, you seem like a nice guy. Anybody give you a hard time about being from the North?"

"Oh, once or twice. A lady come in here, said her father was killed at the Battle of Gettysburg. She said she wouldn't patronize any kind of store run by a Yankee. And I hear rumors about one person or another boycotting my store because of where I'm from."

"And how does that feel, sir?"

Mr. Wheeler looked at Brandon in amazement. Now Brandon remembered that asking someone about their feelings wasn't a usual thing in the early 20th century. But the pharmacist answered his question anyway. "Well, now, not too good. But I got the law and my business to consider ..."

Brandon felt his ice cream start to trickle down his hand. "But how would you feel if you were me?"

CHAPTER ELEVEN

"Not so good, I guess," said Mr. Wheeler, shaking his head sadly. "But I can't change the way things are. Neither can you. Maybe you should go back to England, or maybe you could go North. It's a little better up there for colored folks."

Suddenly, Brandon was angry. "Snipesville is my home," he snapped, "And I'm an American." With that, he walked out, taking two quick licks of his ice cream before he realized he didn't want it anymore. There were no trash cans on the street, so he tossed the half-eaten cone into the dirt road, where it was promptly crushed by a passing wagon. It was then that Brandon remembered he had meant to ask for a job in the pharmacy. That hope was now as squashed as his ice cream cone.

He already knew the one most likely option for employment left to him, and he didn't relish it at all, but what could he do? The phrase "beggars can't be choosers" popped into his head. With a tightening in his stomach, he set out in the direction of the cluster of pine woods beyond West Snipesville, to a place he had never seen, but that he knew was there. He knew Miss Julia would not approve. But he had to do something.

The sun warmed the forest, and Brandon smelled the strong scent of pine before he saw the shack on stilts that told him he was in the right place. Nervously entering the clearing in the woods, he could hear the sounds of activity in the woods, and he saw several men, all black, tending the smoking turpentine still.

To Brandon's left was a small row of wooden cabins. Even by the low standards of housing in Snipes County in 1906, these were miserable hovels. A young dark-skinned woman wandered out of one of them, followed closely by a naked toddler, and she emptied a bucket of steaming water on the ground. She saw Brandon, but paid him no attention. To him, her eyes looked empty.

Now a white man on horseback emerged from the woods and trotted toward him. "What you want, boy?" the man called out. "You looking for work?"

"Yes, sir," he said.

The rider sniffed, then spat on the ground. "You need the Boss Man, then. He should be over yonder, by the still."

It wasn't hard to spot the "Boss Man." He was the only other white person Brandon could see. When the Boss Man saw Brandon, he pushed up the brim of his hat. "Saw you talking to the Woodsrider. You want work?" he said. "This your lucky day. You done turpentinin' before?"

Brandon shook his head. The Boss Man scrunched up his face, and spat in the long pine needles that coated the ground.

"Never mind, we soon learn you to scrape. What your name, boy?"

CHAPTER ELEVEN

"George," Brandon said "George Braith ..."

"Only need your first name for my book," said the Boss Man. "You work hard, like a good boy, you get paid a dollar fifty for the week. You need a place to stay?"

"No, sir," Brandon said. He didn't feel like explaining that he boarded with Miss Julia. He sensed that the less he told this man about himself, the better.

The Boss Man pointed into the woods, to where a small group of workers were dragging metal tools down sections of tree trunk. "Go over there to them, and tell them I sent you. Ask for Willie. Say, you ate? You brung your dinner pail?"

Brandon hadn't even thought of lunch, even though it was around lunchtime, and he shook his head. "Well, then, you learn," said the Boss Man, and he smiled to himself. "Afore you go to Willie and them, go get you some dinner from the commissary, over there." He pointed to a large shack that looked like a garage.

The commissary was basically a very bad grocery store. White sacks of flour and cornmeal, tubs of lard, and a scanty collection of canned foods all caught Brandon's eye, as did boxes of soap flakes, a bunch of kerosene lamps and a couple of hams hanging from the ceiling, alongside assorted woven baskets. An open barrel filled to the brim with rice stood next to another piled high with dried black-eyed peas. There were no luxuries here.

The Boss Man walked behind the counter. "I'll get you a good meal," he said, smiling in a way that Brandon definitely didn't like. Turning his back, the Boss Man busied himself selecting and cutting things, and then wrapped them in paper. When he was done, he dropped the anonymous paper parcels onto the counter, and said, "I got you a hunk of ham, a bit of cheese, some crackers, and lard. That should see you right."

Brandon looked at him warily. "How much does it all cost, sir?" he said.

But the Boss Man waved him aside with a smile. "No charge, I'll just mark it against your pay for the week. Here, here's a flour sack to carry them. Go along now and tell Willie to set you to work."

Wondering what he had got himself into, Brandon gathered up the cloth bag, and headed out to the woods.

"Now where your dinner bucket?" said Willie, a tall man in his forties.

"I didn't know I had to bring one, sir," said Brandon. "The boss let me have this from the commissary." He held up his lunch bag.

"Hoo—ee," Willie laughed, revealing several missing teeth, and he turned to address the other workers. "We got a new one here, boys. This short George, he wet behind the ears, all right. Say, Short George, you know anything about turpentining?"

"No, sir, I don't," Brandon said curtly. He thought he had made that obvious, but apparently Willie wanted to hear him admit his ignorance.

"So the Boss Man sent you to us, I teach you to scrape. You take this scrape iron here," Willie picked up a short metal pole with a triangle of metal affixed to the end, "and you scrape off the rosin, off the tree." He demonstrated, running the scrape iron down the tree trunk. Flakes of dried white gum fell from the bark-stripped tree into a battered tin box attached further down the trunk. "Now, your turn," said Willie, handing Brandon the scrape iron. It looked easy enough, Brandon thought, and he reached up with the tool to rest it against a thick patch of whitened dried resin. As he dragged it down, the end triangle of the scraper iron ran harmlessly over the trunk's surface. Only the tiniest particle of resin came off the tree.

Willie laughed, "Well now, Shorty, I think that's what we call you, Shorty, on account of you come up short."

Brandon was not amused.

By lunchtime, Brandon's stomach was growling, his arms were aching, and a blister was starting on his right thumb. He had scraped hard at several trees, and finally begun to yield results, but it was exhausting work. Willie had also shown him how to empty the Herty cups, little metal containers that collected whatever sap had flowed down the trees. Brandon was scraping the inside of a Herty cup with a little spatula when the Woodsrider stopped by. He grumbled that Brandon was too slow in his work.

"Shorty's learning," Willie replied in a light tone. "I learn him, yes, sir."

"He need to learn faster," said the Woodsrider. "You boys eat dinner now, then back to work."

Brandon opened up his lunch. The ham had a green sheen, the cheese was dry and cracked, and the lard smelled revolting. Willie noticed that Brandon wasn't eating. "Here, have a biscuit," he said, handing him one. "Dip it down in my pail." Brandon was puzzled, but he did as Willie instructed, and allowed his biscuit to touch the floor of the lunch pail. When he lifted it out again, he saw syrup dripping from it. He looked quizzically at Willie. "That's cane syrup," said Willie. "My wife puts some in the bottom of the pail, so's I can dip my biscuits. Ain't that biscuit good, Shorty?"

Brandon licked his fingers and nodded in agreement. He ate his biscuit so

CHAPTER ELEVEN

fast, Willie gave him another.

"So tell me, Shorty," Willie said. "You got someplace to stay, apart from the woods?"

Brandon nodded again, and said through a mouthful of biscuit, "Yes, sir. I'm staying in Snipesville, with Miss Julia Russell. Do you know her?"

Willie shook his head. "No. I don't know nobody. I ain't from here. My wife and me, we was floaters from Florida, came this way looking for work about two years ago. I work six days, and on the seventh I rest. I never been to Snipesville. My wife go there, because she take in laundry."

Brandon was amazed. Two years in the turpentine camp, and Willie had never set foot in town?

"Say, you never seen no commissary before, Shorty? That's where you buys what you needs until you gets paid. Trouble is, by the time you gets paid, you run up a debt at the commissary. Never can pay it off. Never can leave here."

"That's slavery," Brandon said loudly.

Willie hushed him. "You keep your voice down. It ain't the worst place I heard of."

"You're just saying that because you have no choice," Brandon said. "But the truth is, you can't leave, can you, sir?"

"I could," said Willie. "If I run fast enough, and don't think I haven't thought about it. But the Boss Man would hunt me down, on account of I owe a debt. Then I would get whipped, or worse. And I can't take my wife and children if I run. So that is that."

"This is slavery," Brandon repeated bitterly.

Willie didn't reply. He just took a sip of water, and wiped his mouth. Then he said, "So what you doing here, Shorty? On the run from the law?"

"No, sir," Brandon said. "I just needed work."

"Not this kind of work, you don't," Willie said. "I seen your hands. You never worked a day in your life."

"Not true," Brandon blustered. "I was a coal miner ... Once. And I was a servant. And I was a dentist's apprentice."

"Not hard labor like this," Willie said. "No, Shorty, you in the wrong place. You got schooling too, I bet. You read and write?"

Brandon nodded wordlessly.

"Yeah, I reckoned so. Turpentine camp is no place for you, Shorty. You go back to your mama."

"George, what have you done to your clothes? And, forgive me for saying so, but you smell like you've rolled around in pine sap." Miss Julia was shocked,

❖ 299 ❖

and Brandon couldn't blame her. His trousers and shirt were dusty, and he smelled like a Christmas tree. "As soon as you change," she said, "ask Alberta if she can clean them for you."

"Miss Julia, I got a job," said Brandon. "These are now my work clothes."

"But what sort of work is this?" she said. Before he could answer, she gasped. "You're working in the turpentine camp?"

"Yes, ma'am," Brandon said with a nervous smile.

"But George, I told you not to. That's a terrible place."

"I don't have a choice," Brandon said. He turned away, and didn't see her look of deep concern.

Tuesday, February 27, 1906

Brandon had hardly slept, for fear of being late for work, when his alarm clock rang. He skipped breakfast, to Miss Alberta's consternation, and completely forgot to ask her to make him lunch, something he didn't realize until he was halfway to work.

It was a long walk to the turpentine camp in the bleak light of dawn, and when he arrived, the Boss Man was there to greet him. "You late!" he barked. "I gone dock you pay for that. And I see you got no food, neither. Best you stay in the quarters, so you won't be late in the mornings. I'll see if someone can spare you a place, and I'll send one of the women with food. Now go work with Willie and them."

Tired as he was, Brandon's head spun. He wouldn't figure out the significance of what the Boss Man had said until sometime later.

Willie told Brandon that the Woodsrider had declared him too slow at scraping, and so he set him to work instead raking long pine straw needles from around the bases of the trees. "I don't know how he 'spect you to learn, unless you do the work," Willie grumbled. "But orders is orders. You don't argue with him." He lowered his voice. "A few months ago, him and the Boss Man tied a man to a pine tree, and beat him to death. They left him there for days, as a warning to the rest of us. And I seen the Woodsrider whip a man with his bush knife, that's the yard-long knife he carry. That man was bleeding bad, but he managed to drag himself to the highway, and someone picked him up there, and drove him to a doctor in Savannah. He like to have died. Maybe he did die. We just heard the story of what happened to him, but we never see him again."

Brandon carried on raking, but he found that his hands were shaking. He tried not to think about what Willie had said.

CHAPTER ELEVEN

Brandon was still raking, and daydreaming of home, when a young woman came traipsing through the woods toward him, carrying a basket. "You George?" she said. "Boss Man done told me to bring you this."

She lifted the cloth that covered the basket, and Brandon saw a bowl of rice and beans, and a few small whole fish. Sardines. He had learned to eat sardines in Balesworth. "Crunchy eyeball fish," wasn't that what he and Alex had called them in 1940? That seemed a very long time ago now.

"Thank you," Brandon said without enthusiasm. "What do I owe you?"

"Nothing," she said. "Food's from the commissary. I just cooked it."

Brandon hesitated, knowing that to accept the food meant owing more money to the Boss Man. But what could he do? He was hungry, and even if he turned away the girl, he still owed for the food. She said, "Boss Man say you needs someplace to stay. He say you got to stay here, or else you be late every morning. You come stay with us. My name's Weezie."

Brandon said nothing. He just nodded. But now he was truly scared. He hadn't agreed to give up his freedom, but somehow, he suspected, his consent was not required.

Over lunch, Brandon told Willie about Weezie bringing the food, and the Boss Man's message that he had to live in the camp. "That's the way they take us in," Willie said quietly. "First it's a meal, and then it's your rent. Soon, you owe more money than you make."

"I should be okay," Brandon said uncertainly. "I only owe for a couple of meals, and I'm getting paid a dollar fifty for the week …"

"That's what he tell you," Willie said, "but come Saturday, when the Boss Man reckons up the accounts, you find, no matter what, that you owes him. Shorty, you was right. This is slavery. Ain't no escape."

Brandon felt his stomach drop. "I can leave right now," he said, "and not owe him a thing."

Willie shook his head, and spoke quickly in a low voice. "Listen, you owe him already for the food. He have the sheriff at Snipesville come round you up. But if you going to leave, yes, best you do it today, and you run fast and far as you can. You just a boy, Shorty, and you ought not to be here. Don't tell nobody I said so, but you run."

Just then, they heard a horse coming toward them. Willie jumped to his feet, and Brandon followed him. This time, it was the Boss Man who was on horseback. He pointed a whip at Brandon, and said firmly, "You stay with Weezie, she tell you?"

CHAPTER ELEVEN

"Yes, sir," Brandon said, "I'll move in after payday. I still owe my landlady. I have to pay her before I can move in."

The Boss Man grunted and rode on. As soon as his horse had left the clearing, Willie turned to Brandon. "When it's time to go at the end of the day, Shorty, you go. You don't come back."

Even after taking a hot bath and putting on new clothes, Brandon felt the stress and degradation of the turpentine camp weighing on him. He was ashamed to have been fooled by the Boss Man. He took a deep breath as he opened the parlor door, and mentally prepared to tell Miss Julia the whole story. But as soon as she saw him, Miss Julia said, "George, there is no call for you to return to that dreadful place. Robert has found you another job."

Brandon felt his burden of worry and fear start to fall away. "That's awesome, ma'am, what job?"

Robert answered. "My cousin is taking you on at the blacksmiths' shop as an apprentice. You can start tomorrow."

Brandon was bewildered. "But Thomas said he couldn't afford to hire anyone."

"He changed his mind," said Robert. "And he thinks the same as me and Aunt Julia. There is much about you I don't know, George, including how you came by your education …"

"I read a lot of books in England," Brandon interjected.

"Regardless of how you came by it," Robert said firmly, "a young man of your education cannot work in turpentine."

"Yes, but …"

"No buts," Miss Julia said. "George, you must take the job with Thomas. I insist."

Brandon knew the moment had arrived to tell them what had happened. "Miss Julia, Robert, I'm scared. One of the guys I worked with, Willie, he told me the Boss Man …"

"The who?" Miss Julia said, looking astonished. "George, you are normally so well-spoken. Pray tell, what is the gentleman's name? Surely it is not *Boss Man?*"

"I don't know his name," Brandon said. "Everyone calls him the Boss Man, and his henchman is called the Woodsrider. Anyway, Willie said the Boss Man will come looking for me, because I owe him."

"You owe him?" Robert said, his eyes narrowing suspiciously. "I know that men working in turpentine are enslaved by debt, that they are peons, but you have only been employed for two days. How can you already owe your employer?"

Miss Julia was looking thoughtfully at Brandon. "What did you accept from that man?"

Brandon gave her an agonized look. He felt utterly stupid for having been so naive. "I didn't really have a choice, Miss Julia."

She looked at him kindly. "I know you didn't, my dear," she said, "It's not your fault. You are blameless in this. But it is imperative that you tell me the truth. What did you accept?"

He told her about the two bad meals, and she nodded. "Was there anything else?" she said.

"He said I should live in the camp so I could be at work on time."

"I see," Miss Julia said. "Then I think it's safe to assume that he will expect you to owe him advance rent also."

She turned to her young cousin. "Robert, kindly come with me."

"Where are we going, Aunt Julia?" said Robert, getting to his feet.

"To visit Sheriff Bragg," said Miss Julia.

Brandon spent the next anxious hour or so by the fireplace, an untouched cup of coffee sitting at his elbow. He jumped when he heard the front door open, and was greatly relieved when Miss Julia and Robert appeared in the parlor doorway in an obviously good mood.

"All is well," said Miss Julia, setting down her purse. "Sheriff Bragg agreed to take our payment for your debt to this Mr. Brantley at the turpentine camp. The Sheriff agreed with us that three dollars should cover all your costs, and more."

"That's kind of you, Miss Julia," Brandon said, "and I will pay you back as soon as I can. But why would the Sheriff want to help me?"

"Don't worry about repaying me. You have amply repaid me already. Oh, and you might want to thank Reverend Evans, too, next time you see him. Robert and I took him along. The Sheriff regards all of us as respectable representatives of the race, and he was most helpful."

Something was still bothering Brandon. "I'm grateful, but what about Willie, and Weezie, and all of them? They're trapped in slavery. Slavery's supposed to be illegal."

"Those are poor, ignorant people," said Robert. "Reverend Evans sometimes holds services in the camp, and that is all that may be done at present for these wretched souls. There is much drunkenness among them."

"That's easy for you to say," Brandon said angrily. "I'm sorry, Robert, I don't mean to be rude, and I'm grateful for you helping me out. But I'm not surprised if the turpentine workers get drunk. They are desperate. Willie told me the Boss Man last summer ordered that a guy with pneumonia get dragged from his bed, and sent back to work. He died. And Willie saw them beat another man to death just a few months ago."

Robert looked troubled. "I will pray for them all, George," he said softly. "It was brave of you to tell me these things. Thank you."

Brandon was pleased and surprised by this. He was starting to think that maybe Robert wasn't so pompous after all. As though reading Brandon's mind, Robert said, "I shall tell you this. There was much I did not know about Atlanta, as a lad from the country, moving to the big city for college. But now I find that there's much I don't know about Snipes County. That's education, George. It teaches us to think, and to be humble about knowledge, for no matter how much we learn, we thirst to learn more. This is why we need the high school."

"Too true, Robert," said Brandon, with feeling. "Too true."

Chapter 12:
BALESWORTH POLITICS

Thursday, October 19, 1905

Hannah always cleaned Elizabeth's desk very carefully, flicking a feather duster around the piles of letters, papers, and envelopes that tottered on the surface. Or at least that was how she had cleaned Elizabeth's desk, until today. As soon as she walked into the room, she saw that all the papers had vanished. It wasn't hard to see where they had gone: Tiny charred fragments of handwritten letters lay scattered about the cold fireplace. Gingerly, Hannah picked up a few of them with her fingertips, laid them in her palm, and examined them. On one, the word "suffrage" appeared in Elizabeth's neat handwriting, and Hannah sighed.

In Hannah's experience, Mrs. Devenish never talked about feelings, and neither did Elizabeth, her younger self. But that didn't mean she didn't have them. Hannah guessed that Elizabeth was so hurt by what had happened between her and Mrs. Lewis, that she was giving up her women's suffrage work. Verity was right, Hannah thought: Behind that prickly exterior was a deeply sensitive young person.

Hannah was serving tea when Victoria said to her youngest sister, "I'm happy to see you present yourself in the drawing room, dear Elizabeth, but I thought the Balesworth Women's Suffrage Association committee meeting was this afternoon?"

Elizabeth, who was reading a novel, did not reply.

"Won't you be going, Elizabeth?" Victoria persisted.

CHAPTER TWELVE

"I have no chaperone," Elizabeth said absently.

"What nonsense. Why would you need a chaperone for an afternoon visit to Mrs. Lewis's house?"

"Please let us not speak of this, Victoria," Elizabeth snapped. "I am no longer interested in the Association's affairs."

Victoria opened her mouth to say something, and then exchanged looks with Margaret instead. After a pause, she said hesitantly, "Margaret and I are going out this afternoon."

"I don't want to come with you, thanks," Elizabeth said.

"I did not invite you," Victoria said firmly. "I was simply going to ask you to tell Mama when she returns home. We may even return before she does."

"Fine," Elizabeth said. Hannah thought she made it sound like "whatever."

Victoria made her final effort. "Elizabeth, you ought to go out. You need fresh air. Oh, and May?"

Hannah was startled when Victoria spoke to her, and suddenly fearful that she had noticed her keen interest in the conversation. "Yes, Mrs. Halley?"

"Has Mrs. Morris any biscuits? Tea should always be served with cake or biscuits. You ought to know that by now."

Hannah gritted her teeth. She was so looking forward to the glorious day when she could finally quit this job, and tell Mrs. Halley and her family to get their own tea and cookies.

"Where are Miss Victoria and Miss Margaret going off to, I wonder?" Mrs. Morris asked nobody in particular, as she took cookies from a tin, and arranged them on a plate. "I saw them do the same last week, and the week before that. Off they went without so much as a by-your-leave, as though they was off to the races, if you please. Didn't they say nothing, May?"

"No clue," Hannah said. "They don't usually share their social plans with me."

"Mrs. Hughes don't seem troubled by it, so I don't suppose she minds," said Mrs. Morris, closing the tin with a thundering rattle. "Mind you, I don't suppose she wants anything else to worry about. She's got her hands full with Miss Elizabeth, that's for certain. That girl's hardly out of her room, sitting up there sulking. I reckon she only came down today to remind them all that she lives here."

Hannah said, "She just seems kind of down, that's all."

"Yes, she has a touch of melancholy, I'll be bound," said Mrs. Morris. "Or perhaps it's guilt, after what she done to the front window. That were very naughty of her. Now, May, before you take these biscuits through to the drawing room, answer me this. Do *you* know where Miss Victoria and Miss

CHAPTER TWELVE

Margaret are going?"

"I told you, I don't," Hannah said. *But,* she added to herself, *Elizabeth does seem to feel kind of left out. What's the big secret that her sisters are keeping from her? And to think I once thought there was no drama at Willowbank.*

She might never figure our Victoria and Margaret's secret, Hannah thought, but she had an important role to play in what was yet to come. She decided to grab paper and an envelope before Elizabeth destroyed all the stationery in Willowbank.

Friday, October 20, 1905

Elizabeth was not at breakfast, or at lunch. Once again, Hannah had brought her breakfast on a tray, only to later find it left untouched in the upstairs hallway. Now, she was preparing to take up a tea tray, when Mrs. Morris said, "Look, May, I can't watch that silly girl starve herself, and she seems to like you. Why don't you see if you can persuade her to eat something? Here, I made ginger biscuits. They're her favorites."

Balancing the tray carefully on one arm, Hannah knocked at Elizabeth's door.

"What is it?" Elizabeth called out in a muffled voice.

Hannah hovered uncertainly. "It's me. May. I've brought you some tea. And ginger biscuits."

She did not reply, so Hannah opened the door, walked in, closed the door with her foot, and slipped the tea tray onto the dressing table. Taking tea strainer and pot in hand, she poured the golden liquid through the strainer into the cup, then added a tot of milk from the little jug on the tray. "One lump or two?" she said, holding up the sugar bowl, even though Elizabeth couldn't see it because she was lying on the bed with her face pressed into her pillow.

There was a pause. Then Elizabeth said, "Two. Please."

Breakthrough, thought Hannah. She stirred in the sugar, placed a cookie in the saucer, then slid Elizabeth's tea onto the bedside table, and, without asking permission, sat down. In the silence that followed, she inspected the objects on the dressing table: Brushes, combs, mysterious little pots, and two even more mysterious small brown pads. She wondered what those were for.

Hannah also looked at Elizabeth, and processed what she was seeing. Elizabeth Hughes, the future Mrs. Devenish, was a depressed teenager, a *normal* teenager, having a meltdown in front of her maid. *And it's all my fault,* Hannah thought with shame.

She had to find a way to make things up to Elizabeth. But first, she had to persuade her to talk. Hannah picked up one of the mysterious little pots on the dressing table. It was a small white porcelain cylinder, with a pretty country scene painted on it, and a hole in the top, the width of a quarter. With the other hand, she picked up one of the little soft brown pads.

Elizabeth turned her head to look at what she was doing. "You seem perplexed. I assume you know that's a hair-keeper, and the other is a rat."

"That tells me nothing, Miss Elizabeth," said Hannah.

"Surely you know, May? I pull stray hairs from my combs and brushes, and put them in the hair-keeper."

"Eww," Hannah groaned, putting the china pot back on the table. "Why?"

"Well, you see the rat you're holding? That's a little bag that I fill with my hair."

Hannah quickly put the pad down, too. "That's gross," she said. "Why would you do that?"

"Everyone does," said Elizabeth. "All ladies, I mean. How do you think I have such a large pompadour? Do you really think I have that much hair?"

"So you stuff these little rat thingies in your bun to make it big?" Hannah said, and she laughed at the very idea. "That's so bizarre."

Elizabeth smiled, and said, "Yes, I suppose it is. It's only a silly fashion. And it's such a nuisance."

"I know I shouldn't say this, Miss Elizabeth," Hannah said quietly, "but I know you feel bad. And I know things will be okay."

"I don't know what you mean," Elizabeth mumbled, looking away from her.

"Yes, you do," Hannah said, suddenly feeling like she was in dangerous waters, but carrying on regardless. "You know what I'm talking about. You will get over it, well, mostly you will, and you'll realize that some people are just too important to you to drop altogether."

Elizabeth sniffed again, lifting her head from the pillow, and then she sat up, glancing at the cookies. "What are you talking about? There's no use denying that I'm upset, that much is obvious, but this is really none of your business, May."

I know it's not, thought Hannah. *But it kind of is.*

She persisted. "Look, I know you're embarrassed," she said with feeling. "I know exactly how you feel, like you never want to look anyone in the face again."

Elizabeth, grimacing, took a sip of tea, and dipped a cookie in it before taking a bite.

Hannah tried a different tactic. "Somebody I cared about … I mean, someone I do care about, she was kind of like a … another mom to me. She really hurt my feelings. I thought I would die."

But Elizabeth wasn't listening. "She hit me," she said, more in amazement and sadness than in outrage. "She talked to me as though I were five years old.

She made that hideous suggestion to my mother, and she …"

Hannah said, "Look, it's up to you what you want to do, and who you hang out with. I mean, it's different with your mom, you're kind of stuck with her, because she's your mom. But nobody says you should care what anyone else thinks. You're an adult, and you …"

"An adult?" said Elizabeth, looking at Hannah in surprise. "You think me an adult? Of course I'm not an adult. I shan't turn 21 for more than a year, and the law says I remain a child even then, for a woman does not possess a vote, and so long as we have no vote, we are as helpless as children in the eyes of the law. As a woman, I shall *never* cease to be a child in the eyes of English society."

Hannah was anxious to steer the conversation away from women's rights. She said, "Okay, Miss Elizabeth, but why do you care what Mrs. Lewis thinks about you?"

Hannah saw Elizabeth grimace at the mention of Mrs. Lewis's name. But then she mulled over Hannah's question, before saying slowly, "You know, May, that is an excellent question. Who, I beg to know, does that woman think she is?"

Suddenly, and without really understanding why, Hannah found herself defending the difficult Mrs. Lewis. "Be fair, Miss Elizabeth," she said, "you did kind of backtalk her after she was nice to you at the meeting, and you must see why she might be seriously mad about you throwing the brick and getting her involved. But you know what? She cared about you enough to drop everything and come rushing up from Balesworth because she thought something bad happened to you. I see how she talks to you, and it's kind of obvious she thinks the world of you. She's annoying, I can see that, but please, don't drop her."

Elizabeth didn't say anything. And Hannah couldn't help thinking that this entire discussion had turned weirdly familiar. But now that she had said it, Hannah wondered if it mattered at all whether Elizabeth and Mrs. Lewis ever spoke to each other again. Perhaps patching up their relationship wasn't part of her mission at all.

As Hannah came downstairs with the tea tray, she was still thinking. It was she who had given Elizabeth the brick idea, and even if that was an honest mistake, it was also she who had summoned Mrs. Lewis to the house, and ordered Verity to forge a letter that was supposedly from Millie Cooke. *What kind of person am I*, she wondered?

But then Hannah thought to herself, *Did I really just give advice to Mrs. Devenish?* That cheered her up a little, as did the thought that her job was to make sure that Elizabeth married Tom Devenish, not to get Elizabeth to reconcile with Mrs. Lewis. Once again, she thought with relief, *So what if Elizabeth never speaks to the old bag again?*

But suddenly, Hannah felt chilled to the bone. In an instant, she knew she was wrong. If Elizabeth Hughes and Mrs. Lewis never spoke again, then Mrs. Devenish would never learn the whereabouts of George Braithwaite in 1940. And that would be a disaster. George would have a horrible childhood, and he would not move to Snipesville and become the first black doctor, or a friend to three confused time-travelers. Still, awful though this was, it didn't seem to be such a disaster as Verity and her family never being born. But for some reason, Hannah thought, it might even be worse. She just couldn't think why. Hopelessly tied in mental knots, Hannah slammed down the tea tray on the kitchen table so hard, a cup shattered, and Flora gave a little scream.

Saturday, October 21, 1905

In the morning, Hannah found Elizabeth in the garden, snipping at the twigs of a rose plant with a small pair of pruning shears. "What is it, May?" Elizabeth said tersely. She didn't look at Hannah. But Hannah didn't take her abruptness personally. She knew Elizabeth was embarrassed by their conversation yesterday, and she was just glad to see her out and about.

"Sorry to bother you, Miss Elizabeth," she said in a breezy tone. "There's a meeting about politics in Balesworth on Tuesday. It's going to be all young people. In someone's house. I just wondered if you would like to go with me."

"That is out of the question, May," Elizabeth said. "I cannot possibly attend when I haven't received a proper invitation. I can hardly present myself at the door as the guest of my maid."

What a snobby brat you are, Hannah thought. She looked crossly at Elizabeth, who caught Hannah's angry look, and then turned back to her roses, ducking her head slightly, and looking uncomfortable.

Suddenly, Flora, out of breath, was standing at Hannah's elbow.

Elizabeth glanced at her, and said impatiently, "Yes, Flora, what is it?"

"There's a letter for you, Miss Elizabeth," she puffed. "It's on the hall table. Shall I fetch it for you?

Figures that Flora would find a stupid excuse to interrupt our conversation, Hannah thought. *She thinks the whole family belongs to her, including Elizabeth, and she doesn't even like her.*

"No, no, don't fuss so, Flora," Elizabeth said. "I'm perfectly capable of getting the post for myself."

As Hannah followed Flora and Elizabeth back across the lawn into the house, she thought of how this conversation reminded her of what Brandon had said about meeting Mrs. Devenish and Flora during his visit to Willowbank in 1915. *Funny how you step into someone's life, and you only see snapshots of it,* she thought. *And how strange that nobody's life is predictable at all, including mine.*

While Elizabeth took off her gardening gloves in the hall, Flora held the letter under her nose. "Balesworth," Elizabeth muttered, noticing the postmark, and then she added to herself, "What unusual handwriting …" She handed Flora her gloves in exchange for the envelope. Quickly, she read over the letter.

"Is it bad news, Miss Elizabeth?" Flora asked eagerly.

"No, not at all," said Elizabeth, and she turned to Hannah. "May, by a curious coincidence, it seems that I'm invited to a gathering this next Tuesday, in Balesworth. I don't know who has invited me. I can't read the signature. Can you read it?"

Hannah took the letter from her, and glanced over Verity's neat handwriting, noticing that Verity had scribbled Millie's name, and misspelled it in the process, omitting the "e" from Cooke. "It's from Millie Cooke," she said, trying to sound surprised as she handed it back to Elizabeth. "You know Millie Cooke, Miss Elizabeth. She was at Mrs. … I mean, the Association meeting." Hannah stopped herself just in time from uttering the dreaded Mrs. Lewis's name in Elizabeth's presence.

"But I hardly know Millie Cooke," Elizabeth said, knitting her brow. "I've only met her once."

"She's nice!" yelped Hannah.

"I am sure she is," Elizabeth replied shortly. "But the fact remains …"

It was time for Hannah to apply serious pressure. "Miss Elizabeth, I was invited, but I didn't think I could go, because I wouldn't have anyone to go with, and I would be too shy to turn up at a posh lady's house all by myself. Please say you'll come with me? I'm sure it will be fun to get out of the house. And didn't you say at the Association meeting that working-class girls should be more involved in politics? Don't you want to encourage me? I need to be encouraged. Or I might not do anything. Ever."

Elizabeth had listened to Hannah's frantic speech with a smile playing about her lips. After a pause, she said, "Very well." And then, she said anxiously, "You don't think, um, Mrs. Lewis will be there, do you, May?"

Hannah mentally crossed her fingers before she lied. "No, I did ask Miss Cooke about that, and Mrs. Lewis absolutely, definitely won't be there."

Of course, Hannah had not spoken to Millie at all. But since the meeting was for young people, and Millie Cooke wasn't exactly a fan of Mrs. Lewis, *no way has she invited the old bat,* she reassured herself. Then again, that was a problem. She needed to find a way for Elizabeth to reconnect with her mentor.

Sunday, October 22, 1905

"What are you doing here?" The Professor said. "It's Sunday." Hannah was hovering on the doorstep.

"I know. I didn't want to startle you, so that's why I knocked. Look, I needed a day off. I told Mrs. Morris and Mrs. Hughes that my mother was sick."

"Ah, a mental health day," said the Professor, holding the door open for her. "Good idea. Come in, and you can help me make dinner."

"Hannah, peel those for me, please," said the Professor, nodding toward a bunch of carrots lying on the kitchen table. They were covered in garden dirt, and their grassy tops were still attached.

Hannah held the carrots under the kitchen tap, and began to run clear water over them.

"You know, you look very comfortable handling household tasks these days," said the Professor.

"Do I?" Hannah said. "It's not exactly rocket science to wash carrots. But I do have lots of experience now, and I guess it shows. It's made me a more practical kind of person. I just wish I could handle all the thinking stuff as easily as I peel carrots and potatoes. I do try, but my plans never work out, you know. I'll be amazed if can get Elizabeth to talk to Tom and Mrs. Lewis at Millie's party."

"Don't worry. Nobody's plans ever really work out," said the Professor. "And when they do seem to work, it's almost never because it was planned that way. That's the story of my life, honestly."

"Okay, so that's something I would like to know more about," Hannah said, shaking the water off the carrot tops and into the sink.

"What?"

"The story of your life, Kate."

The Professor smiled. "You never used to call me Kate, did you?"

"I know," Hannah said. "Is it okay?"

"Of course it is. But tell you about my life? I wouldn't know where to begin. Look, the important thing is that your plans don't matter as much as you think. Show up, and then allow serendipity to work. It's your presence, your experience, your influence, that are important to the world, not your plans." She looked over at Hannah. "Aren't you going to ask me what serendipity means?"

"No," said Hannah. She shook out the last of the carrot greens, then took the bunch to the kitchen table. Grabbing a large knife, she hacked the roots from the tops. Trading the knife for a small peeler, she returned the carrots to the sink, and began to strip off their skins. "I already know what serendipity means," she said finally. She didn't mention that she had only recently read the word in a book, and looked it up in Elizabeth's dictionary. "Have you got a clean tea towel so I can dry these carrots?"

"Tea towel? I see you're finally learning the local language," said the Professor. She took a linen dish towel from a drawer, and handed it to Hannah. Hannah laid it out on the draining board next to the sink, placed the washed peeled carrots on it, and rolled them in the towel to dry them off.

"And then, of course," the Professor said, "there's the opposite of serendipity, which is looking for things that don't exist."

Hannah started peeling another carrot. "Is that really the opposite meaning of serendipity?" she said.

There was another small silence. "Okay, so maybe not," the Professor admitted.

Hannah said, "You're talking in riddles again. Why don't you just say what you mean?"

The Professor gave her a half-smile, and said, "You look tired, dear."

"Kate went out," said Hannah, the moment Verity entered the kitchen.

"Hannah! What are you doing here on Sunday? I wish I'd known you had the day off. I've been in London. I took communion at St. Paul's Cathedral, and you could have come with me. How are you?"

"Oh, fine, except for having to deal with a crazy family."

"And what crazy family would that be?" Verity said. "Mine, I presume."

Hannah was embarrassed, but Verity reassured her. "We *are* quite mad," she said. "Be grateful you're not related to us."

That comment hurt, strangely, until Hannah remembered something that cheered her up. "But I think I am related," she said. She hadn't meant to say it out loud.

"How can we possibly be related?" Verity blustered. "Don't be ridiculous."

"Look, I'm not one hundred percent sure, and I don't even know if it matters, but it's not ridiculous, is it? I mean, think about it. We all have, like, a bunch of ancestors, right? We all have two parents, but we have four grandparents, eight great-grands, and so on."

"Yes, I suppose that's true," Verity said. "I've never really thought about it. But you and I aren't likely to be related when you're from California, and your surname is Dias. That's very unlikely. There are no Spanish people in my family."

"Portuguese," Hannah corrected her.

CHAPTER TWELVE

"Or those," said Verity. "No foreigners of any kind. We're all English, through and through, all the way back to the Norman Conquest."

Hannah almost laughed. "Are you sure about that?"

"Yes, of course," said Verity, and there was no doubt in her voice. "Why wouldn't I be?"

Hannah's eyes narrowed. "Verity, did you ever take a good look at Mrs. Hughes?"

"My great-grandmother? No. Well, not since I was a small child. I haven't met her here, not yet, and she died when I was still little. Why?"

Hannah said, "She's half-Indian."

"Rubbish," Verity said stoutly. "Of course she isn't."

That's what you think, Hannah thought. "Okay, Verity, you tell me. Who were your great-great-grandparents, Mrs. Hughes's parents?"

"I have no idea," Verity said. "Granny never spoke of them, and I have never looked up the family tree. But I'm sure I would know if they were from India, either of them."

"But you never tried to find out?" Hannah said slyly.

"No, of course not," Verity said. "Why would I? I'm really not that interested."

"Maybe you should be," said Hannah. "You might learn something."

Verity looked at her keenly, and in a subdued voice she said, "Oh, good heavens. You know something, don't you? Oh, blast. Of course you do. You're a time traveler. Now, tell me, how are you and I related?"

"That's just it," Hannah said. "I don't know, it's just a hunch."

"Well, related or not," said Verity, "I'm glad to have this chance to get to know you better, Hannah. I just wish we didn't have this terrible problem to solve." She gave Hannah a brave smile.

"You mean fixing up Elizabeth and Tom? Yeah, I know. And I hate to tell you, Verity, but I figured out I also have to get your granny and Mrs. Lewis to be friends again."

"Why? I can't imagine that's terribly important."

Hannah reminded her of Mrs. Lewis's role in discovering the whereabouts of the young George Braithwaite in 1940, and told of her foreboding feeling that George's rescue was even more important than they thought. Verity looked very serious now. "Well, what are we going to do about it?"

"I don't know. Follow my gut, I guess. My instincts. Kate says I just have to be myself, and do what I think best."

"How strange," said Verity. "It's as though she really doesn't know what to tell you. Kate told me she normally knows how to advise you and Alex and Brandon because she looks up historical documents. I don't really understand

CHAPTER TWELVE

that, because how would she know where to find them? I've been in my college's archive in Cambridge, and there are simply masses of old papers. Tons of them."

Hannah was intrigued. "Kate told you that she figures out what to do from history research? She's kind of hinted about that before, but …" She stopped. "You just asked a good question. How does she know where to look? Verity, she won't tell me stuff like this. She seems to trust you more than she trusts me."

"Yes," Verity said.

"Don't you think that's weird?" said Hannah.

Verity now looked very uncomfortable. "I suppose so," she said. "It's very odd. She talks to me as though she has known me for a long time, but I have never met the woman before. She knows all about me. And Granny. And she seems to know all about you. All of us. She seems to take a special interest in all of us, but why? It's very disturbing, frankly. But, and this is the strangest thing of all, she does seem familiar, somehow. I just have no idea why."

"I know what you mean," Hannah said slowly, "For a long time, I thought she was an evil witch, just messing up our lives for fun. But when Brandon, Alex, and me got stuck in 1752, she was really, really nice to us, and I started to think, okay, so she's really our friend. That's why I've decided to call her Kate, like you do. But honestly, I don't know what to think. I want to trust her. And I feel like I know her, too, but then I realize I really don't know her or trust her at all."

"Kate said something to me about parallel universes," said Verity. "It meant nothing to me at all. Do you know what it means?"

"I've heard of that," said Hannah, thinking hard now. "It's a theory. Something to do with, like, somebody makes a choice, and both choices happen, because somehow a separate universe forms to make them happen."

"So there's a universe in which I exist, but I didn't start smoking?"

"I think so," Hannah said. "And another in which we never met. And another in which …"

"I don't exist?" Now Verity was smiling. "Then everything will be all right. Don't you see, Hannah? No matter what you do, I carry on existing in this universe. Why should I worry about any of the other Veritys, in other universes?"

Hannah wanted to believe that, too. "I don't know," she said. "But Kate is worried. And that worries me, because she's the expert. Maybe it's not so simple. We should do what she says. We should do what I think we should do."

Verity frowned. "I don't mean to be unkind, but that's absurd. Why should you make such important decisions alone, Hannah? You're younger than me, you're less well-educated …"

"No, actually, I'm not," Hannah said calmly. "I was older than you in 1940, so I kind of still am. Also, I may not have started college yet, but I am a pretty experienced time traveler. I've survived all kinds of things. And Kate is better educated than both of us, and this is what she says should happen. I'm inclined to respect that."

"I want to discuss all of this with Kate," said Verity. "Where is she?"

"I have no idea," said Hannah. "I thought she would be right back." She peered anxiously at the door.

Monday, October 23, 1905
By the time Hannah and Verity were ready to go to work in Ickswade, the Professor still had not returned to Weston Cottage. "Should we call the police?" said Verity, as she closed the front door behind them.

"And tell them what?" said Hannah. "What would we tell them, exactly?"

Verity shrugged her shoulders.

The Professor had always arrived and left with dizzying suddenness, but this time, Hannah thought, her departure felt different. How or why that was, she couldn't tell. It just was. Anyway, she felt strangely calm. Her own thoughts and feelings were her best guide to what she should do, and they always had been.

Tuesday, October 24, 1905
Hannah and Elizabeth followed the crooked little lane off Balesworth High Street to Millie Cooke's home. "Oh, what a cool old house!" Hannah said when she saw Waldley Cottage. She could tell it was hundreds of years old, a two-story house with a thatched roof, lots of crooked beams, and a doorway that was too low for most adults to enter without lowering their heads.

"May, don't remark on the appearance of the house," Elizabeth said irritably, "It's common."

"Of course I'm common," Hannah muttered to herself as Elizabeth strode up the front path ahead of her. "I'm a maid, you silly snob."

Standing in the narrow little hall, Hannah could hear the babble of excited young voices from the drawing room. Elizabeth unpinned her massive and elegant hat, while Hannah removed her crushed little black hat. Mrs. Fitch's maid took both their coats, speaking only to Elizabeth to welcome her, and not to Hannah. Yet again, Hannah felt her self-confidence wobble.

The lively chatter died down for a second as the two of them entered the drawing room. Most of the young people looked curiously at Elizabeth: Some didn't recognize her, while others appeared puzzled or surprised by her pres-

CHAPTER TWELVE

ence. Arthur Ingle-Gillis smiled and raised a cup of tea to her. To Hannah's dismay, if not surprise, Millie Cooke looked shocked, her mouth hanging open.

Hannah asked herself how she could possibly have expected nobody to notice that Elizabeth was gatecrashing this party. In fact, the only person who didn't know was Elizabeth herself: She had no idea that her invitation was Verity's forgery. However, it was clear that she knew something was wrong: Hannah saw her suddenly get a "deer in the headlights" look. Mrs. Fitch came forward to greet Elizabeth. "How good to see you again, Miss Hughes," she said smoothly. "I had no idea you had been invited this afternoon. We did so miss you at the last meeting of the Women's Suffrage Association committee. Were you unwell?"

"I am perfectly well, thank you," Elizabeth said stiffly.

"And I'm May!" Hannah cried with slight hysteria, trying to interrupt this dangerous conversation.

"Excuse me, Miss Hughes," Mrs. Fitch said to Elizabeth, glancing furiously at Hannah. "I must see to the arrangements."

Now, Elizabeth turned angrily on her maid. "May, what on earth ..."

But the reprimand was interrupted when Mr. Ingle-Gillis unwittingly came to their rescue. "Miss Hughes! What a tremendous pleasure. I am so pleased you decided to join us after all. Forgive me, but I thought you had quite forgotten my invitation during your last visit to my shop. And who is this? Why, it's your little maid! You brought your maid? How frightfully forward-thinking of you!"

Hannah gazed at him in rapture. He was so tall, dreamy, and charming. He had just saved her from a very difficult situation, and now she wanted him to whisk her away, preferably on horseback. But one glance at Elizabeth, and Hannah's blood froze. Elizabeth was also gazing starry-eyed at Mr. Ingle-Gillis, and giving the rarest of her smiles, the one that included teeth. This was not part of the plan. And it got worse. Mr. Ingle-Gillis now took Elizabeth by the hand, and led her over to a small group that included his friend Mr. Pierce.

Hannah was left standing in the middle of the room, all by herself and feeling awkward. But now she heard Verity calling to her. "Hannah! I mean, May! Over here!" Verity was sitting on a sofa with Millie Cooke, who had her hand to her mouth, barely covering a grin. Clearly, she and Verity were hitting it off. As Hannah sat next to Verity, Millie said, "Good evening, um ... "

"May," Hannah said stonily. She was very tired of being the Amazing Invisible Maid.

Millie smiled. "Yes, of course!" Then she turned to Verity. "Thank goodness Mr. Ingle-Gillis told me he had invited Miss Hughes, or I would have assumed she had arrived uninvited, and wouldn't that have been appalling …"

But Verity had stopped smiling. "Excuse us one moment, Miss Cooke," she said in an icy voice, and she pulled Hannah into a corner of the room.

"I'm so sorry Millie and the others are such ghastly snobs and keep forgetting your name," she said quietly. "The only reason they overlook my being a shop girl is that I'm posh enough to pass muster in their company. It's amazing how many of them are socialists, yet want nothing to do with working-class people. Anyway, I have something I must tell you. I haven't seen her since Wednesday."

"Who?" said Hannah.

"Kate, of course! But I do think she's all right. Some woman called Mrs. Letchmore turned up this morning, and said Miss Harrower has employed her to cook and clean for me. Thank goodness. I've made an absolute mess of the kitchen, and I haven't had a decent meal in days. Kate must be terribly busy to abandon ship like this."

"No, I don't think she is," said Hannah. "She's a time traveler, remember? She could have found a quiet time in her life to come back and see us. It never has been about her being too busy. It's about her wanting us to figure things out by ourselves."

Verity looked about the room. "Hmm, whispering in a corner is hardly good manners, is it? Explain to me later why you think a mature woman like Kate would use children to do her supposedly important work."

Hannah's eyes widened. "Verity, that's a really good question," she said. "In fact, that's brilliant. I can't believe I never thought of it."

"Thank you," said Verity. "Now, if you will excuse me, I must try to detach my young grandmother from the delightful Mr. Inglis or whatever his name is …"

"Ingle-Gillis," Hannah corrected her. "Arthur Ingle-Gillis."

"Whatever his name is," Verity repeated firmly. "Mind you, now I get a good look at him, he really *is* dishy, isn't he?"

Hannah accepted a cup of tea from the maid, and watched as Verity smoothly inserted herself into the group around Mr. Ingle-Gillis. They all looked a little startled when this tall young woman, the spitting image of Elizabeth Hughes, sat next to Mr. Ingle-Gillis and joined in their conversation. But within seconds, Verity had made some witty remark that had the whole group laughing uproariously, including Elizabeth, who then introduced her to everyone.

"How delightful to meet you, Miss Powell!" Mr. Ingle-Gillis said warmly, "Why have we not met properly before?"

"For one thing I live in Ickswade," said Verity, before adding, with a sly smile, "And for another, I work in a grocer's shop." Hannah knew that she was

CHAPTER TWELVE

telling the posh young people that she was not as posh as she sounded. There was a small embarrassed silence, broken when Mr. Ingle-Gillis added hurriedly, "There's no shame in shop keeping, Miss Powell. England is, after all, a nation of shopkeepers. I myself keep a shop."

Verity, however, wasn't going to let him get away with pretending that she was a rich person who played at shop keeping, just like him. "Actually, I don't own the shop," she said. "It's Mr. Baker's …"

But Mr. Ingle-Gillis wasn't interested in her explanation. He had decided that Verity was acceptable, no matter who she was, because she was amusing and pretty. The others immediately followed his lead, chatting amicably with her.

Just as Hannah was assessing the situation, it became much more complicated: Tom Devenish walked in. She had planned on his arrival, of course, but actually seeing him made her a little panicky. She had never been a matchmaker before. Before she could react, she watched in dismay as Tom made a beeline for Verity. Hannah ran over in a panic, and grabbed Tom's arm to stop him, completely forgetting that for a maid to grab a gentleman's arm was absolutely inappropriate in 1905. He didn't resist, however, but laughed. "I say, have we been introduced, Miss … um?"

"Harrower, May Harrower," Hannah said rapidly. She looked around the room. She could hardly allow him to sit with Verity, because he would try to chat her up. What's more, charming Arthur Ingle-Gillis would completely overshadow shy, stammering Tom Devenish in Elizabeth's presence, and that wasn't likely to make Elizabeth find him attractive. Glancing around desperately, Hannah spotted Millie Cooke, who looked like she was ready to go outside for a cigarette. Hannah cried, "Miss Cooke, have you met Mr. Devenish?"

Hannah brought Tom face to face with a highly amused Millie, who said, "Mr. Devenish, I presume? Do tell me how you are, Tom, but be quick about it, because I have to pop outside for a smoke without my aunt seeing me."

Mr. Devenish, clearly trying not to laugh, said to Hannah, "I do indeed know our hostess. The question is, Miss Harrower, do I know you?"

"Of course you do," said Hannah, her brow furrowed. "We met at Mr. Baker's shop. Don't you remember?"

He gave a chuckle. "Oh, yes, I do. You're Miss Powell's friend."

"That's me. And you remember meeting Miss Elizabeth, right? Miss Elizabeth Hughes?"

"Well, of course I know who Miss Hughes is, but we really aren't acquainted. I'm surprised she's here. I had no idea she was invited."

"Neither had I," said Millie, who was feeling about in her purse for her cigarettes, while keeping an eye out for her aunt. "Apparently, Arthur asked her to come."

Putting Tom and Millie together was not working out for Hannah at all. She instructed them, "Hang on, wait here …", then rushed over to Elizabeth and Verity, who were in earnest conversation with their group. Standing on the edge of the circle, Hannah tried to get Elizabeth's attention. Spotting Hannah's frantic gestures, Verity pointed to herself with an enquiring look, but Hannah shook her head, her lips clamped together to mime that it wasn't Verity she needed to speak with. Finally, Hannah tapped Elizabeth on the shoulder. Elizabeth was clearly annoyed to have been interrupted. "What *is* it, May?" she snapped.

"I need to talk to you," said Hannah.

"Is it important?"

"Very."

Wearily, Elizabeth got up and followed Hannah, who immediately rushed her over to Millie. Millie had almost reached the hallway, cigarette and matches in hand, and she did not look pleased to see them.

"Miss Elizabeth," Hannah said, "do you remember Millie Cooke?"

"Yes, of course," said Elizabeth politely, although she also looked a little concerned at Millie's obvious discomfort. "How … ah … How do you do, Miss Cooke? How very kind of you to invite me. It was a pleasant surprise."

Hannah felt her stomach drop. Uh-oh.

Fortunately for Hannah, the situation required an Edwardian lady such as Millie to be polite. "Miss Hughes! Gosh, yes, what a surprise! I mean, a pleasant surprise, of course. I didn't expect you would come."

"Whyever not?" Elizabeth said sharply.

Now Millie looked positively panicked. "Gosh, well, we're in Balesworth, and I know you live in Bedfordshire, Biggleswade, isn't it? So it's a long way for …"

Elizabeth's mouth was set. "I live in Ickswade, actually. But since you and I first met at Mrs. Lewis's, Miss Cooke, you must have known that travel to Balesworth is hardly an impediment to my attendance at an occasion?"

Millie had balled up her fist in stress, and Hannah could see that she was crushing her cigarette. "Well, no. It's just that I, um, I thought you were no longer involved in the women's suffrage movement, Miss Hughes?"

Elizabeth now looked baffled. "But this event is not specifically about women's suffrage, is it?" she said. "It's simply a general discussion of politics, is it not? And in any event, who told you that I was no longer involved in women's suffrage?"

CHAPTER TWELVE

Millie was turning bright pink. She was so obviously embarrassed, Hannah felt bad for her. "I, um, that is …" Millie faltered. "Oh, gosh, here's Mr. Ingle-Gillis!" Once again, Hannah thought, the knight in shining armor had come to a lady's rescue, quite without meaning to.

"I do apologize for interrupting, ladies," Mr. Ingle-Gillis said. "But I must pay my respects to our dear hostess." He took Miss Cooke's hand and planted a kiss on it. Hannah felt jealous.

"Pay your respects?" Millie said loudly. "Good grief, Arthur. I'm not dead."

Everyone who heard her laughed, except for Hannah. She watched as Elizabeth now gazed admiringly at Mr. Ingle-Gillis, while Mr. Devenish made eyes at Verity. This was not going well. At all.

Hannah wondered how she could persuade Elizabeth to talk to Tom, and whether she could take care of Mr. Ingle-Gillis by setting him up with Millie Cooke. Hannah's brain was flying in so many different directions, she was starting to get a headache.

But now, with a rush, Hannah remembered where she had heard of Millie Cooke the first time: Mrs. Devenish had mentioned Millie in her diary, part of which the Professor had shown to Hannah. Since Millie was still known as Millie Cooke in 1940, it was very unlikely that she had married Mr. Ingle-Gillis, or anyone else.

Now that Hannah saw Millie return from her smoking expedition to take back her place on the sofa, she spotted an opportunity, and sat next to her. "Great party!" she said. "Did anyone bring music?"

"It's not really a party, May," Millie said disapprovingly. "That is your name, isn't it? May? I do so wish this were a party. But alas, our speaker arrives soon, and then we shall make terribly serious conversation. I must say, I am still rather surprised to see your Miss Hughes here."

"Are you? But Mr. Ingle-Gillis invited her."

"Yes, apparently he did, but that's not the difficulty," said Millie. "Oh, this is terribly embarrassing. Look, let me ask you a question. I wonder if you could tell me whether Miss Hughes is aware of whom Mr. Devenish has invited as our speaker? This might be rather mortifying for her. Oh, and speaking of the devil, here's our speaker now."

Hannah followed the direction of Millie's eyes, and found herself looking at Mrs. Lewis. The little woman in the enormous hat beamed as the entire roomful of heads turned in her direction. She acknowledged the attention, and then began speaking with Millie's aunt, her friend Mrs. Fitch. She did not seem to have noticed Elizabeth in the crowd. But Elizabeth had noticed her, and she looked appalled.

❖ 321 ❖

CHAPTER TWELVE

Well, thought Hannah, *this is awkward.* She knew immediately she would have to do whatever it took to stop the two women clashing again. Rushing over to Elizabeth, Hannah leaned down behind her, and said quietly, "Miss Elizabeth, I have to tell you something super-important. Please. Do what I say. Whatever you do, don't give Mrs. Lewis a hard time. Just stay quiet. I'll tell you why later."

Elizabeth frowned, but then nodded to show she had understood.

Standing at the front of the room, Tom Devenish called for everyone's attention. He looked shy, as usual, but when he started to speak to the audience, he astonished Hannah with his confidence. "Welcome, ladies and gentlemen. I am sure we are all terribly grateful to Miss Millicent Cooke and particularly to Mrs. Fitch, for kindly hosting us today." There was a murmur of agreement in the crowd. "Miss Cooke has asked me to introduce our distinguished speaker, Mrs. Lewis. An introduction is hardly necessary, since Mrs. Lewis's accomplishments are well known to all in this room. This afternoon, she has very kindly agreed to speak to us on the subject of," and here he consulted a scrap of paper in his hand, *"Progress in the Cause of Women's Suffrage.* Without further ado, may I present Mrs. Lewis."

There was a smattering of polite applause. Mrs. Lewis stood up, looking very important, and graciously acknowledged the crowd with a nod. And then Hannah saw her notice Elizabeth, and a frown cross her face. At that moment, Elizabeth appeared as though she would rather be anywhere else.

Having talked of her political work for at least half an hour (which felt to Hannah like several hours), Mrs. Lewis said, "In conclusion, I hope you will permit me to make one last observation. You are aware, no doubt, of the Women's Social and Political Union. You know of Mrs. Emmeline Pankhurst and her daughters, particularly Christabel, and their followers. They take as their motto *Deeds, Not Words,* and they daringly confront Members of Parliament with a demand for the vote."

To Hannah's horror, Elizabeth cried out, "Indeed!" Her interruption was followed by nervous applause.

Mrs. Lewis gave her a sharp look, but did not allow herself to be rattled. "I do understand that, as young people, you are not satisfied with the pace of change."

"Of course we aren't, Mrs. Lewis," Elizabeth called out. "The question is, what are you going to do to advance the cause more quickly? Writing letters is all very well, but it has hardly been effective, has it?"

For a moment, everyone stared at her. But then Mr. Ingle-Gillis called out

CHAPTER TWELVE

"Hear, hear!", and a couple of brave souls clapped, briefly. Hannah was watching Mrs. Lewis, Mrs. Fitch, and Tom Devenish at the front of the room, and they did not applaud. All of them looked deeply uncomfortable.

Mrs. Lewis quickly recovered herself. "You ask a very good question, Miss Hughes," she said, speaking through gritted teeth. Her words were laden with meaning. "Since you ask, I do not think that reckless confrontation is the best means of achieving one's goals, whatever they may be. Confrontation simply encourages our detractors to dig in their heels."

But Elizabeth wasn't about to back down. "It's worth trying though, is it not?" she said. "Because I see no proof that your assumption is correct, Mrs. Lewis. Gentle persuasion in the cause of gradual change never seems to produce any results at all. Perhaps that is its intent."

Mrs. Lewis stared at Elizabeth. Tom stepped forward to prevent further hostilities between them, and said hurriedly, "I am sure you will all join me in thanking Mrs. Lewis for her informative address."

More polite but unenthusiastic applause followed, but Mrs. Lewis looked furious. Elizabeth looked triumphant. Hannah had her head in her hands.

"I say, May," Millie Cooke said with a chuckle to Hannah, "Perhaps Miss Hughes is the madwoman my aunt thinks she is. Excuse me, but I must go and pay my respects to Mrs. Lewis."

Hannah couldn't believe how badly things had gone. Elizabeth had messed things up. She had done the exact opposite of what she had told her to do. Now, just to rub it in, Elizabeth caught Hannah's eye, gave a slight shrug of her shoulders, and raised her eyebrows, as if to say, "What else did you expect from me?"

When she saw Hannah slumped on the sofa, Verity came and sat next to her. "Hannah, I don't know what you said to Elizabeth earlier, but well done."

"Well done? You're just trying to make me feel better," Hannah said despairingly. "It's a disaster."

"Nonsense," said Verity. "I heard what you say to Elizabeth. You accidentally inspired her to be her own person, and to stand up to the ghastly Lewis woman."

"But that's not what's meant to happen …"

"Are you sure? How do you know?" Verity said sharply. "I told you before, Granny and Mrs. Lewis will fall in and out with each other their entire lives. That's what is supposed to happen. But Elizabeth can't become Granny so long as she's under Mrs. Lewis's thumb. And even if you didn't mean for her to stand up to her, she did it because you told her not to."

Hannah did not feel better. "Maybe," she said. "I'm just not sure they're sup-

CHAPTER TWELVE

posed to be *this* mad at each other. And Tom Devenish didn't look pleased at all. He thinks Elizabeth's crazy. And she's not interested in Tom, anyway. She's only interested in Mr. Ingle-Gillis."

Verity exhaled sharply. "I can't say I'm surprised about that. I mean, poor Tom is no competition for fabulously handsome Arthur, is he? Tom's a wet blanket, what with giving Elizabeth such a nasty look just now. Anyway, cheer up, Hannah. We did make some progress."

"You have to be kidding me," said Hannah. "How?"

"Look, I reckon Millie fancies herself as a bit of a rebel," said Verity, "even though she's really not. So long as she thinks Elizabeth is one, too, it won't take much to persuade her to become Elizabeth's friend. Granny needs an ally, doesn't she? After all, she has a couple of World Wars to win. I mean, if she doesn't take charge soon, who's doing to defeat the Kaiser and Hitler?"

Hannah laughed at this, and she felt a weight taken off her shoulders. "Verity, I remembered where I heard of Millie before. She's in your granny's diary, in 1940. They were friends by then, I guess."

"Ah, good, yes, Granny's diary," said Verity. "You know, I'm under strict instructions from Kate that when Granny dies, in the dim and distant future, I am not to read it, but to take it straightaway to the county archives in Hertford. I suppose I can manage to do that. Oh, I say, look, Elizabeth's putting on her hat. It's time for you to go. Now, buck up, Hannah. You've done very well. As have I, by the way. I have ensured that Tom Devenish is no longer interested in me. I'll tell you about it later. Oh, and I have made social inroads with Mrs. Lewis, who has invited me for tea, if you please. Now, if you'll excuse me, I am going to walk home by myself. You go with Elizabeth. You need more time with her, and that's always easier when you're not under the nose of her dreadful mother. Oh, dear, I suppose I shouldn't say that about my great-granny, should I?"

Hannah laughed. She and Verity were unlikely friends, she thought, but there was a reason that Verity was the best friend she had ever had.

On the way from Millie's house, Hannah and Elizabeth reluctantly found themselves walking alongside Mrs. Lewis. It was Mrs. Lewis who finally broke the embarrassed silence. "Elizabeth, why did you come to this meeting today?" she said abruptly.

Elizabeth's steps faltered, and she replied without looking at the older woman. "I came because I was invited," she said.

"No, according to Mrs. Fitch, you were not," said Mrs. Lewis. "She tells me that your name was not on Miss Cooke's list."

CHAPTER TWELVE

Hannah squirmed, but Elizabeth was offended. "Perhaps Mrs. Fitch was not fully aware of the membership of Miss Cooke's list? I would never show up to an event to which I was not invited," she said. "Incidentally, Mrs. Lewis, Mr. Ingle-Gillis tells me you are considering asking Miss Cooke to take my place as secretary of the Women's Suffrage Association. May I ask why?"

"I should think that was obvious, Elizabeth," Mrs. Lewis said. "You have failed in your responsibilities. You ceased your correspondence on the Association's behalf, and you did not so much as send your apologies for the Association committee meeting."

"I needed a rest," Elizabeth said lamely. "I've been rather tired lately."

Mrs. Lewis pounced on her admission that she was at fault. "Did you really think the Association's work would wait for you to finish sulking?"

"I wasn't sulking," Elizabeth said sulkily.

"Nonsense," Mrs. Lewis snapped. "I don't believe you, Elizabeth. Just like your absurd act of vandalism, throwing a brick through your mother's window, your shirking of your responsibilities is intended to gain my attention. So was your insolence to me this evening, and so indeed is everything else you have done and said of late. It has all been to gain my attention … Or perhaps your mother's."

Walking behind Elizabeth, Hannah saw her put her head down, and she cringed on Elizabeth's behalf. Elizabeth wasn't just embarrassed, Hannah thought. She was crushed.

Mrs. Lewis looked keenly at Elizabeth, and said quietly, "Oh, I see that I have hit the nail on the head. I have, haven't I? Believe me, Elizabeth, you have my attention now. If it is more than you bargained for, then you have only yourself to blame. Now, you must hurry if you intend to catch the next train to Ickswade. Good day to you."

With that, she carried on up Balesworth High Street, leaving Elizabeth and Hannah standing in the dirt. "So how did everything go, apart from that?" Hannah said, trying to sound positive.

Elizabeth glared at her. "Why did you tell me not to speak up to her? Almost everyone else said I was quite right to do so."

Hannah thought quickly. "I think you just saw why, Miss Elizabeth," she said. "She's really mad at you. It wasn't hard to see that coming. It doesn't bother me, and I'm not saying you should always try to make Mrs. Lewis happy, but are *you* happy? You don't look like you're happy. Are you?"

Elizabeth said nothing, and Hannah walked ahead of her toward the railway station. She really wished there was a way to know whether she was doing the right thing.

Chapter 13: TRIUMPH AND DISASTER

Wednesday, February 28, 1906

Alex wasn't prepared for a storm, but it came anyway. Huge spots of rain began speckling the dirt road, thunder growled directly over his head, and he saw lightning strike in the fields. Whipping off his hat, he sprinted the last hundred yards to Thomas's workshop, sending up clouds of beige dust. He was careful not to run directly behind the horse tethered outside the building. But he stopped right before he reached the door, to admire the huge new sign in professional lettering on the roof of the rickety wooden workshop: *E. T. CLARK, BLACKSMITH, CARRIAGE, BICYCLE & AUTOMOBILE REPAIR.*

Opening the door and slipping into the dimly-lit forge, Alex felt a blast of warm air. Brandon, wearing a leather apron and with his sleeves rolled up, was vigorously pumping the bellows, so that the charcoals glowed brightly, flames leapt up, and sparks flew from the fire. He waved to Alex, and then, at a nod from Thomas, paused the bellows. Now Thomas took up his hammer and tongs, pulled a white-hot stick of iron from the fire, and started pounding it on the anvil, with sharp ringing blows. As Brandon and Alex watched, the hot metal bar transformed into a horseshoe. Rain was now pounding the roof, and a steady trickle of water began dripping from overhead. Brandon grabbed an empty bucket and placed it underneath the hole in the roof.

"How are you today, sir?" asked an old man's voice. Alex turned to find Jupe squatting on a short log behind him, his feet planted firmly in the dirt, and steadying himself with his walking stick. Alex squatted next to him. "I been hoping to run into you," said Jupe. "Your granddaddy, he was the one who took me to England, and he had a colored friend who helped me get to Massachusetts. They were only young boys, but they were good men, yes, sir. I owe them my life."

Alex said simply, "You helped save my life, too." Then he realized what he had said. "I mean, my grandfather's life," he stammered.

Jupe was looking at him closely. "If you say so, sir," he said slowly.

Thomas was looking out through the workshop door. "George, the rain stopped. Take Mr. Chumley's bicycle to him. He stay down on East Main, just past the hotel. Someone can tell you the house." Then he noticed Alex. "Are you here to see George, Mr. Alex?"

"Kind of," said Alex. He turned to Brandon and she said quietly, "When did you start working here?"

"Today," Brandon said. "I figured I could learn to be a blacksmith. Maybe a car mechanic, too. So I'm kind of doing a paid internship. Well, an apprenticeship, sort of."

Alex sighed. "Brandon, you know it's not real life, right? You aren't going to become a blacksmith. Why take a dangerous job? Eric and I can give you money. The Professor can give you money. You don't need to do this."

"I know," Brandon said, "But I like earning for myself, and I owe Miss Julia big time. This just feels, um, manly."

"Manly?" said Alex, raising an eyebrow. "Okay, but a blacksmith? You should be a teacher, or something. You're smart."

"And Thomas isn't?" Brandon said, scowling. "I think you're confusing intelligence with education and opportunity. Thomas is an entrepreneur. He can make a lot more money than Robert Gordon ever will."

"Brandon, have you listened to yourself lately?" said Alex. "This isn't what you're about, money."

"Isn't it?" Brandon said, pushing past Alex. "How would you know? And what makes you think black people have a big choice of jobs in Snipesville? I mean, your Mr. Hughes practically begged you and Eric to work for him, and I wasn't even allowed to sweep his floor. Now excuse me. I have a job to do."

With that, he lifted the bicycle propped against the wall, and pushed it out of the workshop. When Thomas saw that Alex wasn't leaving with Brandon, he called over to him, "So, how can I help you, sir?"

"I've come to interview you for *The Snipesville News*," said Alex.

Thomas laughed. "Well, sir, if you don't mind the state of my clothes. Wait a moment while I wash off some of this dirt."

As Brandon pushed the bicycle downtown, he felt lousy. He was not embarrassed by taking on manual labor, whatever Alex might think. He was embarrassed because he felt he had let everyone down: Miss Julia, Robert Gordon, his own ancestors, the community of Snipesville, and maybe his own future. His meeting with Booker T. Washington had not helped. Mr. Washington still had not replied to Miss Julia, and it was getting harder and harder to believe that he ever would. Every day, Miss Julia anxiously awaited the mail to see if there was a letter from the Wizard of Tuskegee, and every day, he remained silent.

That evening, as she poured tea, Miss Julia said, yet again, "I mailed Mr. Washington two copies of my letter. I wanted to be absolutely sure he received at least one of them."

Brandon gave her a glum smile, but said nothing.

"Never mind," she said determinedly. "There is still no cause for despair. At least I need not visit Snipesville every day for my mail, as I had to until last year, when the post office began rural delivery. We're lucky. Our local postmaster would have avoided delivering here if he could. He is greatly prejudiced against colored people."

It wasn't like Miss Julia to ramble on, Brandon thought. Clearly, she was very nervous. Who could blame her? If Booker T. Washington didn't help, what then? But the failure wasn't Booker T. Washington's, he thought. *It's mine. I didn't do a good enough job of persuading him. I was too busy being outraged about what happens at Tuskegee Institute, instead of saying what he wanted to hear.*

Brandon was pretty sure that a black high school would be created in Snipesville eventually, but he was also increasingly certain that it would have nothing at all to do with his efforts. Maybe he had been arrogant to think that it would. He began to wonder whether he had misread God's intentions. Maybe, he thought, he wasn't here to help create a high school after all. Maybe he was here to help out his family in its early days, in some way that had yet to be revealed to him. Surely, it had to mean something that Thomas had offered him a job out of the blue. It wasn't a well-paid job, but it made him useful to Thomas, and to the whole town, and it helped bring money into the black community. Maybe his main role in Snipesville's history was meant to be something humble but necessary, to prepare him for the trial he was now pretty sure he would endure in 1906. But now, he needed cheering up. He decided that after he had dropped off the bike, he would go and say hi to Eric.

Eric sang Alex's praises to Brandon. "I must say, his work is improving. He and I talked about how he could make his articles more interesting, and he was listening. He's determined to write enough copy so that the newspaper doesn't have to depend on wire stories."

"Why's he bothering?" Brandon said. "I mean, what difference does it make?"

"You don't know?" Eric said. "Well, you do surprise me. You see, if Alex is writing nice, upbeat stories about the good people of Snipesville, the newspaper won't be filled with hateful articles from the Atlanta newspapers that encourage racial prejudice."

"I don't read the paper," said Brandon. "But Miss Julia does, and she'll be glad to hear what Alex is doing. She says the stories from Atlanta about the election for governor are just awful."

"They are," said Eric. "I, meanwhile, am doing what I can in my position as the *other* Englishman in Snipesville."

"The other apart from me?" Brandon said.

"Um, no, at least not as far as the white ladies are concerned," Eric said apologetically. "I meant apart from Mr. Hughes. Anyway, I see it as my moral duty to urge the young white maidens of Snipesville whom I encounter to reconsider their views on colored people."

"Hold it right there," Brandon gasped. "You're kidding, right?"

"No, I'm not," said Eric. "How do we change the town unless and until we persuade people to think differently? Surely you must understand that?"

It was hard to argue with Eric, Brandon thought. He was so … sincere. Mrs. Devenish might have said "gormless," but then Hannah always said she could be a little harsh. Still, on this occasion, he was inclined to agree with her. Eric was being an idiot.

"You really think it's that simple, Eric?" Brandon said. "How do you think you're going to get your lady friends to give up all the weird ideas about black people they've been told all their lives? Do you know what will happen if they change their minds and tell their friends and families?"

"Life in Snipesville will get better?" Eric said hopefully.

"Nope. Not for them it won't," Brandon said. "Look, let me try to explain. I met a Freedom Rider once …"

Eric looked blank. "A what?"

Brandon didn't want to describe the entire history of the Civil Rights movement of the 1950s and 1960s, so he kept it simple. "This white lady came to speak at our school. She protested back in the 60s for racial equality. Here's what you need to know, Eric. White Southern women weren't supposed to support equal rights. So when she did, even her family stopped talking to her. Permanently."

"Her family disowned her for that?" said Eric, looking shocked. "Then they were evil. They were …"

CHAPTER THIRTEEN

"They were typical, Eric," Brandon said with a sigh. "When you start arguing against segregation, you're asking white people to give up their privileges, their lifelong beliefs. That's huge."

But Eric refused to back down. "Change is never easy, but it must be done. It can be done. I mean, look at Germany since the War. The Germans have returned to democracy, and we are reversing Nazi brainwashing."

"Eric, I think it's great you're willing to try to change things. But whatever you do, just be careful, okay? What you're doing could be dangerous, especially because you're not from here. In the 1960s, they called people like you *outside agitators*, and …"

Just then, the door opened, and an elderly white woman walked in, ignored Brandon completely, and started complaining to Eric that she had not been receiving her newspaper. Brandon made to leave, but Eric, ignoring the old lady, called after him. "Brandon! I mean, George! Someone left a note for you at the boardinghouse. Hang on, I meant to deliver it to you on the way to work this morning, and I completely forgot." He rummaged around the inside pocket of his jacket, and then handed Brandon a wrinkled envelope. The old woman looked at both of them with a mixture of indignation at being forced to wait while Eric dealt with a black kid, and evident curiosity.

Brandon, well aware that Eric had spoken to him far too much like they were equals, hastily took the envelope and left the building. As he walked along the boardwalk, he tore open the envelope. It contained a short note from the Professor, instructing him to meet her at the site of the future Snipesville State College.

It was almost six, and already it was growing dark. Brandon had done as the Professor's note had instructed, and returned to the clearing in the woods. At first, nothing happened, but as he watched, the forest parted like a pair of curtains, the skies brightened, the temperature rose dramatically, and the college materialized. Once again, he had traveled in time, and once again, by the looks of it, he was in the summer of 1910.

The building seemed deserted. Reaching the second floor, Brandon knocked at the Professor's office door, and when there was no answer, he tried the door handle. It was locked. He didn't have pen or paper with which to leave her a message. But maybe he could something to write with in one of the classrooms? Looking about him cautiously, he quietly approached an open door … And almost jumped out of his skin when he saw the younger Professor standing at the teacher's desk.

CHAPTER THIRTEEN

"Hello, Brandon." She picked up a heavy book and held it up. "Have you ever read Matthew Arnold?"

"No, I haven't," Brandon said without enthusiasm. "I guess you're going to tell me to read him, whoever he is."

"Possibly. He's a 19th century poet. Not my absolute favorite, but my options for teaching poetry in 1910 are a bit limited, and unfortunately, I have to pretend I'm an English teacher this year. Never mind. I can fake it. I would love to have my students read the First World War poets, like Wilfred Owen or Siegfried Sassoon, but I fear they would be disturbed by reading poetry that hasn't been written yet about a war that hasn't yet happened. So we'll do Matthew Arnold and Robert Browning, I think. Nice and harmless, if longwinded."

Brandon wondered if what she was saying had anything at all to do with him. He also knew he had to ask his questions quickly, because he never had much time with her. "Okay, so I worked in a turpentine camp, and now …"

"I know about that," she said. "And about Thomas giving you a job. So what's bothering you?"

"I failed," he said.

"Oh, dear, what a shame," she said distractedly, and began riffing through her poetry book. "What makes you say that?"

"I'm supposed to help make the black high school happen, but it looks like, if it happens, it will happen without Booker T. Washington's help, or mine. I guess."

"Hmm," she said, continuing to leaf through the pages. "If that's what you think you're here to do."

Brandon's head jerked back. "You mean it's not? I got the wrong idea? That's what I was wondering. So what am I here to do?"

"I didn't say it was or it wasn't," she said. "Would you like a book?"

He didn't reply, but she took a volume from the stack on her desk, opened it up to a poem, and handed it to him, tapping on a stanza on the right hand page. As he read, she recited it from memory.

Foil'd by our fellow-men, depress'd, outworn,
We leave the brutal world to take its way,
And, Patience! in another life, we say
The world shall be thrust down, and we up-borne.

"Is that your answer?" Brandon said.

"Well, if Matthew Arnold doesn't appeal to you, I suppose I could quote Kipling," she said. "You'll find him in the book, too.

CHAPTER THIRTEEN

If you can meet with Triumph and Disaster
And treat those two impostors just the same.

Honestly, I can quote Victorian and Edwardian poetry at you all day, Brandon, but my advice is the same. Be yourself. Do what you think best."

"Great," he said sullenly.

"Take the book with you," she said, "but best I give you a bag to carry it. I don't want you seen carrying a book through Snipesville. Sad, isn't it? Pathetic, really, that they feel so threatened by a black kid with a book." Suddenly, her tone hardened. "But don't underestimate them. They're not stupid, and they are dangerous."

"I know," Brandon said. "When does it happen?"

"What?" she said. "When does what happen?"

"We Don't Talk About That," he said.

"Oh, if you don't know, I can't tell you. Sorry. Let me get you that bag." She swept past him into the hallway.

Thursday, March 1, 1906

"Is there any news for Aunt Julia?" Thomas asked Brandon this same question every morning, and Brandon, as he did every morning, shook his head and said "Not yet." There had been no letter from Tuskegee.

"Ah, well," Thomas said. "I guess that's the end of it, then." He jerked his head toward the torn and oil-smeared auto repair manual sitting on the workbench. "Things are slow this morning, George, so you sit a while and study your auto repair. It's about brakes, and if you understand it, maybe you explain it to me. There's a lot of long words in there. I was about ready to take it to Miss Julia to help me."

"Sure, but what happened to the book cover?" Brandon said, holding up the battered manual.

"It dropped off yesterday while I was reading," Thomas said. Brandon wasn't surprised. He had seen how Thomas treated the manual: Balancing it on the edge of a car engine, eating his lunch over it, and generally manhandling it. "No matter," Thomas said. "It doesn't need a cover to be useful. And we might need it soon. Rumor's going round that Mr. Edgar Thompson is planning to purchase an automobile, because I guess the department store is doing good business, and maybe Mr. Duval from the hotel, too, because he's gotta keep up with Mr. Thompson, and his business is booming, too. We should be ready for more new customers, because there ain't an automobile invented that don't need regular repairs. I might be able to pay you more, if you keep working hard."

Brandon smiled wanly. Sure, he was relieved to have escaped the turpentine camp, and working for Thomas was probably the best job he could hope for. But he wasn't happy. If he was to be honest with himself, he was stung by Alex's suggestion that he was somehow settling for something less than he should. Then again, he reflected bitterly, it was easy for Alex to say something like that. There was no shortage of work around town for young white guys, especially those with a little education. For Brandon, meanwhile, even to mention his education in front of white people was downright dangerous. But one thing he had learned from this job was that he hated dealing with dirt and grease. He would never admit it to Thomas, because, somehow, to dislike grime seemed "unmanly," to use that phrase he kept hearing in 1906. But he would just have to put up with it for now. *No*, he thought, *I'm better off working for Thomas, and waiting for this all to be over, one way or another. I'm being myself, aren't I? The Professor can't complain.* Somehow, this thought didn't help.

"Should I get in some charcoal?" he asked reluctantly.

"Oh, I already fetched it in," Thomas said, tutting. "I always forget to leave the charcoal to you. I ain't used to having help. Anyhow, that's all right. Best you study, let me finish the chores. If we figure out what it says about brakes, you can go home early, maybe read something you enjoy." Brandon grunted his thanks, but he really wasn't thinking about what Thomas was doing for him. He was starting to think that Booker T. Washington had been right all along, that what black folks in Georgia in 1906 needed was a practical training in real skills, not a fancy education. What use was an education in Snipesville when there were seldom any jobs for educated black people, and they were supposed to hide their learning?

But now he remembered what Robert had said, about people needing to learn to think for themselves, and to become informed. Maybe if Willie had been able to read and write, he wouldn't have ended up trapped in the turpentine camp. And how could Brandon have kept up his own spirits in modern Snipesville if he had not been able to escape into books? So perhaps W. E. B. Du Bois was right after all. It was so confusing.

Brandon returned his attention to his auto repair manual. And as he read an especially complicated paragraph on brakes, he realized that someone like Willie or even Thomas would never have a chance at a good job in the twentieth century without at least a high school education. He could not give up on the school, he realized. Perhaps it was time to consider boarding another train bound for Tuskegee, Alabama.

When Alex arrived at the end of the afternoon, Brandon had gone home, and Thomas was alone in the workshop. He greeted his visitor warmly. "Mr. Day,

CHAPTER THIRTEEN

how can I help you, sir?" he said. "You got more questions?"

"Actually, yes, I do," Alex said, pulling his notebook from his pocket. "I was wondering … Is Snipesville really a good place for black people? I mean, compared to other places in Georgia?"

Alex didn't see the wave of consternation ripple across Thomas's face. This was clearly not a question he had anticipated. Thomas slowly wiped his hands on a rag. Then he said, "Yes, sir, I believe it is. Now, I can't be sure, because I ain't never lived noplace else. Maybe you should talk to my cousin Robert. He would know better, because he lived in Atlanta for a spell. But I like it here, I surely do. It's my home, and my business is doing fine."

In his notebook, Alex carefully wrote down what Thomas had said. Then he said, "I guess it must be, because you've been able to hire, um, George as a helper, right?"

Again, Thomas looked a little uncertain of how best to answer. But then he said, "Yes, sir, George started working for me, at least for now. Until he finds a better position. Or he moves on."

This was news to Alex. Brandon's job was temporary? He wondered if Brandon knew that. Thomas was looking at him thoughtfully. He said, "Of course, if we open a high school, George can teach there. He's an educated young man, you know that, sir. In fact, we're holding a fundraising picnic for the high school at First African Baptist Church this coming Saturday, around noontime. Trouble is," he said, watching Alex carefully, "we don't have too much money among the colored folk, so I doubt we will raise much in the way of funds."

Alex now had an idea. He was completely unaware that Thomas had planted it there. "Maybe Eric Powell and I can help," he said eagerly.

"Well, that would be very kind, sir," Thomas said, beaming at him.

"Okay, I'll see what I can do. And thanks for the interview. I'll let you know when it appears in the newspaper."

As Alex walked back to the newspaper office, he looked at the "to do" lists on the first page of his notebook and, with pleasure, observed that he had checked off every one of his latest interviewees: Mr. Wong, Mr. Wheeler, Mr. Duval, Mr. Gordon, and Thomas Clark. This, he decided, was going to be great. He would hold up a mirror to Snipesville, and its people would see what it really was and could be: A modern, cosmopolitan little town, with a bright future. In doing so, Alex thought, he would nudge Snipesville toward being a much better place.

CHAPTER THIRTEEN

Saturday, March 10, 1906

The people were dressed in their best clothes, mingling outside First African Baptist Church in the crisp air of a perfect March day. Most of the men had turned up in suits, while others arrived in mismatched and threadbare outfits that were nonetheless neatly pressed. All the men had their shirts buttoned-up to the neck, some with ties or bowties, and most wore the shapeless wide-brimmed hats popular among Snipesville men. Women were dressed in white blouses with puffy sleeves. Some wore simple straw boaters, while others sported large grand hats. Small children, clad like miniature versions of their parents, ran about excitedly.

As he approached this gathering, Brandon smiled. This was his church home, and more than he knew they would ever suspect, these were his people. Spotting Rev. Evans, he offered to help, and was immediately put to work assisting the men of the congregation as they brought the long bench pews outside to serve as tables and chairs for the picnic. As Brandon passed by, toting a pew with the help of another male congregant, Mrs. Evans, the minister's wife, laid out a large platter of carved ham on the large table reserved for the food, and said to Miss Julia, "The good Lord has favored us with this weather, Miss Russell."

Miss Julia, wearing a white pinafore apron, set down a huge basket of fluffy Southern biscuits, loosely wrapped in a cloth, then pushed her spectacles back up her nose. "He has indeed, Mrs. Evans. Now, let me just make sure of something. You say your husband is willing to serve as cashier, is he not?"

"Yes, ma'am," said Mrs. Evans, "and here he is."

Reverend Evans arrived, bearing a glass bowl. "Miss Russell, how much shall we charge for a plate?" he said.

Mrs. Evans tutted. "You should know better," she chided her husband. "Ask them to give what they can, and they will."

He nodded sagely at his wife, and smiled as the first diner ventured forward. Others quickly gathered behind him.

Robert, fastidious as ever, glanced over at Thomas, who had tucked his napkin in at his shirt collar, and was eagerly shoveling ham biscuits into his mouth as fast as he could. Brandon could see that Miss Julia had also seen Thomas stuffing his face, and she looked ready to come over and tell him not to be so greedy. But Caroline Clark beat her to it, as she sat down on the bench next to her husband. "Thomas, you will choke yourself," she complained. "And don't be in such a rush to eat. It's impolite. The ladies have worked hard to prepare the food."

CHAPTER THIRTEEN

"And I sure appreciate their efforts," Thomas said through a mouthful of biscuit, winking at Brandon, who was suddenly reminded of his food-loving father. Robert, meanwhile, looked slightly disgusted by his cousin's appetite.

Caroline said to Brandon, "It looks like everyone in Snipesville is here, don't you think, George?" He agreed, knowing that she meant everyone black was present. Even in modern Snipesville, it felt like black and white people lived in parallel universes that hardly crossed. Now, in 1906, even as Snipesville grew, segregation was growing with it.

Watching a smiling Rev. Evans drop more coins in his glass bowl, Caroline said, "I wonder how much we're raising for the high school?"

Robert, picking up a ham biscuit and inspecting it, said morosely, "We may collect enough to add a few bricks to the foundation."

Brandon, meanwhile, had a biscuit halfway to his mouth when he recognized a white face in the crowd.

"Afternoon, Brandon, I mean, George!" Eric cheerfully offered him a handshake. "Alex mentioned that your church was holding this picnic in aid of school funds, and I thought I would bring some people along. You'll know Mr. Wong from the laundry, of course? And Mr. Duval from the hotel?"

Bemused, Brandon nodded to the businessmen, who both looked ill at ease. "Can I get you gentlemen something to eat?" he said.

"Thank you," said Mr. Duval. He was looking around him helplessly, as though he expected the food to magically leap out at him.

Brandon led the men to the end of the serving line, but, to his embarrassment, Mrs. Evans waved the visitors to the front. Eric stood by politely while Mr. Duval and Mr. Wong waited for the ladies to serve them. Miss Julia beamed at them all. The crowd had grown very quiet when people realized that Mr. Duval, Mr. Wong, and Eric were present, but now the confident chatter had resumed. Eric quickly took charge, and, followed by Brandon, escorted the two men to where Robert, Caroline, and Thomas were seated. Before Brandon could stop him, Eric seated everyone together on the same bench.

But after wolfing down his food, Mr. Duval said to Eric, "I am sorry, I have just remembered that I must meet with my staff at the hotel. I must go."

Eric was dismayed. "Are you sure you can't stay, sir?"

"Quite sure," said Mr. Duval.

"Nor I," Mr. Wong said quickly, as he evidently sensed an opportunity to escape. "Before I go, Mr. Powell, I'll give some money for the school."

"As will I," Mr. Duval added quickly. "With whom should we speak?"

Brandon took charge. "This way," he said, and took them to meet Rev. Evans.

CHAPTER THIRTEEN

No sooner had Mr. Duval and Mr. Wong left the picnic, than Reverend Evans introduced himself to Eric. Eric jumped to his feet at the clergyman's approach, to the astonishment of everyone but Brandon. He extended a hand, which the surprised Rev. Evans reluctantly shook. "Eric Powell, *Snipesville News*," he said. "Delighted to meet you, Vicar."

"He's not a vicar," Brandon muttered, but Eric didn't hear him.

"I hope you don't mind us coming along today, Vicar," Eric said. "I told Mr. Wong and Mr. Duval that Mr. Hughes is already a supporter of Snipesville's colored high school, and so they were eager to contribute."

Mr. Wong and Mr. Duval hadn't looked eager, Brandon thought.

Eric continued, "I'm afraid Mr. Duval and Mr. Wong had to leave early. Perhaps," he joked, "Mr. Wong had *pressing* business?"

"Yes, indeed," Rev. Evans said uncertainly, "But he gave me twenty dollars, and Mr. Duval very kindly left this." He held up the check to Eric, then turned to allow Brandon to see it. Drawn on the Bank of Snipesville, it was written for $50, and signed in Mr. Duval's large signature. "Mr. Powell," said Rev. Evans, "I cannot thank you enough, sir, for drawing this cause to the attention of our leading citizens."

"Delighted to help," Eric said breezily. "I've been talking to a great many people. Mr. Hughes has said the high school is a worthy cause, so we, that is, Alexander Day and I, thought we should use his name to drum up more donations."

Brandon tapped Eric on the arm, and jerked his head in the direction of the door. "Can I talk to you outside?"

"Of course," Eric said, following him. "Is everything all right?"

"Brandon, I don't understand why you're so worried," Eric said plaintively. "Mr. Hughes is very much in favor of a colored high school. He thinks it will add to Snipesville's fortunes, by training workers for the businesses springing up in town."

Brandon was not impressed. "Does Hughes know you've been using his name to get people to contribute to the black high school?"

"Not exactly," Eric said.

"Not exactly?" Brandon said sternly.

"Well, no. Actually, not at all. He's away on business, you see. But since he supports …"

"Eric, no offense, man," Brandon said, "But you know nothing. Was this your idea or Alex's?"

CHAPTER THIRTEEN

"It's hard to say, really," Eric said. "I think Alex came up with the idea of fundraising among local businessmen. He thought it would kill two birds with one stone: Mr. Hughes would love the idea of fundraising for a project that benefits Snipesville, and you would appreciate help for your school, or we thought you would. Inviting along local businessmen to this picnic was my brainchild. But I'm rather disappointed with the response, honestly. Mr. Thompson from the department store, and Dr. Marshburn, the dentist, were very rude when I invited them, which I thought was a bit much …"

"Are you TOTALLY stupid?" Brandon said loudly. "I mean, seriously?"

Eric shrank back from him. When he spoke, his childhood Cockney speech suddenly reasserted itself, and he began dropping his "h"s in alarm. "Blimey, Brandon, that's … That's cheek, that is. I have 'alf a mind to punch …"

"I don't care what you think," Brandon hissed. "You have no idea where you are, do you? Don't you get it?"

"I don't see the 'arm," said Eric,. "What 'arm does it do for them to come 'ere and eat? The women who cook the food down the café are colored, so 'ow's this any different?"

Brandon closed his eyes in annoyance, and then opened them to give the hapless Eric a laser stare. "It's different. I bet you didn't warn them this was a social event where they would be eating with black people. They probably thought they would hand over their donations, everyone would applaud, and they would go. Look, Mr. Wong will probably get away with being here, because Southern whites don't know what to make of Asians. But Duval made a big mistake coming here, and he knew it. And what were you thinking, even asking the Southern white guys? Why would they want to support black people getting any kind of education?"

Eric looked lost. "But … you said … that Booker Washington bloke you keep going on about, you said he's got white supporters."

Brandon said firmly, "Yes, he does. They're white people from the North. Not white people from the Deep South. Don't you get the difference at all? Hey, ever wonder why the whites in Snipesville suddenly built a Confederate soldier memorial now, forty years after the Civil War? Don't you think that it just *might* be to send black people a message? That these white people fought a war to keep these black people enslaved, and that's how strongly they feel about it?"

"Oh," said Eric, looking troubled.

"*Oh* is right," said Brandon. "Even asking for donations is kind of naive when you do it randomly. I mean, I appreciate you're trying to move some of the money in Snipesville into the black community, but you have to be very,

CHAPTER THIRTEEN

very careful. You don't understand this place."

Eric took offense at this, and his posh accent suddenly returned. "Excuse me, Brandon, but perhaps it's you who doesn't understand. Mr. Hughes is planning to build houses in Snipesville to sell to colored people, and I have not heard of any whites objecting to his plan."

Brandon mentally facepalmed himself. "Yes, they know he plans to sell houses to black people who can afford them. I bet a lot of whites aren't happy about that, no matter what you heard. However, they also know he's planning to build a lot more houses that will be rented to poor black people, and that he and they will make a wad of dough out of that plan."

Eric was confused now. "But why won't white people mind colored people living in Snipesville in rented houses?"

Brandon said, "Because the people who live in those houses will be poor, and will work for cheap. Their rent money will go into the pockets of Mr. Hughes and other white investors, and then to the Bank of Snipesville. The Bank will loan that money to well-off white people for their farms, houses, and businesses. Meanwhile, when poor black people see that a few middle-class black people can own houses, that will encourage them to think maybe they can own a house one day, too. They'll stay here, and keep working for peanuts, and never be able to rise unless we find a way to give them an education. That's why."

"That's rather cynical," Eric said stuffily.

"It's also true," Brandon said. "Don't get confused, Eric. The whites who run this town don't actually want black folks to leave. Who would pick the cotton and make the turpentine? Who would clean their houses and cook their food? But they want us to stay here on their terms. Not ours. What they really want is to bring back slavery. Remember, it's only been gone forty years. A lot of people still remember it, or they heard their parents talk about it. And anyway, it isn't really gone."

Eric looked quizzically at Brandon.

"I didn't tell you about me working in turpentine, did I?" Brandon said. "It's slavery, whether you call it that or not. This whole evil place is designed to keep people who look like me from having a good life."

Eric looked long and hard at Brandon. Finally, he exhaled sharply, looked at his feet, and then, looking up, said, "I'm sorry. The only colored person I've ever known well in my life is George Braithwaite, the real George Braithwaite, and that's in England. Things are different there. You're right. I don't understand this place at all, or these people. We, that is, you, me, and Alex, we need to meet with your Professor, and see what she suggests."

"You're still optimistic that this woman you've never even met will help us, huh?" Brandon said. "Good luck with that. She never tells us anything, except in riddles."

"I'm rather good at riddles," Eric said.

"Great," Brandon said. "Because this whole town is one big riddle. Forget the Professor. Let's go make ourselves useful, and see if the ladies need any help washing the dishes."

Miss Julia happily accepted Brandon's offer to wash dishes, but Rev. Evans overheard the conversation, and intervened. "Come now, George," he said, "that is women's work! It is hardly a manly pursuit."

Brandon gave him a tight smile. "Reverend, with all due respect, real men wash dishes. Miss Julia? Show me and Eric what you need doing."

Miss Julia beamed at Brandon, and pointed him toward the water pump in the schoolyard. She politely ignored Eric.

"How are you proceeding, gentlemen?" Robert said, slight mockery in his voice, as Brandon scrubbed with a stick at the plates in a tub of cold water, and Eric, oblivious to people's stares, dried the dishes with a cloth.

"Fine. Why don't you help?" Brandon said curtly.

"Oh, I have already done my share of work here, thank you," Robert said cheerfully. "I don't need to assist the ladies with their feminine tasks. I thought you might like to know how much we raised."

"Yup," Brandon grunted, handing another plate to Eric.

"From the colored folk, around twenty-seven dollars," Robert said.

"And?" said Brandon

"And from the Oriental gentleman, twenty dollars."

"Pretty good," Brandon said, "considering his laundry doesn't look like the most profitable business."

Holding a plate to his chest, Eric looked at Robert. "Don't keep us in suspense, Mr. Gordon. How much did you make altogether?"

Robert's face fell. "Ninety-seven dollars and 32 cents," he said. "It would be enough to keep the school open for a short while, but it hardly helps to complete the building. I have already suggested to Miss Russell that we end the matter here, and that she apply the funds to her elementary school instead. There's no sense in continuing to hope against hope."

Brandon frowned. "It's too soon to give up."

"Hmm," Robert said, "That's what Aunt Julia said, too. We shall see if your optimism is well-founded."

CHAPTER THIRTEEN

Monday, March 12, 1906

As Brandon returned from Thomas's workshop, Miss Julia stopped him in the hall.

"Come to the parlor once you have bathed," she said gently. "We must talk."

Brandon's tie was crooked, and his skin was still damp, when he came into the parlor and found Miss Julia waiting with a fresh pot of coffee, and his favorite cookies, the big sugary rounds that Miss Alberta termed tea cakes but Miss Julia, being a Yankee, insisted were really called snickerdoodles.

While Brandon settled himself on the upright sofa, Miss Julia pushed her glasses up her nose, then unfolded a sheet of paper. *"Dear Miss Russell,"* she read aloud, *"I am pleased to inform you that Tuskeegee Institute has awarded you a grant of $2,000 toward the establishment of an industrial high school in Snipesville, Georgia. Mr. Washington also congratulates you on the appointment of Professor R. H. Gordon as principal of the Snipesville Colored Industrial High School. Truly yours, Booker T. Washington."*

Brandon practically jumped for joy off the sofa, grinning from ear to ear. He knew $2,000 was a great deal of money in 1906. But … "Is it enough to start the school?" he said.

Miss Julia took off her glasses. "I believe it is, especially since the community is providing the labor and some of the materials for the building. And once it's known that Mr. Washington has pledged this sum, both white and colored people are more likely to subscribe, or to increase their subscriptions for the school. George, please understand, this is a triumph. And I have you to thank for it."

Brandon tried to look modest, but he was thrilled. This *had* been his mission, after all. His instincts had not been wrong, whatever the Professor had said. Miss Julia, meanwhile, folded the letter carefully. "Now," she said, "I have more good news. You're a talented and capable young man, George, and you show great promise as a teacher. No, please don't interrupt me. I have already corresponded with Professor John Hope at Atlanta Baptist College. Professor Hope is a friend of mine, and he is also rumored to be the next president of the college. He has promised me that the college will offer you a scholarship, and he would like you to commence your studies this fall. Meanwhile, you will assist Robert and me as we devise a curriculum for our school, one that will satisfy Mr. Washington, and also our own consciences, about the sort of education our young people deserve. I know that we three, you, Robert, and I, are all of one mind on this subject, and I hope that you'll decide to return to teach at the new school upon your graduation. George, do you accept this proposal?"

CHAPTER THIRTEEN

Brandon was astonished. This was a kind and generous offer. It was an amazing offer. He would be a student at the college that was destined to become Morehouse. He would be able to use his brain in the months before he went to Atlanta … . But, he realized with a sinking feeling, this was not his future. It was "George Braithwaite's." He cleared his throat. "Miss Julia, that's awesome. Thank you." He had to think quickly of an excuse to turn her down. "But I don't want to leave my job with Thomas. I just started working with him."

She frowned. "Don't be absurd, George. Your future, your duty, is to study. You are one of Dr. Du Bois's Talented Tenth, and you have a duty to share your talents, and help uplift the race. Now, if you'll excuse me, I must take Mr. Washington's letter to *The Snipesville News* office. Your friend Mr. Day has taken a very keen interest in the establishment of the high school, and I would like him to see it."

With that, she bustled from the room. Brandon calmly poured himself another cup of coffee, and helped himself to the largest tea cake on the plate. So he had succeeded. What he had done would help the people of Snipesville, after all.

Yet, happy though Brandon felt, and much as he tried to think positively, part of him also resented that he had had to worry about the high school. Did Alex ever feel responsible for people in his own community? Did Hannah? Brandon snorted at the thought.

And that led to another uncomfortable thought. Even as they planned for the new high school, *We Don't Talk About That* was coming, and Brandon already sensed that he could not stop it. But how did it even start? Suddenly, with a chill, he wondered what, exactly, Alex was writing for the newspaper. Spotting a copy of that day's *Snipesville News* lying unread on the table next to Miss Julia's chair, he grabbed it. Within half a minute, he was sitting up in his seat, his mouth hanging open, and hearing himself say out loud, "Has he totally lost his mind?"

The boardinghouse mattress was old, lumpy, and sagged in the middle, which was why Alex now woke up in middle of the night, his back aching. Lighting the kerosene lamp by his bed, he had no idea what time it was, and he had neither watch nor clock in his room. He had already finished his latest library book, and having nothing else to keep him occupied, tried counting the thin lines in the white beadboard ceiling. It didn't help.

There wasn't much else to look at: What Mrs. Hudgins called the "fancy" flowery wallpaper in the bedroom made Alex dizzy if he looked at it too long, as did the colorful geometric quilt. He examined the wooden washstand with

CHAPTER THIRTEEN

its mirror, washbasin, and jug, but this substitute for a bathroom was no longer an entertaining novelty. The tall, narrow pine wardrobe, stained dark to make it look like a more expensive wood, put him in mind of an oddly-shaped coffin. Every window was draped with net curtains that were never raised, even during the day. He remembered Mrs. Devenish saying that net curtains were tacky—the word she used was "common"—and he had asked her why people used them at all. She had given him a long and disparaging answer, the gist of which was that net curtains were supposed to provide people more privacy. What was the point of that, he wondered, when the boardinghouse was surrounded by cotton fields?

Perhaps, he thought, he should just try to go back to sleep. He switched off the light, and looked again at the windows. Now, through one of the net curtains, he saw a glow in the distance. Jumping up, he pulling aside the curtain, and there, less than a quarter of a mile away, was the unmistakable outline of a house fire. Sparks and orange flames leaped into the night sky, illuminating the billowing smoke.

Alex grabbed his clothes, and began pulling them on, calling for Eric as he did so.

By the time Alex and Eric reached the farmhouse, the building was burning furiously, crackling so loudly that it was hard to talk over the noise. The lantern that Alex had brought with him hung uselessly at his side, as the blazing house lit up the scene. He had seen this before. He remembered what had happened in 1752.

"I hope to God nobody was at home," Eric shouted. "Do you know who lives here?"

Alex shook his head. "No. Mrs. Hudgins is local, so she'll know. What do you think we should do? There's no phone at the boardinghouse. Should we walk into town and tell someone?"

"No need," Eric yelled, as the sound of hooves and buggy wheels approached. He called out to the driver, "Hello there!"

Wordlessly, the stony-faced white man in the driver's seat pulled the vehicle to a halt, and tied his horse to a nearby tree. He stood for a moment, watching the blaze, and then turned to Eric and Alex. "Who are you?" he said tersely.

"I'm Alex Day, and this is Eric Powell. We work at *The Snipesville News*. I met you a couple of weeks ago, sir."

"I remember you, Day," the man said, speaking through a wad of chewing tobacco stuffed into his cheek. He did not look impressed. "What happened here? Did Mr. McCabe get out of there?"

CHAPTER THIRTEEN

"I have no idea. I'm sorry," Eric said, "But you are … ?"

"Sheriff Bragg," the man said, sounding offended not to be recognized. Alex was immediately on his guard. He had heard that tone many times before in modern Snipesville. Some locals were quick to judge newcomers who didn't instantly know everything about the community, and especially if they didn't know who was in charge.

Now more buggies began to arrive, all of them bearing white men, except for one: After Thomas drove up, he waved to Eric and Alex, and then, with his hat in his hands, walked up to the Sheriff.

"Sir, I just came to see what was going on," he said. Alex could tell Thomas was anxious, but why? And then he looked around, at all the white faces, and saw that some were staring at Thomas, who was the only black person present, and some were staring at Eric, and some were staring directly at him.

"Who are you fellas?" A farmer in dungarees said sharply to Alex. "You a foreigner?"

Alex didn't know what to say. Eric, realizing this, smiled politely at the farmer, then nudged Alex. "Get out your notebook," he said quietly. "We have to report on this for the paper."

"I don't have it with me," Alex muttered, and just then, there was a mighty crash. The house had begun to collapse. The Sheriff spat a long stream of brown tobacco juice onto the dusty road.

"Hey, Sheriff, over here!" a farmer called out. The Sheriff went to see what he was pointing to, and Alex and Eric followed, along with most of the growing crowd. The farmer said, "Sheriff, did you see these here footprints, coming from the house?"

The Sheriff looked closely at where he was pointing, and then turned to address the assembled men. "I want y'all to go to every one of your neighbors, and get me some bloodhounds."

"I got hounds," said one farmer, "but they ain't no bloodhounds. They hunting hounds."

"They'll do," said the Sheriff, although he didn't sound convinced. Now, he turned to Thomas, "Go home, boy, and tell the colored to stay in their houses. You got that?"

Thomas, his face taut and impassive, gave the sheriff a curt nod.

"Come on," Alex said to Eric. "Let's go home. There's nothing we can do."

"You don't have to tell me twice," Eric muttered. "I don't like the way this lot are looking at us."

But as they left, the Sheriff called after them. "You two *gentlemen* headed back to Snipesville?"

CHAPTER THIRTEEN

"No, sir," said Eric. "We're going back to our boardinghouse, Kintyre. It's over there." He pointed up the road.

"I know where Kintyre is," the Sheriff said gruffly. "So that's where you live, huh? I might have questions for you later."

As they walked away, Alex said to Eric, "Okay, now that's not good, is it?"

"No, it's not," said Eric. "Terrifying, in fact. I wish your Professor were here."

Usually, Alex got irritated whenever Eric went on about consulting the Professor. But not this time. "Me, too," he said.

Chapter 14:
THE TRUTH, BALESWORTH, 1905

Wednesday, October 25, 1905

This was Hannah's usual Wednesday afternoon off, but her train to Balesworth was unusually late. When she finally walked into Weston Cottage, she was greeted with smoke in the hallway, and her pulse raced. "Verity!" she screamed, and ran to the kitchen.

Verity was standing by the sink, from which clouds of steam and smoke were issuing. "I am so sorry, Hannah," she said despairingly. "I tried to boil a gammon joint, but I let all the water evaporate. It's ruined."

"Here, let me see," Hannah said. She stepped forward, and inspected the sorry charred remains of the ham. "Huh, I think we can kiss goodbye to the pot too. You must have left it for hours."

"Yes, I did," said Verity. "I put it on this morning. I thought you would be here for lunch, and I didn't think the water would disappear. I mean, I had a lid on it."

Hannah did not comment further. She led Verity away from the ruins of the meal, and said, "So I guess Kate's not back?"

"Obviously not," said Verity. "Mrs. Letchmore comes in most days to char." Seeing Hannah's puzzled expression, she translated, "She cleans the house, I mean. *Char* is not a reference to her cookery, since she's a far better cook than me. Unfortunately, she sent word this morning that she wasn't feeling well, and wouldn't be in today to cook or clean. Hannah, I would suggest we pop out for fish and chips this evening, but it might be quite a few years before Balesworth gets a chip shop. What on earth will we do?"

CHAPTER FOURTEEN

"Verity, we can manage fine. We have flour and lard to make pastry, right? So why don't you run down to the greengrocer's, and get us some potatoes, a couple of onions, and, I don't know, carrots or peas, whatever they have at this time of year. I know quiche is not exactly an autumn food, but it's tasty and easy."

"Quiche?" said Verity, her eyes narrowed in suspicion. "That sounds very French. What's in it? Nothing nasty and foreign, I hope. No frogs' legs or garlic?"

Hannah sighed at 1951 Verity's fear of all things foreign. She described the single-crust pie made with eggs and cheese, and Verity's expression brightened. "Oh, you mean cheese and egg flan! That's one of Granny's best dishes. During the War, we had enough eggs from her hens to make it, but because of rationing, she never had quite enough cheese to make it properly. Don't you remember? She made cheese and egg flan for you in 1940. But you weren't terribly enthusiastic, as I remember."

"Yeah, well, I was pickier back then," said Hannah, marveling to herself that "back then" was just a few months earlier.

Verity said, "How lovely if you would make flan with lots of cheese!"

"If you want cheese," Hannah said, "you better get some. I'll make the pastry and start on the filling, then you can help me peel and chop the veggies when you get back."

"Veggies? Oh, you mean vegetables! Super," said Verity. "I was afraid you would make something like, I don't know, steamed fish in white sauce. I hate steamed fish in white sauce."

"You've got to be kidding," said Hannah. "That sounds disgusting. Remember, I'm not English. I like food to taste of something. Now hurry."

Hannah offered Verity another slice of quiche, but she shook her head. "I feel like an absolute pig for having had two portions already," she said. "Hannah, that was absolutely scrumptious." And then she said suddenly, "She will come back, won't she, Hannah?"

"You mean Kate? I don't know," said Hannah. "But don't panic. We always made it home before, with or without her." Hannah was not as confident as she sounded, but she didn't want to worry her friend. Still, Verity looked troubled.

"I do *want* to go home," she said. "Not right now, but soon. I miss Mummy. I even miss Granny, and she's not exactly a barrel of laughs these days. And I miss Eric, which is a relief."

"A relief, why?" said Hannah, serving herself one last spoonful of mashed potato.

CHAPTER FOURTEEN

"I have been thinking of breaking off our engagement."

Hannah, alarmed, stopped tapping the spoon on her plate, and said, "Why's that?"

"I don't know. I suppose part of it is our talking about Elizabeth getting married, and why that might not be a good idea even if it's necessary. Part of it is what you said, about Eric and I being so young. But there's something else. My mingling with the fascinating young people here gave me second thoughts. You see, I have had doubts about our engagement before. Eric and I never talked of marriage before university, of course—we were far too young. But when I went to Cambridge, I met so many interesting and educated people, and when Eric visited, he just seemed so, I don't know, unsophisticated next to them. I know it's awful, but I grew quite ashamed of him when he came to visit me. Recently, when I started thinking aloud that perhaps the engagement was a mistake, Mummy agreed with me. She likes Eric, but she thinks I should make a more suitable match for myself, but Granny was quite angry with me. She did say she would prefer if we waited a year or two, but she didn't like me criticizing Eric, and she said she didn't want him hurt. She accused me of being an awful snob, which is terribly funny when I think of all the times that she told off Eric for his Cockney accent. Still, and this is the oddest thing …" She paused, and Hannah looked at her expectantly. "You see, despite all my misgivings, I really do miss Eric. Don't look so worried, Hannah. I intend to marry him because that's what's meant to happen, or we think it is. But I also have to decide whether that's the best thing for me."

"You love him, right?" Hannah said gently. "Eric's really a kind and decent guy, and you love him. That's what matters most about people, not if they're popular or rich or clever. Mrs. D.'s right. You need to stop being snobby. You know, that's what I hate most about 1905. No matter what else people have got going for them, practically everyone's a snob. Heck, even Flora's snobby, and she's just a servant like me."

"And are you never snobbish, Hannah Day?" Verity said pointedly.

Hannah thought about it. "Okay, that's a fair question. Sometimes, I guess I am," she said. "All of us are snobby sometimes."

"And you are right that we ought not to be," Verity said, in a softer tone, "And you're also quite right about Eric, Hannah. He is a good man. I just hope he's the right man for me."

Verity sounded emotional, but she quickly collected herself. "Now," she said, sniffing. "How do you propose to reunite Elizabeth with the formidable Mrs. Lewis?"

"I'm not sure," said Hannah. "I'm pretty sure that Elizabeth doesn't really want to cut off Mrs. Lewis, which is helpful. I think she's just trying to figure out how to have an adult relationship with her. She still needs her, you see, because Mrs. Lewis is her role model."

Verity blinked. "I don't think we have those in 1951. What on earth is … what did you say?"

"Role model," said Hannah. "Mrs. Lewis is the person Elizabeth wants to be like when she grows up."

"Oh, I see," said Verity. "Yes, I suppose so. Anyway, I don't think there was ever any question of the two of them making a complete break. They had too much history together, you see."

Hannah furrowed her brow. "So you think that that's important?"

"Of course," Verity said. "Hannah, what's wrong?"

"Nothing," said Hannah. "Not really … It's just … Why was your Granny so mean to me in 1951? Please, Verity, I'm not attacking her. I just don't get it. What did I do wrong? Did she really forget me?"

"Oh, dear, dear Hannah," Verity said kindly. "You're so wise beyond your years, I can never remember that you aren't the grown-up you appear to be. You must have been absolutely crushed by what Granny said to you in 1951." She patted Hannah's hand. "Look, it's nothing to do with you. Granny has always been difficult, and we can both see that more clearly than ever, now that we know Elizabeth. But over the last several months, in 1951 I mean, Granny has been in such a frightful mood. Even though Eric won't admit this, she's upset him, too. We're all very worried about her, actually. We don't know what's behind it. Her mind is just as sharp, but …"

Hannah remembered something her own grandmother had said once about an elderly friend. "Do you think maybe it's because she lost all her friends? That happens when people get old, although she's not that old… "

"Sixty-six is rather old," Verity said.

"Not in my time," said Hannah. "My grandma is in her 70s, and she seems way younger than Mrs. D."

Verity considered this. "How interesting … Let me think … To my knowledge, Granny has never had many true friends. Lots of acquaintances, yes, but she never liked to get too close to adults who turned up in her life. She had one or two old friends from boarding school she would occasionally visit, but they both died in recent years … And Mrs. Lewis died last year."

"So that's it," Hannah said. "She's lonely."

"Gosh, I think you might be right," said Verity. "Not that she would ever tell me, of course, but … Oh, goodness, you are right. That *is* it. She's lonely. No wonder she's upset. And then when we marry, Eric will move out for good, and we shall probably move to London. She wants us to marry, because she is very fond of both of us, but she must dread us leaving, so she's in no hurry to see us go. Gosh. How complicated. And how sad. Poor Granny."

But now Verity sat up straight. "Oh! In the midst of this heart-to-heart chat, I almost forgot."

"Forgot what?" said Hannah

"You remember that Mrs. Lewis invited me to visit her? Well, I haven't done it, because it's not a good idea."

Hannah was taken aback. "Are you crazy? Of course it's a good idea. You can persuade her to be kind to Elizabeth. She'll take you way more seriously than she would take me."

"I'm sorry, but I simply can't," said Verity. "Kate told me early on that, when the time comes, I must not go to see Mrs. Lewis. I didn't know what she meant, but I do now, and here's the thing. She also said that you must go, instead. So you must go to Mrs. Lewis's for tea."

Hannah stared at her. "Kate said that?"

"In so many words," said Verity, "but do you think this is what she meant? I really think you should do as you think best."

"Agreed," said Hannah, "And what I think best is that I had better stop by and see Mrs. Lewis."

Thursday, October 26, 1905

"Mother, tell me again why you object to my taking cookery lessons from Mrs. Morris?" said Elizabeth.

Mrs. Hughes frowned. "We have already spoken of this, Elizabeth. We have servants for such work. You need not play the skivvy."

Hannah, listening in to this drawing-room conversation while ironing in the pantry, took offense. *Mrs. Hughes really is an awful old snob, she thought. Whatever Brandon and Alex are dealing with right now, it can't be snobbier or crazier than this.*

Elizabeth was now replying angrily to her mother. "May and Mrs. Morris may be skivvies, as you put it, but at least they are capable of supporting themselves. I am quite useless. I could not maintain a household if my life depended upon it."

"Of course you could," her mother said emphatically. "You are a lady. Your husband will employ servants, and you will manage them. That will be your duty."

Now Victoria intervened to try to keep the peace. "Elizabeth," she said, "do not let us have another scene between you and Mama." Margaret remained silent as usual, but Hannah, listening, imagined her nodding in agreement with Victoria.

Elizabeth ignored her sisters. "Mother, what makes you think that we will always keep servants? That we will never need to cook and clean for ourselves?"

"You will have no lack of servants if you make a good marriage," Mrs. Hughes said firmly. She clearly had no doubts on the subject. "Please, Elizabeth, stay out of the kitchen. You will hardly find a good husband with work-worn hands."

Elizabeth shot back, "And what if I am widowed, like poor Victoria here? How am I to support myself then?"

"You notice," Victoria said stiffly, "that 'poor Victoria' as you put it, has servants to wait upon her in her widowhood. I am provided for, as you will be, Elizabeth, when you marry."

Hannah heard a long silence, and then Elizabeth said, in an ominous tone, "Then it is time we discussed the truth."

"Oh, please don't," Victoria groaned. "Elizabeth, we have heard more than enough from you about women's rights."

But women's rights was not Elizabeth's subject. "How much longer," she said, "can this family afford the upkeep of three servants, one of whom is absolutely useless?"

In the pantry, Hannah froze, her eyes wide. Taking great care to make no noise, she abandoned her ironing, and moved closer to the wall to better hear the conversation.

"Elizabeth," Mrs. Hughes said weakly. "There is no call for this. Poor Flora has served me, indeed all of us, for many, many years, and I will not hear a word against her. And as for our finances, we shall cross that bridge when we come to it."

"I think we should cross that bridge now," Elizabeth said. "Mother, I took it upon myself recently to examine the household accounts ..."

"How dare you?" gasped Mrs. Hughes, "You wicked girl!" Immediately there was hubbub in the room, as everyone, even Margaret, began angrily criticizing Elizabeth. Mrs. Hughes cried, "My accounts are none of your business. How dare you pry into them?"

"But they *are* my business," Elizabeth said calmly. "It is all of our business, all of us, if we cannot afford the upkeep of this household."

Victoria now asked in a subdued voice, "How bad is our situation, Elizabeth?"

Elizabeth replied in the same serious tone, "We're in great difficulties,

CHAPTER FOURTEEN

Victoria, as I think Mother knows. We must either increase our income, which means one or more of us finding employment …"

"Impossible!" Mrs. Hughes interrupted. "What gentleman of our class would marry a shop girl or a governess?"

"Otherwise," Elizabeth continued, as if her mother had not spoken, "We must lower our expenditures."

There was a silence.

"Or," said Victoria, "we need to reduce the size of the household, and I don't mean by dismissing the servants. Isn't it time you found a husband, Elizabeth, dear?"

"Even if I were to entertain thoughts of marriage," Elizabeth said, "I doubt very many young men would be interested in a plain, gangly bluestocking like me."

Hannah couldn't decide if Elizabeth really thought she was ugly, but how sad was that if she did? Anyway, she was too young to rush into marriage. There was something reckless and immature about the brick incident, and if Mrs. Lewis was right, that Elizabeth had mommy issues, it was probably best she sorted them out before she got married. *Wait,* Hannah thought, pulling a face, *what I am I saying? I need her to get married to Tom Devenish as soon as possible.*

Now Mrs. Hughes said, "Should a gentleman be interested in your hand, Elizabeth, I would be willing to loan you Weston Cottage as a residence."

"You really do want rid of me, don't you, Mother?" said Elizabeth.

Before Mrs. Hughes could reply, Victoria said, "That's all well and good, Mama, but have you considered selling Willowbank, and moving into Weston Cottage?"

Mrs. Hughes did not like this suggestion. "Victoria, I will not, and that is final."

No wonder she's so determined to stay, Hannah thought. As young Sarah Chatsfield, Mrs. Hughes had been forced to leave the luxury of Balesworth House, her enormous childhood home, at a very unhappy time in her life. To her, Weston Cottage was part of a bad memory, and, perhaps more crucially, it was a house too small for someone as important as her.

And suddenly, with that thought, Hannah understood that the immature person in the Hughes family was not Elizabeth. It was Mrs. Hughes, who simply could not come to terms with how her standing in society had fallen since she was a little girl. *Elizabeth is the grown-up here,* Hannah thought. After all, she was realistic about her family's finances, and about the sacrifices it would take to assure their future.

CHAPTER FOURTEEN

As if all this were not enough for Hannah to process, it was Victoria's turn to drop a bombshell. "Mama, Elizabeth … Mr. Collins has asked for my hand in marriage."

"Mr. Collins?" said Mrs. Hughes, clearly astonished. "The solicitor who visited us?"

"Yes, Mama," said Victoria. "I have consented to become Donald Collins's wife." Elizabeth congratulated her sister, but Mrs. Hughes remained silent. Victoria continued. "Presently, Donald lives with his mother, but he has made a suggestion that might be a help to you, Mama. He would like us, after we marry, to become the tenants of Weston Cottage. He would repair the roof, and pay you rent. I know you already have a tenant, because Donald is handling the property for you, but the woman is renting on a very short lease. If Donald and I move into Weston Cottage, at least until we purchase a house of our own, that would help your finances, wouldn't it?"

"Mr. Collins has asked you to marry him?" said Mrs. Hughes, still amazed. "And you have consented?"

"Is that really such a shock, Mama?" Victoria said, sounding rather offended.

Mrs. Hughes shook her head. "No, no, I didn't mean that, Victoria. I meant that I am a little taken aback that you have never mentioned this courtship to me, and that Mr. Collins did not ask my permission."

"Actually," Victoria said sheepishly, "I was rather afraid you might not want me to leave home again. But Donald, that is, Mr. Collins, has asked for and received permission for my hand in marriage."

"From whom, pray?" her mother demanded.

"From Papa," said Victoria.

There was a stunned silence. In the pantry, Hannah put her hand to her mouth to avoid gasping aloud. *Mr. Hughes isn't dead? What?*

"Margaret, shall I tell Mama your news?" Victoria said, followed by a pause in which Margaret presumably nodded in agreement. "Papa has also given Margaret his blessing to marry Mr. Cooper. I'm sorry, Mama. I hope you will see, eventually, that this is good news."

"Victoria … Margaret," their mother said in a strangled voice, "do you mean to tell me that both of you have been in communication with your father?"

"Yes, Mama," Victoria said, taking a deep breath, "I do. Donald and Mr. Cooper thought it best that we have his consent for our marriages, despite his estrangement from us."

In the pantry, Hannah was silently panicking. *Really? Mr. Hughes isn't dead? Really?* Everything she thought she knew about this family had been destroyed in less time than it took to boil a tea kettle. They weren't rich, as she had

CHAPTER FOURTEEN

thought, but had been struggling to stay middle-class. Elizabeth wasn't the immature teenager she had assumed, but a diligent young woman doing her best in a situation she really couldn't handle, with a mother who was a control freak and who didn't have a clue how to manage money. Hannah's head felt like it was about to explode.

She stepped away from the wall, and as she did, she knocked over her iron and ironing board with a great crash. Within seconds, she heard the drawing room door open and close. The pantry door flew open, and Elizabeth, with a face like thunder, slammed it behind her. She stepped over to the wall, and yanked back the tapestry hanging to reveal the open hatch. Closing it, she whirled around to Hannah, leaned over her, grabbed her upper arms, and glared at her, her face inches from Hannah's. "You were listening to our conversation," she whispered furiously. "Don't deny that you opened that hatch. How *dare* you?"

Now Hannah knew that this woman was no longer young Elizabeth. *This was Mrs. Devenish.*

"I'm just doing my job, Miss Elizabeth," Hannah sputtered in a quavering voice, and she wasn't lying.

Letting go of her arms, Elizabeth said quietly, "I want to talk to you. Come upstairs, this minute."

Hannah held up a hand, and said solemnly, "Only if you promise not to hit me when we get there."

Elizabeth looked incredulous. "Why on earth would I hit you? You're not a child. Come along."

When they got to her room, Elizabeth said, "Close the door, May." Hannah did as she was told, although she kept one hand on the door handle, just in case she needed to flee.

"Now," said Elizabeth, "Who do you think you are?"

Good question, Hannah thought. She took a deep breath, and said calmly, "Miss Elizabeth, you're always saying that women should be equal to men. But what's the point of that if everyone isn't equal to each other? I'm a poor person, so I'm supposed to pretend like I don't really live here, and that I don't notice what goes on in this house. Well, guess what? I do live here, and I have ears. You guys were talking about me, so I listened. If you don't want anyone to listen, you shouldn't have servants, or at least you should keep your voices down. Now what's going on? I thought your dad was dead."

Suddenly, the wind seemed to go out of Elizabeth's sails. She sat down at her dressing table, and wiped over her face with her hand, a gesture that in 1940,

Hannah had seen Mrs. Devenish make often in times of stress. Then she said slowly, "This is a very private matter. We do not discuss it with anyone. And at this moment, I cannot say that I trust you. Should I?" She gave Hannah a look that seemed to bore a hole into her soul, the sort of look that Mrs. Devenish gave her. Hannah nodded, and let go of the door handle. Elizabeth motioned to her to sit on the desk chair.

Hannah thought long and hard before she spoke. "Miss Elizabeth, you have to decide for yourself if you can trust me, because you're not going to take my word for it that you should. But I trust *you*. I would trust you with my life." She meant it.

Elizabeth said quietly, "You are the only friend of mine, if I might call you that, who knows about this sordid affair."

"Okay, so Mr. Hughes is not dead," Hannah said. "But that's nothing for you to be ashamed of. Are your parents divorced?"

"Oh, Lord, no," said Elizabeth. "That would be far too expensive, and too shameful."

"So your father just left the family?" Hannah said.

"Yes," said Elizabeth, looking away from her. "It wasn't sudden. He left gradually, beginning five or six years ago, so gradually that we didn't understand what was happening. He spent more and more time in London. I tried to arrange to meet with him, but he said he was too busy. And then he began to cease all contact with us. When I wrote to him at his club, where he was staying, he never replied. I traveled to London to see him, without telling my mother and sisters, but the butler refused me admission. Three years ago, the club returned all of our letters, with a note to say that my father was no longer a member. Today, as you overheard, I have learned that he and my elder sisters have secretly been in touch. I am quite at a loss to understand what's going on."

By now, Elizabeth had tears rolling down her face. She wiped them away, and continued. "Six months ago, Father stopped depositing money in Mother's account. We can manage without his money, I think, but not as we live now. We're barely making ends meet. Victoria and Margaret getting married should help, because it means that Mother won't need all three servants, but she still won't admit that. But that's not my greatest worry now. You see, with both my sisters marrying, my own future will be very different."

"Why?" said Hannah, who was now confused.

Suddenly, Elizabeth seemed to pull herself together. She wiped her eyes on the back of her hand, and pursed her lips for a moment. "May, let me explain. I am the youngest daughter. If I don't marry or find a respectable post as a governess or schoolmistress, then the family will expect me to look after my mother for the rest of her life. I don't relish living with my mother forever, and the thought of being a governess or teacher, cooped up in some family's attic or some boarding school for the rest of my days, is awful. In any of these circumstances, I will be a servant myself, always subject to the rule of others. I do not wish to take a husband just yet. But perhaps it would be best if I did. At least then I shall be able to choose who will direct my life, and it won't be my mother."

That's worrying, Hannah thought. *If she gets married right now, it will probably be to Arthur Ingle-Gillis. He would make her happy, but what would happen to Verity, Eric, George, Brandon, Alex ... and me?*

Standing up, Elizabeth took a cloth handkerchief from her dresser drawer, wiped her face, and blew her nose. "May, I'm sorry I have involved you further in my family's affairs. I should not have told you all this. You are a servant, not a friend. And of course I cannot entirely trust you. You have been eavesdropping on us all."

"Yes, I have," Hannah admitted. "I'm really sorry. I had my reasons, but ..."

Elizabeth gave her a hard stare.

Hannah looked down. "I'm sorry," she mumbled. "No excuses. It was a terrible thing to do."

"Yes, it was," Elizabeth said shortly. "You should be ashamed of yourself."

"I am," Hannah said, and she meant it. Somehow, confessing to Elizabeth about snooping came as a relief, because even though Hannah knew she had very good reasons for listening in, it still felt wrong. "The thing is, Miss Elizabeth, sometimes I do stupid things and say things, even without knowing why. I don't mean to be a bad person ..."

"Oh, but you're not," Elizabeth said in genuine surprise. "Don't be silly, May. You're young, as am I. And I can hardly pass judgment on you. Heavens, I threw a brick through my mother's front window. I am sure you have never done anything quite so stupid as that, have you?"

Hannah couldn't suppress a smile. "No, I haven't. Not yet, anyway."

"Good," said Elizabeth, adding in a mock-angry voice, "because that would be a very wicked thing to do." She gave Hannah a small smile. "Now, be off with you. And please, May, no more eavesdropping. You are privy to our family's greatest secrets, and that is privilege enough. I will trust you to keep what you have learned to yourself. Is that clear?"

"Yes," Hannah said. "It's clear." She was careful not to say that she had agreed to it, and to the extent she did agree, it was as "May," not Hannah. With a sinking feeling, she realized that she did not know when or if she would have to eavesdrop again. When lives might be at stake, Hannah knew, she did not have the luxury of choosing absolute integrity.

As Hannah returned to the kitchen, Mrs. Morris said, "Have you finished that ironing, May? You've taken a long time about it. Now, stop dilly-dallying. I need you to go to the corner shop for me."

Hannah started taking off her apron. "Mrs. Morris, did Arthur Ingle-Gillis ever visit this house?"

"Mr. Ingle-Gillis? The gentleman what owns the bookshop, you mean? No. Why would he? I don't believe he and Mrs. Hughes are acquainted." She returned to running her finger down the list of ingredients on a recipe. "Now go down to Baker's, and get me some onions on account."

As Hannah put on her coat, she thought that if Elizabeth was romantically involved with Mr. Ingle-Gillis, she was keeping it very quiet. *But then she would keep it quiet, wouldn't she?* Mrs. Devenish was always discreet, so it was hardly surprising that Elizabeth was, too. Only … this was the same woman who had just poured out her heart to a maid she hardly knew.

Hannah had always known how complicated and contradictory Mrs. Devenish could be. Now, the mystery deepened.

As Verity rang up Hannah's paper bag full of onions on the cash register, she said, "My great-grandad did a bunk? He left? I thought he died." She was astonished. "Granny never mentioned her father deserting them, although admittedly it's not the sort of thing she and I would discuss. I do wonder, though, if his absconding is something that has changed in time?"

"Maybe," Hannah said morosely, "And I'm worried also about Elizabeth feeling like she has to get married to get away from her mother. I mean, why can't she just move out and get an apartment?"

"How on earth would she do that?" said Verity. "Hannah, don't be stupid. Elizabeth can't live alone. First, she's underage, because she's not even twenty yet. Second, she hasn't got a job to support herself. And third, it's not 1951, when I could, I suppose, leave home and find a horrid little bedsit in London, miserable and odd though such a prospect would be. In 1905, young women are always expected to live under adult supervision. Heavens, look at us two here! You live with your employer, and so far as everyone else knows, I live with my aunt. Look, I just hope you can think of how to bring together Granny and Tom. I daren't stick my oar in, because I'm afraid it's supposed to be your job, and I might muck it up."

"I know it's my job," Hannah said with a grimace. "But I need all your

CHAPTER FOURTEEN

advice, Verity. Things aren't looking good. I mean, you saw Tom's face when Elizabeth harassed Mrs. Lewis at the meeting. He looked really ticked off."

"I know," Verity said, flaring her nostrils. "I told you, he's a wet blanket. But to be fair, he made a better impression of himself to me at the party when I talked with him, even though I was doing my best to kill his interest in me."

"Verity, you *did* say you got Tom to lose interest in dating you, right?"

"Oh, absolutely," said Verity. "He looked very unhappy, and he's not been in the shop since."

"So what did you say to him, exactly?"

"I told him that the only reason I came to these meetings was to find a husband, and that I looked forward to the day when I wouldn't have to think for myself, but would have a man to look after me. Awful stuff. I didn't mean a word of it, of course, but he clearly believed me, and he wasn't impressed."

"Huh," said Hannah. "Well, that's progress. Look, everything's so complicated, I can't make any decisions now. But, as your Granny always says," and here Hannah gave a spot-on impersonation of Mrs. Devenish, *"I shall continue with my enquiries."*

Verity laughed.

Wednesday, November 1, 1905

After a week of thinking hard about what she would say, the day had arrived for Hannah to pay an important visit in Balesworth. She was so nervous that morning, she had knocked over a bucket of soapy water in the hallway, and while she was cracking eggs in the kitchen, she dropped two of them on the floor. She even left behind the lunch basket Mrs. Morris had prepared for her.

Her plan was, she hoped, a clever plan. It was certainly a brave plan, because it involved visiting with Mrs. Lewis.

As she walked up Balesworth High Street, Hannah almost chickened out several times along the way. She was afraid that if she blew it, her meeting with Mrs. Lewis would have bad consequences for Elizabeth. And the chances of her blowing it, she feared, were pretty high. Somehow, she had to persuade the formidable Mrs. Lewis to talk about private matters and, worse, she had to do that while in the guise of the lowly maid, "May Harrower." A little voice in Hannah's head said "Good luck with that," and she shivered. The best course of action, she decided, was to be as truthful about Elizabeth's situation as she possibly could, and just hope that truthfulness worked. On this occasion, she really had no choice but to trust her own judgment, and hope that Mrs. Lewis was the person Hannah believed she was.

Finally, she found herself on the street in front of Oaks Lodge, Mrs. Lewis's house. Should she go to the back door, as a maid would? And that was when Hannah realized: She was not coming to Mrs. Lewis's home as "May Harrower," a lowly maid. She was here as "May Harrower," Elizabeth Hughes's friend, concerned for her welfare. If Mrs. Lewis was the person Hannah trusted she was, she would respect that. If she was not, then none of it mattered anyway. Throwing back her shoulders, Hannah pressed the bell at the front door.

Mrs. Lewis's maid showed Hannah into the drawing room, and introduced her as "Miss May Harrower." But, to Hannah's dismay, Mrs. Lewis was not alone. Millie Cooke was sitting on her sofa.

"Please, do be seated, Miss … um … Harrower," said Mrs. Lewis. "I wish I had known you were coming." Hannah knew that Mrs. Lewis was telling her off for having invited herself to the house, and her confidence evaporated even further. While Hannah removed her hat, Mrs. Lewis instructed her maid to bring tea.

"Now, what brings you here, Miss Harrower?"

"Mrs. Lewis, it's kind of private," Hannah said hesitantly, glancing at Millie.

"I see," Mrs. Lewis said evenly. "And does this private matter concern a mutual acquaintance of ours?"

Hannah certainly hadn't expected the encounter to be this easy. "Yes, it does," she said with relief.

Millie, with a knowing look, gathered up her purse and hat. "Don't worry, Mrs. Lewis, I was about to take my leave." Then she looked curiously at Hannah. "I say, have we met?"

"Yes," Hannah said through gritted teeth, "Twice. Here, and at your house."

Millie gasped. "Oh, gosh, of course! Miss Powell's friend, the maid."

Hannah scowled. Why did she always have to play second fiddle to middle-class people? It was like the world was organized around them, and everyone else was an anonymous and unvalued audience, only needed when unpleasant work had to be done, and never really noticed. What made them think anyone wanted or deserved to live like that?

Millie, sensing she had offended, got to her feet, and addressed her hostess. "It's good to see you again, but I ought to be going. Thank you, Mrs. Lewis. I am gratified by your trust, and I promise you can depend on me."

Mrs. Lewis graciously inclined her head. "Goodbye, Miss Cooke."

After showing out Millie, Mrs. Lewis's maid brought tea, and Hannah and Mrs. Lewis sat in silence while she laid out the tea things and a selection of tempting little cakes. Mrs. Lewis then poured out tea, and said to Hannah, "I am sure you did not come today to discuss the weather, Miss Harrower. You have come to tell me about Miss Powell. I had wondered why she never accepted my invitation to visit. Is she unwell?"

Hannah felt her stomach lurch. Mrs. Lewis thought she had come to discuss Verity, not Elizabeth. Suddenly, the visit seemed like a really bad idea. Trouble was, there was no polite way to escape. She couldn't fake an urgent text as an excuse to leave: It was 1905. She was trapped in Mrs. Lewis's drawing room, with Mrs. Lewis and a plate of fancy cakes. She was going to have to wing it. "I'm not here to talk about Verity Powell," she said, grimacing slightly.

Mrs. Lewis sighed heavily, and drummed her fingers on her knee. Then her eyes met Hannah's. "Now, young woman, you have me at a disadvantage. You are Miss Hughes's maid, are you not?" Hannah nodded. "But you are here today as her friend?"

Hannah nodded again, relieved that Mrs. Lewis possessed Mrs. Devenish's ability to size up a situation instantly.

"Hmm," said Mrs. Lewis. She looked like she was thinking how best to handle this awkward visit. And then, to Hannah's consternation, she said, "You know, I ought to send you home with a flea in your ear."

A flea in my ear? Hannah thought. It was yet another baffling British expression she would have to look up. But she definitely understood the "I ought to send you home" part. Certain that Mrs. Lewis was about to kick her out, Hannah picked up a small iced cake and took a large bite, spraying crumbs all over the sofa. Mrs. Lewis frowned, and handed her a small and expensive-looking plate. Feeling abashed, Hannah took it, and dropped the remains of her cake on it.

After waiting for Hannah to finish what was in her mouth, Mrs. Lewis said, "How is Miss Hughes?"

"Okay, I guess," Hannah said cautiously. She stirred sugar into her tea and, without thinking, placed the wet spoon directly on the tea table. Mrs. Lewis frowned again, and without a word, picked it up and laid it on Hannah's saucer. Hannah cringed. Her intensive lessons in 20th century middle-class manners with Mrs. Devenish had been a while ago now, and it wasn't comfortable to get a refresher course from the daunting Mrs. Lewis.

"Miss Hughes is unhappy, is that what I am to infer?" said Mrs. Lewis. "You are aware that she has abruptly severed all connection with the Association, and with me, by her own choice?"

Hannah replied with a question. "Have you talked to any of the Hughes family since the, um, thing with the window?"

Mrs. Hughes briefly put a finger to her lips, exhaled, and shook her head.

CHAPTER FOURTEEN

"No," she said. "I don't know Miss Hughes's family at all. Her mother does not mix in Balesworth society, and she and I do not pay calls upon one another."

In that case, Hannah thought, *I'm probably your only source of information about Elizabeth.* So this was why Mrs. Lewis was willing to talk with "Miss Harrower", a lowly maid! Hesitantly, Hannah said, "Miss Elizabeth's life is way more complicated than you think."

"Oh? How so?" Mrs. Lewis said sharply.

Hannah took a deep breath. "Her dad walked out on the family years ago."

But to Hannah's surprise, Mrs. Lewis did not seem shocked. "I daresay that is no great secret, and certainly not to me, although I would caution you not to be so indiscreet with others ... Remind me of your Christian name?"

"May," said Hannah.

"Well, May, I was indeed aware of this sorry state of affairs. You see, by an extraordinary coincidence, Elizabeth's father has settled near a pen-friend of mine in America. He has made little effort to conceal his identity. When I learned from my friend Miss Russell that the new mayor of her town was an Englishman named Charles Hughes, I asked her for his description. She sent me a photograph from a newspaper, and I confronted Elizabeth with it. Needless to say, she was greatly distressed, but I assured her of my sympathy and concern."

Hannah was agog. "Mrs. Lewis, the town in America, is it Snipesville, Georgia? Can I see the picture?"

Mrs. Lewis looked startled, but then she collected herself. "What business is it of yours?"

"Please, Mrs. Lewis," Hannah said firmly.

Mrs. Lewis gave her an appraising look, and then got to her feet, opened her desk, and retrieved a folded sheet of newspaper. Sure enough, it was *The Snipesville News* from a few months earlier, and Hannah saw the photograph captioned *Charles Hughes, Mayor of Snipesville.* Even with a mustache, he was recognizable as the man in the framed photograph she dusted on Mrs. Hughes's dressing table.

Mrs. Lewis meanwhile, said, "Put that newspaper down, if you please. There is something else I will tell you, in the strictest confidence. Over the years, I have tried very hard to be a friend to Elizabeth Hughes. But she can be very ..."

"Difficult?" said Hannah

"Childish," preferred Mrs. Lewis.

"Look, I know it looks that way, like she's completely immature," said Hannah. "But she's not. Her mother isn't getting any money from her dad anymore. So Elizabeth has been trying to sort out the family's finances, and Mrs.

Hughes has been trying to get Elizabeth married to someone."

"Someone?" said Mrs. Lewis, looking very uneasy.

"Anyone," said Hannah. "Any guy who will have her. But Elizabeth doesn't want to get married, because she's young, and anyway, I don't think she has a boyfriend. The thing is, now she's found out her sisters are engaged, and she knows that if she stays single, everyone will expect her to look after her mom for the rest of her life, because she's the youngest daughter. She could go get a job, but she doesn't want to be a teacher. So she's kind of trapped, whatever she does, unless she marries someone fast. I think Tom Devenish would be perfect for her, but he seems to think she's totally crazy."

"Oh, dear," said Mrs. Lewis. She rose to her feet and walked over to the cold fireplace. There, she leaned forward, her fingers on the mantle, as though she were praying. "Oh dear, oh, dear."

Hannah said quietly, "Mrs. Lewis, I'm not gonna kid myself that you enjoy a maid coming over to your house and drinking your tea. I'm here because I thought you would want to know. Miss Elizabeth needs your help, but she won't tell you herself, because she's kind of, you know …"

"Willful?" said Mrs. Lewis, turning back to look at her.

"Independent," Hannah preferred.

"Indeed," said Mrs. Lewis, folding her hands. "I cannot imagine she would be pleased to know that you are sharing confidences about her with me. I am not sure that I ought …"

"Tough," said Hannah, and she wondered how that word was magically translated, because Mrs. Lewis's eyes widened slightly at the sound of it. Hannah hurried on. "Look, Mrs. Lewis, I think Elizabeth threw that brick because she was so freaked out. She wasn't just acting out for fun. She's been trying to save her family and herself from disaster. And she's been depressed since you guys fell out. The stuff you and she fight about, it's not that important, is it? And you don't see differently from each other as much as you like to think you do. You might not ever agree with each other on how women should get the vote, but at least you guys agree they should, right? And anyway, she thinks the world of you, and she really respects you, even if she won't admit it. I think she's just embarrassed about, you know, how she's behaved, and that she stopped writing the letters for the Association because she's so down. I think she thinks you'll never forgive her for any of it, and that your friendship is over."

After that exhausting speech, Hannah knew she had very few cards left to play, and much depended now on how Mrs. Lewis reacted to what she had said.

To her dismay, Mrs. Lewis' voice took on a hard edge. "And so she should be embarrassed. She has behaved disgracefully."

But Hannah wasn't going to let Mrs. Lewis off the hook. "Yeah, well, she's also ashamed by what you said to her and her mom."

"I am sure she is," said Mrs. Lewis. "But I won't apologize for remonstrating with her, if that's what you're hoping for."

Hannah was getting desperate. "She's so embarrassed and hurt, she doesn't even want to face you."

"I know that," Mrs. Lewis said firmly, "But until Elizabeth is prepared to swallow her pride, there is nothing I can do. The truth is, I can manage perfectly well without her contribution to my work. Indeed, I have already suggested to Millie Cooke that she take Elizabeth's place as secretary."

Hannah prepared to play her last card. "And there's something else," she said.

"What's that?"

"Millie's aunt, your friend Mrs. Fitch, told Millie and Tom Devenish that they shouldn't invite Elizabeth to their meeting. Mrs. Fitch gave them the idea that Elizabeth is a crazy person. But how did she get that idea?" Hannah looked straight at Mrs. Lewis. In fact, she was bluffing. She didn't really believe that Mrs. Lewis had spilled the beans about the brick incident to her old friend Mrs. Fitch.

But Mrs. Lewis now looked very uncomfortable. "I have no idea," she said quickly, and Hannah realized at once that this morally upright and highly-respected lady was lying through her teeth. It was strangely disappointing to find out that Mrs. Lewis was human, after all.

Hannah took a last sip of tea, and a huge bite of another cake, before deliberately placing the leftovers on the serving plate with the untouched pastries. It was her own little act of rebellion. Then she said, through a mouthful of crumbs and frosting, "Thanks for the tea." Mrs. Lewis shuddered.

As Hannah got up to leave, Mrs. Lewis said, "Thank you, May, for bringing me news of Elizabeth. Let me see what I can do. I will make a promise to you. I will help Elizabeth, if she will let me. After all, someone has to take an interest in that girl and her future. It was brave of you to come to see me, and please don't think I'm not grateful."

Touched by these words, Hannah nodded. "Thank you, Mrs. Lewis."

To Hannah's surprise, Mrs. Lewis didn't ring for the maid to show her out, but instead walked her to the door herself. As she opened it, she said in a kindly tone, "May, you are a clever girl. Tell me, were you always a maid?"

"No, Mrs. Lewis," said Hannah. "I wasn't. Good afternoon, and thanks again for the tea and cake."

As Hannah crossed Balesworth on her way to Weston Cottage, she floated on the cloud of Mrs. Lewis's compliment. *She thinks I'm smart,* she thought. *She likes me.* For the first time, she understood what Mrs. Devenish saw in Mrs. Lewis, and why she would never quite find it in her heart to cut ties with her. Or, at least, Hannah hoped she wouldn't.

Monday, November 6, 1905
Hannah walked up Balesworth High Street behind Elizabeth, but she had no idea where they were going. Elizabeth had said only that it was a surprise.

As they neared the Ingle-Gillis bookstore, Hannah expected they would stop in and say hello to Arthur, but Elizabeth kept on walking. Hannah was surprised, but also relieved. She did not wish to encourage Elizabeth's budding romance with the charming Mr. Ingle-Gillis. All the same, she couldn't restrain herself from peeking through the bookstore's window as she passed, and just as she did, she saw a young woman kiss Mr. Ingle-Gillis on the cheek. Now this was interesting. Elizabeth, it seemed, had a rival. What would be even more helpful would be if she were to find that out. Hannah ran to catch up Elizabeth. "Can't we visit the bookstore, Miss Elizabeth?" she said. "Please?"

Elizabeth looked at her watch. "I don't see why not."

As the doorbell jangled, Elizabeth stopped so suddenly in the doorway, Hannah almost bumped into her. "Good afternoon, Miss Hughes," chorused the voices of Mr. Ingle-Gillis, and a tense young woman. Hannah stepped out of Elizabeth's shadow to see who the girl was. It was Millie Cooke, looking guilty and embarrassed. "You know Miss Cooke, of course?" Mr. Ingle-Gillis said smoothly. "She just visited to …"

"To purchase a book," said Millie. "Yes, gosh, I'm always in here, aren't I, Mr. Ingle-Gillis?"

"Well, I wouldn't say that," he said, looking puzzled, "But it's always a pleasure to see you, Millie. Now, Elizabeth, Miss Cooke was just telling me that you have resigned as secretary of the Women's Suffrage Association. A great pity, but I'm sure you have your reasons. And I can assure you that Miss Cooke here will do her best to follow in your footsteps."

Elizabeth had a look on her face that Hannah knew all too well. It was the same stony expression she would wear on the evening in 1940 when, as Mrs. Devenish, she decided to whip three misbehaving children, one of whom was Hannah. It was an expression of righteous fury. "I did not resign," she said coldly, ignoring Mr. Ingle-Gillis and looking straight at Millie. "I was unaware that you had taken over my duties, Miss Cooke."

Millie looked like a frightened rabbit. "Mrs. Lewis asked for my help," she said in a scared voice. "I suggest you take up the matter with her. Good day, Arthur. Good day, Miss Hughes." With that, she almost ran from the shop. Mr. Ingle-Gillis called after her, "Your book!" But she didn't stop.

Now, Mr. Ingle-Gillis angrily rounded on Elizabeth. "What on earth did you have to say that for?" he roared. Hannah, who was both uncomfortable and fascinated by the developing scene, tried to blend in with her surroundings, which was tricky since she bore no resemblance to a stack of books.

Elizabeth's nose twitched. "I don't know what you mean, Arthur," she said, suddenly sounding to Hannah like a little girl caught in a lie. "It's the truth. And you should know that Millie Cooke has been trying to worm her way into the Women's Suffrage Association and Mrs. Lewis's favor since she arrived in Balesworth."

"Elizabeth, that's absolute rot, and you know it," Mr. Ingle-Gillis exclaimed. "Millie's a good sort, always trying to be helpful. She wouldn't have had anything to do with the wretched Association if her aunt hadn't twisted her arm. When you failed to perform your duties, Mrs. Lewis asked Millie if she would help, and Millie's not about to refuse a request from such a formidable person. If you want your position back, I know Millie would give it you, gladly. But you will have to swallow your pride. Go and make your apologies to Mrs. Lewis, Elizabeth, and stop acting the fool. Oh, and while you're at it, you might also want to apologize to Millie Cooke."

Hannah waited for Elizabeth to explode all over Arthur Ingle-Gillis. But it didn't happen. "I had no idea that you and Miss Cooke were so close," she said in a slightly sarcastic tone. "I'm sorry to have taken up your time, Mr. Ingle-Gillis, but I need no further advice from you. Come along, May." With that, she swept from the store. Hannah, however, lingered, a book having caught her eye.

"Don't be ridiculous," Mr. Ingle-Gillis said to himself. Then he noticed Hannah was still in the shop. "Ah, the little maid," he said with a smile. "Go and tell your mistress that Mr. Ingle-Gillis will welcome her back for pudding whenever she pleases. But that he will expect an apology. Better yet, tell her I should like to take her for tea at the new tea rooms, if she promises to behave. I will shut up shop and meet her there in half an hour. Hurry now."

Seeing Elizabeth stop and gaze into a window a hundred yards ahead of her, Hannah began walking quickly to catch up. But then she slowed her steps. What was her rush? She wasn't going to pass along Mr. Ingle-Gillis's message. The last thing she needed was for Elizabeth to rekindle their romance. But then Hannah felt bad. Not telling Elizabeth the message would be dishonest. And wasn't she supposed to be honest? She walked up to Elizabeth and said reluctantly, "Mr. Ingle-Gillis wants to meet you in the Tudor Tea Room in thirty minutes. If you want."

Elizabeth sniffed. "Does he indeed? Well, it won't change my plans. Come along, May." She looked annoyed, but not nearly as upset as Hannah had feared. That was a good thing, if puzzling.

Now they were headed in the direction of Mrs. Lewis's house. So Elizabeth was going to do as Mr. Ingle-Gillis had told her, and fix things with Mrs. Lewis! But suddenly, Elizabeth crossed the street, and started up the alley that led to the Tudor Tea Rooms. Surely she wasn't going in there … Oh. She was. What was she up to?

As Hannah stood in the tiny hallway of the Tudor Tea Rooms, she looked into the main downstairs room, where she was destined to eat with Brandon and Alex in 1940. Today, however, a waitress in black and white uniform led her and Elizabeth up the narrow little staircase, Elizabeth lowering her head to avoid hitting her large hat on a dark oak beam. Once upstairs, they were directed to a small corner table, where Elizabeth sat facing the wall, leaving Hannah to face the door. Hannah was pleased to notice that the café didn't smell smoky, as it would in World War II. She supposed that was because most of its customers today were women, and in 1905, very few women smoked.

Elizabeth removed her gloves. "Since you're my maid, I'm supposed to make you wait for me outside," she said. "You see, the lovely thing about tea rooms is that a respectable lady need not have a chaperone to visit one."

"You're not going to make me wait outside, are you?" Hannah said anxiously. She didn't want Elizabeth to be alone with Mr. Ingle-Gillis. Plus she had her eye on some scrumptious scones and cakes on the nearby sideboard.

"Of course I'm not, May," Elizabeth said briskly. "I would hardly send you away when I had just invited you in, would I? Now, tea for two, I think, and what would you like to eat?"

"A toasted scone with jam and butter … Oh, wait, what's the green thing next to the scones on the sideboard?"

"Green *thing*?" said Elizabeth, turning to see where Hannah was pointing. "Oh, you mean the tennis cake. That's a fruit cake with marzipan and green icing. A little garish, but rather moreish." She smiled at her own rhyme.

"Sounds great," said Hannah. "What does it have to with tennis?"

"Not a great deal. I suppose it's so named because it's green," said Elizabeth. "Just like a tennis lawn. Would you prefer tennis cake to a scone?"

Hannah was now struggling with her decision, and especially because she

CHAPTER FOURTEEN

saw still more goodies calling her name from the sideboard. Mrs. Morris was a fantastic baker, but she couldn't keep up with Hannah's sweet tooth, and Hannah loved that she could eat sweet things without ever putting on weight because she worked so hard in Willowbank.

"Why don't you have both?" said Elizabeth with a twinkle in her eye. "My treat. Now, I should like some Dundee cake …"

"There's a cake named after Dundee?" Hannah said. "What does that taste like?"

"Well, hopefully not like Dundee," Elizabeth said with a chuckle. "No, it's a dark fruit cake, with whole almonds pressed on top. I'm astonished you've never heard of it."

"I'm game. I'll try some of that too."

"Now you're being greedy, May," Elizabeth said disapprovingly. After weeks of feeling older than Elizabeth, Hannah felt very much in the company of Mrs. Devenish. It didn't matter that at this moment, Hannah was physically older than Elizabeth. She strongly suspected that she would always think of Elizabeth Hughes Devenish as her elder.

But now Elizabeth added kindly, "I'll let you have a little of my tennis cake, May."

The waitress appeared. "Would you care to see a menu, miss?"

"No, we know what we wish to order," Elizabeth said briskly. "We will take a pot of tea for two, two buttered scones with strawberry jam, a slice of tennis cake, and a slice of Dundee cake … Oh, gosh."

"What's wrong?" said Hannah.

"I forgot to go to the bank, and I only have about sixpence ha'penny in my purse," Elizabeth said. She turned back to the waitress. "How much does that come to?"

The waitress tapped her pencil on her notepad as she added up the tally. "Tea for two is sixpence, miss, toasted buttered scones are tuppence each, and a penny extra each for jam, so that's …"

"A shilling, before we even discuss the cakes," Elizabeth said. "Ah. Oh, dear."

"It's okay, Miss Elizabeth," said Hannah. "I've got your back. Here's a shilling. We can at least have our tea and scones."

"Thank you, May," said Elizabeth, taking the heavy little silver coin from her. "I'll pay you back."

"I know you will," Hannah said, and suddenly she felt very emotional. Elizabeth would indeed pay her back, she knew that, and in so many ways. Elizabeth, who was rummaging around in her purse, didn't notice Hannah becoming teary. Quickly, Hannah wiped her eyes, and said, "You seem more cheerful than you've been lately."

"Do I?" said Elizabeth, in a voice that suggested that she knew this perfectly well. "Yes, I suppose I do. I suppose you could say that I have made a decision."

"And what decision is that?" Hannah said.

"None of your business, May," she said, snapping her purse shut. She held up a heavy silver coin. "Look, I found half a crown in the bottom of my handbag. Now we can have our cakes after all, and you don't need to help me."

That's what you think, Hannah thought.

No sooner had the waitress served tea and cakes than Hannah, to her annoyance, smelled cigarette smoke. As Elizabeth poured tea, Hannah glanced around the room for the offending smoker. Looking over by the window, she spotted Tom Devenish holding a cigarette, and he was sitting with Millie Cooke. Hannah wondered how she could not have seen them arrive. Then she recalled that she had spent several minutes focused on picking out pastries. *Right.*

Were Tom and Millie on a date? Surely not, since she had just seen Millie plant a kiss on Arthur Ingle-Gillis. Hannah watched as Millie lit a cigarette, to the scandal of two middle-aged ladies at the next table, who looked horrified, tutted loudly, and whispered to each other. Seeing their reaction, Millie hastily stubbed out her cigarette. *She's worried someone will report her to her aunt,* Hannah thought. For once, she sympathized with a smoker. Why *was* it all right for Tom to smoke, but not for Millie? Then she wondered if what most offended the other customers was Millie smoking, or her sitting unaccompanied with a man. Hannah's thoughts were suddenly interrupted.

"You're very quiet," said Elizabeth. "Don't you want your cake?"

"Sure," said Hannah, hoping Elizabeth would not turn around and see Tom and Millie.

But it was too late. Tom Devenish, was on his feet and coming toward them. It shouldn't have been a surprise: The room was so small, and Elizabeth was so tall, it was hard to hide her. "Miss Hughes?" Tom said, "I wonder if you and, um, your companion would care to join us?"

Elizabeth began to turn her head to see who "us" was, but then she seemed to decide that it was rude to check out Tom's company before accepting his invitation. "That's very kind, Mr. Devenish," she said. "If it's not too much trouble …"

"Of course, it's no trouble at all," he replied. But it *was* trouble, Hannah thought, and now Elizabeth spotted Millie, Millie spotted Elizabeth, and their mutual dismay was obvious. But it was too late for everyone to change their minds: Tom had already helped the waitress transfer Elizabeth's and Hannah's tea, cakes, and chairs to his table.

As they all sat down, there was an embarrassed silence. Finally, Tom said, "Miss Hughes, I'm glad to have this opportunity to speak with you. I have been meaning to apologize to you for my behavior."

"And why would I need an apology from you, Mr. Devenish?" Elizabeth looked genuinely confused.

"Because, um, well, I did not applaud when you asked Mrs. Lewis your very brave question at our meeting at Miss Cooke's house. I wanted to applaud you, naturally, but since it was I who had invited Mrs. Lewis to speak, I was in a rather awkward position, as I hope you will understand."

Elizabeth gave him what Hannah thought of as her Mona Lisa smile. But then she said, "It is I who should apologize to you, Mr. Devenish, and also to Miss Cooke. I should have realized that I embarrassed both of you when I criticized Mrs. Lewis."

"But, dear Miss Hughes, you didn't criticize her," Tom said warmly. "You contradicted her, and that's hardly the same thing. You know, at school, I was once beaten for insolence, purely for having disagreed openly with one of my masters in a matter of opinion. Nothing will ever persuade me that the punishment was just. We must always feel free to speak our minds in political discussion."

Watching Tom Devenish, Hannah saw him now in a very different light. He was not a shy and uninteresting boy. He was a kind and compassionate young man. Suddenly, Hannah found him very attractive.

But now Millie had something to say. "And I must also apologize to you, Miss Hughes, for the same and more," she said, again to Elizabeth's evident astonishment. "I truly never meant to undermine your connection with Mrs. Lewis. My aunt, you see, is an old friend of hers, and she absolutely insisted I offer Mrs. Lewis my help. Truly, I ought to stick up for myself. Heavens, I'm almost twenty-one, you would think … Miss Hughes, I do hope we may be friends. Please, do call me Millie."

Elizabeth smiled again. "And you may call me Elizabeth," she said.

"Is this a private party, or might I join you?" said Arthur Ingle-Gillis, pulling up a chair between Hannah and Elizabeth. Hannah was alarmed by his arrival. What would happen now? Should she drop a cup of tea on him to create a distraction? But Mr. Ingle-Gillis turned to Millie. "So, Miss Cooke, were you confessing to Elizabeth that you are thoroughly under the thumb of your old battleaxe of an aunt?"

Millie tutted, with a smile that told everyone that she instantly forgave him for his rudeness. Who could stay angry at Arthur Ingle-Gillis, thought Hannah, when he was so impossibly gorgeous and charming? Even though she could now see Tom Devenish's appeal, she was still sad that Elizabeth wouldn't marry Arthur, and so be spared the grief of losing her husband in the First World War.

"You see, dear Elizabeth, here's the thing," Arthur said, "You are so busy picking fights with all of us, you never notice that everyone who comes to know you adores you, and thinks you are marvelous. You make Balesworth a better place by your very presence." Hannah watched with concern as Elizabeth visibly melted at these kind words. Arthur continued, "And none of us thinks you should end your connection with Mrs. Lewis simply because the two of you disagree. Of course, this assumes that you *do* disagree."

"What do you mean?" said Elizabeth.

"Oh, Elizabeth, you're an open book," Arthur said. "You really aren't terribly impressed by the Pankhursts, are you? You just fancy the idea of declaring your independence from the overbearing Mrs. Lewis."

Suddenly, Elizabeth's indulgent smile switched off, and she looked away, embarrassed. Arthur stretched out in his chair, and folded his arms behind his head, and to Hannah, he suddenly looked a bit smug, and rather less attractive. "Oh, dear, have I given offense?" he said with an air of mock innocence.

"No more than usual," said Tom, giving him a stern glare. "Honestly, Ingle-Gillis, I must insist you apologize to Miss Hughes."

Arthur Ingle-Gillis suddenly sat up, and pouted. "You are still the perfect prefect, Devenish. One would think we had never left school. But very well, I shall do as I'm bidden. I apologize, Miss Hughes."

But now Hannah had had enough. "Will you guys *please* stop offending and apologizing to each other? Can't you just all be friends? You know, just support each other, and accept each other as you are?"

Everyone noticed Hannah now. "May" was no longer an anonymous presence. They all stared at her. But then Tom said, "May, you are wiser than any of us. Our little band has so much in common. We are bright, educated, young people with progressive, even radical ideas, despite our conventional and privileged middle-class upbringings. And yet, here we are, being conventional and privileged Victorians, and allowing silly misunderstandings and squabbles to come between us. Elizabeth, Mr. Ingle-Gillis is quite right about one thing. We do all admire you tremendously, and I propose we all unite behind you as you continue to strive to bring a young person's sensibility, a breath of fresh air, to the Women's Suffrage Association. What do you say?"

"Jolly good idea," said Arthur Ingle-Gills. "I shall go so far as to promise that

Reid Pierce and I will attend Mrs. Lewis's meetings more faithfully, much as it pains me to say that."

"Thank you," Elizabeth said. "We shall see what Mrs. Lewis thinks of my reprising my involvement with the Association."

"Oh, I'm sure she'll be delighted," Tom said. "Well, perhaps delighted is too strong a word."

Elizabeth laughed despite herself. "I know what you mean, Mr. Devenish," she said.

"Please," he said, "do call me Tom."

Yes, thought Hannah. *Do.*

As Hannah left the Tudor Tea Rooms with Elizabeth, she said, "Thanks for the surprise. The cakes were great."

"I'm glad you enjoyed tea, but that wasn't the surprise," Elizabeth said.

"It wasn't?" said Hannah. "So what was?"

"You'll see," said Elizabeth, as they walked down the alley, and turned right onto the High Street. Hannah followed her to a doorway flanked by a red and white barber's pole. "The tea was a thank you in advance from me," Elizabeth said. "I brought you under false pretenses, you see. I brought you along for courage. You probably don't know it, May, but you are a great inspiration to me."

"I don't understand," Hannah said. "Why are we at a barbershop? They only cut guys' hair."

"That's what you think, May," said Elizabeth, with a wicked chuckle. With that, she went inside.

The stunned exclamations of Elizabeth's family could be heard clearly in the kitchen. "What on earth was that?" said Mrs. Morris, setting down her rolling pin. "Quick, May, hurry to the drawing room and see if they need a doctor."

"No, it's okay," Hannah said, taking off her hat and propping her umbrella in the corner of the kitchen. "Everyone's fine."

"I doubt that," Mrs. Morris said firmly, wiping her hands on her apron. "Flora, you go."

Flora struggled to get out of her chair by the fireplace, but Hannah stopped her. "No, no, you stay there, Flora," she said kindly. "I'll go. But I promise you guys, everything really is fine."

"Excuse me, Mrs. Hughes," Hannah said, "but Mrs. Morris wants to know if everything's all right, and do you need anything?"

CHAPTER FOURTEEN

"May, bring us tea," Mrs. Hughes said tersely.

Elizabeth was standing proudly by the window, showing off her short hair. It was, Hannah thought, a very cool-looking curly bob, and with it, she appeared very modern, and every inch a young version of Mrs. Devenish. Hannah couldn't resist saying something. "Miss Elizabeth, your hair really does look awesome!"

"Thank you, May," Elizabeth said with a grin. "No more rats for me! Ha!" Seeing Elizabeth's expression of delight, Hannah was glad she had complimented her in front of Mrs. Hughes, even though it meant that both she and Elizabeth were now in disgrace.

As she walked back down the hallway with a cheery smile, Hannah noticed the new bicycle parked against the wall.

"It's all good," said Hannah as she entered the kitchen. "Miss Elizabeth got her hair styled, and everyone was kind of surprised."

"Is that all?" Flora said, sighing with relief. "I thought there'd been a murder."

"Me, too," said Mrs. Morris. "Are you putting the kettle on for them, May? Make a pot for us, while you're at it. But I still don't understand what all the fuss was about."

Hefting the heavy tea kettle, Hannah staggered over to the stove, and set it down. She scooped coals from the nearby scuttle, and added them to the drawer under the stovetop. "Hey, who does that bike in the hall belong to?" she said.

"Miss Elizabeth," Mrs. Morris said in an exasperated tone. "Miss Elizabeth only went and ordered it, didn't she? It was delivered this afternoon. You and Flora will just have to do your best to clean around the wretched thing when you do the hall. I'll wager that was the reason they're having a bit of a barney through there."

"You think they're fighting over a bike?" Hannah was amazed.

"Yes, of course," said Mrs. Morris. "Mrs. Hughes doesn't want Miss Elizabeth running around. It's not right for a young lady to go exhausting herself at all hours of the day and night, and Mrs. Hughes is worried …"

"She's worried Elizabeth will get out of this house, and see that there are more interesting people and places out there," Hannah finished for her.

"That's as may be," said Mrs. Morris, suddenly looking a little guilty for having gossiped. "But this is none of our business."

"Before I forget," Hannah said, "Mrs. Hughes wants Flora to serve them the tea. Is that okay, Flora?"

Flora blinked at her. "Why me?"

CHAPTER FOURTEEN

Hannah shrugged. "I dunno. I guess they prefer you."

Flora looked suitably mollified. It had not been the truth, but Hannah felt it was important to set things right, because she sensed that her mission was almost complete. Flora was annoying, but she was harmless, and after giving up her life to serve Mrs. Hughes, Hannah thought, she deserved to feel valued in her old age. She found it sad that the only way Flora felt valued was by Mrs. Hughes's approval, but not everything, she reflected, can be made perfect.

Just then, Elizabeth walked into the kitchen, curly bob and all. When the servants saw her, Flora's mouth fell open, and Mrs. Morris dropped a knife on the floor. "Just to let you know," Elizabeth said cheerfully. "I'm going out, so I don't require tea."

After Elizabeth was safely out of hearing distance, Hannah said, "What's wrong with short hair? Seriously?"

Mrs. Morris stared at Hannah as if she were stupid. "May, have you ever seen a girl with short hair?"

"Yes," Hannah said, without mentioning that it was in the 21st century. She grabbed a knife, and started slicing up a hard-boiled egg.

"You've seen filthy workhouse brats that's had their hair shorn for lice, I'll venture," said Mrs. Morris. "But not respectable girls. A lady's hair is her crowning glory, May, and why would a woman want to look like a man?"

"But Miss Elizabeth doesn't look like a man," Hannah replied. "She looks great."

"We're all allowed an opinion, May," said Mrs. Morris, looking grim as she quickly gathered up and kneaded pie dough. "But some opinions are best kept to ourselves. Now get on with your work. I need this ham and egg pie in time for supper."

What a funny lot these Edwardians are, Hannah thought. Why on earth did they care so much about short hair? Hannah remembered seeing old pictures of "flappers", the name given in the 1920s to young women who wore their hair super-short. But then again, that was the future. This was 1905, and a World War had yet to happen. Maybe Elizabeth was ahead of her time. Or maybe she was just doing another crazy thing because she was stressed. One thing Hannah did know: Elizabeth looked pretty relaxed and happy today, whatever anyone else thought.

Mrs. Morris carried on fretting aloud. "Miss Elizabeth will never find a man now. No gentleman wants a lady who's cut her hair, and that's a fact …" She glanced out the window. "Oh, there's the postman. Answer the door, May."

Hannah shuffled through the mail as she brought it into the hallway, and came across a bright white envelope, addressed in elegant handwriting to *Miss E. Hughes*. As always, there was no return address. Right behind the letter, an identical envelope was addressed to *Miss M. Harrower*. Dropping the rest of the mail on the table, Hannah tore open her letter. Who could be writing to her?

Well, this was a surprise. It seemed that Mrs. Lewis had summoned her to a meeting at Oaks Lodge on Wednesday afternoon. Hannah was very flattered to be invited, and very intrigued. *Why does she want me there?* she thought with a perplexed smile. *Maybe she just needs someone to pass around the sandwiches.*

Wednesday, November 8, 1905

Verity, Tom Devenish, Reid Pierce, Millie Cooke, and Arthur Ingle-Gillis all burst into grins when Elizabeth took off her hat in Mrs. Lewis's drawing room, and revealed her dramatic new hairstyle. Mrs. Lewis hurried over to greet her. "Elizabeth, I am pleased to see you, but, good heavens, what have you done to your hair?"

"Do you like it?" said Elizabeth. "I think it makes me look rather artistic."

Mrs. Lewis rolled her eyes, and gave a resigned shake of her head, leaving Elizabeth to look very pleased with herself. It was at that moment Hannah realized that Elizabeth's haircut was the 1905 version of getting a tattoo.

"You wonder, perhaps, why I have invited you here this evening," Mrs. Lewis said to the assembled group, which Hannah couldn't help noticing was entirely made up of young people. "First, I hope you will all join me in congratulating Miss Cooke, whom I have appointed as secretary of the Balesworth Women's Suffrage Association, following Miss Hughes's much-lamented resignation."

Hannah glanced at Elizabeth, who looked thoroughly put out. What did she expect, Hannah thought? She blew it. She quit. And this was her punishment. All the same, Hannah hoped that Mrs. Lewis had not invited Elizabeth to the meeting simply to put her in her place. Mrs. Lewis meanwhile continued, "Now that I have made this announcement, I rush to add that I have not called you young people together on the matter of women's suffrage. Rather, I have come to appeal to you for your help for an old friend of mine." With that, she held up a letter. Everyone looked at her, intrigued.

"For some years now, I have corresponded with a lady who is actively engaged in the women's suffrage cause in the United States. She has a concern that is just as pressing as that of winning women's right to vote."

This caused a slight sensation in the room. Nobody would have guessed that Mrs. Lewis thought anything was as important as women's suffrage.

She went on. "You see, my American friend is a Negro. Even if American women were to win the vote, she tells me, she would be unable to exercise that right because of the color of her skin. Now, I doubt that many of you have ever met a colored person. And I am sure that some of you are surprised to learn that I have political interests beyond women's suffrage. So I shall tell you something. I am one of those fortunate few who subscribed in my younger years to *Anti-Caste*, an extraordinary magazine edited by the suffragist Catherine Impey for women of all colors from throughout the Empire and English-speaking nations. In the pages of this magazine, we learned from each other through published correspondence, exchanged through Miss Impey. And what Miss Impey emphasized most by the letters she chose to print was the appalling discrimination against Negroes in the Southern United States. Before I subscribed to the magazine, I was a young married lady living in dull old Balesworth, who had assumed that I could never make a difference to injustices anywhere, here or elsewhere in the world. Yet Miss Impey herself lived in Somerset, which, as you know, is very far from London, and yet she was bringing together likeminded people from all over the world. I found her example deeply inspiring."

Everyone looked wowed. "I say," Verity muttered to Hannah, "I never suspected Mrs. Lewis of being such a radical. How very interesting. Good for her."

Mrs. Lewis continued. "Miss Impey's magazine, I am sorry to say, ceased publication some years ago. But it was through *Anti-Caste* that I became acquainted with Miss Julia Russell, and we have remained devoted correspondents ever since. Like me, she lives in a small provincial town. And like me, she is engaged in a wider world through her letters. Like Miss Impey, Miss Russell is an inspiration, and now, she has asked for my help. As you may know, schools in the Southern states of America are segregated by caste. Miss Russell teaches in a Negro elementary school of which she is both headmistress and sole teacher. But despite the pressures of her work, she is not content with her considerable accomplishments. Many of her children, she says, are perfectly capable of continuing on to secondary education, and she would like to begin a high school for them. I am asking you to please consider helping me to help Miss Russell in achieving …"

Suddenly, as Hannah looked on in horror, Elizabeth interrupted Mrs. Lewis. "That's an admirable cause, no doubt, Mrs. Lewis, but surely we have equally worthy causes here in England? My maid, for example, is one of millions of English people who was forced to leave school at the age of 13, simply because we do not provide secondary education for working-class people in this country. I sympathize with the plight of American Negroes, but ought we not to be more concerned with causes that are closer to home? Or is it, perhaps, easier for us to examine the dust in others' eyes, while ignoring the planks in our own?"

Mrs. Lewis looked, Hannah thought, as though she were counting silently to ten, to prevent herself from walloping Elizabeth. Hannah knew that look: She had seen Mrs. Devenish direct it at her. "Miss Hughes, I had thought you would have learned something from your correspondence with other suffrage groups in England," Mrs. Lewis said. "We all learn best when we consider views very different from our own, and when we realize that other people have much to teach us. Those of us privileged to learn from them have a moral obligation to apply what we have learned and to assist them, and others, in our turn."

Hannah wasn't sure she had understood this, but she glanced at Elizabeth, and guessed from the annoyed look on her face that Mrs. Lewis had won this round of their ongoing battles. Mrs. Lewis took up her subject again. "However small the sum we raise, our assistance will be an encouragement to Miss Russell. That is why I have decided to invite Mr. Devenish and Miss Hughes to form a committee with me to raise funds for Miss Russell's high school in Snipesville, Georgia."

A little wave of interest and approval rippled around the room, and Hannah glanced at Tom Devenish, who looked pleased, but not at all surprised by this news. *He already knew*, Hannah thought, with a smile. Elizabeth, however, looked very surprised but also, Hannah was relieved to see, very pleased.

The meeting concluded with a generous tea. Mrs. Lewis's dining table practically groaned under the weight of three-tiered serving platters loaded with little sandwiches, fancy cakes from Balesworth's most prestigious bakery, homemade scones, and even handmade chocolates. "Hmm, chocolate eclairs," said Verity as she picked up a pastry. "This is Mrs. Lewis at her best."

"No, Verity. Mrs. Lewis was at her best when she gave Elizabeth this new job," Hannah muttered, "not when she had her maid put out some cakes. Look, I need to go check on Elizabeth and Tom."

"No need," said Verity. "Look over there."

Hannah looked, and she saw Elizabeth and Tom standing closely together, deeply engrossed in conversation, with eyes only for each other. From there, Hannah cast an approving eye over the roomful of young people, with a happy-looking Mrs. Lewis at the center of the crowd.

"Things are looking up, Verity," Hannah said. "But I won't be satisfied until I know your Granny marries Tom, instead of Mr. Ingle-Gillis. You know what's still bothering me? Elizabeth and Arthur both love literature and poetry and stuff, and she has way more in common with him than she does with Tom."

"Wait, did you say poetry?" Verity said, the eclair halfway to her mouth. "Mr. Ingle-Gillis isn't a poet, is he?"

Hannah nodded.

"He's a poet?" Verity confirmed. "Oh, then, gosh … I *do* know who he is. Granny told me about him. When she was young, she was a good friend of a poet's. They were never romantically involved. She said he wasn't the marrying kind. But it was very sad. He died a few days after my grandfather. Both of them were killed in the trenches in France in the First World War."

Hannah turned to look at handsome and charming Arthur Ingle-Gillis, and kind, sweet Tom Devenish. Her heart ached. *What a terrible waste.*

Verity put a hand on her arm. "Hannah, I can't say that I'm shocked that Arthur died, but apparently you are. I am so sorry. You do know what happened to Granny's generation, don't you? Hundreds of thousands of young men died in the First World War. So many were killed that, after the war ended, there weren't enough husbands to go around."

Quietly, Hannah said, "So that's why Millie Cooke never married, I guess."

"I suppose not. How short life is," Verity said. "And how precious."

And, Hannah thought, this also explained why Mrs. Devenish had never remarried after Tom's death. There weren't a lot of men of her age to choose from, and even fewer who would be keen to adopt two small children. Once again, Hannah looked across the room at the happy young people, and felt like bursting into tears.

"I know it's sad, dear," Verity said, taking her hand. "It makes me sad, knowing that Granny was left alone, and that Mummy and my aunt grew up without their father. But it happened to so many people. Life is like that, Hannah. You can't manage everything. You can't worry all the time about the sad things that might happen. You, me, all of us, we must enjoy the happy times, and the people we care about, while we can, and do what good we can, just as Granny has. We only have one life. And, anyway, look at all of them. They're happy today. That's what matters right now."

"You sound like an old person," Hannah said sadly.

"War," Verity said gently. "War does that to all of us. It makes us realize that every day is important. You lived through the Second World War with us, part of it, anyway. Don't you feel the same way?"

"No, I don't," Hannah said. "I can't pretend I do."

Verity smiled. "Don't pretend. That's what I love about you, Hannah. You keep ploughing on, regardless, being exactly who you are, warts and all, in the peculiar situations in which you find yourself. When we were children, I had no idea how brave you were, but now I do. There you were, a young girl in another country, in another time, and in the middle of a war, no less, and yet you couldn't tell a soul. I think you're extraordinary. I really do."

Now Tom Devenish was approaching. "Miss Powell, how good of you to come," he said. "You know Miss Hughes, of course."

"Of course," said Verity, and gave her young grandmother a dazzling smile. As ever, Elizabeth seemed puzzled by her enthusiasm.

Tom, meanwhile, looked proud. "I'm absolutely honored to have the opportunity to serve on Mrs. Lewis's committee with Miss Hughes," he said. "And Miss Hughes has kindly invited me to have dinner with her family this Sunday."

"Has she, indeed?" said Verity. "How splendid."

Hannah looked forward to serving that meal. But she suspected that the honor would, and should, fall to Flora in the end. Her employment at Willow House would not, she felt, last much longer.

The party was breaking up, and Verity had already left for Weston Cottage. Hannah, waiting for Elizabeth, was thrilled to hear Tom Devenish offer to walk her to the station. But at the exact moment that Elizabeth happily accepted his offer, Mrs. Lewis touched her arm. "Elizabeth, I must speak with you."

"Now, Mrs. Lewis?" Elizabeth said. "May and I were hoping to catch the half past three train."

"This won't take long," Mrs. Lewis said briskly. "Tom, would you mind?"

"Not at all," said Tom. "I'll wait outside. May, would you like …?"

Hannah ignored Tom's hint to wait for him, and remained in the room. She was worried. Apparently, Mrs. Lewis still had some axe to grind, and Hannah had to find out what the problem was. But to her surprise, Mrs. Lewis did not launch into a tirade against Elizabeth. Instead she appeared calm, and rather tired, as she lowered herself onto an armchair, leaving Elizabeth and Hannah standing in the middle of the drawing room. Nodding toward Hannah, she said, "May does not need to be present."

"I would prefer that she remain with me," said Elizabeth. "Anything you wish to say to me, you can say in front of May." Hannah suddenly felt like Elizabeth's bodyguard.

"I don't intend to quarrel with you, Elizabeth," Mrs. Lewis said wearily. "I have done all I can to pour oil on the troubled waters of our friendship."

"I know, and I appreciate your kindness," Elizabeth replied. "But please, do listen to me, Mrs. Lewis, because this is terribly important. Kindly explain something to me. You are a leader in the women's suffrage movement. You claim to believe that women are the equal of men. Yet you treat me like a wayward child."

Hannah really wished she could step in, but somehow, she knew that the situation required her to remain silent. Meanwhile, Mrs. Lewis said, "That's hardly surprising in view of your conduct, Elizabeth. What we in the movement are fighting for is for all adult women to be treated as adults. We are *not* seeking license for Elizabeth Hughes to act childishly."

"I cannot imagine a boy of my age being spoken to in the manner in which you speak to me," Elizabeth snapped.

If Elizabeth had hoped to goad Mrs. Lewis into losing her temper, she was about to be disappointed. Mrs. Lewis spoke slowly and deliberately. "That's utter tosh, Elizabeth, and you know it. You think that I want to treat you as a child? Well, you are wrong. Why do you think I appointed you to my committee? Because despite your irresponsible behavior, I value your work, and your company. And I value them far more when you are calm and self-possessed. No, don't interrupt. This is something I must say to you. You must learn to govern yourself, Elizabeth, or someone else will do it for you. Since your mother does not feel equal to the task, and it certainly won't be me, whatever you might assume, then perhaps it will be your husband, and that worries me very much. It is not wise for a woman to enter upon a marriage without confidence in her own judgment."

Elizabeth put a hand on her hip, and said, "And by 'governing' myself, you mean that I must become meek, mild, and biddable, I suppose?"

Mrs. Lewis tutted. "That is not at all what I mean. I simply mean you to exercise greater tact and discretion. Learn not to express every stray thought that enters your head, and do occasionally consider the feelings of other people. But rest assured, I am not at all interested in keeping you childish, or in forming you into the sort of woman who does as she is told."

Elizabeth looked at Mrs. Lewis with great skepticism.

"Ah, so you doubt my honesty, do you?" Mrs. Lewis said. "Well, let me ask you this. Would you ever describe me as meek, mild, or biddable?"

Elizabeth laughed despite herself. "No, Mrs. Lewis, of course I would not."

"Exactly," said Mrs. Lewis, and Elizabeth's eyes grew wide. "Now I see that you grasp my meaning. You and I are like two peas in a pod, Elizabeth Hughes, although appearances might suggest otherwise. You see, you can never expect to have a peaceful time in your conversation with me, nor should you wish to. We both learn far more from our duels than you seem to realize."

CHAPTER FOURTEEN

Elizabeth looked stunned by Mrs. Lewis's words.

Mrs. Lewis held her chin high. "But, here's the thing. You simply must concede me some ground if I am to be willing to deal with you another day. You have imagined, haven't you, every time we have quarreled, that you have forever alienated my regard for you? No, don't deny it. You were hurt, and you assumed you had ended my fondness for you. You were wrong. But I must be truthful, Elizabeth. When you are so utterly relentless in criticizing my every word, you do take the risk that one day, I shall decide that I have had enough. If you keep pushing me, then one day, I warn you, I may not be there to push. I am not your mother, Elizabeth. I cannot give my word that I shall remain loyal to you regardless of how you behave."

Hannah thought that Elizabeth had stopped breathing. Mrs. Lewis, however, was not done. "Now that I have made my position clear, I will tell you that your loyalty to me touches me deeply, even as your determination to find fault with my opinions and your desperate efforts to gain my attention drive me to distraction."

"I don't understand," Elizabeth said helplessly.

"Oh, I rather think you do," Mrs. Lewis said knowingly. "You're a clever girl. Of one thing I am certain: a difficult girl needs a difficult woman in her life, one who is not her mother, and who can be counted on to offer motherly guidance without maternal prejudice. I accept and am flattered that you have chosen me as that person, Elizabeth. You need a listening and understanding ear. You need sound advice, and sometimes severe reproof. But you should know that I have no interest in crushing your spirit. My hope has always been that I can, in some small way, help you to acquire the self-discipline to be taken seriously as an adult. Unfortunately, this is something that you seem only able to learn from me in the heat of battle. But for both our sakes, I beg you, learn to restrain yourself, and show me respect as your elder, no matter how much you think I provoke you. And in so doing, you will increase my respect for you." Mrs. Lewis folded her hands. "Now, Elizabeth," she said kindly, "are you all right?"

"Yes, Mrs. Lewis," Elizabeth said, looking bewildered. "Perfectly well. It's just that I ... I feel as though you have poured balm onto my soul."

"Why, Elizabeth Hughes," said Mrs. Lewis, beaming, "I do believe that's the kindest thing you have ever said to me."

They had both forgotten Hannah, who had stood staring at them the entire time in absolute wonderment. Both of them suddenly remembered she was there, and turned to look at her. "What are you gawping at, girl?" Mrs. Lewis said in a stern voice, but with a twinkle in her eye.

"Thank you," Hannah said. "I mean it, don't ask me to explain. Just … Thank you. Both of you." Her head swam. For the very first time in her life, Hannah Dias fully understood that she was not alone.

Friday, November 10, 1905

"May, I need a word, please," said Elizabeth. She was holding a sheet of paper, and she looked very serious. Everything for the past week had run smoothly, and Hannah wondered what she could possibly have done wrong. Apprehensively, she followed Elizabeth into the drawing room.

"Please sit down, May," said Elizabeth. Hannah was astonished. She had never expected to be invited to sit in the drawing room. Nervously, she perched on the edge of the sofa.

Elizabeth retrieved her pince-nez glasses, and affixed them to her nose. "Now, what I am about to say is very difficult," she said. "I want you to know that I consider you a friend. My mother has decided to turn over the running of the household to me, at least for now."

"Great," said Hannah, but still not sure where this was going.

"The thing is," said Elizabeth, "that we have too many servants, and I'm afraid it's last in, first out …"

"Wait," Hannah said. "Hold it." She couldn't believe her ears. "You're *firing* me?"

"Not as such, not giving you the sack," Elizabeth said hurriedly. "More … well, letting you go. With an excellent reference, of course. And I have already given notice to Mrs. Morris, too. She's taking a position with Mrs. Lewis, but Mrs. Lewis has no need of a housemaid or kitchen maid, and so …"

Hannah was agog. "You're firing me and you're going to send me out into the cold, cruel world without a job?"

Elizabeth looked very tense. Clearly, this wasn't easy for her. But now, Hannah surprised her. She burst out laughing, and as she did, she lolled back onto the sofa cushions. "I can't believe this," she giggled. "I thought I'd have the chance to quit! Is it too late to tell you to shove this job?"

"I beg your pardon?" said Elizabeth, looking both confused and offended.

"Never mind, Elizabeth," said Hannah. "We're cool."

"That's *Miss* Elizabeth," Elizabeth said. "But I understand that you're upset, May, and I'll overlook it. I have written you a character, and I wish to read it to you." She cleared her throat.

CHAPTER FOURTEEN

"Willowbank"
Church End Road
Ickswade, Beds

Thursday, November 9, 1905

To Whom It May Concern,

May Harrower has been in my family's employ since September, 1905, as a housemaid and kitchen maid. She has carried out her duties with hard work and skill, and is respectful and considerate toward her employers and the other servants.

Miss Harrower is an exemplary employee. More than that, she quickly became a beloved and trusted figure in our household. We are discharging her from our employment with the greatest of reluctance. Unfortunately, the circumstances of our household have changed, and so we regret we are unable to retain her services. We recommend Miss Harrower without the slightest hesitation for any position as a housemaid, parlour maid, or kitchen maid.

Yours truly,
Elizabeth Hughes (Miss)

CHAPTER FOURTEEN

When Elizabeth finished reading it, she handed it to Hannah, who gave her a tearful smile.

That afternoon, Elizabeth walked Hannah to Ickswade Railway Station for the last time. "May, have you ever considered that you might have a different destiny?" she said. "Other than that of a servant?"

Hannah laughed. "Oh, you bet!" Then she remembered that she was supposed to be May Harrower, and she put on a straight face. "Trouble is, the only way out is marriage, if I can escape from the house where I'm working for long enough to find a guy. But I'm sure change is coming for girls like me."

Elizabeth was intrigued. "Are you sure? How do you know that?"

"I just do," said Hannah. "I don't know where, and I don't know when, but it's coming. Don't worry about me, Miss Elizabeth. I won't end up like Flora, I promise. I'll keep looking ahead. And it's been so great getting to know you. Now I have to get on with that other destiny you say I should have, but you've helped me so much."

"Will you allow me to help you in future?" Elizabeth said.

"Oh, I'm sure I will ask for your help one day," said Hannah with a smile.

"In that case, do stay in touch," said Elizabeth.

"I promise I will," said Hannah, "one way or another."

Chapter 15: THE TRUTH, SNIPESVILLE, 1906

Tuesday, March 13, 1906

Eric read over the front page while Alex anxiously awaited his verdict. "Your article about the fire is a bit weak," Eric said. "I suspect a real reporter would have interviewed the police."

"I tried," Alex protested. "I went to see the Sheriff twice, but he was out of the office. It's not like I can call him on his cell."

"Call him on his *what*?" said Eric, baffled.

Alex shook his head. "Never mind. But what do you think of the other articles?"

"Not bad," Eric said grudgingly.

Alex had lived in England in 1940, and he knew this was meant almost as a compliment. He tried to take it as one. But then Eric added, "It's just …" And he paused awkwardly. "Well, I wish you had let me edit your work before the newspaper went to press."

Alex was alarmed. "Why? Did I make spelling mistakes?"

"No, it's not that," Eric assured him. "Well, I did spot one misspelling, but that's not what concerns me. It's just that, well, it does seem rather odd to print your feature story about Thomas on the front page, next to the other important news."

"You know I didn't do the layout, Jimmy did, but what's wrong with it? Oh, you think the story about Thomas isn't important enough to be on the front page? Fair enough, I guess, but no big deal."

Eric held up the newspaper. "Come and have a look so I can show you what

I mean."

Alex looked over Eric's shoulder. Eric pointed in turn to his story on the farmhouse fire, his article about Thomas, and a wire-service article about the campaign for Georgia governor.

"Alex, you have to look at all of these together, to see how readers will see them. Have you actually read the election story?"

"No, not exactly," Alex admitted.

Eric rested his forehead on his hand. "Have you, in fact, ever read *The Snipesville News?*"

"Of course I have," Alex said. Eric looked skeptically at him, and he said reluctantly, "Well, I read my own stories. The other stuff is pretty boring."

"Look, I do sympathize," Eric said. "I'm an absolute stranger to America, and much of what I have seen and heard in Georgia makes no sense to me at all. But the longer I'm here, and the more I read this newspaper, the more I start to understand this place. I can't say I like what I read, but it is useful to know. Perhaps you ought to read *The Snipesville News*, eh?"

"I guess," Alex said without enthusiasm.

"Since you don't seem to grasp what I'm getting at, let me spell it out for you," Eric said firmly, sounding for a moment, Alex thought, very much like Mrs. Devenish. "Most of the articles that Mr. Hughes runs in his newspaper are extremely prejudiced against colored people."

"Oh. You mean he's a *racist*," Alex said. "That's funny. I mean, he probably is, because they all are, but he never talks about black people."

Eric sounded exasperated now. "I have no idea what Mr. Hughes's personal views of colored people are. That's not my point. It doesn't matter. What matters is that he's always printing these awful articles, probably to sell newspapers. I'm sure it's important to report that the men standing for governor are arguing about taking votes away from colored people, but why do the reporters themselves have to attack Negroes in their writing? Of course, it's not just *The Snipesville News* that reprints this rubbish. I read a copy of the Savannah newspaper, and it was no better."

"Yeah, okay, it's all awful," said Alex, feeling stung. "But that's just how it is in Georgia right now. How is this my fault? My article isn't racist."

Eric looked at him pityingly. "Don't you think it's a little more complicated than that?"

Alex did, in fact, think it was a lot more complicated than that. He just didn't want to admit it to Eric, or perhaps even to himself. Looking through the window, he watched as Dr. Marshburn, the dentist, hopped off the far boardwalk with a newspaper clutched to his side. He walked gingerly across the muddy street, and stepped up onto the boardwalk by the newspaper office. Alex had a very bad feeling about this. Now Dr. Marshburn flung open the door. "Hughes in?" he barked.

"I'm sorry?" said Eric.

"Your boss, sir, that Yankee, Charles Hughes."

"He's not a Yankee," Eric protested. "He's from England. And he's in Chicago until tomorrow."

Dr. Marshburn advanced on him threateningly, waving his newspaper. "He's not from Snipes County, and he's a foreigner, just like you. Tell him I want to speak to him the minute you see him." Throwing down the newspaper on Alex's desk, he left, slamming the door behind him so hard, Alex was afraid the glass would break.

Alex and Eric exchanged worried looks. Then, a second later, the door was thrown open again. Now it was Brandon who burst into the office. He looked around, and, satisfied that the three of them were alone, he yelled, "You morons. You totally stupid morons."

That was about the strongest language Alex thought he had ever heard come out of Brandon's mouth.

Wednesday, March 14, 1906

"I read the newspaper when I returned home late last night," Mr. Hughes said sharply as he strode into the office.

"Good morning, Mr. Hughes," Eric said with a forced smile. "We weren't expecting you back quite so soon."

Mr. Hughes ignored him. "You made an absolute mess of everything," he said angrily.

"How?" said Alex.

"Let us begin with the fire. You missed the most newsworthy part of the story. You failed to mention that William McCabe was murdered."

Alex and Eric exchanged horrified looks. "But why do you think it was murder?" Alex sputtered. "We were both there, and it looked like a house fire to us."

"I spoke with the sheriff just now," said Mr. Hughes. "There were footprints on the road leading from the house, and the victim's skull was fractured."

"Ah, now, I can explain the skull," said Eric, clearing his throat. "It probably exploded because of heat from the fire. And of course there would be footprints coming from the house, wouldn't there? People come and go on these dirt roads, and we haven't had rain in several days to wash away their tracks."

But Mr. Hughes wasn't listening. "Sheriff Bragg led a search party with dogs.

CHAPTER FIFTEEN

He's been hunting down the Negro or Negroes responsible, and now he's questioning suspects."

"That's just wrong," Alex exclaimed. "What makes him think black people did it?"

"Don't be a fool, Day," Mr. Hughes snapped.

Alex felt his eyes water. Suddenly, everything caught up with him. He was in sixth grade. He wasn't supposed to be imitating an adult, and writing articles for a newspaper in 1906. He was getting yelled at for asking a perfectly reasonable question.

Eric noticed Alex's sudden silence. He leaned over and said kindly to him, "Chin up, young'un."

Mr. Hughes meanwhile, had sat down at his desk. He ran a hand through his hair, and said wearily, "Look, Day, you're not stupid. However, you are an innocent. This is Georgia. And in Georgia, you do not extol the success of a Negro, unless he is successful in something humble that does not bring him into conflict with the interests of white men. In your article, you describe Tom Clark as hardworking, ambitious … Successful."

"But what's wrong with that?" Alex said, dumbfounded. "It's true."

Mr. Hughes groaned, and then thumped the table with his fist. "I am not a Southerner, Day! I am an Englishman who is tolerated in this town so long as I bring prosperity. But I cannot afford to be seen as weak on the race question. Don't you understand? If people perceive me to favor the Negro, my work here will end, and all I have invested in it will be lost. When white people read of the success of a colored man in his own business, they resent it. If Tom were the fastest tiller of cotton fields, or even if he repaired cars while working for a white man, it would not present a problem. But in your article, he is boasting of his success in owning a profitable new business, and that is a problem."

Alex wanted to argue, but he sensed it was wise to keep his opinions to himself. "I'm sorry," he said, hating himself even as he said it. He wasn't sorry at all. He was mad.

Mr. Hughes gave him a stern look, "I hope you've learned something, Day. I say, though, didn't Jimmy try to stop you from printing this stuff?"

Alex slowly shook his head.

"Humph," Mr. Hughes grunted. "He was probably drunk. If I had anyone to replace him, I would sack him on the spot. Very well, Day, you may proceed with your work. Compile the obituaries."

"Yes, sir," Alex said. Then reluctantly, he added, "I ought to tell you, sir, Dr. Marshburn came by. He's not too happy about something in the paper. He didn't say what."

"I'm sure we both know what," Mr. Hughes said. "I'll speak with him, and assure him it was your innocent and foolish mistake."

Alex swallowed his pride. Again. He had done nothing wrong. Why did he have to do wrong things to please people? Why was he expected to apologize for doing the right thing? He glanced at Eric, who gave him another sympathetic look.

"I will take care of writing for tomorrow's newspaper," said Mr. Hughes.

Thursday, March 15, 1906

Eric held up the new edition of *The Snipesville News* as Alex sat down to his breakfast ham and eggs. "I think you ought to see this," he said. "I walked into town to get it while you were still in bed." He nervously licked his lower lip. "It looks as though Mr. Hughes took it upon himself to write something for the paper. This story here certainly wasn't on the galleys when I left last night, but Mr. Hughes came in as I was leaving. I wondered why he was acting strangely."

ORGANIZED BLACK MAFIA "BEFORE DAY CLUB" RESPONSIBLE FOR ARSON, MURDER OF WILLIAM MCCABE

He handed the paper to Alex, who now saw the front page headline:

He looked up, uncomprehending, and stared at Eric. "Go on," said Eric. "Read the whole article. It gets worse."

And as he read, Alex's eyes grew wider and wider.

Finally, Eric said, "So what is this *Before Day Club?* That can't be true, can it?"

"I don't know," Alex said faintly. "I don't think so. I think he's making it up. I guess we better ask Brandon. This is bad, isn't it?"

"You know what," Eric said slowly. "I'm not sure we should continue to work for Mr. Charles Hughes. I think we should hand in our notice."

"Hand in our notice?" Alex said. "You mean, quit?"

"That's exactly what I mean," said Eric.

"We can't do that. At least, I don't think we should. I know I'm supposed to be doing something here …"

"Then we should at least threaten to resign," Eric said. "We've both done enough, Alex. I don't want nothing … I mean, anything … to do with violence."

Alex looked at his friend's anxious face, and suddenly, saw that Eric really wasn't much changed from the frightened little boy who had been evacuated from London's East End to live with Mrs. Devenish. Eric was no coward, but he had survived desperate poverty, war, and family abandonment, and he had no interest in supporting evil.

"Eric, I want to go home, more than anything," Alex said. "But there's got to be something good I have to do here. It's just that I don't know what it is, and that scares me. Come on. Let's talk to Brandon."

Eric and Alex had found neither Thomas nor Brandon at the blacksmith's shop. The workshop door was locked and bolted. Even Jupe was missing from his usual perch outside. Something was wrong, Alex knew, for the shop to be closed. And now, as the two of them ran toward Miss Julia's house, they could see that the blinds were drawn. Alex felt his heart pumping hard, and his mouth was dry. With Eric right behind him, he dashed up the steps, and banged hard on the door. The reply was silence. He was about to suggest to Eric that they head for Rev. Evans's home, when, from behind the door, Miss Alberta said sharply, "Who's that?"

Alex yelled, "Miss Alberta, it's Alex. I'm Brandon's ... I mean, George's friend. Is he home?"

The door opened a crack. Alberta's eye stared balefully at him from around the door jamb. "He ain't here. Sir, ain't nobody here but me." But then, from behind her, Alex heard Miss Julia's voice say calmly, "It's all right, Alberta. Allow the gentlemen in."

Miss Julia's cluttered little parlor was now packed with people, and chairs had been brought through from the dining room to accommodate all the visitors. Everyone stopped talking and stood up when Eric and Alex entered the room. Among the assembled faces, Alex recognized Reverend and Mrs. Evans, Jupe, and an elderly couple he took a moment to identify as the senior Mr. and Mrs. Elias Thomas Clark. At the center of the room were Robert, Caroline, and Brandon.

"What's going on?" Alex said.

"Thomas has been arrested for fraud," Brandon replied angrily. "And it's your fault."

Alex felt sick, even as he struggled to take in what Brandon was telling him. "But why?" he said plaintively. "I don't understand."

"The reason I was told," Robert said, "is that the engine of Dr. Marshburn's car is broken and cannot be repaired. Dr. Marshburn claims that Thomas must have damaged it when he tried to fix it. He also told the sheriff that Thomas claims to be an auto mechanic when he's nothing of the kind."

"But is that true?" Eric said. "Is Thomas actually a qualified mechanic or not?"

"Eric, it's not that simple," said Brandon. "All these auto mechanics are learning on the job. There's no auto repair schools. Thomas told me the car had big problems, and that's probably why the previous owner sold it. Dr. Marshburn bought it used, even though he claimed it was new."

CHAPTER FIFTEEN

"Then it's Dr. Marshburn who is the fraud," Eric said firmly, "Not Mr. Clark."

Robert gave him a sour look. "With respect, Mr. Powell," he said, "That kind of talk won't help us."

"But I'm right, aren't I?" Eric protested. "Marshburn claimed to have purchased a new car, when it was actually second-hand. That's dishonest."

It was Brandon who had to break the news to Eric. "Eric, this isn't Balesworth in 1951. What's true and honest doesn't matter here. Black people can't go around making accusations against white people, and especially not important white people, even when they're right. Not in 1906. We have to find a practical way to help Thomas."

"And we must do it today," said Robert. "Thomas's situation threatens to become more grave, now that Mr. Hughes has printed that Billy McCabe was murdered, and that it was the work of this Before Day Club. People will believe anything they read in a newspaper."

"But it's not true, is it?" Eric asked. "The Before Day Club, I mean?"

Alex could see the entire roomful of people trying not to roll their eyes at Eric.

"No, of course it's not true," Brandon snapped. "Get a clue. Your Mr. Hughes is making it up. Or else Dr. Marshburn is making it up, and Hughes is printing it, but one way or another, it doesn't matter. Hughes is responsible. He publishes what white people in Snipesville want to read. He doesn't care if it's true or not, so long as they approve of what he writes." The others nodded in agreement.

"You're right," Eric said quietly. "Mr. Hughes ought to know better than to spread such nonsense, and he is being remarkably dishonest. It's wicked."

"It is indeed nonsense," Robert said sternly. "And, as you say, sir, it is wicked. But, again, with respect, Mr. Powell, don't you understand? That won't stop whites in Snipesville from believing it."

Eric was still confused. "The thing is, why will they believe it? Surely enough white people know enough black people here to grasp that the idea of an organized group setting out to kill whites is complete rubbish ..."

Nobody answered him, but Alex noticed that almost everyone in the room gave Eric another pitying look. Robert now turned to Alex. "Mr. Day, I do appreciate that you meant no harm in writing about the ambitions and achievements of colored people in Snipesville. But your articles in *The Snipesville News*, unfortunately, will have stirred envy and prejudice."

Alex was near tears now. "That's what Brandon and Mr. Hughes said. I'm sorry. I didn't know."

"Of course you didn't know, Mr. Day," Miss Julia said sympathetically. "It's madness. You have acted from the highest possible motives. And unlike your employer, you have been writing the truth for the newspaper, as you should."

Robert cleared his throat. "It cannot be helped now, Mr. Day," he said. "I do appreciate that you have been making a gesture of goodwill to the colored people of Snipesville. And this situation, I daresay, would have arisen eventually. As for now," and here he turned to the entire group in the parlor, "this is not the first time that colored folk have been attacked for appearing to rise above our place. We can only hope that calmer heads will prevail among Snipesville's leaders."

"You're expecting important white guys to step in and protect Thomas?" Brandon said. "Good luck with that."

Robert ignored him, and clasped his hands together. "There is something else standing between us and catastrophe. You see, we people of color are needed. Whether we are laboring in the cotton fields and turpentine camps, or repairing the cars of certain eminent men, we are needed. They dare not frighten us away. If any harm befalls Thomas," and here he glanced at Caroline, who looked away from him and shuddered, "they know there is a danger we will leave Snipes County for good."

But Brandon was slowly shaking his head. "You're right that they need us, Robert. We're their meal ticket. But that's still not enough to protect us."

Robert opened his mouth to reply, but now Miss Julia had something to say. "I have written a letter to Mrs. Lewis, my friend in England, to ask whether she could find refuge for Thomas and Caroline."

"Mrs. Lewis?" Eric said, and turned to Brandon. "That's not Mrs. Lewis who's Granny's friend, is it?"

"Her frenemy, you mean, Eric," said Brandon. "Yes. One and the same. Can you believe it? But, Miss Julia, why send Thomas and Caroline all the way to England? Why don't we just help them get to the North?"

"Because slavery ended a long time ago, and the North is no longer a refuge. The arm of Georgia law is long," Miss Julia said firmly. "If Thomas were captured in the North, he would be returned here. But in England, he and Caroline will surely have a sympathetic reception, for there is much concern among the English people about the plight of colored Americans. I cannot imagine that they would accept the forced return of Thomas to Georgia without protest. Mrs. Lewis has the means to draw sympathetic attention to this case, if such should prove necessary."

Brandon looked at her sadly. Miss Julia was clutching at straws. Thomas and Caroline's journey to England would not happen. He knew that. Or would it? With a sudden sense of purpose, he thought that maybe, just maybe, he could change the past, and make it happen. It was worth a try. If the foreboding feeling he had was right, he had nothing to lose.

"I'm sorry we're late," Eric said as he and Alex walked into the office of *The Snipesville News*. "We had a matter to attend to …"

But Mr. Hughes was not alone. "Powell, Day, I believe you know Sheriff Bragg?"

"I got some questions for you boys," said Sheriff Bragg. "You got a moment?"

There was to be an interview. Only this time, it wasn't Alex or Eric who were asking the questions.

When the Sheriff had left, Eric and Alex discussed his visit with their boss. "Like I told the Sheriff, Mr. Hughes," said Alex, "the bloodhounds he borrowed led him to Kintyre because they followed our scent from when we walked to Mr. McCabe's house to see the fire. I don't know why he finds that so hard to believe."

"You're ignoring the most likely explanation," Mr. Hughes said, "Sheriff Bragg is probably choosing what he will believe about you two, regardless of the evidence. You are strangers to this town, after all."

"That's ludicrous," Eric shouted. "Why does that make us automatically at fault?"

But Alex kept quiet. He knew better. He may have misjudged a lot of things, but he knew that Mr. Hughes was right about this. He also knew that he and Eric were in danger. Snipesville people said they welcomed strangers, but they really didn't. Alex knew that, because he had been one of those strangers in the 21st century.

Mr. Hughes continued. "*The Snipesville News* must make it clear where we stand," he said quietly. "This newspaper cannot be seen to have any sympathy with Negro criminals."

"But Thomas isn't a criminal," Eric said furiously. "He's no more a criminal than I am. I appreciate that you are trying to protect us, sir, but we cannot allow a gross miscarriage of justice. Mr. Hughes, I'm appealing to you as a fellow Englishman. Allowing an innocent man to be accused and convicted goes against our ideas of justice and fair play."

"We're a long way from home, Powell," said Mr. Hughes shortly. "A very long way indeed."

Eric wasn't giving up. "But surely, Mr. Hughes, this is not a question of popular opinion. It's a question of right and wrong."

"That's quite enough, Powell," Mr. Hughes growled. "Return to your duties.

CHAPTER FIFTEEN

Day, go to the jail, and see if you can interview Thomas Clark."

"But … but … you just said we're suspects …" Alex sputtered.

Mr. Hughes spoke over him. "After you get your interview, speak with the Sheriff, tell him you're there as a reporter, which you are, and ask him for the latest developments in the case. If he has any concerns, tell him to speak with me. You needn't look so worried. I'm the mayor, remember? The head banker. The newspaper publisher. I *am* this little town. Now, do as I say."

By the afternoon, small groups of white men had gathered on the courthouse lawn. Some stared at Alex as he walked by. He smiled and waved, but they did not respond. They appeared to be farmers, judging from their clothing, and they were outnumbered in Snipesville by the townspeople, who were, he reflected, quite modern. Townspeople had electricity, and plumbing, and telephones. They dressed better than the farmers, so that said something about how modern and progressive and educated they were. Unlike these farmers, he thought, the townsfolk of Snipesville had joined the 20th century. Maybe he shouldn't worry so much about what was happening.

Still, unnerved by the stares, he hurried toward the jail.

It was a nondescript building across the street from the bank, and next to the hotel. Trying to look confident, Alex climbed the steps, knocked on the heavy wooden front door, and asked the Jailer to let him interview Alex.

"Nope," said the Jailer, holding the door open, but not inviting Alex inside. "I can't let nobody talk to Clark without the Sheriff's say-so."

"But I told you," Alex said. "I'm with *The Snipesville News*. Mr. Hughes, you know, the Mayor, he said I should talk to Thomas, and …"

"I don't know about that," the Jailer said brusquely. "You get along now. I don't do nothing the Sheriff don't tell me. I'm just doing my job."

"So where do I find the Sheriff?" Alex said.

"In the courthouse," said the Jailer, pointing a finger across the street.

Alex really didn't want to speak to the Sheriff. He wasn't looking forward to another encounter with the law.

Alex did not knock at the Sheriff's office door, because, as a person of the twenty-first century, he assumed that he would be entering a reception area, and that a receptionist would greet him.

So he was not prepared for what he found when he walked in, which was that he was face to face with the Sheriff, and two other men. To his horror, Caroline Clark was slumped on a chair in the middle of the room, crying. "Caroline!" he blurted out.

CHAPTER FIFTEEN

Sheriff Bragg looked at him strangely. "You know this nigger?" he said, pointing to Caroline.

"No, I mean, yes, I know who Caroline is, but that word you used is wrong. What's going on?"

"What word?"

"That word you used," Alex said. "The "n" word."

The Sheriff drew himself up. "Don't you put on airs and graces with me, boy. You in a heap of trouble as it is. In fact, it's a good job you presented yourself here. You done saved me the trouble of arresting you."

Sharp knocking at the front door put everyone on edge. Brandon peeped out through the blinds, and relaxed when he saw Eric on the front porch. But as soon as he opened the door, his guts clenched again. Eric looked terrified.

"Caroline …" Eric said breathlessly. "She's under arrest."

"She was," Brandon said. "But she's home now. The Sheriff questioned her about the fire. He forced her to confess that Thomas started it."

"Brandon," Eric said hoarsely, following him inside. "The Sheriff has also arrested Alex."

Brandon spun around to face Eric, feeling nauseous. "What? Why?"

"He and I appeared on the scene, remember? On the night of the fire."

"I know, of course you were there," said Brandon. "You guys live close by the McCabe place, and you work for the newspaper." He put his head in his hands, and moaned, "This is crazy. We're making things worse, just being here."

Eric had more bad news. "The bloodhounds already led the Sheriff to the boardinghouse."

"Of course they did. That's not evidence of anything. Those dogs must have been following your trail to and from the scene of the fire."

Eric pressed on. "I know. But after Alex didn't come back to the office, the Sheriff told Mr. Hughes that the dogs found a shoe in the woods. It matches the prints in the dirt road, and the shoe fits Alex."

Miss Julia and Robert were standing in the hallway now, grimly listening to this conversation.

Brandon roared, "That's garbage, they're framing him!"

"Please let me finish!" Eric snapped. "Listen! The Sheriff must have frightened Caroline terribly, because she told him that Alex and Thomas *together* murdered McCabe."

Everyone in the hallway gasped, and then Eric dropped his final bombshell. "She also said that I was involved."

Miss Julia looked deeply shocked. "You, too, Mr. Powell?" she said.

CHAPTER FIFTEEN

"Yes. Mr. Hughes has given me a letter of introduction to help me escape, and he told me to leave town immediately." Eric's lip wobbled now. "But I have nowhere to go. I'm supposed to be at home in Balesworth with Granny and Verity, not trapped in a nightmare in America. Please, do something."

Eric looked so pale, Brandon was afraid he would faint.

As they stood in the cluttered attic of Jupe's house, Eric, who was short, could barely stand up in the middle, the highest point. Brandon said, "I'm sorry, this is the best we can do. We'll push all the junk to one end."

"Don't worry about that," said Eric, sounding calmer now. "It's fine. I'll be fine. Absolutely."

There was a strained pause in the conversation. Brandon could tell that Eric was panicking, but putting the bravest possible face on this desperate situation. "Anyway, it's very kind of old Mr. Gordon to allow me to stay." Eric said politely. "I'm afraid he's putting himself in great danger by having me here."

"That's all right," Jupe's gravelly voice called up from the foot of the ladder. "I'll do whatever you and your friend need, Brandon."

"Thanks, Mr. Gordon," Brandon said. And then he froze. How did old Jupe know his real name? He stepped over to the trapdoor, and looked down. Jupe nodded back at him. "I know who you and Alex Day are," he said quietly. "I always knew. You're a miracle, my miracle, come from Balesworth. Now, it's my time to help you."

Brandon looked down at him, and tried very hard not to cry.

For once, Brandon relished his anonymity. This afternoon, instead of trying to preserve his dignity by walking defiantly through downtown Snipesville with his head held high, he acted very differently. He walked slowly, his shoulders hunched, his arms flopping at his sides, his hat pulled low over his eyes, and a burlap bag hung across his shoulders. He was trying to look as unassuming and inconspicuous as possible. He had prepared several speeches for anyone who might try to get in his way. He hadn't told Miss Julia or Robert what he was doing. It was best, he thought, if they knew nothing, at least for now. He walked in the direction of the courthouse. And then he halted.

Dozens of white men were gathered now on the courthouse lawn at the foot of the new statue of the Confederate soldier. Farmers, their wagons and buggies parked nearby, formed much of the crowd, but now men in suits were also present, men who worked in town as clerks and managers. No one looked happy. They looked intimidating. Brandon, suddenly feeling a cold sweat, pretended to take an interest in the birds roosting in the oak tree on the courthouse lawn.

CHAPTER FIFTEEN

What he was actually doing was deciding what to do next.

Nobody paid him the slightest bit of attention. Judging from their raised voices, some of the men were angry about something, although not at each other. Brandon feared that he knew exactly why they were angry. He could see the jail, just down the street, next to the hotel. He stood up, put his hands in his pockets, and ambled along the dirt road, stepping aside to allow a couple of buggies to pass.

A small thin tree branch lay across his path, and he picked it up. He trailed it behind him in the dirt, to give the impression that he was not doing anything serious. Half a block away, the office door of *The Snipesville News* opened, and Mr. Hughes stepped out. Brandon pulled his hat lower, hunched a little, and continued to walk slowly. Mr. Hughes passed him on the boardwalk without giving him a second look.

It was amazing, Brandon thought, how little attention people pay to someone who acts unimportant. But how was he ever going to get inside the jail? Casually, he strolled up the alley between jail and hotel. There was a door in the side of the jail building, and, on impulse, he pulled on the handle. To his amazement, it opened. He slipped inside.

Thomas and Alex were caged behind bars in adjoining cells, but Brandon was not nearly so astonished to see them as they were to see him. Both of them jumped to their feet.

"Where's the jailer dude?" Brandon whispered. "Is anyone else here?" His stomach felt fluttery, and he was abuzz with adrenaline.

"He's out," said Alex. "And it's only him. His wife died last year, he said. There's no one else here. We only see him a couple of times a day when he comes to check on us."

"He got careless and left the side door unlocked," Brandon said. "Look, we have to get you guys out of here, before those men on the courthouse lawn decide to come in and get you."

"Why would they do that?" said Alex.

Thomas spoke up now. "George is right. We gotta get out of here as soon as we can."

"But how?" Alex said. "The cells are locked." He rattled his cell door to demonstrate.

"Does he keep any keys around?" said Brandon.

"If he did, you think we would know?" Alex said.

Brandon grabbed the bars of Thomas's cell. "I don't know how to cut the bars. Maybe you could, Thomas?"

CHAPTER FIFTEEN

"Of course, if you bring me tools."

"Like these?" Brandon said, pulling out two cloth-wrapped packages from his bag. He quickly revealed a short hacksaw and a small crowbar.

"Well, yes," said Thomas. "But I can't cut without making noise, and the Jailer will be back soon."

"Look, we're just gonna make things worse," Alex said anxiously. "Why don't we just wait for the trial?"

"Because there won't be a trial," said Brandon. "Listen, I have an idea, but first, I gotta run to the drugstore."

The Jailer brought them two bowls of beans, and shoved the first bowl through the meal slot in Alex's cell. Alex took it. Thomas, meanwhile, was lying on his bunk, and did not acknowledge the man's arrival.

"C'mon, boy," said the Jailer, not unkindly. "I got food for you. Come get it." Thomas groaned, and staggered to his feet, as though he were tired or sick.

"This would be a good time," he said loudly. It was a signal. Just as the Jailer shoved the bowl through the slot, Thomas suddenly did what appeared to be impossible: He punched one of the cell bars, and it magically fell away, allowing him to grab the Jailer's belt, and use the other hand to shove out another bar. In a split-second, he had wrapped both arms around the Jailer's thin waist, just as Brandon ran up from behind.

Jumping on the Jailer's back, Brandon put one arm around the man's shoulders to hang on, and with the other, held a folded cloth soaked with chloroform against the man's nose and mouth. Both Thomas and Brandon had the jailer in a bear hug, and within seconds, he had crumpled and fallen to the ground, taking Brandon with him.

"Ow," said Brandon, who had landed hard on the brick floor. As he stood, he looked at the unconscious Jailer next to him. "Sorry, man," he said.

Even as he said it, Thomas was already sawing fast at another bar.

They carried the Jailer to his bed, and, after liberally sprinkling him with some of his own whiskey, emptied the rest of the liquor down the sink, before placing the empty bottle next to the unconscious man. Brandon stood lookout at the side door, while Alex and Thomas slipped outside.

Ten minutes later, Alex and Brandon were out in the countryside, following Thomas southwest on a trail through the woods. "Where did you get the chloroform?" Alex said, pushing aside the tangled brush. "I mean, how did you even think of that?"

❖ 397 ❖

CHAPTER FIFTEEN

"I worked for a dentist in 1915, remember?" said Brandon. "I told Mr. Wheeler the pharmacist that Dr. Marshburn had sent me to get some. Lucky he had it in stock, or I would have had to try to get it from Marshburn himself, and that would have been really hard."

"Huh. I hope we're out of here before they find out you took it. Are we going to Miss Julia's?"

"Of course not," said Brandon. "That's the first place they'll look. We're going to Jupe's house for now."

"That's stupid," Alex said. "I mean, the Sheriff is going to know where we are. Jupe is Thomas's great-uncle, right?"

"I'm counting on the Sheriff to go to Kintyre first," Brandon said rapidly. "Robert is trying to spread the rumor that you're going to be walking with Eric to Clacton to take the train from there today. Thing is, you're not. You're going be hiding with Eric and Thomas in Jupe's attic. Robert is also going to help me get you guys over to Kintyre right after the Sheriff leaves. You'll hide there until he thinks you skipped town. That's when all five of us, you, me, Eric, Thomas, and Caroline, will make our way to Charleston, and try to catch a ship for England."

"That all sounds complicated and seriously dangerous," Alex said.

"Of course it's dangerous," Brandon said irritably. "We're desperate. Look, we'll talk about it some more when we get to Jupe's house."

But Alex was already thinking of something else. "What about the hounds? Won't the sheriff search Jupe's house? What about Caroline? I mean, how can she travel when she's pregnant? You can't think of everything, Brandon."

"Alex, please, enough questions," Brandon said. "I'm doing my best. That's all I can do. Come on, keep moving." Truth was, Brandon was terrified. In movies, plans like these always worked like clockwork. But this wasn't movies. It was real life. As they began to run through the woods, he prayed they weren't seen. He prayed for strength. He prayed for a different outcome than the one he knew was coming. He thought again of the poem the Professor had read to him, of the words of Matthew Arnold. He could hear her reciting in his head:

Foil'd by our fellow-men, depress'd, outworn,
We leave the brutal world to take its way ...

He wasn't going to be foiled by his fellow men if he could help it.

Monday, Late May, This Year:

Ellen Walker, Hannah and Alex's grandmother, was tempted several times to hang up on her bizarre internet conversation with these two elderly British strangers, George Braithwaite and Verity Powell. But she had stayed online because of the riveting story they were telling, the obvious sincerity with which they were telling it, and their accents. Ellen loved all things British. For her to believe their story, however, even in these accents, she would have to start believing in impossible things.

"I'm still trying to understand," she said. "Verity, what do you mean that you know now for sure that the past has changed?"

Verity said, "Last summer, Ellen, you and I met in England."

Ellen opened her mouth to say no, that was nonsense, that she had never met Verity in her life before now. But Verity continued. "I know it's unbelievable, Ellen, but please bear with me. When your grandchildren went to Victorian England, they altered something in Time, so that our meeting never occurred. That is why neither you nor I remember that meeting, Ellen, but the children do, and they told me about it. And something else in time has changed: George here has just learned that he had a strange experience as a teenager, in which he magically found himself here in Snipesville."

But Dr. Braithwaite was shaking his head. "No, Verity," he said quietly. "I didn't just learn about it. I have always known."

"What an extraordinary thing to keep to yourself all these years, George," Verity said.

"Of course I did," said Dr. Braithwaite. "Would you have believed me?"

Ellen cleared her throat. "Please, both of you, put yourselves in my position. How am I supposed to accept anything you've told me? Even if the children tell me it's true, they're only children. Do you have any proof?"

"I hoped it wouldn't come to this," said Dr. Braithwaite. "But there really is only one thing to do. Ellen, I would like you to meet Dr. Kate Harrower."

Now, George and Verity pushed back their chairs to allow a third face to crowd onto the screen in Snipesville. As Ellen was looking at George Braithwaite, he vanished. She heard a scream, and she wasn't sure if it came from Verity, herself, or both of them. In shock, Ellen now looked at the face of Professor Kate Harrower.

The Professor removed her glasses, and smiled at Ellen. Ellen felt her world change forever.

"Hello there, Ellen," said the Professor. "It's all right, ladies. Everything is happening the way it should. George will return, and normal service will resume momentarily."

"I'm on my way," gasped Ellen. The screen went dark.

Thursday, March 15, 1906

At Miss Julia's, Brandon could not rest. His mind was racing. The Jailer hadn't

CHAPTER FIFTEEN

seen him when he and Thomas attacked, and hopefully nobody remembered seeing him go into the jail, or recognized him when he did so. He thought of Thomas, Alex, and Eric in the cold, crowded attic of Jupe Gordon's house. The plan felt too easy, but really, Alex was right. It was too complicated. It depended too much on things happening a certain way. It depended, too, on the angry white people of Snipesville remaining calm for one more day, and how likely was that after the disappearance of the suspects in the death of William McCabe?

He needed to know what was going on downtown, whether the unconscious Jailer had been found, whether people were still gathering on the courthouse square. At first, Brandon hoped that Miss Alberta might spy for him. Nobody would suspect an old woman, and Brandon was sure that she would be willing to help. But even if she was willing, and if she witnessed an angry mob heading for West Snipesville, how could she send warning to him and the others? Miss Alberta was pretty fit for her age—whatever her age was—but it was a long walk to Miss Julia's from downtown, and she would never outpace the crowd. Maybe Robert could spy. But no. That would be too dangerous for him.

Brandon's mind was racing. *I can spy*, he thought. He was young, and nobody associated him with the death of Billy McCabe. If he went barefoot, and dressed in old clothes, and hung back in the shadows, surely he could spy? Nobody would recognize him. It had worked that afternoon ... *Wait, is Jupe's house really safe?*

It was that last thought that sent Brandon running out into the late afternoon, heading for Jupe's attic.

"We should go to Kintyre now," Brandon said to Alex, as Eric and Thomas napped nearby. They were in Jupe's cramped attic. "I bet the Sheriff already looked through there, because Eric and you were his first suspects. But now that Thomas is missing, he's gonna come look here eventually."

"Whoa," said Alex. "How do we know if they already searched Kintyre? Did Robert see anything?"

"No. I'll go to Kintyre and ask," said Brandon. "You know what? Caroline or Mrs. Hudgins might be there."

"Can you trust Mrs. Hudgins?"

"Right now, I don't trust many people," said Brandon, "but Mrs. Hudgins is Thomas's mother-in-law. I don't think she'll give us away. Come on, let's all of us just go."

"This is so dangerous," said Alex. "Look, you made yourself time travel to get to 1906, right? It wasn't the Professor?"

"Kind of," Brandon said.

"Then why don't you try and get us back to the 21st century?"

"I don't know if I can," said Brandon. "And even if I can, I won't."

Alex was stunned. "Why not?"

Brandon drew himself up. "Because I have a job to do."

Alex couldn't believe what he was hearing. "You mean the high school? You can't be serious …"

"No, not the high school," Brandon said.

"Then what?"

"I can't tell you."

"Fine," Alex said angrily. "Get us all killed."

Brandon did not reply.

As the sun was setting, Brandon led the little group into Kintyre, as an anxious Mrs. Hudgins watched. Brandon said, "You're sure the Sheriff didn't say anything about coming back?"

"He didn't say nothing about that," said Mrs. Hudgins. "But what do I do if he does?"

"Go home," said Brandon. "That way, you won't get caught up in this."

Mrs. Hudgins nodded to her son-in-law, and then, pulling a shawl over her shoulders, made her way out of the house. Brandon saw her face crumple with emotion as she brushed past him.

Now Brandon turned to Alex, Eric, and Thomas. "You guys go upstairs and stay quiet. I'm going back to Miss Julia's, to let Robert know what's going on. Get into the attic if you can, and stay upstairs if you can't."

The three men started up the narrow staircase. "Brandon, is it safe for you to go back to Miss Julia's?" Alex called back. "Will you be okay?"

"Of course it's not safe," snapped Brandon. "I told you before. There are no safe choices, or good decisions. I just have to do what I think best, that's what the Professor told me. And since I'm the only kid among us, and the Sheriff maybe doesn't suspect me yet, I can help get us out of Snipesville."

With that, he headed out into the evening. The sky was a blanket of clouds. His first destination was not Miss Julia Russell's, as he had said it would be. He was going to Mr. Hughes's house. He needed to plant some false rumors, to help throw the Sheriff off the trail.

"Eric Powell told me to tell you he's gone, sir," Brandon said, as soon as Mr. Hughes came out onto his front porch. "He left on foot."

"On foot?" Mr. Hughes exclaimed. "I told the fool to take the first train from

Snipesville. Do you know where he's planning to go? Is Mr. Day with him?"

"I don't know, sir," Brandon said.

But now Mr. Hughes was looking suspiciously at him. "Why would you come here and tell me this? You're the boy Robert Gordon introduced to me, the boy who claims to be from Balesworth."

Brandon nodded, afraid to say more.

Mr. Hughes looked hard at him. "Did my wife send you?"

It was a bizarre question, and Brandon was completely unprepared for it. He had to think fast. "I'm friends with your daughter," he said. "Elizabeth."

Judging from the alarmed look on Mr. Hughes' face, Brandon realized that his wild guess had hit the bullseye. Mr. Hughes was Mrs. Devenish's dad. *Wow.*

"What are you and your two white friends?" said Mr. Hughes. "Private detectives?"

Brandon gave him what he hoped was a sophisticated smile. "You could say that."

Mr. Hughes stood very still. "In that case, I suppose now you have what you came for. You have confirmed where I am, and what I'm doing, so now you may leave. Unless, of course, my wife also intends that you ruin my reputation."

"No, nothing like that," Brandon said, still bluffing, because he was still confused. "We just came to find out the, uh, the truth."

"As if my wife were any judge of the truth!" Mr. Hughes grew angry. "Let me tell you something, whoever you are. My wife never told me the truth about her family. She said only that her mother was an impoverished member of the aristocracy. Then my own investigator discovered she was the half-caste daughter of an Indian butler. But there was always something colored about her, and even as my daughters grew older, I could sense that there was something colored about them, too, especially Elizabeth. I see you knew this already. I'm warning you, *boy*. If you spread rumors, or tell anyone in Snipesville that I have another wife, a colored wife, in England, I will kill you. That is a promise. Snipesville is *my* town. These people look up to me. I control everything that happens here."

Brandon refused to be bullied by this desperate man. He stared back at him. "Do you, Mr. Hughes? You sure about that? I wonder if the white people round here know that this is your town. Did you tell them that you're the boss of them, you, an Englishman?"

Mr. Hughes stared at him again. "You will be gone by the end of the day, or else."

Brandon thought about asking what the "or else" was, but decided he would rather not know. It didn't matter, anyway. Throwing Mr. Hughes an angry look, he said, "I'm leaving, and your secret is safe with me, so long as you don't threaten me. Got that?"

"Are you blackmailing me?" Hughes growled.

"Call it what you like," said Brandon. "Just don't threaten me. And you better do what you can to get safe passage for my friends, too. Because I've already written to people in England and they will know if anything happens to us, it will be your fault."

Brandon was making it up, of course, but he noted with satisfaction that what he had said had the desired effect on Mr. Hughes. The self-important mayor, banker, newspaper publisher, and lawyer suddenly looked deeply afraid of a teenage boy.

Miss Julia had news for Brandon. "Robert is at the Sheriff's office now," she said. "He's spinning some story to mislead him. Don't worry, Robert is a clever young man, and held in some esteem among the leading white men."

But when Robert returned, he looked shaken. Sitting down on the sofa, he ran a finger around his collar. "It was probably unwise of me to go downtown. It is a very fraught and possibly dangerous scene. Many white people are gathered in front of the courthouse. They gave me hostile looks, and one man called me something I would rather not repeat, but he asserted that I am, um, *uppity*. I did speak with the Sheriff, and when he told me Thomas had escaped, I think I was able to feign innocence. Of course, he wanted to know if I knew anything about it, and I told him I did not. Apparently, the jailer was only discovered this evening, drunk in his bed. The good news is that the Sheriff is under the impression that Thomas and the others had a long head start in fleeing the county. He's putting all his energies into sounding the alarm in neighboring counties."

Miss Julia looked close to tears. "And after all our hopes for the school …"

"No, it is too soon to give up hope for our school," Robert said. "Aunt Julia, I spoke with Mr. Hughes, and I protested that this so-called Before Day Club is a figment of his imagination. He told me frankly that he is well aware of that fact, that it came from Dr. Hunslow, and that he will print a retraction."

"Robert, perhaps you ought to leave Snipesville, too," Miss Julia said, sniffing.

"I'll take the risk and stay," said Robert. "You are not in danger, and neither are the ministers, or others considered to be the better sort. Neither, I believe, am I. Thomas, I think, will be found to be guilty of having been in the wrong place, at the wrong time. No, the greatest danger is to those who are strangers to the community, and that includes you, George, despite your youth, because

CHAPTER FIFTEEN

although I did not accuse you, you are a stranger, and you are colored."

"Sometimes," said Miss Julia, clasping Brandon's hand, "all we can do is put our faith in God. Let us pray."

With that, she lowered her head and folded her hands. Brandon, Caroline, and Robert joined her.

Under cover of darkness, Robert drove Caroline and Brandon to Kintyre, watching out nervously for witnesses as they approached the old house. Once there, Thomas and Caroline greeted each other in tears. "I can't go with you," Caroline wept. "I'll slow you down." She ran a hand across her swollen belly.

Thomas just shook his head. "You stay here, stay with your mother. Wherever we go, I'll send for you once I'm settled. The family will look after you so long as you're in Snipesville."

"But I told the Sheriff you set the fire," she wailed. "He was going to hurt me and the baby."

Thomas's answer was to wrap her in his arms.

It was a heartbreaking scene, and Brandon felt terrible watching it. Thomas had done nothing wrong except to be a black man who showed a little ambition. That was his crime in Snipesville in 1906.

Brandon turned away to hide his tears, only to find Alex and Eric standing behind him, looking grave. "Look, you guys head upstairs and get some more sleep," he said, wiping his eyes. "We can take turns keeping watch. Robert is leaving Miss Julia's buggy out back, and hopefully we can all fit into it in the morning. We're leaving right at dawn." He didn't tell them that he had another role to play: That of spy.

Brandon could not believe what he was seeing. Hundreds of people, most of them men, and all of them white, were gathered under the electric lights on the courthouse square, their buggies and wagons parked randomly, the horses tethered to any available post. He had no idea that there were this many people in Snipes County. He made little attempt to hide, because he reckoned that hiding in plain sight was the safest thing to do. Still, he stayed well back from the action. Not that the crowd noticed him. They were gathered closely to where the Sheriff was making a speech on the steps of the Confederate soldier statue, saying things that Brandon could not hear. He recognized Mr. Duval from the hotel, standing blank-faced on the edge of the crowd. He also noticed the *CLOSED* signs in Mr. Wong's laundry window, and the offices of *The Snipesville News*. He watched as Mr. Wheeler shut the door of the pharmacy, and gingerly made his way to join the crowd.

Brandon really wished he could hear what the Sheriff was saying. But now he heard boos. Now he saw a man with a shotgun climb onto the statue steps, and order Sheriff Bragg to step aside. Brandon heard the armed man yell, "Never mind the Before Day Club. We're the All Night Club." The Sheriff moved away, his shoulders hunched in shame, and the crowd surged forward. The man with the gun started jabbing a finger westward, toward West Snipesville, and the black community. The whole crowd turned their heads to look.

There was no more time. Brandon was out of options. This was it. He ran.

He took a side street he knew well, toward where the BBQ joint would be one day, past the familiar row of stores, and as he ran, he tried to think of everyone and everything he loved, and wished them all a silent goodbye.

As he rejoined the main road, and turned to look back, Brandon saw them surging down the hill of West Main Street, buggies, wagons, and men on foot, kerosene lanterns bobbing like fireflies. They were moving fast, faster than he was. He ran, and ran. But every second that passed, they drew closer. His only chance was the falling darkness. He prayed he wouldn't trip on the road.

As Brandon ran into the yard at Kintyre, he started hollering to warn the others. He tried to grab the axe resting on the tree stump, but the handle separated from the axe head. He took the wooden handle anyway, and sprinted up the steps, hurling himself at the door. But then he realized that making all this noise probably made it more likely that the refugees would retreat to the attic. He needed them downstairs, or there would be no escape.

As Brandon entered the house, he tried shouting their names, but he was shaking so hard, he could barely make himself heard, or hang on to the axe handle. He heard the horses' hooves behind him, the wheels turning on the dusty road, and the audible yells and curses of the mob. He stopped, and turned, as the last light in the sky faded away.

Brandon returned to the open doorway, holding the axe handle, his only weapon. He was nauseous, breathing heavily, and trembling. Whenever he had imagined himself as the hero at this moment, he realized now, it had been like watching a movie. Now it all seemed terrifyingly real. Now the blazing kerosene lanterns were almost at the fence. Now, as he shifted from foot to foot, he heard someone in the mob laugh, and then just as suddenly the laugh was silenced. His nerve faltered then, and almost failed. He tried to remember what he had told himself all along: This had to be done. And he case he didn't have a chance to do it later, he commended his soul and those of the others to the care of God.

The crowd had started coming through the gate. He could see arms, legs, hats, even moustaches. And he started to recognize faces, and he was shocked by who they were. These were not just ignorant farmers. They were clerks, and shop assistants, and there was the dentist, Dr. Marshburn, and the doctor, Dr. Hunslow. There was Mr. Duval, hanging back, but present all the same. And at the very front of the mob was Charles Hughes, the Englishman, the Mayor of Snipesville. They were all headed toward him. Then they stopped halfway across the yard.

"Move out the way, boy!" cried a man carrying a gun. "You heard of the Before Day Club? Well this here's the All Night Club. You step aside, or you'll get a whipping."

Brandon still trembled, but he drew himself up, and as they advanced up the path, he stared right at them. He was no longer afraid. He was angry. The mob paused again.

Charles Hughes looked at Brandon, and Brandon looked at him. "He's only a lad," Mr. Hughes called over his shoulder, in a forced casual tone.

"He'll be grown soon enough," cried a voice.

"Teach him a lesson!" yelled another voice.

Brandon heard a gunshot, and flinched. Then he heard another, and in the same instant, felt intense pain as a bullet grazed his arm. When he looked, there was a smoking tear in his shirt, and blood.

"Dance for us, boy!" cried a voice, followed by laughter.

"Naw, he ain't worth the trouble," said another. "It's not him we want. It's Tom Clark we want. Where's that boy?"

Brandon, ignoring the burning pain in his arm, looked right at Mr. Hughes, and said loudly, "Is this what you want?"

Mr. Hughes looked away from him, and Brandon thought he saw shame, or maybe, he thought, he didn't. Now the crowd was pushing up the path, and onto the porch. Brandon swung his axe handle wildly, and to his amazement, connected with someone's jaw, felling the man where he stood. "You gonna pay for that boy," said a voice, but Brandon kept swinging, and hit someone else.

Then suddenly, he was pulled backward, the axe handle falling from his hands, and he was sitting on the floor, and someone else was now standing in the doorway. In an instant, he saw it was Thomas Clark. But who still had such a firm grip on his arm? He looked up and gasped. It was old Dr. George Braithwaite.

"No," Brandon screamed out, but it was too late. The mob was surging forward, and Thomas, fighting back hard, disappeared in a tangle of fists and arms and legs. Dr. Braithwaite held Brandon's arm tighter, and Brandon heard him yelling "Hang on …" The old man half-dragged him down the hall, just as Eric and Alex came downstairs.

CHAPTER FIFTEEN

"Who are you?" Eric said to Dr. Braithwaite.

"Never you mind," Dr. Braithwaite yelled. "All of you, hold onto me."

"What?" said Eric.

But Brandon knew. "Just do it!" he cried. Alex and Eric each grabbed one of Dr. Braithwaite's shoulders, as Brandon clung to his forearm.

Lurking in the kitchen doorway, Robert Gordon saw Alex, Brandon, Eric, and the strangely-dressed light-skinned stranger vanish before his eyes. A split-second later, he watched as Thomas collapsed in a heap in the doorway, kicked, punched, and surrounded by angry white men, who now started dragging him across the porch. Feeling his own knees threatening to give way, Robert stepped back into the shadows of the kitchen. Seizing Caroline Clark by the hand, he pulled her through the back door, and out into the inky darkness.

Monday Afternoon, Late May, This Year

Now, nothing. Only silence. Dr. Braithwaite was standing unsteadily in the middle of the living room, old Verity was sitting on a chair at the computer, and Brandon, Alex, and Eric were sprawled on the floor. Only the Professor appeared calm, and she was watching all their faces closely.

Eric was the first to speak. "Hello, where are we now? Granny, what are you …" He was looking at Verity. *He doesn't recognize her,* Alex realized with a start. *He thinks she's Mrs. Devenish.*

Verity knew, too, but she was so happy to see him, she didn't care. "Hello, darling," she said warmly, her eyes filling with tears.

"Gosh, now we must be in the future," Eric said in wonderment. "Because you look older than you do in 1951, if you don't mind my saying, Granny. When is this? The 1960s? Oh, and thanks for rescuing me, Mr …?"

"It's me, Eric," Dr. Braithwaite said gently. "It's George."

Eric looked from Dr. Braithwaite to Verity and back again. "But if you're George, then you must be …"

She gave him a watery smile. "Verity, yes."

"Blimey," said Eric, "You don't 'alf look like Granny."

"So I'm told," Verity said dryly.

Brandon was still lying on the floor, winded by the leap through time, but his arm was healed, and his clothing was back to normal. He scrambled to his feet, and, clenching his fists, glared at Dr. Braithwaite. "I was supposed to save Thomas's life," he yelled. "I was supposed to change things. You messed it up!"

"No, Brandon," Dr. Braithwaite said calmly. "I did what I was meant to do. It was Thomas's job to save *your* life. You weren't supposed to die. Tom saved you, by holding back the crowd. Your job was not to save him, but to get him to the house, to learn for yourself what it is to be willing to give up your life for another. When Thomas could no longer protect you, well, then it was up to me, because, had I not intervened, then, yes, you would have died. And this was never meant to be a suicide mission."

Brandon's shoulders sagged, and he began to cry, in huge heaving sobs. "I failed," were the only agonized words he could get out. Dr. Braithwaite put an arm around his shoulders, and gave him a reassuring shake. "No, you didn't," he said emphatically. "I know you think you did, but you didn't. Brandon, listen to me. This was meant to happen. And you are successful. You were successful on the very first occasion you traveled in time. You see, if you had not been kind to my guardian, Dr. Healdstone, when he was a child, nobody would have inspired him to adopt me, and I would not have been around to save you. It was your kindness to Uncle Arthur that made all the difference." And here Dr. Braithwaite had to pause to fight back tears of his own. "That chain of kindness began with you, Brandon. There you were, a young boy suddenly finding yourself in England in 1915, separated from your friends. Nobody would have blamed you if you had focused entirely on yourself and your own fears. But you didn't. You looked after a little lad who desperately needed attention. Nobody said you had to care, but you did. And it seems to me that this will be the story of the rest of your life, dear boy, because you are a man of character. You, Brandon, are perhaps the greatest hero of, what shall we call our strange tale? I know … You are the greatest hero of 'The Snipesville Chronicles.'" Brandon and Dr. Braithwaite locked eyes, and a look of compassion and understanding passed between them.

The Professor had been quiet through all of this, watching the scene with apparent detachment, but now she recited from Matthew Arnold's poem once more:

> *Foil'd by our fellow-men, depress'd, outworn,*
> *We leave the brutal world to take its way,*
> *And, Patience! in another life, we say*
> *The world shall be thrust down, and we up-borne.*

"What on earth does that mean?" said Verity.

"A lot," said Brandon, wiping his eyes. "It means a lot. Thank you, Professor." The Professor nodded.

Now Alex spoke up. "Dr. Braithwaite? Thank you for saving me, too," he said forlornly.

"And me," said Eric.

Dr. Braithwaite turned to them both. "Alex and Eric, I will say the same thing to you that I said to Brandon. You must know how much I am in debt

CHAPTER FIFTEEN

to you both. You came to my rescue, back in 1940, at great personal risk. You three, and Verity, and Hannah saved my childhood. I only wish I could think of how to repay the ladies."

"Don't be ridiculous, George," said Verity. "You've done that already. You have kept an eye out for all the kids this past year, including Hannah. And you have been my oldest, dearest friend, especially since Eric..." But then she stopped, and at that moment, everyone, including Eric, realized that her next word was to be "died."

Eric stepped forward, and took the old woman's hands. "I don't want to know anything else," he said firmly.

"I know you don't," said Verity. "Dear, dear Eric. How I miss you." She touched his face.

Unnoticed by the others, Kate Harrower gave Eric a long hard look. He vanished. Everyone gasped. "I returned him to 1951, to Balesworth," said the Professor.

"You sent him home, back to his beloved Granny, and to me," said Verity, her voice breaking slightly as she said it. "That's where he belongs, about to be married, and to make me very happy for the rest of my life."

The Professor sniffed, cleared her throat, and then said in a business-like voice, "I need to confirm what has changed in the story. Verity, when did you learn that the kids were time-travelers?"

Dabbing at her eyes with a tissue, Verity said, "Oh, in 1951. Eric and I knew because I traveled to 1905 with Hannah, and he went to 1906 with the boys."

Brandon, still hiccupping, stared at her. He was mystified. "I don't get it," he said. "Until you said something at Hunslow's coffee shop, you know, before I left, I thought you and Eric and Dr. Braithwaite only found out a few months ago that we were time travelers."

"That *was* the story," said the Professor, "but the story has indeed changed. Don't worry, though. It was meant to."

"Verity, if you time-traveled with Hannah," Alex said. "Where's Hannah?"

"Oh, don't worry about Hannah," the Professor said with a smile. "She's fine."

Chapter 16: THE TRUTH, BALESWORTH, 1951 AND SNIPESVILLE, THIS YEAR.

Sunday, May 27, 1951

Hannah awoke in her bed in Weston Cottage, not quite sure how she had got there from the Ickswade to Balesworth train in 1905. Jumping up, she quickly looked herself over in the mirror. She still appeared to be in her early twenties. Racing to Verity's room, she found her friend sitting up in bed. Verity stared at her blearily. "Hannah, I just had the most peculiar dream," she said, in a dazed voice. "But I'm not sure it was a dream …"

"It wasn't," said Hannah. "Sorry, Verity. I should lie to you and say it was, but you're my friend, and I won't lie."

Verity sat up straight and rubbed her face. "No, it wasn't a dream, was it? How absolutely barking mad."

Hannah hurried to Alex's room to see if her brother was there. But in the moment before she walked in, she heard Mrs. Devenish say to herself, "Elizabeth Devenish, you are a bloody fool."

Hannah pushed the door open, and said cheerfully, "I don't think you're a bloody fool at all, Mrs. D. I think you're awesome."

"Don't be impudent, Hannah Day," blustered Mrs. Devenish, trying to cover her embarrassment that Hannah had overheard her. She got to her feet. "And where on earth have you been? I thought you'd walked out."

CHAPTER SIXTEEN

"No, not yet," said Hannah with a grin. "You'll have to work a lot harder than that to get rid of me."

"Hannah," Mrs. Devenish said quietly, "I do want to apologize to you, for what I said. It was cruel and uncalled for, and …"

"And also true," Hannah said. "I won't accept your apology, Mrs. D., because it's not necessary. I'm grown up enough to understand that I'm not Verity, or Eric. I'm lucky to have known you at all. I shouldn't have expected you to give me more of your time and attention."

"I didn't really mind," Mrs. Devenish said quickly. "You just arrived at a difficult time, and that was hardly your fault."

"Do you want me to put the kettle on?" said Hannah.

Mrs. Devenish gave her a long, appraising look, and then she said briskly, "No, I shall make the tea. But you can keep me company in the kitchen if you wish. I would like that … very much." Then she coughed. "You know, I think we should bake scones. You like my scones, don't you?"

"I love them," said Hannah, putting a hand on the old woman's shoulder. Then she said, "I love you, too."

Mrs. Devenish looked slightly shocked. "Oh, now, you're being American. Stop it at once."

Hannah laughed, and followed her, saying, "Of course I'm being American. I *am* American. Hey, can I call you Granny?"

"If you must," Mrs. Devenish said with a heavy sigh.

As Hannah began to follow her downstairs, she heard *psst* behind her. She turned and saw Verity, standing in the doorway of her room. "Look, Hannah," she said quietly. "You just made her day by asking to call her Granny. And she's thrilled that you're here. But she'll *never* tell you these things herself. Do you understand?"

"No," said Hannah, "I'll never understand. But I do accept her the way she is. Will that do?"

"Of course it will," said Verity.

"Thanks," said Hannah. "Now maybe you can help me think of how to explain to her why Alex is missing."

Hannah found Mrs. Devenish pulling cold ingredients for scones from the larder shelves: butter, milk, an egg …

"Granny …" said Hannah, and then she felt silly for saying it. But she persisted. "Granny, I remember Mrs. Lewis talking about you being involved in the suffragettes."

"Not the suffragettes," Mrs. Devenish replied quickly, taking the ingredients to the kitchen table. "I was a suffragist."

"What exactly is the difference?"

Mrs. Devenish looked askance at her. "We didn't chuck stones through windows. They did." Hannah laughed. As Mrs. Devenish weighed flour on the kitchen scale, she said, "I told you about that when first you stayed with me during the War. But I only broke a window that once, and I was simply being a silly girl in a fit of pique at my mother. We never saw eye to eye on, well, anything, really. I was terrified that I would end up looking after her instead of having a life of my own. In the end, of course, I did live with her after I was widowed, but at least that was at a time when I could see it as my decision, and when, honestly, we both needed the company …"

"Is that the only reason you threw the brick?"

Mrs. Devenish said thoughtfully, "No. It's not. I did it also because I was overwhelmed by a great many responsibilities, far too many for a young woman. I made fun of what happened when I told you about it later, but at the time, I really was at my wits' end. And I aimed my cry for help at poor old Mrs. Lewis, whom I adored, and so it was all very foolish really."

Then she fell silent. Hannah felt moved and honored that Mrs. Devenish had told her something so personal. She asked quietly, even knowing the answer but hoping to learn more, "How is Mrs. Lewis these days?"

"Dead," said Mrs. Devenish. "She died late last year. None of us lasts forever—although she certainly tried. She lived to be 95. Women like her usually do. My mother was the same: She lived until 1933. By that time I had moved back here to Weston Cottage, and I brought her with me. The house in Ickswade was far too large for just the two of us, you see, because my daughters had both left home. Of course, I had no idea that only a few years later, I would be looking after Verity, and Eric, and you, and Alexander, and George, *and* Brandon. Having the extra room would have been useful during the War, I suppose, although we managed, didn't we?"

"You remembered Brandon's name," said Hannah. "That's pretty good when you hardly knew him."

"Yes, well, I consulted my diary," said Mrs. Devenish. "It reminds me of many things I might otherwise forget." She tossed spoons of soda and cream of tartar into the flour, and shook it through a sieve, tapping the side with her forefinger to speed it along.

As casually as she could, Hannah said, "That's what I don't get. You had your diary to remind you of me. Why did you pretend you didn't remember me? Why were you so angry at me?"

Without a moment's hesitation, Mrs. Devenish replied, "You never wrote."

CHAPTER SIXTEEN

Hannah's breath caught in her throat.

Mrs. Devenish continued gravely, "I invested a great deal of time and attention in you, Hannah Day, and you didn't bother to stay in touch. I never so much as received a thank-you letter from you."

So this was it. This was what had been bothering her all these years. It was so simple. But how could Hannah tell Mrs. Devenish the truth, that a minute after they had parted in 1940, she had returned to 21st century Snipesville?

"So you just thought I was rude?" she said slowly.

"Of course," Mrs. Devenish said, putting down the sieve.

Hannah took a deep breath. "Didn't you think, maybe, I *couldn't* contact you?"

Mrs. Devenish shook her head. "No. Why on earth would I think that? You know where I live. A letter to Weston Cottage, Balesworth, would have reached me, even from America. But I didn't get so much as a postcard."

There was no point in trying to tell Mrs. Devenish the truth, Hannah decided. She said quietly, "I'm really sorry I hurt you."

"Apology accepted," Mrs. Devenish said shortly. "Now let's carry on. Are you paying attention? You should. I'll wager you have forgotten how to make scones since you left England, and this is the best recipe I know. It was given to me years and years ago by our cook, Mrs. Morris. Here, finish sieving the dry ingredients."

"I've done some baking and cooking," Hannah said modestly, taking the sieve from her. "So you never became a suffragette?"

"No, I told you, I did not," said Mrs. Devenish. "But I must say I am sorry for it. I think the suffragettes were right, you see. All of Mrs. Lewis's resolutions and petitions amounted to little by themselves, but the WSPU's brave acts caught everyone's attention, and made us moderates appear reasonable. People now say women only earned the vote because we carried on the men's jobs during the First World War, but I don't doubt for a moment that the suffragettes' actions paved the way, keeping the question under everyone's noses. Even Mrs. Lewis admitted that to me in an unguarded moment.

"But by the time the suffragettes really went on the warpath, having themselves arrested for throwing bricks through shop windows, and then that poor Emily Wilding Davison woman throwing herself under the King's horse at the Derby, and … well, by that time, I was married with a baby. It wasn't the best time for me to gallivant around the country breaking the law. In any event, the suffragettes were braver than I was. I didn't have their sort of courage. I did write letters to the government demanding an end to forcible feeding, and the release of suffragettes from prison. But that was too little. I ought to have done more."

CHAPTER SIXTEEN

And then she said hesitantly, "I hope you're not disappointed in me, Hannah. I'm afraid that, like most people, I have never been at the center of history. I lack imagination, you see. I am a very practical person, not a leader. Oh, but I do know Annie Kenney, if that impresses you. You know who she is? She was of course a famous suffragette, but these days, she's a very old lady living in Letchworth. My friend Millie Cooke introduced me to her. Poor Millie. She died, you know. In 1944. During the war. She was in a Woolworth's in south London that was hit by a V-2 rocket. Those dreadful things traveled silently. The poor people in the shop never stood a chance. Nearly two hundred died, and Millie was simply one of them. I don't know what she was doing in South London, because she worked at the Women's Voluntary Service headquarters in Westminster, and she lived in Kensington. Perhaps she was visiting people who had been bombed out of their houses, and perhaps she remembered needing something for herself, and so off she went to Woolworth's …" Mrs. Devenish had a distant look in her eyes, and now she fell silent, and stared into space.

"I am so sorry about your friend," Hannah said quietly, deeply saddened to know what became of the chatty, energetic, fun Millie, and sad also for Mrs. Devenish having experienced yet another loss. "But of course I'm not disappointed in you. Who decides what the center of history is? And I don't think it's true that you don't have courage. I think you're very clever and very brave."

"That's kind of you to say, but you only think that because you first met me in 1940, when I was in the prime of life," said Mrs. Devenish, as she cut a blob of white lard into lumps, and dropped them into the flour. "I was much less fearful as a mature woman than I was in my early youth. The First World War changed everything, you see. After losing poor Tom, my husband, and so young, life held few fears for me. Here, rub the fat into the flour. Like this, you see? Fingertips only. Your palms are too warm, Hannah, and they'll melt the fat, which is no good … That's the ticket. Don't be afraid of it. Keep finding the large lumps, and keep rubbing until the mixture looks like coarse breadcrumbs. My goodness, you do have the hang of it, don't you?"

Hannah had used this mixing technique so often before, but she didn't tell Mrs. Devenish. She didn't want to spoil the lesson. She felt the fine flour and lightly sticky lard flowing through her fingers as she gradually blended the dough. It was a very comforting feeling.

"There is something strange I remember, though, that might amuse you," said Mrs. Devenish, picking up the glass bottle of milk. "I never have understood it. When I threw that brick through my mother's front window, it was three years before the suffragettes began their violent campaign. I had the idea from a little maid we employed for a short time, a girl called May. She told me that Mrs. Pankhurst and her colleagues were breaking windows in protest. But they weren't, you see, not for several more years. That was what I have never understood. How on earth did that girl get the idea that they were throwing stones?"

"Maybe the maid knew something you didn't," said Hannah with a smile.

"Perhaps," Mrs. Devenish said uncertainly. "Now here, add the milk … No, no, Hannah, not all of it, just a little at a time. You want your dough to be soft and light, not too sticky. Mix it with your hand."

"Ugh," said Hannah, as sticky dough stuck to her fingers and got under her fingernails. "I hate this bit."

"Don't fuss, Hannah. Just keep stirring. No, don't squash the dough like that, you'll make it as tough as old boots. There, lightly. Just like that. Good. Do you see how the mixture is coming together? If the dough looks ragged, add the tiniest splash of milk, but otherwise, leave well alone. Now, gather it up with your hand … Well done."

"I bet you're grateful to that maid," Hannah said, forming the dough into a ball. "She made you into a suffragette pioneer."

"Don't talk nonsense, Hannah Day," Mrs. Devenish said. "She gave me the idea to throw the brick, which got me into the most awful row with my mother and Mrs. Lewis, that's what she did. She was a clever girl, though. If it hadn't been for her, I would never have mended fences with Mrs. Lewis, or befriended Millie Cooke … or my husband. I was sorry when May left us. We had become friends, you see. Well, as much as one could become friends with a servant. Those were very divided times, Hannah, quite the opposite of how things have been since the last war. I suppose that is why I took such an interest in helping you, because, strangely, you are the spitting image of May Harrower. And because, if I am to be truthful, you reminded me of myself as a young girl. But my goodness, it is all such a long time ago. Working-class and middle-class people, we all knew our places in those days. Quite dreadful, really, thinking of everyone having a place. When all is said and done, we are all people."

"We are indeed, Mrs. … Granny," said Hannah, dropping the dough onto the floured work surface, and patting it gently until it was about an inch deep, as she had seen Mrs. Devenish and Mrs. Morris do so many times before. She grabbed the cutter, and started stamping out rounds.

"Very good, Hannah," said Mrs. Devenish. "I'll write down the recipe for you. You're ready to make them by yourself. You will make scones in America, I suppose?"

"Yes, I will," said Hannah, and then she put an arm around Mrs. Devenish and leaned against her. Mrs. Devenish returned her awkward side-hug.

CHAPTER SIXTEEN

Wednesday, May 29, 1951

Strolling up Balesworth High Street, Hannah wondered vaguely if she should get herself back to 21st century Snipesville. But then she thought better of it. She knew she wasn't ready to time-travel solo. And anyway, she wasn't in a hurry to go home, not knowing what she knew now. She was also asking herself if she should, in fact, go back at all. Ever. Why not stay here in England, in 1951? Mrs. Devenish had offered her a place to live, provided she got a job and paid rent. She liked that idea even more than the thought of going back to 1940 as her real age. Perhaps she could work in a café, or a restaurant. Maybe she could do some traveling.

But if she didn't go back to Snipesville in the 21st century, ever, what would happen to Alex? He would be devastated. And so would her grandparents. She supposed her dad would miss her, even if he barely noticed she existed anymore ….

I can go back to the present day whenever I want and I will still appear to be the same age as when I left. If I want, I could stay in England for decades, she thought. But how would it feel to return home as a teenager on the outside and a middle-aged woman on the inside? Just as she pondered this, Hannah was startled by the touch of a hand on her shoulder.

"How about I buy you a cup of tea?" said the Professor, taking her by the arm.

"Oh, no," said Hannah, suddenly afraid. "You've come to take me away, haven't you? I won't see Verity and Granny … I mean, Mrs. D. … again, right?"

The Professor smiled. "I know you call her Granny now. Don't be embarrassed. It's very sweet, and it makes both of you happy. And why are you worried? You know how to travel in time now. You can see them all again as much as you like, and as your own age if you prefer. Well, within reason, but we can discuss that in due course. For now, though, you do need to come home, but why don't you let me buy you tea first?"

With that, she steered Hannah down a side street, and toward a building that Hannah knew so well. It bore a now-faded sign that read *The Tudor Tea Rooms*. "This is the first place that Brandon and Alex and I ate when we arrived in 1940," said Hannah. "And I came here with Mrs. D. in 1905."

"I know," said the Professor. "But it hasn't been continuously in operation. That's a mistake historians try not to make, to assume that just because something seems not to have changed, it hasn't. You see, the original tea room you visited in 1905 went out of business in 1910, and went back to being cottages in which people lived. It reopened under the same name in 1928, with a new owner, and then it changed hands and went downhill for a while. It survived the War, as you see, but it won't be here in the 21st century.

CHAPTER SIXTEEN

"Oh, the building will be all right, don't worry, it's from the 14th century and people do care about it, at least for now. But the tea room is just a temporary tenant, like everyone and everything in the world, I suppose. In the Fifties and Sixties, Italian coffee houses and burger bars were all the rage, and tea rooms become unfashionable. Some tea rooms managed to hang on, serving an increasingly elderly clientele, but The Tudor Tea Rooms isn't one of them. It will change its name to The Copper Kettle in 1960, and it will finally close its doors in 1962. The building will house an antiques shop in the Sixties, an artists' supply shop in the 1970s, then a toy store, then a real estate agency. After that, in 2010, it becomes a coffeehouse, called Balesworth Brews …"

"I know," said Hannah. "I saw it."

"Ah, but did you know that, later," said the Professor, "it becomes a tea room again?"

"What do you mean later? You mean in the future? How do you know that?"

"Past, present, future, it's all relative," said the Professor. "All about moving around in the same big room. Come on. Let's get tea."

With a clatter, Hannah replaced her teacup on its saucer, and murmured, "She is so grumpy, and so difficult. I should hate her."

Hannah eyed the three-level cake stand loaded with scones, shortbread fingers, little triangular egg and cress sandwiches curling at the edges, and a rather dry-looking slice of Victoria Sponge with a microscopic layer of jam in the middle.

The Professor grunted. "You're talking about Mrs. D. Yes, you always come back to her, don't you? Look, if you want to understand her, it's mostly about her historical context. She's a product of her times. She's basically a Victorian, and yet she's also one of the first modern women, eager to look to the future. You always understood this about her, I think, on some level. But do know that if she had lived in your time, she wouldn't have been quite the same person."

"I've thought about that too," said Hannah. "I mean, I wasn't the same me in 1851 or in 1752 or even in 1940. I mean, I was still me … but … you get it, don't you?"

"Of course," said the Professor. "You're a cultural chameleon, but you're saying that even though you change on your travels, you're still you, deep down inside. And the same would be true, I think, of Mrs. Devenish. I would like to think that some things about her would be the same, no matter when or where she lived. She would always be complicated but lovable."

Hannah couldn't help but laugh. "Complicated, anyway."

"Oh, come on," said the Professor. "What about 1940, when she took in you

CHAPTER SIXTEEN

and Alex, when you showed up on her doorstep in the middle of the night? That night, you learned something you already suspected. She wasn't just an angry old harridan, was she?"

"No," said Hannah quickly, "I never really thought she was. Not even when she spanked me. I mean, you helped me understand that about her. No matter what, she's never told me I'm a bad person, or talked to me like I'm an idiot. She makes me feel like I'm worth making an effort for." And here, Hannah's chin wobbled. "She makes me feel like I'm worth something."

"Well, you are worth something," said the Professor. "And difficult people typically are the best people. We—I mean, Mrs. D., and you, and me, because I include myself in this—we aren't easy to deal with. But we have lots of integrity, lots of decency about us. Some psychology professors studied us. They discovered that nice people, who aren't at all difficult, are much more likely to go along with inflicting real harm on others. Difficult people, on the other hand, stand up for others, even though we can be a bit of a nightmare to know."

"That's a perfect description of Mrs. D.," said Hannah, and she sipped her tea.

"It's also a perfect description of you," said the Professor. "That's a good thing, truly. You take risks, Hannah. You stood up for George Braithwaite in 1940, and for the people of Dundee in 1851, and for your friend Jane in 1752. But, darling, wherever did you get the idea that you're worthless?"

"I never said that," Hannah protested halfheartedly.

"No, I know you didn't say it," said the Professor firmly. "But you absolutely think it."

Hannah did not reply. So the Professor said it for her. "You do stupid things and annoy people? Is that what you're worried about? Of course you do. Anyone good enough or brave enough to take risks does stupid things. But the only stupid thing you absolutely should not do is trust someone—anyone—who makes you feel worthless, even when they think they're being kind to you, because someone who pities you is not your friend. You're not worthless, Hannah Dias. In fact, you are splendid."

Hannah gave her a watery smile. "Thank you," she said.. "I feel like you just wrapped me in the best hug of my whole life. Or maybe second-best, after what Mrs. Lewis said to Mrs. D. in 1906."

"Well, thank you. I don't mind second place. That was quite a speech Mrs. Lewis gave that day, wasn't it? I hope you'll write it down for yourself, so that you remember it. Words, used carefully and sometimes sparingly, give the best hugs of all. That's something Mrs. Devenish knows, too. She understands love, and what it is, and how best to express it. Not that she always gets it right, but

CHAPTER SIXTEEN

who does?"

There was a pause, while Hannah ate half a buttered scone, and thought. Then she said, "I don't get something. How come practically everyone involved in this time travel thing is related to everybody else, except Dr. Braithwaite, Mrs. Lewis, and you?"

"Interesting, isn't it?" said the Professor. "Mrs. Lewis isn't related to anyone, but she's practically a member of the family. She's a huge influence, even on you."

"How?" said Hannah. "I mean, I hardly knew her."

"Oh, I think you know. She influenced Mrs. D., and Mrs. D influenced you," said the Professor. "I suppose I ought to use that word *mentored*, but I can't stand it. Anyway, I'm not sure that mentoring is quite the right word to apply to you and Mrs. Devenish. Or Mrs. Lewis." She laughed.

"Good point," Hannah said, with a giggle. "More like warfare, really." Hannah realized that now, when the Professor was relaxed and smiling, was the right time to blindside her with a question. And this time, she would not let her avoid answering. Her smile fell away, she looked directly into the Professor's eyes, and she said, "How do you know what Mrs. Lewis said to Mrs. D. that day?"

"Ah," said the Professor. She drummed her fingers on the table. "I could tell you I was eavesdropping, but you wouldn't believe me, would you?"

"No, I wouldn't," said Hannah.

The Professor exhaled loudly. "Right. Hannah, what I'm about to tell you ... Well, Verity already knows, because I told her everything in 1905. But it's now the time to tell you."

"Tell me what?" said Hannah, suddenly feeling tense.

"Hannah," said the Professor. "Look at me."

"Yes," said Hannah, looking her up and down.

The Professor tried again. "No, really. Look at me."

So Hannah did. And saw for the first time what she should have seen all along. Without a sound, she slid down in her chair, and only just stopped herself in time from slithering onto the floor.

Verity was sitting on the wooden bench in Mrs. Devenish's garden, reading, when she saw Hannah, and she put her book down in her lap. "Are you all right?" she said. "You look out of sorts."

Hannah nervously licked her lips. "Kate told me the truth," she said shakily.

Verity gave Hannah a sympathetic smile, and held out her hand to her. "Yes, well, I can imagine you're rather rattled by it," she said, as Hannah sat down

❖ 419 ❖

CHAPTER SIXTEEN

with her. "It should take some getting used to, I'm sure, just as this entire peculiar episode is requiring me to rethink everything I thought I knew. But don't worry about me. That was an extraordinary adventure, and I loved almost every minute."

Hannah watched a honeybee hover for a moment by the arm of the sun-bleached old bench, inhaled the smell of cut grass, and listened to the call of a woodpigeon, the sound that always told her she was in England. She looked at Verity, and saw her for the first time, too, as the same soul she had been as a little girl, and who she would be as an old woman. Verity wasn't the easiest of people to know, but then, Hannah thought, what does that matter? *I'm not an easy person either. So what?*

Verity said, "I've come to a firm decision."

"A decision?" said Hannah. "About what?"

"Whether or not I should marry Eric," Verity replied. "As you know, Granny thinks we should wait a little longer, Mummy doesn't think he's good enough for me, and my university friends think me mad."

Hannah would once have said, "But of course you should marry Eric!" But now, she wasn't sure. She thought of Verity's daughter, whom she had yet to meet, but who seemed to be a good person, and Verity's son, whom she had met, and who was awful. She didn't know, honestly, whether the marriage was a good thing or a bad thing for Verity and Eric. She said only, "So what did you decide?"

As soon as she asked the question, she felt her eyes close.

Monday Evening, Late May, This Year

When, with a start, Hannah opened her eyes, she found herself still sitting across from Verity, but on a sofa, indoors. They were alone. And Verity was now a very old woman.

"You finally woke up," Verity said gently, taking her hand. "I saw you fall asleep in 1951, suddenly, before my eyes, and before I had a chance to answer your question, you faded away, like a ghost. Welcome back, Hannah. You're in George Braithwaite's living room. Yes, I did marry Eric, and it was the right thing to do. The only other person I was ever tempted to marry was George Braithwaite, but, well, George isn't the marrying sort. But Eric was. He was sensible and kind. He believed that women and men are equals. And we looked after each other. I was proud to be his wife."

Hannah smiled sleepily. "I'm glad you married Eric ... I'm glad you were happy. I just wish I was."

"And why are you unhappy, my dear Hannah? The time travel must be very difficult."

Hannah swallowed and sniffed. "It is, but that's not the problem. This place, Snipesville, this is my real life. I'm stuck in a town that's all about some weird version of the past. I don't belong here. I belong with you guys in 1940, even though you didn't really want me," and suddenly she said with a sob, "Being with you and Granny was the only good time of my whole life. I was so happy with you."

"Hannah, stop it," Verity said firmly. "Please. We did want you, but, my goodness, what about your own family?"

"My mother died," said Hannah, forcing herself to speak through tears. "Not long … not long before I came to Balesworth the first time."

"I know, dear. Granny told me later. I am so sorry."

In a small voice, Hannah said, "But I didn't tell Mrs. D. … Granny … I didn't tell her everything. I couldn't tell her. I couldn't do it. But I want to tell you."

"Tell me what, darling?"

"She left," Hannah blurted out, her face crumpling. She was saying it aloud for the very first time, gasping for breath between sentences. "My mother left us … My mom left us … She didn't want to see us anymore, not my dad, not Alex, and most of all, not me. She never liked me. Not ever."

Verity laid a hand on Hannah's arm. "Oh, Hannah, surely not … Kate never said anything about this."

"She probably didn't want to. My mom told me she didn't leave because she was seeing someone else, she was just tired of us. She was tired of me. She said I was the worst thing that ever happened to her. Then she died." Now Hannah began to speak rapidly, as everything poured out. "Then we moved to Snipesville. My dad doesn't care what we do. I try to look after Alex, but I can't always be there for him. I only have two friends, Brandon and this girl Tara at school. All the other people we know hate us. I want to go home, but I don't even know where that is." Her voice rose at the end of this frantic outpouring, and she put her face in her hands, and then she broke down completely in great sobs, just as she had on the night that she and her brother had arrived on Mrs. Devenish's doorstep.

"Oh, no," said Verity, holding out her arms, "Oh, Hannah, come here."

As Verity held a sobbing Hannah, she said, "Oh, now it all makes sense, you poor little thing. I cannot imagine. You must be so bruised. No wonder you loved Granny so much. And no wonder Elizabeth confided in you. You're kindred spirits, Granny and you."

Hannah couldn't talk. She could only howl. And as she did, she felt herself let go.

CHAPTER SIXTEEN

Monday Evening, Late May, This Year

Ben Hunslow was worried. Only two days since Snipesville State College's graduation, and already most students and faculty had cleared out of town. Hunslow's Sippin' Snipe was quiet, even by the standards of a Monday evening. The house-made pizza special had drawn few takers, and Ben wondered if Hunslow's Sippin' Snipe would make it through the summer. There was talk, though, of the college becoming a university, and how it would grow … He hoped so. He liked how Snipesville was changing. If the business failed, he would have to move back to Atlanta, and he didn't want to. Atlanta was fun, but Snipesville was home. He wanted to see it do better. Maybe, he thought, he should try harder to make the café a community center, maybe encourage more people to hold meetings here, or just come play board games. That was an idea.

Tonight, Ben's only customers were old Dr. Braithwaite, his elderly white lady friend from England, and three kids. They weren't exactly the exciting, sophisticated, worldly people whom Ben had hoped to attract to his establishment. But at least they were customers, and he was learning to love his customers.

An empty pizza pan sat on the coffee table, a solitary mushroom slice lying upon it. Verity was sitting on the coffeehouse's lumpy sofa. She was holding Hannah's and Brandon's hands, and Hannah was leaning against her shoulder. Hannah had not left her side in hours. Alex sat slumped next to Brandon.

"I should take all of you to hospital," Dr. Braithwaite said quietly, "but I fear we would be subjected to lengthy psychiatric examinations."

"No need for that," Verity said firmly. "Just rest and love. That's what all of them need." She looked down at Hannah, and then at Brandon and Alex. Hannah didn't argue. She didn't feel like talking, or doing much of anything. She just wanted to be looked after, for now. She leaned over Verity and touched Brandon's arm. "You okay?"

"I guess," he said. "Just lucky to be alive. I made a mess of things."

Dr. Braithwaite gave him a stern look. "Now, Brandon, stop that at once. As I keep telling you, you didn't. Listen:

> *If you can meet with Triumph and Disaster*
> *And treat those two impostors just the same*
> *Then you'll be a Man, my son.*

I'm paraphrasing Kipling, but you get the idea."

"The Professor quoted him at me, too," Brandon said. "Look, I understand how triumph was an impostor, but face it, Dr. Braithwaite, sometimes a disaster is just a disaster."

CHAPTER SIXTEEN

Dr. Braithwaite gave him a small smile. "Go look out the window, Brandon," he said. "Look across the street."

Brandon got up, and wandered across the café. Looking outside, he saw the huge mural painted on the building opposite. He knew it, of course, because it had been there since the year he was born. It was fading and chipping off the bricks these days, but at the center of the mural was a middle-aged Robert Gordon, sitting proudly on a chair, holding his walking stick, and surrounded by children and teens, not only black kids, but white, Latino, and Asian, too. Robert Gordon was the symbol of education, of hope, in Snipesville. Brandon choked back tears, and wiped his eyes. He also wondered, just for a moment, why Miss Julia was not also in the mural.

"I think it's time," said Dr. Braithwaite, "that we talked about *We Don't Talk About That.*"

"What?" said Hannah, puzzled. "I don't even know what that means."

"Listen and learn, Hannah," said Dr. Braithwaite. "I wasn't entirely truthful with you, Brandon. I have done a fair amount of reading on what happened in 1906. In that year, tempers were rising here and throughout the South. There was now a generation of black folk with no memory of slavery, who were keen to rise in society. But the more successful and accomplished they were, the more hostile whites became to their success. The Georgia Equal Rights meeting that you attended in Macon, Brandon, was everything that whites feared: Educated black people met to demand that they be treated as equals.

"But even humble Thomas, who took no part in politics, inspired envy and hatred because he started an enterprise that promised to make him a thriving businessman. The race for Georgia governor in 1906 focused on two candidates, each trying to be more racist than the other, to appeal to whites' fears and jealousy. They promised to take away votes from black men, to put blacks in their place. And their speeches, with their heated and hate-filled words, were published throughout Georgia, including in *The Snipesville News*. Now, what happened in Snipesville was dreadful, but what happened in Atlanta was even worse."

Brandon goggled at him in amazement. "The Atlanta Race Riot!" he exclaimed, and he took up the story for his friends. "It was in 1906! How could I have forgot that? I just never kind of connected it."

"When people hear about the Atlanta Race Riot now," said Dr. Braithwaite, "They sometimes assume it was black people who were rioting and looting. But that wasn't it at all. White mobs rampaged through Atlanta, attacking and killing innocent black people. It was a massacre. We don't even know how many people were killed."

CHAPTER SIXTEEN

Brandon nodded. "When I was in Atlanta, it was kind of obvious that something was gonna go down. And what you said, Dr. Braithwaite, about whites feeling threatened by black people? I ate at a café in Atlanta, and the owner's daughter was telling me that the white guy who owned the café across the street was unhappy about them competing with him."

"What was the café owner's name?" asked Dr. Braithwaite, frowning.

"Miss Mattie Adams," Brandon replied promptly.

"I was afraid you would say that," said Dr. Braithwaite. "Mrs. Adams's home and business were attacked and destroyed during the Race Riot. Rioters broke a wagon wheel spoke over Mrs. Adams's head, and hit her with a glass pitcher. The rioters also entertained themselves by smashing up the furniture, and shooting bullets around her grandson."

"Those filthy, evil ..." Brandon seethed

"Ah, but hear this," said Dr. Braithwaite, "Mrs. Adams and her daughter recognized the son of the white café owner in the mob, and they pressed charges against him. You see, stories don't just end, Brandon. And often people don't know how they begin. As you know, but most people don't, before there was a rampaging white mob in Atlanta, there was one in Snipesville. And just as in Atlanta, it wasn't merely a bunch of poor people who rioted. Alex, remember you said you were surprised by all those white men in suits in Snipesville, the bank clerks, and the salesmen, and so forth? They were all there that day, weren't they? The mob who killed Thomas included young people who had escaped from the farm, who had found office jobs in a rapidly-growing Snipesville. And among their leaders were powerful whites, who saw rising blacks as a threat. That was why all of them were so ready to believe that the death of a farmer in a house fire was a deliberate act, and that it was the fault of black people."

"But I'm not black," said Alex. "Neither's Eric."

"Quite true, Alex, but you were in terrible danger."

Everyone looked surprised by that, and Dr. Braithwaite explained. "The mob made no attempt to attack Miss Julia or Robert Gordon, despite their being black and supporting a new high school, because they were respected members of the community. But if Alex or Eric had fallen into the mob's hands, I dread to think what would have happened. You were outsiders, and you were whites who supported black equality, which made you traitors in their eyes. That was enough to put your lives in jeopardy.

"Now, don't think that what happened that day ended with Thomas's death. In the hours after he was killed, the mob rampaged through Snipes County, attacking black people and property. They whipped a poor woman they dragged from her home, and shot and killed an elderly man and his son as they sat on their porch. By the next morning, the mob had dispersed, but how could the black folk of Snipes County know that the calm would last? Of course they couldn't. That very next day, they began to leave Snipes County in droves, headed for the North."

"Isn't that what the whites wanted?" said Hannah.

"Good Lord, no," said Dr. Braithwaite. "They just wanted them to know their place, to do the lowly jobs that white people wouldn't do. They wanted them to work in cotton, and turpentine, and as servants. After the riot, when black folk began packing up and leaving, Charles Hughes and the other city leaders saw they had made a dreadful mistake. Who would buy or rent the houses that Hughes planned to build and profit from in Snipesville? Who would do the essential but low-paid work? Hughes approached Reverend Evans and Robert Gordon, and begged them to use their influence to persuade people to stay."

"Why didn't he talk to Miss Julia?" said Brandon. "She had a ton of influence."

"I don't doubt you, Brandon, but your Miss Julia was a woman, and in 1906, I would guess that even Miss Julia wasn't considered a leader by a man like Charles Hughes."

Brandon looked perplexed. "So what did Robert say to get people to stay? And why would he even do that?"

Dr. Braithwaite smiled. "He was an optimist, remember? And he was clever about it. He told Mr. Hughes that if powerful and wealthy whites helped to build the colored high school, and promised that there would be no more violence, then black community leaders would try to get people to remain. That same day, money was arranged, including a loan from the Bank of Snipesville, and a large donation from Mr. Hughes himself."

"So, Dr. Braithwaite, you're saying that what Robert did worked?" Brandon said. "He and Miss Julia got the high school started?"

"Of course," said Dr. Braithwaite. "You always knew that. You just didn't know how he managed it. And getting it started was only the beginning. The school would have failed if Robert hadn't been a very astute man. He didn't rely on the continued help of local whites, because he knew there was no goodwill there. He also wasn't sure he wanted to depend on Booker T. Washington, because money from Tuskegee always came with strings attached. And anyway, Washington died in 1915. By then, Robert Gordon had appealed directly to wealthy people like Julius Rosenwald. He was a white Jewish fellow, and the founder of the Sears, Roebuck company, which was the nineteenth century version of online shopping. He gave money to create thousands of schools for black kids in the South."

"I guess Robert didn't need the money I raised, then," said Brandon, looking downcast.

"Rubbish," said Dr. Braithwaite. "He needed every penny. Rosenwald's Foundation would only give money to communities that had already raised a fair bit of money themselves.

"Now, Robert Gordon certainly spoke of the "industrial" part of education to his Northern benefactors, but meanwhile, he was up to some quite radical things. He offered plenty of arts programs to students, and he even forged a relationship with a later president of Snipesville State, a white Southern man who was mostly educated outside the South. The two of them quietly arranged for black university faculty to visit Snipesville, which was an enormously radical think to do in the 1930s."

"So he won," said Brandon, looking much more cheerful. "We won."

"Brandon, it's never that simple," said Dr. Braithwaite. "These things are always an ongoing effort. There's no moment in history when one can stop and say, *That's it. We won.* You see, in the 1970s, long after Robert Gordon died, and long after the Supreme Court ordered the integration of public schools in the case of *Brown versus Board of Education*, Snipes County finally integrated its schools."

"That's a win too, then," said Alex.

"Yes, and no," said Dr. Braithwaite. "Many white parents, especially the wealthier people, withdrew their children from public school altogether so they wouldn't have to go to school with black kids. That's why they opened Snipes Academy."

This was news to Alex. "Wow, so that's how SA got started? Did you know this, Hannah? Does Dad know?"

"He might," said Hannah. "Which kind of bothers me."

But Brandon had always known about Snipes Academy, and why no black children from the community attended it to this day. People remembered. And something else was still troubling him. "Why isn't Miss Julia Russell on the mural out there?"

"Well, that's typical," Verity said. "A woman does all the work, and a man takes all the credit."

"I have never heard of your Miss Julia," said Dr. Braithwaite, "but it's not too late to add her to the story. It's never too late. Oh, and while we're on the subject, somebody else important is missing, too."

"Who's that?" Brandon said curiously.

CHAPTER SIXTEEN

"You see, I remember people in the community were very struck by my name when I first arrived here," and here he smiled at Brandon. "Apparently, there was another George Braithwaite who came to Snipesville once upon a time, a young American who had lived in England. He was only a lad, they said. He arrived one day out of the blue, and helped raise money for a high school. He was almost a legend, they said. They told me that Robert Gordon always swore that the night Thomas Clark died, George Braithwaite literally vanished into thin air, before his very eyes. Some said George was a ghost. Others said he was a gift from God. Either way, it was said to be a good omen that I carried his name, and it was why the community worked so hard to persuade me to stay here. Now I know he was you. Well done, Brandon."

"That doesn't make sense," Alex said sleepily. "That's full of time paradox thingies. Isn't it?"

"A great many things are hard for all of us to understand," said Dr. Braithwaite, but he didn't elaborate.

Alex was staring at the television in the corner of the coffeehouse. "Hannah, isn't that dad's bank?"

"Yes, of course it is," Hannah said. "Just across the street."

"No," Alex said, "I mean on the TV news."

Hannah sat up straight now, and leaned forward to read the ticker at the bottom of the screen: *Snipesville Bank Scandal.* "Quick," she called to Ben Hunslow, "turn up the sound."

The gray-haired white anchorman on the Savannah news sounded very serious. "There were several arrests, and our own Sarah Thompson is live on the scene in Snipesville with the story. Sarah? This must be quite a shock."

The reporter, a young dark-skinned woman, indicated the bank building behind her. "Yes, Buddy, people in Snipesville are in shock this afternoon as news breaks of an alleged scandal involving bank and community leaders. Details are just emerging, but according to an FBI spokesman, several arrests have been made today, and I'm told, charges are pending against high-ranking officers of the Bank of Snipesville, which is owned by GrandEstates Bank. I've learned that charges will include fraud, embezzlement, and racketeering, with many accusations going back decades. A spokesman for GrandEstates said their internal investigation had yielded important clues …"

"Dad!" Hannah gasped. She shot off the sofa and out the door, followed closely by Alex and Brandon.

Hannah was the first of them to come running back to Hunslow's Sippin' Snipe. "The police wouldn't let me in the building, and my dad's not answer-

CHAPTER SIXTEEN

ing. Dr. B, would you mind driving us home? Please?"

Monday Evening, Late May, This Year

When Hannah, Alex, Brandon, Verity, and George Braithwaite arrived at the house, there were two vehicles in the driveway, neither of which Hannah recognized. One was a large black car. *This has to be an FBI car,* she thought, *or something like that.* Was their dad already in handcuffs, being read his rights? Her guts clenched. Looking at Alex, she saw he was having the same thoughts, because he grabbed her hand and squeezed it.

When they ran into the living room, Hannah expected to see a scary-looking guy in a gray suit with short hair and a holstered gun standing over a handcuffed Bill Dias. Instead, she found Brandon's mom, dad, and Aunt Marcia, and, to her amazement, her own grandmother from California. She rushed to Ellen, and hugged her, crying, "What are you doing here?"

"I've never packed for the airport so fast in my life," said Ellen. "Your grandfather was speeding so badly, I was scared he would get arrested. There was only one seat left on the flight, and I made it with seconds to spare. And I took a taxi here from Savannah. Have you any idea how much this has cost me?"

"Okay, Grandma," said Hannah, "but why? What's going on?"

"Oh, darling," Ellen said, "I only wish I knew. Look, I'll explain later. But I've had a call from your dad, to say he's being interviewed by the FBI, and not to worry."

"Why wouldn't we worry about that?" Hannah said.

"A very good question," her grandmother replied, before greeting the other new arrivals. "Verity, it's good to meet you in person. Do you know Brandon's parents, Gordon and Dawn, and his Aunt Marcia? They have kindly been keeping me company."

"So you're Verity," said Brandon's mom, stern-faced. "We heard about you from our son. Maybe you can explain what all this is about?"

"Oh, dear," sighed Verity. "I hardly know where to start. And you won't believe me anyway."

Aunt Morticia gave her a gimlet stare. "Okay," she said. "Try me."

"Wait," said Hannah. "Grandma, how do you know Verity?"

Monday Night, Late May, This Year

Hannah felt sick. Was her Dad going to prison? Was there going to be a trial? She didn't want to know. She was afraid of the answers. Mr. Dias sat on the edge of a dining room chair he had brought into the living room, and addressed his children. "Hannah, Alex, I owe you guys an explanation."

CHAPTER SIXTEEN

"Bill," Ellen said sharply, "I think you owe all of us an explanation."

Mr. Dias smiled ruefully at his mother-in-law. "Yes, you, too, Ellen, and Dr. Braithwaite, and, um, Brandon's family, and …" He looked at Verity, frowning.

"Verity," said Verity, extending her hand. "Verity Powell. I'm a friend of George's."

Hannah took Verity's arm. "Verity is our friend, too, mine and Alex's and Brandon's."

Mr. Dias looked puzzled by Verity's presence, but then decided to carry on. "Look, I didn't tell anyone the truth when we moved to Snipesville," he started slowly. "Not even you kids. You probably wondered why I got transferred from San Francisco to a small town in Georgia, but you never asked me. The thing is …. Mr. Marshburn, my boss, was arrested today for fraud. So were several others, including one of the bank directors, Cassius Shrupp."

Here, Gordon Clark shook his head with a smile. "I knew it!" he crowed. "I knew Cassius was a crook!"

Mr. Dias continued. "And they arrested Hunslow, and …"

"Not Ben Hunslow at the coffeehouse?" said Alex, shocked.

"No, this was the bank vice-president, Tommy Hunslow," said Mr. Dias.

"Oh, that's his uncle," said Aunt Morticia. "He's a nasty piece of work."

"Dad, what's going to happen to you?" Hannah cried.

"That's what I'm trying to explain, Hannah. The thing is, you, me, and Alex, we're going to have to leave town."

The kids' eyes grew wide. Brandon gasped, "Why?"

"Are we going on the run?" Hannah said, her eyes swimming. "We have to leave Snipesville?"

"We do have to leave Snipesville," said Mr. Dias, "but we're not going on the run. I did nothing wrong."

"That's what people always say when they're in trouble," Ellen said grimly.

"Yes, I know, Ellen, but I'm not," Mr. Dias said, through gritted teeth. "Let me finish, okay? Here's the story. The true story. GrandEstates Bank promoted me before I left San Francisco. They gave me a new job. You see, our president was worried that there was something fishy about the Snipesville bank we'd just acquired, and he wanted me to find out what it was. We couldn't just close the Snipesville bank, rename it, and hire new people that local folks didn't know, or we would lose customers, because people in small towns don't like to give up their little local banks to some big chain from California. We had to be careful how we handled things. So my boss in San Francisco sent me to investigate."

"You were working undercover," Alex said quietly. "So that's why you weren't put in charge of the bank?"

CHAPTER SIXTEEN

"That's right, Alex," Mr. Dias said. "Turns out, the bank had been turning down a lot of loans to black people for their businesses and mortgages …" Aunt Morticia snorted loudly at this. Mr. Dias continued, "… while the bank's managers and directors had been quietly siphoning off funds for years, even decades, for themselves, their families, and their friends. They were really clever about it. But they weren't clever enough. In fact, they were dumb enough to try to involve me in their schemes, thinking I was just as greedy as they were. I just … I want to apologize to you kids. I saw this job as a way to get you away from bad memories, from the stuff in California … you know."

"The stuff with Mom," Hannah said quietly, and her dad nodded.

"And you brought them to Georgia," said Ellen, unable to keep the anger out of her voice, "to the middle of nowhere …." She turned to the Clarks and Dr. Braithwaite. "I'm sorry, that was rude."

"No apology needed," said Dr. Braithwaite, folding his arms.

"Yes, I did bring them here," said Mr. Dias. "I thought life in Snipesville would be simpler …."

And then Hannah did something completely unexpected. She began to laugh. Everyone stared at her. "I'm sorry, Dad," she said, through her giggles, "but you have no idea …."

"Look, I know you had a hard time this past year at Snipes Academy," her father said, shaking his head. "I didn't anticipate that. But life can be like that. Even adults don't always know what they're getting into."

"You can say that again," Hannah said. "But why do we have to leave Georgia?"

Mr. Dias looked at his daughter in disbelief. "You gotta be kidding me. You hate this place."

"Yes, I do," Hannah said. "But at least I have a life here. I made friends since we got here."

"You mean Brandon? And that girl from school you talk about, Tara?"

"Yes, and all my best friends ever," she said, giving warm looks first to Brandon, and then to Verity, who smiled back at her. "But it's not just them."

"Then who? Look, honey, I know I've been so busy and stressed, I haven't paid enough attention to you and Alex, but I promise I'll make it up to you. I think you retreated into your imagination since we got here because I've been neglectful. Or do you have a boyfriend I don't know about? But …"

The doorbell rang. "Now who could that be?" Mr. Dias said with a sigh, and got to his feet. "Excuse me, folks. And look, you really don't all have to stay."

"Yes, you do," Ellen said sharply to the group. "Don't anyone go anywhere."

"Oh, we're staying," said Mrs. Clark, putting out a hand to touch Ellen's

CHAPTER SIXTEEN

arm. "I'm not leaving until I know what's going on, and what it all has to do with my son."

When Mr. Dias returned, he ushered in Professor Kate Harrower. She was carrying a stack of papers, and dressed in a gray silk suit, the same one, Hannah thought, that she had worn on that fateful day when the three of them had first met her, and the time travel had begun. Could it really have been less than a year?

The Professor beamed at everyone, and sat down on the sofa between Mrs. Clark and Grandma. Alex looked curiously at her, and then at his sister, but Hannah's only reaction to her arrival was a small knowing smile.

Mr. Dias said, "Professor Harrower, maybe you would like to explain why you're here? I didn't quite understand what you said to me just now."

"Oh, I'm here for the same reason everyone else is," she said cheerfully. "To discuss the truth."

He looked dumbfounded. "The truth? About what?"

"I'm a friend of your children's," the Professor said. "In fact, I'm a friend to everyone in this room."

"Not to me," muttered Aunt Morticia, and Brandon's parents looked skeptical, too.

"So, tell me," said Mr. Dias, sitting down. "What's the truth?"

"Why don't you ask your mother-in-law?" said the Professor, and Mr. Dias turned to Ellen.

"Let me get right to the point," Ellen said in her usual matter-of-fact voice. "Bill, your kids and Brandon are time travelers."

Mr. Dias and the Clarks looked dumbstruck. If this were a movie, Hannah thought, someone would now say something like "Is this a joke?" or "That's crazy!"

Mr. Dias said, "Is this a joke? That's crazy!"

Verity cleared her throat, and everyone turned to look at her. "I first met Hannah in 1940, then in 1951, and most recently in 1905. I know it's incredible, and I'm well aware that you don't know me, but do I sound as mad as my words imply?"

Mr. Dias didn't answer. He looked instead to Dr. Braithwaite, who said, "Like Verity, I met your children in 1940. And all of us have just returned from the early twentieth century."

Now the Clarks looked really shocked. "God, have mercy on us," Aunt Morticia exclaimed, putting a hand to her chest.

Dr. Braithwaite continued, looking at the Clarks. "I haven't lost my mind. We could show you Edwardian coins in mint condition, and various trinkets, but that won't prove anything, so you can believe us, or not. But the truth remains the same."

"Oh, I have something for all of you," said the Professor. "Not faked, but we can't prove that, so you'll just have to decide for yourselves." She handed the kids photocopies of newspaper clippings: a picture of Brandon speaking with W. E. B. Du Bois in Macon in 1906, and another of Hannah in a group with Mrs. Lewis and Elizabeth in 1905. The adults gathered around to peer over the kids' shoulders. Mr. Dias glanced at the photos, and said, "Give me a minute." He ran from the room.

When he returned, he was carrying a heavy photograph album.

"That's mine!" Hannah yelped. "It's private!"

"I know," her father said. "But I didn't know what it was, and I thought you might be hiding drugs, or something. When I looked inside, I couldn't understand what it was all about. And then I found out your brother has one too." He opened the album, and laid it on the coffee table for all to view. "See this photo? It looks like you went to one of those re-enactor museums, or something, or had a lot of fun with an editing program."

"No, that's me in 1752," said Hannah.

"And who are these people? This looks like it was taken in England in the 1940s …"

"Does anyone see me?" Verity asked the group.

Mr. Clark pointed to Mrs. Devenish and looked questioningly at her, but Verity said, "No, that's my grandmother. Look over here." She pointed to the young girls standing either side of Mrs. Devenish: "*This* is me… and that's Hannah. There's George Braithwaite, and Brandon …"

"You're asking us to believe in science fiction," said Mr. Dias.

"No, we're just stating facts," Dr. Braithwaite said calmly. "I knew your children, Bill, before you were even born."

Mr. Dias bristled at this. "Look, I know what facts are. My name is William Dias. That's a fact. I'm a Portuguese-American from Sacramento, that's a fact …"

"No, it's not," Ellen said bluntly.

"What?" Mr. Dias looked completely thrown.

"You're not exactly Portuguese-American."

"Yes, I am," he said. "My grandmother was from a family of Portuguese fishermen who settled in Monterey."

"Your grandmother's name wasn't Dias, was it?" she said.

"No, that was my grandfather's family name, but I assumed …"

"You assumed wrong," said Ellen. "Here's a printout of your family history. Have a look."

CHAPTER SIXTEEN

Mr. Dias looked it over, and exhaled. "Wow. The Dias family was Mexican?"

"Not exactly," Ellen said. "Mexican-American. Californians of Mexican descent. And thanks to your grandma, you're also Portuguese-American. You pick."

"It's interesting," Mr. Dias said, handing the paper back to Grandma. "But it kind of pales next to being told that my kids are time travelers."

"My point," Ellen said, "is that we don't always know what we think we know. This evidence could have been made up, the evidence I found about your family tree—but you must admit, it's pretty unlikely. The same is true of the kids' photos and stories. Ask Hannah to talk about 1752."

"Oh, I will," said Mr. Dias. "But not now." He narrowed his eyes at the Professor. "What about you, Dr. Harrower? Where do you fit into all of this?"

"I'm a historian," she said with a shrug. There was a collective silence as everyone stared at her. Finally, she said reluctantly, "And I'm a time traveler."

"Okay, I'll bite," said Mr. Dias, folding his arms. "Let's pretend this is true. Why are my children traveling in time?"

The Professor looked at him hesitantly. "I'm sorry, but I don't know. I do have some theories. It seems that there's some sort of connection between Snipesville and Balesworth, the town where Verity lives. At first, I thought that Balesworth and Snipesville balanced each other, or something, that one was good, and one evil. Snipesville certainly feels different from everywhere else I have ever been, even here in the South."

"Maybe the Indians cursed Snipes County?" Alex said.

"No, that's silly," said the Professor. "People do talk a lot of nonsense about Indians. Still, you are onto something. There's no evidence that Native Americans settled in the area, except for a couple of temporary camps on the river. They pretty much avoided the place. Early European and American settlers also avoided Snipes County. Snipesville itself was just a hamlet with three families until long after the Civil War. Snipesville as we know it today was largely created by Charles Hughes, an Englishman from Balesworth."

"Wow, so he kind of unleashed the evil within?" Hannah said dramatically.

The Professor chuckled. "No dramatic hocus pocus like that, Hannah. Although … I admit it's uncanny that Kintyre plantation house was on the precise spot where the first Robert Gordon built his house in 1752, and both of them were burned down. But that's a coincidence, I'm sure. It's just … Well, it's as though something in the universe is trying to tell us something, but not spelling it out."

"So if Snipesville is weird, what's special about Balesworth?" said Alex.

"Nothing is special about Balesworth, not so far as I can see," said the Professor. "It's really what it seems to be, an ordinary English town. You kept ending up back there because of the people, you see. It's not Balesworth that's the connection. It's the people. That's what leads me to wonder if what has happened to us is also somehow connected to genetics."

Blood and Balesworth, Brandon thought. *Or maybe just blood.*

Mr. Dias's mouth twitched. "Time travel is genetic? You're saying there's a time travel gene?"

"I'm not sure," the Professor said quickly. "I'm a historian, not a scientist, although, honestly, scientists will be the first to tell you that we know very little about how the universe works. If there is a time-travel gene, it doesn't affect everyone who's related, as genes tend not to. Look, whatever is going on, much of it passes human understanding."

"Whatever has happened," said Brandon, "I see God's hand in it."

"Perhaps," said the Professor. "Honestly, I would like to believe that. I can't prove you're wrong, or right, Brandon. And surely that's the definition of faith."

"I think it's magic," said Alex.

"Possibly," said the Professor. "You will have to decide for yourselves. But no question, there is one fact of which we may all be sure. You kids are all distantly related to many of the people you meet in time, including Verity, and to each other."

Mr. Dias frowned. "Of course Hannah and Alex are related to each other, but to Brandon?"

"Yes," Ellen said. "To Brandon."

The Clarks, who had looked shell-shocked through the entire conversation, perked up at this revelation. Mr. Dias looked less pleased. "But how can that be?" he said. "My family, both sides, we've lived in California, from way back. We never lived in the South."

"Yours, Bill, certainly," said Ellen. "But not mine, it seems." She waved print-outs at him. "It's distant, but it's there. The kids are related to Brandon through a common ancestor, a member of the Gordon family, and also through other ancestors, and cousins. Verity is related to me and the kids through several people. I'll show you the charts later."

Bill Dias gave his mother-in-law a condescending smile. "Ellen, are you a time traveler, too?"

She looked at him frostily. "Not that I'm aware, Bill, but as Kate said, it's complicated."

"And are we related to you?" Mr. Dias said to the Professor. "Is there a Harrower in the family tree?"

It was Ellen who answered his question. "No," she said. "There's no Harrow-

CHAPTER SIXTEEN

er anywhere."

Verity now looked long and hard at the Professor. "Perhaps that's because Kate Harrower isn't her real name," she said. "Isn't that right, *Kate*?"

The Professor looked away.

Mr. Dias sighed, and briefly put his face in his hands. Then he looked around the room. "This is all fascinating, but it's seriously bizarre. So, what am I supposed to do with what you just told me?"

The Professor held up the papers she had brought with her. "That reminds me," she said. "I have directions."

"Directions?" said Mr. Dias. "What directions?" He smiled.

She gave him a hard stare. "This isn't funny. This is vitally important. You're all following a script, whether you know it or not, and it's generally wise not to deviate from it too much. How do you think I was able to find your children in time?"

"That's just it," said Mr. Dias, his voice rising. "That's the problem, right there. Look, maybe you have brainwashed my kids, my mother-in-law, and all these people into believing you, but at the end of the day, you're talking garbage."

The Professor turned to Hannah, and said angrily, "Hannah, go and stand next to your father. Go on."

Reluctantly, Hannah did as she was told.

"Now, Bill, hold your daughter's hands."

"What is this, a conjuring trick?" he said, but he held out his hands anyway. Taking them, Hannah looked expectantly at the Professor, and so did Mr. Dias.

"Now, Mr. Dias, look at your daughter, and don't let go of her hands or take your eyes off her for an instant."

"Oooo…kay …," said Mr. Dias, snorting, but he did gaze at Hannah.

The Professor gave Hannah a hard stare, and as she did, Hannah vanished.

Hannah didn't hear her father and the Clark family scream, which was probably just as well. She was now in Balesworth, standing at the kitchen door of Weston Cottage, and, looking through the window, she had a rough idea of when she had arrived. Well, what else was she going to do? She knocked.

"Don't worry," the Professor said. "She'll be back in a moment."

Brandon noticed that Mr. Dias's teeth were chattering.

Sure enough, Hannah suddenly reappeared right in front of her father. "Oh, hi!" she said brightly. "Nice to be back!"

Her father stared openmouthed at her. Hannah turned to the Professor.

❖ 435 ❖

CHAPTER SIXTEEN

"Sorry, Kate, I think I messed things up. I showed up in 1951 again, only this time, I appeared as myself, you know, young. I almost gave Mrs. D. a heart attack."

"I know," said the Professor. "She didn't believe you were a time traveler, did she?"

"Not at first," said Hannah with a sigh. "She said I must be a relation of Hannah's, playing a silly trick on her, whoever I was. She made me a cup of tea, because I think she was trying to figure me out, and then she sent me off with a flea in my ear. But I …"

The Professor interrupted her with a laugh. "Well, at least you got a cup of tea before she kicked you out," she said. "Now, Bill, what are you going to do?"

Mr. Dias looked dazed. "Huh?"

"Now that your work in Snipesville is done," said the Professor, "what now?"

Mr. Dias still appeared to be in a dreamlike state, but he did reply. "I told my bank I'm done with undercover work. They asked me to return to San Francisco, to corporate headquarters. Or," he said reluctantly, "there's a position available in Sacramento."

"Sacramento," Ellen and Alex said simultaneously.

"Good," said the Professor, sounding relieved. "Now, Brandon, you're staying in Snipesville, at least for now. Have you given any thought to where you want to go to college?"

"Yes," Brandon said, "Morehouse."

The Professor nodded again. "Good. Yes, that's right," she said. "But when the time comes for you to go to graduate school, I want you to make sure you chat with me beforehand, all right? Actually, we have to talk this week about you joint-enrolling at Snipesville State College as soon as possible, because you're really well beyond what middle and high school have to offer. I can definitely arrange for you to start in ninth grade, although we may be able to start you sooner."

Unfazed, Brandon nodded. After everything that had happened to him, he felt ready to enroll in a doctoral program. "Okay," he said, "But what about staying in touch with Hannah and Alex? Do we still time-travel together?"

"You will stay in touch," the Professor said. "And Alex?"

"Yes?"

"If you want it, your time-travel days are over."

He exhaled. "Good," he said.

"Good?" Brandon said. "You don't mind?"

"No," Alex said quietly. "I prefer a normal life. Brandon didn't mess up, but I did. Writing that stuff in the newspaper made so many people angry."

CHAPTER SIXTEEN

The Professor gave him a look of enormous compassion. "It wasn't your fault, darling. It really wasn't. You see, you did what you were meant to do, and it simply could not be fixed. But you told the truth, and that's the most important thing."

Alex's chin wobbled briefly, then he sniffed. "That's what Miss Julia Russell said."

"Don't ever lose your integrity, Alex," the Professor said, and Brandon, watching her, could have sworn she was fighting not to cry herself.

"What about Hannah?" asked Ellen.

"Don't worry about me, Grandma," Hannah said. "I've thought about it, and it will be good to be back in California."

"I never knew you missed it," said her grandmother.

"Me neither," said Hannah, "but sometimes, you have to learn the hard way, yeah?"

"Hannah won't be leaving for Sacramento immediately," the Professor said. "First, she must attend summer school."

"Summer school?" said Mr. Dias. "Hannah, why do you have to go to summer school? Are you failing your classes?"

"Her grades are fine," said Professor Harrower. "She's taking an independent study course with me at Snipesville State College on the finer points of historical research and time travel. Mr. and Mrs. Clark, would you mind hosting Hannah for the next couple of months?"

Brandon's parents exchanged glances, and silently nodded in agreement. "She'll be company for Brandon," said Mr. Clark. "He's going to miss you kids."

"Brandon, you must come to California, and stay with us a while," said Ellen. "Although fall or winter break is better," she added hurriedly. "You don't want to be in the Sacramento Valley in summer if you can help it."

"Sounds good," Brandon said. "Anyway, I already have a busy summer lined up."

"You do, indeed," said his father, eagerly seizing on this normal subject of conversation.

"Why, what's he doing?" said Mrs. Clark. "Nobody told me."

"I did promise I would save the funeral home," said Brandon. "Me, Dad, and Aunt Marcia decided to turn it into a nonprofit."

"Well, that wouldn't be hard," Mrs. Clark grumbled. "That place hasn't turned a profit in years."

"That's true," said Brandon, "but now we're going to be able to take donations to keep Aunt Marcia employed, at least until we start drawing more business."

"And how do you plan to do that?" his mother said.

Brandon stood proudly "I'm going to give speeches to groups across Georgia. Write articles. Contact big shots who were raised in the community and who are now in good careers to ask them for donations. We're the last independent funeral home in Snipes County, and we have a proud history of black-owned businesses to uphold. Plus we're there to show loving kindness to folks at the lowest, hardest times in their lives, and we're not in it for the money. I believe people will want to support that."

Mr. Clark led the applause for his son.

Friday, Mid-July, This Year

On the last day of her lessons in history and time travel, Hannah walked into the Professor's office, and was shocked to find her surrounded by cardboard boxes. "What's wrong? Where are you going?"

"Home," said the Professor. "I'm resigning from Snipesville State. Again."

"But I thought this was your home?" Hannah said.

"Not exactly," said the Professor, and Hannah couldn't help marveling how, even now, she was cagey about what she shared. "Look, these books are yours now."

"All of them?" Hannah looked uncertainly at the massive stack of boxes.

"All of them," said the Professor. "There's plenty of room in the house your dad is buying across the street from your grandparents, and I'll ship them to you, so don't worry. They'll arrive in Sacramento before you do."

There was a short silence. And then she said, "Hannah, this is the last time you'll see me."

"No! Why?" Hannah felt panicky.

"Dear, this is the fork in the road we talked about, and some day, when you know that your successor is ready, you too will take your own path, away from hers."

Hannah understood. She just didn't want to, and she blinked back tears. "But can't I see you again somehow?"

"No, I don't think so," said the Professor. "I know you've met a future me before, and I still don't know if she was *me*, or if … Well, I just don't know, let's leave it at that. That meeting was not supposed to happen. But I am glad that you and she were there for each other. Anyhow, don't worry, you are ready to go solo. And it's your decision. If you want to continue, you must train as a historian, because it will make things easier. And if you don't … "

"Then all this will end?" said Hannah.

CHAPTER SIXTEEN

"This path will end, yes. But there are others of us, I do know that, and they will carry on. Multiple Hannahs, multiple Kates, all carrying on. This really is your decision to continue as a time traveler. If you want to do as your brother has done, and call it a day, I do understand."

"No, I want to go on. But suppose I forget what you taught me?"

"You won't," said the Professor. "I gave you a guide for reference, and you promised to keep practicing to stay up to date, and that's really all you need. You have the hang of it. If you make a mistake, don't panic, just try again. It's like riding a bike. You won't forget."

"So what will you do to, um, I don't know what to call it …"

"Separate from you guys? Go off into my own universe?"

"Yes."

"I can't tell you," said the Professor. "But I can say it has to be something that really wasn't supposed to happen. That's why I sent you guys to go find my calculator in 1851. It was too soon. That wasn't in the records, and I didn't mean to lose it."

"So I could, you know, lose a calculator, when it's my turn?"

"You could. But you can do anything, really, that you think best. Look, Hannah, we're talking years, decades in the future. By then, you'll have no doubts in yourself. You will know when it's time, and you will know what to do. I promise. Then, if you wish, you can carry on time-traveling, once you have helped the new kids, just as I plan to do. I'm not retiring. Now, I really must go."

"Kate?" Hannah said.

"Yes?"

"Thank you," said Hannah, and, after wiping her eyes, she gave the Professor a final hug. "I'm sorry I was so mean. I didn't know."

"Of course you didn't know," the Professor said gently. "How could you have known?"

Hannah smiled weakly. "You taught me a lot, about everything."

"Thank *you*, Hannah. I can't say it was always a pleasure for either of us, but I'm glad I got to know you. I really am. You're a fine young woman, and never let anyone tell you otherwise."

Friday, Sept. 1, 1978

A short walk beyond the boys' school, the Professor finally reached Weston Cottage, and she paused to look at it with a mixture of joy for simply being there once again, and sadness for what she was about to do. Unlatching the green garden gate (*that's new*, she thought), she pushed it open with a grating squeak. It snapped shut behind her.

She knew to wait after she rang the doorbell, with its loud ear-grating buzz, because it might take the occupant a while to come to the door. As she waited, she noticed the paint peeling on the trim. But now the door swung open, and there in the doorway stood a very old woman, giving her the smallest of smiles. She was slightly stooped, and not as tall as she had once been. *If I hadn't seen her recently,* the Professor thought, *I would never have recognized her.*

"Goodness gracious," Mrs. Devenish said. Unlike her appearance, her voice had hardly changed. "Well, come along, don't hang about on the doorstep all day. Come in, and I'll put the kettle on."

The huge kitchen was almost exactly as it had been nearly forty years earlier, but with a newer stove from the 1960s, a refrigerator, and a dishwasher. The Professor took a seat at the table, and said, trying not to laugh, "You've got a dishwasher."

"Indeed," said Mrs. Devenish, as she busied herself filling the teakettle. "It was a present from Eric and Verity. I have no idea why they bought it. I didn't ask for another gadget. I don't use it. It's more trouble than it's worth. And Verity is a nuisance. She's always offering to clean my kitchen for me, but as I tell her, if my kitchen needs cleaning, I shall be the one to do it. Or not, as the case may be."

The Professor chuckled. "Here's one more gadget for you," she said, and she handed the small black device to Mrs. Devenish.

"What on earth is this?" she said.

"A present. Touch the little picture of a camera," the Professor instructed. Hesitantly, Mrs. Devenish did so. "Oh, it's a camera," she said. "How extraordinary."

"Yes, it's a camera, and a phone, and a computer," said the Professor. "I can show you how to use it if you like?"

"Perhaps later," said Mrs. Devenish. "If it's not too complicated. Otherwise I shall use it as a plant stand."

But the important thing had already happened, the Professor knew. Now that Mrs. Devenish accepted the phone, decades before smartphones were invented, her own future had changed unalterably.

When the tea was ready, the Professor took up the tray without being asked, and followed the old woman into the drawing room. Mrs. Devenish sat down carefully in her armchair. "I've been thinking about what you first told me all those years ago," she said. "I was rather dubious then, of course."

The Professor looked at her with surprise. This was a subject they had long

CHAPTER SIXTEEN

ago silently agreed not to discuss, to act over the years as though this life of hers were perfectly normal, when it was nothing of the kind. She nodded, and said, "Of course you were dubious. I expected nothing less. I was more surprised when you started to take it in your stride."

"I thought you were a ghost at first. And now here we are again, and how old are you? In your mid-fifties, I suppose? About the same age that I was when you first stayed with me during the War. It has been a while since your last visit."

"Yes, sorry about that," the Professor said, shifting uncomfortably. "Two years ago in your time, I think. I was in my forties, then, and things in my life weren't going well, and I needed your advice. Remember?"

Mrs. Devenish sighed. "I remember, but you're confusing me. Honestly, you must think me ancient now, which of course I am."

The Professor dug in her pocket and pulled out her Snipesville State College business card. "I don't think I've ever shown you this," she said, handing it to Mrs. Devenish. "It's mine, under my professional name."

The old woman put on her glasses, and read it at arm's length. "You have done very well for yourself," she said, in a voice that told the Professor that she did not entirely approve.

"I'm not just about getting ahead in my career, you know," said the Professor. "I've tried to help other people along the way. And I have tried to atone for my sins. Perhaps I've not tried as hard as I should have, but …"

The old woman didn't let her finish. "I'm glad to hear it. But what an odd life you lead. You must have lived all over the place and all over time, much of it by yourself. All the while that you have had the most extraordinary adventures, I've been puttering about here in Weston Cottage, with my cooking and my garden. I cannot imagine what you think you can learn from me." She gave a small, sardonic smile.

"You're right, it is a peculiar life," said the Professor. "I have had some help, though. From you, for one."

Mrs. Devenish frowned. "You're not listening. Don't be ridiculous. I didn't do anything. And it's not as though we ever saw eye to eye. I know you thought me a terrible old dragon."

"No, I never thought that," the Professor protested.

"You really are the most awful fibber," said Mrs. Devenish. "I *am* a terrible old dragon. I certainly had to be during the War, with so many children underfoot. But I suppose all of you turned out all right."

The Professor said, "Hopefully, we will again."

"Now stop saying things like that. It's irritating. Let's not discuss it. Are you well? How are your husband and children? Have you more photographs of

CHAPTER SIXTEEN

your grandchildren?"

For the next two hours, they chatted and reminisced and laughed and ate cake and drank tea.

And then the Professor sat forward on the sofa, and said somberly, "I must tell you something. This will be my very last visit, I'm afraid."

The old woman's face fell. "Oh!" she said. "Well, I didn't expect that you would be calling on me five years from now, but ..."

The Professor nodded. "I know, and I'm sorry. I've helped my successor adjust to her new life. She'll retell our story in her own way. And so I came today to say my goodbye to you." She knew this wasn't the whole truth, but she could not bring herself to say it aloud, to tell the old woman, and herself, the real reason she would not return: Within less than a month, Elizabeth Hughes Devenish would be no more, and this was the time for endings.

"Everything changes the course of the past," said the Professor. "All the time. No straight lines. Few if any certainties."

"I have no idea what you're talking about," Mrs. Devenish complained, bringing her sharply back down to earth. "I do wish you wouldn't speak in riddles. It's very annoying."

"You should talk!" the Professor laughed. "You have never been the easiest person to read. But here's something you will understand, and I'm going to say it whether you want me to or not: Thank you for everything you've done for me."

Mrs. Devenish waved away the compliment. "Nonsense. I did so little."

But the Professor insisted. "You underestimate the value of kind words and attention and caring. Those meant so much to me at very difficult times in my life."

Mrs. Devenish looked at the Professor, and softened. "You give me far too much credit, my dear. You were your own best influence. You ought to be very proud of yourself," she said, and then, visibly struggling with what she was about to say next, she smoothed down her skirt. "As I am proud of you, Hannah Day."

The Professor beamed, and blinked back tears as she rummaged in her purse. "Before I go, I want to show you something else," she said, and pulled out a very old, folded piece of paper, contained in a glossy plastic sleeve. "I've carried this with me, all these years," she said. "It's one of my most treasured possessions."

She took it out, unfolded it, and handed it to Mrs. Devenish, who read it over. "I remember writing this," she said. "You didn't seem very grateful at the time, as I recall."

CHAPTER SIXTEEN

"Well, you had just fired me." The Professor smiled, and Mrs. Devenish handed her back the letter as she stood up to leave. After old Mrs. Devenish struggled to her feet, the Professor made to hug her, paused a moment to reconsider, and then, muttering "Oh, what the hey," gently embraced her anyway.

Mrs. Devenish stiffened, and protested. "Oh, really! You know I don't do that."

"Well, Granny, you should," said the Professor, as she stepped back and gently clasped the old woman's arms. "We should all move with the times."

Mrs. Devenish shook her head irritably, but the Professor saw her suppress a smile.

Pausing on the door step, she turned to Mrs. Devenish, and said in a choked voice, "Goodbye, Granny."

"Now, now," said Mrs. Devenish, embarrassed by this show of emotion. "No need for that. Goodbye, Hannah Day. Look after yourself. And give my love to Alexander, and to young George, or Brandon, or whatever it is that he calls himself now, and to dear George Braithwaite. Goodbye, my dear."

Hannah Dias (who sometimes called herself Hannah Day, sometimes Kate Devenish Gordon Harrower, and sometimes other names) turned away, took a few steps, and looked back again. She waved, and blew a kiss to Elizabeth Hughes Devenish. Then she walked determinedly down the garden path of Weston Cottage for the very last time.

As she reached the gate, she closed her eyes, and by the time she had opened them again, she was on the porch of the home she had named Kintyre, built on the spot where other houses of that name had once stood, to proclaim that it is possible to start anew. This house was where she had lived for twenty years with her husband, Brandon Clark, the greatest mayor in the history of Snipesville, Georgia, and it was where they had raised their children. They spent so little time here now. Brandon was Georgia's junior senator in Washington, D.C., and, so people said, was destined to be an extraordinary president. But that lay in the future.

Acknowledgments

At its most serious, this is partly a novel about apologies, regret, and redemption, so I shall add my own. It took me six years total to write the first three books of *The Snipesville Chronicles*, but, to my horror, this final volume has taken four years to complete, a pace more suited to writing history than to writing fiction. I am so very grateful to those of you who have waited patiently, and who did not simply move on and forget all about Snipesville, as you were absolutely entitled to do. I particularly thank my first young readers, who are now not as young as you were: Those of you who were nine when *Don't Know Where, Don't Know When* appeared are now in college.

I can also report that I'm astonished at how topical are the themes in *One Way or Another*. It certainly wasn't planned that way.

In summer, 2006, I was a tenured history professor who, tired of academic politics and the hamster wheel of my work, sat down to write a novel for my own reasons. I had no idea if anyone would want to read it. I had no idea if I wanted it published. But write it, I did. *Don't Know Where, Don't Know When* turned out to be an unexpected synthesis of fact and fiction, of historical knowledge (both content and discipline), memories of my British childhood, and travels throughout the UK for the past three decades, and imagination. Encouraged by enthusiastic feedback from friends, which I treated with healthy skepticism—even though they were historians and thus normally unashamedly critical—I also started thinking about how best to get the manuscript to an audience—any audience.

But first I went on a time-travel adventure of my own. Shortly after I finished the first draft, I flew on impulse to England, and specifically to the town where I grew up, to visit some of the people who had influenced me most, and who had also influenced the characters of "Balesworth." It was one of the most profound weeks of my life, and I learned more about myself in that short time than I would have dreamed possible.

Shortly after my return to Georgia, however, I had a serious health scare, which strengthened my resolve to get the book into print as soon as practicable. I calculated that if I published it myself, and sold 500 copies to friends, family, and former students, I could cover my costs. I would also not have to wait years for someone in New York to decide that the manuscript was publishable, and that my platform for publishing was sufficiently high. Having satisfied my vanity, I could then return to my career as a historian, leaving the remaining books to molder in the garage.

Of course, nothing in life goes quite as planned. I soon realized that *Don't Know Where, Don't Know When* struck a chord with those who read it. I learned of and met enthusiastic young readers, first in Georgia, and increasingly as far away as New York, San Francisco, the UK, and Australia who had read the story over and over. I also became acquainted with adult readers who had discovered *The Snipesville Chronicles*, and who were just as passionate about this quirky time-travel story as were the kids and teens.

And then, after another health crisis the following year (it was a testing time), I decided that my future lay outside the academy. Although it has been gratifying in the years since to learn of the impact and significance of my scholarly publications, I have never regretted walking away. Working for most modern universities is an ordeal, even with tenure, and I have been infinitely happier and more productive as an independent public historian. I have also finally fulfilled my long-suppressed dream, one to which I alluded in my graduate school application, of reaching a broader public with a love of history and historical thinking.

Throughout this journey, I have received extraordinary support. I write and produce my books, I perform in schools, libraries, and museums, and do most of my own marketing. But I don't do it all alone. I want to thank everyone along the way who has encouraged and assisted my work. Most of all, I thank Bryan Ogihara, my husband, who not only handles the accounts and works alongside me at conferences when he can, but also literally makes my work possible through his practical and emotional support. Our son, Alec, has doubtless led a less privileged life because I renounced my tenured professorship to strike out on my own, but he has never, ever complained, and both he and Bryan have been endlessly supportive. I love them so much.

For a book (or series) to become successful requires massive marketing to create critical mass and large-scale buzz, which is why big publishers invest so heavily in launching books. Otherwise, as in the case of *The Snipesville Chronicles*, it requires great patience (and the luck) that leads to gradual discovery. I have enjoyed the gradual discovery to no end, and I have taken great (if idiosyncratic) pride in the fact that readers continue to find and enjoy these books quite by happenstance. Thank you for continuing to spread the word, giving copies of *The Snipesville Chronicles* as gifts, sending links, and (if you dare) sharing your copies!

Special shout-outs to:

- All the historians whose scholarship was essential to these books, and those humanities scholars who have personally encouraged my work, especially Drs. Cathy Skidmore-Hess, Jonathan M. Bryant, Jennie Goloboy, and Julia Griffin.

- Georgia Humanities, including President Jamil Zainaldin, VP Laura McCarty, and most especially Senior Programs Officer Arden Williams, who have promoted my work throughout the state, and offered me great personal encouragement at every turn.
- Deborah Harvey, graphic designer and friend, for the time and talent she has expended on my books, publicity materials, and me. The success of *The Snipesville Chronicles* would have been inconceivable without Deborah's cover art.
- My former student Kelley Lash, who so kindly helped with the layout of the first three books, and Suzanne Sen, who helped with the editing of this one.
- Librarians (with a special hello to Gordon Baker and Kathy Pillatzki in Henry County, GA) and school library media specialists (among them Jan Perry, Kristi Craven, Cristina Dover, Lori Shiver, and Karen Hickey) who have invited me to visit schools, and who, along with teachers and administrators too numerous to name, have continued to spread the word. I apologize if I have not named you specifically, but do know that if you think this should include you, it does. Thank you.
- Independent booksellers who responded positively to my approach. I thank especially Diane Capriola and author/bookseller Terra Elan McVoy (who thought I was mad to self-publish, and was probably right, but who gave me my first big boost), both of Little Shop of Stories of Decatur, GA, the folks at Park Road Books (Charlotte NC) and The Book Worm (Powder Springs, GA) and most especially, former booksellers Debbie Campbell (The Book and Cranny, Statesboro, GA) and Fran Bush (Booklovers Bookstore of Aiken, SC) who were my earliest supporters in the bookselling community.
- My readers, who continue to share the books and spread the word, and especially my Kickstarter backers, who have helped enormously with the considerable expense of producing this fourth book, and who have enthusiastically supported my growing outreach beyond the Southeast. I am extremely grateful for their generosity, and their considerable patience.

Many Thanks to my Kickstarter Backers:

Commanders of the Order of Snipesville (COS)

Atumpan Edutainment	Patricia Ingle Gillis
Gordon Baker	Mary Keith
Tara Bloyd	Reid Pierce
Lorna Boyd	Fred Richter
Keri Cross	Alexander Clarke Shaffer
Jason Freeman	Nora Shiver
Gina Futch	Rosemarie Stallworth-Clark
Julia Griffin	Cindy Wheeler
Norma Nicol Hamilton	Charles S. Zilinski
Monica Hunt	

Members of the Order of Snipesville (MOS)

Jessica Baldwin	Arlys Ferrell	Hazel Kirby
Brandy Baird	Jennie Goloboy	Robert Laing
Allison Bennett	Yvette Marie Gordillo	Chloe Lyn Lambaren
Loretta Brandon	Dusty Gres	Sue Levine
Michael Braz	A.T. Gritten	Jim LoBue
Jenny Brown	Donald Guillory	Nancy Malcom
Jonathan M. Bryant	Katarina Gurevich	Julie Brinkman McCracken
Patsy Buccy	April Herring	
Monica M. Burgett	Karen Hickey	Ken and Judy Montgomery
Mary Butler	Deena Michelle Holt	N. Mooney
Kevin Chua	Mallorie Hyatt	Jackie Nunn
Kristi Craven	Jessica Keeley	Carlyn Pinkins
David Crockit	Christy Keith	Paul & Katherine Quinnell
Brenda Dartt	Nicole Kemper	
Lauren English	Krystal King	Vicky Alvear Schecter

Dani Skoog	Ellen Torgerson	Ashley Williams
Vicki Stanton	Nick Utley	JoAnn Wood
The Summerlin Family	Meg Walling	Michael Xydias
Megan Taylor	Karen Wells	
Jackson Gerome Temple	James Whittle	

... and all the other backers of the Snipesville Kickstarter of 2014.
Thank you.

Some of the characters in this book are named for generous Kickstarter backers or the honorees they designated. I do stress that all characters are fictitious, even when they are named for real people.

They are:

- Gordon N. Baker, the Georgia-born Dean of Libraries at Clayton State University (and Mr. Library in Georgia), loaned his name to the English proprietor of a corner grocery in turn-of-the-century Bedfordshire.

- Brooklynn Simone, thanks to sponsor Atumpan Edutainment, gives her name to Brandon's cousin in modern-day Snipesville.

- Caroline Cross, daughter of Keri Jones Cross, is mentioned as manager of the Hotel Duval in the 21st century.

- "Arthur Ingle-Gillis" is named in honor of retired Georgia Southern University English professor Patricia Ingle Gillis and her family (some of whom use the hyphen in their name). The sponsored characters were all supposed to be minor, but Arthur, um, got out of hand. Dr. Ingle Gillis also asked me to try to include a custard reference as a private joke to her grandchildren. It was fun to play with!

- Reid Pierce, bibliophile and teacher, was easy to cast as assistant manager of Ingle-Gillis Bros. Bookshop, and Arthur's companion.

- Alexander Clarke Shaffer is a long-time fan of my books, and his mother, Martha, kindly sponsored the use of his name for the character of Alex Shaffer. "Alex Shaffer" is, together with Ben Hunslow, Javarius Evans, Tara Thompson, and, of course, Brandon Clark and his wife, among my beacons of hope for the future of "Snipesville."

- Fan Cindy Wheeler named the drugstore in "Snipesville" Wheeler's Apothecary, and was kind enough to allow me full dramatic license with the fictitious "Mr. Wheeler", a character not even remotely connected to her.

- Charles S. Zilinski is, in real life, a generous young Kickstarter philanthropist in Massachusetts. Making Charles's doppelganger the receptionist/right-hand-man of Mr. Duval helped me drive home the point that, a century ago, many small Southern towns owed their progress to incomers of all kinds.

I owe a great deal to my beta test readers, whom I saddled with a ridiculously long manuscript (250,000 words in its original form), and tasked with telling me if it was understandable and enjoyable. Their praise delighted me, but it was their cogent criticisms which inspired me to make this book far better (and shorter) than it would have been otherwise, whether or not I actively followed their advice. That said, if you didn't enjoy reading it, blame me, and not them! I wish to thank the following advance readers for their thoughtful and helpful feedback:

Elaine Connolly	Terri Nalls
Kristi Craven	Tara Sandmann
Cristina Dover	Lori Shiver
Arlys Ferrell	LaQuita Staten
Cate Godley	Cynthia B. Ward
Dusty Gres	Kimberley Warrick
Kate Gladstone	JoAnn Wood
Nikki Matthews	

I thank everyone else who contributed to this book and to the series in ways large and small. If your name is not listed above or below, I do apologize.

Thanks to...

- My Facebook friends and followers, and especially Tonya Janicke, for coming up with the name "Sippin' Snipe" for "Snipesville"'s new coffee shop. (I added the "Hunslow's" because the first question that locals in South Georgia often ask about a new business is not "Is it good?" but "Who owns it?") Tonya also named the funeral home chain "Eternal Interment".
- Pauline Maryan, volunteer at the Stevenage Museum, for researching when electricity and telephone service debuted in Stevenage, the Hertfordshire town that most closely resembles "Balesworth".
- Robert Greene, University of South Carolina graduate student and scholar of African-American intellectual history, for giving the thumbs up to my interpretation of W. E. B. Du Bois. If I mangled my portrayal of Du Bois's complex relationship with Booker T. Washington, it's not Robert's fault.
- My former student Kevin Chua, a globe-trotting corporate accountant, who confirmed that Bill Dias' investigative role could, indeed, have been a real thing.

- Dana R. Chandler, University Archivist and Assistant Professor at Tuskegee University, who said he couldn't be sure whether or not the hall of The Oaks, Booker T. Washington's house, would have featured a bench or chairs for less important visitors to await an audience. However, he writes, "It is quite possible since that was common at the time." My sentiments exactly.

Notes on Sources

(for adult readers who care about such things)

Young Readers: Please ignore this section.
"Boring" doesn't even begin to describe it. Seriously.
—*Annette*

A Word…
(or, since I am a historian, lots of words)

Having restrained myself from extensive notes on my sources in previous Snipesville books, I'm going to go all out for this last in the series.

Academic historians are required to write history that honestly fits the evidence available. Novelists are not. My work lies somewhere in between. As ever, I remind everyone that my novels are fiction. I do my best, within the limitations of historical knowledge and the genre, to ensure that the *Chronicles* represent the times and places in which they are set. I do make good use of published academic history, but I also inevitably take liberties. "Snipesville" borrows from real places, but it is not itself a real place. Likewise, "Balesworth" and "Ickswade". And the characters are fictitious, including those inspired by (and even named for) real people.

All those caveats aside, I am delighted that my novels give my readers a peek into the rich—but seldom accessible—world of academic history, and even more delighted when you tell me that the books make you think about past, present, and the ways in which they connect. That's what history is supposed to do. We most profitably learn about the past not through instruction and drill, but by osmosis.

If the Chronicles encourage you to learn more about the past, so much the better. In this section, I give a brief and selected overview of further reading, mostly for adults (but as someone who dipped into history books from the age of ten, looking at pictures and reading what she could understand, that doesn't mean I think kids should be forbidden from looking at academic history!) Most academic books are horribly overpriced, but your public library can order them for you, and many are also available cheaply in used editions online. Another world is out there, waiting for you, if you're interested in looking for it. Never be content with textbooks, because they're awful: Memorizing the script you were handed in school is not the point of studying history—there is no test at the end of life. Find what interests you, dig, and be amazed.

General Source on Georgia:
New Georgia Encyclopedia, a project of Georgia Humanities, is a remarkably helpful and constantly improving resource to help you become acquainted with any area of Georgia history.

The Professor's Lecture at Snipes Academy:
If you're interested in learning about enslaved and free black people who spied for the Union during the Civil War, check out this book for young readers: Thomas B. Allen, *Harriet Tubman, Secret Agent: How Daring Slaves and Free Blacks Spied for the Union During the Civil War* (National Geographic Children's Books, 2006).

"Balesworth" and New Towns in England:
I grew up in Stevenage, Britain's first ever New Town, and have very mixed feelings about it, just like Mrs. Devenish! No question, though, the New Towns, which were bold post-war experiments, become more interesting as the years go by. If you decide to visit "Balesworth", Stevenage comes closest to it, and it's worth visiting the "Old Town" and Stevenage Museum (in the New Town). Alas, Weston Cottage does not exist, and if you follow my directions, you'll end up on a bridge overlooking a busy road.

Diversity and Progress in Early 20th Century South Georgia:
I have lived in Georgia for a very long time, but I am not a native Southerner. To this day, most Americans, inside as well as outside the South, have no idea how complex a place it actually is. This is not intended as a defensive statement: It's an invitation to explore, not to label.

Alex's view of Broughton Street in Savannah is based on a fantastic photograph online. Give it a Google: Savannah, Georgia, circa 1905. "Broughton Street, looking east." 8x10 inch dry plate glass negative, Detroit Publishing Company.

As you know, Snipesville does not exist, but lest you think I'm completely making up the technological progress of the town and the diversity of its entrepreneurs at the turn of the last century, rest assured that this theme is inspired by early twentieth-century Statesboro, GA. My Georgia Southern University students and I did quite a bit of reading and research in local history. Statesboro did indeed have electricity and telephones before Stevenage (the primary model for "Balesworth") I was astounded to learn of the diversity of Statesboro's downtown business community more than a century ago: A German-Swiss hotelier opened the Jaeckel Hotel in 1905. A Chinese laundryman set up shop around the same time Jewish merchants established stores, as did an illiterate local man who opened a department store that did, indeed, rely on farmers spending all their money by the time they got downstairs. The first mayor of the city, James Alonzo Brannen, while a native of Bryan County (GA) and not of Britain, had some traits in common with the fictional Charles Hughes: An entrepreneurial spirit that resulted in railroad lines being sent into Statesboro, and a strong marketing plan that attracted capital and business to his adopted hometown. I have taken some dramatic license with Charles Hughes, among them imagining how an Englishman could have ingratiated himself sufficiently to become mayor of a small Southern town. My best defense? It is plausible. Charles Hughes is also partly inspired by Connecticut native Henry Harding Tift, the founder of Tifton, in south Georgia. Tift's home, now housed at the Georgia Museum of Agriculture and Historic Village (formerly known as the Agrirama) in Tifton, is the model for Charles Hughes's mansion, and I highly recommend a visit. At this terrific museum, you will also see the models for "Snipesville"'s covered boardwalk, and "Wheeler's Apothecary." You can also visit the Jaeckel Hotel (model for "Hotel Duval") in Statesboro, but you cannot book a room: It is now Statesboro's City Hall.

As transport connected previously isolated communities, civic boosterism became a huge phenomenon in early 20th century America. Community leaders set out to capture business and tourism with better communications (trains, roads, and telephones), civic architecture (like "Snipes County"'s new courthouse), and hotels (like Hotel Duval). Sinclair Lewis satirized the phenomenon of gosh-darn booster enthusiasm in *Babbitt* (1922). If you have never read Sinclair Lewis, do!

The Good Roads Movement was real, and it held state and national conventions that would have been ideal places for Mr. Hughes to further his quest to put "Snipesville" on the map. You can read about it in Wikipedia, or look up original copies of Good Roads Magazine on Google Books.

Asian-Americans in the South
John Jung's fascinating web site about Chinese laundries is a labor of love. I appreciate his collecting images which helped me to create a plausible description of Snipesville's Progressive-era Chinese laundry: https://chineselaundry.wordpress.com/.

The Rise of a Black Middle Class
Since conflict and disaster tend to be more compelling subjects, the public rarely gets a look at the generally less dramatic but profound topic of the accelerating rise of middle- and upper-class black Americans in the South after slavery. I'm glad to have made it a theme in this book.

I had learned that the Georgia Equal Rights Convention of 1906 was held in Macon, but where? The secondary sources I consulted didn't tell me, and I was on the verge of concluding that the meeting place simply had to be a church (and leaving it at that) when a footnote in John Dittmer, *Black Georgia in the Progressive Era, 1900-1920* led me to the Atlanta Independent newspaper for February 24, 1906 (one of the few surviving issues from that month). I have no idea why I read the society page (not usually my cup of tea) but I did, and lo and behold, there was a letter from a former delegate, who mentioned that the meeting was held at the AME Church in Macon. Deduction led to Steward Chapel AME Church. It subsequently hosted Dr. Martin Luther King, Jr., not to mention Benjamin Mays and Mary McLeod Bethune, and still holds political meetings today. The speeches Brandon hears are quoted from the official program for the convention, which is available online, courtesy of Special Collections and University Archives, University of Massachusetts Amherst Libraries. Search: Georgia Equal Rights Convention program, ca. 1906.

John Hope (1868-1936) was the first black president of what became Morehouse College. You can read more about him online in the New Georgia Encyclopedia, and there is an excellent biography: Leroy Davis, *A Clashing of the Soul: John Hope and the Dilemma of African-American Leadership and Black Higher Education in the Early*

Twentieth Century (University of Georgia Press, 1998) Hope's father was indeed a white Scotsman who had a loving common-law marriage with his African-American partner in Augusta, GA. John Hope and his wife later visited Scotland to see his father's birthplace.

Although I read John Hope Franklin and John Whittington Franklin (eds.) *My Life and an Era: The Autobiography of Buck Colbert Franklin* (LSU Press, 1997) when this book was almost finished, I was delighted to find that it reassured me about my portrayal of middle-class black American life in the early 20th century South. Attorney B. C. Franklin, like "R. H. Gordon", used his initials in public to prevent white men from using his first name as a form of condescending put-down. His son, one of the editors, was the late John Hope Franklin, whom he named for his friend Professor John Hope. The younger Franklin was a pioneering African-American historian, whose classic text, *From Slavery to Freedom*, was among the first books I ever read on American history, as a young teenager in England. I had the distinct honor and pleasure of meeting Dr. John Hope Franklin at a conference many years ago.

In 1906, wealthy barber/insurance mogul Alonzo and Adrienne Herndon and their son Norris were living on the campus of Atlanta University, where Adrienne had been a faculty member in theatre (young Bazoline Usher performed as one of the witches in Mrs. Herndon's production of *Macbeth*). The Alonzo Herndon Home in Atlanta was built in 1910, and at time of writing, it has been reopened to the public after extensive renovations. To learn more about Alonzo Herndon and his family, see Carole Merritt, *The Herndons, An Atlanta Family* (University of Georgia Press, 2002).

Du Bois, Washington, and Black Education:
This has got to be one of the most fascinating subjects in American history, yet it's largely unknown to the public. If you are intrigued by historically black colleges and K12 education in the decades after the Civil War, check out James D. Anderson, *The Education of Blacks in the South, 1860-1935* (University of North Carolina Press, 1988).

Devoted Snipesville readers know that I seldom include famous people as characters, and never more than in passing, preferring to highlight the lives of the vast majority of "ordinary" folk in the past, through dramatized composites. I have made an exception in this last volume in the series for W. E. B. Du Bois and Booker T. Washington. The debate they personified, between liberal arts education and economic development via job training as the best route to progress for black Americans, is of relevance to everyone in modern America. Their contentious and complex relationship is not easy to untangle, and I hope I have done both justice without overwhelming you. If you're interested in finding out more for yourself, and have a high tolerance for long books, I recommend Robert J. Norrell, *Up from History: The Life of Booker T. Washington* (Harvard University Press, 2009) and David Levering Lewis, *W. E. B. Du Bois: Biography of a Race, 1868-1919* (Henry Holt, 1993). I visited Booker T. Washington's home, The Oaks, at Tuskegee Institute National Historic Site on the campus of Tuskegee University (AL), and enjoyed a fascinating tour with Tuskegee graduate and Ranger Vester Marable, himself the great-nephew of eminent sociologist Manning Marable.

The conversation I invented between Brandon and Booker T. Washington is partly drawn from the Washington Papers, Volume 8 (1904-6), BTW to Francis Jackson Garrison, October 5, 1905. However, I am not 100% sure where Washington was in mid-February, 1906. So the conversation with Brandon, which is of course fictitious anyway, may not have been possible.

Scottish-American steel magnate Andrew Carnegie did indeed accept an invitation from Washington to come to Tuskegee for the 25th anniversary celebrations, as this photo demonstrates: http://www.corbisimages.com/stock-photo/rights-managed/IH156957/andrew-carnegie-at-tuskegee-institutes-25th-anniversary. However, I was unable to find the invitation itself, or a record of when it was sent.

Bazoline Usher (1885-1992) was a real person, and one with whom I have become fascinated. I have tried very hard to do her justice, borrowing attitudes from the evidence I have been able to piece together, including her contempt for the hapless Lizzie Pingree (Miss Usher is quoted in Lewis, *W. E. B. Du Bois* describing Miss Pingree, wonderfully, as "a fluffy kinda somebody" (p. 211)) I had a very happy time exploring the transcripts of interviews with Miss Usher at the Atlanta History Center, with particular thanks to the lovely Sue VerHoef and her equally friendly and helpful colleagues for drawing several uncataloged materials to my attention. Taught by W. E. B. Du Bois at Atlanta University, where she started in the prep department at age 14, Miss Usher graduated with a degree in mathematics, and became a teacher. She later did graduate work at the University of Chicago, before returning home to complete her Master's degree at Atlanta University. She had a long career with Atlanta Public Schools, retiring as Director of Negro Schools in 1955. Miss Usher was better educated, and a very different person, than the fictional "Mrs. Devenish," but they remind me very much of each other: They shared a birth year, a Victorian sensibility, and a commanding presence that comes through, in Miss Usher's case, in the extant sources. You notice I call her "Miss Usher".

"R. H. Gordon" is very loosely based on what I have learned over the years about William James (1872-1935), a Morehouse graduate who served as principal of schools, including the industrial high school for black children, in the early 20th century in the small town of Statesboro, GA. Last time I looked, there's a mural of William James as an old man, surrounded by kids, in downtown Statesboro. William James forged a relationship with Marvin Pittman, the white president of South Georgia Teachers' College (today Georgia Southern University) and helped arrange for Tuskegee Institute professors to visit Statesboro in the 1930s.

Racial Segregation and Discrimination:
There are far more academic books available on segregation than the public ever suspects. Visit a university library, and you will see what I mean. I recommend an oldie but goodie as a highly readable introduction to racial segregation in the South: C. Vann Woodward, *The Strange Career of Jim Crow* (Oxford University Press, 1955 and later editions). I also recommend a well-written popular history on the turn of the century South: Douglas Blackmon, *Slavery by Another Name: The Re-Enslavement of Black Americans from the Civil War to World War II* (Anchor, 2009)

The National Association of Colored Dentists mentioned by Dr. Marshburn was and is real. It's now known as the National Dental Association, and membership is open to all.

Violence Against Black Americans:
Here's a subject that could not, unfortunately, be more timely at the time of publica-

tion. My former student Holly Timmons Baldwin had miraculously kept her research folder on the Statesboro lynchings and riot of 1904 from our historical methods class, and she was kind enough to send her materials all the way from South Korea, saving me a great deal of time refreshing my memory in the archives. I am very grateful to her. The terrible events in Statesboro in 1904, and what led to them, formed much of the inspiration for the events of Chapter 16. I often fearlessly tackle heavy historical issues in Snipesville, but I have pulled my punches here, given that some of my readers are nine or even younger. Awful though the events of Chapter 16 are, I barely hint at how appalling lynchings could be. It's a disturbing and traumatic subject, and yes, historians have written at length about it. For readers from middle school on up, I do recommend further reading. The most accessible book on lynching is probably Laura Wexler, *Fire in a Canebreak: The Last Mass Lynching in America* (Scribner, 2004) For a more specific look at lynching at the turn of the century, I recommend W. Fitzhugh Brundage, *Lynching in the New South: Georgia and Virginia, 1880-1930* (University of Illinois, 1993) and Amy Louise Wood, *Lynching and Spectacle: Witnessing Racial Violence in America, 1890-1940* (University of North Carolina Press, 2009).

I am so sorry that I can't invite you to take the late historian Clifford Kuhn's Atlanta Race Riot walk. Dr. Kuhn, a lovely and accomplished man, helped to me grasp the scale of the city in 1906, as well as the explosive horror of that terrible event, which took place two years after white men in Statesboro and Bulloch County, Georgia, lynched two black men accused of setting a fire that killed a family, and rioted through the countryside. These riots by whites against blacks, as well as the Wilmington, NC riot and coup of 1898 that "Robert Gordon" mentions, all took place in the same broad context of the rise of segregation, urbanization, racial discrimination, modernization, class tension, and a manipulative yellow press. Dr. Kuhn's untimely death has left a hole in public history in Atlanta: His free monthly walk was a gem, and it was a memorable gift to all who took it.

On the Atlanta Race Riot and its aftermath, I recommend David Godshalk, *Veiled Visions: The 1906 Atlanta Race Riot and the Reshaping of American Race Relations.* On the Wilmington coup, I suggest starting with the "Wilmington Riot" episode of the PBS documentary *The Rise and Fall of Jim Crow*: http://www.pbs.org/wnet/jimcrow/stories_events_riot.html

Jupiter (Jupe) Gordon's Return to Georgia:
My rule for historical fiction is to use real events whenever possible, and informed conjecture in making things up. In other words, it all has to at least be plausible, meaning that it could have happened (except for the time travel, of course).

Jupe's odyssey may seem unlikely, but his story pales compared with the colorful true story of abolitionists, former slaves, and all-around great people Ellen (1826-1891) and William Craft (1824-1900). They escaped to England, where they continued to agitate against slavery, raised a family, and then, after nearly 20 years, returned to Georgia after the Civil War to start a school for freedpeople in southeastern Georgia. They came under increasing pressure and harassment as Georgia became ever more segregated and hostile toward black citizens in the late 19th century. Read more about them in New Georgia Encyclopedia (online) or in William and Ellen Craft, *Running a Thousand Miles for Freedom: The Escape of William and Ellen Craft from Slavery* (University of Georgia

Press, 1999).

Could Jupe have brought a white wife back to Georgia? Could Caroline Clark have had a white mother and black father? Absolutely. People at the end of the Civil War had no crystal ball, and Reconstruction promised to change the South quickly, and forever. But the promises were not kept, and the federal government's abandonment of black Southerners in 1877 caught out a lot of people. For more on "interracial" couples in the South, see Charles F. Robinson, *Dangerous Liaisons: Sex and Love in the Segregated South* (University of Arkansas Press, 2006). Laws were passed against "miscegenation" (black-white couples) precisely because they existed. Couples made up of white women and black men were rarer than white men and black women, but among the cases Robinson cites is that of Pace v. Alabama (1881) (p.51), the prosecution of Tony Pace, who was black, and his white common-law wife, Mary Ann Cox, with whom he had several children. See also Carter v. Montgomery, an 1875 case from Tennessee (p.52), Robert Hoover and Sarah Elizabeth Smith of Talledega, AL (1876) (p.53), Thomas and Mary Dodson (Arkansas, 1895) (p.54). The State of Georgia amended its Constitution after the Civil War to prohibit interracial marriage forever (p.24), but it passed a law with stiffer penalties for such relationships in 1927, which strongly suggests that they persisted, despite the threat of prosecution. More scholarly work is needed on Georgia, but evidence from other states shows that, although many laws were passed and people harassed, interracial relationships never ceased.

Women's Lives and Women's Suffrage

Miss Julia Russell

Miss Julia Russell is fictitious, but she represents black women who have been given insufficient attention and credit for their role in promoting civil rights, whether because of class or (as in Miss Julia's case) despite it. As an upper-middle-class woman with a strong missionary streak, "Miss Julia" draws on those women (and men), black and white, who came South in the aftermath of the Civil War to do what good they could among people released from slavery. After two decades in Georgia, I can say that simply knowing that such people existed is a considerable source of comfort and support to me personally. "Miss Julia" also owes more than a little to suffragist and civil rights activist Mary Church Terrell (1863-1954). Terrell is one of those figures who gets a passing mention in Black History Month, and who (along with the even more impressive Mary McLeod Bethune and Ida B. Wells) merits a closer look. Her autobiography, *A Colored Woman in a White World*, is an engaging and enjoyable read.

Middle-Class Young Women in Edwardian Britain

Without overburdening the reader, I have tried, through my depiction of life in Willowbank, to summon up the world of middle-class Edwardian domesticity, which was suffocating even (and perhaps especially) in an all-woman household. Much of "Elizabeth Hughes Devenish"'s character is Victorian in nature, such as her resistance to hugging. But what I had sensed about "Mrs. Devenish" from the beginning of the series, and have tried to depict, was that she was basically a modern person, chafing against the repressive environment in which she had grown up. In this book, of course, she gets considerable help from Hannah in pushing the envelope. For Elizabeth's rebellion, I consulted historian Carol Dyhouse's *Girls Growing Up in Late Victorian and Edwardian England* (Routledge, 2014). For a more readable and much more affordable interpretation of these ideas, written for the public, I recommend Carol Dyhouse's *Girl Trouble: Panic and Progress in the History of Young Women* (Zed Books, 2015)

I also reacquainted myself with Vera Brittain's diary, published as *Chronicle of Youth* (1982), and her classic memoir, *Testament of Youth* (1933), both of them good sources on the pre-First World War adolescence of a middle-class girl.

Might Elizabeth have cut her hair in 1905? Yes, but she would have been a pioneer. Increasing numbers of women started bobbing their hair in the 1910s, likely in response to the suffragette movement. The trend accelerated during World War I, as the old order came crashing down. For a girl like Elizabeth Hughes to have cut her hair in 1905 would have been very radical, but not unheard of.

Suffragists and Suffragettes

If my frequent mentions of Emmeline Pankhurst and her movement inspire your interest in them, so much the better. I'm not a huge fan of the 2015 movie *Suffragette*, preferring the slower-moving 1970s BBC classic *Shoulder to Shoulder* as a dramatic re-telling of the militant Edwardian suffrage movement. Sadly, the BBC has yet to release it on DVD.

Here's a great article on *Shoulder to Shoulder*, which also gives a good critique of the program, including mentioning that suffragists (the real-life counterparts of "Mrs. Lewis" and "Elizabeth") don't get all the credit they should for their unglamorous work, in large part because women sitting at desks writing letters doesn't make for thrilling storytelling: http://blogs.lse.ac.uk/politicsandpolicy/why-remember-shoulder-to-shoulder/.

Having established in *Don't Know Where, Don't Know When* that "Elizabeth Hughes Devenish" was a suffragist, not a militant suffragette (with the exception of one unfortunate incident involving a brick and her mother's front window) I challenged myself in this book to represent the moderate suffragists as entertainingly and sympathetically as possible. I am particularly fascinated by the complex relationship between those women who promoted gradual change, and the radicals, a particularly timely subject now. This is a factor also in my growing interest in the interplay between the ideas of W. E. B. Du Bois and Booker T. Washington. Young people like Elizabeth Hughes and Millie Cooke (not to mention R. H. Gordon and Thomas Clark) surely struggled with deciding which way to go in order to make the world better, just as many people do today, and that internal struggle is one of the subtexts of *One Way or Another*.

To learn more about the women and organizations who inspired my writing of Mrs. Lewis and her moderate (and fictitious) "Women's Suffrage Association", see David Rubenstein, *A Different World for Women: The Life of Millicent Garrett Fawcett* (Ohio State University Press, 1991). If the Pankhursts really capture your imagination, check out June Purvis, *Emmeline Pankhurst: A Biography* (Routledge, 2002)

Real-life Victorian English activist and publisher Catherine Impey, whose work so inspired "Mrs. Lewis" and helped connect her with "Julia Russell", is the subject of Caroline Bressey, *Empire, Race and the Politics of Anti-Caste* (Bloomsbury Academic, 2013)

Edwardian Domestic Servants and Shop Girls

Social and economic inequality were so pronounced in Victorian and Edwardian Britain that even middle-class families could afford at least one servant. My family fell on both sides of the divide: My paternal great-grandfather employed a maid, while my maternal great-great-grandmother was a maid. In recent years, British house museums have placed much more focus on the lives of servants, which has helped me better imagine the settings and perspectives of the majority who lived and worked in grand houses. Indeed, at the extraordinary Ickworth House in Suffolk, which I visited in 2015, guests begin with an extensive tour of the massive service areas "below stairs", interpreted for the 1930s, before they are directed to see the splendors of the family quarters. For "Willowbank", I also drew inspiration from Audley End, the Edwardian terraced houses at Beamish Museum, and the eponymous Willowbank, a small Victorian family-run B&B in Scotland in which I stayed regularly for over a quarter century with the lovely Penman family, Sandra, Claire, and the late and much-missed Alex Penman. The real Willowbank still has its servant callboard in the former kitchen.

For Hannah's experience as a maid, I relied additionally on several books on servant life in Edwardian and Victorian England, including the account of Elizabeth L. Banks (1872-1938) a daring young American writer who posed in various roles in late 19th century London, including as a maid. Her work is published (and free as an e-book, since it's in the public domain) as Elizabeth L. Banks, *An American Girl in Victorian London*. Hannah's exchange with Margaret Hughes over the closing of the bedroom window is borrowed directly from an incident that actually happened to Banks.

Verity, as a highly-educated middle-class young woman from 1951, must have been quite a novelty among shopgirls in 1905 "Ickswade". For the mood, layout, and stock of an Edwardian grocer's shop, I have drawn on my many visits to Beamish and The Black Country Living Museum, Britain's premier outdoor museums.

Random Stuff:
Brandon's tricky train journey from Chehaw to Tuskegee to meet Booker T. Washington is heavily based on the real experience of a African-American author and activist Charles Chesnutt (1858-1932). See Journey to Tuskegee (1901): http://www.chesnuttarchive.org/works/Essays/visit.html

The mule on the railroad line near Chehaw, Alabama? Yes, that happened: Western Alabama v. Turner (1909) in the *Report of Cases Argued and Determined in the Supreme Court of Alabama*, Volume 170 (Google Books) A train struck an "iron grey" mule near Chehaw on Sept 27, 1909. The farmer (plaintiff) claimed the driver was negligent because the train could have slowed down. Lawsuits are a wonderful source for small incidents as well as weightier matters.

The scenes at the turpentine camp drew heavily on the oral histories and videos at the web site of "Faces in the Piney Woods: Traditions of Turpentining in South Georgia" produced by the South Georgia Folklife Project at Valdosta State University, Georgia. The site: http://ww2.valdosta.edu/turpentine/

A Note on "Ellen Walker"'s Genealogy
I know many of you would like to see the family history charts compiled by "Ellen Walker", Hannah and Alex's grandmother. I hope to include them in a future edition of this book, but I will add them to the website (AnnetteLaing.com) before then. If you want to see how everyone was related, stay tuned.

About the Author

Dr. Annette Laing was born in Scotland, raised in England, spent many years in California, and many more in rural Georgia. She was professor of early American and transatlantic history at Georgia Southern University, before resigning in 2008 to concentrate on her work as a public historian. As well as being author of *The Snipesville Chronicles* series, Annette presents "Non-Boring History" programs for kids, teens, and families, in schools, libraries, and other settings. She also speaks regularly at teachers' conferences. Annette and her family live in Atlanta.

To learn more about Annette and her work, and sign up for her newsletter, visit AnnetteLaing.com.